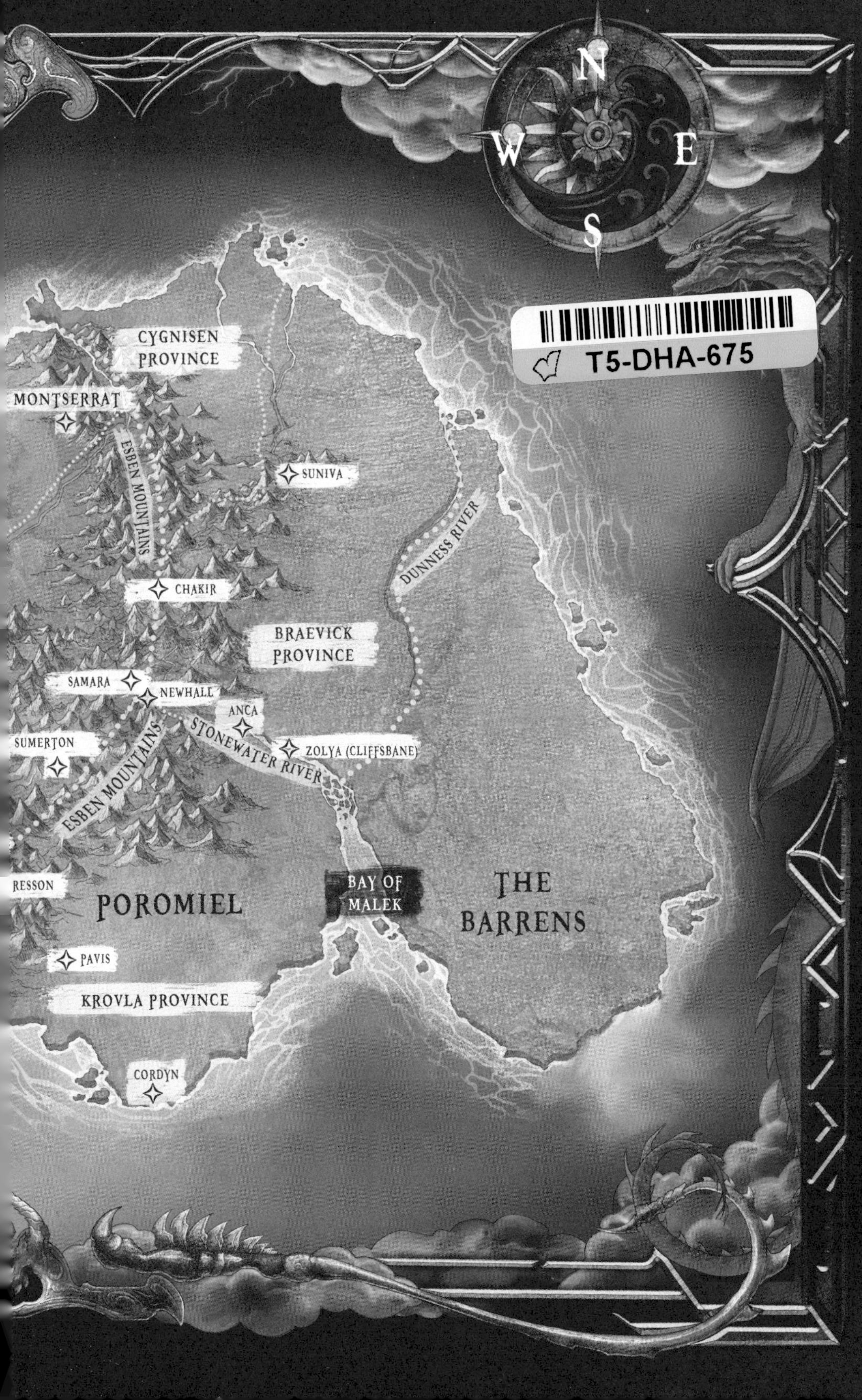

N
W E
S

CYGNISEN PROVINCE

MONTSERRAT

ESBEN MOUNTAINS

SUNIVA

DUNNESS RIVER

CHAKIR

BRAEVICK PROVINCE

SAMARA

NEWHALL

ANCA

STONEWATER RIVER

ZOLYA (CLIFFSBANE)

SUMERTON

ESBEN MOUNTAINS

RESSON

POROMIEL

BAY OF MALEK

THE BARRENS

PAVIS

KROVLA PROVINCE

CORDYN

ONYX STORM

ONYX STORM

#1 *NEW YORK TIMES* BESTSELLING AUTHOR
REBECCA YARROS

Entangled Publishing, LLC
644 Shrewsbury Commons Ave., STE 181
Shrewsbury, PA 17361
rights@entangledpublishing.com

Red Tower Books is an imprint of Entangled Publishing, LLC.

Visit our website at www.entangledpublishing.com.

Edited by Alice Jerman
Cover art and design by Bree Archer and Elizabeth Turner Stokes
Cover stock art by Peratek/shutterstock, Romolo Tavani/Shutterstock,
VRVIRUS/Shutterstock, Dmitr1ch/GettyImages, KBL-loss/shutterstock,
stopkin/shutterstock, yanng/Depositphotos, Liu Zishan/Shutterstock,
Next Mars Media/Shutterstock, and Laslo Ludrovan/Shutterstock
Sprayed edge design by Bree Archer
Edge stock art by KBL-loss/shutterstock, stopkin/shutterstock,
and yanng/Depositphotos
Interior art by Bree Archer
Endpaper map art by Melanie Korte
Target Edition Inserts by Elizabeth Turner Stokes
Interior design by Britt Marczak

Standard Hardcover ISBN 978-1-64937-715-9
Deluxe Edition ISBN 978-1-64937-418-9
Target Exclusive Edition ISBN 978-1-64937-860-6
eBook ISBN 978-1-64937-694-7

Manufactured in China

10 9 8 7 6 5 4 3 2 1

RED TOWER BOOKS™

THE EMPYREAN SERIES

Fourth Wing
Iron Flame
Onyx Storm

MORE FROM REBECCA YARROS

The Things We Leave Unfinished
Great and Precious Things
The Last Letter

To the ones who don't run with the popular crowd,

the ones who get caught reading under their desks,

the ones who feel like they never get invited, included, or represented.

Get your leathers. We have dragons to ride.

NAME	BONDED	SIGNET/SPECIALTY
		(if applicable)
VIOLET SORRENGAIL	TAIRN AND ANDARNA	LIGHTNING WIELDING
XADEN RIORSON	SGAEYL	SHADOW WIELDING, READING INTENTIONS

SECOND SQUAD, FLAME SECTION, FOURTH WING

NAME	BONDED	SIGNET/SPECIALTY
IMOGEN CARDULO	GLANE	MEMORY ERASING
QUINN HOLLIS	CRUTH	ASTRAL PROJECTION
RHIANNON MATTHIAS	FEIRGE	RETRIEVING
SAWYER HENRICK	SLISEAG	METALLURGY
RIDOC GAMLYN	AOTROM	ICE WIELDING
SLOANE MAIRI	THOIRT	SIPHONING
AARIC GRAYCASTLE *(AKA Cam Tauri)*	MOLVIC	NOT MANIFESTED

AVALYNN, BAYLOR, AND LYNX - *FIRST-YEARS WITH UNMANIFESTED SIGNETS*

CATRIONA CORDELLA	KIRALAIR	MANIPULATING EMOTIONS
MAREN ZINA	DAJALAIR	

BRAGEN, NEVE, TRAGER, AND KAI - *GRYPHON FLIERS*

WORLD LEADERS

KING TAURI THE WISE - *THE KING OF NAVARRE*
HALDEN TAURI - *FIRST IN LINE FOR THE NAVARRIAN THRONE*
QUEEN MARAYA - *THE QUEEN OF POROMIEL*
VISCOUNT TECARUS - *FIRST IN LINE FOR THE POROMISH THRONE*

Onyx Storm is a nonstop-thrilling adventure fantasy set in the brutal and competitive world of a military college for dragon riders, which includes elements regarding war, hand-to-hand combat, blood, intense violence, brutal injuries, gore, murder, death, animal death, injury rehabilitation, grief, poisoning, burning, perilous situations, graphic language, and sexual activities that are shown on the page. Readers who may be sensitive to these elements, please take note, and prepare to face the storm…

The following text has been faithfully transcribed from Navarrian into the modern language by Jesinia Neilwart, Curator of the Scribe Quadrant at Basgiath War College. All events are true, and names have been preserved to honor the courage of those fallen. May their souls be commended to Malek.

Securing Basgiath and the wards has come at great cost, including General Sorrengail's life. Strategy must adjust. It is in the realm's best interest to ally with Poromiel, even temporarily.

—Recovered Correspondence Of General Augustine Melgren
To His Majesty King Tauri

PROLOGUE

Where in Malek's name is he going? I hurry through the tunnels beneath the quadrant, trying to follow, but night is the ultimate shadow and Xaden blends seamlessly into the darkness. If it wasn't for our dragons' bond leading me in his general direction and the sporadic disappearance of mage lights, I'd never think that he's masked somewhere ahead of me.

Fear holds me with an icy fist, and my footing grows unsteady. He kept his head down this evening, guarded by Bodhi and Garrick while we waited for news about Sawyer's injury after the battle that nearly cost us Basgiath, but there's no telling what he's doing now. If anyone spots the faint, strawberry-red circles around his irises, he'll be arrested—and likely executed. According to the texts I've read, they'll fade at this phase, but until they do, what could possibly be important enough for him to risk being seen?

The only logical answer sends a chill up my spine that has nothing to do with the cold stone of the corridor seeping in through my socks. There hadn't been time for boots or even my armor after the *click* of the closing door woke me from a restless sleep.

"Neither of them will answer," Andarna says, and I yank open the door to the enclosed bridge as its counterpart on the far end snicks shut. Was that him? *"Sgaeyl is still…incensed, and Tairn smells of both rage and sorrow."*

Understandable for all the reasons I can't allow myself to dwell on yet, but inconvenient.

"Do you want me to ask Cuir or Chradh—" she starts.

"No. The four of them need their sleep." No doubt we'll find ourselves on patrols for any remaining venin come morning. I cross the freezing expanse of the bridge with increasingly uncertain steps and jolt at the view outside the windows. It had been warm enough for thunderstorms earlier, but now snow falls in a thick curtain, concealing the ravine that separates the quadrant from Basgiath's main campus. My chest clenches, and a fresh wave of seemingly endless tears threatens to prickle my painfully swollen eyes.

"It began about an hour ago," Andarna says gently.

The temperature has fallen steadily in the hours since… *Don't go there.* My next breath shakes, and I force everything I can't handle into a neat, mentally fireproof box and stash it somewhere deep inside me.

It's too late to save Mom, but I'll be damned if I let Xaden get himself killed.

"You can grieve," Andarna reminds me as I pull open the door to the Healer Quadrant and enter the crowded hall. Wounded in every color of uniform line the sides of the stone tunnel, and healers dart in and out of the infirmary doors.

"If I wallow in every loss, that's all I'll ever have time for." I've learned that lesson well over the past eighteen months. Passing a set of clearly intoxicated infantry cadets, I cut through what's become an expanded sickbay, searching for a blur of darkness. This part of the quadrant didn't sustain any damage, but it still reeks of sulfur and ash.

"May your mother be remembered! To General Sorrengail, the flame of Basgiath!" one of the third-years calls out, and my stomach twists tighter as I forge ahead without reply.

When I approach the corner, then turn it, I see a patch of darkness enveloping the right side of the wall for a stuttering heartbeat, and then the stairwell to the interrogation chamber appears, flanked by two groggy guards. Shadows slip down the steps.

Fuck. Usually I love being right, but in this instance, I was hoping otherwise. I reach for Xaden mentally, but there's only a thick wall of chilled onyx.

I have to get past these guards. What would Mira do?

"She would have already slain your lieutenant and been confident in her choice," Andarna answers. *"Your sister is an* act first, ask questions later *kind of rider."*

"Not helpful." What little I'd eaten for dinner threatens to reappear. Andarna's right. Mira will kill Xaden if she finds out he's channeled from the earth, regardless of the circumstances. But confidence? That's not a bad idea. I muster every ounce of arrogance I can scrounge up or fake, straighten my shoulders, lift my chin, and stride toward the guards, praying I look steadier than I feel. "I need an audience with the prisoner."

The two men glance at each other, and then the taller one on the left clears his throat. "We're under orders from Melgren not to allow anyone down these steps."

"Tell me"—I tilt my head and fold my arms like I'm strapped with every dagger I own...or am at least wearing footwear—"if the man directly responsible for your mother's death was a flight of stairs away, what would you do?"

The shorter one looks down, revealing a cut beneath his ear.

"Orders—" the taller one starts, glancing at the ends of my sleep-loosened braid.

"He's behind a locked door," I interrupt. "I'm asking you to look the other way for five minutes, not give me the key." My gaze darts poignantly to the key ring hanging on his bloodstained belt. "If it had been *your* mother, and she'd secured the kingdom's entire defense system with her life, I promise I'd afford you the same courtesy."

The tall one blanches.

"Goverson," the short one whispers. "She's the lightning wielder."

Goverson grunts, and his hands flex at his sides. "Ten minutes," he says. "Five for your mother, and five for you. We know who saved us today." He motions toward the stairwell with his head.

But he *doesn't* know. None of them realize the sacrifice Xaden made to kill the Sage...their *general.*

"Thank you." I start down the stairs with wobbling knees, ignoring the pungent scent of wet earth that claws at the outer edges of my composure. *"I can't believe he came down here."*

"He probably seeks information," Andarna notes. *"I cannot blame him for wanting to know what he is."* The longing in her voice startles me on multiple levels.

"He isn't a soulless venin. He's still Xaden. My Xaden," I snap, holding tight to the only thing I'm certain of as I make my way silently down the stairs.

"You know what channeling from the earth does," she warns.

Know? Yes. Accept? Absolutely not. *"If he'd completely lost himself, he would have drained me at any number of points tonight, especially while I slept. Instead, he ensured our safety and risked exposure to sit at my side for hours. He channeled from the earth* once. *Surely we can repair wherever his soul may have... cracked."* It's the most I'm willing to admit. *"I already know what Tairn thinks, and the possibility of fighting both of you is exhausting, so please, for the love of Amari, be on my side."*

The bond directly between us shimmers. *"All right."*

"Really?" I pause on the stair, splaying my hand on the wall to catch my balance.

"I am as unknown as he is, and you still trust me," she says. *"I will not be another battle you have to fight."*

Oh, thank gods. Her words seep into the marrow of my bones, and I hang my head in relief. I hadn't realized how badly I needed to hear that until she said it. *"Thank you. And you have every right to know about where you come from, but I have no doubts about who you are."* I start down the remaining steps, sure of my footing. *"You alone should make the choice to find your family, and I'm worried that Melgren—"*

"I scorched the venin during the battle," she interrupts in a rush of words that run together.

"You…did." My brow puckers as I spiral downward toward the interrogation cells. I'd been too shocked at her appearance, the way her scales had shifted, to think about the burning dark wielder. As far as I know, we've never caught one on fire. Tairn hadn't said anything, either.

"I've been thinking about it all night. Magic feels different when I change color. Maybe my use of power in that moment altered the venin, weakened her enough to blister." Andarna slows enough to enunciate her words, but not by much.

"That could alter…everything." Muffled voices sound beneath me, and I quicken my pace. *"It's definitely worth investigating later."* Not that I'm willing to risk Andarna by shouting that she might be our newest weapon, especially not when the rumor has already circulated that we'll seek an alliance with Poromiel. What could be worse than leadership endangering Andarna? The whole Continent's leadership seeking to do the same.

"You can fight it all you want, but that power streaming through her veins?" Jack taunts, his words growing clearer as I near the final few turns. "There's a reason the higher-ups want her. A little brotherly advice? Fall in line and find someone else to fuck. That infamous control of yours so much as flickers in her direction—"

"I would *never*," Xaden retorts, his voice lethally icy.

My heart rate doubles and I halt just before the last curve in the stairwell, keeping out of sight. Jack's talking about *me*.

"Even you don't get a say in which parts of us are taken first, Riorson." Jack laughs. "But speaking from personal experience, control goes quickly. Just look at you, freshly fed from the source and already down here, desperate for a cure. You will slip, and afterward… Well, let's just say that silver hair that has you so besotted will be gray like the rest of her, and those weak-ass initiate rings in your eyes won't just last a few days—they'll be permanent."

"Not going to happen." Xaden bites out every word.

"You could deliver her yourself." Chains rattle. "Or you could let me out and we'll do it together. Who knows, they might let her live just to keep you on a leash until you turn asim and forget all about her."

"Fuck you."

My hands ball into fists. Jack knows Xaden's channeled. He'll tell the first person who questions him, and Xaden will be arrested. My mind spins as the two start to argue only yards away, their words blurring in the whirlwind of my thoughts. Gods, I could lose Xaden just like—

I can't. I won't. I refuse to lose him, for him to lose *himself*.

Fear fights to rise and I snuff it out, denying it air to breathe or grow. The only thing stronger than the power prowling within me is the resolve stiffening my spine.

Xaden is *mine*. My heart, my soul, my everything. He channeled from the earth to save me, and I'll scour the world until I find a way to save him right back. Even if it takes bargaining with Tecarus for access to every book on the damned Continent or capturing dark wielders one by one to question, I'll find a cure.

"We'll *find a cure*," Andarna promises. "*We will exhaust every closer resource first, but if I'm right and I somehow altered that venin inadvertently while changing my scales, then the rest of my kind should know how to master the tactic. How to change* him. *Cure* him."

My breath stutters at the possibility, the cost. "*Even if you're right, I'm not using you—*"

"*I* want *to find my family. We both know the order to locate my kind is inevitable now that your leadership knows what I am. Let us do so on our terms and for our own purposes.*" Her tone sharpens. "*Let us follow every possible path to a cure.*"

She's right. "*Every possible path may require breaking a few laws.*"

"*Dragons do not answer to the laws of humans,*" she counters in a tone that reminds me of Tairn. "*And as my bonded, as Tairn's rider, you no longer answer to them, either.*"

"*Rebellious adolescent,*" I mutter, forming half a dozen plans, half of which might work. Even as their rider, there are still some crimes that would demand my execution…and that of whomever I trust to involve. I nod to myself, accepting the risk, at least for myself.

"*You'll have to keep secrets again,*" Andarna warns.

"*Only the ones that protect Xaden.*" Which currently means preventing Jack from revealing this conversation without killing him, since we can't afford the manhunt the death of our only prisoner would cause.

"*You sure I shouldn't ask Cuir or Chradh—*"

"*No.*" I start down the stairs. There's only one other person besides Bodhi and Garrick I *can* trust to prioritize Xaden's best interests, only one other person who can know the truth in its entirety. "*Tell Glane I need Imogen.*"

~~I will not die today.~~
I will save him.

—Violet Sorrengail's personal addendum
to the Book of Brennan

CHAPTER ONE

Two weeks later

Flying in January should be a violation of the Codex. Between the howling storm and the incessant fog in my goggles, I can't see shit as we cut through the blustering snow squall above the mountains near Basgiath. Hoping we're almost through the worst of it, I grip the pommels of my saddle with gloved hands and hold tight.

"Dying today would be inconvenient," I say down the mental pathway connecting me to Tairn and Andarna. *"Unless you're trying to keep me away from the Senarium this afternoon?"* I've waited more than a week for the invitation-disguised order to come from the king's council, but the delay is understandable given they're on the fourth day of unprecedented peace talks happening on campus. Poromiel has publicly declared they'll walk after the seventh day if terms can't be reached, and it isn't looking good. I only hope that they'll be in an agreeable mood when I arrive.

"Want to make your meeting? Don't fall off this time," Tairn retorts.

"For the last *time, I didn't fall off,"* I argue. *"I jumped off to help Sawyer—"*

"Don't remind me."

"You can't keep leaving me off patrols," Andarna interrupts from the warmth and protection of the Vale.

"It isn't safe," Tairn reminds her for what has to be the hundredth time.

"Weather aside, we're hunting dark wielders, not out for a pleasure flight."

"You shouldn't fly in this," I agree, looking for any sign of Ridoc and Aotrom, but there's only walls of white. My chest tightens. How are any of us supposed to see topography or our squadmates, let alone spot a dark wielder hundreds of feet below in this mess? I can't remember a more brutal series of storms than the ones that have battered the war college in the last two weeks, but without—

Mom. Grief sinks the tips of her razor-sharp claws into my chest, and I lift my face to feel the stinging bite of snow against the tops of my cheeks, focusing on anything else to keep breathing, keep moving. I'll mourn later, always later.

"It's just a quick patrol," Andarna whines, jarring me from my thoughts. *"I need the practice. Who knows what weather we'll encounter on the search for my kind?"*

"Quick patrols" have proven deadly, and I'm not looking for reasons to test Andarna's fire theory. Dark wielders may have limited power within the wards, but they're still lethal fighters. The ones who didn't escape post-battle have used the element of surprise to add multiple names to the death roll. First Wing, Third Wing, and our own Claw Section have suffered losses.

"Then practice evenly dispersing enough magic to keep all your extremities warm during flight, because your wings won't hold the weight of this ice," Tairn growls into the falling snow.

"'Your wings won't hold the weight of this ice,'" Andarna blatantly mocks him. *"And yet yours miraculously carry the burden of your ego."*

"Go find a sheep and let the adults work." Tairn's muscles shift slightly beneath me in a familiar pattern, and I lean forward as far as the saddle will allow, preparing for a dive.

My stomach lurches into my throat as his wings snap closed and we pitch downward, slicing through the storm. Wind tears at my winter flight hood, and the leather strap of my saddle bites into my frozen thighs as I pray to Zihnal there isn't a mountain peak directly beneath us.

Tairn levels out, and my stomach settles as I tug my goggles up to my forehead and blink quickly, looking right. The drop in altitude has lessened the intensity of the storm, improving visibility enough to see the rocky ridgeline just above the flight field.

"Looks clear." My eyes tear up, assaulted by both wind and snow that feels more like tiny projectiles of ice than flakes. I clean my lenses using the suede tips of my gloves before snapping them over my eyes again.

"Agreed. Once we hear the same from Feirge and Cruth, we'll end today's endeavors," he grumbles.

"You sound like making it three straight days without encountering the enemy is a bad thing." Maybe we've really caught and killed them all. As cadets, we've

slain thirty-one venin in the area surrounding Basgiath while our professors work to clear the rest of the province. It would be thirty-two if anyone suspected one of them was living among us, though—even if he's credited with seventeen of the kills.

"I am not comforted by the quiet—" Wind whips overhead with a *crack*, and Tairn's head jerks upward. Mine immediately follows suit.

Oh no.

Not wind. Wings.

Aotrom's claws consume my vision, and my heart seizes with panic. He's dropping out of the storm directly on top of us.

"Tairn!" I shout, but he's already rolling left, hurling us from our course.

The world rotates, sky and land exchanging places twice in a nauseating dance before Tairn flares his wings in a jarring snap. The movement cracks the inch-thick layer of ice along the front ridges of his wings, and chunks fall away.

I draw a full but shaky breath as Tairn pumps his wings with maximum effort, gaining a hundred feet of altitude in a matter of seconds and barreling straight toward the Brown Swordtail bonded to Ridoc.

Wrath scalds the air in my lungs, Tairn's emotions flooding my system for a heartbeat before I can slam my mental shields down to muffle the worst of what streams in through the bond.

"Don't!" I shout into the wind as we come up on Aotrom's left, but as always, Tairn does whatever he wants and full-on crunches his jaws within what looks like inches of Aotrom's head. "It was clearly an accident!" One that would usually be avoided by dragons communicating.

The smaller Brown Swordtail *squawks* as Tairn repeats the warning, then Aotrom exposes his throat in a gesture of submission.

Ridoc looks my way through the band of snow and throws up his hands, but I doubt he sees my shrug of apology before Aotrom falls away, heading south to the flight field.

Guess Feirge and Rhi reported in.

"Was that really necessary?" I drop my shields, and Tairn's and Andarna's bonds come flooding back at full strength, but the shimmering pathway that leads to Xaden is still blocked, dimmed to an echo of its usual presence. The loss of constant connection sucks, but he doesn't trust himself—or what he thinks he'll become—to keep it open yet.

"Yes," Tairn answers, declaring the single word sufficient.

"You're almost twice his size and it was obviously an accident," I repeat as we descend rapidly to the flight field. The snow on the ground of the box canyon has been trampled into a muddy series of paths from the constant patrols second- and third-years are flying.

"It was negligent, and a twenty-two-year-old dragon should know better than to close himself off from his riot simply because he's arguing with his rider," Tairn grumbles, his anger lowering to a simmer as Aotrom lands beside Rhi's Green Daggertail, Feirge.

Tairn's claws impact the frozen ground to Aotrom's left, and the sudden landing vibrates every bone in my body like a rung bell. Pain explodes along my spine, my lower back taking the brunt of the insult. I breathe through the worst of it, then accept the rest and move on. *"Well, that was graceful."* I jerk my goggles to my forehead.

"You fly next time." He shakes like a wet hound, and I block my face with my hands as ice and snow fly off his scales.

I tug at the leather strap of my saddle when he stills, but the buckle catches along the jagged, shitty line of stitches I put in after the battle, and one of them pops. *"Damn it. That wouldn't have happened if you'd let Xaden fix it."* I force my body out of the saddle, ignoring the aching protest of my cold-cramped joints as I make my way across the icy pattern of spikes and scales I know as well as my own hand.

"The Dark One didn't cut it in the first place," Tairn responds.

"Stop calling him that." My knee collapses, and I throw my arms out to steady my balance, cursing my joints as I reach Tairn's shoulder. After an hour in the saddle at these temperatures, a pissed-off knee is nothing; I'm lucky my hips still rotate.

"Stop denying the truth." Tairn enunciates every word of the damning order as I avoid a patch of ice and prepare to dismount. *"His soul is no longer his own."*

"That's a little dramatic." I'm not getting into this argument again. *"His eyes are back to normal—"*

"That kind of power is addictive. You know it, or you wouldn't be pretending to sleep at night." He twists his neck in a way that reminds me of a snake and levels a golden glare on me.

"I'm sleeping." It's not entirely a lie, but definitely time to change the subject. *"Did you make me repair my saddle to teach me a lesson?"* My ass protests every scale on Tairn's leg as I slide, then land in a fresh foot of snow. *"Or because you don't trust Xaden with my gear anymore?"*

"Yes." Tairn lifts his head far over mine and blasts a torrent of fire along his wing, melting off the residual ice, and I turn away from the surge of heat that painfully contrasts my body temperature.

"Tairn…" I struggle for words and look up at him. *"I need to know where you stand before this meeting. With or without Empyrean approval, I can't do any of this without you."*

"Meaning, will I support the myriad of ways you plan to court death in the

name of curing one who is beyond redemption?" He swivels his head in my direction again.

Tension crackles along Andarna's bond.

"He's not—" I cut off that particular argument, since the rest is sound. *"Basically, yes."*

He grumbles deep within his chest. *"I fly without warming my wings in preparation for carrying heavier weight for longer distances. Does that not answer your question?"*

Meaning Andarna. Relief gusts through my lips on a swift exhale. *"Thank you."*

Steam rolls in billowing clouds from his nostrils. *"But do not mistake my unflinching support of you, my mate, and Andarna for any form of faith in him."* Tairn lifts his head, cueing the end of the conversation.

"Heard." On that note, I trudge toward the trampled path where Rhi and Quinn wait. Ridoc gives Tairn a wide berth as he does the same to my right. My nearly numb, gloved fingers fumble with the three buttons on the side of my winter flight hood, and the fur-lined fabric falls away from my nose and mouth as I reach them. "Everything good on your route?"

Rhi and Quinn look cold but uninjured, thank gods.

"Still…alarmingly routine. We didn't see anything of concern. Wyvern burn pit is still just ash and bone, too." Rhi picks a clump of snow from the lining of her hood, then pulls it back up over her shoulder-length black braids.

"We didn't see shit for those last ten minutes, period." Ridoc shoves his gloved hand into his hair, snowflakes slipping off his brown cheeks without melting.

"At least you're an ice wielder." I gesture to his annoyingly flake-free face.

Quinn pulls her blond curls into a quick bun. "Wielding can help keep you warm, too."

"I'm not chancing it when I can't see what I might strike." Especially having lost my only conduit in the battle. I glance at Ridoc as a line of our Tail Section's dragons launch for their patrol behind him. "What were you arguing with Aotrom about, anyway?"

"Sorry about that." Ridoc cringes and lowers his voice. "He wants to go home—back to Aretia. Says we can launch the search for the seventh breed from there."

Rhi nods, and Quinn presses her lips in a firm line.

"Yeah, I get that," I say—it's a common sentiment among the riot. We're not exactly welcome here. The unity between Navarrian and Aretian riders crumbled within hours of the battle's end. "But the only path for an alliance that can save Poromish civilians requires us to be here. At least for now."

Not to mention, Xaden insists we stay.

"He remains because Navarre's wards protect you *from* him." Tairn blasts another stream of fire when I ignore him, heating his left wing, then crouches before launching skyward with the others.

The courtyard is nearly empty when we enter through the tunnel that runs under the ridgeline separating it from the training grounds. In front of us, snow tops the dormitory wing, the centered rotunda that links the quadrant's structures, and all but the southernmost roofline of the academic wing ahead to our left, where Malek's fire burns bright in the highest turret, consuming the belongings of our dead as he requires.

Maybe the god of death will curse me for keeping my mother's personal journals, but it's not like I wouldn't have a few choice words for him should we meet, anyway.

"Report," Aura Beinhaven orders from the dais at our left, where she stands with Ewan Faber—the stocky, sour-faced wingleader of what little remains of Navarre's Fourth Wing.

"Oh, good, you all made it back." Ewan's voice drips with sarcasm as he folds his arms, snow falling on his broad shoulders. "We were so worried."

"Prick was barely a squad leader in Claw when we left," Ridoc mutters.

"Nothing this morning," Rhiannon replies, and Aura nods but doesn't deign to say anything. "Any news from the front?"

My stomach knots. The lack of information is agonizing.

"Nothing I'd be willing to share with a bunch of deserters," Aura answers.

Oh, screw her.

"A bunch of deserters who saved your ass!" Quinn offers a middle finger as we continue past, our boots crunching on the snow-covered gravel. "Navarrian riders, Aretian riders… We can't function like this," she says to the group quietly. "If they won't accept *us*, the fliers don't have a prayer."

I nod in agreement. Mira's working on that particular issue—not that leadership knows or will allow the use of whatever she's learned, even if it saves the negotiations. Pompous assholes.

"Devera and Kaori will be back any day. They'll sort out command structure as soon as the royals ink a treaty that hopefully pardons us for leaving in the first place." Rhi cocks her head as Imogen walks out of the rotunda in front of us, her pink hair skimming her cheekbone as she descends the stone steps. "Cardulo, you missed patrol."

"I was assigned elsewhere by Lieutenant Tavis," Imogen explains, not missing a beat as she comes our way. Her gaze jumps toward me. "Sorrengail, I need a word."

I nod. She was on Xaden duty.

"See that you're present tomorrow." Rhi walks past Imogen with the other two, then pauses halfway up the steps and glances over her shoulder as the others head inside. "Wait. Is Mira due back today?"

"Tomorrow." Anxiety ties a pretty little bow around my throat and tugs. It's one thing to form a plan and quite another to carry it out, especially when the consequences could involve the people I love becoming traitors…again.

"Every possible path," Andarna reminds me.

"Every possible path," I repeat like a mantra and straighten my shoulders.

"Good." A slow smile spreads across Rhi's face. "We'll be in the infirmary when you're done," she promises, then walks up the remaining steps to the rotunda.

"You told the second-years what Mira's up to?" Imogen whispers with a sharp bite of accusation.

"Only the riders," I retort just as quietly. "If we get caught, it's treason, but if the fliers do—"

"It's war," Imogen finishes.

"Ridoc, did you freeze this door shut?" Rhi shouts from the top of the steps, yanking on the door handle of the rotunda with her full body weight before marching through its counterpart to her left. "Get back here and fix it, *now*!"

"Right. Telling them was a solid choice." Imogen rubs the bridge of her nose as Ridoc laughs hysterically from inside the rotunda. "The four of you are a fucking nuisance. It's going to be a miracle if we pull this off without getting ourselves executed."

"You don't have to be involved." I stare her down in a way I never would have dreamed of eighteen months ago. "I'll do it with or without your help."

"Feeling snarky, are we?" A corner of her mouth tugs upward. "Relax. As long as Mira figures out a plan, of course I'm in."

"She doesn't know how to fail."

"I can see that." Snow blows across our faces as Imogen's eyes harden. "But please say you didn't tell your fearsome foursome *everything* about why we're doing this."

"Of course not." I shove my gloves into my pocket. "He's still pissed at me for 'burdening you' with the knowledge."

"Then he should stop doing stupid shit that needs to be covered up." She rubs her hands together in the cold and follows me up the steps. "Look, I needed you alone because Garrick, Bodhi, and I talked—"

"Without me?" My spine stiffens.

"About you," she clarifies unapologetically.

"Even better." I reach for the door.

"We've decided you need to rethink your sleeping arrangements."

My grip tightens on the handle and I contemplate slamming the door in her face. "I've *decided* you can all go fuck yourselves. I'm not running from him. Even in the moments he's lost control, he's never hurt me. He never will."

"That's what I told them you'd say, but don't be surprised if they keep asking. Good to know you're still predictable even if Riorson isn't."

"How was he this morning?" Heat rushes over my face as we walk into the empty rotunda, and I push back my hood. Without classes, formation, or any sense of order, the academic wing might sit abandoned, but commons and the gathering hall are congested with aimless, worried, agitated cadets hoping to survive the next patrol and looking to take their frustrations out on someone else. Every single one of us would *kill* for a Battle Brief.

"Surly and stubborn as always," Imogen answers when we cross into the dormitory, quieting as we pass a group of glaring second-years from First Wing, including Caroline Ashton, which means the truth-sayers cleared her. Lucky for us, the steps leading down to the Healer Quadrant are blessedly empty. "You consider telling him what we're up to?"

"He's aware we'll be sent to find Andarna's kind. As for the rest? He doesn't want to know." I nod at a pair of approaching Aretian riders out of Third Wing when we reach the tunnels but wait to speak until we're out of earshot. "He's worried about being an unintentional leak—which is ridiculous, but I'm respecting his wishes."

"I can't wait for him to discover you're leading your own rebellion." She grins as we walk across the enclosed bridge to the Healer Quadrant.

"It's not a rebellion, and I'm not...leading." Xaden, Dain, Rhi—they're leaders. They inspire and command for the good of the unit. I'm just doing whatever it takes to save Xaden.

"Including the mission to find Andarna's kind?" She throws open the door to the Healer Quadrant, and I follow her in.

"That's different, and I'm not leading as much as I am selecting a leader. Hopefully." I glance down the cluttered tunnel, past the quietly sleeping patients dressed mostly in infantry blue, and spot a group of hooded scribes moving among them, no doubt still working to get accurate accounts of the battle. "Sounds the same, but it's not."

"Right." The word drips with sarcasm. "Well, message delivered, so I'm done with this conversation. Let me know when Mira gets back." She walks off toward main campus. "Give Sawyer my best, and good luck this afternoon!"

"Thanks," I call after her, then turn toward the infirmary. The scents of herbs and metal hit my lungs as I enter through the double doors. I wave at Trager on my right, who's among the healing-trained fliers doing their best to help where they can.

He nods back from a patient's bedside, then reaches for a needle and thread.

I continue quickly to the nearest corner, moving from the healers' paths as they scurry in and out of the curtain-lined bays where rows of the injured rest.

Ridoc's laugh sounds from the last bay as I approach. The pale blue curtains are tied back, revealing a pile of discarded winter flight jackets in the corner and every other second-year in our squad crammed around Sawyer's bed.

"Stop exaggerating," Rhiannon says from the wooden chair near Sawyer's head, shaking her finger at Ridoc, who's sitting on the bed, right where our squadmate's lower leg used to be. "I simply told them that it was our squad's table and they needed to—"

"Take their cowardly asses back to the First Wing section where they belonged," Ridoc finishes for her with another laugh.

"You didn't really say that." A corner of Sawyer's mouth quirks upward, but it's far from a true smile.

"She did." I'm careful not to step on Cat's outstretched legs on the floor beside Maren as I move into the cramped space, unbuttoning my flight jacket and tossing it onto the pile.

"Riders get offended by the weirdest things." Cat arches a dark brow and flips through Markham's history textbook. "We have far bigger issues than tables."

"True." Maren nods, plaiting her dark-brown hair into a four-strand braid.

"How was patrol, anyway?" Sawyer scoots to a more upright position without any help.

"Quiet," Ridoc answers. "I'm starting to think we've gotten them all."

"Or they've managed to flee," Sawyer muses, the light fading from his eyes. "You'll be chasing them down soon."

"Not until we graduate." Rhi crosses her legs. "They're not sending cadets beyond the borders."

"Except Violet, of course, who will be off seeking the seventh breed so we can win this war." Ridoc glances my way with a shit-eating grin. "Don't worry, I'll keep her safe."

I can't quite tell if he's teasing or serious.

Cat snorts and flips another page. "Like they're going to let you go? Guarantee it'll be officers only."

"No way." Ridoc shakes his head. "It's her dragon, her rules. Right, Vi?"

Every head turns in my direction. "Assuming they put us on orders, I'll provide a list of people I trust to go." A list that's been through so many drafts, I'm not even sure I'm carrying the right one.

"You should take the squad," Sawyer suggests. "We work best as a team." He scoffs. "Who am I kidding. You'll work best as a team. I'm barely climbing stairs." He nods to the crutches beside his bed.

"You're still on the team. Hydrate." Rhi reaches across the bedside table and over a note that looks to be in Jesinia's handwriting to grab a pewter mug.

"Water's not going to grow my leg back." Sawyer takes it, and the metal handle hisses, forming to his grip. He looks up at me. "I know that's a shitty thing to say after you lost your mother—"

"Pain isn't a competition," I assure him. "There's always enough to go around."

He sighs. "I got a visit from Colonel Chandlyr."

My stomach hollows. "The commander of the retired riders?"

Sawyer nods.

"What?" Ridoc folds his arms. "Second-years don't retire. Die? Yes. Retire? No."

"I get that," Sawyer starts. "I just—"

A shrill scream echoes throughout the infirmary in a knee-wavering pitch that's reserved for something far worse than pain—terror. The silence that follows chills me to the bone, apprehension lifting the hair on the back of my neck as I unsheathe two of my daggers and turn to face the threat.

"What was that?" Ridoc slides off Sawyer's bed, and the others move behind me as I step outside the bay and pivot toward the open infirmary doors.

"She's dead!" A cadet in infantry blue stumbles in and falls to his hands and knees. "They're *all* dead!"

There's no mistaking the gray handprint marking the side of his neck. *Venin.*

My heart seizes. We haven't found them out on patrol—because they're already *inside*.

The rarest of signets—those that rise once in a generation or century—have manifested concurrently with an equal twice in our records, both critical times in our history, but only once have the six most powerful walked the Continent simultaneously. As fascinating as that spectacle must have been, I would rather not live to see it happen again.

—A Study on Signets by Major Dalton Sisneros

CHAPTER TWO

"*They're within the walls!*" Tairn bellows.

"*Already figured that out.*" I swap my daggers for two alloy-hilted ones at my thighs and move quickly to hand one to Sawyer. "None of us die today."

He nods, taking the blade by the hilt.

"Maren, protect Sawyer," Rhiannon orders. "Cat, help whoever you can. Let's go!"

"Guess I'll just...stay here?" Sawyer calls after us, muttering a swear word as we take off sprinting between the rows of infirmary beds.

We're the first to make it to the doors, where Winifred holds the wailing infantry cadet by his upper arms. "Violet, don't go out there—" she starts.

"Lock the doors!" I shout as we run through.

"Like that's going to stop them?" Ridoc challenges as we enter the tunnel, then all three of us skid to a halt at the sight before us.

The blankets on every overflow bed down the hallway have been thrown back, revealing desiccated bodies. My stomach plummets. How did this happen so fast?

"Oh shit." Ridoc draws another dagger at my right as two more riders sprint through the infirmary doors behind us, both from Second Wing.

I reach for Xaden and find his shields not only up but impenetrable.

Frustrating, but fine. I'm perfectly capable of fighting on my own, and I have Ridoc and Rhi with me.

"You do not have a conduit," Tairn reminds me. Which means I can't pinpoint my lightning strikes, especially not indoors.

"I've always been far more accurate with daggers than my own power. Warn whoever's riders guard the wardstone."

"Already done," he replies.

"Check the bridge!" Rhiannon commands the two from Second Wing, and they take off toward the Riders Quadrant.

"Bring their bodies outside once you're done killing them so we can roast them for fun," Andarna suggests.

"Not right now." I calm my breath and concentrate.

"Eyes open," Rhiannon says, her voice as steady as her hand as she pulls an alloy-hilted dagger and moves to my left. "Let's go."

Then we move as one, quiet and quick as we make our way down the hall. I keep my eyes forward as Rhi and Ridoc check left and right respectively, and their silence tells me all I need to know. There are no survivors.

We follow the curve of the tunnel, passing the last cot, and a scribe flies out of the stairwell ahead, his robes billowing behind him as he runs toward us at full speed.

I flip the dagger in my hand and pinch it by the tip, my heart starting to beat double-time.

"Which way did they go?" Rhi asks the cadet.

The scribe's hood falls back, revealing red-rimmed eyes with spiderwebbed veins at his temples. Nope, definitely *not* a cadet. He reaches beneath his robes, but I've already flicked my wrist by the time he grabs the pommel of a sword.

My dagger lodges in the left side of his chest, and his eyes bulge in shock as he falls gracelessly to the tunnel floor. His body shrivels in the span of a heartbeat.

"Damn. Sometimes I forget how good you are at that," Rhi whispers, scanning our surroundings as we move forward.

"How did you know?" Ridoc asks in the same hushed tone, quickly kicking the husk of a body over and retrieving my blade.

"A scribe would have run toward the Archives." I take the blade back and wrap my hand around the hilt. "Thanks." The alloy's hum of power is a little dimmer but still there, hopefully capable of another killing blow. How many of them had Imogen and I seen on our walk to the infirmary without even realizing? "That's how they fed without notice. They're dressed as scribes."

Two figures in cream robes approach from the opposite side of the tunnel, mage light shining on their first-year rank, and I prepare to throw again.

"Drop the hoods," Rhi orders.

They both startle, and the cadet on the right lowers her hood quickly, but there's a slight tremble in her counterpart's hands as she complies, her wide blue eyes locked on the body at my feet. "Is that…" she whispers, and her friend wraps an arm around her swaying frame.

"Yes." I lower my blade, noting that neither of them carry red in their eyes or at their temples. "Get back to the Archives and warn the others."

The women turn and run.

"Up or down?" Ridoc asks, facing the steps.

Someone shouts beneath us.

"Down," Rhi and I say simultaneously.

"Great." Ridoc rolls his neck. "Down the stairwell to the torture chamber where an untold number of freshly fed dark wielders wait. Good times." He takes the lead, switching his dagger to his left hand and lifting his right in preparation to wield as Rhiannon steps in behind me.

We edge down the stairs rapidly, keeping our backs to the stone wall, and I send up a silent thanks to Eran Norris for building Basgiath with stone stairs instead of wooden ones with the potential to creak…or burn.

"Pay attention to the present, not the past," Tairn lectures.

Metal clangs beneath us, the pitch varying from the *ting* of colliding blades to the ear-grating rasp of steel scraping against stone. But it's the maniacal laughter mixed with grunts of pain that has me hurrying faster, has power rising, crackling along my skin.

"Control it!" Tairn orders.

"Quiet time," I remind him, throwing my shields up to block him, knowing he can still push through if he wants.

"Stop playing with your kill and help us get this door open!" someone demands from below. If they want a cell door open, they're definitely *not* on our side. They've come for Jack.

"How many guards are on Barlowe?" Ridoc whispers as we near the turn in the staircase that will expose us to whomever waits beneath.

"Two—" Rhiannon's answer is quickly muffled by the sound of a low and painful scream.

"Make that one," I reply, readying my right hand to throw.

The antechamber of the brig comes into view, and my gaze flies over the all-too-familiar space, taking quick stock of our situation.

Two dark wielders dressed in scribe robes yank at the unmoving door handle to Jack's cell, while a female pulls her ruby-hilted sword across the neck of a second lieutenant who's been pinned to the thick table with daggers through his hands, and a fourth stands at the edge of the shadows.

Her long silver braid swings free of her hood as her attention whips in our direction, and her eerie red gaze jumps to mine and widens slightly under a faded tattoo on her forehead. My blood chills when a smirk tilts her mouth, distorting the red veins at her temples, and then she...disappears.

I blink against the sudden breeze that rustles a loosened strand of my braid, then stare at the empty space she'd occupied. At least I think she had. Am I seeing things now?

Rhi gasps behind me, and my focus jolts to the imprisoned guard. Blood floods the table from the rider's wound, and I swallow back the burn of acid in my throat, catching sight of two corpses to the left, one in cream, the other in black.

The female with the jeweled sword at the table pivots, her short blond hair smacking her sharp cheekbones as she turns in our direction, revealing branches of red veins at her temples.

I flick my wrist just in case this one disappears, too.

"Riders—" Her alarm dies with my blade lodged in the middle of her throat.

Ridoc rushes the two at the door, but they're ready, one drawing a sword that Ridoc blocks with a thick band of ice.

I throw my remaining dagger at the other as I jump the last two steps, but the dark-haired venin moves unnaturally fast, dodging the strike. My blade bounces off the stone wall behind him as I run toward the rider bleeding out on the table.

Fuck!

Rhi leaps over the female's body, headed for Ridoc, and I continue on, keeping an eye on the one I missed.

The venin swings his arm, and a shape flies toward me.

"Drop, Vi!" Ridoc shouts, throwing his hand out, palm down, and a chill sweeps over the front of my legs as spikes rush at my face.

I hit my knees and slide along a small sheet of ice as the mace whips over my head, slicing through the air with a whistle.

"Not the silver hair!" the dark wielder with the sword bellows, and I scramble to my feet, slipping on the blood-covered stone. "We need her!"

To control Xaden? Fuck that. I'll never be used against him again.

"Mine, now!" Rhi shouts, and when I glance left, she's swinging the mace at its previous owner, giving me time to get to the twitching rider on the table.

"Hold on," I tell him, reaching for his throat to staunch the bleeding, but I pause as his last breath rattles his chest and he falls limp. He's gone. My heart clenches for all of a beat before I draw two more daggers and turn toward my friends.

The black-haired venin moves in a blur, ducking beneath the mace Rhiannon swings, then appears before me like he'd been standing there all along.

Fast. They're too damned *fast*.

My heart jolts as I jerk my dagger to his throat, and he studies me with sickening excitement in his red eyes. Power floods my veins, heating my skin and lifting the hair along my arms.

"Ah, the lightning wielder. You're a long way from the sky, and we both know you can't kill me with that knife," he taunts, and the veins along his temples *pulse* as Rhi sneaks up behind him, her alloy-hilted dagger poised to strike.

Shadows quake at the edges of the chamber, and a corner of my mouth rises. "I won't have to."

His eyes flare in confusion for all of a millisecond before shadows explode around us, immediately devouring every speck of light in a sea of endless black I instantly recognize as *home*. A band of darkness wraps around my hips and yanks me backward, then brushes my cheek gently, steadying my galloping heartbeat and quieting my power.

Screams fill the chamber, followed by a pair of thuds, and I know without a doubt any threat to my life's been extinguished.

A heartbeat later, the shadows retreat, revealing the shriveled bodies of the dark wielders on the floor, alloy-hilted daggers embedded in their chests.

I lower my weapons as Xaden strides toward me from the center of the room, the hilts of the two swords he keeps strapped to his back peeking above his shoulders. He's in thick winter flight leathers, devoid of any markings but his second lieutenant rank, and speckled with tiny dots of water that tell me he's been out in the snow.

Second lieutenant. The same rank as Barlowe's guards had been.

The same as Garrick, who's standing at the base of the steps behind Xaden, and almost every other officer temporarily stationed here to protect Basgiath.

My heart stutters and my gaze rakes over Xaden's tall, muscled frame, searching for any sign of injury. Gold-flecked onyx eyes meet mine, and my breath stabilizes only when I realize he's unharmed and there isn't a single trace of red to be found anywhere near his irises. He may technically be an initiate, but he's nothing like the venin we just fought.

Gods, I love this man.

"Tell me something, Violence." A muscle in his square jaw ticks as he stares down at me, rippling the tawny-brown skin of his stubbled cheek. "Why is it always you?"

• • •

An hour later, we're dismissed from the debrief with the commandant of the Riders Quadrant, Colonel Panchek, and sent on our way.

"He doesn't even seemed fazed that they were working to *rescue* Barlowe instead of going for the wardstone." Garrick shoves his hand through his short dark hair as he descends the staircase of the academic wing ahead of Xaden and me.

"Maybe it's not the first attempt." Rhi glances back over her shoulder at Garrick. "It's not like we're getting briefed every day."

We aren't safe here, not that we ever really were.

"Panchek'll notify the other leadership, right?" Ridoc asks as we pass the third floor.

"Melgren already knows. There were only two of us down there." Xaden glances pointedly at Garrick's hand, where his rebellion relic peeks out from the sleeve of his uniform.

"I'm just grateful for the wards Sorrengail put in place before she left." Garrick doesn't bother to clarify that he's talking about my sister. "Barlowe can't hear or see a thing outside that chamber unless someone opens the door, so it's not like he's gathering new intel. From the look of the stones he's drained within the cell, he'll be dead within the week."

Xaden tenses at my side and I reach for him mentally, but his shields are thicker than the walls of this fortress.

"It's not *always* me," I whisper to Xaden, brushing my hand against his as we continue down the wide spiral staircase, approaching the second floor.

Xaden scoffs, then laces his fingers with mine and brings the back of my hand to his perfectly sculpted mouth. "It is," he replies just as quietly, punctuating the remark with a kiss.

My pulse jumps just like it does every time he puts his lips on my skin, which hasn't happened much in the last couple of weeks.

"You know, that whole slay-them-in-darkness thing was badass" — Ridoc lifts his finger — "but I totally had him."

"You didn't." Xaden strokes his thumb over mine, and Garrick's shoulders shake with a quiet laugh as we descend the final flight of steps to the main entrance.

"I was *about* to have him," Ridoc argues, shaking that finger.

"You weren't," Xaden assures him.

"How could you possibly know that?" Ridoc drops his hand.

Garrick and Xaden exchange a look of sheer exasperation, and I fight a smile.

"Because you were on one side of the room," Garrick says, "but your blade was on the other."

"A problem I was in the middle of solving." Ridoc shrugs, reaching the ground floor with Rhi.

Xaden pauses, tugging my hand in wordless request that I stay with him, which I do.

"We should check on the others." Rhi glances up at me. "You headed to the great hall?"

I nod, and nerves jumble in my stomach.

"You're ready. You've got this," she says with a flash of a smile. "Want us to walk you over?"

"No. Go check on the squad," I reply, and Garrick stills a step beneath us. "I'll find you afterward."

"We'll be waiting," Ridoc promises over his shoulder as he heads to the left with Rhi, disappearing around the corner.

"Everything all right?" Garrick turns our way and studies Xaden's eyes.

"It will be if you give us five minutes alone," Xaden answers.

Concern knits Garrick's brow as he glances at me, but he quickly smooths his expression when I nod.

"For fuck's sake. You trust her to babysit me at night, don't you?" Xaden narrows his eyes on his best friend.

"Don't act like *I'm* the reason you need to be supervised," Garrick fires back.

Shadows creep across the step at our feet.

"It's fine," I quickly assure Garrick, keeping my hand entwined with Xaden's much larger one. "I'm fine. He's fine. *All* fine."

Garrick glances between us, then pivots and moves down the steps. "I'll be close by," he warns, turning the corner to the right, toward the sparring gym.

"Damn it." Xaden pulls his hand from mine, then leans back against the wall, his swords clinking against the masonry. His jacket falls open as he rests his head on the stone window frame. "I never realized how much I like alone time until I didn't have any." His throat works and his hands clench at his sides.

"I'm sorry." I cross the foot of space between us, stepping between his feet and lifting my hand to the side of his neck, right over the magically inked lines of his mark.

"Don't be. He has every right to worry about leaving me alone with you." He covers my hand with his own and lowers his head, slowly opening those eyes I can never get enough of.

"I trust you." *Not a trace of red to be seen.*

"You shouldn't." He wraps his arm around my waist and tugs me against his body. The contact instantly heats my skin and makes my stomach flip in the best possible way. "I'm pretty fucking sure the only reason he and Bodhi aren't sleeping at the foot of our bed is that they know I would have killed them for it before, let alone now."

Not that we're doing anything in that bed besides sleeping. I might trust him, but he sure as Dunne doesn't trust himself, at least not enough to let go of control in any form.

"In the spirit of transparency, I should tell you they'd like me to reconsider our sleeping arrangements." I splay my other hand over his warm chest.

His eyes flare, and his arm tightens around me. "Maybe you should."

"That's not happening. I told Imogen to get fucked."

A smile ghosts his mouth. "I'm sure you did."

"They'll stop hovering as soon as you're cured." My gaze skims the carved line of his jaw, then along the rise of his cheekbones to the locks of his black hair that have fallen over his forehead. He's still him. Still mine.

His muscles tense beneath my fingers. "You ready to meet with the Senarium?"

"Yes." I nod. "And don't change the subject. I will find a way to cure you." I put every ounce of my determination into the words and lift my eyebrows at him. "Let me in." It isn't a request. To my surprise, he lowers his shields, and the shimmering onyx bond between us solidifies. *"You wielded your signet today. Behind the wards."*

He nods, dropping his hand from mine and fully wrapping his arms around me. *"I channeled from Sgaeyl."*

I savor the feel of his body against mine but don't push my luck for a kiss. *"Did she tell you we were in trouble?"*

His gaze falls away and he shakes his head. *"She's still not speaking to me. Flying is awkward as fuck."*

My chest threatens to crack under the weight of the sadness in his tone. *"I'm so sorry."* I slide my hands around the small of his back and hug him, turning my head so his heart beats beneath my ear. *"She'll come around."*

"Don't count on it," Tairn warns with a growl down the mental pathway that only belongs to us, and I blatantly ignore him.

Xaden lowers his chin to the top of my head. *"She knows I'm not...whole. She senses it."*

I startle and pull back, lifting my hands to hold his face. "You're whole," I whisper. *"I don't know what you paid to access that power, but it didn't change you—"*

"It did," he counters, sidestepping down a stair and out of my arms.

I can only think of one way to prove it didn't. "Do you still love me?" I hurl the inquiry at him like a weapon.

His gaze snaps to mine. "What kind of question is that?"

"Do. You. Still. Love. Me?" I enunciate every word and lean right into his space just to prove that I'm not intimidated by him.

He cups the back of my neck and pulls me within inches of his face—close enough to kiss. *"I could reach the rank of Maven, lead armies of dark wielders against everyone we care for, and watch every vein in my body turn red as I channel all the power in the Continent, and I would still love you. What I did doesn't change that. I'm not sure anything can."*

"See? You're still you." My gaze drops to his mouth. "Telling me you're capable of horrible things while still loving me is pretty much your idea of foreplay."

His eyes darken, and he hauls me closer until only his own obstinance separates our lips. "That should scare the shit out of you, Violet."

"It doesn't." I rise on my toes and brush my lips over his. "Nothing about you scares me. I won't run, Xaden."

"Damn it." He drops his hand and retreats a step, putting space between us again. *"With my shields up, I didn't know you were in the interrogation chamber until I was halfway down the stairs."*

"What?" I blink. "Then how did you know to come help?"

Silence stretches between us, and a prickle of apprehension makes me shift my weight, aggravating my lower back.

"I sensed them," he finally answers. *"The same way they sense me."*

My stomach pitches, and I reach for the wall, splaying my palm over the rough-hewn stone to keep my balance. "That's not possible."

"It is." He nods slowly, watching me. *"That's how I know I've changed, how Garrick and I have managed to slay more than a dozen of them this week. I can feel them calling to me, just like I can feel the source pulsing beneath my feet with its incomparable power…because I'm one of them."* His eyes narrow. "Scared yet?"

Sometimes I worry about Violet. She has your sharp wit, quick mind, and steadfast heart paired with my bullheaded tenacity. When she finally and truly gives that heart, I fear it will overrule the other gifts you've given her and logic will cede its voice to love.
And if her first two liaisons are any indication of what we might expect... Gods help her, my love, I'm afraid our daughter has atrocious taste in men.

—RECOVERED, UNSENT CORRESPONDENCE OF GENERAL LILITH SORRENGAIL

CHAPTER THREE

Xaden can *sense* them.

My fingernails bend slightly when my hand flexes along the grout line, holding on for dear life as my mind spins. But just because he can sense them doesn't mean he gave up part of his soul, right? It's there in his eyes, watching me, waiting for me to reject him, or worse, push him away like I did after Resson.

Maybe it's more dire than I thought, but he's still whole, still him. Just with... heightened senses.

I shove my stomach right back where it belongs and hold his stare. "Scared of you?" I shake my head. "Never."

"You will be," he whispers, looking over my features like he needs to memorize them.

"Your five minutes are up," Garrick says from the base of the steps. "And Violet has a meeting to get to."

Xaden's expression shifts into something dangerous as he glares at his best friend and leans away from me.

"She told you we think you should sleep somewhere else, didn't she?" Garrick rolls his neck like he's preparing for a fight.

"She did." Xaden starts down the steps, and I follow. "And I'll tell you the same thing she said to Imogen. Get fucked."

"Figured." Garrick turns a pleading look on me, and I smile back as we walk out of the academic wing and into the surprisingly empty rotunda, crossing between two dragon pillars. "Thought you'd at least be logical, Violet."

"Me? You're the ones acting based on feelings and with no evidence whatsoever. My decision to trust him is based purely on the facts of our proven history."

"As much as I appreciate the concern," Xaden drawls, his voice edging on icy, "you try to dictate the occupants of Violet's bed again, and we're going to have problems."

Garrick shakes his head at his best friend but drops the subject as we make our way to main campus, passing through the chaotic cleanup near the infirmary.

The death roll in the Infantry Quadrant will be painfully long tomorrow.

"For someone who's about to face the highest-ranking aristocracy in the kingdom, you seem pretty calm, Sorrengail," Garrick remarks as we cross onto the thick red carpet of the administration building.

The hallway is cramped with people in tunics of various colors waiting for talks to resume, identified only by the heraldry embroidered on cross-body sashes that remind me of our dress uniforms. Our own provinces are easy to recognize, and I even spot Braevick's as heads begin to turn in our direction.

"I've known this was coming and have a plan. Two weeks is a lot of time to overthink every possible scenario," I reply as the crowd slowly parts to the side of the hall in what I've come to think of as the Xaden effect. I can't blame them for staring. He's gorgeous. I can't blame them for backing up, either. He's not only terrifyingly powerful, he's known to be responsible for splitting Navarre's riot and providing weapons to Poromiel.

Safe to say not every gaze trained on him—on any of the three of us—is friendly.

"You're sure this is what you want?" Xaden asks as we approach the massive double doors of the great hall.

"It's what she wants," I tell him, and one of the guards adorned with the crest of Calldyr slips into the hall, no doubt to announce our arrival. *"And it's what we need. You still up for coming with?"* I glance at him. *"Even beyond the wards?"*

The magical barrier is doing more than protecting us from him—it's protecting him from himself.

His jaw flexes. *"Even beyond the wards,"* he confirms as we reach the doors and the remaining stone-faced guard in infantry blue.

"I assume you're expecting me?" I ask the guard.

"You will wait to be escorted, Cadet Sorrengail," she replies without looking my way.

Pleasant.

"I'm starting to think twice about this meeting," Garrick says from Xaden's other side, his gaze scanning the heavily armed crowd in the hallway. "She's been invited to appear before the Senarium alone, and we haven't exactly been pardoned for leaving Basgiath and taking a large portion of the riot. Brennan might be sitting in on the treaty negotiations on behalf of Aretia, but we don't have a seat on the council. Anything could happen to Violet in there."

"Already thought about that," I assure him. "They need me alive for Andarna's sake if not Tairn's. I'll be fine."

"She has Lewellen in there representing Tyrrendor and can set the whole damned place on fire with a wave of her hand," Xaden adds, folding his arms and glowering at the guard. "I'm more concerned for their safety than hers."

The door on the right opens, and the other guard walks through.

My stomach twists when General Melgren appears in the doorway, his beady eyes narrowing as he looks down his beak of a nose at me. "Cadet Sorrengail, the Senarium is ready to receive you." His gaze darts to Garrick, then Xaden. "Alone."

"I'll be right out here" — Xaden's tone slips into menace — "deterred by these wooden doors that hang an inch off the ground."

"Subtle." I fight the tug at the corner of my mouth.

Melgren gestures me inside but doesn't take his eyes off Xaden.

"Never going to be," he replies as I walk into the hall. *"I have every faith in your ability to protect yourself, but say the word and I'll rip the doors off their hinges."*

"You're such a romantic." I quickly take in the new furniture arrangement of the familiar room, finding a long trestle table running the length of the hall with dozens of chairs, no doubt to accommodate the negotiations. Six nobles dressed in lushly embroidered tunics and gowns sit facing me at the closest end, representing each of Navarre's six provinces. I know them all thanks to my mother, but only the one on the far left offers me a tired smile as I approach the center of their grouping and place my hands on the back of the chair.

Lewellen.

"Any last-minute additions?" I ask Andarna as Melgren walks around the table and sits to the right of the Duchess of Morraine.

"Nothing that comes to mind," she responds.

Here we go.

"Let's make this quick," the Duchess of Morraine snaps in a high-pitched voice from the right, a giant ruby jostling along her collarbone when she heaves a sigh. "We have three days to save these negotiations and need every hour of it."

"I couldn't agree more — " I start.

"We've been briefed by General Melgren and conferred with the king," the Duke of Calldyr interrupts directly across from me, stroking his short blond beard. "As of this moment, you will be assigned to a—" He glances at Melgren. "What did you call it?"

"A task force," Melgren supplies, sitting eerily still as he studies me.

"Task force," the duke repeats. "Which will embark on a quest to find and recruit the seventh dragon breed with an aim to increase our numbers and hopefully provide insight into killing the venin."

I reach into the pocket of my uniform and pull out two folded pieces of parchment. I hold up the first. "Should we agree to participate, this is a list of Andarna's demands."

The Duchess of Elsum raises her dark brows, and the Duke of Luceras recoils.

"You are not in a place to make demands," the Duchess of Morraine admonishes. "While we owe your mother a debt of gratitude, you are still considered a deserter."

"A deserter who saved this college, our wards, and our kingdom, not to mention took on *multiple* venin within these walls a few hours ago, all of which I've done without falling under Navarrian chain of command." I tilt my head. "Makes it hard to assign me to anything, as none of you commands the Aretian riot. And they're not my demands, they're *hers*."

"The return of *our* riot is a matter still in negotiation." Melgren glances down the table at Lewellen. "This assignment is being made in good faith, with the understanding that the riot will remain at Basgiath. Lewellen, seeing as you've secretly represented Aretia for years—which is a separate issue this council has yet to address—perhaps you'd be willing to read *her* demands."

The rebuke has most of the aristocrats shifting in their seats.

Lewellen holds out his hand, and I give him the folded list. Step one, complete. A smile tugs at the corners of his lined mouth as he reads. "Some of these are quite…unique."

"As is she," I reply, launching into step two. "I will take six riders—"

"*You* will take no one," Melgren interrupts. "*You* are a second-year cadet who will only be allowed to participate because we need your dragon. It has already been decided that Captain Grady will lead the task force, due largely to his experience behind enemy lines."

My stomach sinks. "My RSC professor?" No, no, no, this is *not* how this was supposed to go. I grasp the list that has Mira's name inked at the top.

"The same." Melgren nods. "He's been made aware, and you can expect to hear from him once we've settled the Poromish alliance and its requirements and he's configured the squad of his choosing."

His choosing. Power rises within me, simmering in my blood. "Which will at least include Lieutenant Riorson, correct?"

The aristocrats all look to Melgren.

"Riorson's involvement will be at Grady's discretion." Melgren stares back at me, unflinching.

"Tairn and Sgaeyl can't be separated," I argue.

"Which would suggest Riorson will be among his selections," Melgren states with about as much emotion as a tree. No wonder Mom liked him so much. "But again, it's at the captain's discretion."

Captain's discretion. My blood *hums.* "Determining the members of the squad is one of Andarna's demands." In every scenario I'd thought through, Andarna's compliance had always been the card I'd mentally played.

"Then it's one that won't be met." Melgren folds his hands in his lap. "It's a nonnegotiable military operation, not a class field trip."

"We won't go," Tairn states.

"We have to go!" Andarna argues, her voice rising.

The parchment crumples in my hand. *"She's right. We have to go."* Andarna deserves this, first and foremost. But if there's any chance they know how to defeat the venin or how to cure Xaden, then we truly have no choice. *"Every possible path."* Which means we have to give.

"Shall we consider the matter settled?" the Duke of Calldyr asks.

Absolutely the fuck not.

"It is," Melgren states.

"Only if you meet the rest of Andarna's demands." I lift my chin. "I think both she and Tairn have shown they're more than willing to walk—if not fly—away from Basgiath."

Melgren's nostrils flare, and I bite back a crow of victory. "We will consider approving her other requests."

"Then it's settled," the Duke of Calldyr announces. "Excellent. This development should help smooth negotiations."

"At least letting the fliers *enter* the quadrant would help," I add, frustration burning in my chest.

"When they can't even wield to protect themselves?" Melgren scoffs. "The riders will eat them alive."

"Isn't that one of Poromiel's arguments against leaving those additional forces with us?" the Duchess of Morraine asks, and Melgren nods.

They aren't *forces.* They're cadets in need of the protection of the wards.

The duke scratches his neck. "We'll think on it. The fliers handling themselves in the quadrant would go a long way toward smoothing that negotiation point."

My thoughts exactly.

"You're dismissed, cadet," Melgren orders.

"I'll walk you out," Lewellen says, pushing away from the table and rising to his feet.

I slip the mangled list into my pocket and cross the cobblestones to the door, trying to pick up the pieces of my shattered expectations. There's no telling if we'll be able to trust whoever Grady selects for the squad.

"I'll work on these," Lewellen says quietly, raising the list of Andarna's demands. "And in the meantime"—he reaches into his tunic and retrieves a palm-size missive—"I was asked to give you this privately."

"Thank you," I respond out of habit, taking the parchment.

He knocks twice on the door, and I depart through the one the guard gestures me through on the left.

Opening the missive, I walk into the hall, recognizing Tecarus's sprawling handwriting.

You have three days to hold up your end of our bargain.

Fuck. That's not an option. I look up and find every member of my squad waiting, a wall of black and brown holding back a sea of colorful tunics and gowns.

"How did it go?" Imogen asks.

"Give her a second," Rhi lectures.

My gaze sweeps over them as the door shuts behind me, and then I lock eyes with Xaden, who is crossing the distance between us. "The plan went to shit."

Which means the one I'm holding in my hand can't fail.

• • •

Morning light pours in through my window, and I slowly blink awake to the sound of the campus bells chiming eight times. Snow sits stacked on the sill, but the skies beyond are blue for the first time since solstice.

Holy shit, I didn't just sleep, I slept *in*. Maybe it was hitting the gym last night with Imogen, or the emotional letdown after I'd vented with Rhi and Tara about why Grady was the worst possible choice to lead Andarna's mission, but I didn't wake once, thank gods. I must have drifted off after settling into bed with the book on Navarrian imports predating the Trade Agreement of Resson that Jesinia had tossed at me when I'd shown up to visit Sawyer, still seething. Lifting my head from the pillow, I spot the closed book on my nightstand, my page marked by one of Xaden's daggers.

A slow smile curves my mouth at his thoughtfulness. Guess I'd been asleep by the time he made it to bed after his daily meeting with Brennan, Lewellen, and, as of yesterday afternoon, Duke Lindell, who fostered Xaden and Liam.

I turn under the warmth of the blankets, fully expecting to find Xaden wide awake given the hour, but he's fast asleep with one arm curled around his pillow and the other with its freshly pink scar lying on the blanket between us. My heart clenches, and staring seems the only logical action, if only for just a few moments. Gods, is he beautiful. His face is softened in sleep, and all the tension he usually carries in his jaw, his shoulders, is strikingly absent. The last week has been hard on him, being constantly torn between his duties as a rider and navigating the responsibility he carries for Aretia in a space that doesn't recognize it. I fight the urge to touch him. He's slept like shit since the battle, too, and if he can get even just another few minutes, he should have it.

As slowly and silently as possible, I scoot toward my side of the bed and sit up, letting my feet dangle just above the floor. My hair is still partly damp from braiding it right after my bath last night, and I make quick, quiet work of running my brush through it so it has a prayer of drying before it's time to head out into the cold. Once I set the brush back on the nightstand, I stretch with a speed a sloth would be proud of—

A band of shadow wraps around my waist a second before my hair is swept to the side and Xaden sets his lips to the juncture of my neck and shoulder in an open-mouthed kiss.

Oh, *yes*.

I gasp as an immediate flare of heat races down my spine at the lash of his tongue, the scrape of his teeth, and my head falls back against his shoulder. He moves straight to the hypersensitive spot at the side of my neck like my body is a map only he has the key to, and I spear my fingers into his hair as my back arches. Damn, he knows exactly how to take me from the ground to sky-fucking-high in less than a handful of heartbeats.

"Mine," he growls against my skin, and his hand skims the hemline of my nightdress before dragging it up my thigh.

"Mine," I counter, tightening my grip in his hair.

He laughs into my neck, the sound low and intoxicating as his hand crosses over the juncture of my thighs, then grabs hold of my hip and tugs.

My fingers slip from his hair, and the room spins before my back hits the center of the bed. Then he's all I see, rising above me with a wicked smile in nothing but loose sleeping pants, sliding his hard thigh between mine. "Yours," he says like a promise, and my breath catches at the intensity in his eyes.

Gods, it feels like my chest is going to crack open when he looks at me like that.

"I love you so much it hurts." I slide my hands down the warm, bare skin of his chest, my fingertips ghosting the scar over his heart and down to the rigid lines of his stomach.

He draws a sharp breath through his teeth. "Good, because that's exactly how I love you, too." His thigh moves between mine with exquisite friction, and then he's *all* over me, erasing every one of my thoughts except how I can get him closer.

His hands stroke every curve, and his mouth caresses every inch of skin down to my neckline. Need races through my veins like flame, igniting every nerve ending, then flaring bright as his teeth graze the tip of my breast through the fabric of my nightdress.

I whimper and lace my fingers behind his neck. *Holy shit* do I need this man.

"That's one of my favorite sounds." His words wrap around my mind as his hand glides up my thigh, slipping under my nightdress to toy with the line of my underwear, and I fucking melt. *"Second only to those little gasps you make in the moments before you come."*

His knuckles brush over my clit through the infuriating layer of fabric between us, and my hips rock as his mouth moves to my other breast. There are too many damned clothes between us.

He lifts his head to watch me as his fingers dip beneath the barrier of my underwear. Then he's *right* there, stroking and teasing, slipping over my clit, and finally, thank-fucking-gods, giving me the exact pressure I need.

"Xaden," I moan, and my head thrashes on the pillow as power whips through me, racing down every bone, every vein, every inch of my skin.

"Changed my mind." He slides two fingers inside me. *"That's my favorite sound."* His fingers stroke deep, then curl upward as he withdraws just enough.

My breath hitches, and a corner of his mouth rises into a smirk that has my walls clenching around his talented fingers. Power hums, spiraling into a tight coil within me, and my hands slip to clutch his shoulders, pressing into his rebellion relic.

"How do you want me to take you, Violet?" His brow furrows as he adds his thumb against my clit, and the energy gathering within me vibrates. *"Here on your back with me above you? Before me on your hands and knees with your ass in the air? Against the wall so I can drive harder? Astride so you can control the pace? Tell me."*

Control? That's only an illusion when it comes to being with him. The second he touches me, I'm his to do with however he wants.

"All of it." I'm on fire in the sweetest way possible, and his words fan the flames. I don't care how he gets inside me, I only care that it's right. Fucking. Now.

His eyes flare. "I can feel it. I can feel *you*." He stares for a second longer, then lowers his head to mine, hovering an inch or two above my lips, and quickens the pace of his fingers, winding me so tight I know the only way I'll survive it is to shatter. "Bright and hot and fucking perfect."

And I want all of him, his cock, not just his fingers. I can feel just how hard he is against my thigh, and I need him moving within me, with me, unraveling, wild and unhinged. I just can't find those words, not when he's set on making me speechless.

I grasp for the shimmering onyx that connects our minds and pour my pure, acute need into it as my breath comes faster and faster.

"Violet," he groans, and lines etch between his brow as his jaw flexes, as if he's holding himself back.

Why would he be fighting this? Fighting us? I'm his, but he's mine, too. Doesn't he remember how good we are together? Holding the bond with a viselike grip, I recall the armoire cracking against my back, the sublime feel of him pounding into me, hard and so damned deep, both of us lost in the other, breathing the same heated air, living for nothing but the peak of the next thrust.

The power coiled within me starts to *burn*, flushing my skin and threatening to incinerate everything I am if I don't let it go. Gods, how it would feel to have that soft brush of his shadows all over my skin, enveloping me with a thousand caresses as he—

His forehead falls against mine, and he trembles, sweat beading on his forehead. "Fuck, *love.*"

There's something about hearing that guttural groan, all rasp and desperation, that hurtles me over the edge with the next stroke of his fingers. I try to hold it close, but power snaps, and light flashes to my left as I shatter. Shadow floods the space for a stuttered heartbeat as pleasure crests in waves, pulling me under and dragging me to the surface again and again.

I catch the scent of burned wood, and Xaden whips both his hands to the headboard above me. The torture twisting his face sobers me up in less than a second. He looks like he's in unbearable pain.

"Xaden?" I whisper, reaching for him.

"Don't." It comes out half demand and all plea.

My hands fall to my chest, and when I trip down our bond, it's faded and *sealed* by a wall of chilled onyx. "What's happening?"

"I need space." He bites out the words.

"All right." I get out from under him and scurry off the bed, immediately spotting the scorched crack in the nightstand. At least I'm getting better at not setting the trees on fire. "Is this far enough?"

"Not sure the isle kingdoms would be far enough," he mutters, slowing his breathing.

What the fuck? "I'm sorry?" I watch in utter confusion as he gathers his control, then nods like he's certain of himself again.

"I forgot." He slowly lets go of the headboard and sits back on his heels, gripping his thighs, then letting his hands fall at his sides. "I woke up and saw you sitting there, and it was the most natural thing in the world to reach for you, but I'm not *natural* anymore. Fuck, I'm so sorry, Violet."

Oh. "I forgot, too." The second he put his mouth on me. "You have nothing to apologize for, and don't say you're not natural—" *Wait.* My mouth curves. This is a totally solvable problem. "In fact, I think you just did us a favor." I take a single step toward the bed, and his head snaps in my direction. "Nothing bad happened, Xaden. You just had your hands all over me, inside me, and I'm perfectly fine. Give me two seconds to crawl across this bed, and you'll be gloriously fine, too."

His eyes slide shut, and he gestures to the headboard. "Not fine."

My gaze narrows on the dark wood, and I have to lean in a little to finally see two faint marks of discoloration, barely a shade lighter than the original stain, right where his thumbs had been. I cover my stomach with my hand like that can keep it from sinking.

Did he just channel?

There are two reasons rider cadets are not given the
same summer and winter leave as others:
Firstly, civilians do not react well to dragons
casually roaming their villages.
Secondly, raising tigers for war requires locking their
cages lest they turn on each other…or you.

—SHARPEN THE TALON: A PROFESSOR'S GUIDE
BY COLONEL TISPANY CALTHEA

CHAPTER
FOUR

I shake my head at the two subtle marks.

"That's nothing. It's barely there." And his eyes look exactly the same from this distance. Whatever he did wasn't even close to what had happened during the battle.

"Because I stopped." He climbs off the far side of the bed and retreats until the backs of his thighs hit my desk. "The second your power rose, I felt it and remembered why I'd promised myself I wasn't going to touch you. And I thought, if I could at least take care of you, that would be enough for me, but then I was so fucking close…" He white-knuckles the edge of my desk and brings his gaze to mine. "I can't afford to lose control around you. Not even the edge of it." He glances toward the headboard. "Not like that. Not at all."

My chest aches, and I breathe deeply to slow my racing heart. If he truly channeled… "Can I come over there? I won't touch you."

He nods. "I'm all right now. Firmly under control."

I cross the cold floor in my bare feet and put myself directly in front of him, sighing with relief when I don't find a trace of red in his eyes. "No red."

His shoulders dip. "Good. I locked it down pretty quick and didn't even feel myself taking anything, but I obviously did."

"Sandpaper takes more than you did." I look back at the headboard just to be sure I wasn't imagining things. "I can barely see it, and only because I'm *looking*."

"I took it without thinking. Without choice. And if it had been you?" He tucks my hair behind my ear. "I would never have forgiven myself." He heaves a heavy sigh.

The ache in my chest only sharpens. "Are you going to go all broody and try to pull away from me? Because fair warning, I'm not going to let that happen."

"No." The corners of his mouth rise. "I just think we've been right to steer clear of activities where I can't be trusted to keep control. It's the only way you're safe, and as much as I want you to run, I'm too selfish to give you up."

I nod slowly, since it's not like I'm going to argue with what's obviously his line.

"And just so you know, that memory of yours was *really* fucking hot. I loved every second of it." He swallows and grips both sides of the desk again, like he already regrets his decision.

My brow knits. "I'm not quite sure how I even did it. Is the thought sharing an inntinnsic thing? Or a bond thing? It's happened more than once with us."

A corner of his mouth rises, and his grip relaxes. "No fucking clue. I've never tried it with anyone else." His smirk shifts to a full smile, and I breathe a little easier. "The first time, I was sitting in tactics and couldn't get you out of my damned head. Then you reached out, struggling to wield when you'd all but set the whole campus on fire the night before, and I just let the memory play, partly to help you, but mostly so you'd be in the same hell I was in." There's zero guilt in the admission. "Now let's get dressed. We probably slept through breakfast."

We get ready in relative normalcy considering what just happened. I wrap my knee quickly, going above and below my kneecap to hold it in place, then finish dressing. By the time I slip my armor on over my undershirt, Xaden is there, lacing it on just as efficiently as when he takes it off, though one takes considerably longer than the other. "You were out late last night," I say as he works his way to the tie. "Anything to do with Duke Lindell being here?"

"Yeah." He tugs gently, and my shoulders straighten.

"Makes me glad you're sleeping here," I note, and his fingers still. "All three of the highest Houses of Tyrrendor are here, two of whom are known to hold allegiance only to the province, and the third is suspected." I glance over my shoulder at him. "Was it not Lindell who made sure you and Liam were trained to enter the quadrant?"

Xaden nods. "It was, though Lewellen had a hand in it, too."

My brows rise. "I'm sure it's crossed Melgren's mind that he could wipe the slate clean. There's a lot of chaos in these halls and almost no one of rank to notice." *Be careful.* I say those two words with my eyes.

He nods again, then goes back to situating the corset, and I face forward. "Killing me isn't required to annihilate the Tyrrish aristocracy. Officially, I'm just a lieutenant who has no place in any of the negotiations, and yet I'm supposed to speak for Aretia, according to your brother. All done." He ties the corset strings, then shocks the shit out of me by placing a kiss beneath my ear before he walks to the weapons rack by the door.

"Thanks. Do you want to?" I ask, tugging my uniform top on and buttoning it.

"Sit in on the negotiations?" he asks, shrugging on his back sheaths.

"Speak for Aretia. All of it." I cross the room, starting to braid my hair into its usual coronet on my way to the desk, and he looks at me with an expression I can't read. "You said you were happy with the way things were running, but I don't know if anyone ever…asked you."

His brow furrows. "The Assembly runs Aretia. I just own the house, which is probably a good thing, since I'm…well, venin. Great on the battlefield, but not a good governing quality."

I lock every muscle to keep from flinching, then continue braiding.

"Anyway, we're trying to work out the terms of the riot staying, and Lewellen seems to think he can at least get my father's sword back from Tauri, but it all feels tangled. If we don't stay, Poromiel walks. If Navarre can't protect the fliers here at Basgiath, Poromiel walks. If anyone murders anyone—which happens a lot around here—"

"Poromiel walks," I guess, reaching for the pins on my desk to secure the braid in place, and most *definitely* noticing that he used the term *we*. It's on the tip of my tongue to tell him I'll be actively working on one of those things in the next forty-eight hours, but he doesn't want to know, and losing control a few minutes ago isn't going to help that stance.

"Exactly, and two of the third-year fliers had a run-in with First Wing last night near the great hall that left everyone bloody." He starts sheathing his daggers along his thighs. "If Tauri isn't willing to take civilians, then Poromiel has nothing to gain by promising not to attack our outposts. The only incentives are weapons and keeping the fliers safe."

"Both of which can be achieved by an alliance with only Aretia," I note as Xaden begins putting *my* daggers in place, slipping them into the sheaths at my thighs and the ones sewn into my uniform along my ribs.

"Now who sounds like the separatist?" His mouth quirks. "If we had stable wards, maybe. But we know they're faltering, and even if they weren't, the last time Tyrrendor attempted to secede, it didn't go—" He cocks his head to the side like he's listening, then storms toward the door, whipping it open. "Are you fucking kidding me? Neither of us has even used a bathing chamber yet."

Ah, there's the hard-ass everyone else gets. I don't fight the urge to smile.

There's a huge part of me that likes that I'm the only one who gets his softer edges. "Who is it?" I ask, grabbing my flight jacket off the back of the chair.

"You're in there with *my little sister* and you're asking me if I'm kidding *you*?" Brennan snaps back. "Usually, I consider myself pretty understanding about the fact that you sleep in her bed, and I look the other way when you two attach yourselves at the face, but we have a meeting in thirty minutes and I need to talk to you before then."

"Good morning, Brennan," I call out, slipping my arms into my flight jacket.

"Hey, Violet," he answers.

"I have a patrol," Xaden says.

"He does," Garrick adds from somewhere behind Brennan.

"How many people are out here?" I duck under Xaden's arm, and my brows rise. The hallway is *packed*. Brennan, Garrick, Lewellen, Bodhi, and Imogen are all waiting. The days of negotiation have worn on both Lewellen and Brennan, darkening the circles under Brennan's eyes and thickening the salt-and-pepper stubble on Lewellen's strong jaw, as though he's been too tired or too busy to shave. "Did someone die? Why didn't any of you knock?"

"Because she's mean." Garrick nods toward Imogen, who's leaned up against the wall to my right.

"She needs to fucking sleep." She cocks her head to the side at him. "Given how rested you look, I'm guessing you got *plenty* of that in Nina Shrensour's bed last night. How disappointing for her."

"Damn." Bodhi fights to smother a laugh.

A slow smile spreads across Garrick's face, and a dimple pops in his left cheek. "Careful, Imogen. You sound a little jealous."

"Who the hell would be jealous of a *flier*?" Her pointed glare promises a quick death.

"Right." Brennan rubs the bridge of his nose, and Lewellen walks away, shaking his head. "Look, we just need Riorson."

"Seriously, figure your shit out, kids. We're in the middle of a war," Mira says from the end of the short hallway, her cheeks red and goggle lines still fresh in her skin.

I instantly grin. "You made it!" Thank you, Amari, we have forty-eight hours and a shot.

"I thought you were due back tonight at the earliest." Brennan raises his reddish eyebrows.

"Teine was feeling spry." Mira's smile could cut glass, but at least she's trying. It took her months to let him back in after she found him alive. Who knows how long she'll need to get over losing our mother on what she considers to be Brennan's watch. "I bring news and a few missives."

I need everyone to leave *now* so I can know exactly what that news is.

"Thank you," Brennan says to Mira, then turns to Xaden. "This is more important than patrol."

Xaden's hand skims my lower back as he walks into the hall, then follows Brennan to the main hallway, where Lewellen waits, Garrick close on his heels.

"Anything I should know about?" Bodhi asks, two lines appearing between his brows as Mira slings her pack from her shoulder.

"We're good," Brennan assures him as the foursome turns the corner and disappears.

"Good to feel needed," Bodhi mutters, stepping closer as Mira completes our own huddle. "Guess we'll be taking the patrol, Imogen."

"Did you figure it out?" I ask Mira, unable to take another second.

"First, Felix sent a gift." She retrieves a conduit from her bag and hands it to me with a smile.

"Oh, thank the gods." I sigh with relief as my fingers curl around the metal-rimmed glass orb that gives me a semblance of control over my signet.

"And then there's this." That little spark of hope behind my ribs fans straight into a flame when Mira pulls a wooden, runed practice disk from her satchel. "Trissa's a genius."

My jaw drops. There are three runes tempered into the disk, one for levitation in the middle, then two in overlapping layers for what appear to be sound-shielding and warmth. The outermost line—warmth—is broken by a small green shoot of new growth. "How did you do it?" It's almost impossible to keep my tone down.

"After being nearly blown up and hurled like a projectile"—a smile lifts the corners of her mouth—"we altered the material the rune is tempered into without destroying it, truly changing its form. Turns out Kylynn is an agrarian," Mira says.

"Battle-Ax is a plant wielder?" I whisper.

"You don't have to whisper, Vi." Mira grins. "The sound shield is still active even though we nullified the warmth rune. It should cover us to almost the edge of the hall."

"Are you sure?" I ask.

"I'm sure. It's cool to the touch, and…" Mira places a gold coin over the center of the levitation rune, and it *floats*. Nullifying a rune is mind-blowing. Figuring out how to do it without affecting the others? Incredible. "We've got it. It's not without risk, but we can do it."

My heart starts to pound. "We can save the negotiations." The fliers will stay, and I can keep my deal with Tecarus.

"If they agree," Imogen says slowly, "which you know they won't."

"Incoming," Bodhi announces, tilting his chin toward the hallway. Brennan slowly makes his way toward us, his gaze focused on the floor like he's deep in thought. "We're heading out."

"Don't tell the others yet," Mira rushes, shoving the disk in her pack at her feet. "We have to give the Senarium a chance to do the right thing, and the fewer people who know, the fewer people who are executed for treason."

Bodhi and Imogen both nod, and I blink as they start walking away. "Hey, what did you need? Why were you waiting?" I ask Imogen.

Bodhi crams his hands in his pockets and continues walking, and Imogen glances sideways at Brennan as they pass. "Just wanted to make sure you were… getting some sleep," she calls back as they turn the corner and disappear.

Bodhi. Garrick. Imogen. My stomach tightens. They were checking to make sure Xaden hadn't killed me.

"You look like shit," Mira says as Brennan reaches us.

"I feel like shit." He rubs a hand over his face. "Poromish politics are nothing like ours. I only have a few minutes before I need to get back in there and beg Cygnisen to stay at the table. Neither side speaks the language of middle ground."

"I would think not wanting to be killed by venin would encourage them to learn quickly," Mira states, tilting her head just like our mother, which tightens my throat.

"You would think." He shakes his head. "The only thing everyone can agree on is that the fliers will be allowed to tour the quadrant today with their squads' first-year riders—apparently they're not as threatening—and the task force going with you," he says to me.

"Where exactly is she going?" Mira snaps, moving to my side.

"We're being sent to find the rest of Andarna's kind," I answer for Brennan.

"You *what*?" Her eyes widen to impossible proportions.

"Andarna wants to. I should have told you before you left, but the Empyrean hadn't approved it yet." Guilt thickens my throat at her stricken expression. "She was always going to go. At least Andarna was able to make some demands this way."

"You let this happen?" She glares at Brennan.

"Mira—" I start.

"Quiet, *cadet*, the officers are speaking," she snaps.

Rude.

"Beyond our needs, Queen Maraya hopes the seventh breed might know how to defeat the venin, given the age of Andarna's egg." He's not far off from our own train of thought. "Mira, that hope is all that's keeping Poromiel at the table, and we're still negotiating for flier safety and conferencing with Navarre for the Aretian cadets to stay. You know, behind the functioning wards. This is more complicated than it looks."

Mira bristles. "Simple question: Did you tell them over your dead body is our sister flying through what's likely enemy-controlled, wyvern-filled territory on a *fool's errand*?"

"They should worry more about what will happen when we do find them," Tairn growls. *"If a den of our kind chose to leave—chose to hide—they will not welcome our intrusion."*

"You don't know that." Hurt laces Andarna's argument.

"You are naive to assume otherwise." His tone sharpens, and Andarna slams our pathways shut. *"She needs to prepare herself,"* he says. *"And so do you. There's every chance this mission will kill us."*

Or it could save us all. Freaking pessimist.

"He couldn't say no." My grip tightens on the conduit. "Aretia needs another of Andarna's kind to fire their wardstone."

Mira whips her face toward mine, horror widening her eyes before they quickly narrow back on our brother. "Is that why you sent me off to evaluate the status of the wards? So you'd know how long you have before using our sister like a gaming chip?"

"That is *not* how it happened." His jaw ticks. "I'm trying to support what she wants."

"It's *not* happening. We have six months, Brennan!" She digs into her pack and retrieves a bundle of missives, then shoves them at his chest, hitting him right next to his Aisereigh name tag. "Given the rate they're diminishing, I calculate six months before total collapse if we're lucky. Finding Andarna's kind could take *decades*. By the time she finds them—*if* she finds them—Aretia's gone. You'd be risking Violet's life for nothing."

My stomach hits the floor. Six months? I figured we'd at least have a year or two before the wards gave out. That path's timeline just got complicated, but I'll be damned if Xaden loses his home twice.

"Six months." Brennan's gaze darts between Ridoc's and Rhi's doors as if he's performing calculations in his head.

"No. This is the kind of mission riders don't return from." Mira draws back, studying our brother like he's a stranger.

Well, that's comforting.

"This is bigger than the three of us. Hundreds of thousands of civilians are under attack in Poromiel." He shoves the missives into his chest pocket and sighs. "Of course I don't want her in danger, and they won't let me go with her. I already asked."

"Find another way." Mira shakes her head. "You can't trade Violet's life for strangers."

"Now you sound like Mom." The words fly from his mouth, and to his credit, he immediately winces when both Mira and I gasp. "Shit." He hangs his head.

"You dare mention our mother when you won't even wear it?" She grabs the runed disk from her pack and throws it at our brother, smacking him square in the chest. He fumbles to catch it. "Look at what I've been doing this week, *Lieutenant Colonel Aisereigh*. Not sure Mom would approve."

Crap. This is *not* the cool, calm plan we discussed presenting to our brother.

His brows knit as he studies the disk. "I don't understand."

"We found a way to keep the fliers at Basgiath safely," she says.

He keeps looking at it, and I see the moment the truth hits him. The blood drains from his face, and his mouth slackens. "You want to—"

"Yes. And you should find a mirror," Mira interrupts, earning his attention. "Sacrificing members of our family for what's considered the greater good is a weapon straight out of Mom's arsenal." She walks away without another word.

I pat his shoulder. "Take it to the Senarium."

"They'll never agree."

"You and I both know it's the only way to forge this alliance."

He nods. "That's what I'm afraid of."

Never forget that dragon riders have been selected, trained, and even bred for cruelty. Expecting mercy from a rider is a mistake, for none will be given.

—Chapter One: The Tactical Guide to Defeating Dragons by Colonel Elijah Joben

CHAPTER FIVE

A few hours later, I'm pretty sure this has been the longest day of my entire life. The gathering hall is less than a quarter full and the perfect place to wait for news, so that's what the three of us do while Sawyer naps and the first-years tour with the fliers: sit—with our backs to the wall in case some Navarrian rider decides they want to make a point—and wait for Brennan and Mira to bring news.

Xaden hasn't returned, either.

Not knowing if more venin could be running around campus is terrifying, but at least if there are, Xaden will sense them. The thought is oddly comforting.

"That venin by Jack's cell had silver hair," I mutter, setting my dagger to an apple and peeling it in one long ribbon. "That's weird, right?"

"Everyone's hair eventually turns gray. That's the least weird thing about yesterday's attack. How long are we supposed to wait to see if they charge us with treason?" Ridoc drums his fingers on the thick oak table. "Let's just go with plan B already before another group of scarily coordinated dark wielders tries to break Barlowe out again."

"It's called plan A for a reason. Be patient," Rhi lectures from Ridoc's right, skimming through the book of Tyrrish knotwork Xaden gave me back before I knew it was meant to prepare me for runes. "I highly doubt the Treaty of Aretia was written in a matter of hours."

"The initial phase was thirteen days of negotiation." I finish peeling the apple as a first-year comes running through the arched double doors, then set my blade down as the gangly guy makes a beeline to a full table in First Wing's section, immediately spreading what appears to be a tasty bit of gossip. "When are the first-years going to be done?" I ask.

Whatever rumor First Wing has caught wind of spreads quickly, rippling outward from the center table down the line in a fascinating display of turning heads and scrambling cadets.

"No clue," Rhi says, turning a page. "I'm just hoping it's a peaceful bonding experience, since I'm fairly certain there's some kind of love triangle going on between Avalynn, Baylor, and Kai. Which I normally wouldn't stress about; it's not like Aetos cared who any of us were fucking last year—"

"So not true." Ridoc snorts and shoulder bumps me.

I glance over at the next table to make sure Dain didn't hear, but he's clearly engrossed in conversation with a group of third-years, including Imogen and Quinn.

"—but they keep..." Rhi wrinkles her nose. "Squabbling. It isn't helping integrate the fliers in this hostile environment, and it's screwing with their interpersonal dynamics."

Ridoc's fingers pause, and he takes note of the pattern I've been watching. News spreads from person to person, and riders start scurrying out of the hall. "You seeing this?"

I nod and sheathe my dagger, leaving my apple uneaten. "Rhi."

She closes the book and looks up.

"You think they'll win?" a brunette in Third Wing asks excitedly, slamming her pewter mug down on the table across from us.

"No fucking way. It'll be a bloodbath," the guy next to her replies, catching my gaze and quickly averting his as he gets up from the table, grabbing his flight jacket and abandoning his drink.

"Something's happening." A quick glance down the tables makes my skin crawl. The only riders left in the gathering hall are Aretian.

All three of us rise as a stocky cadet barrels through the double doors, and I spot first-year rank and his name tag, *Norris*, a second before he throws his hood back, revealing his familiar face.

"Baylor?" Apprehension slithers between my shoulder blades at the panic in our squadmate's brown eyes, the worry creasing the dark-brown skin of his forehead.

"They're here!" he shouts over his shoulder, and Sloane races in behind him.

I grab my jacket and slip out from behind the table to meet the first-years in the middle of the gathering hall. "What's wrong?"

"You have to do something." Sloane stares past me to Rhiannon. She hasn't been able to look me in the eye since she siphoned the life out of my mother.

"First Wing grabbed one of Tail Section's fliers in the courtyard, and they're forcing a challenge."

My stomach hurtles to the floor. If so much as a drop of flier blood is shed, it could end the peace talks.

"Beinhaven's insisting at knifepoint," Baylor all but growls.

A *wingleader* is orchestrating this? There aren't enough four-letter words in the world. Article Four, Section Four…we need another wingleader.

"Let's move," Rhiannon orders, and they sprint toward the door, Ridoc sliding past me as I turn back to the third-years.

"Dain!" I shout, and his head jerks up, his familiar brown eyes finding me instantly. "We need you." Without waiting for his response, I take off after my squad, shoving my arms into my coat.

Dain catches up before we hit the far side of commons, and the rest of the Aretian riders aren't far behind him.

We burst through the doorway of the rotunda into the courtyard, and my gaze sweeps over the crowd, taking stock of the situation. There's a clear division in the mass gathered in front of the dais, with most Navarrian riders standing to the left, at least half of them wearing sickening smirks while Caroline Ashton appears to take bets near the far staircase. The rest hold back the angry crowd of Aretian riders and fliers arguing directly in front of—

My heart lurches into my throat.

Aura Beinhaven stands centered in front of the crowd, holding one of the daggers she usually keeps strapped to her upper arms against the tan neck of a terrified first-year flier.

And there's no leadership in sight.

"Find your squads and de-escalate at all costs," Dain orders over his shoulder as we race down the steps and into the swarm.

"If only we were taught those techniques," Ridoc mutters.

"They're at the front. Follow me," Baylor tells us, then pushes through the crush like it's nothing, leaving us an easy wake to follow in. The snow has stopped, only to be replaced by a bitter chill as the sun sinks behind the mountains.

"Let him go!" Cat's voice rises above the others as we reach the front of the crowd, and when Baylor steps aside, I spot Maren holding Cat back from the line of Navarrian riders guarding Aura, her arms hooked around her best friend's waist.

"Feel free to accept the challenge, since he won't." A third-year out of Second Wing holds the tip of her sword less than a foot from Cat's stomach.

"Happy to!" she shouts.

Holy shit, this place is a tinderbox just waiting for a single flame to set it ablaze.

Palming a dagger, I move before my common sense can get the better of me and put myself in front of Cat, lifting my chin at the third-year. "This isn't how we treat our fellow cadets."

"They're *not* cadets!" she sneers.

"I didn't hear you complaining when they were carting your little sister to the infirmary during the battle." Imogen's shoulder rubs against mine as she edges in, urging me back. "But if you're going to raise blades"—she draws her sword—"then you'll do so against someone your own year, Kaveh."

Quinn pushes through on my other side, forcing Neve—one of our third-year fliers—behind her and setting the head of her labrys on the ground, squaring off against a guy out of First Wing who seems twice her height. "I kicked your ass our first year, and I don't mind doing it again, Hedley."

I take the opportunity and spin, putting my forearm at Cat's collarbone and forcing her back into the safety of our squad.

"I'll fight!" she shrieks.

"You can't." I grasp Cat's forearm with my empty hand. "Cat, you *can't*. If you fall—"

"You'd be so sad to lose your rival, wouldn't you?" Her dark eyes narrow on mine. "Or are you more intimidated by the thought that I could win and once again prove why I'm the better match for—"

"Oh, shut up." It takes everything I have not to shake her. "You can't wield behind the wards, so stop trying to manipulate my emotions. There's no winning here. If you bleed, we have no chance at an alliance, and I'm not willing to lose a squadmate over Second Wing's assholery. You win and harm a rider, you'll confirm everything they fear about you."

Her expression softens, and for a second, she looks just like her older sister. "They're never going to accept us."

"*They* don't have to," I assure her. "We already have."

"Challenge! Challenge! Challenge!" The chant comes from the left and quickly catches along the row of Navarrian riders.

Shit. Nothing like mob mentality.

"This coward won't accept the challenge of a senior wingleader!" Aura shouts over the crowd, using lesser magic to amplify her voice. "But I'll be merciful and accept another. Pick your champion or watch him die."

"This goes against the Codex!" Dain elbows a Navarrian cadet from Third Wing in the head and pushes through the line. "Challenges are only issued in the presence of a combat master."

"On what authority do you object, Aetos?" Aura snarls.

The crowd quiets, but the silence feels more dangerous than the chanting had been as everyone turns to watch the interaction.

"Stay here," I order Cat, then shove my way between Imogen and Quinn.

"Article Four, Section Four." Dain approaches Aura with his hands up, exposing his palms. "'A wingleader has the authority and duty to maintain—'"

"Article Two, Section One," Aura shouts, raking the edge of her dagger along the flier's throat. "'Riders outside quadrant chain of command can't interfere with cadet matters.' *You* are no longer in the chain of command."

The Navarrian riders mutter in agreement, and tension rises like the bubbles in a simmering pot, one degree away from boiling. The quadrant has made us far too comfortable shedding each other's blood.

My grip tightens on my dagger as color fills my peripheral vision. I look up to see both gryphons and dragons landing along the thick stone walls of the courtyard.

Great, just what we need in this situation: fire and talons.

"Are you here?" I ask. There are no black scales among the dragons, but I spot Cath behind the dais.

"Are you in danger?" Tairn asks, and I feel Andarna's presence, but she remains silent.

"Not exactly, but—"

"Then I trust you can handle it."

"Injuring a flier will jeopardize this alliance," Dain argues, and I nod like he needs the encouragement.

"Who said we want it?" Aura drags the edge of her blade under the flier's chin, and he winces but doesn't move. "They haven't crossed the parapet. They haven't climbed the Gauntlet. They won't even accept a challenge. We do not tolerate cowards!"

The Navarrian riders cheer, and I use the opportunity to dart between the two standing guard in front of us, finding myself quickly flanked by Ridoc on my left and, surprisingly, Aaric on my right. The first-year is almost as tall as Xaden, and his menacing glare keeps Kaveh and Hedley silent as they stand with Quinn's and Imogen's weapons at their backs.

"I'll accept!" Kai shouts, the first-year flier charging through the line on the right, and every head turns as Rhi and Baylor quickly drag him back.

Bone crunches ahead of us, and my focus whips to Dain, who shoves Tail Section's flier toward the line as Aura stumbles backward, disarmed, blood streaming through her fingers as she covers her nose.

"This ends now!" Dain's shout echoes off the stone walls.

"We don't answer to deserters!" Aura spits blood into the snow and straightens. "You no longer speak for Fourth Wing, Aetos. You're nothing here."

Dain takes the insult with a lift of his chin, and I crack open the door to Tairn's power, welcoming the heat that floods my veins, warming my cold-cramped muscles and exposed hands.

"Fourth Wing!" Ewan Faber steps out of the crowd near the steps. "Prepare to defend your senior wingleader!"

"Fuck me," Aaric mutters, drawing his sword as Ridoc does the same at my left.

Weapons rise at the edges of my vision, but I keep my gaze locked on Aura and adjust my grip around my dagger. I may have some very mixed feelings when it comes to Dain, but there's no way under Amari's sky that I'm going to let Aura harm *any* Aretian rider, let alone my oldest friend.

"We answer to Aetos," Ridoc shouts down the line, pointing his sword in Faber's direction. "And there's more of us than there are of you."

"Only in Fourth Wing!" Iris Drue announces, the leader of First Wing moving to Faber's side. "First Wing stands strong! Stands loyal to Navarre!"

A cheer rises from the left.

"Not sure I'd brag about being in the wing that produced Jack Barlowe!" Ridoc counters.

"Ridoc!" Rhi hisses.

"I'm done," he promises as Dain shoots a glare his way.

"Really missing the professors right now," Aaric says under his breath.

"Challenge Aetos!" someone yells from the left, and a new fear wraps its fingers around my heart and squeezes. There's no single person in the courtyard with the authority to command us all. The only thing more dangerous than a quadrant full of arrogant killing machines is a *leaderless* quadrant, and if Dain accepts the challenge and…falls, an alliance with Poromiel won't matter—we'll tear each other apart from within.

Now would be a *great* time for Xaden to lower his fucking shields.

"The Dark One cannot unite what he broke."

"Stop calling him that."

"You blame us for Barlowe, but you're the ones who left!" Aura motions at our side of the formation, displaying her bevy of patches beneath the one that indicates her fire-wielding signet as she stalks toward Dain.

Dain draws his dagger and drops it in the snow, facing Aura unarmed. "I'm not raising my blade against you, Beinhaven."

"That's a…choice," Aaric says quietly. "He's going to *talk* her down?"

One by one, I flex my fingers along the hilt of my dagger, prepping my hand for movement as power hums within me.

"Yes, we left," Dain continues, his hands closing into fists. "But we also returned."

Aura reaches for her shoulder as if forgetting she already used and lost that dagger, but she doesn't draw the sword at her hip. "Did it occur to any of you that they only attacked because they knew we weren't at full strength? That your desertion allowed the wards to fall in the first place?"

Ouch.

"We chose truth," Dain shouts back, a vein bulging in his neck. "We chose to defend the helpless—"

"You chose to break the riot! Fracture the quadrant!" Aura counters, pointing her gloved finger at Dain's chest as she approaches him with slow, methodical steps that elevate my pulse. "And then you bring home the very enemy we've spent *centuries* fighting, the enemy that killed my own cousin in one of their raids! And you think we should welcome them into the heart of the kingdom they've been trained to destroy?"

The Navarrians mutter in agreement.

"I think our boy is losing this one," Aaric whispers. "He's good, but he's no Riorson."

Xaden hadn't just led Fourth Wing, he'd commanded the respect—and fear—of the entire quadrant. My jaw clenches. But he isn't a cadet anymore, and the entirety of the Riders Quadrant will only answer to one of its own. *He can't unite what he broke.*

"Xaden can't fix this," I murmur, mostly to myself. Fuck it, I hate when Tairn's right.

Mercifully, he keeps silent.

"We need the fliers!" Dain holds his ground.

"*You* need them!" Aura's voice edges on bitterness as she takes another step toward Dain. "*We* fought to save Basgiath! We were steadfast in our defense! We never wavered!" Another chorus of cheers resounds as she turns to the quadrant like a politician.

"He can't win the crowd. She's going to really challenge him," Aaric warns, his gaze darting over the audience of dragons and gryphons, and I suddenly remember *exactly* who he is.

"Any chance you have an affinity for public speaking?" I ask Aaric, undoing the first button on my flight jacket as the heat builds. "It certainly runs in your family."

"Was it the shunning of my birthright in favor of a high probability of death that gave me away?" he responds, his tone dry.

I take that as a *no.*

"What do you say? Their strongest against our strongest?" Aura taps her bloody hand over her heart. "I'll make you a deal, *wingleader.* Defeat me, and your fliers live to see the morning. Fail to rise to the occasion, and we'll stain this courtyard red."

The Navarrians' roar of approval rattles my teeth.

"Dain isn't the strongest," Andarna points out.

"Dain can take her in hand-to-hand." Nepotism isn't the only reason he earned his rank, and wielding isn't allowed in challenges. I watch every motion as Aura tugs at the fingers of her glove instead of reaching for another dagger or her sword. My stomach tenses. There's only one reason she'd need her hands bare.

Fire trumps memory-wielding every time.

Aura gestures to the hard-packed snow between them. "Let this serve as our mat. What would our combat master say?" she asks the crowd.

"Begin!" the whole of First Wing calls out.

"I'm not fighting you, Aura!" Dain roars.

"I'm fighting *you*!" Aura fidgets with her glove, and I flip my dagger, holding it by the tip. "Or have you really turned coward? Just another rebel who needs to be marked as such?"

Marked. Rage narrows my eyes.

"Dain isn't the strongest!" Andarna repeats, and this time, I get the point.

I am.

Aura whips off her glove and flares her hand. I throw, releasing my dagger a second before flame erupts from her palm.

The steel pins her glove to the wooden support of the dais.

Aura gasps, and the flame dies before it can touch Dain, her head tracking the loss of her glove before whipping toward me. Her eyes narrow. "Sorrengail."

"Violet, no," Dain protests.

"'Rebel' is so…outdated. We prefer the term 'revolutionary,'" I inform Aura, taking a measured step in her direction and welcoming the crackle of sizzling power in my fingertips. "And if you're going to wield, then it's me you'll be dealing with."

CHAPTER
SIX

"**Y**ou dare—" Aura turns to fully face me, yanking off her other glove.

"I dare." I lift my open palms skyward, and heat streaks along my arms as I release a wave of power, forcing it upward and letting it go.

Lightning splits the sky, flashing bright above our heads and branching outward into the clouds. Thunder follows instantly, so loud it shakes the masonry.

The crowd quiets, and Aura's mouth hangs for a moment before she lowers her hands.

"You see, Dain's too honorable to wield in a challenge, but you'll find that my sense of morality has learned to...waver." I retrieve another dagger and shake it in her direction. "You lift your hand against him again, and the next one goes through it. He's the reason you're alive. The reason you're *all* alive!" Power thrums through me, buzzing with readiness, and I slip my left hand into the pocket of my flight jacket and remove the conduit.

"Violet," Rhiannon warns softly from my right.

"Shh, it's more fun when she blows shit up," Ridoc whispers.

I turn slightly and draw on lesser magic to allow my voice to carry to the Navarrian riders while keeping an eye on Aura. They've closed in, taking this situation from dangerous to lethal. "The only reason you survived the attack is because we gained access to the knowledge Navarre purposely hid from us. We stole it. We translated it. We saved your ass." Warmth streaks down my arm, the conduit beginning to hum. "And yes, we expect you to recognize that we need this alliance to survive what's coming for us!"

"You expect us to trust them?" Caroline calls out.

Aura retreats a step, eyeing my conduit.

"You have to," I answer, pushing against the heat that flushes my skin as power gathers within me again. "But more importantly, you *can*. They've fought by our side for months, even after we've spent centuries condemning their people to death because we're unwilling to share the one resource that could have saved them. We don't have to like each other, but we do have to trust each other, and we can't keep doing this, can't keep accepting needless casualties in the quadrant in the name of strengthening the wing, not when every single one of us is needed in this war."

"It's their war!" Aura challenges. "Do you really believe we should weaken our wards, endanger our own people just to arm theirs? You choose Poromiel over Navarre?"

"We can choose both." I slip my dagger back into place and free my hand to wield.

Aaric lifts his sword as Ewan Faber comes a little too close.

"The riders who came before us failed to protect the innocent just because they were on the other side of our border," I argue. "They lied and hid. *They* were the cowards! But we don't have to be. We can choose to stand together and fight. Leadership is locked behind doors right now trying to forge a treaty." My gaze skims over the riders who stayed when we fled for Aretia three months ago. "But they're failing, just like every generation before us has failed, and if we do the same…" I shake my head, fumbling for words. "You've seen what's out there. Either this alliance begins right here with us, with *our* generation, or we will be the last dragon riders and gryphon fliers on the Continent." Sweat beads along the back of my neck, my temperature rising with every second I keep my power ready. "Well?" I ask.

Silence falls, thick and heavy, but no one moves.

"Is this what you do when we give you a break from classes?"

Everyone turns toward the rotunda at the sound of Devera's voice. The professor stands with her feet braced apart, flanked by Professors Emetterio and Kaori. All three look in desperate need of a bath and a good night's rest.

Thank you, Dunne. I force the Archives door to Tairn's power shut and note the steam rising from my hand before the conduit dims.

"Sorrengail is right," Devera shouts. "There is every chance we will all meet Malek in the coming months, but you must decide if you'd rather die fighting each other or facing our shared enemy." She rocks back on her heels. "Go ahead and choose. We'll wait."

"Die now or die later, what's the difference?" someone from Second Wing asks.

"Die now, and the scribes will call your name in the morning." Emetterio shrugs. "Choose to fight your common enemy, and there's a chance you'll live to graduate. Personally"—he scratches his beard—"I like our odds. The last time a shadow and lightning wielder fought side by side, they managed to drive the venin back into the Barrens for a few hundred years. We'll figure out how to do it again."

I fumble the conduit and nearly drop it. Xaden and I are the first of our signets to live simultaneously since the Great War?

Heads turn my way, and one by one, every weapon lowers.

"You do your dragons—and gryphons—proud." Devera nods. "Vacation is over. Your professors are returning in the next twenty-four hours, and if I were you, I'd concentrate on getting a good night's sleep before Emetterio here decides you should run the Gauntlet just for fun. We are done waiting for the nobles. Battle Brief is at nine a.m. sharp, treaty or no treaty." She looks pointedly at our group. "And that includes *every* cadet, no matter what color leathers you prefer. You're released from whatever it was you thought you were doing here."

The cadets disperse, passing by our professors as the three walk our way, and then the winged ones take to the sky. I can't help but note that the cadets are still separated between Navarrians and Aretians. At least no one's trying to kill each other.

We keep our fliers' backs toward the dais until the Navarrians are gone, and then our squad brings up the rear.

"I can see it sometimes," Cat says, pulling up her hood as she walks ahead of me. "Why he chose you. Nice speech. Took you long enough to step in, though."

"You're welcome," I mutter to her back, but the tiniest of smiles curls my lips.

"Never thought I'd yearn for a simple day of classes." Ridoc throws his arm over my shoulder as we walk. "Maybe a good old session of Parapet."

I spot Xaden off to the side of the rotunda steps with Lewellen, Brennan, and Mira, and my stomach flips. They must have news.

"Our classmates trying to kill each other isn't exactly original," Sloane says, passing by as I slow at the tense look on Brennan's face.

Guess it's not *good* news.

"Did you really just stand there and watch all that happen?" Rhi asks as our professors approach.

"Yes." Devera wipes off her flight goggles, then stretches the leather band behind her head. "It was bound to happen at some point, and at least this was a controlled environment," she finishes over her shoulder.

"I feel so protected." Ridoc puts his hand over his heart. "Nurtured, even. Wouldn't you agree, Violet?"

"You pretty much described how Violet was raised," Dain says, coming from behind us with Aaric as the rest head inside with the remainder of the squad.

He looks at me. "Thanks for stepping in. Thought she was going to torch me there for a second."

"Thanks for coming without hesitation when I said we needed you." Our eyes meet, and for a second, it hits me how different things might have been if he'd shown the same faith in me during my first year as he did today. Not different enough to change the way I feel about Xaden, though.

"Always will." He offers me a hint of a smile before turning toward the dormitory.

When I look over to Xaden, I find him watching, his scarred eyebrow rising as his gaze jumps to Dain before finding mine again.

My eyes narrow. Is that… No, it can't be jealousy, can it?

Rhi glances at Ridoc and Aaric, motioning with her head. "Violet, we'll catch up with you later."

"We need to speak with you as well, Aaric," Brennan notes, looking like he's aged five years in the last few hours. He's not exactly standing close to Mira, either, causing my heart to sink.

Ridoc's arm slides off my shoulders. "Oh, come on. Why does Aaric get to stay? He's a first-year."

"Do not make me drag you," Rhi warns, holding up a single finger, and Ridoc acquiesces with a sigh, moving forward and leaving the six of us on the rotunda steps.

"Let's take this inside." Brennan surprises me by heading down the steps and cutting a diagonal path toward the academic wing.

Moving to Xaden's side, I study the stern lines of his face as we follow Brennan, the others close behind us. "Everything all right?" I ask quietly, feeling his shields locked firmly in place. "Are *you* all right?"

"Good speech." He takes my hand, lacing our fingers.

"She was going to kill Dain." My voice drops to a whisper. "They really do hate us."

"Doesn't change the fact that we're here. Especially now that we've reached terms for the riot to stay." Xaden catches the door before it can close behind Brennan, then holds it as I walk through, his fingers slipping from mine.

"That's good, right?" I glance his way as we enter the deserted sparring gym. "And you didn't answer my question."

"Talk to your brother first." He folds his arms when we reach the edge of the first row of mats, where Brennan waits. As the others join us, we form a loose circle.

That doesn't bode well. Anxiety coils in my stomach like a snake poised to strike as I take in the older riders' somber expressions across from us.

Aaric slides his hands into his pockets at my left. "Let me guess. Halden complicated negotiations?"

I fucking *blanch*.

"Your brother certainly didn't help," Lewellen notes, scratching the bristles along the underside of his jaw.

"Halden's here?" I manage to ask.

"Rode in this morning with a company from the Western Guard." Aaric shoots me a knowing look, which I return with a quick glare.

"Great." His temper is the last thing we need at the negotiating table.

Mira studies Xaden and me intently, but she keeps quiet.

"Your secret is still safe, by the way," Lewellen says to Aaric, "though you might consider putting your father out of his misery. He has half his personal guard searching for you."

"Shows how effective they are, don't you think?" Aaric grimaces sarcastically. "So do you carry news? Or were you just gathered to hear Violet's speech?" His attention jumps from person to person, no doubt cataloging the tiniest details of every shift in expression as he's been raised to do. He's always been the most observant of his brothers. "She was quite moving."

"We heard." Brennan offers me a flash of a proud smile. "And saw."

"She'd be a great politician," Aaric continues. "Or a general, maybe? Definitely nobility."

"With that speech? At least a duchess." Xaden shifts his weight, brushing his elbow against my shoulder.

I shake my head. "No thank you to...any of that. I have no love for politics, nor am I good at dealing with the Senarium." I look around. "Okay, someone needs to start talking."

"Lieutenant Riorson?" a rider with a messenger sash interrupts, calling out from the doorway.

"Be right back." Xaden's hand skims my lower back as he answers the summons.

"Your mission was discussed at the negotiating table today in hopes they would give us an extension," Brennan says, "and given the participants at hand..."

That snake of anxiety strikes hard and true.

"Halden," Aaric guesses, his emerald-green eyes narrowing slightly in speculation toward my brother. "Halden's going with her, isn't he?"

My jaw *unhinges*, then snaps shut at the apology filling Brennan's eyes. "No fucking way." I shake my head. "You cannot be serious." I refuse to even *think* about it.

"They're serious," Aaric says without looking in my direction. "Poromiel would accept a Sorrengail without question, so if you need a royal capable of speaking for Navarre, they must think you're headed to the isle kingdoms or northward." He tilts his head, studying the older riders. "That about cover it?"

I'm going to be sick.

"Why are you ill?" Andarna asks.

"Halden?" Tairn muses slowly, and I swear I can feel his nonexistent eyebrows rise.

"So, we kill him if he makes her uncomfortable," Andarna suggests. *"Problem solved."*

"You cannot kill the heir to the throne." Even though I've been tempted myself a time or two.

"You really are the wisest of them, aren't you?" Lewellen huffs a sardonic laugh. "Our kingdom would have benefitted from *you* being the firstborn, Your Highness."

"It's Aaric," he corrects, folding his arms. "Is that why you wanted me here? To see if I'd announce myself, since Halden wants to go gallivanting off on dangerous missions? Make everyone feel good and cozy that there's still a spare?"

"Perhaps." The duke smiles at Aaric.

"Admirable attempt, but I'm only here for my squad. I'll dismantle the family business before I rejoin it," Aaric quips.

"Your prince doesn't want to play." Mira arches a brow at Lewellen. "Now, tell Violet the rest, or I will."

The comment reminds me: "Andarna's demands?"

"Right," Lewellen says as Xaden returns, still stern-faced but now holding a rolled parchment as he fills the space at my side. The duke pulls Andarna's list from his pocket. "You already know point two is now in the hands of Captain Grady. But you won point three. The Senarium has agreed that all those who flew for Aretia will be welcomed back with a full pardon for their treason and sedition within the now-negotiated accord with Aretia"—he glances at Xaden—"which will be signed in the morning once the scribes finish drafting it. Personally, I think you scared the shit out of them by threatening to leave yesterday, Violet. Good job. Point four, Andarna will not submit for any examination—"

"Because that was never going to happen anyway," she chimes in.

"And five, she will be granted access to hunt in the king's forest whenever she pleases."

"That one was just for fun."

"You skipped the fliers." I straighten my spine and look to my brother. "Keeping them safe and our squads intact is first on the list." I narrow my eyes. We only have two days left. *And we gave you the solution.*

Brennan presses his lips into a flat line, and my stomach rolls.

"That particular matter didn't make it to Poromiel's table." Lewellen folds

Andarna's list and puts it into the front pocket of his hunter green tunic. "Your sister argued valiantly and displayed astonishing capability, but the Senarium voted six to one, and the safety of Navarre's borders is not to be tampered with."

Mira crosses her arms.

Prickling heat rolls down Andarna's bond, and my hands curl, my nails biting into my palms. "What about the alliance?" Without it, the deal with Tecarus falls apart.

"It's failed," Lewellen announces unemotionally, as if reading from the death roll.

"Because the fliers aren't safe here." I bite out every word at my brother.

"Because treaties like this take *time*, and we won't figure this out before their queen's deadline in two days." Brennan rubs his thumb along his chin. "Flier cadets will be safe in Aretia while we still have wards, and hopefully Queen Maraya can force her nobles back to the table at a later date," Brennan promises, his shoulders sagging. "Politics are complicated."

Fuck that. How can *our* nobles let them walk away without an alliance, knowing we have the means to protect the fliers?

"We still have the means," Andarna reminds me.

Right. Plan B: treason. Guess that path chooses itself.

"When you put it that way." I force my shoulders to relax and my hands to fall peacefully at my sides. "I guess it's back to Basgiath business as usual tomorrow, and I should prep for our mission—or is research as out of my control as the team members?"

Mira's eyes narrow in my direction, like she's the inntinnsic in the room and not Xaden.

"Every resource, including the royal library, will be made available to you," Brennan promises.

"Oh good, because *books* will keep her safe." Mira shoots Brennan an icy look.

The right books will.

"Well, as fun as this has been." Aaric nods at me, then departs without another word.

"He'll come around." Lewellen sighs, then turns to Xaden with a smile so proud it borders on teary. "Enjoy your win, Xaden. Delaying the alliance is unfortunate, but we won. Your father would be proud."

"I highly doubt that." His tone is sharp.

What? I reach, but his shields are tighter than ever. Did he get his father's sword back? Why wouldn't he be happy about that?

"We'll leave you to tell her the good news. I really am sorry we couldn't make the alliance work." Brennan gives me an awkward, apologetic smile, then heads out, taking Lewellen and Mira with him.

I wait until the door shuts behind her before I turn to Xaden. "What did you win?"

Every muscle in his body seems to tense even more, if that's possible. "I didn't *win* it. Didn't even ask for it. I'm the last person…" He shakes his head and stuffs the rolled orders into his breast pocket. "Lewellen and Lindell told them it was the price of keeping the riot here, and the Senarium gave in. That's how scared they are of losing our numbers. They actually agreed to give it back, and I wish they hadn't. Not now. Not when I'm like…this." He points to his eyes as if they were still red, but I only see him. "My father wouldn't be proud. He'd be horrified." Every word is short. Clipped.

"I don't believe that." It's impossible not to be proud of him, not to love him.

"You didn't know him. There was only one thing in this world he loved more than me." He looks away, and I start to rethink my assumption about the sword.

"What did the king give you?" A blade wouldn't worry him like this.

"I've been trying to think of a way out of it for the last hour. The king sanctioned both Lindell and Lewellen for their roles in hiding Aretia—just like they predicted this morning—so they're not options. And I can't reject the agreement, or everyone will know something is wrong." His tortured gaze finds mine, and my heart clenches. "The only solution I can think of is you. You'll be the first to sense when I lose the rest of what makes me…me." Slowly, he tucks a windblown strand of my hair behind my ear.

"You won't." I have enough faith in him for the both of us.

"I will. This morning showed me it's just a matter of time and reason." He nods with a certainty that sours my stomach. "It's not fair, and you might hate me for it later, but I need you to make me a promise." His warm hand cups the back of my neck as his eyes search mine. "Swear you'll sound the alarm if I go too far, that you'll keep it safe, even if it's from me."

"What—" I start, but the gym door opens, and I look over my shoulder to see Garrick waving a rolled parchment.

"The *Earl* of Lewellen said you'd be in here. Orders aren't optional, Riorson, even for nobility. We need to go."

"Promise me," Xaden says, stroking his thumb under my ear and completely ignoring his best friend.

"You're leaving?" I swing my gaze back to Xaden's, realizing that's why the messenger had tracked him down. "Now?"

He leans in, blocking out the rest of the world. "Promise me, Violet. Please."

He'll never go too far, never lose his soul, so I nod. "I promise."

Xaden's eyes slide shut for a heartbeat, and blatant relief shines from their depths when he opens them. "Thank you."

"I know you can hear me." Garrick raises his voice. "Let's *go*."

"I love you." Xaden kisses me hard and fast, and it's over before I can even process it's actually happened.

"I love you, too." I grab his hand as he withdraws. "Tell me what the king gave you."

He takes a deep breath. "He gave me back my title and the seat in the Senarium."

Holy shit. My lips part.

"Not just Aretia, either…he gave me Tyrrendor," Xaden says slowly, like he can't believe it, either.

And he doesn't want it. My chest clenches. "Xaden—"

"Don't wait up." He presses a kiss to the inside of my wrist, then strides toward Garrick. "I'll be back by eight a.m. to sign that accord," he calls back over his shoulder. "Try to stay out of trouble while I'm gone."

"Be careful." He's *the* Duke of Tyrrendor. This is so much bigger than how I feel about him now. There's an entire province depending on him.

I need to find a cure, and that means saving the alliance tonight…

Even if it means I'll be a traitor by morning.

If I'm to be court-martialed for helping Braxtyn defend his people, then I shall welcome the trial. All who channel from dragon and gryphon alike should flourish under the wards, and now Aretia will be that haven should one of the others ever return.

—JOURNAL OF LYRA OF MORRAINE
—TRANSLATED BY CADET JESINIA NEILWART

CHAPTER SEVEN

"I want to be on the quest squad," Ridoc whispers at my side as we cross the enclosed bridge to the Healer Quadrant, my heart strangely steady considering what we're about to do.

"For the last time, there's no *quest squad*," Rhi hisses at him as the bells announce midnight's arrival, muffling the sound of rusty hinges as Imogen opens the door ahead of us. "There's a very small, very skilled group going with Violet to find Andarna's kind."

"Sounds like a quest squad to me. Given Riorson's recent promotion, he should be able to pull some strings with Grady, right?" Ridoc checks over the daggers sheathed along his right side, like he's afraid he might have missed one. Hopefully we won't need them. "What do we all think?"

"I think you should shut the hell up before you get us caught and killed," Imogen says over her shoulder, walking into the mage-lit tunnel.

Ridoc rolls his eyes and glances in my direction as we cross into the Healer Quadrant. "Still sounds like a quest squad."

"If I had a say, I'd take you," I promise, pulling the door shut once we're all inside.

The tunnel is empty—all the beds have been cleared since yesterday morning's attack, which feels like a decade ago. We find the darkest stretch between mage lights and lean against the wall just out of sight of the infirmary doors.

"Now we wait," Rhi mutters, drumming her fingertips on her folded arms.

It isn't long before we spot Bodhi and Quinn making their way toward us from the opposite direction with Maren in their wake, pillow lines etched on her face.

"You ready to do this?" Bodhi asks me, keeping his voice down as he reaches us. "You really *want* to do this?"

"No second thoughts," I assure him, lifting my chin. "Whatever it takes."

He nods and glances over our party. "Everyone know their assignment?"

"I don't," Maren whispers, looking at us like we've lost our minds. "Is this some kind of hazing ritual?"

"It's best you don't know until we need you." I pull the vial of concentrated, purple valerian root tincture from my left pocket. "It's for your own safety—and plausible deniability—that you trust us. For now, just stay here with Imogen."

Maren glances at each of us as if deciding, then nods.

"Then let's go." Bodhi gestures toward the infirmary, and I take the lead.

Gods, I hope I've thought of everything. If one thing goes wrong, we're fucked.

The five of us approach the infirmary doors, and I knock lightly four times. *Please be here.*

"Remind me how you know this guy?" Bodhi whispers.

"I saved his life during navigation last year," I answer, then hold my breath as the right door opens silently.

Dyre pops his head out, his brown eyes crinkling as he smiles. "I did everything you asked. Come on in." He holds the door open, and we all slip inside as quietly as possible.

"Thank you for taking the extra shift on quick notice and helping us." I hand him the vial. "Here's another dose in case you need it. The other healers have to stay asleep until we bring him back."

"Understood." He takes the vial. "But you know I can't do anything if someone comes out of the critical care chamber."

"It's a risk we have to take." We leave him standing watch at the door and silently make our way down the row to Sawyer's bay, mage lights casting multiple shadows as we pass the sleeping injured.

Sawyer's sitting upright but doesn't say a word as we pile into his brightly lit bay, just lifts his eyebrows and sets down his pen and parchment on the bedside table.

Bodhi closes the curtains and throws out a line of blue energy that encapsulates us in a bubble. "Sound shield is active. You feeling up to a trip across campus?" he asks Sawyer.

"Took one earlier today as part of rehab. I can make it for the right reason."

Sawyer nods. "Is this why Dyre told me to stay awake?"

"We need you to help with that plan we discussed." I take the seat near the head of his bed. "Mira found a way. It involves altering the very material a rune is tempered into without destroying it."

He leans back against his headboard. "Then you're fucked, because I can't think of a single rock or earth wielder in our history."

"I'm pretty sure it's mostly iron," I say slowly.

His mouth falls open and hangs there for a few seconds. "No." He shakes his head, then looks to Rhi. "Find someone else. There are at least a dozen metallurgists in our ranks." He folds his arms over his black shirt.

"Not here." Ridoc moves to the other side of the bed, then rummages through a set of drawers. "They're all stationed on the border with just about every other rider we have right now."

"Then wait for them," Sawyer argues. "I'm...I'm not good enough for something like that."

"You have to be." Rhi sits at the foot of his bed.

"Sliseag won't even..." He shoves his hand through his unruly brown hair. "I don't know if I can."

"You can." I lift my brows and look pointedly at the mug on his bedside table that bears his handprint.

"I am not the rider you want for this, Vi. Not sure I'm even a rider anymore. Wait for someone else."

"Waiting won't matter," Bodhi says beside Rhi.

Sawyer's shoulders sag. "Leadership doesn't approve."

I shake my head. "If we don't do this tonight, the negotiations are done. Fliers will be escorted to Aretia tomorrow."

"They're going to tear our squad apart?" Sawyer's gaze jumps from me, to Bodhi, to Rhi, as if hoping one of us will correct him.

"Not if you do something about it." Ridoc tosses Sawyer's uniform top on the bed. "Now, I love you like a brother, and I get that you lost your leg, and we respect however you're feeling about that, but you're still one of us. You're still a rider, with all the benefits and shit that come with wearing black. So with all the love in my heart, put your fucking uniform on, because we *need* you."

Sawyer picks up his uniform and rubs his thumb over his metallurgy patch, then down across his Iron Squad one. My heart counts out the long seconds it takes for him to nod. "Someone hand me my crutches."

A few minutes later, five of us walk out of the infirmary, including Sawyer.

"Where's Quinn?" Maren asks, pushing off the wall.

"Making sure no one notices he's missing," Bodhi answers.

"Good to see you dressed appropriately," Imogen says to Sawyer. "It's a long way, including two sets of intentionally difficult stairs, so if you need help, we've got you."

Sawyer glances down to where Ridoc tied up his empty pantleg to the knee. "Noted," he says with quiet determination. "Let's go."

We make our way up the spiral steps into the main campus, then down the hallway to the northwest turret, narrowly missing one guard patrol in infantry blue by ducking into a healer classroom midway, and then another in scarlet tunics by piling into the stairwell as they turn the corner.

"It's busy out here," Sawyer remarks between quick breaths, his back pressed against the stone wall. Sweat beads his forehead, and he's lost a little color.

"You good?" I ask him as we near the three-minute mark.

He nods, and we keep going.

"Every noble on the Continent is in residence," Maren notes. "Maybe you should have done this with Riorson. He would have been able to lend some shadow aid."

"He's not exactly aware of what we're doing," I tell her as Imogen walks down a couple of steps in front of us. *Any chance he shows up?* I ask Tairn.

They are out of range, he answers. *He will not be your problem tonight.*

"Give me sixty seconds to knock out the guards, then come down," Imogen orders, disappearing around the first curve.

"Do I get to know yet?" Maren asks.

"No," Bodhi and Ridoc answer simultaneously.

And how does the Empyrean feel about this? I tap my fingers on my thigh, counting out the seconds.

You have the full support of the Aretian riot. We will find out how the others feel in the morning.

So we're begging forgiveness instead of asking permission. Understood.

We start down the steps, Bodhi and me taking lead. "Xaden's going to be pissed," I whisper so the others don't hear.

"Which is why you're going to be the one to tell him when we pull it off," he answers with a grimace. "He won't kill *you*."

We wind our way down, keeping a pace Sawyer seems comfortable with, and my chest grows tighter with every step. There should only be two guards on tonight, which is absolutely no challenge for Imogen, but the anxiety doesn't let up until she comes into view, waiting for us on the bottom step with her arms folded.

"We have a slight problem," she says, her mouth tensing as she steps aside. "I wasn't sure you'd want me knocking out this particular guard."

Mira walks into the center of the chamber and tilts her head at me in an uncanny imitation of our mother.

My stomach hits the floor. "Shit," I mutter.

"Shit is about right." Mira puts her hands on her hips. "And to think, I figured I was overreacting when I dismissed the guards and took their place."

"How did you know?" I meet her in the middle of the tunnel, noting that she stands between me and the entrance to the wardstone chamber.

"Because I know *you*." She levels a withering look on me, then glances over my shoulder. "You pulled that rider from his sickbed?"

"I'm the one who gets to say how 'sick' I am," Sawyer counters from behind me.

"Right." She swings her attention back to me. "You shouldn't do this."

I lift my chin. "Are you going to stop me?"

Her eyes narrow slightly. "Can you be stopped?"

"No." I shake my head. "You were there when we gave our word that the fliers would be educated with the riders. If Navarre wants us, then they take *all* of us."

"And you're willing to risk the wards our mother gave her life to power to keep your word?" She lifts her eyebrow.

"You're the one who told me this can be done." I skirt the question as the others move to stand beside me.

"Which is something I'll have to live with." She looks at each rider. "You're all aware that if we fail, the wards could fall? And if we succeed, there's every chance we'll be charged with treason and executed by dragon?"

"That's not happening," Tairn assures me with a low growl.

"I'm sorry, what?" Maren looks down the line from the right.

"Relax." Imogen knocks her with an elbow. "Your only job is to wield. You'll be clear of the rest."

"We know the risks," I tell Mira. "If the wards fall, then it looks like there's a mass migration to Aretia, and I'm truly on a ticking clock to find Andarna's kind. But they won't, because you found the solution, and you're never wrong. So I'm asking you again: Are you going to stop me?"

She sighs and drops her arms at her sides. "No, but only because I know you'll just try again, and I might not be here to make sure it works next time. You have the best shot with both of us." She pivots on her heel and disappears through the entrance to the ward chamber.

With Bodhi keeping watch, the six of us make our way into the narrow passage, Maren and me holding Sawyer's crutches as Rhiannon and Ridoc shuffle sideways with Sawyer's weight braced between them.

Only when we enter the massive chamber housing our kingdom's wardstone do I fully comprehend what Mira had meant by *us*.

"This little venture tells me you've been hanging out with Riorson too long,"

Brennan says, waiting beside Mira in front of the massive iron pillar and its eerie black flame.

Guess this is now a family affair. The corners of my mouth rise. "You're the one leading a revolution with him. Maybe you rubbed off on me." I keep my gaze on my siblings, ignoring everything else about the chamber in the name of self-preservation.

"And to think, you could have been wasted on the Scribe Quadrant." He flashes a smile, but it falls quickly as he gets serious. "Henrick, you're with Mira. She'll help you through the process. Flier—"

"Maren Zina," she corrects him.

"Great. Zina, you prepare to wield whatever lesser magic you're most comfortable with. You three"—he points at Rhi, Ridoc, and me—"don't touch anything."

"And you?" I ask.

"I'm here in case it all goes to shit." He glances back at the stone. "Wouldn't be the first time I've mended it."

I hand Sawyer his crutches, and all of us sit in one long line to begin the nail-biting process of waiting. The very future of this war will be determined in this room, just like it was a couple of weeks ago. I close my eyes to avoid the stone, but there's no blocking the scent of the chamber or the memory of my screams.

I'll get to see him soon. Her voice floods my head, breaking through every barrier I've thrown in grief's way to keep from feeling it, and slicing into my heart like the rusty edge of a jagged blade. *Live well.*

"Vi?" Rhiannon wraps her arm around my shoulders.

"I couldn't stop her," I whisper, forcing my watery eyes open as Sawyer lifts his hands on the left. "She was right there, and I couldn't stop her."

"Your mother?" she asks gently.

I nod.

"I'm so very sorry, Violet," Rhi says quietly, laying her head on my shoulder.

"I'm not even sure if I miss *her*," I admit in a broken whisper, "or the chance we had at eventually…being something. Maybe not what you and your mom have, but *something*."

"You can feel both." She takes my hand in hers and squeezes, and my chest lightens as we watch a spot on the top line of runes differentiating Navarre's wardstone from Aretia's bubbling outward. It's working.

Both our heads swivel right, toward Maren, and the flier stares down at the small rock in her palm, then shakes her head.

Well that's disappointing.

"Onto the next," Mira orders.

"Kind of wondering what protection we just took off," Ridoc mumbles as

Sawyer lifts his hands again, sitting to our left.

Sawyer's arms begin to shake, and I continue squeezing Rhi's hand. "Maybe we pushed him too hard," I whisper to her.

The next line on the stone bulges outward, then splits for a terrifying heartbeat before melted metal oozes from the wound. Oh...crap.

"Gamlyn!" Brennan barks as Ridoc throws up his hands, hurtling a ball of ice toward the stone. It makes contact with a hiss, and Ridoc holds it there as steam bursts skyward, then fizzles and dies.

"Maybe this wasn't such a great idea—" he starts.

"Hey, everyone," Maren says.

I whip my head in her direction so fast the room spins and find the stone twirling above her hand. My breath rushes out, taking the form of a relieved laugh.

"Mira?" Brennan asks.

My sister is already walking toward the wardstone, her hands splayed open. "They're still intact. We need to be sure that Barlowe is still *contained*, seeing as he's our only test subject, but I'm ninety-nine percent sure the protections against dark wielders are still in place."

"We did it!" Ridoc bounces to his feet, throwing his fists in the air. "Fuck yes, Sawyer! Fuck you, Senarium—the fliers can wield! They can *stay* with their squads!"

I grin like a kid. In eight hours, the accord for the riot to stay will be signed, and we'll be whole.

"What now?" Maren catches the rock.

"Now we stand trial for treason," Sawyer manages between gulping breaths. But when our eyes meet, he's smiling just like I am.

"No. We won't." My smile widens. "Maren, I need you to listen to me very carefully."

• • •

The next morning, my heart races and the Battle Brief room buzzes with a mixture of excitement, trepidation, and outright fear as we take our seats. Rhi and Ridoc claim the spots to my right, while Maren holds a seat empty for Cat between her and Trager to my left.

"Keep an eye on him," Rhi orders Aaric as he escorts Kai and the other first-years down the steps at the edge of the room.

Aaric nods, and I notice Baylor and Lynx covering their backs while Sloane and Avalynn lead the way, keeping Kai protected at every angle.

"I've never done this without a notebook." I brush the dust off the desktop in front of me as Cat works her way down our row.

"I'm sure our things will be sent," Rhi says. "At least I hope they will. Guess it depends on how the Assembly takes the news that Riorson didn't heed their wishes for the riot to return."

"He doesn't have to heed their wishes." Cat slides into the seat next to Maren and pulls her braid over her shoulder. "He's not just the heir to Aretia anymore. He's the Duke of Tyrrendor as of eight this morning, according to my uncle."

Thank you, Amari, it's signed. I shift my weight, looking for a position that takes a little pressure off my lower back, and breathe deeply to try and slow my heart rate.

"You all right?" Rhi asks, her eyes narrowing on a group out of Navarre's Fourth Wing as they fill the seats ahead of us.

"Fine." I roll my neck. "Just didn't get enough sleep last night and now I'm paying for it."

"—because you took my fucking pen!" the second-year ahead of us seethes, lurching over the seat of the girl next to him. "You always take it, and I've had it!" He snatches the pen and settles back into his seat.

I shoot a look at Cat's smug face. "Don't."

"What? I was just testing things out." She smothers a smirk. "You said we couldn't tell anyone, not that we couldn't play."

Maren snort-laughs, and I can't help but fight my own smile. At least she's not fucking with me, and the Navarrians do kind of deserve it.

"Welcome to Battle Brief," Devera announces as she descends the steps to our left, and the room falls quiet. "I understand you've been led by Colonel Markham in my absence, but that ends today." She reaches the raised stage at the base of the room and leans against the table. "Even if we only have one day with our flier colleagues, we will be proceeding—"

"Professor Devera!" The auburn-haired professor of the fliers, Kiandra, all but runs down the steps, and our squad shares quick glances as she conveys something to Devera behind her hand.

"Excellent," Devera says, smiling wide. "For everyone who doesn't know, this is Professor Kiandra, and she'll be leading Battle Brief with me from now on, given the news that our nobles are back in active negotiation for an alliance."

A roar of approval overpowers the disgruntled Navarrians.

"When did you tell your uncle?" I ask Cat.

"About twenty minutes ago, just like you asked," she answers. "He works fast."

Which means we have a matter of minutes. I drum my fingers on the desk and stare up at the inaccurate map of Navarre. Everything's about to change.

"With that in mind"—Devera raises her voice, and we quiet down—"let's discuss structure. To keep it easy, you stay where you have always been. If you find it awkward to serve in a squad with those who made a different choice this fall, then feel free to lodge your complaint with Malek."

"That's not fair!" a third-year yells out behind us. "With the addition of the fliers, Third and Fourth Wings are considerably larger, which gives them an advantage during War Games."

"Yes." Devera tilts her head. "Get over it. We're not playing games anymore; we're preparing you for *war*."

"Do you think they forgot what happened two weeks ago?" Ridoc whispers.

"I think it's possible they forgot what they had for breakfast," Rhi replies.

"First and Second Wings will only be smaller until the rest of the flier cadets arrive from Cygnisen," Devera continues. "At which time you will welcome them."

"Fuck." The guy ahead of us sinks lower in his chair.

"Next issue: we have too many wingleaders among us," Devera continues, and I glance over my shoulder at Dain, who stiffens in his seat a few rows back with the third-years. "It has been determined that leadership shall align with the wing's...population." She lifts her eyebrows. "Therefore, Iris Drue, you retain leadership of First Wing, Aura Beinhaven retains Second Wing, while Third Wing remains with Lyell Stirling, and Fourth Wing will be led by Dain Aetos."

Thank *gods*.

The room explodes in applause and shouts of disagreement.

"This matter is not up for discussion!" Devera's magically amplified voice shakes the desktop, quieting the room before she continues. "If you are unsure who you report to or if you're still in command, a full list of cadet leadership will be posted in commons this afternoon."

The briefing room door flies open and slams into the wall so hard I hear stone crack as we all turn to face yet another commotion.

"Violet Sorrengail!" Colonel Aetos shouts from the doorway, his face a mottled shade of red as his narrowed eyes search the briefing room.

"Here." Bracing my hands on the edges of my seat to fight a sudden wave of dizziness, I rise to stand as four riders follow Aetos in.

"Vi," Rhiannon whispers.

"No one say a damned thing," I reply under my breath. "I'll be fine."

"You are hereby charged with high treason against the kingdom of Navarre!"

Maybe not.

While many preach loyalty to Hedeon above all others, especially in Calldyr Province, I find that favoring Zihnal has universal appeal. Everyone wants wisdom but *needs* luck.

—Major Rorilee's Guide to Appeasing the Gods,
Second Edition

CHAPTER EIGHT

B eing arrested for treason doesn't exactly come as a shock, but Colonel Aetos delivering the accusation is a blow I didn't see coming.

"Dad?" Dain stands.

Aetos's head swivels toward Dain, and his mouth twists into a sneer. "I have no son."

I gasp, and hurt flashes across Dain's face before he schools his features and straightens his shoulders. "As Cadet Sorrengail's wingleader—"

"Request denied," Colonel Aetos snaps.

"We can't just sit here," Ridoc argues quietly.

"You can and you will." I make my way down the row and glance up at Dain. "I'm all right."

"You're far from all right!" Aetos growls.

The world rocks beneath my feet, and I curse my lack of sleep as I climb the steps to Aetos and the four lieutenants posted at his side. One of the women gestures toward the door, and I hold my head high as I walk by Aetos, somehow managing not to vomit when I see his rank has been raised to *general.*

Aetos keeps pace at my side in the hallway. "You're as good as dead for what you've done."

"I will only speak to the Senarium."

"Good thing they're gathered. It will make for a quick trial." After a silent procession through the quadrant and into the main campus, Aetos escorts me past a barrage of guards and cadets from other quadrants and into the great hall, entering the room just ahead of me. "I have brought the traitor!"

He steps aside to reveal the long table set for negotiations to resume. The members of the Senarium sit to the left side again, all dazzling in their choice of clothing this morning, with the exception of the one in rider black.

Xaden turns in his seat at the end of the table and lifts his scarred brow as shadows brush across my mind. *"What happened to not getting into trouble?"*

"I never promised that." I hold his gaze, noting the circles under his eyes. *"You look tired."*

"Just what every man wants to hear from the person he loves." He drums his fingers on the table, drawing my attention to a scrap of fabric in front of him—my lightning-wielder patch. *"I've decided I'm done not knowing what you're up to."*

"Good choice."

"You really fucked with the wards?"

"Someone once told me the right way isn't the only way." I use his own words from my first year against him, and his mouth tightens.

"As you can see, we have the evidence we need to place you at the stone," Aetos declares as he reaches the table. "I ask that the Senarium quickly pass judgment." He glances at Xaden. "Unless your newest addition needs to recuse himself for his *proximity* to the traitor."

"Remove yourself if you can't be silent, Aetos." The Duke of Calldyr leans back in his chair and runs a hand over his short blond beard. "You have no purview here."

Aetos stiffens at my side, then retreats with the other riders, leaving me to face the Senarium.

"Do you have a plan, Violence?" Xaden asks, and though a muscle in his jaw flexes, the shadows in the room stay put. *"I'm assuming so, since this patch's seams look cleanly cut."*

"Has anyone reported if the capabilities of the wards were damaged beyond allowing the fliers to wield?" the Duke of Calldyr asks.

"Did you sign the accord for the riot to stay?" I ask Xaden just to be sure.

"They're intact against dark wielders." Xaden's fingers still. *"I wouldn't be sitting here if I hadn't."*

"Then I have a perfect plan."

"How would you know?" The Duchess of Morraine turns in her seat.

"Because I would know," Xaden replies to me alone. "We haven't been swarmed, and Barlowe remains in our interrogation chamber. The wards are holding." He tilts his head and gives me the same look of anticipation he does when we step on the mat to spar. *"I'm eager for the show."*

"I'll save everyone the fuss of organizing a trial and execution." I point to the patch I cut off my uniform last night. "That's mine. I was the one who orchestrated altering the wardstone. I'm the reason that the fliers can wield and that you now have a clear path to negotiate an alliance. You're welcome."

The confession is met with six pairs of raised eyebrows and one sexy-as-hell smirk. *"Guess we're not going for subtlety."*

"No time for subtlety, and no evidence to convict anyone else in case it went awry."

"I…" The Duchess of Morraine looks to her peers, her giant ruby earrings smacking her golden-brown jawline as she swings her head back and forth. "What do we even do with that?"

"Nothing," Xaden answers, watching me like I'm the only one in the room. "Cadet Sorrengail, and whomever she acted with, committed the crime last night, and as of this morning, every single one of you and our king signed their pardons."

I nod.

"Brilliant, reckless woman." His gaze heats, and I fight a smile.

"So there's nothing we can do?" The Duchess of Elsum leans forward, her long brown tresses brushing the table. "She alters our defenses and then, what? Goes back to class?"

"It would seem so." The Duke of Calldyr nods slowly.

"Seems the young woman pulled off quite the feat," a new voice says.

I glance to my right, then do a double take at the woman standing in the north doorway of the hall. The silver of her intricate, armored breastplate flashes in the morning light as she walks forward, her smile crinkling the light-brown skin at the edges of her dark eyes. She wears a pair of scarlet breeches with a shortsword sheathed at her hip and a sparkling tiara atop her riotous curls, its delicacy a striking contrast to her weaponry. *Queen Maraya.*

"Your Majesty." I bow my head like my father taught me.

"Cadet Sorrengail," she says, and I look up to find her mere feet away. "I've heard much about the Continent's only lightning wielder, and I am pleased to see the compliments were not spoken in hyperbole." She glances sideways at the Senarium. "I assume she's free to return to her duties, as surely your king will arrive at any minute to continue our negotiations."

"There's not a thing we can do to her." Xaden pockets my patch, and the others slowly agree, four of them with more than a little anger in their eyes.

"Excellent." Queen Maraya offers the Senarium a smile, then pulls me aside and lowers her voice. "Viscount Tecarus spoke of the deal you made. You truly risked your king's wrath, your kingdom's defenses, all to keep my fliers here?"

"Yes." My stomach clenches. "It was the right thing to do."

"And in return, you only asked for unfettered access to his library?" She studies me closely, but I hold her gaze.

"It's the best on the Continent and our best hope for any historical record of how we defeated the venin centuries ago." *And how we can cure them.*

"Tell me you didn't do this for me." Xaden's chair creaks against the stone floor.

"I thought we promised never to lie to each other."

"You endangered yourself—" His tone tightens.

"And I have no regrets." The sooner he gets it through his head that I'll do anything in my power to cure him, the easier this will be on both of us.

"Fascinating." The queen's smile warms. "But his is not the best. Mine is. I have thousands upon thousands of volumes secured in my summer home, and you are now welcome to any and all of them. I'll have my steward send you a full catalog, though I warn you, we have yet to come across any such historical record."

"Thank you." Hope fills my chest. If I don't find it, Jesinia will.

She nods once, then heads toward the table, effectively dismissing me.

I quickly take my leave, escaping before King Tauri—or Halden—can appear.

"This discussion isn't over," Xaden warns as I rush into the hallway, nearly taking out Rhi and Ridoc in the process.

"But it is for now." I catch my balance as the door slams behind me. "What are you doing here?" Every second-year in our squad seems to have pushed their way through the guards.

"We were kind of worried they'd haul you behind the school and turn you to ash." Ridoc rubs his hand over the tattoo of a dragon on the side of his neck.

"I'm fine. Anything we did up until this morning has been pardoned. Did you skip the rest of Battle Brief?"

"There wasn't much to brief us on, since information is coming in from the border at a trickle. One active combat zone that they know of—" Rhi pauses, her eyes flying wide. "Vi."

"You will face consequences!" Aetos roars from the left and I pivot, putting myself between him and my friends as he charges down the thick red carpet at us. Anger rises, swift and strong, bringing power rushing to the surface of my skin.

"Not from you she won't." Brennan steps through the line of guards directly in front of me and shakes his head.

"You." Aetos recoils. "This whole time…"

"Me." Brennan nods, and I move to his side.

"You lost." My fingers brush the hilt of a dagger at my thigh as I glare up at the man I'd once considered a role model. "You tried to kill us at Athebyne, sent assassins after me in the fall, and even sicced Varrish on me, and I'm still here. You *lost*. We're pardoned. We're here."

"And yet I'm the one the king appointed to take over as commanding general of Basgiath"—he gestures to the busy hall around us—"so maybe it's *you* who has actually lost, *Cadet* Sorrengail."

My heart gallops, the edges of my vision turn dark, and I wobble. *No.* Anyone but him. *Anyone.* I shake my head as Brennan grasps a fistful of fabric at the back of my uniform, steadying me.

"You're unfit to sit at her desk," Brennan snaps.

"But here I am." He stands a bit taller. "The Senarium may abide by the pardon, but I assure you that you will not get away with altering a stone none of us fully understand—with endangering our kingdom."

"But here *I* am," I reply softly, anger quickly replacing shock. "Your threats are just threats. I'm no longer the scared first-year, unsure if I'd survive Threshing or be capable of wielding." I take a single step in his direction. "One of my dragons is among the most powerful on the Continent, and the other is the rarest. I didn't realize it last year or even a few months ago, but I do now: you can't afford to kill me."

His face—so like Dain's—twists into a scowl.

"You can't afford to lose either of my dragons, let alone my signet, and you sure as Malek can't afford to lose Lieutenant Riorson's—or should I call him the Duke of *Tyrrendor*?" I hold out both arms at my sides, exposing my torso. "Do your worst, but we both know I'm now beyond your reach, General." Slowly, I let my arms fall.

"Do my worst?" Heaving breaths raise and lower his shoulders as he looks to Brennan, then behind him. "I know exactly where to strike in order to bring you to heel, cadet. Your siblings may be out of my chain of command, but your friends are not."

My stomach dips.

"You second-years seem pretty loyal to one another." He drags his gaze back to mine. "They'll pay each and every time you disobey an order or step out of line, starting now." His head tilts as he stares past me. "You want to play with matters of war? Then you won't mind serving on the front." He glances at Rhi. "Squad leader, every second-year under your command is hereby ordered for two days of duty at the outpost of Samara, to begin tomorrow morning." A cruel smile curves his mouth as he addresses me. "The fighting there is...rather intense, but surely your *signet* will keep your squadmates alive, and two days should get you back before your dragon feels the loss of his mate."

"Tomorrow morning?" My lips part. "But it's at least an eighteen-hour flight for a gryphon, and they'll need breaks." It's more like twenty hours total, and they'll be exhausted by the time we get there.

"Then I guess you'd better get going. I hope to see you all return...intact."

Calling cadets into active service in times of war may only be
authorized by the Commanding General of Basgiath.

—ARTICLE EIGHT, SECTION ONE
THE DRAGON RIDER'S CODEX

CHAPTER
NINE

Twenty-two hours later, the six of us report to Lieutenant Colonel Degrensi
in Samara's courtyard, bleary-eyed and swaying with bone-deep tiredness.
We're not the only ones exhausted. The lieutenant colonel has definitely seen
easier days. His cheeks are gaunt, and dried blood cakes the side of his neck.

The fortress should feel familiar thanks to how many times I visited Xaden
while he was stationed here in the fall, but the scene around us makes the place
nearly unrecognizable. The western wall looks like a dragon crashed through it,
demolishing nearly a quarter of the structure, and wounded in various states of
distress line what's left as healers in bloody smocks move between them.

"Not a dragon," Andarna corrects me. *"A wyvern."*

We flew over what remained of their burned bones a few fields away.

"Try to get some rest," I tell her.

"I'm the only one who slept on the way here," she argues. *"And this thing
itches."*

*"Leave your harness on. There's no telling how quickly we might be forced
to leave."*

"I'm not wearing this when we find my family," she grumbles.

"Then fly farther," Tairn growls. *"Some of us are trying to sleep."*

Lieutenant Colonel Degrensi finishes reading the orders Rhi carried, then
looks up at us over the paper. "They really gave command of Basgiath to *Aetos*?"

"Yes, sir." Rhi holds her shoulders straight, which is more than I can say for
the rest of us.

Cat and Maren look like they've been through a hurricane, and Trager can't quit yawning. Same goes for Ridoc. And after spending all night in the saddle, I'm all but leaning on him to keep upright. Every muscle in my body hurts, my hips are screaming, and my head pounds in time with my heartbeat.

"And he invoked Article Eight to send me cadets?" Degrensi glances down our line, his gaze lingering on the fliers.

"Yes, sir." Rhi nods.

"Wonderful. Well, his intel is old." Degrensi crumples the orders into a ball. "Fighting ended yesterday, and even if it hadn't, I'm not apt to send cadets into battle." He points to the gaping hole in the fortress. "The biggest wyvern crashed through as the wards came back up, but once our perimeter fell, venin didn't need magic to get inside the post anyway. Nearly lost our power supply killing them off. We managed to repel them across the border, but the front is just over the hill." His gaze drifts toward the fliers. "The casualties are far worse beyond the wards."

"They always are," Cat comments.

"Has Newhall been affected?" Maren's face draws tight. "It's a small village on the Stonewater River about half an—"

"I know where Newhall is," Degrensi interrupts, clearly ready to be done with us. "As of this morning's report, it remains standing."

Maren's shoulders sag, and Cat wraps her arm around her.

"What about Poromish civilians?" Trager asks. "Are you"—he flinches—"we offering them refuge?"

Degrensi slowly shakes his head. "We're under strict orders not to allow anyone in unless something in negotiations changes, but we crossed the border and fought with your people up until the horde departed yesterday."

"You have our gratitude," Cat says. "Not everyone would do the same."

He nods. "For transparency, don't expect the others to be friendly, especially among the riders. This potential alliance isn't overly popular." Lieutenant Colonel Degrensi turns his attention to me. "We were all grieved to hear of the loss of your mother. She was an outstanding commander."

"Thank you. She prided herself on it." I adjust the straps of my pack on my shoulders to give my hands something to do.

He nods. "Do me a favor and ask that dragon of yours to stay out of sight. You are both formidable weapons, but you're also a giant target. The enemy may see this as their opportunity to attack en masse and dispatch you both from our ranks, and we can't afford to draw more daggers from the armory if we want to keep the wards in place. Not much we can do if he's already been spotted, but let's avoid additional opportunities."

"Yes, sir," I respond.

"I agree only as a matter of your safety," Tairn mutters, adding something about the insolence of humans.

"Lieutenant Colonel!" a rider in dusty leathers shouts from the gate. "We need you!"

Degrensi bobs his head at the rider, then looks back at us. "Look, I don't really care what you did to piss off Aetos; I'm too busy fighting a war to discipline cadets." He gestures at the mess around us. "So, find whatever space you can and rack out. Get some rest. Then make yourselves useful wherever you see fit." There's a small but noticeable limp in his stride as he leaves us, heading for the gate.

We're left facing more than a few questionable stares from passing soldiers and riders, some downright hostile.

"How are we supposed to sleep knowing most of these riders would happily put knives in our backs?" Maren asks.

"We can take watches," Trager suggests, pulling a piece of feather fluff from his light-brown hair. "Once I get some sleep, I'll offer to help the healers, too."

"If they'll accept it," Cat notes, crossing her arms when a captain in rider black glares our way from across the bailey. "They'd probably put a knife in your back in gratitude."

"Violet?" Rhi glances my way. "You know the outpost better than any of us."

My gaze slides toward the southwestern turret, and a tired smile tugs at my lips. Even hundreds of miles away, he's still taking care of me and doesn't even know it. "I know where we'll be safe."

• • •

I can't find it. Panic seizes my heart as I throw items from the wooden chest at the foot of my four-poster bed, growing more and more desperate with each minute that passes.

It has to be here.

Heat scorches the side of my face as blue flames burst through the window of my chamber, and the blast knocks me backward. I crash into the full-length mirror, and glass rains down, nicking the top of my head. I throw myself onto my hands and knees and crawl toward the chest as fire catches my curtains and screams sound in the hallway behind me.

Panic threatens to seize my muscles. I'm out of time, but I can't leave them. They're all I have left.

Every inch is a fight, my body refusing to obey the simple command to *move*, and sweat beads on my forehead as the flames spread to the linens on my bed.

"What are you doing?" someone shouts behind me as I reach the trunk, but I can't afford the time to turn, not until I've found it. Pillows, an extra blanket, the books my father sent with me — I discard them all, flinging them into the fire like sacrifices as I burrow deeper into the bottomless chest.

"We have to go!" Cat sinks down to her knees beside me. "They've already taken the hall. We need to fly!"

"I can't find it!" I try to yell, but it comes out nearly silent. Why can't I scream? Rail against the cruelty, the perpetual anxiety of impending doom? "Get yourself out! I'll follow."

"I can't leave you!" She grabs me by the shoulders, soot covering half her face, and fear waters her dark-brown eyes. "Don't make me try, because I can't."

"You have to live." I rip away and dig back into the chest. "He'll choose you. I know he will. You're the future queen of Tyrrendor, and your people need you." She hasn't lost her crown. She'll fight for what's hers.

"I need *you*!" she yells, then gasps and throws herself over me as heat roars against our backs. Wood crackles and breaks, and then the heat changes, coming at us from every direction.

"Just another—" My fingers fumble, then finally grasp the miniature painting, and I register their soft smiles, the playful honey-brown eyes of my family before clasping the art to my chest. "Got it!"

Cat yanks me to my feet, dragging me toward the door, and we both startle as the beams of my bed come crashing down. Embers fly, singeing my hand, and the painting slips from my grip, catching fire on its way to the ground.

"No!" I scream as Cat tugs me backward, and as the flame engulfs the portrait, it's no longer a painting…it's them. My parents. My family. They're *burning*.

"Stop!" My throat can't force the word out as I'm pulled away to the sound of their screams, their tears, begging me to save them. "No! No!"

I come awake and jolt upright in bed, gasping for air and blinking off the remnants of the nightmare as sweat drips down the back of my neck.

Late-afternoon sun streams in through the window, lighting the bedchamber that had been Xaden's, the one he warded so only he and I could get through. My heart races as I glance over the sleeping faces of my squadmates. Thank the gods that Xaden used the same warding technique on this room as he had on mine at Basgiath — I'd pulled my squad through one by one.

Trager's sleeping up against the door, using his pack for a pillow, and Ridoc is out a few feet away with his dagger mere inches from his fingertips.

"Vi?" Rhi whispers, sitting up beside me and rubbing the sleep out of her eyes. "You all right?"

I nod, spotting Maren and Cat curled with their backs against each other in the center of the room on makeshift pallets. We're all accounted for. There's no fire. No immediate danger. As much as I miss Sawyer, I'm glad he's not in harm's way. Clearly we're too close to the front for my peace of mind with dreams like that. "Just a nightmare."

"Oh." She lies back down in the spot I'd usually sleep, and I fall onto Xaden's now sweat-soaked pillow. "Basgiath? I get them sometimes, too."

"I think so." It's been months since he's slept here, but I swear I catch a hint of mint as I turn my head toward Rhi, keeping my voice low. "But Cat was there, and I was trying to find this painting of my family, but it was weird, and then they were burning." I sigh. "Which makes sense, considering my mother turned herself into an actual flame."

Rhi grimaces. "I'm sorry."

I scoff lightly, remembering the dream. "And I told Cat she had to live because *she* was the future queen of Tyrrendor."

Rhi's eyes widen, and she smothers a laugh with her hand. "Now *that's* the real nightmare."

"I know, right?" My smile slips. "What's in your nightmares when you have them?"

She smooths the piece of black silk covering her hair. "Usually, it's that you don't save Sawyer, and I can't get to him fast enough because I make the wrong call—"

"You two are not as quiet as you think," Ridoc mutters. "What time is it?"

"Probably time for us to get up," Rhi says.

The rest of the squad stirs, and we take turns in the bathing chamber before filing into the hallway, ready to make ourselves useful. A pair of riders—one wearing major rank and the other captain—approach as I shut Xaden's door, their footsteps as weary as their eyes.

"Maise says they have less than an hour," the major says, wrapping a bandage around her hand, then shoving her short blond hair out of her eyes. "Came out of nowhere."

Maise. I know that name.

"Mated to Greim," Tairn reminds me.

Right. They've been mated for decades and are able to communicate at a far longer range than Tairn and Sgaeyl.

"We're stretched too thin." A line of stitches puckers on the captain's cheek, and he shakes his head. "If they're smart, they've already evacuated Newhall."

We all step back against the wall so they can pass.

Well, all except Maren, who blocks their way. "I'm sorry, did you say Newhall?"

"Yes," the captain replies, looking at Maren like he's tasted something sour.

"Why is it being evacuated?" Maren rushes, her brow furrowing.

The officers share a knowing look, and the rest of us come off the wall in front of the pair as Cat quickly crosses behind Trager to reach Maren. "The area is under attack. It's odd for venin to target such a small village, but scouts reported smoke."

Maren inhales sharply, and Cat hooks her arm through her elbow.

"You have people there?" The major's tone softens, pity in her gaze.

Maren presses her lips between her teeth and nods.

"It's where her family fled," Cat answers. "It's not more than half an hour from here. Are we flying?"

"We?" The captain looks at each of us—pausing at my braid—before addressing Cat. "*We* are running on little to no sleep and have already lost one rider this week. Half our riot is patrolling to the north and the other half is pushing burnout, so as harsh as it may sound"—he shoots the major a look I can't quite decipher—"the village is too small to risk any more casualties to the unit."

My breath abandons me.

"So we just leave them to die?" Trager's voice rises. "Why? Because they're Poromish?"

"Not because they're Poromish. Because *we* can't help." The major's words grow shorter. "Not all of us wield lightning." She glances at me. "If we want to save the towns, the cities, the denser areas of population, then an unfortunate part of war is knowing we'll lose some of the villages. If you don't pick up strategic concepts in your third year, then you'll certainly learn fast once you graduate." The pair walks around Maren and Cat, their footsteps heavy as they depart.

"If any of us are still alive by the time they graduate…" The captain's voice fades.

"My family's there," Maren whispers, her face crumpling. "Why didn't my parents go south when Zolya fell? They would have been safe in Cordyn. Or they could have gone back to Draithus."

"Shh." Cat rubs Maren's arm. "I'm sure they'll get out."

Maren shakes her head violently. "What if they're already dead?"

My stomach churns as I look to Rhi. "Tairn and I can make that flight faster than half an hour if we break from the squad."

"It's not like we haven't seen battle," Cat adds. "We *fought* our way out of Cliffsbane."

Rhi stiffens. "Aetos invoked Article Eight, so we're legally clear, but there are so many unknowns," she whispers to herself. "Number of venin? Wyvern? But the civilians…"

"Look, it's only a fight if we make it one." Ridoc glances at the fliers. "Narrow the scope of the mission. We extract Maren's family. We save as many civilians as we can. We get out."

"Without knowing what we're up against, we can't just—" Rhi starts.

"We defended Basgiath," Cat snaps.

Rhi's mouth snaps shut.

If it were Mira and Brennan in danger, I'd go, especially with that nightmare so fresh in my mind, but there's a reason I'm not the squad leader and Rhi is. "Vote," I suggest. "I get it—ordering us into a war zone could be catastrophic and we're just cadets, so vote. That's what we did at Resson."

None of us mention that Liam and Soleil didn't come home.

Rhi nods. "All in favor—" Every hand goes up, including hers. She sighs. "Well, Degrensi did tell us to make ourselves useful. Let's go be of use."

Weather is the one great equalizer in battle, equally detrimental or favorable to both sides given the conditions. Without our wielders swaying that element to our advantage, we are at its mercy.

—Tactics, a Modern Guide to Aerial Combat
by Major Constance Cará

CHAPTER
TEN

Forty minutes later, the sun disappears as Tairn and I drop between the snow-tipped ridgelines, descending thousands of feet into the warmer valley that houses the Stonewater River. The sun always sets so early this time of year. Power hums in my veins, ebbing and flowing with every heartbeat. I'd almost forgotten how wild magic feels beyond the wards, how accessible. Tairn's power seems endless, deeper than the oceans I've never crossed, wider than the vast sky above us.

"Maise saw us depart," Tairn warns, tucking his wings. My stomach rises as he plummets, following the terrain at a nauseating speed. *"She's relaying an order to return immediately."*

"Can you ignore her?" We're easily five minutes ahead of the other dragons and ten ahead of the gryphons, who travel with Andarna despite my pleas for her to stay behind.

"I do not answer to Maise." He levels out over the river, a notable tailwind helping to maintain his speed. His wings beat so close to the rapids that I half expect to feel the splash of water as we curve around the bend. In a few months, this river will be the most treacherous on the Continent with spring runoff, adding to the region's already unpredictable weather compliments of the abrupt change in altitude.

Smoke rises in thick plumes ahead of us, joining the storm clouds while simultaneously smothering the village beneath. My heart jolts with a rush of adrenaline and dread. *"Ahead."*

"Yes, I, too, have eyes. We're five minutes out." He tips right to fit through a bottleneck in the water-carved canyon, and my weight shifts, the belt of my saddle keeping me in place.

Once we're through, I rip off my gloves, shove them into my right front pocket, then scan both sides of the raging river for signs of life. *"I need you to slow down. I can't tell if those are people or trees."*

"You ask for speed and then complain when I provide it." But he slows as the landscape shifts into the high plains.

"This is the only logical path they'd take to—" I spot a line of civilians hiking toward us on the southern bank of the river. *"There!"*

"I have relayed to Feirge. The gryphons and Andarna will stop there first as planned," Tairn tells me, then picks up speed again. *"One minute. Prepare yourself. The pressure is dropping. We fly toward a storm."*

Sure enough, my ears pop as I shove my wrist through the leather strap that will keep the conduit secure. Quickly, I unbutton my flight hood, letting the warmer wind rip it from my face for the sake of visibility as we fly toward the smoke-and-flame-engulfed village. Civilians flee from a gate in the western wall, and the acrid scent of smoke fills my lungs, growing more pungent with each beat of Tairn's wings.

A shape breaks through the pillar of smoke—

"Wyvern!" I grasp the conduit in my left hand, then throw open the door to Tairn's power, increasing the flow from a trickle to a rush. It envelops me, fire streaking through my veins, embers burning in my bones as the conduit glows, siphoning off the excess.

"Do not channel more than you wield!" Tairn warns as the wyvern flies straight for us, its gray, leathery wings riddled with holes.

"I'm fine." If I miss the first time, those fetid teeth will be in reach of Tairn. I force myself upright against the wind, my core tightening to keep me steady as I lift my right hand, then take aim and release the power with a *snap.*

Lightning flashes, illuminating the clouds above for less than a heartbeat before tearing through the sky and striking the wyvern in the chest. The beast screams as it falls, and Tairn passes so closely overhead that I catch the scent of charred flesh.

There's no time for relief as two more burst through the smoke.

We're outnumbered, and while Tairn is bigger, they are faster.

"High ground," Tairn warns before banking right and climbing, putting the village behind us.

I turn as far as the belt on my saddle will allow and raise my hand, welcoming the burn as energy gathers within me, but— *"They're on us!"*

Too close to strike without endangering Tairn.

The larger wyvern's enormous jaw opens, revealing bloodstained teeth, and its tongue curls as it lunges with a burst of speed. *"Tairn!"*

Tairn dips his wings at an angle, catching the wind, and I hurtle forward in the seat at the sudden decrease in speed as he swings his massive tail. Bone cracks, blood spurts, and the wyvern spins off to the right, missing the lower half of its jaw.

I can't pivot fully, but I take aim at what I can see of the one still pursuing us, then unleash with a *crack*…and miss.

"Fuck." I reach—

"If you remove that belt, I will unseat you over the river and let your meager gods sort you out," Tairn warns, then banks left, giving me the perfect view.

I release another strike, guiding it with the motion of my hand, and it hits true, severing the wyvern's head from its neck. *"Got it!"*

Fuck yes.

But unless those three wyvern are on a scouting patrol—unlikely, given the flaming village—there has to be a creator nearby. I face forward and lean into the turn, casting my focus downward. The demarcation line is clear this high above the village. Half is devoid of color, drained of all its magic, and in the center of the village stands a single figure in flowing dark robes, her light hair—silver?—whipping in the wind.

It's her. The dark wielder from Jack's cell. My grip tightens on the conduit.

She looks toward us, lifts her hand, and wiggles her fingers as if *waving.* A sick feeling squeezes my stomach. *"I think…she was expecting us."*

This is a trap.

And we flew right into it. My heart drops at the realization, but it doesn't change the fact that Maren's family is in danger.

"Above!" Tairn bellows, and I look up as two wyvern emerge from the swirling storm system.

I lift my hand, but there's no time. They're already here.

Tairn punches his tail forward, *underneath us*, swinging his body in a way I've never experienced, and I fall backward, my stomach lodging in my throat as the ground takes the place of the sky and the strap pulls tight across my thighs, holding me upside down long enough for my heart to pound in my ears twice.

Snap. Bone fractures, and Tairn rolls right, dragging the broken-necked corpse of a wyvern with us, then releasing it once we level. I force my stomach back where it belongs and prepare to strike the other as it lunges for us.

It snaps its jaws, teeth clashing mere *feet* from Tairn's shoulder as it misses, cutting at least two years off my life. I extend my arm—

"Do not!" Tairn orders, and a second later, brown scales consume my field of

vision as Aotrom clasps the wyvern's head between his teeth and *bites* as we pass.

The wind roars like a beast, blocking out any other sound, and Tairn banks hard, whipping himself back around. My face contorts into a grimace at the force my body absorbs with the maneuver, and I fight to remain conscious as we turn toward the battle.

Aotrom's tail curves up, the poisonous barb jabbing into the belly of the wyvern— I blink. A scorpiontail?

It's not Aotrom.

"Chradh," Tairn explains as the wyvern falls from the dragon's grip.

"What the fuck is Garrick—"

"Tornado!" Tairn warns a second before a wall of wind hits hard enough to knock the breath from my lungs and drags us into its swirling vortex.

We're flung like a rag doll, and the roar of the storm vibrates every bone in my body. Tairn snaps his wings shut, and I hold fast to the pommels and duck my head as debris flies by, terror locking my muscles as we're thrown round and round and round as though we weigh *nothing.*

Oh Malek, I am not ready to meet you.

"Violet!" Andarna shouts.

"No!" Tairn bellows as we're spun to a near vertical position.

"Stay back!" I shriek, and fear burns through my bones like acid as we're ripped outward by centrifugal motion. She can't get caught in this. It has every chance of killing us and will damn sure take her life.

We're flung out of the storm like a projectile, hurtling backward through the air toward what I think is a mountainside. Tairn opens his wings in a burst, slowing our speed from meteoric to lethal in a move so sudden, my head whips backward and my ears ring. His roar shakes my ribs as he snaps his wings shut and contorts his body in an attempt to twist.

His side hits first, the collision stunning me breathless and knocking boulders loose around us with a cracking sound. Something slams into my knee and Tairn's wings snap over me a moment before I hear a second thud of impact.

The bond goes dark.

NO.

"Tairn!" I scream, terror locking every muscle, stealing every thought but one: *he can't be gone.*

We fall down the ridge in a graceless, limp skid. Deprived of sight, I can only hear the grate of rock against scale, feel the jarring hits as we crash through obstacles and continue downward.

"Tairn!" I try again, mentally grasping for him, but there's...nothing.

"Violet," Andarna cries. *"I can't feel him!"*

"Stay back!" I repeat as we fall down and down and down. Is there a cliff

beneath us?

I should have heeded Tairn's warning about the storm. Is he all right? Has he...

"Don't think like that!" she wails.

My heart thunders a staccato beat as we plummet, and I throw my hands from the pommels and spread them over his scales. I can't feel him breathing, but that doesn't mean he isn't. He has to be all right. I'd feel it if he wasn't, right? Panic fights to close my throat. This isn't how he ends, how *we* end.

Liam only had minutes after Deigh ceased breathing, but he *knew*.

"Choose to live," I beg Andarna in a rush. *"You're the only one of your kind, you have to live. No matter what happens to us."*

Oh gods, *Xaden*.

"Stay with me," she pleads, her voice breaking. *"You both have to stay."*

We free-fall for the length of a heartbeat, my stomach rising, and I prepare for my final breath.

Earth claims us once more in a rough embrace, and this time, we grind to a stop.

Tairn's wings fall open, and I'm left dangling at a ninety-degree angle to the ground, gasping dust-filled air. He's fallen onto his side.

I can't see his head from this angle, so I drop any semblance of a shield and fully reach for him. There's a glimmer of thread where our bond should be, but it's enough to flood my system with hope as something crashes behind me. A glimmer means he isn't dead. My own heartbeat means he can't be—

His chest shudders and his breaths begin a deep, steady pattern.

Thank you, gods.

"He's breathing," I tell Andarna.

"Sorrengail!" Footsteps race toward me.

"Here!" I reply, my abs straining to keep position while I fight with the belt of my saddle.

Garrick's chest heaves as he appears ten feet beneath me, his hood blown back and blood dripping from the right corner of his hairline. "You're alive." He braces his hands on both knees and leans over, and I can't tell if he's catching his breath or going to be ill. "Thank you, Dunne. Tairn?" He looks up, giving me a quick appraisal and blanching.

"Knocked out... What's wrong?" I ask.

"Your knee is a fucking mess."

I glance down at my leg, and a scream works its way up my throat as the agony hits, like it waited until I could see exactly how fucked I am to make itself known. My flight leathers are torn at my right knee, and my mouth waters, bile rising quickly as I realize my kneecap isn't where it's supposed to be. Searing pain hurtles up my leg and spine, stealing logical thought as it consumes me, coming in waves that match my heartbeat.

"Is it broken?" Garrick asks.

Seconds tick by as I concentrate solely on pushing the pain back into a box I can manage, then force my toes to move one by one. "I think. Just. Dislocated. Can't fix it." Nausea rolls through me with every breath. "At this angle."

He nods. "Drop, and I'll catch you. We'll get you sorted on the ground."

"Chradh?" I ask, getting a firm grip on the belt. My weight is holding the damned buckle closed.

"He's slowly coming to." Garrick looks back over his shoulder. "Stubborn ass turned and took the impact on his stomach. Saved my life, but an outcropping halfway down knocked him out temporarily."

That must be what happened to Tairn. That second impact I heard was his head.

Shit. The silver-haired venin is still out here, and both dragons are as good as defenseless without us, at least until the others arrive. "Drop me, and I'll kick you in the face." I grit my teeth through the pain. I'm not dying today, and neither is Tairn.

"Let's be honest. You're not kicking anyone with that knee." He lifts his arms up, and I'm filled with the most illogical longing for Xaden to be standing in his place. "Come on, Violet. Trust me."

I heave up, pushing against the pommels to shift my weight, then wrench the strap through the buckle and fall like a stone. The scream I'd held back rips free as he catches me, the world erupting in shades of red pain at the collision.

"Do you want me to put it back in?" he asks, holding me as carefully as he can.

I nod, and he quickly sets me on my feet and crouches in front of me, holding on to my waist to keep me upright. The scabbards of the swords he wears strapped to his back drag through palm-size hail stones to scrape the rocky ground.

"Extend it slowly," he orders, keeping his hazel eyes on my knee. I turn my head, biting into the collar of my jacket to keep from screaming again as I straighten my leg. "This won't be pleasant. I'm so sorry," he says as he slides my kneecap back into place.

"Don't be," I manage to gasp, the pain immediately sliding to a level where I can at least think somewhat properly. "Wrap is in my pack." The rhythmic sound of Tairn's breathing calms my heartbeat, but I can't see anything beyond his dark scales to my left and hunks of granite to our right with us all but wedged up against the mountainside.

He retrieves the fabric, then holds me steady as I do my best to stabilize the joint. Pain flares as I test my weight on the limb, but it's miniscule compared to what could happen to Tairn if we don't start moving, so I tie off the fabric and call it good. It'll do until I can get to a healer or Brennan—but we need to get out of here alive first.

"You're good at that," he says. Dipping down, he slings an arm around my upper back, and I throw mine over his shoulder.

"Lots of practice." We make our way beside Tairn's back, careful not to step on his wings, and finally clear his tail as the tornado winds its way eastward. "Your head is bleeding right above your scar from Resson."

"Good. Hate to damage the other side of my perfect face," he jokes. "Don't worry about me. It's nothing a couple of stitches won't fix."

"The others approach," Andarna says. *"They do not know Chradh is with you, and I have not told them."*

The Brown Scorpiontail blocked out his riot?

"Tell them to go for Maren's family first. You stay right where you're at until we know what's going on."

There's a definite grumble in her response as I stagger forward with Garrick's help, taking a central position between Tairn and Chradh, who looks like he might be missing a few scales along his jaw.

"The others are on their way," I tell Garrick. "And I'm pretty sure that venin knew we were coming."

"That's…great." He grimaces. "I've flown through some shit, but never been through a tornado before," Garrick says, scanning the horizon. We're at least a mile south of the village.

"Me, either." The smoke rises in a steady column again above the town. I reach for Tairn's power, but as expected, the scorching Archives I've come to depend on sputter with darkness. "Want to tell me what you're doing here?"

"They made it." Garrick tenses and pointedly looks toward the western end of the village as Feirge and Aotrom cross the moonlight. Kira, Daja, and Trager's gryphon, Sila, follow soon after, all of them bearing their riders and fliers respectively. "Maren's family, right? That's what Major Safah relayed."

"That's why *I'm* here. You're supposed to be with Xaden." There's no point confirming what he already knows. "Eight hours away."

"Yeah, well, the second he heard you were charging off into danger, he became…unreasonable." A muscle in Garrick's jaw ticks, and I pull my arm from his shoulder so he can stand straight, shifting my weight to relieve the pressure from my right knee as much as possible. "I've never seen him like that." Garrick shoots a worried look my way. "Ever. I don't even want to think about what he would have done if he'd been out here beyond the wards, because I thought he was going to rip the stones from the wall. He's always prided himself on control—he has to when he wields that much power—and I'm telling you, he *lost* it when he heard you were crossing the border, Violet. He's...not himself."

My chest tightens. He'd been annoyed, even angry when I flew for Cordyn with my siblings a few months ago, but hadn't come close to *losing* it. "Because Aetos sent us to—" The words die on my tongue as I process what he said. "He knew I was crossing the border? Maise." I end on a whisper, staring up at the side of Garrick's face. "How did you get here?"

"It's not important." He draws a sword with his left hand.

"Maise saw us leave maybe forty minutes ago, and you're already *here*. You're a wind-wielder, and there's no fucking way you pushed a hundreds-of-miles-an-hour tailwind at Chradh, so how did you *get* here?" My voice rises with my temper, and lightning strikes twenty feet in front of us, charring the ground as thunder booms simultaneously.

I startle, then wince as my knee cries at the sudden movement.

"Damn, Sorrengail, you didn't have to—" he starts.

"I didn't." I shake my head.

"I did."

Our heads whip right, and the silver-haired venin walks toward us, her purple robes billowing in the breeze. She doesn't bother to look at Tairn as she passes mere yards in front of his hind claws, just keeps those eerie red eyes pinned on us. On *me*.

Wait. She did...what? Lightning?

Blood drains from my face and I throw up my shields, drawing on Andarna's power.

Holy Dunne, she wielded *lightning*. But venin aren't supposed to have signets...let alone *mine*.

Dread pins my heart to the ground, but my hands are fast as I unsheathe and fling two daggers at her chest.

She waves her hand left and right, and the knives fall mid-flight. "Is that any way to thank me?"

Fuck. I should have brought the mini crossbow Maren gave me.

"Thank you for what, exactly?" Garrick raises his sword and moves to my side as I reach for Tairn's power again, finding a dim hum.

"Now wouldn't be a bad time to manifest a second signet," I tell Andarna as the dark wielder approaches. My heart thunders like a drum. All the venin has to do is palm the earth and the four of us will be desiccated in seconds.

"As if I control how you use my power?" Andarna counters.

Second signet. My gaze darts toward Garrick, but a glance is all I can afford with the dark wielder sauntering toward us.

"Not killing you, of course." The dark wielder cocks her head to the side and runs her gaze over me in blatant appraisal, then pauses about ten feet away. The scarlet veins beside her eyes remind me of a masquerade mask topped by the faded tattoo on her forehead, and the red glow around her irises is ten shades brighter than Jack's. A Sage, probably…maybe even a Maven, and were it not for the physical signs of her lost soul, she'd be stunningly beautiful, with high cheekbones and a full mouth, but her skin's eerily pale. "Though I must say I'm disappointed you were so easily lured from your wards." She tsks at me. "Shame the girl's family raised weapons at me, or they might have lived." She shoots a warning glance at Garrick, but he doesn't lower his sword.

The girl's family… My hands curl into fists.

"You killed Maren's family?" Rock and ice crunch under my boots as I take two steps toward her. "To lure *me*?" Anger curdles my stomach.

"Only the parents." She rolls her eyes. "I left the boys as a sign of goodwill, though you can't say the same about my wyvern, can you?"

"Goodwill?" I shout. Maren's going to be devastated.

"Violet," Garrick warns, but he keeps with me step for step.

"Careful with your tone, lightning wielder." The dark wielder flicks her wrist, and Garrick rises in the air in a nauseating reenactment of every one of my nightmares. His sword drops to the ground, and he scrambles for his throat. "You, I'm curious about. I'll even admit to wanting, considering all that power, not to mention being an effective leash. But him?" She shakes her head, and Garrick begins to kick.

Leash. That's exactly what Jack called me. She knows about Xaden.

"Let him go!" I draw another dagger and shove every hint of fear aside. Nothing's happening to Garrick on my watch. "This might not kill you, but it will hurt like hell."

"Let's not compare weapons." She reaches for a knife sheathed in the belt of her gauzy purple robe and reveals just enough of its green tip to seize my breath for a heartbeat. "Our paths are too intertwined to begin with such hostility. I know: you answer a single question and I'll return the walker to the ground. That seems a civil start to our relationship, don't you think, *Violet*?"

"Ask it." I feel Andarna hovering along our bond, alert and hopefully nowhere near us. *"Warn the others."*

"They're coming." Frustration sharpens her words.

"You prize his friend's life over information. Interesting." She shoves the knife back into its sheath. "I'm Theophanie, by the way. Seems only right that you know my name, seeing as I know everything about you, Violet Sorrengail."

Fucking *awesome.* "Because of Jack?" It's the only logical explanation.

She shrugs in a dismissive gesture that reminds me of the Duchess of Morraine. "Bonding one dragon is…enviable. All that power just *given* to you."

Her mouth tightens. "But two is unheard of. Aren't you the luckiest girl on the Continent? Or maybe that's me, being close by when your morningstartail was spotted."

"Is that really your question?" My fingernails cut into my palms as Garrick's kicks become more desperate.

"Just an observation." Her gaze flicks toward Garrick. "For good faith." She turns her hand and Garrick crashes to the ground beside me, wheezing as he draws breath. "Now tell me, which chose you first? The one who gifted you the power of the sky? Or the irid?"

In the hope and excitement this new development of the bonds between dragons, gryphons, and their humans brings, I wonder who has stopped to contemplate the nature of magic's balance. Do we not risk the equal rise of the very powers we seek to wield?

—Recorded Correspondence of Nirali Ilan, Commanding General, Cliffsbane Fortress, to Lyra Mykel, Deputy Commanding General, Basgiath War Camp

CHAPTER
ELEVEN

"Irid?" I blink and fight like hell to keep my face blank.

"Yes, your irid." Theophanie surveys the sky, then the landscape behind us as Garrick staggers to his feet, sword in hand. "Some do not believe, but I knew as soon as the cream-robed scholars whispered about the seventh breed in your war college. Pity I had to leave so abruptly. One hasn't been seen in centuries, and I was so hoping to set…eyes on her." She finishes the statement like the threat it is, bringing her crimson gaze to mine.

Andarna. Terror races up my spine and lightens my head.

"Irid," Andarna whispers. *"Yes. I remember now. That is what my kind are called. I am an irid scorpiontail."*

"Fly for the wards!" I scream mentally. *"She's not here for me. She wants you."*

"I will not abandon you," she roars.

"Everyone on the Continent needs you alive. Now fly.*"* My fingers brush the conduit hanging from my wrist, but it's of no use to me without Tairn's power. I need to stall, give Andarna enough time to escape. "She's out of your reach."

"Hmm." Theophanie studies my face. "Disappointing, but it wouldn't be fun if I caught my prey on the first attempt. You truly don't know what she is, do you?" The dark wielder's mouth curves into a delighted smile that instantly sickens my stomach. "What a prize you've won. Sometimes I forget just how short mortal memory can be."

Mortal. As opposed to what? *Immortal?* How fucking old *is* she?

She moves sideways, toward the village, and Garrick and I both mimic her movement, putting ourselves between her and Tairn. "When the shadow wielder comes to us—"

"He won't," I snap. Power hums, filling me at a trickle as the sound of wingbeats fills the air.

Tairn's waking up, but whatever's coming at us is coming *fast.*

"He will," she says in that same infuriatingly certain tone Xaden uses. Lightning cracks like punctuation, branching through the cloud overhead.

She didn't even have to lift her hands. Holy shit, I'm outmatched in every possible way.

"And when you come with him, you will remember that I let you live today and choose me, not Berwyn, as your teacher." She retreats step by slow step, extending her arms out at her sides.

Maybe venin lose their minds with their souls, but humoring her gives Andarna more time to flee. "And why would I do that?"

Power comes flooding back, scalding my bones, and I let it gather and coil.

"Besides the fact that he's subpar and you'd be chained to him, powerless to resist his orders?" She sneers in disgust, then schools her features. "I'll let you keep *both* your dragons while giving you what you want most in the world." Her gaze drops to the conduit as wind pulses. The others must be here. "Control and *knowledge.*"

Tairn swivels and his head snaps toward Theophanie, but his teeth close just short of her feet as she's plucked off the ground by the claw of a wyvern. Its gray wings beat fast and hard, blasting us with wind and carrying its creator from the battlefield.

"Holy shit, we're actually alive," Garrick says, lowering his sword. "She left us *alive.*"

"Are you all right?" I ask Tairn, my voice cracking.

"I am not deceased." He gains his feet, his talons digging into the rocky soil.

Relief pricks at my eyes, and my vision wobbles.

"Do not dehydrate on my account," he lectures. *"It takes more than weather to fell me."* His golden gaze drops to my knee. *"Wish I could say the same for you."*

"Yeah, you're just fine," I mutter, then turn toward Garrick, who's already picking up one of my lost daggers. "You don't have to do that."

"You're not exactly in a position to walk," he reminds me, scooping up the second.

"Did *you*?" I ask quickly as the wingbeats grow louder. "She called you a walker."

He'd traveled a thousand miles in *minutes*, and there's only one way I've read about to accomplish that, but no one has done it in centuries.

Garrick wipes the back of his hand across his temple, and it comes away bloody. "Yeah, and she called you a leash." No wonder he's best friends with Xaden. They're both excellent at dodging questions.

"You have a second signet, don't you?" And like Xaden, he hid the strongest one.

"So do you." He hands back my daggers and sways. "Or at least you will."

"Thank you." I hold his gaze while sheathing the blades and wade through the significance of what he's concealing. "You know the last time someone wielded distance—"

"Never said I did," he interrupts, looking toward Chradh with a flash of a smile as the Brown Scorpiontail lumbers to his feet. "Scared me there for a second." He scoffs. "Yes, I know how much energy it takes. Trust me, you're missing far more skin than I am."

"You should go." I motion toward Chradh and my knee throbs as the adrenaline starts to wear off. "Now, before they get close enough to see you. I know he's blocked out the riot, so your secret is still safe if you leave in the next few seconds."

Garrick's gaze swings to mine, clearly torn. "Getting you into the saddle—"

"Thank you for risking exposure by coming to help me, but *go*." I lift my brows. "My squad will help me."

Garrick tilts his head like he's listening, then nods. "You'll come straight back to Basgiath?"

I nod. "Run."

He stays a second longer, then takes off sprinting toward Chradh. He launches in the shadows, flying out of sight as my squad nears.

"Did you know?" I ask Tairn.

"We do not gossip about our riders."

Good point. If they did, Xaden would be dead by now.

• • •

"*This is ridiculous,*" I tell Tairn as he descends not into the flight field but straight into the courtyard of the quadrant twenty hours later.

"So is thinking you can hobble back from the flight field." Screams sound from the dozen or so cadets who run for the safety of the dormitory wing as Tairn lands in the mud. At least it's stopped snowing.

"Violet!" Brennan charges past the fleeing cadets, his brow pinched with worry.

"Did you seriously tell my brother?" I glare at Tairn, knowing full well he

can't see me.

"Of course not." Tairn snorts, and steam covers the dormitory wing windows.

"I told Marbh," Andarna announces, landing on Tairn's right, her scales as black as his.

"I'm fine!" I call down to Brennan, ripping the belt free and cursing when the stitches catch again. Biting my lip keeps me from crying out as I force myself out of the saddle. *So much for not gossiping."*

She snorts, and I begin the humiliating exercise of scooting over Tairn's back on my ass while she looks on.

Tairn dips his shoulder when I reach it, and I fail to smother the sharp gasp of pain as I lift my right leg so I can slide down. "How about you go get me a set of crutches, and I'll—"

"How about you get down here," Xaden says, standing where I'd expected to find Brennan. My heartbeat jolts. Gods, he looks good, staring up at me with the kind of intensity that used to rattle my nerves when I was a first-year. He lifts one arm, and shadows rush up from beneath Tairn and solidify as they wrap around my waist. "Now would be preferable." He crooks his fingers at me. "I would do the same for any wounded rider."

"I somehow doubt that." I slide down Tairn's leg, and the shadows turn me sideways at the last second and lift me into Xaden's waiting arms. "My, my." I brush a lock of dark hair off his forehead, then hook my arms around his neck and settle against his chest, ignoring the throbbing protest of my knee as it bends. "What else can you do with those shadows, Lieutenant Riorson?"

He locks his jaw and keeps his eyes straight ahead as he carries me away from Tairn and past Brennan, who holds the door to the dormitory wing open.

"Commons is closest," Brennan says, quickly catching up to Xaden.

Every line of Xaden's body is rigid as he follows Brennan through the rotunda and up into commons. Tension radiates off him in waves of shadows that swirl like footprints as I look back over his shoulder, and when I reach out mentally, he has me blocked.

"You're angry," I whisper as Brennan charges ahead, ordering cadets out of a meeting room to the right of the announcements board.

"Anger does not fully describe my current feelings," Xaden replies, striding through the door into the windowless chamber. Shadows shove all six chairs on this side of the long, coarse table out of the way, and he sets me on the surface with extreme care, then retreats, putting his back to the wall.

"I did exactly what you would have in the same situation," I argue, bracing my weight with my palms as Brennan moves to my knee, leaving the door open. "If you would—"

Xaden lifts a single finger. "Not. Yet."

My eyes narrow on him as Brennan slices through my wrap with a dagger. "And I thought you were headed home?" I ask my brother.

"Just helping put the finer points on the alliance." He grimaces at the black-and-blue expanse of my knee. "Lucky for you, I'm still here. Twenty hours in the saddle didn't exactly help the swelling, Vi."

"Neither would have trying to dismount at Samara." I wince as Brennan prods the joint.

"I brought some arinmint with me. I'll have it steeped in milk to help speed the deep healing." He nods to himself. "It helped after you were poisoned."

"You brought arinmint out of Aretia?" Xaden glowers at my brother.

"Breaking the law in front of the *duke*," I try to tease my brother, but the pain makes my words pitchy and it falls flat. Fuck, that hurts. My leg throbs twice as hard without the wrap.

"I'm well versed in how to use it. You know they don't take too kindly to walking out of negotiations when you speak for your province, right?" Brennan spreads his hands over the joint and looks over his shoulder at Xaden. "You're not just a rider anymore and should probably get back—" He blinks as Xaden delivers a withering glare. "Never mind. I would not want to be you," he says under his breath at me, then closes his eyes.

"It's not her fault!" Garrick shouts as he races through the doorway, all but skidding to a stop at the foot of the table.

"Oh?" Xaden asks.

"Crossing into Poromiel was definitely a choice." Garrick shucks off his flight jacket and drops it on the nearest chair. "But the tornado? A regional hazard. The dark wielder—"

"You've already pled her case. Twice." Xaden's tone is almost bored as he folds his arms.

"I don't need to be protected from him." I shake my head at Garrick as heat envelops my knee, then glance Xaden's way. "I own my decisions."

"Well-the-fuck-aware." Xaden closes his eyes and leans his head back against the wall.

"She's here!" Rhiannon calls out from the doorway.

Second-years flood into the room, including Maren and her two little brothers, who seem glued to her side.

"You two sit," Maren says gently to the boys, and Trager pulls out two chairs across the table for them. The twin boys are seven, with her ochre complexion, dark hair, and honey-brown, grief-stricken eyes, which must be why the two feel so familiar to me. They were also silent every time we stopped on the flight here. She crouches in front of them. "We'll get it all sorted out. I promise."

"Sit down," Trager says to Cat, pulling out another seat.

"I'm fine." She wobbles and rubs the back of her neck.

"You're swaying where you stand." He gestures to the chair. "Sit."

"Fine," she grumbles, all but falling into the chair. "Maren, you too."

Every single one of us is exhausted.

"You disobeyed a direct order?" General Aetos storms into the room, then startles at the sight of Brennan and Xaden.

The heat intensifies at my knee, and the pain lessens slowly as Brennan mends the stressed ligament and swollen tissue.

"We were ordered to make ourselves useful, and did so"—Rhiannon steps between Aetos and the rest of the squad—"sir." The title doesn't come out like a compliment. "Our early return was signed off on by Lieutenant Colonel Degrensi, given that they did not have a mender at the outpost and are already overwhelmed with wounded. Surely you're satisfied now that Cadet Sorrengail is wounded. We completed your punishment."

"And we'll do it again." Ridoc kicks back in his seat, throwing his feet up on the table. "And again, and again."

Aetos's face flushes. "I'm sorry, cadet?"

"He said we'll do it again." I lift my chin and note the shadows creeping across the stone floor toward Aetos. "We make decisions as a squad. We'll take whatever punishment you want to give us as a squad. What we won't do is stand by while civilians die, regardless of what citizenship they hold. And before you ask, every single dragon and gryphon agreed."

Hatred flares in Aetos's eyes, but he quickly glances at Brennan. "You have no right to be here, Aisereigh. This is a quadrant matter."

"It's Sorrengail," Brennan says without opening his eyes. "And even if Article Two, Section Four of the Basgiath Code of Conduct didn't allow for menders to be granted access to all areas of campus—which it does—well, I don't answer to you."

My throat clogs when I spot the newly sewn name tag on his uniform.

"And who answers for them?" Aetos points to the boys. "King Tauri has refused to open our borders."

Even now? I struggle to keep my jaw from dropping. How is that not part of the negotiations?

A corner of Aetos's mouth rises, as if he knows he's won. "They'll have to be returned home. Immediately."

My gaze swings to Xaden, and I find him already watching me. I lift my brows and he sighs, then turns his head toward Aetos.

"As we're concluding this round of negotiations this afternoon, Lieutenant Colonel Sorrengail will happily take the boys home—" Xaden starts, and Maren gasps. "To Tyrrendor, seeing as they are now Tyrrish citizens."

"Since when?" Aetos stiffens, and the heat in my knee dissipates as Brennan lifts his hands.

"Since I said so," Xaden answers with icy authority.

"Ah. I see." If Aetos gets any redder, I'm afraid he might pop. "And with the negotiations wrapping up this afternoon, I expect you and Lieutenant Tavis to be joining the Eastern Wing as ordered, so there won't be any need to remind you that commissioned officers aren't readily welcomed within the quadrant, nor encouraged to fraternize with cadets. The leniency you *enjoyed* this fall will not be extended under my watch."

No. My heart sinks. Xaden won't be allowed to come and go as he pleases like he did in Aretia, which means we'll be separated. And on the border, there's every chance he'll have to pass beyond the wards, where his access to magic won't be limited.

"I doubt Sgaeyl would agree," Xaden warns in a tone that reminds me just how little guilt he feels when it comes to killing enemies who get in his way.

"Your dragon is always welcome in the Vale. You're simply not welcome in the quadrant." Aetos's focus snaps to Garrick. "You and Lieutenant Riorson will depart by tomorrow afternoon for the Eastern Wing as ordered."

"As General Melgren ordered," Garrick responds with a slight nod. "Seeing as we're under his chain of command. Or at least I am." He glances back at Xaden. "Not sure about His Grace over here, since it's been a few centuries since any sitting member of the Senarium has worn black, but I'm pretty sure he commands Tyrrish forces now."

Xaden doesn't deign to reply.

"I don't care who orders whom as long as you get out of my war college." Aetos straightens his lapel. "For the rest of you, classes resume tomorrow." His gaze finds mine and lights with nauseating cruelty. "I'm afraid I'll have to leave you, seeing as my belongings are currently being delivered to the commanding general's quarters. Have to say, there's a lovely view from the personal office."

The comment hits as intended, and my chest threatens to crumple at the thought of Aetos living in the space Mom and Dad used to share.

Brennan straightens to his full height, and Aetos backs away with a smile, disappearing into commons.

"I fucking hate him," Ridoc says, rocking forward and putting all four legs of his chair on the floor. "How did Dain turn out halfway normal with that prick as a father?"

"Language," Maren hisses, though I doubt the boys heard her, considering they've both nodded off.

"He had ours, too," Brennan replies to Ridoc.

"Until he didn't," I mutter.

"Is she mended?" Xaden asks without bothering to look at Brennan, his eyes locked on mine.

"She is," I note with a smirk, then bend my knee damn near painlessly.

"No pain?" Brennan asks, swiping the back of his hand across his sweaty forehead as he looks at me.

"Nothing more than usual." I flex the joint again. "Thank you."

"Get out," Xaden orders without looking away, but I'm more than aware he isn't talking to me.

Everyone stills.

"Let me rephrase," Xaden says slowly. "Everyone get out *now*. And close the door."

"Good luck, Violet," Ridoc calls back over his shoulder as Rhi pushes him out the door with the others, Maren and Cat carrying the twins, and in under a minute, I hear the distinct click of the door shutting.

"You can't seriously be angry with me," I start as Xaden surges off the wall, coming at me with the force of a hurricane. "You've never once begrudged my autonomy"—he reaches over me, takes my hips in his hands, and yanks my ass to the edge of the table, turning me to face him—"and I'm not going to tolerate you starting now. *What* are you doing?"

He grasps the back of my neck and slams his mouth against mine.

You might be angry when you realize I didn't wake you to say goodbye.
But it's only because I no longer fully trust my ability to walk away.

—Recovered Correspondence of His Grace, Lieutenant Xaden Riorson, Sixteenth Duke of Tyrrendor, to Cadet Violet Sorrengail

CHAPTER TWELVE

Oh. *Oh.* I part my lips, and he consumes my world.

He kisses me hard and deep, takes my mouth like this might be the only time he can. It's that note of desperation, the graze of his teeth along my lower lip that has my hands flying to his hair. I push my fingers through the dark strands and hold on for dear life, pouring everything I feel into the kiss.

Heat and need collide low in my stomach, coiling tighter with every stroke of his skilled tongue. He hasn't kissed me like this since before the battle at Basgiath—not even in our bed, and gods, I've missed it. It's as carnal as sex and as intimate as waking in his arms.

My heart pounds, and I part my knees. He fills the space and kisses me deeper, bringing our bodies flush but nowhere close enough to satisfy either of us. His fingers tunnel through the lower portion of my braid, and he tilts my head, finding that perfect angle that makes me whimper mindlessly.

"Violet," he groans against my mouth, and I fucking *liquefy*.

I shrug out of my flight jacket and hear it hit the table, but losing the layer doesn't relieve the insistent heat threatening to burn me alive. Only Xaden can do that. His hand flexes on my hip, then strokes over the curve of my waist as he sucks on my bottom lip, and I moan at the shiver of pure want that dances up my spine.

I reach for his uniform top and skim my fingers along it before yanking the soft linen undershirt free from his pants. My hands are met with warm, soft skin draped over ridges of hard muscle, and I trace the two lines along the edges of his stomach until they disappear into his leathers.

He drags a breath through his teeth, then thoroughly kisses every thought from my head, holding me in the acute state of madness only he can provoke, then driving me higher until we're a tangled mess of tongues and questing hands.

His mouth skims my jaw, then the sensitive line of my throat, and I gasp when he targets the spot he knows will turn me molten, then lingers, ensuring my complete meltdown.

"You…" My head rolls back to give him better access, and he takes it. Fire races through my veins, and power quickly follows in a one-two punch that knocks my common sense clear off the Continent. "Xaden, I need you."

Here. A table in the gathering hall. Against the wall in fucking commons. I don't care where or who sees as long as I can have him right now. If he's game, then I am, too. A low sound rumbles in his throat before he wrenches his mouth away.

"No, I need *you*." He brings his face to mine, and too many emotions to name flicker in the depths of his eyes.

"You have me," I whisper, lifting my hand to the side of his neck, just over his relic. His pulse thrums beneath my fingers, just as fast and hard as mine.

"There was an hour where I wasn't sure I did." His fingers slip to the nape of my neck, and then he pulls away, retreating two precious steps that feel like miles as cool air rushes in to take his place, chilling my heated cheeks. "Sgaeyl didn't even tell me. Chradh told Garrick." He shakes his head. "I wasn't just angry, Violet. I was *terrified*."

The tortured look on his face makes me swallow, and I lean forward to grasp the edge of the table. "It's the same choice you would have made—the choice we *did* make, and I'm all right."

"I know that!" His voice rises, and shadows don't just jump; they flee.

Well, that's different.

He rakes his hand down his face and breathes deeply. "I know that," he repeats, softer this time. "But the thought of you being out there, beyond the wards, facing down a known attack of venin, triggered something in me I've never felt before. It was hotter than rage, and sharper than fear, and cut deeper than helplessness, all because I couldn't get to you."

My lips part, and an ache takes root in my chest. I hate that he's going through this.

"I would have killed anything and anyone in that moment to reach you. No exceptions. I would have channeled every ounce of power beneath my feet without hesitation if it would have landed me at your side."

"You'd never kill civilians," I counter with a hundred percent certainty.

He takes another step backward. "If I'd been there, beyond the wards, I would have drained the very earth to its core to keep you safe."

"Xaden…" I whisper, every other word failing me.

"I'm well aware that you can handle yourself." He nods and retreats again. "And logically, I respect your choice. Hell, I'm proud of your decision to save Maren's family. But something is broken between here"—he taps the side of his head—"and here"—he repeats the motion above his heart. "And I can't control it. You are on orders to find Andarna's kind, and I'm on orders to the front, and I can't even trust myself enough to touch you."

"You just did." My fingers scrape the rough wood and I shift my weight as I fight the selfish need to close the distance between us, remembering the thumbprints on my headboard. He might feel like he's spiraling, but he just displayed complete control.

"And that's good enough for you?" His gaze heats as it wanders over my body. "One kiss. No hands. Fully clothed. That's what you want from me from now on?"

What a loaded question, especially when my body is still humming for him. But every instinct tells me to tread carefully. "I want whatever you're able to give, Xaden."

"No." His scarred eyebrow rises as he slowly walks back to me. "You forget that I know your body as well as my own, Vi." His thumb ghosts across my lips. "Your mouth is swollen, your face is flushed, and your eyes…" He skims his tongue over his lower lip. "They're all hazy and leaning more toward green than blue. Your pulse is racing, and the way you keep shifting your weight tells me that if I were to strip these pants off you right now, I'd find you more than ready for me."

I bite back a whimper. If I wasn't before, I sure as hell would be now.

"A kiss isn't enough. It never is with us." His fingers find the bottom of my coronet braid, and he tugs, tilting my face toward him. "You want me the same way that I want you. Wholly. Completely. With nothing but skin between us. Heart, mind, and body." He brushes his mouth against mine, stuttering my breath. "All I want is to lose myself in you, and I can't. You are the only person in the world with the power to strip me of every ounce of my control, and the only person I can't fathom losing that control with." He lifts his head. "And yet here I am, unable to keep three fucking feet away from you."

"We'll figure it out," I promise, struggling to calm my heartbeat. "We always do. You'll learn how to keep your control while I find a cure."

"And if we have to draw the line at a kiss?" His gaze drops to my mouth.

"Then that's the line. If it means I don't get to have you in my bed until I find a way to cure you, then I guess that's just extra incentive for me to work quickly, isn't it?"

He releases my braid and stands at his full height. "You really think you can, don't you?"

"Yes." I nod. "I won't lose you, not even to yourself."

He leans in and presses a kiss to my forehead. "I can't stay on the front," he says softly. "I might be one of the most powerful riders on the Continent, but out there I'm also the most dangerous."

"I know." My spine stiffens as I contemplate everything that can go wrong out there and what just went *right* for me. "Speaking of powerful…"

He tips my chin back to look in my eyes. "What is it?"

"Garrick's a distance wielder, isn't he?" I don't bother hinting around the question.

A moment of silence passes between us, but I see the confirmation in his eyes. "Are you pissed I didn't tell you?"

I shake my head. "You don't owe me your friends' secrets." My brow knits. "But twenty hours of flying gave me some time to think. You. Garrick." I tilt my head. "And I once thought I saw Liam…"

"Wield ice," Xaden says, stroking his thumb along my chin.

I nod. "How often do second signets accompany these particular relics?" My fingers trail down the side of his neck.

"Often enough to be sure Kaori can't possibly have accurate records, but not too completely that anyone questions why I only present with one," he answers. "Our dragons came looking for us. They knew what they were doing."

"Giving you a better chance of survival?" I rest my hand over his heart.

"If you wax sentimental. More like building their own army." A corner of his mouth rises. "More signets equal more power."

"Right." I take a deep breath, knowing we still need to talk about Samara. "The report Rhiannon gave at Samara left some things out because we didn't want to contribute to misinformation or look like we don't know what we're talking about. What did Garrick tell you?"

"You mean besides the fact that the dark wielder toyed with you and let you go?" His eyes narrow. "Not much beyond what arrived in the report, which pissed me off because I could *tell* he wasn't being fully honest. He's never been able to lie to me. What did you leave out?"

"Am I talking to the man I love? Or the Duke of Tyrrendor? Either way, this could be really embarrassing." Heat creeps up my neck. If I sound a false alarm, I'll look like a fool.

"Both," Xaden replies. "I don't want to be different people to you. Anyone else? Fine. Just not you. You're stuck with all of me, and all of me is quite capable of keeping your confidence. I'll use Tyrrendor to protect you, not you to protect Tyrrendor."

"I've already told you I'm happy to protect your home." My hand fists the fabric of his uniform. "She wielded lightning," I whisper, and his brow furrows. "Xaden, I think we're wrong. I don't think they're limited to lesser magics. I think maybe…they have signets, too."

"I believe you." He doesn't so much as flinch. "What else did you leave out?"

. . .

Over the next week, our professors display just how accomplished they are at making everything at Basgiath feel almost routine, like we're not in the middle of a war. Physics, RSC—with a new professor, since Grady is busy organizing the quest squad and researching where to go—math, and magics. All classes have resumed save one: history.

Guess we're still waiting for Cygnisen's cadets to arrive before beginning that one.

If the third-years weren't gone half the time staffing the midland posts, it might even feel like we never left except for the fact that the fliers have joined us. When Cygnisen's fliers arrive, we'll be near maximum capacity in the dorms, which only makes me realize just how many dragons have stopped bonding in the last century.

"This came to Treifelz last night," Imogen says, stifling a yawn and handing me a folded, sealed missive when we meet at the bridge to the Healer Quadrant. Can't blame her—she's been up all night at the midland post.

Dawn breaks through the windows, but the mage lights give more than enough brightness to make out her name as the addressee. "I don't think this is meant for me." My eyebrows rise as I read the name of the sender. "Especially coming from Garrick."

"Right, because Garrick writes to *me*." She rolls her eyes and stretches her shoulders before pulling open the door into the tunnel. "Everyone knows Aetos is going to read anything with your name on it."

I break the seal and smile at Xaden's handwriting, but it quickly slips.

V—

We fought in Fervan last night, called by an attack upon civilians. It is with deepest regret that I delay my return in favor of rest. I walked the edge of burnout, but the lives we saved were worth the cost, and Garrick has informed the healers I'll be in quarters, recovering, until further notice. Lewellen is standing in as proxy in case the Senarium orders any emergency meetings.

It is worse than we imagined beyond the wards, but I have a solution in mind to prevent future burnouts. Is it just me? Or does my pillow smell like you?

Yours,
—X

My steps slow as we make our way down the tunnel, dread thickening my throat, and I pause at the top of the staircase that leads to the interrogation chamber and stuff the letter into the breast pocket inside my uniform. "He slipped."

Imogen tenses. "He said that?"

I shake my head. "He was careful with his wording, but I'm sure. There's no other reason he'd need to lock himself away in his quarters to recover from a near burnout unless he's waiting for his eyes to return to their normal color."

"Fuck." She starts down the steps, and I follow. "We need to get him off the border."

"I know. And I need to find a cure."

"You're sure this is how you want to go about it?" Imogen stifles another yawn.

"Every possible path," I tell her, running my hands down my sheaths to make sure each dagger is in place, as well as a vial or two. "He's the only direct source of information we have. You sure you're up for this? I completely understand if you're too tired." They're running the third-years into the ground.

"I could do this shit in my sleep." She unbuttons her flight jacket. "You meet with Grady yet?"

"Next week." I sigh. "He's still *researching* before he'll deign to meet with me, but he sent a first draft of the squad yesterday, and the only rider I know on it is Aura-fucking-Beinhaven, because—get this—she's a trustable companion of my own age and the most powerful fire wielder in the quadrant."

"Does he know you've already almost killed her this month?" She lifts her brows.

"Don't think he cares. He has no idea where to start, either, which I only know because he tried to get his dragon to question Andarna. And that's *after* reading my report stating everything she remembered about her first hundred years in shell, which—like most dragons late to hatch—is nothing."

"How did that go for him?" Imogen asks, her brow scrunching.

"Tairn removed a dozen of her neck scales, and Andarna left teeth marks in her tail."

"We'll collect enough next time to make you new armor," Andarna promises.

"From his dragon? Thank you, but no," I reply.

A smile tugs at Imogen's lips. "Got exactly what she deserves." Her smile falls. "I agree you need experienced riders on the squad, but it's hard to trust judgment like that."

Emery and Heaton both look up from their card game as we come around the last turn. "You brought Sorrengail with you this time?" Emery asks, lifting his brows.

"Clearly," Imogen replies.

We cross the stone floor, and I look away from the bloodstained table as we approach.

"Why do I feel like you only visit when we're on guard?" Heaton sets their cards on the table. "Also, I win."

Emery looks at what Heaton's laid down and sighs. "You have unnaturally good luck with cards."

"Zihnal is with me." Heaton grins and scratches the magenta flames dyed into their hair. "Both of you going in?" They glance over our weaponry. "He probably has twenty-four hours left at this rate, but I can't vouch for what he's capable of."

"I've got this." I pat the vials strapped to my upper biceps.

"I do not doubt that. Nolon and Markham usually arrive at seven to start their daily questioning, so be quick. And I wouldn't expect much. He's usually silent." Heaton unlocks the cell door, then steps out of the way. "You have visitors."

I walk into the doorway but stop abruptly, causing Imogen to curse behind me.

Jack doesn't just look like shit; he looks like *death*. He's sprawled on the same stone floor I nearly bled out on a few months ago, but there are thick shackles around his wrists and ankles anchoring him to the wall behind the slab of a bed they must have reconstructed after Xaden blew it apart. Jack's blond hair hangs oily and limp, and the pallid skin of his face has sunken into his skull, reminding me far more of a corpse than a human.

Then again, maybe he really isn't human anymore.

And what would that make Xaden?

I breathe deeply, then step through the wards Mira created, magic tingling at the back of my neck as Jack lifts his red-rimmed eyes in my direction. They're still glacially blue at the center of the iris, but the red has blurred the edges. "Jack."

Imogen comes in behind me, then shuts the cell door, locking us in. It's a shitty but necessary evil to make sure Heaton and Emery don't hear what's discussed.

I breathe in through my nose and out through my mouth, pretending this isn't the cell where Varrish shattered my bones for *days*, but the smell of damp earth and old blood sets my teeth on edge.

"What could you possibly want, Sorrengail?" Jack croaks through cracked lips, not bothering to lift his cheek from the floor.

Imogen leans back against the door, and I crouch in front of Jack, just out of reach in case he decides to test the limits of his tether. "To make an exchange."

"You think out of all the interrogations, the *mendings*, that I'll finally break for you?" Hatred shines from his eyes.

"No." I don't bother telling him that he's broken for Xaden multiple times already. "But I do think you want to live." I reach into my pocket and retrieve the tiny medallion of alloy from my conduit. The shiny, heavy metallic substance is smooth and hot in the palm of my hand, dimly humming as I hold it out for display. "It's imbued with enough power to keep you alive for at least another week."

His gaze snaps hungrily to the metal. "But not enough to fully feed me."

"I'm not helping you escape, if that's what you're asking." I sit on the floor and cross my ankles beneath me. "But answer a few questions for me and it's yours."

"And if I'd rather meet Malek?" he challenges.

"*Does* your kind meet Malek?" I counter, setting the alloy just out of reach and pulling one of the glass vials from my arm strap when he doesn't respond. "You're a day away from finding out, but if you'd like me to end your suffering, I came prepared to do so." The glass clicks against stone as I lay it next to the alloy.

"Is that…" He stares at the vial.

"Powdered orange peel. Simple, yet effective in your case, given how close your body is to giving out. Merciful, too, considering your actions resulted in my mother's death. But I'm not so merciful as to leave you with a dagger."

A sneer lifts his mouth as he pushes himself to sit up in a macabre display of angular, emaciated bone. Chains rattle against stone, and I'm relieved to see my estimate was right. There's three feet between us, but he can only cross half of it. "You were always too merciful. Too weak."

"True." I shrug. "I have always struggled when confronted with a suffering animal. Now, unlike you, I have somewhere I need to be, so choose."

His gaze drifts to the alloy. "How many questions?"

"Depends on how long you want to live." I push the silver-hued substance toward him, keeping it just out of reach. "Four for today." One of which I already know the answer to, just to make sure he isn't bullshitting me.

"And I'm supposed to trust that you'll give it to me?" He glances toward Imogen.

"You're far better off with her than you are with me, asshole. I'll happily sit here and *watch* you die," Imogen replies.

"First question," I start. "Can you sense each other?"

He stares at the alloy, then swallows. "Yes. When we're new, we're not as adept at hiding ourselves. I'm told it's so we'll be found and raised by an elder, usually a Sage, but in rare cases a Maven may take interest." A corner of his mouth lifts. "Initiates, asims—we're all traceable to one another, but the great hall could fill with Sages and Mavens and I'd never know. Neither would you." His eyes sparkle, and red veins pulse at the corners of his eyes. "Makes you wonder who's been channeling here for years, doesn't it? Who's been trading information for power?"

My heart jolts into my throat. "Do you have to be taught to channel? Or can you turn evil all on your own?" I ask, refusing to give him the satisfaction of admitting that I'm now terrified of who might walk among us.

"Ask what you really want to know." His voice turns raspy, and I ignore the instinct to hand him his untouched glass of water from his uneaten breakfast tray. "Ask me when I turned, how I turned. Ask why only initiates bleed."

I absorb that information and move right along.

"Do you have to be taught?" I repeat. Xaden did it on his own, but I need to know if we're in danger from every random infantry cadet who didn't have the guts to cross the parapet.

His breath rattles, and he drops his focus to the alloy. "Not if you're already experienced with the flow of magic. Someone who has never wielded would require instruction, but a dragon rider or gryphon flier?" He shakes his head. "The source is there. We just have to choose to see it, to bypass the gatekeepers and take what's rightfully ours." He lifts his hand, but the chain brings him up short. "Power should be accessible to everyone strong enough to wield it, not just who *they* see fit. You conveniently see me as the villain, but you're bonded to two."

I blatantly ignore that insult. "Do you know their plan?"

He scoffs. "Does a first-year command the wings? No. We're not as stupid as you assume. Information is need-to-know. What a waste of a question. One more."

"Last question." I push the alloy to the edge of its current stone. "How do you cure yourself once you channel from the source?"

"Cure?" He looks at me like I've lost my mind. "You talk like I'm diseased, when what I really am is *free*." He wavers. "Well, free in part. We trade some of our autonomy in the exchange for unfettered access to power. Maybe you see it as a loss of our soul, but we aren't burdened by conscience or weakened by emotional attachment. We advance based on our own capabilities, our own talents, and not at the whim of some creature. There's no *cure* because magic does not negotiate, and we do not wish to *be* cured."

The utter disdain for the question hits like a blow to the stomach, knocking the air from my lungs. At some point, will Xaden stop *wanting* to be cured? "I keep my bargains," I manage to say before tossing the alloy his way.

He catches it with surprising quickness, closing his fist and then his eyes. "Yes," he whispers, and I watch, transfixed, as his cheeks plump and fill with color. The cracks in his lips disappear, and there's a bit more substance underneath his shirt. His eyes flash open and the veins pulse beside his eyes as he flings the alloy back at me.

I catch it, immediately registering its emptiness, then pocket the medallion and slip the orange peel into my armband before standing.

"Do come again," he says, sitting back and raising his knees.

"About a week," I reply with a nod as Imogen walks to my side. Our time is nearly up, but there's one more question I need to ask. "Why me?" I add. "Surely they've offered you the same reward. So why answer my questions and not theirs?"

He narrows his eyes. "Did you scream for Riorson to save you when they locked you down here and broke your bones?"

"I'm sorry?" Blood drains from my face. He did *not* just ask me that.

Jack leans forward. "Did you cry for Riorson when they strapped you to the chair and watched your blood fill the cracks between the stones on its way to the drain? I only ask because I swear I can feel it when I lie on the floor—all your pain singing to me like a lullaby."

I flinch.

"There." Jack's smile sharpens and chills with sickening excitement. "That look right there is why I chose to answer your questions, for the satisfaction of us both knowing that I can still cut you and I don't have to lift a blade."

I breathe in the scent that haunts my nightmares and glance around the cell, half expecting to realize this has all been a hallucination and I'm still locked into the chair, and half expecting to see Liam, but all I find are desiccated, gray stones, drained of any and all magic.

"Do you really think this is the only room where I've felt tormented? Pain isn't new to me, Jack. She's an old friend I spend most of my days with, so I don't mind if she sings to you. Honestly doesn't even look like the same chamber with how you've redecorated. It's a little monochromatic for me." I step to the side. "Imogen, I'm ready to go."

"And what's to keep me from telling your favorite scribe that you've been feeding the enemy?" Jack's smile widens.

"Hard to talk about something you don't remember." Imogen steps into his space, and his grin slips.

Four minutes later, we emerge from the staircase and find Rhiannon, Ridoc, and Sawyer waiting in the tunnel.

"For fuck's sake, can't you four do *anything* by yourselves?" Imogen mutters.

Upon failure of three exams, Jesinia Neilwart has been removed from the adept path and stripped of all its responsibilities and sacred privileges as of January 15. Under protest, I transfer her command to Professor Grady at his over-authoritative request.

—OFFICIAL RECORDS: SCRIBE QUADRANT,
COLONEL LEWIS MARKHAM, COMMANDANT

CHAPTER THIRTEEN

"What?" Rhiannon shrugs and pushes off the wall. "We didn't tag along while Violet played inquisitor. We respect boundaries."

"Do you even *have* boundaries with one another?" Imogen shoots a look at the three of them. "If you're all going with her, then I'll excuse myself from what I'm sure will be a fascinating trip to the Archives. See you at formation." She gives Rhi a mock salute and heads left, toward the quadrant.

"He basically said we could be surrounded by venin and never know it," I tell them.

"That's super comforting," Sawyer replies.

"You look good," I add, noting the color in his cheeks as he balances on his crutches. "Fresh haircut? Clean shave?"

"It's almost like he got up early and prepared for the visit," Ridoc teases as we head down the tunnel, keeping Sawyer at our center.

"Shut up." Sawyer shakes his head. "I was up early trying to fit a godsawful hunk of wood to my leg because it's the only time the wood-carver had available. I'm starting to think I should just make something myself."

"You should. And I bet the thought of seeing a certain scribe made the hour tolerable." A smile pulls at Rhi's mouth to my right.

"Do we give you shit about whatever you have going with Tara? Or the fact that Riorson and Sorrengail fight like an old married couple?" Sawyer glares in our direction, then Ridoc's, but there's no hiding his immediate blush, even in the mage lights. "Ridoc bedhops like a fucking frog, but no, let's give *me* crap."

We make it a few steps before none of us can smother our laughs.

"A frog?" Ridoc grins from Sawyer's left. "That's the best you can do? A frog?"

"Tara and I are old news." Rhi shrugs. "Leadership is hard on both our schedules. We're together when we have time, but it's not like we're seeing other people." She shoots a sideways glance my way. "But he's right, you and Riorson bicker like you've been married fifty years and neither of you wants to do the dishes."

"That is not true," I protest as Sawyer nods.

"Agreed," Ridoc says. "And it's always the same fight." He lifts his hand to his chest. "I'll trust you if you stop keeping secrets!" He drops the hand and scowls. "It's my secretive nature that attracted you, and why can't you just stay out of harm's way for five fucking minutes?"

Rhi laughs so hard she nearly chokes.

I narrow my gaze on Ridoc. "Keep talking, and I'll plant my dagger somewhere that prevents all frog-like activity."

"Don't hate on me for being the only truly single one out of us and enjoying every minute." We round the corner and the enormous, circular door to the Archives comes into view.

"I bet leadership secretly loves that you're with Riorson," Sawyer says to me, shifting his grip on the handrail of his right crutch. "Legacies usually make for stronger riders, and with as much power as you two wield? Melgren will probably escort you both to a temple of your choosing the second you're commissioned."

"Doubt Loial would let me in," I mutter. "Can't remember the last time I stepped foot in her temple." I'd stopped praying to her years ago, along with Hedeon out of pure spite. Love and wisdom hadn't exactly shown up when I'd needed them to.

"If the general even waits that long." Rhi lifts her brows. "Riorson's already graduated."

"Not something we've discussed." I shake my head. "And I'm not against it in the future, but I'm more focused on living until graduation. What about you?"

"Maybe one day," she muses. "Just saying that you're lucky Melgren hasn't yanked you out of Battle Brief and personally seen to the arrangements in hope that your kid will be the next one with battle foresight in twenty-one years." Rhi bumps my shoulder.

"Shame he's so short-sighted," Ridoc says as we pass the first-year scribe sitting guard at the door.

The scent of parchment and ink hits my lungs, welcoming me home. I stare down the stacks that line the right side of the cavernous space like my father might walk out at any second.

"We're here to see Cadet Neilwart," Rhi tells the first-year scribe manning the entrance table, which marks the invisible line only those in cream robes are allowed to cross.

The cadet hurries off as Ridoc pulls out a chair for Sawyer, and our friend sits in the same exact place I'd spent years of my life preparing to enter this quadrant.

"You all right?" Rhi asks quietly.

I nod and force a quick smile. "Just caught up in my head."

"Relax, Violet." Ridoc takes the seat next to Sawyer. "It's not like the fate of our world rests on you finding whatever's left of the irids." He rubs the back of his neck. "Do you guys think it's short for iridescent?"

"Yes," the three of us simultaneously reply.

"Damn. Let's go back to picking on Sawyer." Ridoc leans in his chair as Jesinia walks our way, her arms full of leather-bound tomes.

A third-year steps into her path, and she skirts him. The incident repeats with a second-year a few rows closer to us.

"They're worse than riders." Sawyer's knuckles whiten on the crutches as he arranges them against the table.

"They really are," I agree, noting with pride that Jesinia keeps her head high as a third-year blatantly glares her way from the first row of study tables.

I narrow my eyes at him, and he flinches when he notices.

"I'm petitioning Grady to be on the quest squad," Ridoc says, signing as Jesinia reaches us. "Think he'll say yes?" He raises his brows in her direction.

She sets six books down on the table and lifts her hands. "Is Violet in need of an ice wielder?" she signs.

"She could be," Ridoc says and signs. "Guess it all depends on your research."

"No pressure," she signs and rolls her eyes, but they soften the second her gaze lands on Sawyer. "You didn't have to walk all the way down here," she signs, and Ridoc translates. "I would have come to you."

"I. Wanted. Here," Sawyer signs slowly.

Rhiannon and I share a grin. He's learning quickly.

Two lines of worry appear between Jesinia's brows, right beneath the line of her cream hood, but she nods, then looks at me. "I've brought you six tomes I think may be of some use," she signs, and Ridoc translates for Sawyer quietly.

"Do you need me to bury bodies?" I ask, my hands moving quickly to sign. "Because Andarna will happily roast some scribes if they're acting like assholes."

"*Gladly,*" she chimes in gleefully.

"*No,*" Tairn rebukes. "*Don't encourage her.*"

Jesinia glances back at the cadets who are gathering to start their day. "I have seen enough bloodshed," she signs. "And I can handle the punishment meted out for my desertion of the quadrant."

"Punishment?" My stomach sours.

"They kicked—" Sawyer starts but signs the word "push" instead and drops his hands. "Damn it," he swears at the ceiling. "Ridoc?"

"I've got you," Ridoc says and signs. "And I promise, I won't make any sexual plans for you later."

Jesinia's eyes widen.

"Gods help us," Rhi mutters, then quickly signs it. "Ridoc!"

"They're the ones losing out," Ridoc says and signs.

"And to think," I sign to Jesinia, keeping my mouth shut, "it was almost just the two of us at this table."

She presses her lips between her teeth, fighting a smile.

"As I was saying." Sawyer shoots a glare at Ridoc as he translates. "They kicked her out of the adept program. Made up some bullshit tests they knew she'd fail."

My stomach sinks. I knew Markham would find a way to punish her for choosing Aretia, but never imagined he'd expel his brightest scribe from the path where she's so desperately needed.

Jesinia's attention snaps from Ridoc to Sawyer, and I wouldn't wish the look she gives him on my worst enemy. "That was not your information to share," she signs.

Ridoc repeats.

"That one, I understood," Sawyer mutters. "They needed to know, based on your new orders."

"I disagree," she signs back, then blatantly looks away, her gaze finding mine. "Do not worry about me. I'm not out there fighting venin." She spells out the word.

"I'm so sorry," I whisper and sign.

"Don't be." She shakes her head. "I've been given the one assignment with which they know I can be trusted—helping you with research. Well, officially under Grady, but it's really you."

And they narrowed her scope of knowledge? It takes all the grace in my body to swallow the boulder of anger rising in my throat. "I didn't want that for you."

She makes a face at me. "Oh please," she signs. "I'm left on my own with a treasure trove of royal tomes no one has read in at least the last four hundred years. Look at me suffering." She rolls her eyes and smiles.

"Did you find mention of the irids?" Ridoc asks.

Jesinia blinks once, giving Ridoc a look I've seen enough times to wince on his behalf as she begins to sign. "Yes, in the second tome I pulled."

"Really?" His face lights up.

"Absolutely," she signs, her face completely deadpan. "It was recorded that when the last irid hatches and bonds the cadet born of rider and scribe, she'll be gifted with two signets."

"You're kidding!" he signs excitedly. "There's a prophecy?" He turns toward me. "Violet, you're a—"

I shake my head quickly, wrinkling my nose.

Ridoc sighs and lifts his hands toward Jesinia. "You really are kidding, aren't you? There's no prophecy."

"Oh, you're so fucked," Sawyer whispers.

Jesinia leans over the table slightly in his direction. "Of course there's no prophecy." She signs with abrupt motions, her eyes narrowed on him, and this time Rhiannon translates for Sawyer. "Just research. I've barely finished translating Lyra's journal and now have six hundred years of personal accounts to read through. Do you really think I found the answer in the first week of accessing the vault, or that I wouldn't have gone straight to Violet with that information?"

I rock back on my heels.

"I was hoping," Ridoc says and signs. "And you're kind of scary when you're angry."

"I am not some oracle high off whatever they're serving in the temple that day. I am an extremely educated scribe. Treat me as such, and I won't get angry," she replies, then turns toward me. "Now, I gathered these six for you to read, which mostly cover the southernmost isle of Deverelli, since that's the last isle we had communication with. Figured that's where you might start, but I'll warn you that Grady has requested tomes about Emerald Sea exploration in the north." She pushes the tomes across the table and lifts her hands again. "Honestly, I'm appalled with what isn't in the vault. Thank gods Queen Maraya sent her list for you, because we're missing..." She cocks her head to the side. "I don't even know what we're missing. I was reading General Cadao's journal yesterday, and a whole section of pages is ripped out after he notes that there may have been an outside isle supporting the second Krovlan uprising." She drops her arms in exasperation. "I can't research what we don't have."

"The second Krovlan uprising was supported by an isle kingdom?" I say and sign slowly just to be sure I have it right. "But that was in the four hundreds, right? And it was assumed that Cordyn sent soldiers. We severed all communication with most isles after they sided with Poromiel around 206, and they in turn killed every emissary we sent in the centuries that followed, so how would General Cadao know that?"

"Exactly," she signs. "I can only think of one scribe who might have that answer." She lifts her brows at me.

Oh. I blink, quickly processing the information, then swearing as I reach the inevitable, damning conclusion.

"Is it you?" Rhi asks me, simultaneously signing. "Oh no. Is it *Markham*?"

I shake my head. "My father. And all his research, the work he had yet to publish, is now *really* hard to access." My shoulders dip. I'd been so focused on getting out of Mom's quarters with her journals after she died that I'd completely forgotten what my father had left hidden.

"Hard to access like we need Aaric and a midnight mission?" Sawyer asks, and Ridoc translates.

"Hard to access like we need Dain to betray his father." Which is highly unlikely.

"After disowning him in front of the quadrant, that shouldn't be hard," Rhiannon says, lifting her brows as she signs.

"And it's not like Dain hasn't already betrayed him," Sawyer adds.

I shake my head. "He left Navarre, not his father, and believe me when I tell you there's a difference." I glance at the books, then back up at Jesinia. "Thank you for these and all the work you're doing. I'll start here."

. . .

Three days later, I'm in Battle Brief still pondering the Dain problem as Devera flicks her wrist and the largest map of the Continent I've ever seen unfurls over the quadrant's rendering. And it's a terrifying sight.

"I'm guessing they delivered that with our things from Aretia yesterday," Cat notes from my left.

"There is way more red on that map than I'm comfortable with," Rhi remarks, tapping her pen on her notebook.

The damning color spans from the Barrens, up the Stonewater River, and ends just short of Samara before spreading along the wardline, like the enemy is searching for weaknesses. But Samara still stands. Xaden's safe, at least for now. He's been gone more than ten days, and Tairn is at his wits' end, which makes two of us. Every day he's out there, he risks his soul and sanity. Either he has to produce that solution he promised, or we have to find a way to get him off the border.

Most of Braevick is saturated with red flags, especially along the Dunness River, but Cygnisen hasn't been recently attacked…nor have they sent their cadets yet.

Braevick's capital—Zolya—fell months ago, but the kingdom's seat of power, Suniva, still stands in the province's north. I can't help but wonder where Queen Maraya's summer house—and her library—are. And hope they're at least well protected.

"Cordyn's still safe," I whisper to Cat.

"For how long at this rate?" Her mouth purses, but I don't take it personally. My sister is stationed in Aretia. Hers is beyond the wards.

"As you can see," Devera says, quieting the room, "there is a defined, supported assault happening along the wards, centered at the Samara outpost. We believe it's simply because it's the straightest path that leads to here—the hatching grounds."

I lift my eyebrows. It's not like her to give us the answers.

"Our knowledge of the venin up until this point has been somewhat… impeded," Devera admits.

"That is an understatement," Ridoc mumbles under his breath.

"And I'm sure some of you have been frustrated at the lack of instruction for the last couple of weeks. If you reach beneath your seats, you'll discover why we've been waiting."

I bend at the waist like every other cadet, finding a thick, canvas-bound book under my chair and retrieving it. I blink through the head rush as I sit up too quickly, then glance at the plain spine before flipping to the table of contents. "*Captain Lera Dorrell's Guide to Vanquishing the Venin*," I read. "*Venin, A Compendium*, and…more. Look, they made us a little anthology."

"You've already read them all, haven't you?" Rhi asks, thumbing through her copy.

"All but the last. *Dark Wielders and Dark Times.* Tecarus sent them to me in Aretia."

"My cousin Drake wrote the compendium." Cat preens.

"Yes, we get it, Cat. You're better." Ridoc glances at Rhi. "We need a copy for Sawyer."

Rhi nods. "We can't let him fall too behind or he'll struggle to get caught up when he decides to return."

"Haven't seen too many one-legged riders around here." Cat slips her anthology under her notebook. "Or…any. Maybe you should ask him what he wants before making assumptions."

She has a point, so I don't snap at her for the first comment.

"The cadets in the Scribe Quadrant have worked tirelessly over the last couple of weeks, printing enough copies for you each to have one." Devera sits back against the table. "Nothing in this book is new to the fliers, of course, so I expect you all to pass the first test of your new history class with flying colors." She gestures to Kiandra. "This particular course will be taught by Professor

Kiandra and, for the sake of speed and convenience, will take place in this room on Tuesdays and Thursdays. As our runes expert has declined to come to us, you will also be rotating in two-week cycles to Aretia for rune intensives. Check with your section leaders for the new schedule regarding sharing the flight field and your rune dates."

A class-wide grumble fills the room, even from the third-years behind us. I glance over my shoulder and note Dain in the top row. He's been gone so often I haven't had a chance to ask him about helping me get to Dad's research.

"Don't complain," Devera warns, lifting her finger. "We're only adding three classes to the schedule, all of which will save your lives."

"Three more classes?" Ridoc moans, and the sentiment is echoed around the room. "On top of quest squad research?" He glances my way. "I'm only halfway through the first Deverelli text as it is."

A smile pulls at my mouth that he's jumped in with both feet, regardless of knowing there's absolutely no chance of him going.

"I mean it. Whiners don't wear black," Professor Devera snaps. "Read the book and live. Don't and die." She sighs, then squares her shoulders and looks around the room. "I do, however, regret to inform you that a crucial piece of information surfaced during printing and therefore is not included. It has now been confirmed by three different sources that high-level venin—we believe Sage and Maven—can and do wield signets."

Silence falls thicker than the snow outside, every cadet besides those of us who already knew freezing completely. It took them *ten days* to confirm?

"I know," Devera says with uncharacteristic gentleness. "It's a shock. I'll give you a second to sit with it."

I spot more than one head dropping in the rows ahead of us, like we've just been handed our defeat. I can't blame them; most of us have only been taught to battle fliers with lesser magics.

"And that's all the time you get." Devera stands. "Welcome to the new face of battle, where we are not only outnumbered in the sky but now equally matched on the field in terms of the skill of our opponents. You can and should expect to face a dark wielder with the same abilities as your friends, your squadmates"— she glances my way—"and yourselves."

Another murmur rises, and Professor Devera silences it by raising her hand.

"With that in mind, the nature of challenges will change under the supervision of Professor Emetterio to include wielding in order to better prepare you for actual combat." Her voice rises above the growing number of worried conversations. "But death is no longer an acceptable outcome when you face your classmates. The days of settling your scores on the mat are over. We need each and every one of you to survive to graduation."

"Easy to say when you're not facing Sorrengail," Caroline Ashton calls out.

Fair point. I have no business wielding on a challenge mat.

"We aren't going to throw you to the wolves," Devera tells her. "The third class you'll be adding will be a hands-on approach to prepare you for signet-against-signet combat. You'll have a rotating roster of professors to benefit from all signet types, and the Eastern Wing has temporarily loaned us their most powerful rider to start your instruction."

My throat tightens, and my heart starts to pound.

"And on that note." Devera gestures to the door at the back of the room, and I turn so fast my vision swims. "Look who just arrived."

Xaden stands next to Professor Kaori in the doorway, casually leaning against the frame with his arms crossed, with a tiny, yet undeniable tilt to his mouth as our eyes lock.

I smile instantly. Thank you, gods, he found a way to stay within the wards by teaching—

Teaching.

Oh shit. Article Eight, Section One of the Basgiath Code of Conduct.

My face falls, and Xaden tilts his head as shadows brush against my shields. *"What's wrong?"* he asks when I let him in.

"Everyone, welcome our newest member of your leadership team. Professor Riorson," Devera announces.

My ribs strain, as if they can hold my heart together if they just squeeze tight enough. *"I think our relationship just ended."*

Though fliers only wield lesser magics, in my vast experience with the Northern Wing, they are formidable opponents in both mindwork and hand-to-hand. Take heed, younger riders: do not unseat against them unless forced to do so.

—Tactics part II, A Personal Memoir by Lieutenant Lyron Panchek

CHAPTER FOURTEEN

"**A**bsolutely not," Xaden responds before Kaori leads him away, but there's a slight roaring in my ears as Devera goes over the changes to our academic schedule and how we'll be paired for Xaden's new class, which she labels *Signet Sparring.*

We're dismissed a few minutes later.

I'm fine. This is fine. I'll think about it later. For now I stay focused on the goal directly in front of me, who happens to be halfway down the hall by the time I file out of Battle Brief with the rest of my squad.

"You don't look happy," Rhi notices, shooting me a sideways glance. "Why? You two will get to see each other all the time now."

"Sure." My nod is a little forced. "Every time we have class." I bounce up on my toes, but I'm still too short to see past the crowd of cadets. "I need to catch up to Dain."

"Dain? Xaden shows up and you're talking to Dain?" Rhi puts the back of her hand to my forehead. "Just making sure you're not running a fever."

"After that announcement, I'm not really sure I can handle seeing Xaden right now, to be honest," I tell her quietly so Cat doesn't hear. Gods, she's going to *gloat* over this. "And I haven't seen Dain in days. I need to ask him…" I lift my brows.

"Right." She nods as we pass two third-year classrooms, then peers ahead. "He's in Professor Kaori's office doorway, talking to Bodhi. You going to tell me what's going on with Riorson?"

"Thanks. Article Eight, Section One, Code of Conduct." I speed ahead, weaving through the river of cadets.

"Ouch. Don't be late to flight tactics!" she calls after me.

To my relief, Dain hasn't moved by the time I reach the deep arch of Kaori's doorway and step out of the current so I don't hold anyone up or get trampled.

Dain glances my way, then gives me his full attention, leaning up against the closed door and making room for me. "Vi?"

"I'm sorry to interrupt, but you've been at midland posts for days and I need to talk to you." I adjust the straps of my pack on my sore shoulders. Imogen has been relentless with the workouts this week, and my solo wielding sessions are taking a toll on my arms, too.

"You're not interrupting," Dain assures me. "We're just figuring out the flight field scheduling issue."

Bodhi glances between us. "Need some privacy?"

"Not from you." I shake my head.

"Ah." He gestures to his spot, and I swap places with him as he puts his back to the crowd. "That should be a little quieter for you."

"What's going on?" Dain asks, lowering his voice.

I push aside any lingering apprehension. This might be my only shot. "I need your help, and I know it's asking a lot, so I'm just going to lay it out there and then give you some time to decide." The hall empties gradually behind Bodhi.

"That sounds ominous." Dain searches my eyes. "Are you in trouble?"

"No." I shake my head. "I need something my father left in my parents' quarters before he died. It's nothing that needed to be burned or anything like that."

"Research?" Dain guesses, his expression softening.

I nod. "It's...hidden, and the quarters of Basgiath's commanding general are warded so only their line, by blood or marriage, can pass through, and now that bloodline is no longer mine."

"Right." His throat works. "You'd be better off asking my father yourself. I'm not exactly his favorite person at the moment." He blinks, quickly masking the pain that flashes through his eyes. "He's just a few rooms down with Panchek right now."

"I'm more concerned that he might not give it to me," I say slowly. "He mentioned last year that he wanted it, and I'm scared he'll keep it for himself, or that he or Markham will redact the information."

Dain folds his arms. "So you want me to help you steal it."

"Yes." There's no point in lying.

"Not sure he really considers me part of the bloodline—" Dain starts, but then the door opens behind him.

"Well, that didn't take you long," Kaori says with a laugh, then looks over his shoulder. "I don't think they're here for me." He turns back to us. "Make it quick, cadets. He has a meeting to attend in about ten minutes. Now, if you'll excuse me?"

We part, and Professor Kaori heads into the empty hall.

"Professor Riorson." Dain's tone isn't exactly respectful as Xaden fills the doorway.

My pulse leaps and I drink in the sight of him, stubbled cheeks, full lips, and gorgeous eyes. There's no hint of red to be seen.

"Violet." Xaden ignores Dain and his cousin, his voice sliding over my skin like velvet. "A word in private?"

"Not a good idea." I shake my head slowly.

"I'm certain I've had worse ones." He holds out his hand.

"You're now a professor." Clutching the straps of my pack keeps me from reaching for him. "I'm a cadet."

"And?" Xaden glowers at me.

"Oh shit," Dain says quietly. "Article Eight, Section One of the Code of Conduct."

"Wait. You two broke up?" Bodhi's voice rises.

"Yes," I answer.

"No," Xaden says at the same time, glaring at his cousin, then jerking his gaze to mine. "No," he repeats.

"I mean...if you're our new professor, then the Code applies. At least for as long as you hold the position," Dain muses. "And I can't think of a single piece of Codex that overrides it."

"No one asked you, Aetos," Xaden warns.

"Don't blame me. I didn't write the Code." Dain backs into the hall with his hands up. "Nor did I accept the job."

Xaden tenses.

"Well, I have class, so good luck handling this one." Bodhi hurries after Dain.

Xaden waits half a second before grabbing the right strap of my pack and tugging me into Kaori's room. So much for getting to class on time.

He lets me go and closes the door behind us.

"Garrick didn't come with you?" As stalling tactics come, it's a lazy one, but it's all I have as I retreat toward Kaori's desk, avoiding the two chairs sitting in front of it. The office is one of the bigger ones, boasting two arched windows and a built-in bookcase with tomes stacked haphazardly to fill every possible inch.

"Considering he was dangerously close to my side when I lost control, we decided the babysitting program wasn't as effective as we'd hoped." Xaden leans against the wall to the left of the door, his shoulder resting along the frame of a painted rendering of the First Six's dragons.

But not seven.

"You're here now, so it won't happen again." I brace my palms on the desk and jump to sit on its edge. "I made myself a promise that I would do anything to save you, to cure you, so if that means we can't be—"

"Do not finish that sentence." He walks my way, and my heartbeat increases with every step he takes. "You're already the deadliest here, so it's not like I have to worry about grading you fairly. This changes nothing."

"We live by the Codex—" I try again.

"I live by *you*. When have I ever given a fuck about the Codex or the Code of Conduct?" He cradles my face and leans down, resting his forehead against mine. "I am yours and you are mine, and there's no law or rule in this world or the next that will change that."

My eyes slide shut, like that might stop my heart from falling even harder for this man. "So what do we do?"

"Kaori thinks we can get an exemption. I just have to ask Panchek here in a few minutes." His thumbs graze my cheeks, and I slowly open my eyes, clinging to the hope that he might be right. That it could just be that easy.

"No matter what, we have to keep you here. You were only on the border for a week." *And look what happened.* I don't have to say what we're both thinking.

"I know." He lifts his head. "And the worst part is I don't even remember reaching for the source or taking the power during the battle. It was simply *there*. If Sgaeyl hadn't…" His chest rises with a deep breath. "She spoke to me for the first time—'yelled' is a more accurate term—and I snapped out of it, but the damage was done. I let you down."

"You didn't." I clasp his wrists. "We'll figure this out. And if Panchek agrees to the exemption, I have a few things I need to catch you up on."

He nods. "I'll meet you in your room—"

The door opens, and I drop my hands, but Xaden doesn't move an inch.

"Ah, Professor Riorson," Aetos says from the doorway. "Kaori mentioned you might be in here, so I thought I'd handle the awkward business of you inevitably asking for an exemption to the Code of Conduct so you don't embarrass yourself in front of Colonel Panchek."

My stomach dips. I don't need Melgren's signet to know this battle isn't going to go our way.

"General Aetos." Xaden's hands slide from my cheeks in a slow caress, and then he turns to face the commander. "I'm formally requesting an exemption in regard to Article Eight, Section One, on the grounds that this is a previously existing relationship and the post is temporary."

"Denied," Aetos responds without sparing a second. "I'll obey Melgren's order and give you the position, even though I think there are riders better suited for it, but make no mistake, Riorson, I don't want you here. Pardon or no pardon, title or not, I won't forget that you murdered the vice commandant in cold blood a few short months ago and ripped this institution apart. Your attachment to Cadet Sorrengail gives me the perfect excuse to kick you off my campus, and I will joyfully take it should you break the Code of Conduct, *Professor*. It may be General Melgren's army, but it's my school. Do you understand?"

Gods, I fucking hate him.

"That you're an asshole? Absolutely." Xaden holds up his finger. "And insulting you isn't against the Code of Conduct. I checked."

Aetos flushes scarlet and snaps a glare in my direction. "Farewells are over. Get to class, cadet."

"Nothing changes. We just do what we're best at," Xaden says.

"Steal half the quadrant's riot and run for Aretia?" I slide off the desk, anger stirring my power to a simmer.

"No, smart-ass. Sneak around. At least for now."

"For now," I agree as General Aetos clears the doorway just in time for me to pass through. "Just so you know who to hate," I say over my shoulder once I'm in the hall, "Xaden didn't kill Varrish. I did."

Aetos stiffens and his eyes bulge as Dain steps out of the shadowy archway directly across the hall.

"Come on, Violet. I'll walk you to class." Dain looks at his father like the man has abandoned his dragon to die on the battlefield.

We walk silently until we reach the stairwell.

"The blame isn't solely yours. You struck the final blow, but we both know I killed Varrish," Dain says quietly as we descend to the third floor. "You could have told him, maybe used the information to help you get that exemption."

"And how would that help you?"

"Oh, I'm beyond help when it comes to my father." He huffs out a miserable laugh. "And my father is clearly just...beyond help in general."

"Dain," I whisper, hating that he looks like how I felt about my mother last year.

"He'll be in Calldyr next weekend." Dain nods as if making a choice. "We'll get your father's research then."

It feels like anything but a victory.

• • •

The next Monday, I contemplate slamming my head against the twelve-person table that fills what Mom had called the "planning chamber" on the second floor of the administration building. It would probably be a better use of my time than listening to Captain Grady and Lieutenant—shit, I've already forgotten his name—argue about possible locations to search in front of the map of the Continent that hangs between the two windows.

My favorite part of the map? The hand-drawn, shapeless blobs that are supposed to represent the isle kingdoms to the south and east. It's taken me exactly three minutes of this "meeting" to decide that no one knows what the fuck we're doing.

Jesinia has rolled her eyes twice from the left end of the table, where she sits with a stack of books, quill, and parchment, keeping record of the meeting and who's now officially been chosen for the mission.

"Please tell me you're almost here," I say to Xaden as the shadowy bond between us strengthens with proximity.

"Climbing the stairs," he replies.

"Northward is obviously the answer." Grady signs simultaneously as he speaks, just as everyone has since the beginning of the meeting, then scratches a beard that isn't as neatly trimmed as he usually keeps it.

"Yes, we should absolutely venture into undiscovered territory," Captain Anna Winshire mutters sarcastically in the seat to my right. She's a talkative infantry captain with strawberry-blond hair, quick brown eyes, and serrated blades strapped to both her shoulders, but other than the myriad of ribboned awards for valor sewn onto her uniform, I can't figure out why she's been chosen for the squad.

In fact, I can't figure out why *any* of them have. There are at least three older riders I've just met for the first time sitting across from me, and the one I already know—Aura—is as far away as possible on the right side, closest to the map. But at least Halden isn't here, and he wasn't on the draft roster, either, which is a relief. Maybe they've decided against a royal representative after all.

Grady's still arguing with his team. "North is—"

The door swings open at my left, and Xaden steps in.

Every head turns in his direction, but mine whips fastest. The last four days have felt like an eternity. Being close to him without having the kind of access I'm used to is frustrating as hell. I'm constantly aware of where he is when his shields are down, and even when they're up, I find myself looking around every corner in hopes there's something more to the shadows.

With Xaden sleeping in the professors' quarters, turns out that sneaking around isn't just hard, it's impossible. There's a Navarrian rider watching everywhere I go.

The library? Ewan Faber has one convenient eye on the squad.

The dormitory? Aura finds a sudden interest in late-night hall patrols.

Going to visit Sawyer? Caroline Ashton and her minions trail along behind.

"This is a closed meeting," Lieutenant Forgot-his-name says, drawing his dimpled chin back in indignation.

"I forgive you for failing to invite me," Xaden replies, sinking into the chair on my left.

I bite back a smile. He might think he's changed, but that comment is undeniably him.

"We're not taking a *separatist*—" the lieutenant starts to argue, his hands moving almost violently as he signs.

"You already are," I interrupt with a sweet smile.

Jesinia tucks her chin into her robes, and I know she's muffling a laugh.

"We can waste time arguing," Xaden says, "or we can just agree that Tairn isn't going anywhere without Sgaeyl and move on."

Quill scratches across parchment as Jesinia quickly takes notes, but there's a definite smirk on her mouth still.

Captain Grady's jaw flexes, but I have to respect that it's his only outward display of annoyance. Anyone with a set of bars on their shoulders should have predicted this, but I'm curious to see how he'll handle it considering how illogically our squad has been formed. "Fine," he finally says. "Cadet Neilwart, please add his name to our roster." He glances down the table. "Everyone here has been chosen for this mission because I trust them. Make your introductions if you haven't," he orders the others, then turns to look at the map.

"Captain Henson," the woman with tightly woven black braids to his right replies, nodding. "Air wielder."

"Lieutenant Pugh." The next man narrows his pale blue eyes. "Farsight."

"Lieutenant Foley." *Ah, that's his name.* "Agrarian."

"Cadet Beinhaven." Aura lifts her chin. "Fire wielder."

"Lieutenant Winshire." Anna smiles. "Infantry liaison."

"Lieutenant Riorson," Xaden replies. *"It's like he pulled a list of the most common signets and started choosing names."*

"And there are no fliers or Aretian riders." I fiddle with my pen. *"Doesn't exactly speak to the spirit of alliance."*

"Why no shield signets?" Xaden asks. "Clearly we'll be out beyond the wards, unless you think there's an entire den hiding within Navarre's borders that the Empyrean doesn't know about."

"You were able to hide one," Foley snaps.

"Thinking the Empyrean wasn't aware for six years tells me all I need to know about where your and your dragon's priorities are." Xaden shrugs.

"Stop," Grady orders. "And I've asked General Tinery for a particular shield wielder. Just waiting on a response."

Xaden's brow knits for a millisecond, just long enough to let me know he's digging around people's intentions. "You could just ask me. Mira Sorrengail is the only rider proven beyond the wards, and she's stationed in Aretia."

I grip the pen. Mira had been my first choice in this mission to begin with... if they'd asked me.

"Which is the Southern Wing and clearly under the command of General Tinery." Pugh glowers at Xaden.

"Except for Tyrrendor," Xaden replies, "which as of the Second Aretia Accord now falls to the reigning house." He cocks his head to the side. "Well, really Ulices and Kylynn, but they answer to me."

Quill rasping against parchment is the only sound as some jaws are picked up off the floor and others lock.

I sit back in my chair and fight the urge to smile. *"Have to say, the casual flex of power is pretty hot."*

"Don't," he warns. *"I'm barely keeping my hands to myself as it is. If you knew how often I think about sneaking into your room..."*

My pulse quickens.

"Is this what I can expect, *Lieutenant Riorson?*" Grady asks, color rising in his neck. "You pulling title into military matters? There's a reason aristocrats don't wear black."

"Happens more often than you think," I mutter, signing it discreetly to my friend.

Jesinia lifts the quill and doesn't record my smart-ass remark, but she definitely fights off a laugh.

"Depends on how those matters are handled," Xaden threatens, his hand motions sharpening as he signs and his tone slipping into that dangerous calm that makes the lieutenants across from us shift in their seats and my gaze flicker his way.

The hair rises on the back of my neck. There's a flash of something...cold in his eyes, but it's gone with a single blink. Huh.

"You and I are going to have problems," Captain Grady warns.

"Probably." Xaden nods.

Grady breathes deeply as the flush creeps to his jawline. "As we were saying. We've been given six months to find the seventh breed. The Senarium has ordered that we report back between searching potential sites to keep them informed—"

"What a fucking waste of time," Xaden says.

"—which means selecting our first search areas within easy flight," Grady continues.

"Just wait, it gets better." I pick up my pen and roll it between my forefingers

and thumb to keep myself busy. *"I miss your hands."*

"Same." He keeps his eyes on the map, but a band of shadow curls up my leg beneath the table and wraps around my upper thigh. *"And your mouth, especially if that's all I'm allowing myself."*

It's on the tip of my mental tongue to tell him he doesn't have to limit himself, but I'm sure drawing more power from the earth on his last mission isn't exactly evoking confidence in his self-control.

"And I've chosen to begin along the northward coastline," Captain Grady finishes.

Xaden's brows hit the ceiling.

"Told you it got better."

Captain Henson drums her fingers on the table. "Why?"

Grady clears his throat. "Basing our operation at the coastline gives us access to magic. Plus, the Emerald Sea is largely unexplored—"

"Because sailors don't return from the deepest waters," Henson retorts, then looks my way. "Where would your dragon like to search?"

"Cadet Sorrengail isn't in charge," Aura interrupts.

"You're only here because I chose not to kill you for going after my wingleader," I reply. *"This is a mistake. The only people I trust in this room are you and Jesinia, and she's reporting the missions after we return, not going on them."*

"Agreed." Shadows swirl along the base of the wall. *"Mira should add some balance, but not enough."*

"The last known communication we have with any isle kingdom is Deverelli," I say into the awkward silence. "From what I've read, the merchant isle trades in more than goods. If there's information to be had there, we can buy it for the right price. We should search all possible avenues, not just the north."

Jesinia subtly nods as she records what I've suggested.

Everyone across from us starts speaking at once.

"They'll kill us if we go there."

"Splitting our forces weakens the squad."

"Dragon-haters, all of them."

"If the dragons were on the isles, one of them would have bragged."

"Or used them in an assault," I mutter mentally.

"What do you know?" Xaden asks, and the band of shadow *strokes* my inner thigh.

Fuck, it's hard to think when he does that. *"Records of the second Krovlan uprising have been ripped out of General Cadao's journal, and Jesinia thinks an officer hinted that an isle kingdom was involved hundreds of years* after *we severed contact. General Aetos asked me about my father's research on the subject last year—"*

"Feathertails." Xaden's jaw ticks. *"I vaguely remember him mentioning something about it on our way to the flight field."*

"Exactly. Dragons mentioned with isles tells me we should look south." I watch the others descend into shouting, their hands flying as they sign, and Aura is the shrillest of them all. Pretty bold coming from a cadet. *"I don't know the contents of Dad's research, but I do remember him suddenly going secretive with it about six months before he died. If he'd wanted Aetos or Markham to have it, he would have left the information in his Archives office."*

"As opposed to?" He glances my way as the shouting only grows.

"It's in their quarters." I wince. *"General Aetos's quarters. Don't worry, Dain's agreed to help me find it."*

Xaden cracks his neck. *"'Don't worry' and 'Dain' do not belong in the same sentence."*

"Silence!" Grady shouts, his complexion fully ruddy. "Aside from already provided logic, Deverelli requires too high a price for an audience. South is not an option," he says to me, then turns toward Captain Henson. "And as for the Emerald Sea, perhaps dragons are the reason sailors don't return. Until further notice, assume we will fly northward in the next month. Prepare your supplies. This meeting is adjourned."

Fuck. Every bone in my body says to fly south.

"Stay," Xaden says. *"I'd kill for thirty seconds with you."*

"Absolutely." A freaking *hug* sounds great.

Xaden and I hang behind as everyone files out, even Jesinia, but Aura Beinhaven waits at the door like a nursemaid, her brow arched as I gather my things.

"Yes, Aura?" I ask as I close my pack.

"Just waiting to escort you back to the quadrant." She looks pointedly at Xaden. "Wouldn't want you getting in trouble or doing something I'd have to report to General Aetos, seeing as Grady chose me as your *companion* and all."

More like a fucking chaperone. "Do you mean Panchek?"

She shakes her head. "Aetos made it clear to the wingleaders that the Code of Conduct is to be followed to the letter." Her eyes narrow. "Naturally, we've passed that order down through the chain of command. Turns out there are lots of us happy to make your life as miserable as possible."

"Great." I force a smile and the shadow slips from my thigh as I walk past Xaden, keeping even my eyes to myself so she doesn't have anything to report.

"We'll get time," he promises.

"You're safe here. That's all that matters."

At least until we go northward.

Some combat signets are fearsome, but any rider can be brought low
by two things: lack of a shield...or a group effort. Never give the
enemy the advantage of surrounding you.

—Gryphons of Poromiel, a Study in Combat
by Major Garion Savoy

CHAPTER
FIFTEEN

By the time it's our squad's turn to descend the stone steps of the Infantry
Quadrant's outdoor amphitheater on Friday, it's been another four days
since I've seen Xaden, and he keeps his shields up so frequently that we may as
well just start writing letters again.

Carved into a northern ridgeline just west of the Infantry Quadrant, the
half-dome arena is more fighting pit than lecture hall. It's capable of seating all
thousand-plus infantry cadets, but this afternoon the magically warmed space
only holds our squad, Caroline Ashton's from First Wing, and the devastatingly
beautiful man standing in the middle of the flat base of the amphitheater,
impatience carved on every line of his face. I've always loved him in uniform,
but there's something about seeing him in tight-fitted sparring gear, swords
strapped across his back, that makes me instantly wish this was a private
teaching session.

"This is incredible," Sloane says ahead of me. "The snow is piled up along
the edges, but it feels like summer in here."

"Weather ward?" Lynx guesses, ruffling the melting snow off his short black
hair.

"I'd guess there's a little more to it than that." Given the way the magic
pulled at me like a sticky piece of toffee while walking through, I'm sure weather
isn't the only thing we're keeping out.

Shadows brush against my shields as I strip out of my winter flight jacket midway down the steps, and I crack open just enough of my defenses to let Xaden in.

"I've missed you." His gaze devours me, but he does a good job of quickly looking away.

"Same." I lay my jacket on the first row of stone seats beside my classmates, leaving me in traditional sparring gear. *"Is this where you've been hiding out?"*

"Welcome to your first session of Signet Sparring, in what I like to call the pit," he announces as we reach the base of the steps. The floor is laid in an arched cobblestone pattern of various shades, but only five or so feet are visible before the mat begins. "Those who can wield, keep your feet on the rock but—and I cannot stress this enough—off the mat. Those who cannot, take a seat in the first row." He gestures to the terraced stone behind us, and cadets move. *"If by hiding out, you mean constructing incredibly complex wards that might make even your sister proud, then yes. And it's not like you've been accessible. Bodhi says you're either reading with Andarna as a backrest or wielding alone in the range."*

An hour a day, that's what I've promised myself. No matter how cold it is or how tired I am, I'm on the ridgeline with Tairn, practicing smaller, more concise strikes until my arms feel like jelly.

"I spend a lot of time in the library, too." I roll my shoulders, then take my place between Ridoc and Rhiannon, keeping two rows back from the mat as I secure the strap of the conduit through the loop on the left side of my waist. *"Quest squad may be headed north, but I'm still reading everything I can find on Deverelli, which isn't nearly enough."* And the tomes on dark wielders both Queen Maraya and Tecarus have sent, though there's been no hint of a cure or mention of a dragon ever torching a venin like Andarna did. Maybe it's a good thing I can't spend all my nighttime hours with Xaden, or I wouldn't be flying through books like I am.

"Let's go. It shouldn't be this hard to sort yourselves out." His gaze wanders to mine. *"Quest squad?"*

"Ridoc gave it a nickname and it stuck." I shrug as the other squad fills in to the right of our third-years, standing in our mirror image, oldest at the center of the arc. *"Aetos leaves for his trip to Calldyr soon, so we've been preparing to get into my parents'—"* I wince. *"His quarters."*

"Need my help?" He scans over our line, no doubt assessing strengths and weaknesses.

"No, but I'll let you know if that changes." I bend my left knee, testing to be sure the wrap is still in place. Doesn't matter how often Brennan mends me, that particular joint never stays healed for long. *"Any chance you can sneak away to Chantara this weekend? We're dragging Sawyer out."*

"I hope you have a great time, but watching you across the pub sounds like

torture." His jaw ticks. *"I think we had more time together when I was stationed at Samara."*

"Agreed, but you're safe here." I take stock of who we have on the floor. On Rhiannon's right, Bragen and Neve—the third-year fliers—stand with Imogen and Quinn, and to Ridoc's left are Trager, Cat, Maren, Baylor, Avalynn, Sloane, and Kai. Aaric and Lynx are seated behind us, and it catches me off guard to realize that all four of the first-years in the First Wing squad are sitting, too.

Dragons are taking their time when it comes to channeling.

"Safe is starting to feel overrated." He looks toward First Wing. "You done gossiping among yourselves?"

"We were just saying that we're not sure someone who graduated less than a year ago makes the best teacher." Loran Yashil folds his arms. The cocky third-year with bright-purple locs is one of the best fighters in their wing.

"Oh shit," Rhiannon whispers.

A corner of my lips rises. They've earned whatever Xaden is about to dish out.

"Let's see if you can take me down and settle that worry right now." Xaden crooks his fingers. "You're a metallurgist, right?"

My heart twinges. "Sawyer should be here, too," I whisper to Rhi.

"Yeah, well, everything I've tried to convince him has failed." Her mouth tenses.

Shit. "You're doing your best. I didn't mean—"

Her shoulders dip. "I know."

"Metallurgist." Loran nods. "So these are nice and sharp." He walks onto the mat, drawing the sword from his hip and a dagger from his waist.

"Good for you." Xaden claps twice but keeps his feet planted apart on the mat. "I hope they help."

Loran lifts his sword and circles Xaden to the left. "Are you going to draw a weapon?"

"We'll see." Xaden shrugs, his eyes tracking Loran's movements. "Now do us both a favor and don't hold back. Begin."

Loran charges, and my ribs tighten like a vise around my lungs.

Xaden doesn't move.

Loran runs until he's three feet from Xaden, then thrusts his sword forward, keeping his dagger tucked at his side.

My breath catches as Xaden lets the blade come within inches of his chest, then sidesteps and slams his left fist on top of Loran's wrist. Loran shouts as the sword falls, but he's already pivoting toward Xaden before the blade hits the mat, his left arm swinging in an arc that's aimed at slicing open Xaden's jugular.

Xaden grabs hold of Loran's forearm and spins, yanking the appendage behind Loran's back and driving his elbow upward until Loran cries out in painful frustration. Then he plucks the dagger from Loran's hand and releases him with a shove forward.

"The fucking *nerve* on that one," Ridoc mutters, shaking his head. "If he'd waited a second later…"

But he didn't, because he knew exactly what Loran intended.

A slow smile spreads across my face. *"I've always loved watching you on the mat."*

"I know." Xaden rolls his neck. *"I've used it to my advantage a few times."*

Of course he has.

Loran stumbles but, to his credit, immediately turns to face Xaden again.

Xaden flicks the dagger, and it lodges in the mat between Loran's feet. "You threw too much energy into the charge. Using brute force instead of finesse is a first-year tactic." He cocks his head to the side and studies Loran with a look that's almost bored. "Now that we've proven I'm capable of kicking your ass without breaking a sweat or holding steel, what do you say we get to the point of the class and wield?" Xaden lifts his arms at a ninety-degree angle, palms up.

Loran swallows and keeps both eyes on Xaden as he retrieves his weapons.

"Begin," Xaden orders.

Loran shifts his weight, and there's a definite sheen of panic in his eyes as he circles Xaden again. To my utter consternation, the man I love doesn't even look as Loran creeps around his back. No, instead of following his opponent's moves, Xaden looks my way and fucking *winks* as Loran attacks from behind, the sword transforming, lengthening as he strikes.

In fact, he holds my gaze unflinchingly until Loran raises his blade a few feet from his neck.

Then Xaden glances down at his left, where the blade's shadow stretches past his boot, elongated by the afternoon sun, and lifts a single finger.

The shadow rushes back on Loran and within a heartbeat wraps around his throat and arm.

Xaden steps to the side as Loran falls to his knees in the very space Xaden had stood, and the sword falls, too, abandoned as Loran grabs for the shadows tightening around his throat. His face blotches, and the other squad starts to shift uncomfortably before Xaden drops his hands.

The shadow falls back into position, and Loran gasps for air.

"I'm either completely in love with your boyfriend or utterly terrified of him," Ridoc says under his breath. "Not sure at the moment."

"Both," Cat answers from his left. "You can be both. Trust me."

"You shouldn't be either," Trager mutters.

Ridoc glances my way and rolls his eyes.

I bite back my smile. "I'm never scared of him." Xaden's eyes find mine, and my pulse skips. "And he's not my boyfriend."

Rhi snorts and Ridoc offers me a sarcastic thumbs-up.

"Agreed," Xaden says. *"That's far too casual a term for what we are."* His gaze drops to Loran, who's still heaving for breath on the mat. "Get up."

Loran staggers to his feet and runs his hand over the purple bruise forming on his throat.

"I have two swords and four daggers strapped to me," Xaden tells him. "And you didn't think to heat them? Twist them? Manipulate them in any way?"

"I used my sword—" Loran starts.

"Foolish choice. Get back to your squad." Xaden dismisses him, and Loran retrieves his weapons before retreating. "I'm sure you all noticed the weather ward we have in place to keep you nice and comfortable for these first few lessons, but what you don't see is that the area of the mat has been protected by the best ward-weavers in Navarre."

He flares his hands and shadows run from his feet, expanding in every direction in a cloud of darkness that flies toward us, only to slam against an invisible barrier and flow upward. They withdraw with unnerving speed, clearing the air in front of us in a matter of heartbeats.

"With only a couple of exceptions"—he glances my way—"whatever you wield will stay between the opponents on the mat, and I'm assured your signets will *not* leave the amphitheater or endanger the campus, so when I tell you not to hold back, I mean it, because the venin won't. Next?"

One by one, he sets just about everyone on their ass.

They put a fire wielder against him, and he dodges the flame, her own shadows taking her out at the knees with a flick of his wrist.

Quinn steps up and creates two versions of herself, and when shadows tug her feet from under her, the real Quinn falls and the projection dissipates.

Rhiannon has her own blade plucked from her grasp and lifted to her throat by a wisp of shadow.

Caroline barely gets her hands up before Xaden knocks her backward with a stream of shadow that propels her across the mat and forces her onto the stone.

Neve steps onto the mat gripping her daggers, then uses lesser magic to levitate them.

"Now that's fun," Xaden says with a grin as they race toward him, only to be grasped by shadow and returned with their tips poised to strike above her collarbones.

She puts up her hands, and the shadows fall, dropping the blades to the mat.

"Point made?" Xaden asks as Neve retrieves her blades and steps back into line. "I never need to draw a sword because *I* am the weapon. I'm just good with blades for the fun of it."

"No," Loran says, his voice still hoarse. "You handing everyone their ass on the mat isn't anything new from last year."

"Correct." Xaden lifts a scarred brow. "Up until now, when we spar or challenge, our priority has been to beat our opponent at all costs. That means we train in private, we find an edge—" A corner of his mouth lifts. *"Like poisoning our opponents."* He slides his hands into his pockets. "And we keep our tactics secret because we need that edge on the mat. The difference between my position as a cadet last year, even as a wingleader, and now is that as your teacher, I want to give you *my* edge. I want you to learn, not just from me but from one another. I'll help expose the weaknesses in your signet so that when you come up against a dark wielder with such a power, you will have already practiced how to defeat them. Each of you has something to learn, and I'm here to keep you safe while you do it."

"And what about the ones who can't wield signets?" Caroline asks. "They're just the practice dummies?"

Cat scoffs. "We're far from helpless." She turns a withering glare on Caroline. "You can try your water wielding on me, but I'll already be in your head, turning your own emotions against you."

"She's good at it, too," I admit, shifting the majority of my weight to my right leg.

"You'll find that mindwork can be just as deadly," Xaden agrees. "And if you haven't learned how to shield, I suggest you spend some time with Professor Carr before facing off against a flier or anyone wearing a classified patch." He glances at Imogen.

"And you're going to teach us how to defeat *you*?" Aaric asks from behind us.

A corner of Xaden's mouth slowly curves upward. "I can teach you to try, but there's only one person capable of taking me down one day, and it isn't you, Graycastle."

My cheeks heat as heads swing my way.

"Let's get back to it while you have some relative privacy. As of next week, the infantry cadets will be sitting in so they stand half a chance on the battlefield." Xaden scans the line. "Gamlyn, you're next."

Ridoc ends up caged by a set of icicles of his own making.

Sloane retreats from the arena with her hands tied in shadow behind her back after not even *trying*. I glance at her rebellion relic and wonder if she's hiding a second signet, too.

Neither Cat nor Maren get close before they're off the mat and sent stumbling in our direction, but Cat is the only one of the pair who looks momentarily devastated at having failed.

"You're going to get over him at some point, right?" Trager mutters as Cat falls back in line. "Seems like a waste of time to chase someone who doesn't want you when there are plenty of people who do."

Cat's gaze snaps in his direction, and I lift my brows.

Go Trager.

And then Xaden lifts his brow at me. "No exceptions, Sorrengail."

"Now *this* is what I've been waiting to see." Caroline bounces on her toes like a child.

"Do me a favor," I say to Xaden, unfastening the conduit's leather strap at my hip and hooking it over my wrist so the orb fits comfortably in my palm. Then I take three steps forward onto the mat and open the door to Tairn's power with a hell of a smirk. "Don't let me hurt you."

It is hereby suggested strongly that neither bonded dragon nor gryphon shall be allowed to land or hunt in a one-mile vicinity of the village of Chantara in order to sustain the endeavors of our sheep herders through this surge of demand.

—POSTED BULLETIN, VILLAGE OF CHANTARA
TRANSCRIBED BY PERCIVAL FITZGIBBONS

CHAPTER SIXTEEN

"**A**rrogant, are we?" His flash of an undeniable smile is there and gone before I can fully succumb to its knee-wobbling effect. "Let's see how you do in the dark."

Shadows fill the mat and devour every ounce of sunlight, leaving me in complete and total darkness in every direction I look. Challenge accepted.

"This is playing dirty." I lift the conduit to just above my shoulder and release a steady flow of power from my left hand. The orb crackles, catching the tendrils of lightning as it imbues the alloy at its center and illuminating the area directly surrounding me.

"You already have the upper hand," he replies, and a strand of shadow caresses my cheek but doesn't take form any closer to the conduit. *"I'm just leveling the playing field."*

I walk forward, catching a glimpse of him before he fades into darkness once more.

"Strike," he orders.

"And chance actually hitting you? I think not." My left arm heats, and I grit my teeth against the strain of sustaining the power flow. It's so much easier to strike than trickle.

"Use our pathway to track me down." His lips brush the back of my neck, and a jolt of awareness races down my spine, but when I spin, he's already gone.

"That's cheating." I walk left, then forward, then turn around again, completely lost as to which direction I'm facing.

"It's using every tool at your disposal," he points out. *"Come on, Violence. Live up to the nickname. I could have killed you a dozen times over by now because you're reluctant to strike."*

"And I could kill you with a single, non-hypothetical strike." I open my senses, but it's impossible to concentrate on our pathways while my body channels continuously. Fuck it. It's not like I can see through this anyway. Lowering my arm, I cut the flow of power from my fingertips, and shadows rush over me, cooling my heated skin.

I focus on our connection, on the bond, and obey the subtle, barely perceptible tug that comes from my right.

"Good." The bond strengthens when he talks, and I change directions slightly, following the connection. *"I can wield from anything that casts a shadow, but no one knows the strongest threads are always my own. If you can sort through them, feel their difference, you'll be able to track where I am in the darkness."*

"Is that really what you need me to learn?" I run my hands through shadow, but it all feels the same.

"You have to learn the difference for both our sakes." The bond surrounds me in the same instant that he wraps his arms around me from behind, and a stronger shadow—his—tilts my chin toward my shoulder and up. *"Only you."*

His mouth finds mine in the darkness and he kisses me long and slow, like we're the only people in the world, like our time is infinite and there is nothing more important than hearing my next sigh. It's utterly decadent, thorough, and only makes me want more. My pulse leaps, racing faster with every stroke of his perfect tongue.

"Strike," he demands, his fingers sliding down my stomach and slipping under my waistband. *"Or someone might think I'm taking it easy on you."* He nips my bottom lip.

"Easy is the opposite of what I want from you." Power rises, humming through me with insistent demand, and I lift my right hand, aiming my palm toward the sky of the open amphitheater.

Xaden vanishes from behind me a second before I release the strike.

Light flashes, illuminating the arena as lightning streaks upward, through the barrier of the wards and into the clouds above, and I hear the other cadets' collective gasps before the darkness descends again.

"You're astounding," he says, already one of the shadows.

"Why only me?" I ask, turning endlessly to find him.

"You need to be able to find me." Shadows rush against my skin, and less than a breath later, they're gone, leaving me stumbling near the front of the mat,

staring at Xaden's retreating back as he climbs the stairs. "Class is over. I expect you all to come prepared next session," he says over his shoulder.

"Why only me?" I repeat, more than aware of the other cadets staring as I find my balance, studying me as if hoping to discover a mark, since Xaden walked away unscathed. *"Xaden!"*

He doesn't so much as pause his ascent. *"Because you're the only one capable of killing me."*

• • •

"**A**nd then there's Violet," Ridoc says the next afternoon, waving his mug of ale as we sit at the corner table of the Six Talons pub in Chantara. "Scaring off the *professor* with a lightning strike. He got the fuck out of there and left her stumbling around in the dark."

Sawyer laughs. Really, truly laughs, and I don't care if it's from his second mug of ale or if Amari herself dragged it out of him, I'm just relieved to hear it. For a second, it feels like we have him back, like we're all...us.

The door opens across the room, and snow blows in before someone manages to shut it against the insistent wind. The noisy pub is crowded with villagers and cadets looking for a Saturday escape. I spotted Dain at the bar earlier, trying his luck with a second-year healer, and Ridoc has already fought off three separate attempts to pilfer the three chairs we've saved across the table for the fliers.

The group of us visited a few temples after lunch, but the fliers have been gone for hours worshipping. If they're not back soon, we'll miss the last wagons back to campus.

"Riorson had my own dagger at my throat," Rhi says, shaking her head like she still can't believe it. "I always knew he was powerful, but I never realized he could..." She drifts off.

"Kill everyone in the room without getting up from his seat?" I finish for her, lifting my lavender lemonade to take a sip. *And he thinks I need to know how to kill him.*

The normally sweet drink tastes bitter in my throat.

Maybe he slipped on the border, but he isn't *gone*. One mistake does not equal losing your entire soul.

"Exactly." She nods. "Have you always known that?"

"Yep." I set my mug down. "Well, not always, but definitely after he busted into my room and killed Oren and the others during our first year."

"What are we discussing?" Cat asks, setting a mug down on the table and taking the seat directly across from me. She shrugs out of her snow-covered jacket as Maren and Trager do the same.

"Riorson's ability to wipe out…well…everyone," Ridoc answers, taking his coat off Maren's seat as Sawyer moves his crutches to lean them against the wall behind him.

"Ah." Maren settles in next to Cat and looks her way. "That's…kind of new, right?"

Cat stares down into her mug. "He wasn't as powerful when we—" She cuts herself off and takes a drink.

"Our signets can grow," I say to fill the awkward silence. "We spend our lives honing them and figuring out our limits. A third-year is way more powerful than a first, just like a colonel can wipe the floor magically with a lieutenant."

"And he never scares you." Cat stares at me over the table. "That's what you said yesterday. He *never* scares you."

"I get scared *for* him, but I haven't been scared *of* him since Threshing." I run my finger along the top of my mug.

"Because your lives are connected." She tilts her head, like she's trying to understand.

"Because he'd never hurt me." I take another drink. "He had his reasons for wanting me dead, and instead taught me how to strike a death blow on the mat—and that was way before Threshing."

"Speaking of signets, I'm starting to worry." Rhi quickly changes the subject. "Sloane is a siphon. Avalynn began wielding fire last week, and Baylor has manifested farsight."

Like Liam.

"But Lynx and Aaric haven't manifested yet, and the clock is ticking," Rhi finishes.

"What happens if they don't manifest on your timeline?" Trager asks.

"The magic builds up and we kind of…explode." Ridoc makes the correlating motion with his hands. "But it's the end of January. We have months before it gets dangerous. Vi didn't manifest until what? May?" Ridoc asks me.

I blink, remembering the first time Xaden kissed me against the foundation walls. "It was actually December. I just didn't realize it."

"That doesn't comfort me," Rhi says, frowning over her mug. "The last thing we need is Lynx or *Aaric* exploding on us."

My chest tightens.

"Remind me not to stand next to either of them in formation," Cat drawls.

"Better than one of them manifesting as an inntinnsic," Ridoc mutters. "Could you imagine executing—"

"No," Rhi snaps, then shudders. "I can't. And neither should you." She glances at Maren. "So. How was temple?"

"Our offerings were received," Maren answers with an easy smile. "I believe

Amari will watch over my brothers in Aretia. I really can't thank your family enough for taking them in, Rhi."

"Are you kidding me?" Rhi waves her off. "My mother loves kids, and my dad is thrilled to have two little boys running around the house. I'm really sorry that they couldn't stay here with you, though."

Maren drops her gaze. "Me too, but Basgiath isn't exactly friendly for raising kids."

Cat rubs her shoulder.

"Your temples to Malek and Dunne are disproportionately large compared to the other gods' here," Trager notes, leaning back in his chair. "Except Amari, of course."

"It's a regional thing," Sawyer answers, pushing up on the arms of his chair and readjusting his weight. He seems more comfortable wearing the new wood-and-metal prosthesis he's been working on but hasn't been up for discussing it, so we haven't pushed. "This close to Basgiath, war and death are on most minds."

"So true," Ridoc agrees.

"Your scribes don't pray to Hedeon for wisdom?" Trager asks me, leaving his ale untouched long enough for Cat to reach over and steal it with a sly smile.

"Knowledge and wisdom are two different things," I answer. "Scribes are careful not to ask for what should be earned."

"So you weren't a frequent patron when studying to enter that quadrant?" He scoots his chair in when some drunk cadets try to squeeze past behind him and side-eyes Cat for stealing his drink, but there's a tilt to his lips.

"My mother was never temple-minded, which is odd, considering you'd think she'd favor Dunne. And I preferred to spend what worship time I had in Amari's temple." I glance down at my nearly empty mug. "And then once my father died, I frequented Malek's, though I probably spent more time yelling at him than praising."

"I personally prefer Zihnal," Ridoc adds. "You can get through any situation with luck."

"And ours must have run out, because here comes the wingleader," Rhi notes with a quick glance my way.

The fliers look over their shoulders, and we all quiet as Dain waits for a group of cadets to walk by before reaching the corner of our table.

"Vi." He still has that flat, tortured look in his eyes, and I hate that I can't take it away.

"Dain?" My hands tighten on my mug. I'd rather he be a dick again, even obnoxious in his certainty, over this hollow version of himself.

"Can I talk to you?" His attention sweeps over the others at the table. "Alone?"

"All right." I push away from the table, leaving behind my lemonade, and follow Dain into the dim, deserted hallway that leads to the pub's private rooms. My stomach clenches as he pivots to face me.

"I've spent the last few days reconning the security on Dad's quarters, and there's no way to sneak other people in without getting caught." He slides his hands into the pockets of his flight jacket.

My heart sinks. "You won't help me."

"I told you I would, and I will." His mouth tightens. "It's just going to require you to trust me enough to let me retrieve the research and bring it out myself. Preferably tomorrow night, since my father will be gone."

Shit. All he'd have to do is hand that research over to his father and Dain would be back in his good graces. My only assurance that wouldn't happen had been going with him. The history between us, both good and bad, thickens the air.

"It's up to you," he says with a hint of a shrug. "Either you trust me or you don't."

"It's not just that," I rush. There are so many ways this could go wrong. "If they catch you with it, or the cadets who constantly follow Xaden and me spot you handing something over secretively—"

"I've got that figured out," he interrupts like I've insulted him. "What's your choice?"

I weigh the pros and cons in less than a heartbeat, then sigh. "There's a secret compartment under my father's desk in the study. The latch is in the far back of the center drawer of my mother's."

He nods. "You'll have it by Monday morning."

For better or worse, my fate rests in the hands of Dain Aetos.

My brightest light, I meant to prepare you but only had time for half
the lessons you need, half the history, half the truth, and now time
runs short. I failed Brennan the day I watched him walk the parapet,
failed Mira when I could not stop her from following, but I fear my
death will fail you. Your mother and I trust no one, and neither can
you.

—RECOVERED CORRESPONDENCE OF LIEUTENANT COLONEL ASHER SORRENGAIL
TO VIOLET SORRENGAIL

CHAPTER
SEVENTEEN

"Thadeus Netien," Captain Fitzgibbons reads from the dais the next morning,
his voice carrying over the formation in the snow-packed courtyard as he
holds the death roll in front of him. "Nadia Aksel. Karessa Tomney."

Hearing the names of every member in active service who has died the
previous day takes longer than the typical quadrant death roll, but I appreciate
the change. It feels right to honor those losing their lives. It also serves to remind
me that though Major Devera has called a moratorium on killing one another
within our walls, there's an enemy just waiting to do so the second we leave.

There's an enemy who thinks I'm going to come to *her*.

"Melyna Chalston," Captain Fitzgibbons continues as the icy wind gusts,
tearing at the scroll and stinging the tips of my nose and ears. "And Ruford
Sharna."

I blink.

"From Third Wing?" Ridoc's head swings left, as do Quinn's and Imogen's
in front of us.

"Fell from his seat during maneuvers yesterday," Aaric says from behind us.
"According to their Tail Section, Haem couldn't see to catch him in the snow."

It was an accident. Somehow that makes it feel even worse.

"We commend their souls to Malek," Captain Fitzgibbons says, and a few announcements later, formation breaks.

We all head toward the dormitory wing, and Sloane grabs my elbow as we reach the door.

"I need to give you something," she says, staring at the ground. "Follow me?"

"Sure." Talking to me is at least a start.

She leads me through the rotunda, up into commons and to our small quadrant library on the right. It's empty this time of morning, and I wait at the last group of study tables as she quickly ducks behind the first set of tall bookshelves.

"You can look at me, you know." I unbutton my flight jacket. "My mother made her choice. You didn't."

"Not exactly." Sloane pushes a loaded library cart out of the aisle. "I felt her power. I could have rejected it. Stopped it, even." She rolls the cart directly in front of me. "But I wanted the wards up, wanted to live, so I let it happen." She ends on a whisper.

"That's a pretty valid emotion." Especially considering that my mother had overseen the execution of hers. "And I'm not angry—"

"Did you know that I have Archives duty?" she interrupts, crouching down to the bottom shelf of the cart. "I thought it was kind of fitting, seeing as Liam always went with you when you had it."

"Do you like it?" I manage to ask as my throat squeezes in on itself.

"Well, this morning it gave me a chance to see Jesinia." She stands, pulling a large black canvas bag with her.

"Thank you." I sling the straps of the bag over my shoulder, noting its exceptional weight.

She nods, then finally drags her gaze to meet mine. "It wasn't out of revenge, I swear. I'm sorry I didn't stop her."

My hands clasp around the thick canvas straps, knowing she isn't talking about Jesinia. "I'm glad you didn't. Powering the stone was going to take someone's life. If I had succeeded, Xaden, Tairn, Sgaeyl, and I would all be dead. The world needs Brennan, Aaric is…irreplaceable, and I wouldn't trade you for any ward, Sloane. My mother made the choice she had to. You were the tool, but she gave her own life."

Her next breath shakes. "Anyway, Jesinia said to tell you that two of the tomes were her selection and the other was passed along to her from leadership first thing this morning."

Dain. A smile spreads across my face. Not only did he come through, but he did it in a way that no one potentially watching either of us would suspect. I hold the bag tighter. This could be my father's final body of work. "Thank you."

"Rumor is you're headed northward." Sloane folds her arms.

"Unfortunately, that rumor may be true." I grimace.

Her face puckers. "Seems an odd place to search, given how cold it is. Don't know about Tairn, but Thoirt hates the cold."

I nod. "Makes sense, since Thoirt is a red. Many of their line's ancestral hatching grounds were along the limestone cliffs at the edge of the Dunness River. My gut tells me north is the wrong direction, but Tairn doesn't mind the cold, and most browns prefer it, so maybe Grady is onto something." Andarna isn't a big fan of snow, either, but maybe she isn't stereotypical of her kind.

"I hope for all our sakes he is," Sloane says.

"Me too." But I can't ignore the little voice of intuition insisting we should head south.

When I get the package back to my room, any hope I'd felt since finding Dad's research slips into pure frustration as I unwrap it from its parchment to find the locking mechanism that holds the thick, leather-bound book closed. It's a six-letter lock, and if I get the answer wrong, there are six vials of ink spaced equidistantly around the edges of the paper, ready to destroy whatever my father left inside. Even worse, there's a rune in the center that looks suspiciously like the one that makes things end badly if magic tampers with a lock.

Definitely need to spend more time studying runes.

I pick up the scrap piece of parchment Dad had stashed in a roll beneath the lock and read his formal handwriting again.

First love is irreplaceable.

Fuck. Nothing Dad wrote was ever this simple. So what the hell is that supposed to mean?

• • •

"**A**re we wasting time by overthinking this? It's obviously Lilith, right?" Ridoc asks as we descend the steps into the pit a few days later.

"Dad would have wanted me to overthink. And if I'm wrong, we ruin whatever's in there." I tuck my jacket under my arm and scan the bottom of the amphitheater in hopes of seeing Xaden.

"Maybe we're not thinking fatherly enough," Rhi muses.

"Good idea. So maybe it's Bren—" Ridoc counts out on his fingers. "Never mind, that has too many letters. Mira is too short, but what about Violet?"

"Honestly, it's not like my dad to make it about himself. Both Lilith and Violet are too obvious." We pass by the infantry already seated in the middle of the terraced rows and spot Calvin, the squad leader of one of the infantry units we'd been paired with during RSC. I nod, and he returns the gesture.

"Fine, then who was Brennan's first love?" Ridoc asks as we near the bottom of the steps.

"There's nine years between us. It's not like he was filling me in on his romantic exploits—" I pause as Ridoc shuffles into his seat beside Maren. "Though I do remember Mira saying he'd been in a relationship with a rider a year or two older than him."

"Guess that runs in the family." Ridoc shucks his jacket.

"Are you guys *still* trying to figure out the password to open that damned book?" Cat asks, leaning forward and earning a backward glance from the first-years seated ahead of us.

"Obviously, or they wouldn't be talking about it," Trager says, resting his elbows on the rise behind him and leaning back.

"Space much?" Neve shoves his arm off the rise with her boot. "What book?"

"The one Violet's father left her that everyone seems to think might have some information about where Andarna's kind went," Cat answers. I shoot her a look, and she shrugs. "What? No one on the squad is going to hand you over, and you obviously need some more opinions before you're comfortable enough to actually try and input a password."

Fair point, but still.

"Fine, who's Mira's first love?" Rhi asks, her gaze darting between Avalynn, Kai, and Baylor, who are seated as far apart as possible.

I think, tilting my head and fastening the conduit's bracelet over the raw band of skin around my wrist. An hour of wielding a day is definitely helping me pull down more precise strikes, but my body is *over* it. "I'm not sure she's ever really been in love. Or if she has, she's never said anything to me about it."

"You hadn't even seen Xaden when your dad met Malek—" Ridoc stares at me and sighs with complete exaggeration. "Hello, who is *your* first love?"

Oh, that's not happening.

I set my hands in my lap and notice more infantry pouring in above us. Nothing like being humbled in front of an audience. "My father couldn't stand the first guy I really dated and never knew about the second."

Aaric turns his entire torso around to look at me. "How many letters?"

I narrow my eyes. "Six."

He lifts two sandy-brown eyebrows. "I mean…it fits."

"Absolutely not." Heat stings my cheeks.

"Hold on." Ridoc's head swings between the two of us. "Is the first-year entitled to information we don't have—"

"Good afternoon." Xaden's voice fills the amphitheater as he strides in from a tunnel on the right, dressed in sparring gear that immediately has *all* my attention. Surprisingly, Garrick is at his side.

"Ooh, Imogen is going to love having class today— Ow!" Ridoc reaches for the back of his head.

"Riders, if you'll take your positions as you did last class." Xaden motions to the rings of cobblestone outside the mat. "Hopefully no one gets performance anxiety, because as you can see"—he gestures to the seats behind us—"we have a full house today."

"Not sleeping well?" I ask him, noting the circles beneath his eyes. Abandoning our coats, my squad heads for the edge of the mat, mirrored by First Wing.

"A certain hazel-eyed rider kept me up last night talking." He turns and says something to Garrick, who nods. *"Which I didn't mind, since my bed is too cold without you physically in it and too quiet without you screaming my name."*

Oh, he wants to play? A corner of my mouth lifts.

Game on. *"I miss Aretia, miss sleeping next to you. Find a way to sneak me in and I'll keep that bed at precisely the right temperature for you to get some...rest."* I roll my shoulders and stretch out my arms, just like my squadmates are doing.

"If I find you in my bed, there's no resting, trust me." Xaden turns toward the front of the mat, bracing his feet apart and folding his beautifully toned arms. "Lieutenant Tavis here is an incredibly powerful wind wielder—"

"Don't forget that I know exactly how to knock you out for the night—" I drop my arms and Xaden shoots me a warning look, but the edges of his mouth curl up.

"—and has agreed to let you try your best to bring him—" He full-on smirks. *"Knock me out? You're usually the one begging for mercy a few orgasms in—"*

"Want to see begging? All I have to do is swirl my tongue around the tip of your—"

Xaden coughs like he swallowed a nonexistent bug, and Garrick glances sideways at him. "Down," he finally finishes. "Lieutenant Tavis is willing to be your sparring dummy." He rolls his neck and chances a look in my direction.

I simply smile. *"You started it."*

"I'd give anything to be able to finish it." Xaden's fingers curl. *"You're going to be the death of me."*

"So you keep saying." I try *not* to think about the other ways that statement can be interpreted.

The fire wielder steps up first, and Garrick blows her own flame back at her.

"That's...unnerving," Ridoc mutters, and Imogen masks a smile to my right.

"We go as a team," Rhiannon says quietly by my side. "They never said it had to be one-on-one."

I nod. "Good idea."

Rhiannon relays orders quietly.

The metallurgist—Loran—learned from his last attempt, and within seconds, Garrick unclips the harness across his chest and the scabbards fall from his back before he blasts Loran to his ass with air.

"You ready to join in, Second Squad?" Garrick asks, crooking his fingers directly at Imogen.

"You don't want anything to do with these." She lifts her hands.

"Why don't you put them on me and we'll see?" A corner of his mouth tilts and a dimple pops in his cheek.

"Oh gods, just stop flirting and fuck already," Ridoc says.

Every head slowly turns in his direction.

"I said that out loud, didn't I?" he asks me in a hushed whisper.

"Oh yeah, you did," I reply, patting him on his back. "Garrick's going to blow you off the mat."

"Now *that* I might enjoy, depending on the method he chooses—" Ridoc winces. "I'm going to stop talking now."

"You might want to keep the inside voices *inside* while we're up there," I agree, following Rhiannon, Cat, and Quinn onto the mat, hauling Ridoc behind me when he hesitates.

"How exactly is this fair?" Garrick asks.

"We're never alone on the battlefield, are we?" I tilt my head to the side.

His face tightens, obviously getting my meaning.

"We fight as a squad," Rhiannon says from the center of our group, and Ridoc moves to my left.

"Solid point." Xaden retreats to the back of the mat. "Begin."

Rhiannon lifts her hands beside me, and two of Garrick's daggers appear in them.

"Nice," Garrick admits with a slight smirk, then flicks his hands upward.

Ridoc steps forward simultaneously, throwing a wall of ice that's instantly battered by a gust of wind that rivals the tornado Tairn and I got caught up in.

The edge of the ice chips at the assault, and chunks barrel my way.

I spin toward our squad and tackle Rhi to the ground as the ice flies overhead so near I can hear it whistle.

"Too close!" Xaden bellows, and I look up to see him taking a step in Garrick's direction, rage etched in the hard lines of his face.

"Don't! I'm fine!" I stagger to my feet as Quinn squeezes her eyes shut and turns her palms toward the sun.

"He nearly took off your fucking head." Xaden looks at Garrick in a way I've never seen, like his best friend has suddenly morphed into prey, and there's that cold edge in his eyes that prickles the hair at the back of my neck.

My power rises in response, and I welcome it with open arms, savoring the quick rush of heat and the hum of energy in my veins.

"My head is still firmly attached." Through translucent ice, I see two Quinns appear on Garrick's sides. "Give me his blade." I pivot toward Rhi and hold out my right hand, which she promptly fills with Garrick's dagger.

To my shock, Garrick stares at one Quinn, then the other, and then his head pivots between the two quickly, repeatedly.

Cat.

"You're going to have to be fast," Rhi warns.

"No worries there." The second the wind dies, I step around Ridoc's ice, then throw Garrick's own dagger close enough to scare him but not cause any real damage. Heat flushes my skin as power builds, demanding to be set free.

His hand whips upward and a wind gust knocks the blade off course, causing it to land about twenty feet to the right behind him.

Fine, that works, too.

He starts to redirect, bringing his hand toward the front of his body again, but mine is already skyward. The conduit siphons off just enough power to give me the control I need, and I release the rest, pulling the power downward in a precise flick of my wrist.

Lightning scorches the air, rending it with a flash of brilliance that strikes true, flaring bright as it spears from the sky, then disappearing as quickly as it came. The thunder swallows a few of the gasps and screams from the seats to my right, but I keep my eyes on Garrick and my hand held skyward.

His eyes widen at me. "You really did it."

"I did." The conduit hums in my left hand.

"Hate to tell you, Sorrengail, but not only did you leave yourself exposed, you also missed." He grins.

"Did I?" I look pointedly to the smoking hilt of his melted blade behind him, and he follows my line of sight, visibly tensing when he spots the ruined dagger. "If I wanted you dead, you'd be dead."

"By Malek, I fucking love you," Xaden says.

"And if I'm exposed, *fine*. The rest of my squad is alive." I shrug.

Xaden's gaze cuts to mine.

Garrick turns back toward me, his mouth hanging slightly agape, and someone begins to slowly clap from the top of the steps.

I look up—along with just about everyone else—and my balance wobbles. No. No. *No.*

Sandy-brown hair falls recklessly over his left eye as he starts down the steps, and I know it's illogical, but I swear I can see just how green those eyes are from all the way down here.

"Help Aaric hide," I tell Xaden. *"Now."*

"*Done.*"

A royal herald puffs out his chest from the edge of the back row. "His Royal Highness, Prince Halden."

Every cadet rises to their feet.

"Sit," he says loud enough for his voice to carry over the amphitheater and motions downward with his hands. I know that look on his face all too well. He's perfected an expression of relatable annoyance at the fanfare, when really, he *lives* for this shit. "Impressive," he tells me, passing the first row and the rock wall that separates it from the arena and stepping onto cobblestone.

Breathe. Just breathe.

"Your Highness, you'd be safer in the seats—" Garrick starts.

"And yet, I think the view is much better from right here." He slides his hands into the pockets of his professionally tailored dark-blue infantry uniform and smiles. "Please, don't let me stop you."

Garrick looks back, I'm guessing at Xaden, but I'm too busy keeping my gaze locked on Halden so I don't draw any accidental attention to Aaric by checking. Garrick nods and looks to the line of riders. "Next."

Our squad walks off the mat, and instead of filing in with the second-years, I take the empty place next to Halden, noting that one of the two guards stationed close behind him is Captain Anna Winshire.

She isn't just the infantry liaison for the quest squad; she's Halden's. I'd been naive to assume he'd removed himself from the task force, and if Halden ever realizes that Xaden is the reason his twin isn't breathing... Well, he won't be as understanding as Aaric. *This is bad.*

"What are you doing here?" I ask, glancing over at him.

He doesn't seem as tall as I remember—definitely a couple of inches shorter than Aaric—but he's just as strikingly beautiful as the last time I saw him. His high cheekbones, the mouth tilted in a permanent smirk, and the perfect proportion to his features are enough to turn heads, but his eyes are the real showstopper. They're as green as summer leaves. But man, do they wander.

"Learning, of course, like everyone else in this arena." He flashes a smile, and the edges of his eyes actually crinkle. "Never figured you for rider black, but power looks good on you."

"Don't." I shake my head and face the match.

Garrick blasts the remnants of Ridoc's wall away with a gust of wind, and Caroline Ashton takes the mat, bringing the fire wielder with her.

Xaden's gaze narrows as it jumps between Halden and me, and then he turns his attention to the sparring match.

"I don't mean in the arena." I hook the conduit to the strap at my hip. "What are you doing at Basgiath? It's not exactly alumni weekend." *Please don't say going northward with us.*

"Straight to business?" I feel the weight of his stare as he studies my profile. "You aren't going to ask how I've been? My brother's missing, you know." He sounds exactly zero percent worried.

"Is he?" I fold my arms. "Or did Cam just need some space from your ego?"

Both Caroline and the fire wielder fly backward, landing on their asses before sliding to the edge of the mat.

"What made Second Squad's assault effective was the use of mindwork," Garrick reminds the First Wing squad. "Quinn and Cat worked together to fuck with my head, giving Sorrengail enough time to strike."

"Not that she needed it," Trager calls out, and he's right. I could have struck at any moment. I simply waited until I could be certain of my accuracy.

A smile quirks at the corners of Xaden's mouth.

"Seriously, though." Halden tsks. "No hello? Not even a compliment on the tailoring of my uniform? Or the fresh haircut? I'm heartbroken, Vi."

"You'd have to own a heart to break it," I immediately counter. "And the only hair I remember is your professor's covering your face when I walked in on her riding you. It was auburn, right?"

The next batch heads up, this time armed with fliers as Xaden changes position, moving slightly to the left.

"Ouch. You wound me." Halden rubs his chest. "Yes, I cheated, but you have to remember, I was still suffering from the loss of my twin. I was…"

"Stupid? Thoughtless? Cruel?" I suggest. "Grief doesn't excuse any of that. Never did."

He sighs. "And here I thought you'd thank me for offering to step in and agree with you in regard to your upcoming mission."

"How so?" My brow scrunches.

He reaches into his uniform pocket and retrieves a missive bearing the broken wax seal of Viscount Tecarus. "Here. Grady is taking too long and has yet to present a clear path that satisfies my father. I like this option."

I take the parchment, and my eyes widen. "It's addressed to me."

"Don't get caught up in the details." He shrugs unapologetically.

My mouth tightens as I open the folded parchment.

Cadet Sorrengail,

As per our agreement, here are your requested tomes. I've also handpicked a selection from my personal library I hope you'll find educational. In regard to your search, King Courtlyn of Deverelli has agreed to a single meeting—noble blood only—for the reasonable price of the Amelian Citrine. Queen Maraya has agreed to gift the gem to him but will not be responsible for its retrieval from its display in Anca.

Please let me know when you have the citrine in hand so I can schedule our visit.

In service,

Viscount Tecarus

"You're doing a library exchange with the man first in line to the Poromish throne? Guess you didn't leave the scribes entirely behind," Halden muses as I finish reading.

"You shouldn't be reading my messages." I fold the parchment and tuck it into an empty dagger sheath along my ribs.

"Lucky for you I am."

"Lucky? You're kidding." I scoff as Garrick sends another rider flying.

"I wouldn't kid about your upcoming mission. Or you." He looks my way. "I did some research—"

"You mean had someone do your research?" I counter.

"Same thing." He smirks. "The Amelian Citrine is a lesser-magic amplifier worn by one of the members of the first drift. If you're willing to retrieve it, I'm willing to order Grady to change courses."

"It's not that simple. Anca is in occupied territory." I'm just not sure if it's *still* occupied, or one of the cities they drained and moved on from. Either way, it's beyond the wards, and even *going* there is a risk to Xaden.

"Like I said, if you *want* to go, I'll step in on your behalf. I owe you at least that, and title overpowers rank every day." He clears his throat. "Tell me, is it true what they say? You and...Riorson?" He says Xaden's name with cringe-worthy disgust.

"If you're asking if I'm in love with him, then the answer is wholeheartedly yes." I glance Xaden's way and find his eyes already on me. "If you're prodding to see if we're still together, then let me assure you, we're adhering to the Code of Conduct in the way you never bothered to do. You can report *that* to your father."

"I wasn't asking for my father, Vi. I was asking for *me.*"

"You what?" I forget all pretense of watching the sparring match, giving Halden my full attention.

"I never told you I was sorry." His face softens, and his gaze skims over my face like he's noticing every detail that's changed. "And I should have. If you're not with Riorson—"

"I am in love with him." I bristle. "I haven't so much as *thought* about you in years. Don't chase just because you like a challenge. You'll lose."

Halden scoffs. "Anyone who's ever dated a rider knows their first priority—

their first love—is their dragon. Once you accept that, another man hardly feels like a challenge."

My lips part. He's right. Our first priorities are our dragons. They're *irreplaceable*.

"Besides, with all this time we have coming up together on this mission, I thought maybe you'd at least be willing to have a quiet dinner with me?" His smirk slips. "Tell me you don't let your non-boyfriend control you. Allow me to apologize properly, the way I should have three years ago."

He lifts a hand toward the loosened strands of my braid, but never makes it.

Shadows blast straight through the wards and hit Halden in the chest like a battering ram, sending the crown prince of Navarre flying backward—straight into the rock wall.

Shit.

I cannot imagine sustainable life beyond the Emerald Sea. No ship has ever survived the tempests that form its ice-tipped waves, and the only sailors who return from her exploration do so defeated.

—The Last Admiral, a Memoir by Admiral Levian Croslight

CHAPTER EIGHTEEN

"Halden!" I rush to kneel by his side, and the shadow evaporates like it was never there. "Are you all right?"

"My prince!" Anna jumps to the cobblestone, panic filling her eyes, as his second guard joins her. "Oh, Halden, are you…"

Not just his guard? My eyebrows rise as I glance at her hair. Yep, redheads are definitely his type.

Halden waves her off as he visibly fights for breath, and both guards retreat.

Thank you, Malek, Xaden didn't kill him. There isn't even a crack in the rock above his head. "Give it a second, and you'll be able to breathe," I promise Halden, praying his ribs aren't broken.

Bootsteps approach from behind me, and a wave of glittering onyx wraps around my mind like a caress.

"Sorry about that," Xaden says, his tone implying otherwise. "I was blocking a potentially lethal blow to the first-year and seem to have knocked the wind right out of you."

I arch an eyebrow and slowly look over my shoulder at him. *"Seriously?"*

"He was going to touch you." The glacial rage in his eyes has mine widening. *"Right, because that's the mature response."*

Halden sucks in a breath, then another. "Quite. All. Right."

"It wasn't a response, it was… It simply was." Xaden crouches behind me as Halden pushes himself to sit upright. "Let's get three things straight, *Your Highness.* First, I have remarkable hearing thanks to the shadows at your very

feet. Second, I don't control Violet. Never have. Never will. But third, and most importantly—" He lowers his voice. "She really, honestly *hasn't* thought about you. At least not since the second she set eyes on me."

I'm going to fucking *kill* him.

. . .

A-I-M-S-I-R. An hour later, I'm still seething as I sit with Rhi on my bed, turning the fingernail-size bronze dials until each letter is visible in the book's locking mechanism. My finger hovers over the tiny lever that will either open the book...or destroy it.

"I can't do it."

"We could talk about how your non-boyfriend threw your clearly *ex*-boyfriend into the wall instead," Rhi says. "Or even chat about how you've never mentioned you were in a relationship with the *prince*."

"Never seemed important." I shrug. "He was just Halden to me like Aaric is...Aaric, and I promised myself I wouldn't give him an ounce of my headspace when he turned out to be the asshole everyone warned me he was."

"A prince? A duke? Clearly you have a type," she teases. "Did Xaden know?"

I shake my head. Halden didn't have Xaden arrested, but there was a definite gleam of promised revenge in his eyes when he strode up the stairs with his guards.

Class ended shortly after that.

"That explains the wall," she muses.

Xaden's complete and utter lack of control over his temper because he's venin is what explains the wall, but I'm not exactly going to say that to her, so I change the subject. "Aimsir. It's the right answer," I say, mostly to myself. "My father's world rotated on the axis of my mother, and they didn't meet until their third year. Her first real love would have been Aimsir, and she was irreplaceable. Our entire family's happiness rested on her health and survival."

"You don't have to convince me." Rhi sits with one leg bent under her and her hands outstretched toward the book.

I rest the tip of my finger against the lever. "You think you can save my ass if I'm wrong?"

"I've never tried to retrieve six vials' worth of liquid...or any liquid, but I think I can grab enough that at least *all* of your father's work won't be ruined." She flexes her fingers, then sighs. "And if that rune activates...well, there can't be too much power stored there. Probably just enough to destroy the book."

"Probably." I nod. "I can tell you I'd rather climb the Gauntlet again than be wrong about this."

"Then don't be wrong."

I'm not. *Lilith* is the obvious answer, and therefore it's the wrong one. Anyone else would have entered it without a second thought and ruined the book. No, he left this for *me*.

I press the lever.

It sinks into the mechanism, and my heart stumbles over its own beat when I hear the metallic *click* of the device unlocking. The book opens, and the six vials of ink pivot to lie flat along the pages, their contents perfectly sealed. "Thank you, Zihnal."

"I think that one might be better directed to Hedeon, but I'll take whatever god is with us," Rhi says, scooting closer as I rotate the book so we can both read.

"*A History of the Second Krovlan Uprising* — Draft, by Lieutenant Colonel Asher Sorrengail," I read, smiling at the familiar sight of his formal handwriting.

"All of that for a history text." Rhi shakes her head. "You Sorrengails are something else."

I flip the next page and suck in a sharp breath at the first words.

Dear Violet,

It's written, but I can hear his voice say it so clearly in my head that my eyes immediately sting.

"Not just a history text, then." Rhi wraps her arm around my shoulders. "How about I give you some time with your dad? I'll knock when we need to head out for flight maneuvers."

I nod silently in thanks, and Rhi leaves through the door, closing it behind her.

I want to read it all instantly, yet simultaneously limit myself to a single line so I can save another for tomorrow and then the day after, like I have with my mother's journals. I could make it last, keep him with me as long as possible.

But I need the knowledge now, so I lift the book onto my lap and begin.

Dear Violet,

It's my most sincere hope that you are reading this by my side, laughing at the glorious mess that is a first draft, but I fear that may not be the case. If I now walk alongside Malek with your brother, then guard this manuscript carefully. But if the worst has happened and your mother has joined us, then you must protect this knowledge with your very life. Within these pages, you'll find my careful study of the second Krovlan uprising, but my daughter — remember what I taught you about history: it is simply a collection of stories, each influenced by those that happened before and steering the ones to come. I wrote this study so it could be read by others but understood by you. If time is sweet, peruse at leisure; you'll find the connection between the uprising and the pursuit of feathertails to be both alarming and enlightening. But if time has indeed run out and you seek the weapon to defeat those you've only learned about through lore, then abandon your robes and ride for Cordyn. You have always struggled with Krovlish, but I made sure Dain would be capable should you need him...should he not choose to cross the parapet this summer. If he follows in the footsteps of his father, you must find the strength to let go of your affection for him. From Cordyn, book passage to Deverelli—you will be safe beyond the reach of magic there—and quietly seek the merchant Narelle Anselm. Take her the rarest item you possess—be sure it's truly exceptional to be given what you need. Do not send another in your stead. Should you travel under the banner of Navarre, beware their king—he bears grudges and speaks only in profit. I'm so sorry this falls to you, my brightest light.

Trust only Mira.

Love,
Dad

I read the page over and over, committing it to memory even as my mind races. How would he have known a merchant in Deverelli? *Seek the weapon...* Did he know about Andarna? About the rest of her kind?

For the first time in my life, it dawns on me that maybe I didn't know my father as well as I thought I did.

Narelle Anselm. I relay the information to Tairn and Andarna.

"Safe beyond the reach of magic?" I ask them, then fold the parchment and hide it back in the book.

"There is no magic beyond the Continent. It is why we dragons remain," Tairn tells me. *"Why it is surprising the irids left our shores."*

"I know what to bring with us," Andarna adds.

"I have come to the same conclusion," Tairn growls, *"but do not wish to spend my time with nursery gossips."*

"Do you truly think the isles are our best chance of finding your kind?" I ask.

"I think it's a better plan than flying north until we expire," Andarna answers.

"Agreed," Tairn chimes in. *"If the captain is so convinced, then split the squad in two, but we will head for Deverelli."*

Someone knocks.

I startle, then quickly lock the book and shove it under my pillow before crossing to the door and opening it.

Xaden stands at the threshold, his hands gripping the frame on both sides, his flight jacket unbuttoned, and his head bowed.

My immediate elation is slain by logic.

"What are you doing?" I whisper, trying to look past him to see if there's anyone else in the hallway who could report him.

"Did you love him?" The question is a low rumble of sound.

"Someone is going to see you!"

"Did. You. Love. Him?" Xaden lifts his head and pins me with a look that borders on feral. "I have to know. I can handle it. But I have to know."

"Oh, for Amari's sake." I grab the lapels of his flight jacket and yank him into my room, and he flicks his wrist, shutting the door behind him. The loud *click* tells me he's locked it, too. "I was with Halden *years* ago."

"Yeah, I picked up on that." His brow knits as he nods. "I picked up on *a lot* of things he was thinking."

I blink. "That's not how your signet—"

"Did you love him?" he repeats.

"Holy shit." My hands fall from his jacket. "You're actually jealous."

"Yes, love, I'm *jealous*." He splays his hand over the small of my back and tugs me toward him. "I'm jealous of the armor that holds you when I can't, the sheets on your bed that caress your skin every night, and the blades that feel your hands. So, when the prince of our realm walks into my classroom and starts talking to the woman I love with what can only be considered intense familiarity, and then has the audacity to ask her *out* right in front of me, naturally, I'm going to get jealous." He brings our bodies flush.

"And put him into a wall?" My hands skim the cold skin of his neck to cup his chilled cheeks. He's been outside for a *while*.

"I told you I would." His gaze bores into mine, and my pulse skips. "Back in Aretia, remember? Right after I put you on my throne, spread those beautiful thighs—"

I slip my thumb over his perfect mouth. "I remember." And so does my body, which is instantly heated.

He nips the pad of my thumb, and my hand falls away. "I told you I'd feel jealous and then I'd kick his ass. I might have turned, but I'm still a man of my word when it comes to you."

"You're Xaden Riorson." I rise up on my toes and press a kiss to his chin. "Shadow wielder." Another at his jaw. "Duke of Tyrrendor." My mouth brushes just beneath his earlobe. "Love of my life. You have nothing to be jealous of."

His hand flexes along my spine, but then he steps back, putting a few feet between us. "Did you love him? Violet, you have to tell me." The sharp edge of desperation in his voice does me in.

"Not the way I love you," I admit softly.

He retreats until his ass hits my desk, then stares at the floor. "You loved him."

"I was eighteen." I search my memories, trying to think of a better word to describe what I'd felt for Halden, but come up blank. "We were only together about seven months—a little before his Conscription Day until December. I was infatuated and enamored, and at the time, that rush of utter beguilement was what I knew of love. So yes, I loved him."

He grips the edge of the desk, and his knuckles pale. "Fuck. And he's going with us. I caught that, too."

"Yes. And I get it." I cross the distance between us. "It's *really* hard for me to see you anywhere near Cat—"

"I never loved Cat." Xaden's head whips up. "Sure, the idea of"—he swallows like he might puke—"Halden putting his hands on you makes me want to put him *back* into the wall, especially given the fact that he can touch you and I can't, but knowing he's been here—" Xaden puts his hand just beneath my collarbone. "Has me considering murder so there's no chance of him worming his royal ass back in."

"He can't touch me." I lift his hand and press a kiss to the center of his callused palm before putting it back above my heart and holding it there. "This will only ever be yours. You could leave me or even meet Malek, and it still would be. I've made my peace with knowing there's no getting over you."

He moves faster than I've ever seen, and in a blink, his hands are full of my ass and I'm up against his chest. "Stop me if I cross the line."

That's the only warning he gives before his mouth is on mine.

He lays claim to every inch of my mouth like it's the first time, with deft, skillful flicks and plunges of his tongue that devastate me in the best possible way.

The second he surges forward, I can't bring myself to care *why* he's kissing me like tomorrow doesn't exist. The world tilts, I feel the bed beneath my back, and I only care that he never stops. We can live right here, never taking it a step further as long as he keeps his lips against mine.

My hips arch up as he settles between my thighs, and the weight of him feels so damned good that I moan. Limiting ourselves to the kiss only makes it that much more intense, like we're both desperate to elicit every sensation possible in the simple yet infinitely complex connection of our mouths.

Madness. This need between us is always the sweetest madness. He is the craving I'll never sate, the rush I'll never get enough of. Only him.

I hook my ankles over the small of his back and kiss him with every ounce of longing that's built within me over the last few weeks. He sucks my tongue into his mouth, and I whimper as heat flushes my skin and addles my mind.

"I love you," he says against my mouth and rolls his hips.

"I love you." The confession ends on a gasp as I feel just how hard he is for me. My hands slip down his muscled back over the leather of his flight jacket. "I miss you."

"Violet," he groans, his hands capturing mine, pinning them above my head—

No. Not his hands.

Shadows.

My breath hitches. He holds me as a more-than-willing captive while he kisses me over and over, a heady combination of urgency and demand paired with determined restraint.

He slides the backs of his fingers down my neck, and goose bumps rise on my skin as pure, electric need runs the length of my body. "Fuck, your skin is so damned soft."

My only answer is a whimper, then a moan when the caress is followed by his mouth.

"Yes." My hands tug at their bonds, and I arch my neck for more.

"Still just a kiss." He works his way down my throat and grasps my hip—

He rolls away from me so quickly that I almost go with him, and I'm left staring at my ceiling, gasping for breath, but at least he's in the same condition.

"Fuck." He throws his forearm over his eyes. "Please have mercy and say something—anything that distracts me from how damned good you feel in my arms."

I blink, trying to force my mind to function, and the soft bands of shadow retreat, freeing my wrists. My heartbeat slows just enough to allow logic to creep its way in, and I shove my hands back under my pillow to keep from reaching in his direction.

The book. "My dad left me a letter. He needs me to go to Deverelli."

His head whips to me and I slowly turn mine, locking our eyes. "Then we'll go."

My body isn't big enough to contain how much I love this man. "We'd have to go under the pretense of searching for Andarna's kind, and I think that's what he's alluding to, but I could be wrong. I have to read the research."

His brow furrows. "You still think we should search the isles, right?"

I nod.

"Then it seems like we can accomplish two goals with one trip."

I ghost my tongue over my swollen lower lip. "Searching the isles means we'd need the audience with the king, which requires leaving the wards to get an artifact for the King of Deverelli *and* calling in help from Halden, so it's not that easy a choice—"

"It is. If my dad left *me* a letter..." Xaden rolls up onto his elbow. "You can tell me all the ways it's going to be shitty, and I'll still say let's go."

"The artifact is in occupied territory."

His face tightens. "And if I ask you to stay behind, all cozy and safe while I get it?"

I shake my head.

"Yeah. That's what I thought." He sighs. "At least it will be a chance to evaluate how we function in this squad Grady has put together. When do you want to leave?"

"As soon as possible."

The gem given to you upon graduation from Cliffsbane should always be worn close to the heart, but if you have not mastered your control, it will only amplify your downfall.

—CHAPTER THREE, THE CANON OF THE FLIER

CHAPTER NINETEEN

Four nights later, our riot of eight—now including Mira, thanks to Halden throwing his royal weight around—crosses the border at Samara, and magic slips free of the wards' cage. Power expands in every direction, running like a current that rushes around me, beckoning me to play...or destroy. My skin tingles as we slip down into the valleys through the Esbens, and I'm struck with the oddest urge to try and pluck strands from the very sky and weave runes.

"It feels like there's more power out here than usual," I tell Tairn as we dive along a ridgeline.

"There's actually less—the venin saw to that," he replies. *"But you grow more powerful every day, more capable of recognizing what once was entirely invisible to you."*

"I could recognize it," Andarna chimes in. *"If you ever let me come with you."*

"With Theophanie hunting you, you're far safer at Samara." I grip the pommels as Tairn levels out along the riverbank, sticking to the shadows the overcast night has provided. I swear, there's a permanent bruise just below my sternum from trying to sleep in the saddle. This thing could use some modifications before we head to Deverelli.

"But you're not," Andarna argues, her voice fading the farther we fly. *"I can burn venin."*

"I've told you a dozen times, first fire burns the hottest, which could explain the phenomenon," Tairn replies. *"This mission is dangerous enough without adding a desirable target for any lurking dark wielders."*

"They're all busy to the south…" Her voice trails off as the connection is severed.

"We have about twelve hours before you'll start to feel the pain of distance from Andarna," Tairn reminds me as we cut through the night, opening the conversation to Sgaeyl and Xaden's pathways.

I have no desire to test the three-to-four-day limit that riders and their dragons can be apart, nor to suffer the fatal consequences. Three hours to Anca. One hour to locate the citrine. Three hours back. A third of the riot stationed at Samara launched an offensive against a known stronghold just north of the fortress an hour ago, which allowed us to slip through the red line on Battle Brief's map unnoticed by the enemy. Everything is going according to plan.

Three hours later, it feels almost a little too easy as we land in the desiccated village square of what had once been Anca. *Definitely not occupied.* Other than evading two patrols of wyvern by staying low, we haven't seen a single enemy, only sparse villages and dimly lit encampments of civilians between the land the venin drained in their advance toward Samara. Tairn sets his claws down first as usual, despite being told to hang back in formation by Grady, and the rest follow suit around the withered remains of a clock tower.

"Just because I accepted the terms of the mission does not mean I like them." Tairn grumbles low in his chest as I bundle my flight jacket with the pack at the edge of my saddle and dismount.

"I know." My feet hit the ground, and everything feels…off without the presence of magic. According to our latest intel, wielding within drained territory isn't just challenging, but it seems to draw venin, so I let the conduit fall along my wrist, keeping it close just in case everything goes to shit. *"Stick to the plan. I'll let you know when we have it."*

Tairn bends, then launches high above the crumbling two-story buildings, and is quickly joined by the rest of the dragons, two of whom bear the riders Grady chose to do recon from above—Pugh and Foley.

Xaden strides past the clock tower, heading my way. He's done a good job of masking his discomfort, but I can see the struggle in his eyes and the curl of his fingers.

"You should have taken the sentry assignment," I tell him as Grady gathers the others to my left.

"I wasn't leaving you on the ground." Our hands nearly brush as we turn and walk toward the group, but we're careful not to touch, especially with how Aura Beinhaven narrows her eyes in our direction. *"And it's not like I'm risking anything as long as I remain calm, cool, and collected within the perimeter. The magic is long since drained."*

Which is why the dragons are in the sky, flying over the land the dark wielders left untouched in their haste to reach Samara.

"I can't tell…" Grady flips the hand-drawn map over. "Her handwriting is atrocious."

"It looks like that way," Captain Henson notes, leaning in to see and pointing across the village square.

"Which is why you should have brought Cat like Violet asked." Mira plucks the map straight out of Grady's hand and studies it.

"Gryphons can't keep up," Grady reminds us. "And this mission will serve as a trial run for all those that follow. An extra member would have thrown off the dynamic."

"What fucking dynamic?" I ask Xaden. *"I loathe Aura, don't really trust Grady after he fed us the serum during RSC training, and don't know the rest of them."*

"Calm. Cool. Collected." Xaden slides his hands into his pockets.

"Really? I don't see a prince or his guards here, let alone anyone representing Poromiel. And stop whispering like they can hear you." Mira rotates the map and lines up the landmarks Cat sketched out. "The area is deserted, and we'll be fine as long as our sentries intercept any wayward patrols and no one wields." Mira points past my right shoulder. "It's this way."

"I'll take that, *Lieutenant.*" Grady snatches the map back.

"If I didn't know better, I'd think you were setting the mission up to fail." Mira offers a cutting smile.

"Let's go." Grady glares my sister's way, then stalks past me in the direction she pointed.

"If it makes any difference," Captain Henson says, glancing at Mira as she passes, "I agree with you."

"I don't." Aura pushes up the sleeves of her uniform and runs by. "We can't trust the fliers."

"And yet it's their artifact that Cat is helping us find," I mutter as we follow.

"Cool. Calm. Collected." Xaden scans every building we pass.

"New mantra since becoming duke?" Mira asks, surveying the remains of what looks to have been a marketplace on our right.

"Just trying not to explode on Grady and ruin our little trial run here," Xaden replies.

The village is silent as we walk the abandoned streets, passing the desiccated remains of people every block or so. It reminds me of a sandcastle. The structure is there, but so delicate that even a harsh breeze might crumble the colorless structure.

We turn at the next intersection, entering narrow columns of residential rowhouses with barely enough room for wagons to pass each other in the street. Some of the houses connect to ones across the way with covered bridges, creating a tunnel effect every twenty feet or so.

"Ironic that they built these so tight to keep dragons from fitting between them, and yet it's dragons that might save us," I remark, studying what's left of the architecture.

"A gryphon would fit with no problem as long as its wings were tucked," Mira notes.

"This is the one." Grady stops in front of an expansive house.

"Was it the plaque that says *Home of Amelia, First of the Drifts* that gave it away?" Xaden asks, nodding toward the right side of the door.

Grady's mouth tightens. "You know your places. Let's go." The front door creaks loudly enough to wake the dead as he swings it open, and everyone freezes.

My stomach does its best to displace my lungs, and I clench my fists when power immediately rises in my veins, responding to my fear.

"They can't hear us," Mira repeats, then clasps my shoulder as she walks by, heading to Grady and Henson.

"Be right back," Xaden says, but there's no usual brush of his hand or shadow along my lower back because Aura is watching like we might just start making out at any second.

The four officers disappear into the creaky house, leaving Aura and me in the middle of the street.

"I'll take south," I tell her, moving toward the doorway, then facing in that direction.

"Fine." She puts her back to me, and we begin watch.

Rumblings sound from within the house, and moonlight illuminates the cobblestone street.

I look to see the clouds breaking as the wind picks up.

Shit.

"Stay out of sight," I tell Tairn.

"I am as the night." He sounds more than a little offended. *"It is Dagolh you should worry about."*

Aura's Red Clubtail.

"Any luck?" I ask Xaden.

"This whole place is a museum, and Cat only remembers that it was on display upstairs in a protective case. Not sure if you've noticed, but there's a lot of upstairs," he answers.

I glance up at the five stories that look ready to topple at any second. "We're going to be out here awhile." This is exactly why we should have brought Cat. Maybe being here would have triggered the memory of exactly where it was displayed.

"Great." Aura shifts nervously behind me, her shadow swaying near my feet.

"You scared?" I ask as nicely as possible.

"We're hundreds of miles from the wards, standing in a fucking cemetery," she snaps. "What do you think?"

"As someone who has spent my share of time beyond the wards, it's healthy to be nervous." Something rattles up ahead, and I tilt my head, focusing in that direction. A glass bottle rolls down the gently sloped hill of a street, propelled by a gust of wind before lodging itself in a doorway four houses over. "See? That's—" I glance over my shoulder, then whip my entire body around to face Aura. "What the fuck?"

"Just being prepared." She stands with her hands raised, a flintstrike device between thumb and forefinger, fear pinching her face.

"That"—I motion to her hands—"is an *un*healthy, mission-dangerous amount of fear. Put them down. Away. Gloves on. You need to remind yourself that wielding is the *worst* possible thing we could do."

"No." She lifts her chin. "Getting drained is far worse. I'm not about to be caught off guard. In fact, you should stand ready, too."

"Absolutely not." I shake my head and turn my back on her. "My orders are not to wield unless there's an imminent threat of death, and I hardly think that bottle constitutes such."

"As your senior wingleader, I'm *ordering* you to stand ready," Aura seethes. "What use are you as our 'greatest weapon' if you can't wield at a moment's notice?"

"The only rank that matters out here is cadet, so with all due respect, fuck off." I shrug and roll my shoulders, trying to dispel the tide of energy pushing against my Archives door. At least that means Tairn has located some undrained land.

"Found it!" Mira calls through an open window.

I blow out a sigh of relief.

The door across the street swings open with an ear-screeching creak, and my head whips toward the sound, fear launching my heart into my throat as a figure steps out of the shadows—

"Vi, watch out! Aura's going to—" Xaden starts.

"Don't!" I pivot and throw myself at Aura, but the damage has been done.

Fire sparks and spews from her hand like dragon flame and engulfs the doorway.

We land in a tangle of limbs, and I narrowly keep from smacking my head on the stone of the stoop as a wave of heat blasts the side of my face, lighting up the night. Dread seizes my heartbeat, but I cut it off before it can take hold or, worse, freeze me with fear.

"Get off me!" Aura bellows, shoving me aside as the figure stumbles forward into the moonlight and *screams*.

I gasp, and for a millisecond, fear wins.

Captain Grady is on fire.

"No!" Aura scrambles across the stone as he kneels in the center of the street. Every inch of the leathers that should help protect him is covered in foot-high flames.

And we don't have a water or ice wielder on the ground.

"*Xaden!*" I yell, gaining my feet and running toward the captain. "Aura! Take off your flight jacket!" We can smother the flames. We have to.

His shriek etches itself into my memory as he collapses, and I wrench Aura's flight jacket from her hands and throw it over him, hoping to put out the fire. The scent of charred flesh turns my stomach, but it's quickly overpowered by thick, cloying smoke coming from the building behind him.

Xaden gets to me first, yanking me back from the captain, and shadows stream from our feet to smother the flames as the screams cease, but the fire in the building ahead of us *roars*. "Fuck."

All three of us look up as the wind gusts.

My heart drops to the ground as house after house catches fire, spreading down the street. The land, the buildings, the very wood they're built with may be drained of magic, but they go up like *kindling*.

"Riorson!" Mira shouts, barreling out of the house behind us, Henson close on her heels. "Do it! We're as good as dead already!"

I wrench out of Xaden's arms and stumble toward Grady as shadows rush up the sides of the buildings, but the flames have already licked their way across the bridges. We're in the middle of a fucking tinderbox.

"Sir!" I drop in front of Grady, but he doesn't move.

"He's dead," Xaden announces like it's the weather forecast. "And I can't…"

I look over my shoulder to see sweat beading on his skin as he shakes his head, lifting his hand again and again, directing shadows over one building and then the next, but there's no earthly way to keep up with what the wind is spreading. Every cinder, every gust sends another structure up in flames.

Captain Henson battles what she can, but even the best wind wielder can't control the drift of ash and ember.

The sky cracks, and my eyes jerk upward. The bridge connecting both halves of the house comes crashing down, engulfed in flames. I move to push Xaden out of the way, but Mira's standing between us, her arms raised and fingers splayed.

A pulse of blue emits like a mage light, and the bridge cracks overhead, splitting in two and falling on either side of us.

"We have to get out of here." Mira hauls me to my feet, then yanks a stunned Aura up by her collar. The senior wingleader just stares wide-eyed at the spreading destruction.

"I can do it!" Xaden shouts, raising shadow after shadow.

"Let it go," Henson orders. "The best we can hope for is a clear path to the village square for evac."

Xaden's arms tremble, and fear stabs deep within my chest, chilling me to the bone. If the land he stands on hadn't already been drained…

I put myself in his face, uncaring that everyone can see, and grasp his cheeks in my hands. "Let it go," I beg. "Xaden, you have to let it go. We need to get out of here."

His tortured eyes lower to mine, reflecting the flames in their onyx depths.

"Please." I keep my gaze on his. "There's no stopping this. There's only surviving it."

He nods and lowers his hands.

Relief fills my next breath, but that's all the time we're allowed.

"Run!" Mira shoves at us both, and we break into a sprint down the narrow street.

Pain shoots from my ankles up to my knees, but it doesn't matter, not when both sides of the street are catching fire slightly slower than we're running.

"Focus and get to the town square," Tairn orders, and I do just that—focus.

Dragons can't fit down these streets. We have to make it to the square or we're dead.

Every ounce of my energy goes into the placement of my feet so I don't roll my ankles on the stone, the movement of my breath, the space between us as Xaden keeps pace beside me.

Mira hurries ahead, turning corner after corner with a certainty I could never possess in this maze of a village, and we follow, running for our very lives.

"There!" Mira shouts, pointing as the clock tower comes into view at the end of the street and wings beat overhead. "No!" she yells. "Tairn first!"

I shake my head and run faster. "Go! If Teine is here, then go!"

"I'm not leaving—" she starts to argue.

"Go so we can!" Henson yells.

Xaden throws his arm out, catching me in a skid as Mira races into the courtyard to meet Teine's arrival. Their run-on mounting is flawless, timed to the peak of perfection, and Mira is already climbing the clubtail's foreleg as Teine flies over the village.

Henson nods as if talking to her dragon, then looks back at Aura. "You're next. One minute out."

The flames start catching the houses behind us.

"This is my fault." Aura clenches her fist to my right and looks to the courtyard with wide, frightened eyes. "Grady is…gone. They'll know we're here. There's no hiding a fire like this."

"All that matters is that we get out," I tell her. "Don't think about anything else."

"Overhead!" Xaden shouts as wings block the moon.

"We're not the only wings in the sky," Tairn warns, and ice prickles the back of my neck.

"Go!" Henson orders Aura, pointing toward the courtyard. "Dagolh is on the approach."

"Wait!" I shout, but she's already sprinting toward the clock tower. "Tairn says we aren't alone."

"She'll make it," Henson says in a voice that doesn't quite convince me.

Scorching heat flares at my back, but I keep my eyes forward as Aura races into the open.

A claw reaches for her, and I hold my breath for them to make contact. The claw curls in the same way Tairn's does right before he scoops me up—

The talon emerges somewhere near the middle of her spine.

Blood gushes from the wound, but Aura's scream is silenced as the wyvern drags her lifeless body into the sky. Not too far overhead, a dragon bellows.

Xaden's arm tightens around me, supporting my weight when my knees try to buckle.

"Tairn…"

"Sixty seconds," he says, urgency lacing his tone.

"Damn, they got here fast," Henson mutters, rocking back on her heels. "All right, Riorson, you're up—"

They got here fast? That's all she has to say?

"We do not answer to you," he says without taking his eyes off the courtyard.

The moon catches on a flash of navy-blue wings, but instead of landing, Sgaeyl streaks overhead, flying fast and hard for the wyvern that's just picking up altitude.

"What in Dunne's name…"

"And *she* damn well doesn't take your orders," Xaden says to Henson.

Sgaeyl lunges, then seems to rake her claws into the wyvern and *climb* its back. Her head darts left, then right, and the creature's wings snap free.

"Remind me to never piss her off," I mutter as the wyvern falls, crashing somewhere at the edge of the village.

A corner of Xaden's mouth rises.

"Approaching," Tairn announces.

"Take us both." I grab Xaden's hand. "Run with me."

Xaden's brow furrows for a heartbeat, and then he nods.

"I am not a horse," Tairn fires back as Xaden and I run for the courtyard, the

heat at our back flaring to unbearable temperatures.

"They patrol in pairs," I shout down the pathway that connects all four of us. *"Take. Us. Both!"* My boots pound against the stone, and ahead, I see Sgaeyl banking back in a steep turn.

We hit the open air, and I block out the very real possibility that the wyvern's partner will see us first, sprinting harder for the widest place where Tairn can grab us.

"I'm here," he says down our shared pathway.

"Trust me," Xaden demands, and I can't tell which one of us he's talking to, but I instantly nod. He pivots with alarming speed, putting himself in front of me, then hauls me up against his chest, bringing our heads level. *"Hold on."*

I throw my arms around his neck, the conduit bouncing against his back as he pitches his arms outward, and bands of midnight-black shadow wrap around us both, binding me to him.

Familiar wingbeats sound over the flames in the scant heartbeats before we're plucked off the ground, Tairn's claws hooking over Xaden's shoulders and yanking us into the night.

Wind tears at my eyes as we fly toward Sgaeyl, but another pair of wings approaches from the right on an intercept path. Two legs, not four.

"On your right," I warn Tairn, then turn to Xaden. *"You'd better be damn good with these shadows."*

"I have you," Xaden promises, and the bands tighten.

Power floods my body as I throw open the Archives door, and heat stings my skin. Gods, if I channel too much while attached to him...

"He's been a great deal closer when you've wielded," Tairn reminds me, and—

Nope, *not* thinking about how he knows that.

I fumble for a second to clasp the conduit and hold it away from Xaden's skin, then let the energy surge to a breaking point and focus entirely on my right hand.

Power *snaps*, whipping through me and departing all in the same heartbeat. Lightning strikes and I yank it downward from the sky with my finger, taking aim. Heat singes my fingertip, but I hold the bolt as long as tolerable, then set it free.

Straight into the wyvern's back.

The creature plummets and Sgaeyl roars, blasting its corpse with a stream of fire as it falls past her. She pitches back to follow as Tairn banks left, taking us from the path that leads along the river and heading due west.

We fly like that for another few minutes, just long enough to be sure we're safe, then land to take our respective seats and launch again.

Tairn leads us low, through the shadows of the mountains and up the ridgelines. Two and a half hours later, we cross the wards a hundred miles south of Samara.

We make it back to the fortress with three hours left to spare of our twelve-hour limit.

"I can't believe you let him die," Lieutenant Pugh mutters as we walk under the portcullis at Samara.

Xaden turns on him and pins him to the wall with the weight of his forearm. "Beinhaven was a scared cadet who thought he was venin. What the fuck is your excuse? Where were you when that wyvern skewered her?"

"We were patrolling north." The man's complexion favors a tomato as he forces out the words, but neither Mira nor I intercede.

"You were needed above the village." Xaden removes his arm, and the lieutenant slides down the wall.

Henson and Foley help Pugh stand, then walk away from us into the courtyard, and Mira holds up her hand once their backs are to us, so we stay right where we're at.

"I got there first," she says, turning to face us and dragging a long chain from the inner pocket of her flight jacket.

A thumb-size stone I'm guessing was once the color of a citrine now rests in its setting, cracked, hazy, and smoke-hued.

"Shit." My shoulders dip. "If Courtlyn doesn't accept that, this all will have been for nothing."

"That's not why I'm glad I got there first." Mira hands me the necklace, then reaches into her pocket again, drawing out a folded piece of parchment. "This is."

Clutching the necklace in one hand, I take the parchment in the other, noting that it's addressed to *Lightning Wielder*.

"It was sitting next to the necklace," Mira says as I open it, and Xaden tenses at my side.

Violet,

Just a reminder that while I want you to come of your own free will, I'm capable of taking you whenever I wish. Why do you not ask me for the answers you so desperately seek?

—T

"Theophanie." My stomach hollows.

Either she knows I'm looking for Andarna's kind...

Or she knows I'm looking for a cure.

Xaden stiffens to the point of statuary. "She knew we'd be there."

Well shit, there's *that*, too.

Perhaps the point of this is not to deny rebellion,
but to only go to war with those you trust implicitly.

—Subjugated: The Second Uprising of the Krovlan People
by Lieutenant Colonel Asher Sorrengail

CHAPTER TWENTY

Upon our return, I spend a few days reading every single book on Deverelli Jesinia can find to prepare for my progress briefing with the Senarium. Between those, classes, the tomes Queen Maraya sends at my request, modifying my saddle, and the hours I spend wielding on the snow-capped peaks above Basgiath, I fall into bed exhausted every single night.

By the time Friday arrives, I've devoured *The Dark Side of Magic*, *Red Regalia*, *The Scourge of our Times*, and the nightmare-inducing *A Study in the Anatomy of the Enemy*, none of which brings me the answers I need for Xaden.

Neither does Jack. He's all too happy to tell me about asim progression, how channeling from the earth happens as easily as breathing beyond the wards, but he won't give up the name of his Sage or give me anything other than trivial information about them. And he's sure as Malek not telling me how Theophanie knew we'd go for the citrine or what answers I'm searching for.

But once I finally make my way through my dad's manuscript for the third time and scour the research that behemoth requires, I have an inkling of a thought of where he might have been headed in his hypothesis. I keep it to myself, partially because I'm scared to be wrong but mostly because I'm terrified I'm *right*. When Varrish mentioned last year that he thought the research dealt with feathertails, I never imagined it would lead in *this* direction.

"I want to go," Ridoc says as we walk down the plush red carpet of the administration building, headed for the great hall.

I search for the right words and try to quell the vat of nausea that is my stomach. Presenting to Halden is bad enough, but I skipped breakfast knowing the entire Senarium waits for me, most likely to assign a new commander.

And I'm not accepting one.

"It's not going to happen," Rhi says with a sigh from his other side. "She's going to have a fight on her hands as it is, and they won't let you miss class, anyway. They're not even letting us in that room."

"I can keep you safe," he insists, turning to me, an unpeeled orange in his hands.

"Pretty sure Riorson will keep her safe," Sawyer notes, walking on Rhi's right with the help of his crutches and his latest metal prosthetic leg. He's even rejoined classes this week, though he has yet to make it to the flight field.

"And Mira." I'm taking Dad's letter to heart.

A foursome of infantry cadets steps aside so we can pass, and the massive double doors to the great hall come into view. Cat stands near the threshold, smiling up at a tall flier I've never seen before.

He looks to be a couple of inches shorter than Xaden, with a lean build and a quick smile. His hair is as dark as Cat's, reflecting the same blue mage light that catches on the hilt of the blade he carries at his side and the V of daggers sheathed at his chest.

My eyebrows rise. I figured when I asked her to join this meeting with someone she trusts, she'd choose Maren, but I'm all for her moving on if it means she's going to stop staring at Xaden constantly. Though I kind of hoped Trager had a shot with her.

"Hey, will you just try?" Ridoc's voice doesn't only tense up, it rises, causing all dozen people in the hallway to glance our way.

"What's this really about?" I reach for his upper arm, and the four of us pause ten feet shy of the door.

"I just...need to go." He looks away and grips the orange in both hands. "One of us needs to go with you. Ever since..." Pain flashes through his dark-brown eyes as he brings his gaze back to mine. "Ever since Athebyne, one of us has been by your side." He lifts his finger. "Except the time you snuck out on your little siblings-only trip to Cordyn. The school splits, and we go with you. Basgiath falls under attack, and we're there. Heading into Poromiel for Maren's brothers? It's us. We get separated, and you either get dragged into an interrogation chamber and tortured for days or nearly roasted by Aura's fire, and I know I can't be the only one who thought, if Liam had been here, keeping watch over you, it never would have happened." He swings that finger toward Rhiannon and Sawyer. "You both know it crossed your minds."

A lump grows in my throat. "I appreciate it, I do. But I don't need anyone keeping watch over me."

"I didn't mean it that way." He covers the orange with both hands. "I just think bad things happen when we aren't together. Rhi can't go—she has an entire squad to lead—and Sawyer is still recovering, which leaves me. And if Riorson had been a hundred percent sure of his ability to keep bad things from happening, he wouldn't have assigned Liam to our squad in the first place. The guy is powerful, but he's not infallible."

If he only knew the truth. Gods know who they have waiting behind these doors to replace the ones we lost, but I'm already sure I can only trust two of them—Mira and Xaden.

"And you are?" Sawyer asks, leaning on his crutches.

Ridoc's eyes narrow. "I'm just as good of a fighter as any of you, and while you've been focused on rehab and Rhiannon is chasing first-years to keep them in line, I've been the one reading every fucking book Jesinia shoves at me and spending extra hours training—" The skin on the orange *splits*. "It really pisses me off when you guys act like my sense of humor somehow lessens my ability to show up for our squad."

"Ridoc," I whisper, staring at the orange. "What did you do?"

"I've been trying to tell you." He hands me the fruit, and it immediately chills my hands. "You aren't the only one who's been spending hours honing their signet."

Using my thumb, I peel back the rind. The fruit of the orange is frozen solid beneath it. "How did you do it?"

"I've always been able to draw water out of the air," he says. "Plus, I get bored waiting for Sawyer to wake up when he rests—no offense—and if there's one thing healers are good at, it's leaving fruit lying around. I realized I could freeze the water in the fruit."

My lips part as my mind spins through the implications.

"Sorrengail, are we going in or what?" Cat yells from down the hall.

I look up at Ridoc and whisper, "Are you trying to tell me that you can freeze the water in someone's *body*?"

He rubs the back of his neck. "I mean, I haven't tried it out on anyone, or anything living, of course, but...yeah, I think so."

Well, that's unsettling. And glorious. And horrific. All of the above, really.

"Holy shit, man." Sawyer moves in closer. "Can other ice wielders do that?"

"I don't think so?" Ridoc shakes his head. "Turns out there's only a few of us who can even pull the water from the air."

"Sorrengail!" Cat snaps.

"Yeah, you're coming with me." I push the orange into Ridoc's hand, then motion toward the door. "Though it has nothing to do with the ice—there's no magic where we're headed—and everything to do with the first point you made."

"Bad things happen when we're not together," he says quietly.

Only go to war with those you trust implicitly.

I nod, and we head down the hallway.

"It's about time." Cat rolls her eyes, but her friend opens the door on the right, and I catch a quick glimpse of his name tag as we walk in. *Cordella.*

Her cousin?

Half the tables and benches in the hall have been pushed to the sides, leaving an open space in front of the long center table, where the members of the Senarium sit facing us, and they're not alone. Aetos and Markham flank Halden, who sits in the center of the group, listening to whatever lies Markham whispers.

Xaden occupies the left end of the table, his chair turned toward me, his legs outstretched as if this meeting determines the flight schedule and not the future of the Continent, his eyes locked on me.

"You all right?" I ask, my gaze flickering toward Halden.

"He's still breathing, so I'd consider that a win," Xaden answers, looking rather bored, but the shadows around him have sharp edges that contrast the blurred ones down the table, the natural result of multiple light sources. *"They're set on their course, so you'd better determine ours."*

"Ah, Cadet Sorrengail." Halden's smile lights up his eyes, and he leans away from Markham. "Right on time."

"Actually, we're missing someone." I glance around the room, noting that for once in her life, Mira's late. It's also impossible to miss Foley, Henson, and Pugh sitting farther down the table—all that's left of our task force—and one addition: Captain Jarrett.

"As I see it, there are two extras in the room." The Duchess of Morraine shoots a disdainful look over my shoulder.

"They're here at my request." I lift my chin. "As is Cadet Gamlyn."

Ridoc stays silent at my side.

"You can't be serious—" the duchess starts.

"I'll allow it," Halden says, lifting his hand. "Recent losses have been regrettable, but a month has passed and it's time to act. You have the citrine, and a meeting has been set with King Courtlyn. Command is being transferred to Captain Henson." Halden gestures to the rolled parchment in front of him.

"Is he fucking serious?" I glance at Xaden.

"Entirely." A corner of his mouth lifts. *"Have fun eating them alive."*

I cross the freshly mopped floor and take the scroll, then step back so I'm in line with Ridoc and give my orders a quick read. We will leave for Deverelli the day after tomorrow, meet with the king to try to negotiate an alliance, secure a foothold for expanding the search if we don't find Andarna's kind there, then report back, all under the command of Captain Henson and executive officer Lieutenant Pugh.

While Markham and Melgren search Aretia for any *clues* we have missed.

"Did you read this?" It takes all I have not to crush the orders. *"They want to search Aretia."*

"They can get fucked."

"No," I say to Halden.

"I'm sorry?" Halden leans forward.

"I said *no*." I rip the orders in half. "No to your commander. No to your selections. No to searching Aretia. *No*."

"I warned you," Xaden says down the table.

Halden stiffens, and the Duke of Calldyr shifts in his seat before narrowing his eyes on me. "Captain Jarrett is an excellent addition and the best swordsman we have among the riders."

"That's overly generous, considering I watched Lieutenant Riorson kick his ass without even trying a few months ago at Samara." Power ripples through my veins, but I keep my anger at a simmer. "We tried it your way—"

"And clearly succeeded," Halden counters. "Or are you not in possession of the artifact?"

"We lost two riders out there because you saddled me with a squad full of people who don't know or trust one another. Yes, I have the artifact, and I'll take it to Deverelli, but only with a squad of *my* choosing." I hold my shoulders straight and catch Ridoc nodding out of the corner of my eye.

The door opens behind us, and the familiar rhythm of quick, efficient steps bolsters my courage toward pure audacity.

"Sorry I'm late," Mira says, bypassing Cat and her cousin to stand at my right. "Hell of a headwind out of the north. What did I miss?"

"I think Violet is about to lose her shit," Ridoc whispers.

"This"—I toss the halves of the scroll at Halden, and he catches them with the same reflexes that make him lethal on the battlefield—"is not the plan, and they"—I gesture toward the seated riders—"are not my squad."

Xaden's smirk deepens, and he settles into his seat like he's ready for a show.

"Searching Aretia is the first logical course of action, considering it is the only area we have no information on—" Markham starts, his cheeks leaning toward ruddy.

"You don't speak," I snap, meeting his gaze for the first time in months. "Not to me. As far as I'm concerned, you have the credibility of a drunkard and the integrity of a rat. You dare complain about missing six years of information on Aretia when you've hidden *centuries* of our continent's history from public knowledge?"

Halden's brows rise, and Mira shifts her hand to the pommel of her sword.

"You cannot speak to a superior officer, let alone the commander of a quadrant, with such disrespect!" Markham roars, coming out of his chair.

"In case you missed it when I crossed the parapet, I am *not* in your chain of command," I fire back.

"But you are in mine," Aetos warns. "And I speak with the authority of Melgren."

Fury gets the best of me. "And I speak with the authority of Tairn, Andarna, and the Empyrean. Or did you forget that two *dragons* also lost their riders?"

"If I wasn't in love with you already, I would be now," Xaden says, crossing his ankles.

"Sit, Markham," Halden orders, a note of surprise in his tone. "You tried and failed."

Markham sinks into his chair.

"We'll give this one shot. Name your squad for the Deverelli mission, Cadet Sorrengail," Halden says. "But know that if you fail, we'll assign another commander, and refusing to continue will negate the terms of the Second Aretia Accord."

The one that gave Xaden back his title.

I swallow the lump in my throat. No pressure or anything.

"Accepted." I straighten my shoulders. "For the Deverelli mission, my squad will consist of Lieutenant Riorson, Lieutenant Sorrengail, Cadet Gamlyn, Cadet Cordella" — I glance back over my shoulder to get his rank — "Captain Cordella, Cadet Aetos, Prince Halden, and whatever favorite guard follows you in case you stub your toe," I say to Halden. "When we succeed, I reserve the right to switch out members after the first expedition."

"Absolutely not." Aetos shakes his head. "You'll take only commissioned officers, *no fliers*, and Riorson is out of the question."

Halden lifts his hand, and Aetos quiets.

Xaden stills to the point I have to glance to see if he's breathing.

"I'll take whomever I wish," I counter. "As third in line for the throne, Catriona's capable of speaking for Poromiel—"

"And the *captain*?" the Duchess of Morraine asks, her face twisting like she's scented something sour. "You need two fliers?"

"Cadet Cordella deserves to have someone she trusts, too." I tilt my head at Halden. "Dragons don't carry humans who haven't crossed the parapet or climbed the Gauntlet, so you're lucky gryphons are kinder in this regard, or you'd never keep up. Lieutenant Sorrengail is the only rider capable of creating her own wards. Cadet Aetos is the only rider I trust who speaks fluent Krovlish—

which is the second most common language used in Deverelli. Cadet Gamlyn is dedicated to my personal safety, and even if Lieutenant Riorson weren't the deadliest rider in the whole of our forces"—I glance at Aetos, then Halden—"which he is, you know Tairn and Sgaeyl cannot be separated, and there's no telling how long we'll be forced to travel. I'm tired of arguing this point."

"He's a professor at this war college," Aetos sputters.

"He is my choice."

Halden sits back in his chair and looks at me like he's never seen me before.

"He hasn't," Tairn reminds me. *"He no longer knows you."*

I stare straight at Halden. "And the Tyrrish kept contact with Deverelli up until the last century. Who better to reopen those lines of communication than the Duke of Tyrrendor himself?"

Xaden's surprise barrels down the bond, but he remains unnaturally still.

"You may read my father's book whenever you want," I tell him.

"Riorson holds a seat in the Senarium," the Duchess of Morraine argues. "He can't just *leave*. He doesn't even have an heir should...tragedy befall, though I might be persuaded to agree to his absence should he consider my daughter's proposal."

"Proposal?" The blood runs from my face.

"One of about a dozen since they gave me the title back. Nothing to stress over." A soft strand of shimmering onyx brushes against my mind.

My heart lurches. We have very different ideas of stress.

"At least say what you mean, Ilene." Halden sends a sideways glance her way. "You don't trust him and would like to see your bloodline in not only Morraine but Tyrrendor."

"He led a rebellion!" She slams her hands on the tabletop.

"My father led a rebellion," Xaden says without taking his eyes off me. "I took part in a revolution. There's a difference in the words, from what I'm told."

I catch my mouth curving.

"Besides, arguing makes no difference." Xaden sits up. "I'm going. Lewellen will speak for me in my absence while taking counsel from my only living blood relative—Cadet Durran. Lieutenant Tavis has been co-leading my classes and will step into the role of professor to teach them fully while we're gone until it's time for the next professor to rotate in."

"If I give my permission," Halden retorts.

Wrong move, Halden.

"I ask permission of *one* person on the Continent, and it sure as Amari isn't you." Xaden slowly turns his head to look down the table at Halden, and breathing becomes irritatingly difficult.

"I speak in my father's stead," Halden bites out through gritted teeth.

"Right. Because *he's* the one I defer to." Xaden's gaze swings to me. "When would you like to go?"

"We fly for Deverelli as soon as His Highness is ready." I look Halden straight in the eye, counting on his absolute inability to read my face or sense the fear that he'll retaliate against Xaden with the power of the crown.

Halden stands, as does everyone at the table except Xaden. "Let's at least keep *that* part of the orders intact. We depart the day after tomorrow." He leaves through the northern door, followed by everyone who stood.

"No snide remarks," I say to Ridoc with a quick smile. "I'm proud of you."

"I kept the inside thoughts inside," he replies with a flash of a grin as Xaden approaches.

"You really had to prick his temper?" I ask as he reaches us.

"No." Xaden's gaze flickers to my mouth. "I did that just for fun."

"Drake Cordella?" Mira shouts, and the three of us turn as she charges across the room toward Drake. "As in the nightwing drift?"

He gives my sister a charming yet cocky smile. "You've heard of me?"

"You were instrumental in bringing the wards down in the Montserrat offensive last year." Her eyes narrow.

"I was." His grin expands.

She knees him straight in the groin.

Oh *gods*.

"Ooh." Ridoc winces. "He's going—"

Drake hits his knees, and Cat gasps.

"—down," Ridoc finishes.

"You must be Mira Sorrengail," Drake manages to say, pain etched in every line of his face.

"Guess you've heard of me, too." She crouches down to his level. "If you ever endanger my sister's life again, my blade will replace my knee. Got it?"

To his credit, he lifts his head and sucks a breath in through his teeth. "Heard."

"Excellent." She pats him on the shoulder and stands, dismissing Cat with a glare before turning my way. "You get one chance to form your own squad, and you choose your ex, your current lover, the quadrant's resident smart-ass, two people who have tried to kill you in the past year—one over said current lover—and *whatever* Dain is? These are your choices for the most important mission any rider could possibly undertake?"

"I'm glad someone said it," Tairn chimes in.

"And...*you*." It's not my finest comeback.

"Don't forget Halden's guard," Ridoc adds. "I'm sure they'll be super useful."

She flat-out rolls her eyes at him, then heads toward the door. "I'll need to provision here, but it looks like I'll have time to read the next volume in that series you love," she says to me over her shoulder.

Mom's journals. I nod and soak up the victory for one sweet second.

We could be only *days* away from having everything we need: Andarna's family, a cure for Xaden, and whatever it is my father wants me to retrieve from that merchant in Deverelli.

The day after tomorrow can't come fast enough.

Tyrrendor was the last to cut contact with the isles. The province has a reputation for its cunning leadership, but in this case, I would add: astute.

—SUBJUGATED: THE SECOND UPRISING OF THE KROVLAN PEOPLE
BY LIEUTENANT COLONEL ASHER SORRENGAIL

CHAPTER
TWENTY-ONE

We stop at Athebyne the first night, testing the gryphons' limits with speed and endurance. Then we push them to their max with twenty-four hours in the saddle, pausing only to feed and water the winged ones before reaching Cordyn as dawn breaks.

Everyone thinks the torturous day is to prepare the gryphons for the flight across the sea.

Only Xaden knows the real reason: even though he made it through the night unscathed, I'm terrified to let him touch the unwarded ground more than absolutely necessary.

We fly over swaths of scorched and desiccated land, evading venin with the help of the intel Drake brought. Part of me can't help but feel like we're evading the fight, even though I know we're searching for the way to end it.

"The gryphons cannot keep up," Tairn warns me as we descend toward Tecarus's palace. *"Especially when carrying the bulk of two humans."*

"Carrying" is a loose term for the baskets Halden and his guard dangle in, held by the gryphons' claws.

"Are you offering to carry one of them?" I ask, fighting off the sleep that has weighted my eyelids for the past three hours. The drastically warmer climate isn't helping, either.

"I'm suggesting we continue onward with only riders and fliers." The beats of his wings are slow, almost lazy in deference to the gryphons and Andarna,

who unclasped from her harness an hour ago *just in case* we were spotted and escorted to the palace.

"As much as I would love that, he speaks for Navarre." I reach for my flask, only to remember I emptied it a couple of hours ago.

"He will not matter when we find the irids. Only Andarna will."

"Well, as soon as you make contact with them, I'm happy to ditch the prince. Until then, we're stuck with the humans for clues." I look right, catching glimpses of Andarna in the pulses between Tairn's wingbeats. *"You feeling tired?"*

"Hungry," she responds. *"Kira says they have a plethora of goats, since the environment is not as suitable for the fleece of sheep. Perhaps they have superior food along with the superior weather."*

"We're well aware you aren't a fan of the snow." I grin into the warm wind as Tairn approaches the expanse of Tecarus's fighting pit instead of the grassy terrace he chose during our last visit.

"Perhaps you are like Sgaeyl's kind," Tairn notes. *"They favor the warmer climate."*

That's right. The hatching grounds of the blues used to be near here before the Great War.

Guards notice our arrival and rush to the highest terrace of the fighting pit as Tairn lands in the center of the field, snapping his wings closed while Andarna touches down less gracefully to his right.

Within moments, our five dragons and two gryphons cover every available foot of the field.

I detach one of my packs but hesitate to leave the second strapped to the back of the saddle.

"It is safer that I carry it," Tairn reminds me, dipping his shoulder impatiently.

"It means you can't detach the saddle." I don't want him uncomfortable.

"As if I would disparage my family name by being unprepared should the enemy—"

"Got it." I undo my strap, then beg my body to comply as I climb out of the seat. Muscles, tendons, ligaments—they all creak and pop as I dismount, and my knees nearly buckle when I hit the ground.

I can't help but shoot a glare at Cat as she springs up the stairs to meet the two waiting flier guards like she hasn't been airborne twenty-four hours straight.

"Can I take mine off?" Andarna asks, swiveling her head to gnaw on the metal strap across her shoulder.

"No!" Tairn and I shout simultaneously.

"No," Andarna mocks. *"Fine. I seek sustenance."*

"You will wait until our welcome is assured," Tairn orders, and Andarna huffs a breath of steam in his direction, then sits on her back legs and glowers. *"Pick your*

tail up off the ground right now. *Where do you think we are? The Vale?"*

I adjust the straps of my pack over my summer-weight flight jacket and bite back a laugh when Andarna blasts a short stream of fire at Tairn's back leg as she rises to all fours.

"I'm not dignifying that with a response," he snarls.

Ahead of us, Sgaeyl springs into the air, and my brow furrows as Xaden watches her fly away, his features schooled in that carefully controlled mask he loves so well.

Aotrom, Teine, and Cath all stay put, but Kiralair launches along with Drake's gryphon, Sovadunn.

"How are you feeling?" I ask once I reach Xaden, noting that Mira is already halfway up the steps of the arena, blade drawn.

"I should be asking you that." He rolls his neck and drags his gaze from Sgaeyl's retreating form to sweep over me, lingering on my hips and knees like he can see how sore they are. "Your body can't be happy after that long in the saddle."

"I'm…" I pause — we both do — as Halden climbs awkwardly out of the four-foot-tall basket Kira deposited in front of us. "I'm better off than whatever's happening there."

The prince curses when his pack catches on the thick weave of the carrier as he exits, the fabric holding him prisoner. Instead of lifting the bag over the barrier, Halden wrenches it free, tearing the strap clean off.

"Clearly it was common sense that attracted you to the heir." Sarcasm drips from Tairn's tone.

"I was eighteen and he was handsome. Give me a break." I wince, noting that Halden doesn't exactly rush off to help Captain Winshire, the redheaded guard, out of her basket.

"Kingdom seems to be in good hands with that one." Xaden glances at the drained stones that surround the pit as we walk toward the others waiting ahead. "Think anyone will notice if I sleep out here on these stones until we're ready to go?"

"Yes." My voice quiets as we approach Dain and Ridoc, both of whom stare awkwardly as the captain refuses any offers of help and stumbles all five feet ten inches of herself out of her basket to Halden's left, then strides up the steps after him in speedy annoyance. "But I'll sleep out here with you if you want. If it's what you need." I'll do whatever it takes to lessen his risk.

"Save that worried look for someone else. As long as there's no reason to wield, I'll be fine, just like last night." Xaden reaches for my hand and squeezes, then lets it go before Halden sees.

Dain and Ridoc both gawk at our surroundings as we climb the stairs out of the pit. It's slightly cooler than when we were here last, but the humidity has the leather of my flight jacket sticking uncomfortably to my skin.

"Is this where you got the idea for using the sparring pit at Basgiath?" Dain asks over his shoulder when we finally reach the top.

Xaden nods, scanning our perimeter.

The second I spot Tecarus—in what are obviously his bed robes—hugging Cat on the nearby patio, Tairn and Andarna launch from the pit and the others rapidly follow suit. Mira stands to the side and sheathes her blade, offering a narrowed glance of warning to the two flier guards accompanying Tecarus before Drake clasps the tall one on the right in a friendly, back-slapping hug.

"Let me know if he has any venin locked away in a box as a surprise test," Tairn says, flying in the same direction Sgaeyl took.

We cross the last rows of drained stones imported from the land that borders the Barrens as Halden and Anna reach the patio.

"Will do. Don't let her eat anything—or anyone—she isn't supposed to." A bead of sweat drips down my spine, and I adjust the weight of my pack on my aching shoulders again, cringing at the slight slip I feel in the right joint as my head starts to swim in an annoying wave of dizziness. Exhaustion, dehydration, and heat are never a winning combination for my body.

"You're such a centenarian. Perhaps my kind will not be such killjoys. Perhaps they will feast as they see fit. Perhaps they will— Ooh! What is that*?"*

"A Mammoth Red-Horned Tortoise and absolutely not*! The shell will embed between your teeth, and I will not carry you and a festering tortoise shell— Get back here!"* His voice fades as they fly out of range.

Xaden tenses the second we step off the drained stone and onto the strip of grass that separates the pit from the occupied marble patio leading into the palace's dining room. *"I'm all right,"* he assures me as we reach the group.

We fill in the empty places in the small circle, putting me next to Halden, who somehow manages to still look regal…and haughty in a crumpled infantry uniform.

I wince when the rising sun glints off the golden royal insignia beneath his name tags, catching me in the eye, and quickly look down at the austere black of my flight jacket. I've never worn one made for actual combat before—only training. There's no name tag, no patches, nothing beyond my hair to give away who I might be if I fall behind enemy lines, only two four-pointed stars indicating my rank as a second-year cadet.

"There's the boy!" Tecarus grins at Drake, then glances over the rest of us, his gaze catching on Halden. "Your Royal Highness." He bows his head. "We were not expecting such an esteemed guest."

"We appreciate your hospitality, Viscount." Halden does that condescending head-tilt of a nod that always grated on my nerves. Guess it still does. His hand rises to the small of my back, and I stiffen. "We were hoping to rest for the day, perhaps two depending on the condition of the gryphons, before continuing on to Deverelli."

Shadows rise up the back of my thigh, curling around my hip, and I sidestep toward Xaden, effectively losing Halden's hand in the process. *"Still all right over there?"*

"It would help if your fucking ex kept his hands to himself," he hisses, the shadow firmly gripping my hip.

"Deverelli?" Tecarus asks, his eyebrows nearly hitting his hairline before his gaze swings my way. "You have the artifact."

My lips part—

"We do," Halden answers for me.

Gods, I always hated that about him.

Dain shoots me a look that borders on an eye roll, reminding me that he'd never been Halden's biggest fan.

"Of course," Tecarus says slowly, his attention dropping to the shadows lingering at my hip. "Well then, let's get you comfortable." He turns toward the palace in a flurry of brocaded fabric, and my shoulders dip with exhaustion as we follow him into the dining room. "Forgive the additional security. We are one of the only major cities left standing in the south," he tells us as we round the end of the enormous table and through the doors into the airy palace.

I'd almost forgotten just how breathtaking this place is.

It's built for the movement of air. For beauty, and art, and light. Even the white marble floors shimmer, reflecting the dawn just like the winding pools that flow through the space beyond the wide, central staircase. The palace won't stand a chance should the venin venture this far south.

Whoever built it had to have known that.

Mira pauses at the base of the white steps, looking down at the black pillar barely visible in the level below us through the open staircase. Like last time, it has quite the crowd milling around it.

"Of course, with the number of fliers in residence, our rooms are limited," Tecarus says, drawing the belt of his heavily brocaded robe tight as he starts up the steps. "Would you mind doubling up? We have a few rooms available on our top floor." He looks over his shoulder at the landing. "With the exception of you, Your Highness. Naturally, we can accommodate private quarters for you."

Shit. There's no way I'll make it up two more flights of stairs when this one is already killing me. My knee protests every step, and I curse the humidity and keep climbing even though it feels like the ground rocks beneath my boots.

"Naturally." Halden's tone borders on terse. His fatigue is showing, and if he hasn't changed in the years we've been apart, it will only shorten his temper.

"Your room remains empty as well, Riorson. Or should I say *Your Grace*?" Tecarus adds as we reach the floor we stayed on previously. "I can't help but notice you're not wearing the insignia of your rank." He pauses in the middle of the wide hallway, bringing the entire group to a halt.

I could just about cry as I realize we're right in front of the room Mira and I occupied during our last visit, and I spot the set of doors beyond that I know are Xaden's. How am I going to make it to the top floor? *"Will you still keep me if I have to crawl up the stairs?"* I ask Tairn.

"You're not crawling," Xaden answers.

Wrong pathway. Gods, I really am in trouble.

"Shiny things make good targets," Xaden says to Tecarus from my left as Halden edges in on my right. "And I've never been one to confuse a title with power."

Oh, for fuck's sake. Is he really starting shit with Halden right now? I go to roll my eyes, then blink. Is this what Xaden went through when Cat showed up this past fall?

Ridoc snorts behind me, and I hear the distinct sound of a smack against leather—no doubt Dain's hand against my squadmate's shoulder. I'm glad I can't see Mira's face. Amari knows she's exasperated as all hell back there.

"But how am I to know on what authority you visit me?" Tecarus turns toward us with a flourish, flashing his impossibly white teeth with a political smile. "As a lieutenant? Merely a rider? A professor? The Duke of Tyrrendor?" He taps his fingers together. "Or perhaps as the beloved of the one rarity I can't seem to convince to join my court." His gaze falls to me, as if I need the reminder of his proposal to join his *collection* as his on-call guard dog in return for the privilege of growing old with Xaden and our dragons in the peace of his estate in the isles. "That offer still stands."

"As does my answer." I sway slightly and breathe deeply to beat back the darkening edges of my vision. I need rest and I need it *now*. This time the shadows at my hips are supportive instead of territorial, and when I glance down, they're so thin they blend into my leathers, nearly impossible to see. *"Thank you."*

"What authority do I hold here? Let's ask our prince. What do you say, Your *Royal Highness*?" He levels a look that could wither a fucking *tree* on Halden.

Apprehension prickles the back of my neck.

"I'm not sure I understand the question." Halden's jaw ticks and his fists clench.

"His temper could trigger your power," I warn Xaden as Tecarus smiles with pure glee at the obvious mayhem he's created.

"His temper is exactly what I'm counting on." Xaden drops his focus to the royal insignia. "You understand completely. Am I here as a professor? Or the duke? Or—"

"Obviously you're a fucking duke," Halden snaps. "Lewellen made sure of it, didn't he? The second most powerful title in the godsdamned kingdom goes to a *Riorson* of all bloodlines."

"Don't be an ass—" I start, but the shadows tug gently in a bid for silence, so I give it to him.

"So, I'm not here with the authority of a professor," Xaden clarifies, masterfully ignoring Halden's blatant insult.

"You have *no* authority," Halden seethes, color infusing his cheeks as he steps toward Xaden, his boots nearly reaching mine in the process. "I am the ranking officer here."

"Xaden, he's going to blow. He'll swing." Walls. Mirrors. Tables. Breakables. Whatever's close, really. There was a reason guards never volunteered to be assigned to Halden. The same reason Alic had been such a bully and Cam—Aaric—had avoided them both as much as possible.

"So, not a professor." Xaden's eyes narrow, and my whole body tries to sway, held upright by Xaden's shadows.

"No!" Halden's shout echoes down the hallway. "Not a fucking professor—"

"Just wanted to clear that up," Xaden interrupts, then lifts me into his arms. "We'll see you once we're *rested*." He takes off past Tecarus, striding down the hall.

"What are you doing?" I hiss.

"Doubling up as ordered," Xaden says, throwing open the doors to his room and then kicking them shut once we're through.

"I cannot believe you just did that!" I slide down the length of his body and ignore the way mine ignites as he grips my hips and turns, pinning me against the door. It's blissfully solid behind my back.

"Really?" He lowers his head to mine. "Of all the things I've done, *that's* the one you can't believe?" His voice softens, and he lifts his fingers to the side of my neck. "That's what I thought. Your pulse is racing. I counted at least twice that you almost collapsed out there." He lowers his head to mine. "Did you really want to *crawl* up the stairs?"

"No," I admit.

"Now you don't have to." He presses a kiss to my forehead. "You just rode for two straight days with only twelve hours of rest. I knew you needed to get off your feet and lie down, and I could have just given you my room, but selfishly…"

I look up at him.

"I'm done sleeping in a bed that doesn't have you in it." His thumb strokes along my pulse.

Hope ignites in my chest. If he's willing to sleep in the same bed again, then maybe there's a chance he'll eventually trust himself enough to put his hands on me, and not just because he's jealous that Halden exists. "I'm good with that."

I'm rewarded with a hint of a smile, then swept up against his chest, the rhythm of his heart a perfect drum beneath my ear. I feel like shit, Xaden is slowly losing pieces of himself, and we're a thousand miles from Basgiath, yet that steady beat makes everything somehow tenable.

It feels so right to be in his arms.

"Because it is," he says, holding me tighter.

I blink and pull back to look at him. "I didn't say that out loud."

His brow furrows. "Then you must have thought it down the bond, because I wasn't pushing into your intentions."

My heart races for a different reason. *No. But...maybe.* "Or your signet is growing."

His eyes flare.

Someone knocks at the door.

"Fuck," Xaden mutters, and I push against his chest. "Don't be—"

"Let me down." I'm facing whoever's on the other side of that door on my feet.

"—stubborn." He sets me down, then locks his forearm across my ribs to hold me upright as I face forward. "Ready?"

I nod, and his arm twists along my left side. The gold-handled door opens, revealing Tecarus, his two guards a respectable distance behind him.

The viscount's knowing gaze jumps between Xaden and me, but he doesn't bother with pithy commentary.

"Make it quick," Xaden orders without explanation.

"The prince cannot arrive in a *basket*," Tecarus says, folding his hands in front of him and wrinkling his nose in distaste. "It is unseemly for royalty, and in a culture that values rare items, shrewd trades, and luxury, he'll never be granted an audience if *he* is seen as the item being delivered."

"What do you propose?" I ask, ignoring the sinking in my chest and the lightening in my head.

"It's a two-day journey by my fastest ship," Tecarus says, his brow furrowing as he studies me. "Which would make it what? A twelve-hour flight due south?"

"We estimate sixteen with the gryphons and what your texts have provided about historical wind patterns," I answer, blinking back the darkness. It's been a long time since I pushed myself this hard, and fuck am I paying for it.

"I'll leave within the hour with the prince," Tecarus offers. "It appears you may need the rest—"

"She's fine," Xaden interrupts. "I'm the one feeling a little clingy."

I bite back a smile.

"Right." Tecarus laces his fingers. "I suggest you land at my estate on the northern coast about twelve hours after we'll arrive. It's about ten miles east of the capital, though they measure distance in—"

"Leagues," I interrupt. "I read everything you sent." And everything my father wrote.

"Excellent. The rest of the shoreline is rather…shall we say…defended, and I'll need to prepare the king for the arrival of dragons or we'll return home with fewer of them."

My stomach pitches.

"Trust me, our riot will return intact." There's an edge of warning in Xaden's tone, and his forearm flexes.

"I'm already worried about one hotheaded aristocrat," Tecarus chides. "Should I add a second to that list?"

"They come for our dragons, and it's not the aristocrat they'll be dealing with." Xaden's voice drops to that lethal calm that's a touch more terrifying than a shout.

"Tell me you'll help control him." Tecarus's gaze lands on mine.

I lift my chin. "What makes you think he's the one you'd have to worry about?"

Tecarus sighs. "I'll see that you have a map." He brings his laced fingers to his chin. "You are prepared to lose your abilities when you cross the ocean?"

"We are," Xaden replies. *Definitely prepared to get a second of relief.*

"It will be fascinating to see if your powers reemerge once on land. And you've brought the requested artifact for the audience?" Tecarus asks.

"Halden's carrying it. He'll be taking the audience," I answer. This one time, Halden's enormous ego works in our favor. His insistence on being the only Navarrian to meet with the king frees Xaden and gives us time to seek out the merchant my father mentioned.

"Excellent." Tecarus nods. "A word to the wise…" He glances between us. "I may collect rarities, but King Courtlyn absconds with them. Do not wander off from each other, do not advertise what a rare jewel you are, and at all costs—do not make a deal you cannot keep."

• • •

Nearly twenty-four hours later, my access to magic fades to all but a trickle at the edge of the coast as we fly over by the colors of dawn, trading power for sunlight. The loss is stunning, immeasurable in a way that, for an instant, makes me pity Jack Barlowe.

For the first time since the night Tairn and Andarna channeled to me, I feel… small, naked even, stripped of the power that's come to not only embolden me over the last year but define me.

A shivering chill sweeps over my skin with the next gust of wind, and Andarna shrieks high above. My head whips in her direction as the sound echoes from those around us.

Tairn drops unexpectedly, his wingbeats faltering, and I fall forward, fumbling for the saddle's pommels. My hands make impact, jarring my wrists but catching my body weight just before my stomach makes contact as Tairn levels out over the ocean. *"Are you all right?"* I scan the sky for Andarna.

"Startled. We draw on magic for strength," Tairn explains. *"I hadn't realized how dependent we truly are—"*

Andarna sinks rapidly on our right, her wings beating a furious but futile pace.

"Hook on," Tairn orders.

"I'm. Quite. Capable." She loses altitude with every second, plummeting toward the rippling water beneath us.

"I have no desire to scent salted scales. Once you're wet you're on your own," he warns, then picks up his head, swiveling it back and forth in a reptilian manner.

"What's wrong?" I ask.

He dives toward Andarna without warning, and her sigh of acceptance comes out with a huff of a snarl as his shoulders tighten, and I hear the metallic *click* of the harness locking into place. Her added weight makes him dip for a breath of a second, and then his massive wings beat harder, lifting us toward the riot.

Andarna is suspiciously quiet.

"Tairn?" I prompt, my stomach souring with unease.

"I can't speak with Sgaeyl." He clips out each word. *"Or any of the others. Our communications have been severed."*

I reach for the glittering onyx bond, but even though Tairn is still there, Xaden isn't.

We're already cut off.

It was whispered in academic circles that Cordyn had supplied troops and weaponry for the second Krovlan uprising, but the research has led me across the Arctile Ocean to Deverelli, known to our kingdom as the treacherous isle of merchants, who to my surprise may not have been the source of the arms, but perhaps the broker.

—SUBJUGATED: THE SECOND UPRISING OF THE KROVLAN PEOPLE
BY LIEUTENANT COLONEL ASHER SORRENGAIL

CHAPTER
TWENTY-TWO

Holy *shit* it's hot here, and by my estimates it must only be around nine o'clock in the morning as we approach an endless line of white beaches preceded by splotches of alternating turquoise and aqua waters.

Soft green hills rise directly behind the beach, dotted with stone structures. The perplexing color reminds me of the last batch of wool when the weaver's dye has lost its potency: it's muted, almost faded, and its lack of color is made obvious by the contrast of the water. The closer we fly, the farther forward I lean in my seat, wholly, completely fascinated. The hills aren't *dotted* at all.

"That's the city, isn't it? Hidden in the trees?" My fingers curl in excitement around the pommels of the saddle. The area is a thriving port, with four central piers and several smaller ones.

"It appears to be." Before we get close enough to make out the people, Tairn banks left, taking us east.

"Let me out of this thing before anyone sees," Andarna demands.

"Not until we're out of range of those cross-bolts." Tairn looks pointedly toward a long stone wall a quarter of the way up the first hill, armed with a dozen of the largest cross-bolts I've ever seen, all loaded with shining, metallic tips.

Dragon killers.

For once, Andarna doesn't argue.

"Given this is an isle dedicated to peace, they're certainly prepared for war." My stomach tenses. It's been centuries since any Navarrian has stepped foot on this isle, and if we've overestimated the viscount's sway with the king, there's every chance those cross-bolts will head in our direction.

We fly between the beach and a barrier island, where the water is a breathtaking shade of blue I've never seen, and I can't help but stare, trying to commit it to memory as we slowly descend to a hundred, then fifty feet above the ground. Reading about this place has in no way truly prepared me to see it.

Despite the exhaustion, I don't want to so much as blink for fear of missing a single thing. Although after flying all night, I'm more than prepared to modify this saddle even more for sleeping when we get back to Basgiath.

"According to the map you were given, the estate ahead belongs to Tecarus," Tairn says as we pass by a grouping of elegant manors on the mainland, each with its own dock and a ship that announces its owner's status and wealth. Tairn shifts his shoulders, and the click of the harness sounds a second before Andarna appears off his right wing, hers beating double-time to keep up.

A group of creatures darts beneath us in the water, jumping into the air in a series of graceful leaps that almost make up for the flurry of people yelling and running back into their homes as we fly over.

"I wonder what they taste—" Andarna starts.

"No." My protest catches me by surprise. *"They're dolphinum, and they're just too pretty to be your snack."* Even prettier than the drawings I've seen.

"You're going soft." Andarna snorts.

We touch down in the sand in front of a sprawling two-story manor that reminds me of a smaller version of Tecarus's palace in Cordyn. Its tall white pillars leave a portion of the structure open to the ocean breeze, but the thick stone walls that surround the rest tell me it's weathered storms here, too. Palm trees—tall, wispy things with broad leaves of the same muted, pale green adorning their tops—line a path to the house, and I check to make sure that's indeed the standard of Cordyn flying on a docked ship before I dismount, taking the extra pack we've kept with Tairn until now.

The sand is so fine I can't help but drop down and run my fingers through it with a smile. It's nothing like the rocky texture along the river at Basgiath or the coarse, grainy beach of Cordyn. This makes me want to strip my boots off and walk barefoot.

Andarna lifts her claw and shakes it beside me, sending grains of sand flying in a cloud as the others land in a flurry of activity around us. *"It's going to get between my scales."*

"And now you understand why I didn't let you eat that tortoise," Tairn mutters,

his head perpetually swiveling, taking in our surroundings. *"We'll need to hunt before we fly back. And we're no longer alone."*

A middle-aged man stands in the doorway of Tecarus's manor, his short-sleeved, belted white tunic and matching pants contrasting his brown skin as his arms tremble, his mouth hanging open while he stares at Tairn and Andarna.

"I'll figure out where to do that without causing a war." I stand up as Ridoc stomps forward, then startle when Aotrom roars.

The Deverelli man screams and runs back into the house.

"Great first impression," I mutter, brushing the sand off my palm.

Andarna snorts, then prances off toward the water, her wings tucked in tight.

"Do not go any deeper than your claws!" Tairn lectures, his tail nearly taking out a tree when he pivots to watch her go. *"I swear, if you get in over your head, I'll let you drown."*

Aotrom roars again, getting everyone's attention, including Tairn's.

"I don't know what you're saying!" Ridoc turns toward Aotrom.

The Brown Swordtail opens his mouth and roars louder, blowing back Ridoc's dark-brown hair and covering my friend in a layer of goopy saliva.

Gross.

Ridoc slowly lifts his hands and scrapes the slime off his face. "Yelling at me doesn't help. It's like shouting in a language I don't speak."

A vise of foreboding clamps down on my chest, and my gaze swings toward Tairn, then past him to where Sgaeyl and Teine survey our surroundings restlessly. Mira walks our way, rubbing the back of her neck, but Xaden stands at the edge of the water, facing away from the estate.

"I think it's just us," I say to Tairn, spinning slowly to take it all in.

"Just us how?" he asks.

Kira rakes her claws through the sand, and Cat is on her knees next to her, holding her face in her hands while Drake kneels at her side. Sova, his gryphon, shakes his silver head back and forth like he's trying to clear it. Cath guards the west point of the property, his tail flicking in agitation, and Dain looks down as he walks our way.

Something's off with *everyone*.

"I think we're the only ones who can speak to one another." My feet sink into the sand as I trudge my way over to Mira, and I rip open the buttons of my jacket as the heat starts to cook me from inside my leathers. "Can you talk to Teine?"

She shakes her head. "We lost the connection as soon as we left the Continent."

"I…" I swallow hard, then lower my voice. "I can still speak to Tairn and Andarna."

She blinks, then looks over the group quickly. "From the state of everyone else, I'd say you're alone in that department." Her brow furrows. "Do you think it's because you're bonded to two? Or is it Andarna?"

I shake my head, my focus straying to Xaden's back. "I don't know."

"Either way, I'm glad you still have the connection." She gently squeezes my shoulders. "Being cut off from magic is…"

"Disorienting." I grimace.

"Yes." She nods. "But losing the bond?" Her face puckers for a second before she masks the emotion. "Well, I guess you'd know, since they shoved that serum down your throat."

"Not only is everyone going to be on edge, it'll make coordinating anything a bitch, considering they're cut off from each other," I say, glancing up at Tairn, who's backed away to take a position that puts him equally between Sgaeyl, Andarna, and me.

"Guess we'll have ample opportunity to try these out." Mira swings her pack from her shoulder, then retrieves several leather pouches before picking the one marked with a circular protection rune I don't recognize and replacing the rest. "Trissa sent these as a test to see if runes will work out here." She unbuttons the pouch and hands me a palm-size slice of what appears to be lilac-colored quartz, tempered with the same rune that labels the leather. "That one is supposed to shield you from sunlight. Carry it while we're here for me, would you?" She lifts her brows. "Quietly, of course."

I nod and slip it into my pocket. Having some—or any—form of power out here would put us on a more familiar footing, but it opens the door to a kind of trade I'm not sure any of us wants to contemplate.

"You made it!" Tecarus shouts with glee from the doorway, his arms outstretched in ostentatious welcome as he walks toward us in a fuchsia tunic embroidered in heavy gold. "Prince Halden hasn't awakened yet, but I was able to secure an emergency meeting with a chancellor to the king upon our arrival last night, and you'll be thrilled to know that your creatures may hunt in the valleys three leagues south of here where there is an abundance of wild game. Humans are *not* to be on the menu."

"Understood," I tell him and immediately turn toward Tairn. *"I'd rather you go now so you're at full strength than chance something going wrong—"*

"Agreed." He arches his neck and lets out a short bark of a sound that makes me lift my brows but does the trick of getting everyone's attention. *"Do not die while I am gone."*

"I'll do my best."

He bends a little deeper than usual given the sand, then launches skyward, his wings creating a gust of wind that weaponizes the sand around us. I throw my forearm up to protect my face and leave it there for the next few seconds as the others follow Tairn's lead.

When I open my eyes, it's just us humans on the beach: riders dressed in black, fliers in brown leathers, gawking Deverelli on either side of what appears to be Tecarus's property line, and one rather pompous viscount.

"The prince has an audience with His Majesty this afternoon, so I'm assuming you'd all like to rest before you…" Tecarus cocks his head to the side. "I suppose do nothing, since King Courtlyn will only speak to aristocracy." He crinkles his nose at Ridoc. "You need a bath."

"We need horses." Ridoc scoops a fingerful of slime out of his ear and shakes it off his finger.

"I'm sorry?" Tecarus steps out of the slime's path.

"Violet wants to visit the market. Something about buying books," Dain answers as he catches up, taking a spot to Ridoc's right.

Tecarus nods. "Of course. You'll keep a low profile?"

"As low as possible," I agree.

He tells us where to find our assigned rooms, and after we thank him, I head toward the water. My boots sink in the sand with every step until I reach the zone where it firms just above the waterline.

Xaden stands with his feet apart, swords strapped to his back, and arms crossed, but when my shoulder brushes his elbow, I look up to find his face completely, totally relaxed.

I close my eyes tight, then reopen them just to be sure I'm not imagining things. Nope, he's really staring out at the water like we're in the valley above Riorson House and not in enemy territory, completely cut off from magic. "Hey," I say gently.

"Hey." He tilts his head down toward mine and gives me a soft—but real—smile.

I almost ask him how he is, since he can't talk to Sgaeyl and our own bond is blocked, but it seems like a shitty thing to do after that smile. "Everyone is heading up to take naps before we ride out to find the merchant. Halden is set to meet the king at three, so we can get a good four hours of sleep in if you want."

"I'm going to stay out here for a little bit. You go." He turns toward me and cups the back of my neck. "You need the rest and definitely need to get out of the sun for a bit. Your nose is turning pink."

"Tecarus gave us the same room…"

"Because he values his life." He tucks the loose strands of my braid behind my ears. "Get some sleep. You need it. I'll be up in a bit."

"Do you want me to sit out here with you?"

His grin deepens. "When you clearly need to rest? No, love, though I appreciate the offer. It's hard to explain, but I'm just going to take a little time to myself to soak in this view." He grabs my hand and brings it to his chest, where his heart pounds in a steady rhythm that feels slightly more relaxed than it was in Cordyn—than it has been in weeks, really. "Can you feel it?"

"It's slower," I whisper.

"There's no magic here." He tugs me against him. "No power. No lure. No taunting reminder that I can save *everyone* if I just reach for it and take what's offered. It's only...peace."

For the first time since fetching the luminary, I seriously debate Tecarus's offer.

The uprising suddenly failed overnight on December 13, 433 AU, in what has been called the Midnight Massacre. The foreign troops disappeared, and the rebels were killed in their beds by Poromish forces. It is not their disappearance that strikes this scholar as particularly vicious but their obvious betrayal. There is a saying in Deverelli: *The word is the blood.* When they make a trade, broker a deal, it is considered law. I cannot help but wonder what part of the deal the Krovlan rebels did not uphold.

—Subjugated: The Second Uprising of the Krovlan People
by Lieutenant Colonel Asher Sorrengail

CHAPTER
TWENTY-THREE

"This is a ridiculous way to travel," Ridoc says for the dozenth time, hauling himself upright in the saddle after slipping yet again as our horses navigate the uneven stone streets of Matyas, Deverelli's capital city.

I smother a laugh, but Cat doesn't offer Ridoc the same kindness from two rows back with Mira as we ride the tree-covered fairways. We're arranged mostly in pairs with the exception of Drake, who is solo ahead of Xaden and me.

The city is even more stunning than I imagined from the air. Built under the canopy of enormous trees, only its tallest structures are visible when flying. The rest feels like a hidden treasure, and we haven't even journeyed up the hill where the palace—and Halden—is. The roads have been primarily residential until now, with structures far and evenly spaced, growing closer together the nearer we come to the ports and city center, and in the last mile, every single one of them has been built out of stone.

"I'm sorry, but I find it hard to believe that a dragon rider draws the line at a horse," Cat says with another laugh as we pass what appears to be a tea shop, judging by the painted sign outside the door.

"Hey, horses *bite*," Ridoc says over his shoulder, and a woman jumps away at the sight of us, placing a palm over the neckline of her embroidered white tunic.

"And dragons do what, exactly?" Drake calls back.

"You'll never know, since you'll never be allowed to ride one," Mira snaps in a bored tone before returning to her usual side-to-side perimeter sweep. She's been on alert since we left the manor, even though I've assured her Tairn's within range and he can set this whole place on fire within minutes if I call for him.

What we really need is a freaking communication rune for the others—if such a thing exists.

Drake's eyes narrow on Mira, then Xaden, whose mouth has curved into a smirk. "I'm surprised you didn't fight me for the lead position, Riorson."

Xaden scoffs, and the smirk transforms into a smile as we pass under a patch of dappled sunlight. I stare at him like it's first year all over again. He's in a short-sleeved uniform top like the rest of us, baring those gorgeously toned arms, but it's really the relaxed posture, the ease of his smile that have me utterly transfixed and, I can admit…a little confuddled. Xaden Riorson is a lot of things, but *happy* isn't usually one of them. "It's perfectly fine if you die first, Cordella. I'm exactly where I want to be." Then the man fucking *winks* at me, and I almost fall off my damned horse.

I tighten my thighs on instinct to keep from sliding out of the saddle, and the sable mare prances beneath me before I remember to relax. The dizziness has always been worse in the heat, and it's definitely not doing me any favors today.

"See? Violet prefers dragons, too," Ridoc says.

"I'm fine." I roll my shoulders to keep my pack—and its very precious cargo—in place.

"She's always been a good rider," Dain argues on my behalf.

"Did you two ride a lot when you were younger?" Xaden asks as we pass by a tavern, and more than one mug of ale spills onto white tunics at the outdoor tables at the sight of us.

My jaw drops and my head whips in his direction.

Leather creaks, and when I glance back, sure enough, Mira is leaning forward in her saddle.

"What?" Xaden looks at me, then lifts his brows and glances back at the others. Cat stares at him like he's grown another head. Dain's wearing two lines between his brows like he can't quite figure out if this is a trick question, and Ridoc grins like he's got front-row tickets to a play. Xaden's gaze jumps to mine for a second before returning to the road as we take the fork to the right, leading to the market and port according to the rather remarkable signage jammed between the cobblestone and a large tree. "Am I not allowed to ask about your childhood?"

"No," I blurt. "Of course you are."

"It's just that you usually act like I didn't grow up with her," Dain answers casually. "Like we weren't best friends."

"I'm so fucking glad I got on this horse," Ridoc says, gripping his reins tighter.

I send a look his way that I hope tells him I'm reevaluating my decision to put him in this squad in the first place.

"But to answer your question," Dain continues, just as at ease on his horse as Xaden is, "yes, we rode whenever our parents' duty stations allowed for it. Not the years they were up in Luceras, of course."

"Fuck that was cold," Mira says.

"It was," I agree, cringing at the memory. "Riding was hard on me when I was out of practice, and falling always sucked, but it gave me a sense of awareness of my body, too. What about you?" I ask Xaden as we curve onto a bustling street.

"I think I rode before I walked." He flashes me a quick smile. "It's probably one of the things I missed most once I crossed the parapet, actually. Horses go where you ask them to for the most part. Sgaeyl…" He glances up at the trees as if he can see her in the sky above us, a look of longing on his face. "She doesn't really give a shit where I want to go. I'm just along for the ride."

"Man, do I feel that," Dain mutters, and I laugh.

"Look alive," Drake calls back, and the mood of the squad instantly shifts as the street grows crowded with horses, wagons, and pedestrians carrying baskets in their arms and strapped to their backs. The only blades I see are the ones we carry.

Stone shops line both sides of the congested double-wide street. Their doors are open to the breeze, their wares and produce displayed on carts in front under vibrant cloth awnings for what looks to be a mile straight ahead, and from what I read, I know this area branches off to the south, into a gold and spice market, and farther up the hill where the financial sector perches like an overlord.

We're a half mile off the beach, but the scents of salt and fish are thick in the air, and I understand why business is done under the canopy of the trees. I can't begin to imagine the smell or how quickly things would spoil in the sun in this climate.

Everywhere I look, there's a purchase being haggled over, a fruit I've never tasted, a flower I've never smelled, a bird I've never heard. It's a sensory feast, and I consume it like a starved woman.

"Anyone feel like our home is a completely dreary shithole?" Ridoc asks as traffic pauses us outside a cloth merchant, and I find myself staring at a bolt of shimmering black silk so diaphanous it's almost silver.

It wouldn't last a day against the dragon-scale armor currently covering my torso.

"Speak for yourself," Xaden says, swinging his leg over and dismounting next to me. "Aretia is the second most beautiful thing I've ever seen." He hands me his reins, turning those gorgeous, gold-flecked onyx eyes into weapons capable of melting the underwear straight off my body as he looks up at me. "And my home is the first."

Unh. Yeah, I flat-out liquefy.

"You're laying it on thick, Riorson." But I still smile when I take the reins.

"I'm going to ask about our merchant. Don't leave without me." He glances back at Dain. "Let's go, Krovlish." Offering me another precious grin, he disappears into the store, followed quickly by Dain.

"Is that the same guy?" Drake asks Cat, turning around in the saddle. "That cannot possibly be the same fucking guy."

I try not to look, but fail, and when I glance over my shoulder, I catch a glimpse of her shrugging and quickly looking away.

"Maybe this is who he could have been if his dad hadn't led a whole rebellion and fucked him over by getting executed and having him thrown into the quadrant and making him responsible for all the marked ones at the age of what? Seventeen?" Ridoc muses.

"Yeah," I agree, my eyes on the door. "That." And yet...if all of it hadn't happened, would we still be us? Or is the miracle of our relationship the result of a precise combination of tragedies that broke us both so completely that when we collided, we became something entirely new?

"Or it could just be that he loves Violet, so he's not a dick to her," Mira says, eyeing a puckered-browed Deverelli man who scurries back into a dressmaker's shop at the first sight of us, dragging a woman along with him. "Guess we're more visible than we thought."

"We're the only ones in black," I mutter.

"Fire-bringers!" the man accuses in the common tongue, then slams the door shut, rattling the glass.

"Rude." Ridoc adjusts in his saddle.

"And wrong," Cat mutters. "Some of us just want to fuck with your feelings, not burn your house to the ground."

I huff a laugh, but Ridoc full-on snorts.

Xaden strides through the cloth merchant's door with Dain, tucking a black velvet pouch into the front left pocket of his uniform as he comes down the three stone steps. "She's a dealer of rare books, two streets up the hill."

Stunned, I hand him back his reins, and he mounts quickly. "It can't be that easy."

"It can," he says, tapping his pocket. "We don't share a currency, but gemstones seem to speak in every language." He looks over his shoulder. "Good job, Aetos."

"Was that a compliment? What the fuck is going on?" Dain asks, his gaze flying to mine. "Did you give him something?"

I shake my head, and Drake starts us forward.

"Fire-bringer" is hurled as an insult in our direction more than a few times as we make our way down the rows of shops and up the two streets where Xaden and Dain were directed. The flurry of activity dwindles from the urgency of a daily produce-and-goods mercantile district to more varied and niche shops by the time we reach the second street. When we stop in front of Tomes and Tales, there's ample room next to the trunk of an enormous tree for the horses to wait.

The shop itself is two stories, built in various shades of gray stone, and unlike the streets below, none of its sides touch the buildings around it. From the outside, it looks to be the same size as the bookstore I visited in Calldyr with Dad, a little larger than the library in the Riders Quadrant, but nowhere even an eighth of the Archives.

"You're on," Xaden says from the ground, reaching up for me.

I swing my leg over the sable mare and dismount into his arms, noting how he takes his delicious time sliding me down the length of his body.

He keeps our eyes locked, and the heat I find there, the need that flares as my hands drift down his chest make my breath catch. I reach for our bond out of reflex to tell him how much I want him back in my bed, and my hands fist the fabric of his uniform when I remember it's blocked here.

"I miss the bond," I whisper before I can think better of it.

"Me too. But you don't have to say what you're thinking for me to know," he whispers, his hands slipping from my waist to my hips. "I can read it in every line of your body. Your eyes are a dead giveaway, too." Under my fists, his heartbeat accelerates. "Always have been. You have no idea how many times I almost fucked up on the sparring mat when I caught you watching me."

He says this *now*? When I can't just drag him into the nearest room and lock the door? Suddenly, the last six weeks feel like an eternity.

"I swear to Amari, you two get one inch closer and I'm going to throw a bucket of water on you," Mira warns, breaking the spell.

I fall forward, leaning my forehead on Xaden's chest right between my fists, and feel his laughter rumble as he closes his arms around me.

"Do riders get nicknames once they earn their wings?" Drake questions Mira. "Because I'm pretty sure yours would be Killjoy."

"Are we doing this or not?" Mira asks, clearly ignoring him.

I nod and sigh with resignation as I step out of Xaden's arms. "Ridoc, Drake, Cat, please stay with the horses and be ready to run if this goes badly. Mira, Dain, and Xaden, you're with me. Hopefully we'll be out quickly."

Ridoc dusts off his summer-weight uniform and gathers the reins. "I'll be nearby."

"I know," I reply. The reassuring way he said it makes my brow furrow.

"What?" Mira asks, spotting my face.

"Just wondering if we did the right thing letting Halden go by himself to see the king." My stomach sinks as I consider every way it could go wrong.

"Didn't exactly give us a choice," Ridoc says. "Courtlyn only allows aristocrats to enter."

"Even if he did, we can't be in two places at once." Mira nods toward the bookshop.

Right.

None of us draws a blade, but our hands remain loose and ready as we walk the short cobblestone path to the staired entrance midway down the south side of the shop. Mira enters first, mainly because no one seems to want to argue with her, and Xaden follows me in last, mainly because I don't think he'll ever trust anyone without a rebellion relic to ever truly cover his back.

The scents of dust and parchment fill the thick air as soon as our boots hit the hardwood floor, and I immediately understand why there isn't another shop on the side. Windows stretch from floor to ceiling, allowing natural light to pour in over the rows of bookshelves taller than I can possibly reach that jut out lengthwise from the wall on my right, matching their three-foot-long counterparts on our left, leaving a lengthy, clear aisle to a single counter. The titles are stacked haphazardly, but none touch the backs of the shelves, allowing for air to circulate. It's beautiful...but hot as hell.

If I'd thought the heat outside the shop was stifling, then the temperature inside—without the breeze—is truly oppressive. Sweat immediately beads beneath my armor and along the side of my neck.

There are a few customers browsing toward the narrow staircase in the back and a woman who appears to be in her sixties with a pert nose and a slicked-back salt-and-pepper bun behind the counter, licking her umber fingers every few seconds as she flips through the pages of a ledger, but I don't see anyone in the stacks to the right, so I nod toward the counter when Mira looks back at me.

We make our way down the aisle that opens into a small seating arrangement, and Dain keeps his eye on the customers in the back—a pair of men who have definitely taken notice of us. I glance over my shoulder as we approach the counter, finding Xaden has slipped behind the last shelf on the left and is currently leaned against the wall, wearing his usual expression of apathetic boredom.

Go figure, he's found what seems to be one of the only patches of shadow in the place to wait while I sort out whatever my father sent me here to find.

Dain moves to the edge of the counter, earning the shopkeeper's attention and placing himself between Mira and the customers, while Mira backs herself to the far edge of the seating group, setting a perimeter.

In a bookstore.

I manage to keep from rolling my eyes.

The shopkeeper's gaze darts from Dain to Mira to me before she closes the ledger and places it under the counter.

"Dain, could you ask her—" I set one hand on the counter for balance.

"I speak the common tongue," the woman says. "*We* are educated here in Deverelli."

I blink. "Right. Well, I was just wondering if you happen to know anyone by the name of Narelle."

Her eyes flare, and my stomach jumps into my throat when she glances over my right shoulder.

Mira.

"Fire-bringers!" someone shouts.

I draw two blades in the breath it takes to whip toward my sister.

Two assailants charge from the back shelves—the ones I'd previously, foolishly thought empty—and Mira sighs when one of them, a woman who looks to be my age, lifts a serrated dagger at her.

"If we have to," Mira says, drawing her own as the older man, someone closer to Brennan's build and age with spiky black hair and what seems to be a standard-issue white-and-gold tunic, runs down the aisle. Rage fills his eyes as he rushes toward me, two longer, serrated blades pointed in my direction.

I flip one of my daggers to the tip and prepare to throw, angling my body so the shopkeeper remains within sight.

The guy will be here in four seconds.

Three.

Two.

Xaden takes a single step, then kicks a large armchair straight into the man's path. It hits him square in the stomach, and his breath gushes out, but he regroups quickly, turning a glare in Xaden's direction with raised blades.

"You don't want to do that." Xaden shakes his head.

The guy shouts a battle cry, then draws back his right arm, and I flick my wrist. The dagger lands in his shoulder, and the man howls as crimson streaks down his white tunic and his blade falls to the floor.

"I warned you," Xaden says as the man hits his knees. "Your error was changing your assessment to targeting *me* as the threat and letting your eyes off *her.*" He takes his time walking over to the man as Mira punches her assailant in the face, knocking the woman unconscious. Then Xaden plucks the blades from the man like they're toys. "I *knew* some of you carried blades. There's no society in the world that doesn't keep some kind of cutting tool, and eventually... well, we all cut, don't we?"

Dain clicks his tongue, and I turn in his direction to find both his dagger and sword out, the shorter of the blades pointed at the shopkeeper and the longer at the customers. "I would stay back," he tells the men, who have drawn their own serrated daggers. "In fact, if there's a back door, I would find it and I would leave."

They scurry to do so.

The injured man falls forward, catching himself on his good hand before collapsing on his stomach, and Xaden leans over him.

"This is going to hurt," Xaden warns before retrieving my dagger from his shoulder. To his credit, the man doesn't scream or complain when Xaden wipes the blade clean on the back of his white tunic. "You really shouldn't raise a blade if you're not prepared to receive one."

Mira sheathes her daggers and steps over the unconscious woman. "Well, that was annoying. Are you protecting something? Or do you just really hate riders?" she asks the shopkeeper, who has backed herself into the corner as far as she possibly can.

"Only fire-bringers in this store looking for Narelle," the shopkeeper answers.

Protecting something. Got it.

The stairs creak, and the angle of Dain's sword changes as our heads swing collectively.

The man groans, and out of the corner of my eye, I see him struggle to get off the floor.

"No, no. Staying down is a safer bet for everyone involved," Xaden warns him. "She only wounded you, but I'll kill you if you take another step toward her, and it turns out that's bad for international relations." I glance his way as someone descends the steps, and he arches his scarred eyebrow. "I'm giving diplomacy a try. Not sure it's for me, though."

The man goes utterly limp.

Dain hesitates as a hunched figure rounds the end of the staircase.

The shopkeeper yells something in Krovlish, and I blink. "Did she just call her—"

"Mom," Dain confirms with a nod. "She said, 'No, Mom. Save yourself.'"

"We're not here to kill anyone," I tell the shopkeeper as her mother walks into the light, leaning heavily on a walking cane. Her hair is silver, and the lines of her face have deepened with time, but she has the same pert nose as her daughter, the same deep-brown eyes and round face. "You're Narelle," I guess.

Dain lowers his sword as she approaches, then sheathes it as she completely skirts around him, taking in the scene of what I assume is her shop.

She studies Xaden through thick glasses, then Dain, Mira, and finally me, her gaze lingering on my hair before she finally nods. "And you must be Asher Sorrengail's daughter, here to collect the books he wrote for you."

My heart *stops*.

She won't understand why you've kept her in the dark. You left too soon, left too many of your plans unfinished. Now we can only hope the bond between our daughters is strong enough to endure the paths they've chosen. They'll need each other to survive.

—RECOVERED, UNSENT CORRESPONDENCE OF GENERAL LILITH SORRENGAIL

CHAPTER TWENTY-FOUR

"Books?" I whisper, my fingers curling around the dagger I realize is still in my left hand.

Narelle tilts her head. "I did not stutter." She looks pointedly at the armchair. "Put that back in its place."

Xaden lifts a brow but does as she asks, then crosses the small section of the room and sheathes my dagger at my hip.

"Thank you," I whisper.

He brushes a kiss over my temple, then takes the empty spot at my right side.

"Get off the floor, Urson—you're bleeding everywhere. Take your sister to the back and wake her up. Did I not say you were ill-prepared to carry a weapon?" Narelle lectures as she avoids the spilled blood. "Please forgive my grandchildren. They took our task of protecting the books from any riders who aren't...you a little too seriously." She sinks into the chair. "Thank you, young man," she says to Xaden, then gives him a second look before glancing at Dain. "My, the Continent does have some fine-looking men."

A corner of Xaden's mouth quirks upward, and I can't help but silently agree with her.

"Mom." The shopkeeper rushes to her side, no doubt still worried we'll attack her mother. Urson hurries to do Narelle's bidding, helping his sister off the floor as she reluctantly comes to from Mira's last punch. They disappear into the back, and I almost feel bad for them until I remember that they attacked us.

"I'm ninety-three, Leona, I'm not dead." She waves her daughter off. "Or what is it you Amaralis say? I have not yet *met Malek*. He's your god of death, is he not?"

My brow furrows at the unknown term: *Amaralis*.

"Isn't he everyone's god of death?" Mira leans back against the nearest row of bookshelves.

I shake my head. "Deverelli don't worship gods."

"It's why we're considered the most neutral of the isles. Perfect for trade." Narelle shrugs. "What you call gods, we call science. What you call fate, we call coincidence. What you call the divine intervention of love, we call…" She flourishes her hand. "Alchemy. Two substances combined to make something entirely new, not unlike what's between the two of you." She glances between Xaden and me and sets her hand on her chest.

My heart twists. If she only knew how close she was to my very thoughts earlier today.

She wiggles her finger at Xaden. "I heard you saying you'd kill my grandson if he took another step toward your beloved, young man. How illogically, toxically romantic of you. Have to admit, that kind of confident violence isn't what I pictured when Asher talked about you, but the brown hair, those…I guess they're brown eyes, and how utterly smitten he predicted you two would eventually be for each other? Well, he described you almost perfectly, Dain Aetos."

Oh, fucking kill me now.

My mouth opens, then shuts.

Xaden raises both eyebrows and presses his lips between his teeth.

Dain rubs the back of his neck.

Mira snorts once, covers her mouth with her hand, then doubles over *laughing*. "I'm sorry," she forces out and straightens, quickly masking her face and clearing her throat, but she slips again, her shoulders shaking. "I can't. I just can't. I need a second." She walks behind the row of shelves, hopefully to compose herself.

My face feels like it's been blasted by dragon fire.

"How would you like this to go?" Dain asks me as Narelle glances among the three of us, her silver brows knitting.

"Just like it's gone for the last eighteen months," Xaden answers, losing any and all trace of the niceties he showed Dain an hour ago. "Everyone assumes she'll wind up with you, but it's my last name she ends up wearing on her flight jacket in formation."

"Seriously?" Words absolutely *fail* me that he would go there. It was *one* time. Fine, twice if I count the return trip from Samara after we got back together.

"Glad to see you're feeling like yourself again." Dain leans back against the counter. "But we don't have last names on our flight jackets."

"And yet you get the fucking point." Xaden's jaw ticks.

Narelle's gaze narrows on Xaden through her thick lenses. "You aren't Dain."

Xaden shakes his head.

"I'm Dain." Dain raises his hand briefly.

"And he is?" Narelle asks me.

"Xaden Riorson." I lift my chin as if I'm answering to my father for my choice. "And he's mine, even when he's being a possessive ass."

"Fen Riorson's son." Narelle drums her gnarled fingertips on the armrest. "Asher certainly didn't predict *that*."

"He would have if he'd ever met him." I reach for Xaden's hand and lace our fingers.

"Our mother knew," Mira says, taking her place at the end of the bookshelf. "She wasn't enthusiastic about it or anything, but she knew love when she saw it. But she certainly never told us about our father coming here."

"She wouldn't have, would she?" Narelle shifts in her seat. "When did he die?"

"A little less than three years ago," I answer gently. "His heart failed."

Narelle's face crumples for a few sorrowful breaths, but she nods through it as if having a conversation with herself, then lifts her head again. "Your father risked all your lives to hide away his life's work with the sole purpose that you find it, Violet. He left the last of it with me almost four years ago with explicit instructions that you only be given it if you had attained the intelligence and understanding you would need to comprehend it."

I stiffen.

"That's…" Dain shakes his head.

"That's Dad," Mira says slowly.

"You've got this." Xaden squeezes my hand.

I fight to swallow the sudden lump in my dry throat. "He told me to bring you the rarest item I possess." An ironic laugh bubbles up. "And I thought…" I shake my head, realizing the work we've gone through to haul the satchel all this way has been for nothing.

"You thought it's Deverelli, so naturally, we trade in goods, treasures." Narelle folds her hands in her lap.

"He meant my mind." I glance at Mira, but her gaze is locked on the floor. "That's why he said not to send another in my stead."

"The books are only for you," Narelle confirms, and Leona perches on the arm of her mother's chair. "I have three simple questions, and if you're capable of answering them, the books are yours."

"Arrogant to think you have any right to keep something our father wrote for Violet based on your judgment." Mira's tone could grate stone.

"It's fine," I assure her, refusing to waver, even in this heat. "Ask."

Narelle shoots my sister a withering look and then turns her attention to me. "He left a manuscript for you. What is the title?"

"*Subjugated: The Second Uprising of the Krovlan People* by Lieutenant Colonel Asher Sorrengail," I answer. "Which you already know that I know. How else would I be here?"

She taps her forefinger in obvious impatience. "In chapter fourteen, your father alludes to the Krovlan uprising falling apart because of Deverelli but does not go into specifics. Any"—her gaze skims over my black uniform—"scribe worth her wisdom wouldn't have been satisfied with his speculation. So tell me, what's your hypothesis?"

Out of *everything* in the book, that's what she asks?

"Easy. Krovla didn't keep their part of whatever deal they made with Deverelli. Rather than lose their reputation, Deverelli withdrew their brokerage, hence the removal of the other isle's troops, and then told the Poromish king regent where to find the rebels. End of rebellion." I shrug.

"Not good enough." She shakes her head, and my stomach sinks. "Why did it fall apart? What was brokered?"

"That's not fair—" Dain starts.

Narelle lifts a hand, demanding his silence. "She knows the answer."

I sigh. "I...have an idea. I just don't like being wrong." Or, in this case, right.

"You're among friends." Her smile implies otherwise.

Fine. Sweat drips down the back of my neck, but I gather up the courage to look like a fool. "I think they promised dragons and couldn't deliver."

"They what?" Mira squawks.

Xaden tenses, and Dain pivots fully to face me, his eyes impossibly wide, but Narelle's slow smile tells me I'm either horrifically wrong—or tragically right.

"Present your proof," she says in a tone that reminds me eerily of Markham. "Convince that one." She points to Dain.

I tighten my grip on Xaden's hand, and his thumb strokes over mine. "Public Notice 433.323 acknowledges a failed border breach attempt by Krovlan forces near the outpost of Athebyne on December eleventh, 433 AU, two days before the Midnight Massacre. The only other record of that event exists in the journal of Colonel Hashbeigh, the commander of the outpost, who oversaw the interrogations." I look over at Dain. "Dad drilled that into me while he was working on the manuscript, and I didn't understand why then, but obviously I get it now. I think it was the year you were obsessed with the tactics of defeating Emerald Sea piracy or something."

Dain stiffens. "It was a really big problem in the fifth century."

I keep from rolling my eyes. "Stay with me here. We were on the couch. Dad was pacing in front of the fire, and you thought it was ludicrous that the soldiers had crossed into Navarre to acquire *tailfeathers*, remember?"

He winces. "Right. Yes. And your father told me I was a lost cause if I ever wanted to take the entrance exam for the Scribe Quadrant if I couldn't remember to apply my superior linguistics skills to all areas of analyzing important historical data. Not that I ever wanted to be a scribe, but still. Good times. Thank you for the reminder."

"Is this going somewhere, or are we just enjoying a moment of nostalgia?" Xaden asks.

"Apply your superior linguistics skills, Dain," I prompt him. "The interrogation was recorded in the common tongue—"

Dain's eyes widen. "But the raiders spoke Krovlish, and descriptors follow nouns in Krovlish. They were hunting feathertails. Dragons."

I nod. "I think Deverelli brokered a deal with Krovla and an unnamed isle that the isle would provide the army and Krovla would provide dragons. When they were unable to do so, the deal fell apart, the Midnight Massacre happened, and Krovla remained a part of Poromiel."

Dain folds his arms across his chest. "They were dealing in dragons." He looks over to Narelle. "I believe her. It's just going to take me a minute to absorb it. One does not just…deal in dragons, let alone take babies to isles that don't have magic. Not when you risk the wrath of the Empyrean."

"Oh, wait until you realize that your dad knows my dad's book has *something* to do with feathertails, which means Dad knew to stop trusting him at some point," I add.

Dain's face swings my way, and his stricken expression makes me wish I could take the words back.

"Third question," Narelle announces, and it feels particularly cruel, given what she's just put me through.

"Ask it." My tone leaves something to be desired.

"What made you leave the prince?" She tilts her head to the side, and her eyes light up like we've gathered for tea and gossip.

"I'm sorry?" I lean forward, like it's at all possible I could have misheard her.

"The prince?" She clasps her hands together. "Your father knew it wouldn't last, but I'd like to know the final straw."

"Any chance you want to swoop down and set this shop on fire?" I ask Tairn.

"As the Dark One said, it doesn't bode well for international relations," he answers.

"I would," Andarna offers. *"But then you wouldn't get your books."*

"I…" The weight of every stare in the room flushes my skin so hot, I feel on the edge of burnout without even a hint of magic. "I left him because I found him in a delicate situation with one of his professors."

Narelle leans forward and lifts her eyebrows. "He was having sex with a professor?"

"Mom!" Leona chides.

"What a fucking asshole," Dain mutters. "Why didn't you tell me?"

"What were you going to do? Punch out the crown prince of Navarre?" I counter.

Dain's brow furrows.

"Yes," Xaden answers. "Still might."

"So you left him in a jealous rage even with the crown of Navarre in your hands?" Narelle prods. "Did he come begging your forgiveness? Did you take him back?"

I can definitely see why she owns a bookstore, and which genre might just be her favorite. "I've never sought a crown, and besides, it's not in Halden's nature to beg forgiveness of anyone. I closed the door and didn't bother speaking to him until a few weeks ago. He didn't love me, not in the way I deserve to be loved, and no amount of power is worth staying with someone who doesn't love you."

"You know your value," Narelle says softly with a nod. "Your father would be proud. Get her the books."

Leona stands, then leaves us waiting in the seating area while she disappears into the back, and I deflate with relief, sagging against Xaden's side.

Mira slips her empty pack off her shoulders, then sets it on the unoccupied chair next to Narelle. "I'll carry them for Violet, unless of course you think my father would have a problem with that. Promise not to read them or anything." Her biting tone sends a shiver of guilt straight up my spine. Why was Dad so adamant only I collect them?

Narelle simply smiles and crosses her ankles in front of her. "And that right there is why he didn't leave them for you, dear. We all have a part to play in what's coming for us; this one is simply hers. While he was busy raising Violet for this particular mission, your mother was raising you. I wonder what legacy you've inherited."

Mira's eyes narrow.

We leave the bookstore ten minutes later with six tomes written by my father. And every single one of them is passcode-locked.

• • •

Later that afternoon, I lean my head back against the rim of the carved wooden bathtub in the chamber adjacent to the bedroom Xaden and I have been given and listen to birds I can't identify chirp outside the window above my feet. I'm too short to see the spectacular view of the water, but the sky isn't bad, either, softening with the colors of an approaching sunset.

What time is it? I wonder if Halden's back. If he's managed to secure permission for us to use Deverelli as a home post to visit the other isles or broached the subject of the seventh breed. I reach for the bond to ask Xaden, only to sigh with frustration at the instant reminder that we don't work that way here.

The breeze picks up the white curtains and billows them toward me as the water chills to a temperature that might make me reach for hot water at Basgiath but is definitely welcome here in Deverelli.

Though my toes are pruning, telling me it's time to get out.

"Vi?" Xaden knocks on the door.

"You can come in." A slow smile spreads across my face.

It slips completely when he opens the door and leans in wearing nothing but a towel wrapped around his hips. Gods, is he perfectly beautiful. Wet hair. Still a little scruffy. Water droplets clinging to the lines of his muscles. Abs for days and days and *days*.

"Just letting you know I'm back..." The words die as his gaze catches on my bare shoulders, which is all I'm pretty sure he can see given the height of this tub. Well, my shoulders and my very wet, very unbound hair. "Damn. Just...damn."

"I said you should have stayed and had a bath in our room. Lots of space in here. You didn't need to go borrow Ridoc's." I tap the copper pipe at the foot of the tub with my toe. "They really do have some pretty fabulous plumbing."

"Yeah." His eyes darken and his grip on the door handle whitens. "I figured it was polite to give you time to soak your muscles to help recover after all that riding."

"Polite? How very kind of you." I gather all my hair in my hand and pull it over my left shoulder so it's ready to wring out, then hit the lever with my foot to start draining the tub, trying to focus anywhere but on him and that incredible body he insists on walking around in.

"And do you feel recovered?" His voice lowers.

"A little exposed after being interrogated about my intelligence and my love life, but otherwise fine." Reaching to the right, I grab the soft white towel I left on the little bench as the water empties with a gurgle, then turn my back to Xaden and stand, quickly wrapping the towel around me.

"You're fine," he repeats. "Not dizzy. Not sore. Not tired? Because we just flew all last night."

"I'm not sure I want to go climb the Gauntlet or anything"—I lean left, wringing my hair out over the tub—"but yes, I'm feeling as good as it gets." Clean, fed, and ready to curl up with the man I love.

"Good," he says against my ear, and I gasp with surprise as he grabs hold of my waist and turns me to face him. "Because I'm done being polite."

His mouth crashes into mine.

The most useless word in the language of aristocracy has always been and will forever be: love. Marriage is a necessary evil to secure the line. Nothing more. Save love for your children.

—Confiscated Correspondence of Fen Riorson
to Unknown Intended Recipient

CHAPTER
TWENTY-FIVE

I abandon my towel and my common sense, throwing my arms around his neck and pouring my whole heart into the kiss. Who cares if we're in a house full of servants and a viscount I don't trust? If Xaden has set sexual limits between us the last six weeks? He's kissing me like I'm the only air he can breathe, and that's all that matters—all that I can *allow* to matter.

My wet feet slip on the tile, and then there's nothing beneath them as I'm lifted to his chest. The sensation of my bare breasts against his damp skin makes me gasp around his tongue.

He groans, holding me with one hand under my ass as I wrap my legs around his waist. I nudge his towel straight to the floor before locking my ankles, leaving us skin to skin as he kisses me senseless, robbing me of logic and replacing it with pure *want*.

Our mouths collide again and again without finesse or seduction. There's no flirtation or coy games here. No, it's all hunger and blatant, naked demand. It's fucking perfect, unrestrained, and absolutely greedy.

The room moves, or maybe that's us. Either way, the lighting changes, and I find myself perched on the edge of the small breakfast table a few feet from the bedroom window. I rip my mouth from his to scan our surroundings, but Xaden cups my chin and pulls me right back.

"No one can see at this angle. I checked," he promises, then goes right back to kissing me, wiping every protest out of my head with the indulgent stroke of his tongue.

Wait. He checked. He's thought about this.

Oh gods, this might actually happen.

Heat and need rush through me, bringing every nerve to blaring life. It doesn't feel like it's only been six weeks since I've had all of him above me, below me, within me—it seems like it's been *years*.

He winds my wet hair around his hand, then tugs my head backward gently, breaking the kiss and setting his lips to my throat. Every touch of his lips sends a jolt of *yes* straight down my spine, and they quickly gather into an aching knot of *please* right between my thighs.

My nails rake into his hair and I arch for more, whimpering softly when he delivers, toying with me expertly. He uses his firm lips, soft tongue, and rough stubble to their every advantage, until I'm pretty sure he could get me off by just kissing my neck.

"I love your skin," he says, working his way down to my collarbone. "You're so damned soft."

My pulse jumps and my hands drift to the strong line of his shoulders, touching every inch of his warm skin that I can reach. I want to lay him down on that bed and lick every single line that he's kept hidden away from me for the last six weeks, but there's no way I'm going to chance him stopping this for a change of position.

He abandons my hair, then brings both hands to cup my breasts. I suck in a swift breath when he lowers his mouth to one peak and then uses his tongue and teeth to worship it. Holy *shit* does that feel good. My body is positively starved for his touch, and it's all I can do to stifle a flat-out moan when he moves to the other.

"Shh," he whispers with a playful smile. "Wouldn't want anyone to hear."

It's the smile that does me in, a fear that borders on frenzy breaking through the haze of pleasure he's building. "You can't tease me." I shake my head.

His hands shift to my hips and he stands to his full height, his brow creasing as confusion fills those gorgeous eyes looking down at me.

"I mean, you can," I immediately blurt, my hands falling to the table. "It's just that I want you, *need* you, and I'm trying really hard to respect the whole no-sex aspect of the rules we laid down, and if you tease me—"

He fucking *smirks*, and I debate going back to the throwing-daggers-at-his-head stage of our relationship. "There's no magic here."

"Yes, I know." I fold my arms over my breasts and move to close my thighs, but he's standing between them.

"There's no magic here," he says again, lowering his head, ghosting his lips over mine. "I can fuck you as many times as we want, as many times as you can take, and I can't lose control."

"Oh." My whole body draws tighter than a bowstring, and my breath catches.

"Oh." He runs his thumbs up the insides of my thighs and locks his eyes on mine. "Does that sound like something you'd be interested in?"

I run my tongue over my lower lip, and his hands flex. "Only if you are. I feel like…" I swallow. "I just don't want to push you for something you don't feel comfortable doing."

He takes my hand and wraps it around the length of his hard cock. "Does that feel like I'm not comfortable?"

I squeeze my hand on reflex, and he moans low in his throat, his eyes sliding shut. My core clenches at just how hot, how thick, how perfect he is.

"Fuck, Violet, you do that again, and this will be over in *minutes*." There's an edge of desperation in his eyes when they open, and he hisses through his teeth as he guides my hand away from his body. "Me holding back from you has been purely for your sake, not mine, trust me. I want you from the second I wake until the moment I fall asleep. I *dream* about you."

My lips part and warmth spreads throughout my chest. "I love you."

"I love you." He cups my knees. "And here, I don't have my fucking powers. Don't get me wrong, there's part of that I am very all right with—"

My stomach drops. The venin part.

"But no shadows," he continues, "no intention, no lesser magics? I can't even create a sound shield to keep everyone in this house from hearing what you sound like when you come, and that feels…" His jaw flexes.

"I know," I whisper, skimming the back of my hand along his stubble. Not having that constant stream of power buzzing beneath my skin makes me feel… less than whole.

"And I can't talk to Sgaeyl," he adds. "I can't even sense *you*, which is killing me. But in return for all that shit?" His scarred brow rises. "I get to do my favorite thing in the world, which happens to be fucking you. Now, I have about six weeks to make up for, and love, we're wasting time."

I brace my hands beside me and smile when his eyes darken at the sight of my body. "Well, if you insist."

A slow smile curves his mouth, and he pushes my knees farther apart. "I insist."

My laugh abruptly transforms to a moan when he sinks to his knees and sets his mouth on me.

Oh. *Fuck.*

He doesn't tease or toy—no, he immediately swirls his tongue around my clit and sinks two fingers inside me. "Damn, I've missed your taste."

"Xaden!" Pleasure jolts through my system like power, buzzing in my veins and landing low in my stomach. I slam my hand over my mouth to catch my next moan as he starts to move those exceptionally talented fingers, his tongue working in rhythm to play my body like an instrument created just for him.

Tension gathers and coils, and it's all I can do to stay upright, to keep balanced with one hand and stifle my moans with the other. I waver, my body swaying, and Xaden reaches for my mouth.

I pull his hand to my lips and press a hard kiss to his palm as my hips begin to rock against his face and other hand, chasing the high I can feel approaching with every thrust of his fingers, every flick of his tongue.

But I want more. I want him inside me, his arms around me, his voice in my head... We can have all but the last and it's more than enough.

It's good. So fucking good. My breath catches and my thighs stiffen.

He curls his fingers and lashes his tongue against my clit, and I *unravel*. My climax hits hard and fast, and I shout against his palm as white-hot pleasure pulls me over the edge in bright waves that hit again and again, robbing me of breath as they race through me.

He coaxes the aftershocks from me relentlessly, working my body until the last of them shudder through.

"I have no words for the havoc that mouth can wreak. Get up here." I kiss his wrist, and he stands, dragging his thumb along his lower lip. My temperature rises another degree and my breath hitches as my gaze rakes over him.

Mine. It's the only word that comes to mind as I devour the sight of him.

"Keep looking at me like that..." he warns, prowling toward me. He slides his hands beneath my thighs and lifts me farther back on the table.

"And you'll what?" I lie down, bringing my heels to the surface as he climbs onto me, bracing his weight on his palms.

"Good point." He lowers his mouth to mine, and his arms tremble slightly. "I need you."

"I'm right here." I lift my knees to bracket his hips and reach between our bodies to bring the head of his cock to my entrance. We both inhale at the contact, and his eyes flare.

"Are you sure? You know what I am," he says slowly, and a flicker of something that looks like fear crosses his face.

"I know *who* you are." I cradle his cheeks with my hands. "*Now*, Xaden. You have six weeks to make up for, remember?"

He nods, keeping his gaze locked with mine, then shifts a hand to my hip and drives into me in one long thrust, taking me inch by inch by inch until he's all I can feel. The pressure, the stretch, the feel of him is so perfect that my foolish eyes prickle because I've missed this connection so *damn* much.

"Are you all right?" His eyes widen and his hips jerk back.

"I'm fine!" I wrap my legs around him. "I just missed this."

"Me too." He drops his forehead to mine and rolls his hips, sinking into me. We both moan.

"I miss being inside your head." He withdraws, then snaps forward again, and I see *stars*. Pleasure shoots through my very bones as he begins that deep, slow rhythm I can never get enough of. "I love having every part of you when we're like this."

"Same." I wind my arms around his neck and hold on, arching to meet every delectable thrust as sweat quickly slicks our bodies. "I love when you talk to me..." My fingers slide over his lips. "Even when your mouth is otherwise occupied."

He grins, but it slips when I swivel my hips and he groans. "Fuck, you feel so damned good. I'm never giving you up. You know that, right? You had your chance to run. You should have run, Vi." He punctuates each claim with a harder, deeper thrust that has me straining for breath, for reasonable thought that goes beyond *more* and *yes* as wood creaks beneath us.

I pull his mouth down to mine and breathe through the keening pleasure that's building within me again, deeper and hotter than before. "I'm never running. It's you and me, no matter what."

"You and me," he repeats, sweat beading on his brow as his hips drive me into the table, and it creaks, starting to rock with us.

"Just don't stop." I'm pretty sure stopping might kill me. I hold tight with my arms, my legs, clinging to him with everything I have as he lowers his weight to his forearm, cushions the back of my head with his hand, and drives into me, taking me higher and higher.

Wood snaps a second before gravity shifts, and my stomach hollows as we fall.

My skin only touches his on impact.

He has me held against his chest with one arm, while his other and his knees took the brunt of our mishap.

"Are you all right?" I ask, my face buried in his neck.

"I'm fine. We fell three feet, not thirty." He laughs, rolling us off the destroyed table and onto the hardwood floor, careful not to crush my ankles. Then he picks up right where he left off, except this time I'm close enough to the bedrail to push back against him for leverage.

"Hold on." He reaches over my head, retrieves a pillow, then slides it under my hips. The next thrust hits such a sweet spot that I can *taste* it.

He muffles my cry with his mouth as I arch up for him again and again, savoring every breath through his gritted teeth, every strained line of his incredible body, every drugging kiss as the pleasure spins tighter and tighter between us.

And gods help me, I hold on as long as humanly possible. I don't want it to end, don't want to go back to the endless wanting. A whimper escapes my lips as I fight the pressure, the oncoming wave I know I can't avoid, not when every roll of his hips drives me toward it.

"You have to let go for me, love." Xaden nips my lower lip.

"I'm not…" I gasp, my body twisting beneath his. Fuck, it feels too damned good.

"You are." His hand drifts down my stomach. "I don't need to be in your head to know why you're fighting it. This isn't the only time, Vi. We have all night. Come for me."

All night sounds better than any heaven I know of.

I sink my fingers into his hair as he strokes my hypersensitive clit with the precise pressure he knows I like, and I *shatter*. I fly apart at the seams as the orgasm surges through me in arching pulses. He swallows my moans with a kiss as the waves break again and again, and then he puts me back together with soft strokes of his hands as I come back down.

"So beautiful," he whispers against my mouth, and only when I fall against the floor, a trembling, happily content mess, does he kiss me like he's searching for his own soul and finds his own completion with a few final hard thrusts and a low groan.

I hold him tight as he rolls us to the side, his back to the destruction, and he cradles my head on his biceps.

I trace the line of the scar across his brow as my heartbeat settles and commit the contours of his face to memory again while he watches me with a glazed, soft expression. There's too much of us missing here for this to truly be *us*, but it's a version that I want to cling to, where he isn't plagued by the threat of turning, where he isn't telling me that I have to learn how to kill him. "We could just stay here," I whisper.

His brow twitches, and he pushes my hair back from my face. "Here as in this room?"

"Here as in Deverelli." I run my fingers along his jaw. "I can take Tecarus's offer…if Tairn and Andarna agree. I'm sure they would if it means you stop all progression until I can find a cure. You and Sgaeyl could stay here while I do the research—"

He slides his thumb over my lips. "She's in pain."

I blink.

How could I have missed that? Guilt weighs down my shoulders.

"All the dragons are, I think, not that they'll admit it, but I don't think they can survive—or at least thrive the way they do at home—away from magic. I could never cause Sgaeyl pain." He skims his callused hand down the side of my neck and over my ribs to settle on the slope of my waist. "And I could never let you abandon everyone you love."

A boulder lodges in the middle of my throat.

Someone knocks.

"Hey...uh..." Ridoc says through the door.

My face flushes, and I cover my mouth with my hand.

"We're all good," Xaden calls out with a wicked grin, stroking my hip.

"Yeah, that's...great," Ridoc says. "No, I'm not—" His voice muffles.

"Look, we have a problem here," Cat snaps.

"Shouting it through the door isn't going to help," Dain says.

"Get away from there!" Mira lectures, and both Xaden and I scramble to our feet. "Violet, answer the door."

How many people are crowded into that hallway?

Xaden's faster to the bathroom than I am, and he throws my towel through the doorway, making sure I catch it before striding out with his own wrapped around his hips.

"You can't answer the door like that," I hiss at him, covering myself and bemoaning how long it will take to get my clothes on.

"Neither can you, and I'm sure as fuck not offering the sight of you in a towel up to Aetos after hearing that your father basically planned your wedding to the asshole," Xaden retorts just as quietly, his hand on the doorknob.

I recognize defeat and step toward the wall, out of sight, as Xaden opens the door.

"To what do we owe the honor of a visit from every single one of you?" he asks. "I thought two of you were flying the southern route to confirm there aren't any irids hiding out here?"

Silence answers.

I lean left, just enough to see Xaden glance over his shoulder. "Yes, the table is broken. Now, what do you need?"

"You two totally broke it, didn't you?" Ridoc asks on the edge of laughter. "Like that armoire no one was supposed to notice getting hauled out of her room during first year?"

"The what?" Mira's voice rises, and I lean against the wall, letting my head fall back in mortification.

"What could be so fucking important that you're trying to ruin my *one* evening?" Xaden snaps.

"A messenger came," Dain says. "King Courtlyn has decided to *keep* Halden."

My stomach pitches.

"Too fucking bad for Halden." Xaden shrugs.

"Xaden!" I lift my brows at him, and his mouth tightens.

"We're flying out as planned, but Tecarus needs you," Dain continues. "You're the only *aristocrat* they'll let in."

"You have to go," I whisper.

Xaden looks my way, and too many emotions to count cross his beautiful face. Want. Desperation. Pleading. Frustration. Anger. Resignation. "Fuck. Fine." He slams the door in their faces. "*We* have to go."

In the first twenty-four hours of removal from source magic, the subject—an asim—presented as even-tempered. But withdrawal quickly revealed the subject's true nature, requiring the subject's immediate transfer to stage two of the study.

Her results can be found with group thirty-three B under the category: DEATH BY FIRE, and subsequently group forty-six C under the category: DEATH BY POISON.

—A STUDY IN THE ANATOMY OF THE ENEMY BY CAPTAIN DOMINIC PRISHEL

CHAPTER
TWENTY-SIX

Deverelli is beautiful by sunset, or at least it would be if I could concentrate on taking the time to really appreciate the isle.

Instead, I'm focused on exactly how close Tairn thinks he can fly to the treetops without actually crashing into one as we race along the hillside ahead of Sgaeyl.

To Andarna's disdain, Tairn ordered her to remain behind for her own safety.

"You're sure we're out of range of the cross-bolts?" I ask, hunkered down against the pommels of my saddle, my pack weighing me down, as if my slight stature could possibly affect his aerodynamics.

"They are made not to rotate this way but to defend the shoreline. They woefully underestimate our intelligence."

Still, the existence of the cross-bolts means this isle wants to do us harm. And it possibly already is.

"Are you in pain? Is Andarna?" I ask as I spot four enormous gray pillars ahead, supporting the remnants of an aqueduct as they curve around the hillside, marking the path to their palace.

"What would make you ask that?" His gruff tone answers for him as he crosses over an open space that looks to be in the arts district from what I

remember reading, and a chorus of shouts sounds then vanishes as we pass by.

Sorry, but if you abduct our royalty, we scare the shit out of you with our dragons. Seems pretty fair to me.

"Why didn't you tell me?" Guilt for even suggesting to Xaden that we stay, for not realizing it, settles on my shoulders.

"You live in pain. Do you feel as though you need to alert me every time your knee twinges or your joints slip?" Even his wingbeats change, becoming more staccato. *"There have been several moments, even here, when your heartbeat has elevated and you have approached unconsciousness, yet you have not made special note."*

I lean with him as he banks left, following the centuries-old aqueduct. *"That's just everyday life for me. This isn't normal for you."*

"Andarna shows no sign of trouble. I am inconvenienced, annoyed, and cut off from my source of power, strength, and my mate's thoughts, but I am still Tairneanach, son of Murtcuideam and Fiaclanfuil, descended from—"

"All right, yes, I get it. You are superior in all ways." I interrupt him before he can get through his whole pompous lineage like I don't have it memorized by now.

We level out, following the topography, and I take in as much of the layout as I can before we're too far overhead. Tairn's size is a distinct advantage in battle, but it's a pain in the ass when I'm trying to see what's below me.

The palace is unlike anything I've ever witnessed. Not only is the four-story structure carved into the hillside, but so is a hundred-yard meadow ahead of it. It's truly spectacular, a feat of engineering when it was accomplished a thousand years ago, and testament to their traditions that it's still their seat of power and hasn't faded to ruin like so many of the ancient castles of kingdoms past on the Continent.

Soft blue light glows in orbs down a central path of the clearing, lighting our way as the sun sinks behind the hills and we descend toward the muted green grass. The space is wide enough to support the width of two dragons with fully extended wings, but probably four if they held them retracted.

"Do you know where you're going?" Tairn asks as we approach, his wings flaring to slow our descent.

"The majority of their formal spaces are outside, according to what I've read, as are the king's chambers, just beyond the first row of trees, so in theory…yes." I position my body for landing as he flies over a platoon of panicked guards bearing what appear to be silver-tipped spears, then sets us down to the left of the row of incandescent blue orbs. *"Not that they're going to let me in."*

Sgaeyl and Xaden land to the right.

Shouting ensues as I unbuckle my belt and move for Tairn's shoulder.

"No changes to the plan?" I ask, steeling my nerves for what's bound to be a contentious confrontation.

I want my fucking power back, and I want it *now*.

"None. I will be with you all the way, Silver One."

His promise reassures me as I dismount, the weight of the pack jarring my spine on impact. I shake it off, then walk toward Xaden, who's already waiting for me at the center of the path between the rows of blue orbs. His swords are strapped to his back, but his daggers are within easy reach, and he carries the same oversize pack he's hauled with us from Navarre, which he'd told me was for *just in case.*

I guess an isle kingdom kidnapping your prince qualifies as *just in case.*

I can't help but do a double take at one of the orbs as I walk by, stepping into the path. The blue glow isn't from a single light source, but dozens of large, bioluminescent insects with translucent wings, all feeding from— A smile breaks across my face. "They're Fallorinia moths."

"What?" Xaden's boots crunch on the rocky path as he walks my way.

"Fallorinia moths." I touch the cool glass orb. "We don't have them on the Continent, just their sister species. They light up when they feed from honeycomb. I read about them in *Sir Zimly's Guide to Deverelli Fauna*, but I had no idea they harnessed them for light. It's brilliant. Poisonous but brilliant."

"Of course you did," Xaden counters. "But we should probably concentrate on the dozen pissed-off guards headed our way."

"Fair point." I throw my braid over my shoulder, cursing that I hadn't had time to put it up as usual, and turn to face the approaching horde of angry white-clad Deverelli. I'm guessing we have less than ten seconds, and those spear tips look mighty unfriendly. My hands dangle near the sheaths along my sides, but Xaden stands with his feet braced apart, his arms folded across his chest as if he isn't that concerned.

But his eyes sweep across the group methodically, no doubt putting them all into threat categories. I focus on the fox-like woman on the right who keeps flaring her nose and stepping off the path like I like I won't notice, and her male counterpart on the left, doing his best to fade into the shadows, not realizing he's in the presence of a master.

"Look, more blades," Xaden says. "And here I thought you were a weaponless society."

The one in the center with a blue sash steps forward and starts shouting. I can only pick out a few words, two of which are *stop* and *kill*.

"We could really use Dain right about now," I whisper.

"I could live the rest of my life without ever hearing you say that again," Xaden replies.

We could really use the bond, too.

"Do any of you happen to speak the common tongue?" I ask when the serrated silver blades of their raised spears are about five feet from our chests.

They pause, and I shoot a warning look at the nose-flarer on my right.

"You are forbidden to enter the palace of King Courtlyn the Fourth," Blue Sash declares, jabbing his blade in our direction but not close enough to merit a reaction, "ruler of Deverelli, master of the trade, keeper of the troths, justice of the tribunal, and heir of the antiquities."

By the time he finishes, it's hard to keep my brows level.

"Sounds humble," Xaden says. "Can't wait to meet him."

"You won't be." Blue Sash steps forward, blade raised.

My hands flex near my sheaths as the woman on my right swings her blade back and forth between me and Tairn's slow but steady approach. His head is low, almost even with the ground, and his wings are tucked in tight for protection. If I wasn't his, I'd probably be shitting my pants.

"We will," Xaden counters with a bored sigh. "And I'm trying *really* hard to be diplomatic, since that's the role I've been handed, but let me put this in terms you'll understand. Your king kidnapped our asshole of a prince, and there's a large part of me that wouldn't mind him staying here and annoying the shit out of *you* for the rest of his miserable life, but that would make things difficult back home for someone I have…complicated loyalty toward, so I'm going to need the prick back."

Aaric.

Blue Sash's brow puckers, but his blade doesn't lower.

"Now," Xaden orders. "I have *much* more important things to see to this evening."

Flare Nose to my right swings her blade fully at Tairn and pulls back her arm, preparing to thrust with a full-on battle cry.

I draw my blade the same second Tairn drops his jaw and roars, the sound shattering every glass orb within a dozen feet of us and leaving my ears ringing.

"Was that really necessary?" My right ear won't work for a month.

"No, but I found it amusing."

The guard drops her spear and stands there, shaking like a leaf for several seconds before she slowly turns around to face us, her brown eyes wider than should be physically possible, her bronzed skin suddenly rather wan.

I tilt my head at her. "They don't like it when you do that."

Trembling, she drags her gaze to mine, then collapses to sit on the ground.

There's a definite quiver in Blue Sash's arms, but I give him credit for still holding his blade. "You. May not. Enter."

"I'm Xaden Riorson, the Duke of Tyrrendor." Xaden inclines his head. "He's probably expecting me."

Blue Sash blinks, then looks in my direction. "And you are?"

Well, shit. My mouth opens—

"My consort," Xaden replies casually. "Violet Sorrengail."

What the actual fuck? My jaw snaps shut so hard my teeth click. I want our bond back and I want it back right now. He can't just announce things like that without at least a discussion.

"Are congratulations or commiserations in order?" Tairn lifts his head.

"Shut up." I sheathe my dagger to keep from chucking it at the man I love.

"In that case." Blue Sash raises his spear fully upright, and the others follow his lead. "If you'll divest of your weaponry here, we'll escort you to the table."

"That's not happening." I shake my head. This place took my lightning and my bond. Malek himself would have to pluck my daggers from my sheaths before I give them up.

"What she said," Xaden agrees.

Blue Sash blusters. "We do not believe in weaponry—"

"Unless you're...you," I say slowly. "Have you seen the size of their teeth?" I gesture toward Tairn and Sgaeyl. "Then there's the fire. Our blades are the least of your worries."

Tairn huffs a blast of steam scented with sulfur, and Blue Sash lifts his chin, ordering the others to stay where they are, then leads Xaden and me down the path.

Sgaeyl and Tairn follow alongside us until we reach the first barricade of the clearing, two thick rows of palm trees marking the formal entrance to the outdoor palace.

"Your creatures remain here," Blue Sash demands.

"We'll pass that request along," Xaden replies.

"We can see right over these," Tairn notes.

"Remember, diplomacy is plan A." I reach for Xaden's hand and move closer to him as we walk on the orb-lit path, passing what looks to be an open-air receiving room on the left with various seating arrangements, and a music room on the right with instruments waiting for their musicians.

"No walls," Xaden notes. "No ceilings. What do they do when it rains?"

"Awnings." I point to the long wooden rails that run the length of the room, ready to shelter its occupants with fabric. "And *consort*?" I whisper. "We aren't married."

He fucking *smirks.* "I've noticed. But 'girlfriend' is missing that *permanent* tone. If it makes you more comfortable, *consort* is used pretty loosely in Navarrian aristocratic circles. Pretty sure the Duke of Calldyr has had four different consorts in as many years. The designation just gets you the invitation into this place, plus gives you the protection and privileges of my title—"

"I don't need the protection and privileges—" I shake my head as we pass another row of palms.

"Ouch." He lifts his hand to his chest. "Never thought you'd reject me."

I roll my eyes. "It is not the time for this." Jokes have to wait.

"When would be?" The next look he gives me is a hundred percent serious.

My feet nearly stumble along with my heartbeat. Just the idea of *really* having forever with him makes my chest ache with a longing that doesn't belong on a possible battlefield. "When we're not risking death—"

"We're always risking death." He strokes his thumb over mine.

"True," I admit as we walk onto a flagstone floor, entering the palace's dining hall.

The room is laid out in two rows of eight circular tables, each seating ten finely dressed Deverelli on backless chairs, all outfitted in a riot of pastel colors and lightweight tunics and gowns. The table linens are embroidered, the place settings extravagant with golden cups and crystal chalices, and jewels glitter in the soft blue light that emanates from the center of every table and the posted orbs that run the length of the room, illuminating the rows of guards—and their blades.

At the end of the open-air chamber, there's a raised dais with a U-shaped table for five. A man I can only assume is the King of Deverelli sits at its center, twirling a bejeweled dagger in his hands and staring at Halden on the right end of the table like he hasn't decided if he's going to use that dagger on him or not.

There's no sign of Captain Winshire, but Tecarus looks like he'd rather be anywhere than between Courtlyn and Halden.

"Fuck," Xaden mutters.

"He's…younger than I thought," I say about the king. By about four decades or so. Courtlyn only looks to be a few years older than Xaden and me. He's handsome, with deep golden-brown skin stretched over high cheekbones and a strong jaw, cunning brown eyes, and shoulder-length black hair, but the speed with which he locates Xaden and me and quickly appraises us leaves me a little queasy.

Xaden's hand tightens around mine, and he leans down to brush his lips against my ear. "The shadows here are not mine. I know your skill with a dagger. I'm not discounting your ability to protect yourself, but for the good of my sanity while I try to get Halden out of whatever mess he's created, will you please stay by my side?"

I nod. How can I not? He's not asking me to hide behind him, nor did he leave me with Tairn to keep me safe. He's just asking me to stay close.

And honestly, there's nowhere else I'd rather be.

He squeezes my hand once, then lets go, freeing us both in case we need to fight, and we move forward as Blue Sash beckons, clearly exasperated with the time we're taking.

King Courtlyn waves off the couple on the left as we approach, listening to whatever Tecarus whispers in his ear, and servants scurry to replace the plates and cups as the couple departs.

"They don't shake hands," I tell Xaden quietly as we walk down the aisle. "They don't mince or waste words. They speak in double meanings only when it's convenient to them. They value status, wealth, knowledge, and secrets—anything that can be traded. If you break your word once, you're never trusted again."

"Say what I mean. Don't lie. Act like a rich, entitled dick. Got it." He nods.

Rage shines in Halden's gaze as it meets mine when we reach the last set of tables, and his fist closes around his gold fork.

I send him a silent, subtle plea to keep his shit together, and he places the fork on the table and clenches his jaw.

"The Duke of Tyrrendor," Blue Sash announces loudly, gesturing to the four steps that lead up the dais on the left, "and his consort, Violet Sorrensail."

Close enough.

Xaden walks up the steps first, his gaze sweeping the floor, the chairs, the table, and even the place settings before he reaches back with a hand. It's unnecessary but sweet, so I take it and walk up after him. "It's Sorrengail," he corrects Blue Sash.

I take the seat on the end, and Xaden takes the one closest to Courtlyn's right.

"What did you do?" I ask Halden across the divide.

"Straight to the point," Courtlyn says, rolling the jeweled dagger. "I enjoy this."

"What makes you think I did anything?" Halden challenges, leaning over his plate.

"Previous history."

Servants step up behind the other three occupants and remove the dishes.

"I'm sorry to say that you missed the dinner portion of the evening," Courtlyn announces, "but dessert will soon arrive."

"What did you do, Halden?" Xaden repeats for me.

"Exactly what I was sent here for." Color flushes Halden's cheeks and he slams his palms down on the table. "I reestablished diplomatic connections with Deverelli and asked for their permission to use Tecarus's manor to launch a search mission with a riot of dragons in return for the artifact he requested, and when that was not enough, I offered—"

"What was *not* yours to give!" Courtlyn lunges across Tecarus and plunges the dagger into Halden's hand.

Holy. Fucking. Shit. My stomach churns.

"*Your Majesty!*" Tecarus balks, the blood draining from his face.

I drop my hand to Xaden's knee and squeeze to keep from screaming the way Halden does as he stares down in shock.

Xaden tenses but wears his mask of bored indifference like a professional.

"Stop wailing like a child." Courtlyn sits back in his chair, then takes a drink of red wine from his crystal goblet.

Halden sucks in breath after breath, staring at his hand, but the screaming ceases.

"Pull it out, wrap your hand, get it stitched by a healer, and you'll be fine in a fortnight," Courtlyn lectures. "The cut is between your bones, in the fleshy part. No tendons. My aim is very good." He lifts his goblet at Halden. "You're lucky I respect Tecarus, because what you've done is unforgivable."

"The dagger was mine to give," Halden bites out, staring at the jeweled blade. It looks to be antique, with a silver handle and emeralds the size of my fingernails adorning the hilt.

"No, it wasn't." Courtlyn shakes his head.

"It's mine," Xaden says, and it takes everything I have to keep my features schooled. "Or rather, it should have been. It's the Blade of Aretia, appropriated for the royal vault by Reginald during the Unification."

"Yes!" Courtlyn's goblet swings Xaden's way as three servants climb the steps around us, one on each side. "Fascinating how he chose this particular… gift, knowing it might provoke your emotions. Normally when it comes to such heirlooms, we'd consider possession ownership, but in this case, His Highness's word was already broken, hence why I could not make his deal. I'm fascinated to learn how much he is worth on the ransom market, or perhaps I'll entertain classic blackmail. Surely King Tauri will be amenable to quite a few things should his son remain in residence."

"You can't just keep him," Tecarus argues.

"Why not? Weren't you telling me you wanted to keep that one?" Courtlyn points at me.

"I did not break my word!" Halden growls and grabs hold of the dagger's hilt as the servants put down a covered dish in the center of each side of the table. Looks like we're sharing dessert.

"I hope you don't mind waiting a moment," Courtlyn says, and the servants wait, their hands poised on rounded copper covers. "My little ones have arrived." He gestures down the aisle, and I inhale a sharp breath.

Tairn growls and Andarna perks up, taking notice along the bond, her golden energy intensifying as three pure-white panthers stalk toward us. I've only ever seen their kind illustrated in books, and never in white. They're graceful and elegant and so very beautiful, and the closer they get…the more I'd like them to stay in the books. Their paws are *huge*.

Wind rustles the trees at my back, and a chill runs the length of my spine.

This entire palace is outdoors, and they have the run of it.

I have no desire to be their dinner.

"Aren't they magnificent?" Courtlyn asks, his tone marveling like a proud father. "Shira, Shena, and Shora. I've raised them from cubs myself. All hunters. All vicious. All adept at sniffing out a thief." He turns a pointed look Halden's way.

My stomach sinks, and my heart begins to pound.

"Pull it out and bandage that hand *now*," I tell him.

Xaden moves to push back from the table—

Courtlyn raises his hand. "Do it for him, and any chance of us striking a deal is off." He sets his goblet down. "I need to know you can uphold your end of a bargain even when it's unpleasant to do so, just as your father did."

Xaden nods once, his face an unreadable mask, but his leg tenses under my hand.

Guess my father wasn't the only one keeping secrets.

"Now, Halden!" I have no problem yelling at the heir. The panthers are halfway here.

Halden yanks the dagger free with a hiss, then sheathes it like it's *his* and quickly binds the wound with his napkin, field-dressing it as best he can.

"Now that that's done." Courtlyn turns to Xaden. "I assume you would like the same deal he asked for?"

My hand tightens on Xaden's knee.

"I can't agree, seeing as I have no idea what Halden requested," Xaden says. "But we'd like to reopen diplomatic channels and secure permission to use Viscount Tecarus's manor as a stopping point for a riot of no more than eight dragons and an equal number of gryphons for the purposes of a search party, which would entail securing hunting rights of wild game for said creatures and a promise of safety for all parties."

Courtlyn rolls the stem of his goblet between his thumb and forefinger. "To whom do you owe your loyalty, Your Grace? Your father was a rebel. From what I hear, you are cut from the same cloth, and yet you've been restored to your title, so to whom do you swear your fealty?"

I reach into the right side pocket of my pack for the conduit out of sheer habit as the panthers approach the dais, splitting to surround us. The familiar weight of the orb is comforting in my hand, and I swear I can feel a hum, a swift rise in heat that I know is only in my head, but it's soothing all the same.

"Navarre," Courtlyn continues, "or Tyrrendor? Lie, and this discussion is over. We've fared quite well without the Continent."

Xaden tilts his head, studying the king. "Violet."

My heart skips into double time.

"My loyalty is to Violet first above everything, every*one* else," Xaden says. "Then Tyrrendor. Then Navarre in the moments it's worthy—usually when Violet is in residence."

It's a reckless answer given what hangs in the balance, and now is absolutely not the time, but damn if it doesn't make me love him even more.

"Interesting." The king stops twirling his glass.

"I'm assuming with our deal, trade would begin again," Xaden says, "which would be mutually beneficial, since I'm sure you've heard we're in a war with the venin. Should you decide to become our ally—"

"Oh, we've never involved ourselves with venin." Courtlyn shakes his head. "War destroys isles, blocks economies. Supplying those at war, however…that's where the money is. We remain neutral in all things and always have. It's how we've maintained trade, commerce, growth, and knowledge for the world no matter what god you worship or magic you can access."

"But they've been here, right?" I narrow my eyes slightly, noting that there's now a panther perched directly behind me. I lean forward to look around the servant who is still holding our dish shut. "Did you defeat them?" *Or cure them?*

Courtlyn glares. "To imply that our isle is weak, conquerable, is a line you do not want to cross. Such an assumption is disastrous to an economy that is built on safe, stable trade. People do not invest in unstable isles." He snaps his fingers.

The panthers leap onto the dais with an ease that speaks to nightly routine.

"I will not stand for you being devoured by a house cat," Tairn growls.

"Stay put and keep Sgaeyl with you," I shout down the bond, and my knuckles whiten around the conduit as the panther pushes between Xaden and me, its soft coat brushing against my arm.

"Shora's lovely, don't you think?" Courtlyn says to Xaden, an indulgent smile curving his mouth, then continues toward Halden without waiting for an answer. "I hope you don't mind, but they're used to eating with me. Your Highness, do remember that Shira earned every bit of her special dinner today." He lifts his hands, palms up, and crooks his fingers.

The servants remove the copper covers, then duck off the dais.

Oh gods, it's a giant slab of red meat that has to have been carved off the largest cow to have walked this isle.

The panther—Shira—chuffs low in her throat, flicking her tail, and I can't help but wonder if this is how the infantry cadets felt that day on the field when Baide found us.

Xaden's hand covers mine and squeezes, and I look over to find him staring, stone-faced across the table, then track his gaze—

Captain Anna Winshire's head lies on the plate between Halden and Tecarus, her short, strawberry-blond curls unmistakable.

My jaw slackens. Oh, *Malek*, Courtlyn has killed Halden's personal guard… and is serving her to his *cat*.

I'm going to be sick.

Bile rises in my throat, and I swallow quickly, breathing in through my nose and out through my mouth, but all I smell is meat and blood.

"Don't watch," Xaden whispers, and I wrench my gaze away.

"Eat," Courtlyn orders, and the panthers *pounce*.

Paws land on the table between us, and a massive maw opens, snatching the meat off the plate and dragging it, leaving a bloody trail on the white linen as she hauls her meal to the dais, then to the floor.

The others follow suit.

When I look across at Halden, he stares at his empty plate, completely stricken.

"Aren't they beautiful creatures?" Courtlyn asks.

I blink away the shock and set the conduit on the table. Death and I are old friends, and it's not like I really knew Anna. But the audacity is truly unparalleled.

"You murdered my guard," Halden says slowly.

"Your *thief* was found in my treasury," Courtlyn counters, "with six stolen treasures on her person and a list of five more she had yet to attain written in *your* handwriting."

My stomach lurches, and my gaze jumps to Halden's. "You didn't."

"They are all items that belong to *us*!" He pounds his chest and stands, his chair falling back against the dais. "It is not stealing to take back what is rightfully ours!" A vein in his neck bulges.

Guards move in toward the edge of the dais, forming a perimeter around the panthers, and I slip my hand from beneath Xaden's and reach for the sheaths at my lower thighs, beneath the tablecloth.

"It's about to turn to shit," I warn Tairn. *"Communicate that to Sgaeyl however you can."*

He rumbles in acknowledgment, and palm trees sway in the distance.

"Rightfully yours?" Courtlyn challenges, his voice rising in a sinister melody.

"What's the penalty for thievery here?" Xaden whispers.

"From a royal house?" I focus inward. "Decree twenty-two…" I wince. "No, twenty-three, is death." I've studied, but I'm nowhere near a legal expert.

"Is Halden complicit under their laws?"

"Their system isn't like ours. Their decrees can contradict each other, and

Courtlyn sits on their tribunal, so..." My words trip over themselves. "I don't know. Maybe."

I might want to strangle Halden myself, but I can't let him be executed here for *stealing*.

"Those items are mine, received as goods bartered for services rendered over the last century, as you well know!" Courtlyn shouts, and the diners fall silent at their tables, leaving only the sound of the panthers devouring their dinners.

Wait. The last *century*? My shoulders fall and my mind whirls, recalling Aaric's words from last year when I asked what Halden was going to do about what was happening beyond our borders. *I'm here, aren't I?* Aaric had implied that Halden wasn't going to act.

But this is so much worse.

Halden didn't just know; he's been playing a starring role.

"You took advantage of our desperation," Halden accuses. "Accepted priceless magical artifacts under unfair terms, and now you execute my personal guard when we seek to rectify your outright theft with a genuine agreement? Fuck you! We want no part of you, your deception, or this godsforsaken isle!" Halden surges forward, shoving his section of the table over, and it topples into the void of the center.

Oh. *Shit.*

Courtlyn's gaze turns to ice, and my ribs feel like they're twisting inward as I watch everything we've worked for fall apart in a matter of seconds. Tecarus jumps backward, then quickly scrambles down the steps, and I don't blame him in the least.

Halden has fucked us over. The sour taste of betrayal fills my mouth, but a bitter flood of metallic anger carries it away with the next heartbeat.

"Enough, Halden!" Xaden stands and I slowly do the same, monitoring the guards around us, the panthers behind us, and those in the crowd reaching beneath the linens for what could be hidden weapons.

"He is a thief, and he impugns my honor in front of my entire court!" Courtlyn shouts at Xaden, but he points his finger toward Halden.

"He no longer speaks for us." Xaden swings the pack from his shoulder, setting it atop the table with a *clang*. "If you will not accept the deal with Navarre, then accept it with Tyrrendor, and I'll assure you the only riots on your shore will have Aretian riders and their flier counterparts, who will abide by your laws and respect your customs, and in return, with my utmost gratitude for your trust—" He unbuttons the top flap of his rucksack and pulls it back slowly, revealing an inch of an emerald-studded hilt that steals my breath. It looks too much like the dagger to be a coincidence.

My heart stutters. That can't be. He can't. I won't let him.

"No." I grab hold of Xaden's hand, preventing him from showing the rest of it. "If that's what I think it is, then absolutely not."

"Vi…" He shakes his head, searching my eyes, and I know I'm not the only one longing for the bond that usually makes these moments easy for us. "It might be the only way to forge an alliance and save the prick."

"You've sacrificed enough. I've got this." I slip my heavy pack from my shoulders and set it beside his.

"Absolutely not!" Halden shouts.

Xaden gives him a look that clearly says he's had enough of his shit.

"I alone have the authority to speak for Navarre!" Halden rages, taking two threatening steps toward the king. "You do not make deals with provinces, let alone the son of a traitor who blackmailed his way into a title. I am the only voice of our kingdom!" His hands curl into fists, and the binding around his right floods crimson.

Courtlyn sighs, then reaches for his goblet and takes a drink. "I've heard enough, and this grows tedious. Tecarus may live. Kill the rest."

Sometimes diplomacy is best served at swordpoint.

—Journal of Captain Lilith Sorrengail

CHAPTER
TWENTY-SEVEN

Guards move in and everything goes to complete, immediate shit.

Xaden draws both his swords, then surprises the hell out of me by tossing one across the gap to Halden, who catches it with his left hand in the same breath that I palm two of my daggers.

We are *not* dying tonight.

"Try not to kill anyone," Xaden says, even as the first of the guards charges up the steps between the panthers. "International relations and all."

"Tell *her* that." I glance down at the panther, thankful she's still occupied. *"Do not overreact,"* I warn Tairn, hoping it's not my final request. *"We still need this deal."*

"I resent the implication that I am given to melodramatics," he replies, but there's a distinct, plate-rattling roar to my left that causes more than a few guests to shriek as Xaden clashes blades with the guard, then kicks him clean off the stairs with a boot to the center of his chest.

I whirl to the left as a guard climbs the end of the dais without stairs and pull a move from Courtlyn's own book, thrusting my dagger through her hand and yanking it out. She shouts, falling backward, and when I rise, I find two more guards have managed the same maneuver behind us, filling the space between Xaden and me.

Bone crunches and a body flies around the guards, but there's easily a half dozen more waiting beyond the panthers.

The closest guard has at least a foot on me and fifty pounds, and if the scars on his forearms are any measure, he's no stranger to fighting. But he's no Xaden.

I charge before he can take a fighting stance and let muscle memory take over, my first cut landing deep in the outside of his thigh before I duck close, avoiding the swing of his long spear. They aren't made for close combat, and I am.

He misses, thrusting the spear into the table, shattering glass, and giving me the time to regretfully slice the tendons behind his knee. It's a long-lasting injury for a warrior, but at least it won't kill him.

He bellows, toppling sideways and falling from the dais, but before I can get up, pain explodes at the back of my head, and I'm yanked upward...by my godsdamned braid.

A battering ram of an arm shoves my chest onto the bloodied plate between our packs, and my face narrowly misses a sharp shard of glass. The spear shattered my conduit. "Do your dragons scream before they die, fire-bringer?" the guard hisses in my ear as she leans over my back. "Does it take them minutes to perish after you do? Or is it instant?"

Anger storms through my veins, heating my skin from the scalp down in a flood of smelted rage. "Your ignorance is staggering."

Gods bless my flexibility, I swing my left arm behind my back and stab deep into her arm.

She shouts, jerking upright, and I shove the heel of my hand against the table and throw every ounce of my energy into jolting backward, slamming my head into her face. Bone crunches, and her weight disappears.

I turn, only to meet the stunning blow of an elbow against my cheekbone. Skin splits, my ears ring, and I fall back against the table, blinking the stars out of my eyes as a hand grabs hold of my throat and squeezes.

"Violet!" Xaden yells, and I slash my blade across the offending arm and thrust my knee in a move even Mira would be proud of. The man falls and I cough for my first breath as the dais shudders.

I lift my blade toward the giant on my right, but the pommel of a sword reaches his temple first. The man collapses, and Xaden shoves him off the platform with his foot.

"That is enough,*"* Tairn declares.

"She holds her own," Andarna argues. *"Oh. Perhaps there are now too many."*

"Stop playing and end this! It's the only way to kill their mounts!" Courtlyn shouts from behind us.

Xaden reaches for my face with his empty hand, cupping my chin and turning my cheek toward the blue light as a dozen more guards pour in from behind Courtlyn. I take a precious second to make sure Halden's still alive. He's on the ground, chest moving, eyes closed—I think he might be unconscious, but I don't see any blood.

"Xaden, behind us," I warn as he studies the wound that has begun to throb.

When he doesn't answer, my gaze jumps to his, and my breath falters.

I've seen him in battle before, seen the icy rage that comes over him, even the killing calm. I've witnessed the transformation from man to weapon, watched strategy overtake compassion—just like we're trained for.

But this...whatever's swirling in those onyx eyes is a tempest I've never beheld. It's one step past fury, as though Dunne herself has stepped into his eyes and now peers back at me. He's Xaden, but he's...not.

"Xaden?" I whisper. "It's nothing. Really. I've had worse on a sparring mat."

"They're all fucking dead." His vow lifts the hair at the back of my neck, and the guards rush the table simultaneously with their weapons drawn, obviously having learned from the last failed assault.

Two on...twelve. *Shit.*

I startle and pull back to fight, but Xaden whips his arm around my waist and yanks me against his chest. His sword hits the table, and to my complete and utter surprise, he presses a soft kiss to the top of my forehead as an axe—

Metal hits the ground.

Screams sound around us, and I jerk my head left, finding Xaden's outstretched hand mid-twist. The unmistakable sound of cracking bone follows, and every guard surrounding us drops to the floor, their heads twisted at unnatural angles.

Wisps of barely there shadow dissipate, and the band around my waist falls away with a familiar caress.

No, no, *no.*

Silence falls, thicker than the cloying, humid air, and my heart cries, demanding some other answer than the one my brain already knows because there's only one logical explanation for what just happened—but even that can't be possible because there's no magic here.

Tairn bristles along the bond, and Andarna shudders. I can feel them both, closer than they should be, but there's still no bond to Xaden.

"Y-y-you..." Courtlyn stammers. "What have you done?"

I drag my gaze along the wall of rustling palms to the left, over the scattered dead Deverelli guards and the panthers that happily investigate them, and across Xaden's chest, finding nothing but the same on the other side of the table.

He's killed all dozen of them.

It's only muscle memory that sheathes my daggers.

Something falls from his hand, hitting his abandoned sword with a metallic *clink.* I grab the small object on impulse and close my fingers around the pebble-size piece of alloy from my conduit. Agony cracks my soul clean open, as if I can give Xaden some of what he's just lost as I register the alloy's chill, its complete and total lack of energy before shoving it in my front pocket.

"They hurt you," he whispers without apology. "They were going to kill you."

The why of it doesn't matter. Not right now. Not when we're surrounded on an enemy isle, escorted by riders who don't know what Xaden's become, and facing down Navarrian royalty who would gladly see him dead.

Why is a matter for later.

"Violet." The plea in his whisper pulls me together faster than anything else could, and I jerk my head up. His eyes are tightly closed as he rubs the bridge of his nose.

"Come here," I say quietly, rising on my toes and cupping the side of his face, lifting my hands to his temples to shield him from view. Courtlyn's chair squeaks on the dais. "Look at me."

Xaden's eyes flash open. Red rims his irises and consumes the gold flecks I adore so very much, but he's still him behind these eyes. I force my body not to react, then pull his forehead to mine. "I love you and we need to get you out of here, so you have to trust me. Do not move until I tell you."

He nods.

"Sit down. Put your head in your hands and stay there." I let him go, and he does exactly as I ask, keeping his head low as if he's ashamed of what he's done.

"I need help," I tell Tairn and Andarna.

"We're ready," Tairn replies. Thank gods they're always in my head.

"Andarna, when it's time, be gentle." For once, I don't even want to lecture her about not staying home when she's told, though she'd better have her harness on if this doesn't go as planned.

"Is your lightning gentle? Do I critique your work?" She huffs.

Courtlyn still stands behind the table, one of the panthers at his side, panic etched in every line of his face as the court mutters in muted tones of hysteria behind us.

"I need you to get Sgaeyl as close as possible," I tell Tairn, then offer what I hope is a contrite smile Courtlyn's way. "Our most sincere apology, but in Navarre, riders are trained to kill when you attack us, and our restraint can only be pushed so far. As you can see, the duke feels some remorse, but you did just try to murder two of our kingdom's nobles." I cringe. "Not a good look for negotiations. Shall we begin round two? I'll lead this time."

"We have no magic." Courtlyn's eyes widen, and his gaze darts over the room, as if he's deciding whether or not to call for more guards.

"Watch your words," Tairn warns. *"Sgaeyl is here. It's getting cramped behind these trees."*

"And yet here we are. Did you know that I'm a lightning wielder?" I cock my head to the side.

Courtlyn swallows. "Tecarus mentioned something along those lines."

"What happened?" Halden sits up with perfect timing, rubbing a growing lump on his head.

Courtlyn's chest rises and falls more rapidly with every second, and I watch the panic build within him like a breaking dam ready to burst. I drop my right hand to my sheaths and wait for him to explode. "Shira!" he bellows, snapping faster than I expected.

"Violet!" Halden shouts, and Xaden's back turns to stone beneath my hand, but true to his word, he doesn't move a muscle.

Neither do I.

"No!" Courtlyn shrieks, his eyes locking behind me in horror. His mouth falls agape, and the group of Deverelli erupts into full-blown multitoned cries of distress.

"You stay put and she lives," I warn him as people run for their lives, emptying out the hall.

"Well, holy shit," Halden says with lifted eyebrows, wobbling as he stands.

I look over my shoulder, and a slow, proud smile spreads across my face. Andarna stands with her front claws atop the bodies of the guards, her wings tucked in tight, her black tail flicking back and forth as she holds Shira delicately between her front four teeth, the snarling cat's claws safely tucked outside so she can't cause any damage. Andarna even has her lips puckered so the little cat doesn't get drenched in dragon saliva. How thoughtful.

"Shira…" Courtlyn cries.

"You see, that's *my* little one." I pivot toward Courtlyn with a grin, wrinkling my nose. "Raised her from a juvenile—well, Tairn and Sgaeyl have, really, but you get the point. Now, Andarna doesn't eat our allies—it's a whole thing her elders are trying to teach her—but you know how adolescents are. Never really know if they feel like listening on any given day." I shrug. "So we can negotiate, and I will give you the rarest treasure found anywhere on this world and Shira will walk away in need of a good bath, or I can call Tairn and Sgaeyl in here, and they can all have little panther snacks before we fly back to the Continent. Your choice. But either way, you should know that dragons outlive their riders, so had you succeeded in killing us, all you would have done was *really* piss them off before they scorched everything in their paths and flew back to tell the rest of the Empyrean what you'd done. I'm willing to let the Duke of Tyrrendor depart in good faith that you won't try to attack us again if you're ready to begin."

Courtlyn's face falls, and for the first time since we walked in, he actually looks his age as he glances at Xaden. "Agreed."

"My king!" someone yells from behind me.

"It's fine, Burcet!" Courtlyn calls back. "My trade minister will stay for negotiations, along with finance and"—he looks their way—"foreign."

"As it should be." I nod, then hold out my hand to Halden. "Bring me *both* of his weapons."

Halden's head draws back in offense.

"Now," I add, just in case he thinks I'm kidding.

"Way to fuck up the negotiations, Riorson." He glares and tosses them over.

The steel lands on the table with a clatter, and I make quick work of sheathing Xaden's swords at his back and packaging the dagger in his bag with the Sword of Tyrrendor.

"All ready." I tap Xaden's back and he stands, turning away from Courtlyn and Halden before swinging his pack over his shoulder.

He keeps his head low but opens his eyes to look at me. "I'm not sorry, but I am."

"I love you." I cup the sides of his face and choose my words carefully. "Sgaeyl is just behind the trees. Take the heirlooms back to Aretia and handle whatever business you might have there for the province." My throat tightens as I hold his gaze, beating back the physical instinct to fight or flee at the glimpse of red. I rise up quickly and press a hard, quick kiss to his mouth. "I'll see you at Basgiath in a week."

"A week," he promises, and then he goes, hanging his head as he descends the dais, then lifting it when he passes Andarna and striding through the trees like the arrogant ass he is.

I pivot back to Courtlyn, noting that his three ministers are picking their way toward us.

The king's gaze narrows on me in a glare that's equal parts hatred and appreciation. "Are you nervous now that your *reckless* one has departed?"

I clear my throat, and the ground shakes as Tairn steps *over* the trees, lowering his head so that the table linen moves with his breath. "No, not particularly. Dragons are known to have short tempers, and Andarna's jaw is probably getting a little tired, so we should speed this along, don't you think?"

Courtlyn nods.

"Same terms as the duke stated while I sat beside him earlier this evening, and I will add that Xaden Riorson is to be pardoned of any crime you would accuse him of regarding tonight's activities, considering he was provoked and attacked by your guards, and he is to be allowed to return to Deverelli as a member of our riot at any time." I flash a smile.

Courtlyn blusters, and his ministers call out protests as they make their way toward the dais.

"Or we can go home, and I can ask King Tauri how he feels about tonight's actions and go from there." I shrug.

"Accepted," Courtlyn bites out.

"Excellent. Now, I expect you will accept the citrine as payment for the alliance but agree you should be compensated for the prince's crimes." I unclasp the top of my pack and remove the hard metallic shards of shell I've carried all the way from the Continent. The smallest pieces cover my palm, and the largest section would easily fit a medium-size dog. I set the base on the table and its pieces inside, marveling at how the shades of color graduate from the darkest onyx on bottom to the brightest silvers on top, each ring of hardened scales nestled within the next yet never separate, creating a smooth outer layer with no ridges that only cracks when the hatchling is ready.

"A dragon egg shell." Courtlyn drags out the words, less than impressed. "As amazing as your beasts are, once you've seen one shell, you've seen them all."

"Not this one." A corner of my mouth lifts, and I run my finger along the inner edge, picturing her biding her time for hundreds of years, listening, waiting. A charge of energy runs up my arm, and I lift my brows at the sensation. "This is the only shell of its kind. It belongs to the one and only irid we have on the Continent. The seventh breed of dragon. It is Andarna's kind we're searching for."

"You expect me to believe—" Courtlyn starts, then stands completely awestruck, staring at Andarna.

I glance back and see she's chosen to blend with the vegetation so it appears Shira is hanging in midair, suspended by an unknown pointed vise. "Yes."

"And this is her shell." Courtlyn leans closer.

"It is. She gave me permission to gift it to you." I push the heavy structure toward him.

"I'm starting to drool," she warns me.

"Just a little longer. You're doing great."

Courtlyn nods, inspecting the shell. "Yes, yes." His head pops up. "One condition. He"—his finger swings toward Halden—"never steps foot on my isle again or his life is forfeit."

"Done."

"Violet!" Halden argues.

"Done," I repeat to Courtlyn.

"Then the deal is struck." Courtlyn bows his head.

"The deal is struck." I bow mine, and Andarna spits Shira out. The panther bolts past us, taking her sisters with her.

"You will begin at Unnbriel, will you not? It is the closest main isle, after all." Courtlyn waits for me to nod, then eyes Andarna's shell before stepping around the table toward me. "If you are amenable, there is another trade I might be able to broker for you."

"I'm listening."

There are times I look at Parapet, at the very act of Threshing and marvel that dragons have not been to Unnbriel. What we call treacherous is their idea of primary school.

—Unnbriel: Isle of Dunne by Second Lieutenant Asher Daxton

CHAPTER TWENTY-EIGHT

"You can't be serious," Rhi whispers next to me three days later in Battle Brief as Professor Devera questions first-years about the fall of Vallia, a midsize city two hundred miles west of the Bay of Malek.

Not only are the venin moving in Krovla again, but in the eight days we were gone, Cygnisen's flier cadets arrived. Battle Brief is now beyond standing-room-only capacity. Even the steps serve as seating.

"She's absolutely serious," Ridoc responds from Rhi's other side, cracking a giant yawn that I immediately catch and repeat, fighting and failing to stifle it with my hand.

God*damn* am I tired. Every muscle aches, my stomach can't decide if it wants to eat everything or expel it all, and I'm starting to see double when I try to focus on the map. We flew in this morning from Athebyne and were rewarded for pushing our limits by being sent straight into Battle Brief on General Aetos's order. At least I managed to secure my father's books in my room and heard from Imogen that she'd kept my prisoner alive first.

"He wanted you to trade your and Xaden's...services...for weaponry?" Sawyer asks, leaning forward from Ridoc's right and adjusting the top of his prosthesis. "I thought Deverelli was neutral. They don't even have an army."

Xaden. My hand clenches around my pen as I scribble the nearly mid-February date on my notes. How many more times can he slip before the rings around his irises become permanent and the veins at his temples turn red? For a second in that bedroom, I thought I'd found a temporary answer to stay his progression, but even on an isle without magic, he hadn't been safe.

"Or perhaps the isle hadn't been safe from him," Tairn interjects.

I ignore the jab.

"Could you keep it down?" A brown-haired flier with a Cygnisen shoulder patch and third-year rank turns around and glares at Sawyer, and though I hate his scowl, I have to admit, the glasses really work for him.

"Turn it back around—" Ridoc starts, then pauses to appreciate the flier. "Well, *hello* Cygnisen. Have you been properly welcomed to Basgiath yet?" He cranks up a smile I've seen enough times to know he'll be coming out of someone else's bedroom tomorrow morning.

The flier scoffs. "I don't do second-years."

"Good thing I fuck like a third." Ridoc grins. "Plus, I'm on quest squad, which gives me an additional boost of desirability."

That earns him a second glance and a flash of interest before the flier turns around in his seat.

"Where *do* you get the confidence, Gamlyn?" Maren asks from my left.

Ridoc snorts. "Survive the Gauntlet. After that, you're well aware one rejection isn't going to kill you." He leans toward the flier. "By the way, third-years usually sit up top, but if you want to be close to me, that's all right, too."

The flier tilts his head and drums his pen on the desk.

I smother a laugh, and Sawyer shakes his head.

"Tell Sawyer about the Deverelli Army," Ridoc reminds me, settling back in his seat as a first-year fumbles an easy question about high-ground strategy.

"Oh, right." I yawn again and open the Archives door to a crackle of power in hopes it will keep me from falling asleep. Have to admit, it's nice to be *me* again. "They have one. They just call them guards. So yes, they have weaponry to trade, they just don't advertise it."

"Wanting you as a weapon is weird. They don't have magic," Cat says from Maren's left. "You're scary with lightning, Sorrengail, but without it…" We all look her way, but she just shrugs. "What? You were *all* thinking it. I just said it."

"Is there something more important than enemy troop movements going on up there, Iron Squad second-years?" Devera asks, and the lecture hall quiets.

Heat creeps up my neck, and I sink in my seat.

"I mean…" Ridoc scratches the side of his head. "Sorrengail's kind of responsible for saving the entire Continent right now, so maybe—"

Rhi's hand slams over his mouth. "Absolutely not. You have our apology, Major."

Devera arches a sardonic brow and leans back against the desk. "And how was your trip to Deverelli, cadet? Have you saved us all?"

Leather jackets creak in every direction as heads turn my way.

I clear my throat. "I believe the prince is debriefing leadership, but we've brokered a deal that will allow us diplomatic access to the isle as a launching ground for further searches." And I personally secured Courtlyn's silence on what Xaden did by promising my own like a sacrifice, adding a gentle reminder that I wouldn't want our new ally to appear *weak*.

"Is that all we should discuss?" she asks, her expression uncomfortably close to my mother's, and I nod.

"Of all the shops in the merchant isle, she made us visit the *bookstore*," Cat adds with an exasperated sigh, tapping her pen on her notebook, and I breathe a little easier with the transfer of attention.

"That sounds like our Violet." Devera flashes a smile. "Since you're so talkative today, Sorrengail, why don't you tell us what about the offensive in Vallia is so concerning." She gestures behind her at the map.

Shit, I really should have been paying attention. I scan the map for the length of two heartbeats, noting that some flags that had once been red are now gray, and the red has retreated from the north of Braevick and on the whole is moving nauseatingly southwest.

"It shows southward movement," I answer. "Once we raised the wards in Aretia, the venin changed course, leaving conquered territory like Pavis to concentrate on Poromiel's border with Navarre in what we now know was an offensive meant to strike the Basgiath hatching grounds. Moving southwest shows a change in strategy." They're less than a day's flight from Cordyn by wyvern, but there's a lot of undrained ground to cover if feeding is their only goal. But if that were the case, the map wouldn't look quite so premeditated.

"Your best guess on that strategy?"

My stomach turns. "They somehow know about the Aretian wards and they're moving into position for the inevitability of them falling."

A murmur ripples through the room.

Devera nods. "That's what I think, too."

My blood runs cold. But *how*?

• • •

The next week passes in a blur. I've never had to work harder...or worried about Xaden quite so much.

He should be back by now. The Senarium expects us to leave in a week for Unnbriel, and I'm getting nervous. Eight days should be enough for the circles around his eyes to fade, right?

Unless he's progressed to asim. I shove that thought as far away as possible.

When I'm not learning in class, pushing burnout in the range, freezing my ass off in flight maneuvers, practicing with the mini crossbow Maren gifted me, working every muscle to its breaking point with Imogen, or listening to Andarna go into exhaustive detail on why Tairn is the worst—period—mentor—period—ever—period, I'm reading my dad's books with whichever members of my squad can spare their time. It takes Dain and me two evenings to decode the clues Dad left to open the passcode-locked books, and once we do, I can't even tell my sister, since she's taken personal leave for the first time in her entire career.

And whenever I'm not doing any of that? I'm in the fighting pit with my squad, either for our own instruction or joining the rest of the quadrant in what's quickly become our favorite activity—watching the shit get kicked out of one another in hopes of learning something.

This afternoon, every second- and third-year in our squad is seated on the bottom left rows of the amphitheater with a book from Jesinia in their lap while two other squads from Second and Fourth Wing practice in front of us under the guidance of Professor Carr, who's rotated in to teach today. Garrick and Bodhi look on from just beneath us, leaning against the wall, both shaking their heads every now and then when they, too, look up from their books.

A second-year goes flying in a blast of fire, and every single one of us looks up as the guy lands on his ass, flames still rising from his hair.

"You're up." Bodhi jabs Garrick, and he takes off at a sprint onto the mat. A flick of his wrist and the flames snuff out, deprived of oxygen.

"Letting them get a little close, don't you think?" Garrick asks Professor Carr.

"Oh, this is going to get good." Ridoc sets the Continent's most redacted volume on Unnbriel's warlike customs in his lap, and Sawyer follows suit beside him. Sawyer hasn't joined us in flight maneuvers, but I'm glad he's feeling up to sitting in on classes. It bodes well for his return, if and when he's ready, or even just ready to talk about it.

"Ballsy," Rhi agrees from my other side, using her thumb to mark her place in a book about weather patterns throughout the isles.

Professor Carr narrows his eyes on Garrick and folds his arms. "A scar would remind him to wield a little faster next time. It's not like he's dead."

"Flame never should have *touched* him," Garrick argues.

"Clearly you haven't *taught* enough to know the best methodology," Carr snipes. "Having powerful friends doesn't make you a good instructor."

Garrick's jaw ticks as he steps off the mat with the smoking second-year, and the guy goes back to his squad.

"He's an asshole," Bodhi notes, then leans back against the wall and returns to reading his assigned collection of early fables from Braevick. He's looking for tales of dark wielders cured by love, or good deeds, or dancing naked under a full moon after drinking the venom of a rare snake only found on the farthest isle during a lunar eclipse, or…something.

Anything.

I adjust the blank leather cover disguising Dad's book and reread the passage on trial by combat for different levels of entrance to Unnbriel's court, then roll my left shoulder with a wince. Pushing into my stiff trapezius muscle doesn't help soothe the protesting joint, either.

"You were too hard on her last night," Garrick grumbles at Imogen, grabbing his book from Bodhi.

For all that *we're* reading, I can't begin to contemplate what's on Jesinia's desk.

"Fuck off," Imogen mutters behind me, flipping a page aggressively.

"I'm fine." I spare a glance at both of them, then continue down the page. My father's observations on the combative isle are sharp, almost clinical, but lack his usual insight. There's a marked difference between this book, written when he was twenty-three and straight out of the Scribe Quadrant, and the manuscript he left for me in his office.

But when did he visit the isles? Or have the time to transcribe the rudimentary dictionaries that have quickly become the bane of Dain's existence?

"She's rotated every single one of her joints at least three times in the last hour." Garrick's tone sharpens. "I'd say that means you need to lighten up—"

"Nope." Imogen flips another page. "You're not taking your frustrations with Carr out on me. If Violet thinks we're doing too much, she'll tell me."

I glance over my shoulder to see her twirling her forefinger, suggesting Garrick turn back around, while Quinn leans over her shoulder, reading a volume Queen Maraya sent on venin and their medicinal uses.

Given how difficult it was to get our hands on these books, it's wild to think that Garrick could probably *walk* straight from here to wherever her library is.

I blink, then lean forward, bracing my elbows on the wall right above Bodhi's head. "Hey, Bodhi?" I whisper so only the two of us can hear.

"Hey, Violet?" he answers, looking up.

"What's your second signet?" I lower my voice even more.

He lifts his brows, then glances in Garrick's direction. "Don't have one."

"As in you don't have one that I get to know about but will eventually see you wield, or don't *have one* have one?"

A corner of his mouth lifts into a wry smile that reminds me of his cousin's. "Don't have one. Just like Xaden. Why?"

"Curious," I admit. "And selfishly hoping you'd be able to do something cool like keep Halden from speaking." Gods only know what he'll do at the other isles after his performance on Deverelli.

"If I could, would that mean I get to go on the next expedition?" His eyes light up.

"Heads up," Garrick says, and we both look forward as a first-year with a rebellion relic steps into the pit with Timin Kagiso—the newly promoted wingleader for Second Wing. "Let's try to keep anyone else from burning."

Go figure another fire wielder was Second Wing's executive officer when Aura died.

"On it." Bodhi sets his book on the wall and takes a step closer to the mat near the end of the squad.

"Still can't believe they made Stirling the senior wingleader," Sawyer mutters, glancing up the rows to where Panchek watches with other members of leadership.

"Better than Iris Drue," Cat notes as she works out a knot in Trager's shoulders. "Pretty sure she'd murder every flier in their bed if she could."

"True," Sawyer agrees, his attention shifting up the steps. "I thought you all had physics right now."

Rhi and I both follow his line of sight as Lynx, Baylor, Avalynn, Sloane, Aaric, and Kai descend the steps on our right. The first-years are here.

"Got out ten minutes ago," Sloane replies, her gaze darting over us—or rather, our books. "We came to help."

"Excellent." Rhi jabs her thumb over her shoulders. "Empty row behind the third-years. Take a seat and watch."

"That's not what I mean." Sloane crosses her arms and lifts her chin in a way that reminds me of her older brother. "You're in charge of your mission now, right?"

"Yes." My stomach sinks.

"We want to help." She gestures to the books.

Ridoc shakes his head. "First year is hard enough without adding all this into it."

I'm with him.

"You're one dragon short of even pairs," Avalynn says, completely ignoring Ridoc. "You know, in case you need to split up for some reason."

Rhi cocks her head to the side.

"Odd numbers don't bother me—" I start.

"What Sorrengail is too nice to say is first-years aren't going," Imogen says.

"Or helping," Garrick adds over his shoulder.

"Didn't ask you," Baylor challenges, glaring in Garrick's direction. "Last time I checked, we're the actual Iron Squad and you're a substitute teacher."

"That's not a fight I'd pick." I lift my brows at Baylor.

"Unless you'd like your ass kicked," Garrick offers with a flash of a smile.

"Sit or move," Dain orders, walking down the stairs. The circles under his eyes have my brows knitting. Between decoding my dad's clues, studying for his own classes, and his duties as wingleader, he's taking on too much, and I'm a major reason for it.

"We're trying to help," Sloane argues, her cheeks flushing a second before her narrowed gaze drops away from Dain.

"You can help by staying alive," Dain counters, sliding in to sit on the edge next to Rhi and taking out Dad's separately bound dictionary for Unnbriel from his pack. "Carr tells me you're refusing to train your signet."

"You what?" I shut my book.

"You really going to mourn the loss of another Mairi?" Sloane fires back at Dain.

"His death will *always* be on my head. Yours will not." Dain's tone sharpens. "I don't coddle first-years anymore, so train. Your. Signet."

"Asshole," she whispers, and the flush in her cheeks deepens.

I lift my brows at the look she shoots him, mostly because I can't tell if she wants to stab him in his seat or—

"Fuck," Garrick mutters, and all our heads turn toward the pit as fire erupts from Wingleader Kagiso, streaming toward the first-year.

Bodhi takes three quick steps onto the mat, then turns his hand, and the fire dies. An argument immediately ensues with Carr, but I ignore it and pivot my focus to Sloane.

"Why won't you train?" I ask her.

"Would you train if all you did was destroy things?" She drags her gaze from the pit. "Kill people?"

Power hums along my bones, hot and insistent. "I don't know," I say quietly. "Would I?"

She glances at Rhi.

"Don't look at me. I agree with her." Rhi shakes her head and flips to the map section of her book.

Sloane's shoulders fall. "I just want to help in a way that doesn't suck the magic out of something. And I highly doubt you lot would have been content to sit aside last year while your second-years went off and saved the Continent."

My words fail, and Aaric lifts a single brow behind her, taking note of my speechlessness.

"Solid point," Sawyer says slowly as another first-year enters the pit against Kagiso.

"Liam—" I start.

"Made his choice," Sloane reminds me. "We're making ours." She folds her arms. "And he would want me to make sure you're as prepared as you can be, even if that means none of us go with you."

Rhi and I exchange a look, and she nods.

"Fine." I pivot in my seat and grab the heavy pack at Imogen's feet, then rifle through for the most innocuous-looking texts. "Here you go." I hand the stack to Sloane. "Read these and write up a one-page report on each—"

"Oh for *fuck*—" Kai groans from two steps back.

"No whining. You said you wanted to help," Rhi interrupts as Bodhi returns to the wall.

"And get them back to me as soon as you can," I finish.

"Thank you." Sloane gives them to the others, then glances at me, Rhi, and Dain before following the rest of her squad up the steps.

Aaric waits, holding a tome on mythology. "Scribes haven't released your mission report yet. How badly did it go?"

Ridoc scoffs. "Your arrogant brother—"

"Give us a second," I cut him off quickly, then set my book on my seat and scoot past Rhi and Dain to get to the steps.

"Halden was Halden," I tell Aaric, lowering my voice. "He did Halden things and caused Halden-style ramifications, none of which are your fault."

A muscle flexes in Aaric's jaw, and his grip tightens on the book. "He get anyone killed?"

I nod. "His guard, Captain Winshire."

He looks toward the pit. "Did he jeopardize your mission?"

"No. Halden got himself banned from Deverelli, but I was able to accomplish what I needed to." It just cost Xaden… *Gods*, I don't even know how much it cost him this time.

Aaric nods, then looks back at me with eyes that are identical to his brother's and a gaze that couldn't be any more different. "Are you in over your head, Violet?" he asks quietly.

"No." I swallow.

He narrows his eyes, then nods before following his year-mates up the steps.

I turn to find the second- and third-years engaged in a heated debate, all gathered so tightly around Rhi that I can barely see her in the center.

"I think you fly from Deverelli to Unnbriel, then—" Trager starts.

"*Back* to Deverelli, then Athebyne, then here?" Cat interrupts. "You have no idea how fucking long that flight is. Then you double that journey for Hedotis, then Zehyllna, Loysam, and the minor isles? No." She shakes her head. "No. Even using Deverelli as a base, it's a waste of flight time."

I lean over Dain's shoulder.

"I fucking hate when you're right," Dain mutters.

Rhi drags her finger across the map. "You have predominantly westerly winds until you hit this latitude." She points to the northern coast of Deverelli. "At which point, they shift, so every time you're coming back to report, you're facing a headwind."

"Dragons can take it," Maren notes quietly.

"Gryphons can't," Bodhi finishes, looking over the wall alongside Garrick.

"So basically, we're fucked," Ridoc notes. "It will take us way longer than five months to search all the isles."

Numbers fly through my head. The major isles aren't the issue. It's the dozen minor isles that border the Cerlian Sea that pose the conundrum. This last trip took eight days, and that was just to Deverelli.

"Interesting read?"

I spin toward that voice. My heart jolts at the sight of Xaden on the lowest step, then settles as I take my first deep breath since he walked away more than a week ago. "Hi," I whisper, taking in every single detail of his face before locking my gaze with his. The whites of his eyes are clear, but something about the color...

"Hi," he replies, looking me over the same way I just did to him.

"You look good." I reach for the bond and nearly melt with relief when I feel his shields give way for me. Glittering onyx wraps around my mind in a familiar wave, and I drop my barriers. *You feel good, too.*

"I slept," he answers. *And I feel oddly...well.* He clears his throat. *Funny thing about that bedroom.*

In Aretia? I brace my hand on the rough edge of the wall to keep from tugging on the edges of his flight jacket and yanking him against me.

His gaze drops to my mouth and heats. *I used to love it, and now I can't fucking stand it when you're not there.*

I missed this. I lean into the bond, like I can somehow burrow into it if I try hard enough, bury myself in us. In terms of intimacy, this is even better—

Than sex, Xaden finishes, and I find myself nodding instead of lecturing him about reading my intentions, but that wasn't...

My eyes widen. Has he been honing his signet like Ridoc?

"News from home?" Bodhi asks behind us, and I startle.

"Not unless you want to hear about how Riorson House needs roof repairs or how the oldest Sorrengail sent the largest med bag I've ever seen for the next expedition." Xaden looks past his cousin to Garrick. "I just need Professor Tavis." I step forward, but he retreats out of my reach, shaking his head. "We're at Basgiath."

Right. Back to the rules.

"*Later?*" I move out of the way so Garrick can slide by on the steps, and the sun catches on the amber flecks in Xaden's eyes as he nods before walking away.

Amber.

It's only sheer force of will that keeps me from chasing him down. Instead,

I turn back toward the argument that's continued around Rhi.

"Then skip Deverelli and just fly straight there!" Bodhi points to the isle of Unnbriel.

"The gryphons won't make it!" Cat shouts.

My focus darts island to island. Ten days here. Twenty days there. A month round trip once we're toward the outer reaches of Loysa and the minor isles. A sour feeling takes hold of my stomach, and it begins to slowly churn. The problem is reporting back to the Senarium between trips. Xaden doesn't have enough time, and neither do the Aretian wards.

"The Empyrean will side with whatever choice you make," Andarna promises, but Tairn is quiet, no doubt occupied with finally being able to talk with Sgaeyl after their period of forced silence.

We have to go, and we have to go *now.*

"So we fuck the rules." I raise my voice, and everyone quiets.

Cat throws a practice disk onto the map, and I recognize the sound-shield rune she's tempered into it.

I glance her way thankfully, then look to the others. "We supply and we go. We leave for Unnbriel as planned, but then we…disobey direct orders. We don't fly back between isles. We don't report or return until we find her kind."

Rhi's brows rise to impossible heights. "That could take a month."

"Or longer depending on weather," Maren guesses.

"They'll court-martial you," Sawyer reminds us. "It's probably the right plan, but you go against direct orders…" He cocks his head to the side. "Then again, it's hard to court-martial the squad that comes back with the seventh breed."

"Excellent point." Ridoc nods. "Do we still have to take Prince Pompous?"

"Yes." Dain leans forward and braces his forearms on his knees. "Some of the isles won't talk to us without him. Hedotis immediately comes to mind."

"This is…" Bodhi's eyes narrow on me. "Come down here." Magic ripples as I cross the sound shield and step down onto the outer cobblestone rings of the pit. "What's going on, Sorrengail? Because I'm all for fucking rules, ignoring orders, and bucking protocol, but this rush—"

"His eyes." I clench my fists and lower my voice to softer than a whisper. "From the alloy in Deverelli…the flecks in Xaden's eyes didn't go back to gold. They're still amber." We have to find a cure before people start noticing or he worsens.

Bodhi's features slacken. "Shit," he says quietly. Hope fades from his expression, but I refuse to let it steal mine. "Well, I have what you asked for." He reaches into his pocket and hands over two vials that have been marked *S* and *A.* "I can get more if you want it."

Serum and Antidote.

"Thanks." I quickly pocket them before anyone can see. "I'm not planning on using them on—"

"I'm just glad you recognize you might *have* to," he interrupts.

"We'll find a cure," I promise with far more certainty than I feel.

Bodhi's mouth tightens. "I'd kill to go, but you need to take Garrick with you."

Neither of us say what he means.

Take Garrick in case you don't.

Someone shouts on the mat, and both our heads jerk in that direction.

Kagiso shoots another blast of fire, sending a shrieking second-year scrambling backward, but Carr doesn't intervene as the flames creep closer and closer to the terrified brunette.

"Help her," I whisper.

"I've been ordered to stand down." Bodhi tenses as her screams intensify and she drops to her hands and knees.

The next blast of flames comes within inches of her.

"Wield!" Carr shouts. "Defend yourself!"

The second-year out of Claw Section splays her hand wide on the mat and *screams*. Color drains in a circle around her hand, leaving the mat gray.

Oh *shit*. My stomach clenches and I stare, stunned.

She's turning right in front of us. Or has she been one of them all along? Xaden would have sensed her, right? He was *just* here. Or would she have sensed him? I palm my dagger.

Gasps and shrieks sound in the stands behind us.

"Carr!" Panchek orders.

The professor moves faster than I've ever seen him, brandishing an alloy-hilted dagger and driving it straight through the cadet's back, into her heart.

Just like that. She's *dead*. Executed. No questions, no chance to cure her, nothing.

Bodhi shudders. "Take. Garrick."

In a culture that worships the goddess of war exclusively, blood is the preferred sacrifice and cowardice is the ultimate sin.

—Unnbriel: Isle of Dunne by Second Lieutenant Asher Daxton

CHAPTER
TWENTY-NINE

It takes ten days to put plans in motion and get everything together, and the time wears on me like the steady drip of water in the interrogation chamber, grating on my very last nerve. I sit through every class as instructed and practice wielding until my arms drop from exhaustion, but I can't quit watching Xaden's eyes in case their flecks change back to gold whenever I see him during Signet Sparring.

They never do.

By the time most of us have gathered on the flight field in the foggy predawn hours of the first Saturday of March, my anxiety to get moving feels like insects under my skin. I hate that we've lied to Halden that this is only the Unnbriel trip, but there's a growing part of me that just doesn't care.

He's a fucking liability.

After a surprisingly easy discussion with Cat, our squad has grown to include Trager and Maren—partially because of Trager's healing training, but more so we can split if we need to. Given the look on Mira's face as those in our squad approach the lines of waiting gryphons and dragons, she's not too pleased about the development. Guess I forgot to mention that part in my missive.

"Where have you been?" I ask, breaking away from the group in hopes of getting any form of privacy. They quickly disappear into the thick fog.

"On leave," she answers. "While you've been back here making plans to disobey direct orders from the Senarium, which of course is your prerogative as mission commander." She glances at the oversize pack currently murdering my spine, then the one sitting at her feet. "The missives were clever. Subtle, even.

The packs? Not so much."

"The fact that you were *on leave* was all Panchek would tell me when I asked how to get a letter to you. You disappeared." My eyes narrow and I exhale a puff of steam into the freezing air. "And we can't help the size of our packs when we have to carry—"

"Are you worried about not getting enough supplies in Deverelli?" Halden asks from behind me.

Mira quirks an eyebrow upward, managing to say *I told you so* without moving her mouth.

"More worried you're going to fuck something up again," Xaden remarks, and I pivot to see him walking toward us with Garrick out of the mist.

Halden's spine stiffens. "You don't get to talk to me like that, Riorson."

"Oh, good. I was wondering when you two would start arguing." Mira folds her arms in front of her chest.

"Or you'll what? Get yourself banned from another isle? Sit off the coast on Tecarus's ship? You're already dead weight, *Your Highness*. Are you really going to be a detriment, too?" Xaden stops at my side but keeps his hands to himself, just like he's done since he returned. *"Everyone here?"*

"Dain is on his way."

"I'm not going to apologize for conducting Navarrian business while in Deverelli—" Halden starts.

"How about apologizing for keeping mission-essential information from those of us responsible for the fucking mission?" Xaden counters, stepping into Halden's space, shadows swelling around his feet. "If it wasn't for us, you'd be dead."

Shit.

I glance over at Garrick, who looks back at me like I'm the one supposed to do something.

"Let him kill the prince," Andarna suggests, and I hear her halter jingle about twenty feet behind me. *"He does not represent us well."*

"He will not be a problem," Tairn assures us.

If only I felt half as certain.

"Well, we're off to a great start," Drake notes, sauntering by on his way to the line of gryphons, where the other fliers wait in the heavy fog. I can barely see their shapes from here.

"Get out of my face," Halden orders.

"Must kill you that you can't make me." A corner of Xaden's mouth rises. "Why don't you scurry into your little basket?"

"Fuck off." Halden's cheeks redden, but he retreats a single step.

"I honestly don't care if you kill him," I say to Xaden down the bond, *"but*

you will. Wasn't that your line when I nearly took off Cat's head in Aretia?"

"He's going to get you killed," Xaden retorts. *"This isn't going to work."*

"I'm not dying on Halden's account."

Ridoc walks out of the fog from my left, takes one look at Halden and Xaden, and makes a beeline for my side. "Kind of feels like Threshing, doesn't it? Exciting. Terrifying. We know we have to go, but there's every chance we're about to have our asses handed to us."

"I did not enjoy flying straight through to Athebyne," Halden announces into the fog. "We'll only fly halfway today—"

Fog swirls with the beat of another pair of wings, and the ground shudders as a dragon lands to the left, just behind Ridoc.

Halden gawks and stumbles backward.

The fog obscures all but the outline of claws until the dragon lowers his blue snout to ground level and chuffs a deep breath in Halden's direction.

What the fuck is Molvic…

My stomach lurches.

"I told you the firstborn would not be an issue," Tairn reminds me.

"Molvic?" Ridoc leans forward slightly, like there's any mistaking the scar that runs across the Blue Clubtail's snout.

"No!" I roll my shoulders, drop my pack, and run past Xaden and Halden, straight into the fog. "Don't do this!" I make it less than thirty feet before I find him walking toward us at Dain's side.

"I'm not going to sit aside and watch while Halden gets you all killed," Aaric says, tugging the strap of his rucksack to tighten it. For Dunne's sake, he doesn't even have a battle-ready flight jacket.

"This isn't what you want," I remind him. "Don't let your brother's actions force your hand"—I swing a pointing finger at Dain—"and don't you let him do it!"

Dain puts both hands up, palms outward at his chest. "How in all that's holy am *I* to blame for this?"

I fumble for an answer. "He's a first-year and you're the wingleader!"

Dain rubs the bridge of his nose and pushes his fingers outward, over the heavy, dark circles under his eyes. "Vi, I think he outranks me in this department."

"You sure you want to do this?" Xaden asks, so close I can suddenly feel the warmth of him at my back.

"Want? No." Aaric shakes his head. "But I need to. And as much as I don't mind Halden making *your* life fucking miserable, I do mind him condemning the Continent to death by dark wielder because he can't take a deep breath and count to three when he gets mad."

"Sounds great to me." Xaden's hand brushes the small of my back. "You good with this?" He glances my way.

I study the set of Aaric's chin and the determination in his green eyes, then nod in defeat. "We're all allowed to make our own choices, and if this is yours, I'll support it."

Aaric nods, and Xaden and I fall into step with him and Dain, heading for our dragons…and Halden.

"Looks like you won't be needing that basket after all," Xaden says as we make it back to where Mira waits with Ridoc, Garrick, and Halden. "We found ourselves another prince."

Halden's jaw hits the ground as his widened gaze locks on his little brother.

"Don't look so surprised," Aaric says in greeting.

"Don't look…" Halden shakes his head slowly. "You've let us run all over this kingdom searching brothels and gaming houses for you, and all the while, you've been *here*?"

"The fact that you went searching *your* favorite haunts for *me* is just the start of where you went wrong," Aaric replies.

"You're a *rider*?" Halden shouts.

"As the dragon would imply." Ridoc points to Molvic.

"He could have let you think he was dead," Mira mutters.

"He's *going to be* when our father hears—" Halden starts.

"Fuck off and tell him." Aaric shrugs. "Or don't. I really don't care. I crossed the parapet because I was sick of sitting by knowing you and Dad weren't going to do *shit* about the dark wielders, and I'm not going to sit by now and watch you run our only hope into the ground. I'll be going as the royal representative."

Halden stiffens. "Absolutely not, Cam."

"He goes by Aaric, and he absolutely will," I counter, earning myself a menacing glare from my ex that doesn't even faze me. "You're banned from Deverelli and have the temper of a two-year-old on a good day, Halden. Aaric is a rider. He'll keep up with us in the air and on the ground, and having been in his squad for the last eight months, I can promise you that he knows how to keep his shit together when things go badly."

Halden's glare shifts to Aaric. "It was you who breached the royal vault."

"Yes." Aaric nods.

"Father blamed *me*." Halden takes a step forward, and a tiny twinge of guilt nips the back of my neck, since our past is most likely the reason he took the heat. "Did you stay in Basgiath? Or fly with the rebels?"

"You already know the answer," Aaric replies.

Halden turns as red as Sliseag. "Go back to the quadrant. I'll be the only royal—"

"Good luck getting a gryphon to carry your basket again," Aaric says, then walks toward Molvic without another word.

"Well, as awkward as this has been..." Ridoc lifts his brows.

"I'm sure you know your way off the flight field," Xaden says to Halden, but the prince's gaze is locked on the claws of the blue dragon.

"Violet." Halden lowers his voice and slowly looks my way. The plea in his eyes hits me straight in the chest.

"I won't let anything happen to him," I promise.

Halden nods once. "I'll hold you to it." He looks at each of us in turn, and the promise morphs into a threat. "All of you."

. . .

We spend a day at Athebyne and another at Cordyn, resting the gryphons between legs of the journey. They're far less winded without the baskets to carry, but without magic to bolster their strength, we need to take two days to rest in Deverelli before continuing onward.

That second day convinces Mira of what she'd already guessed on our first trip: some runes work off the Continent. Now to narrow down which ones and figure out *why*. We're each supplied with a handful of multicolored quartz disks to test. I'm grateful not to be sunburned—though I can't tell if it's the amethyst disk or the same rune on one of the daggers Xaden gave me last year—but annoyed to all shit that runes are the only thing Mira is willing to talk to me about.

The southwestern Deverelli coastline falls away in the early hours of the eighth day of the trip, and the color shifts from aqua to midnight blue as we head over the open sea.

And that's all I see on the horizon—water.

If it weren't for ships beneath us making their own journeys, I'd be more than a little apprehensive about flying into nothingness.

"Save your nerves for when we reach Unnbriel in nine hours," Tairn tells me. *"And save* yours *for when the winds shift,"* he instructs Andarna, who's clipped in below.

Gods, I hope the maps my father included are accurate. Dragons aren't exactly boats. They can't just float if they get tired, and nine hours from now will put our total flight time at twelve.

Gryphons aren't fond of anything over eight.

The air current shifts sometime around noon, giving us a tailwind as the clouds clear, and Andarna relishes in her freedom unclipped from Tairn, off to his side. Her wingbeats are strong, but the difference in her left wing is far more visible without magic for strength. Each beat strains the tendons to gain full extension, and it isn't long before she's dipping slightly.

Worry wraps her prickly fingers around my throat when Andarna pitches in a gust, but I keep my mouth shut as she climbs back into formation.

"Do not lose altitude," Tairn warns her. *"There is no telling what weaponry arms the merchant vessels beneath us."*

"Do you ever tire of your own voice?" she questions, soaring a little closer to Sgaeyl.

"Never," he assures her.

With nothing to do for the next eight hours but hold on, I listen as Tairn recites the lore of his breed from the first of his line up to Thareux, the first black dragon to ever successfully bond, back during the Great War, then stops.

Apparently the story is no longer worth telling once humans are involved.

The sun has slid into the angles of afternoon by the time Tairn catches sight of land.

"Thirty minutes!" he announces to Andarna and me, then lets loose a roar that vibrates my teeth to alert the others.

I pivot in the saddle to check our formation. Everyone is where they should be, with the exception of Kiralair, who is drifting back from her guarded position in the center, toward Aotrom's snout. *"Just in time, too. Kiralair is fading."*

"Had to bring the gryphons," Tairn mutters as I turn forward again and the hilly coastline comes into view.

The sea transitions from dark blue to white-capped teal crashing on cream-colored beaches along what appears to be a port city a few miles in front of us.

"That must be Soneram." We've definitely found the isle of Dunne. I can make out the tiered walls of defenses—including cross-bolts—from here, and they haven't changed much from what my father detailed in his drawings. *"Let's avoid being skewered, shall we?"* I ask Tairn.

Tairn huffs and surges ahead of the others, then banks right and leads our formation along the northeastern shoreline, giving the port city a wide berth.

I block the afternoon sun with a hand on my forehead and scan the coast, noting the end of the city walls. *"There's another town in two or three miles, then nothing for at least forty."*

As long as they haven't expanded in the thirty-plus years since my father wrote his book.

We pass the town and its substantial fortifications, and after we travel another ten minutes without sight of habitation, Tairn turns inland, breaking formation and flying ahead of the others.

"Stay with Sgaeyl," he orders Andarna.

Andarna huffs in annoyance.

"Stick to the plan," I remind her.

"I loathe the plan," she replies.

The beaches are rockier here, the narrow strip of sand strewn with boulders before it gives way to hills of thick vegetation that roll as far as I can see.

All of it is the same muted green as Deverelli.

"That one," Tairn says, locating a suitably large clearing about halfway up a hillside a few miles inland from the coast, and after a perimeter sweep, we finally land in the dead center of the meadow.

Birds launch from the trees in a riot of color, quickly fleeing.

A low rumble resonates through Tairn, not quite powerful enough to be a growl but definitely loud enough to warn anything that might consider making us dinner as he slowly rotates, scanning the edges of the trees and sweeping his tail through the waist-high grass.

"This will do," he says once he's completed a turn.

Moments later, the rest appear overhead, Sgaeyl leading formation. Their wings cast shade over the clearing momentarily, flaring to slow their descent before they land around us.

The ground shudders as they make impact, Andarna to the right and Sgaeyl to our left. Teine, Aotrom, Cath, Chradh, and Molvic touch down behind us, and the gryphons fill in the spaces as we form a large circle.

Every set of teeth and talons faces the trees.

"Hear that?" Tairn lowers his head and stalks forward.

The jungle around us is unnaturally silent. *"The animals here recognize you as predators, that's for sure."*

"Good." He dips his shoulder and I start the process of dismounting, leaving all but the essentials strapped behind the seat of my saddle.

Everyone strips down to our undershirts—or in my case, my armor—to accommodate the suffocating heat and humidity that rivals Deverelli, and then we make quick work of securing the site and locating a nearby stream for fresh water. Then Cat and Trager take off into the woods to hunt while half the riot launches to do the same.

"We're alone for now, but we won't be for long," Mira says as Teine follows Tairn and Aotrom into the sky. "Someone will see them."

"Good. Once Aaric meets with their queen, we can move on." I skim my hand over the pale green meadow grass and pick up a sizable rock to line the firepit with. "Chances of an alliance here are slim. Given how painful it is for the riot to be separated from magic, I doubt Andarna's kind settled here."

"What if they learned to live without magic?" Mira asks, rotating a beaded bracelet of what looks like black tourmaline on her wrist and watching Ridoc and Garrick build a fire as Dain constructs a cooking spit with Maren and Aaric.

"I don't know if they can," I admit softly, my eye catching on the bracelet. Something about the knotwork holding the metallic beads tickles the back of my brain, and I swear I can smell parchment for the smallest of seconds before I look away. "Tairn isn't exactly offering up details on how it affects their lifespan."

"Are he and Sgaeyl having some kind of mate drama?" Mira picks up a rock of her own.

"Not that I know of. Why?" I ask, and we start back toward the center of the clearing.

"They haven't hunted together the entire trip." She tucks her stone under her arm and picks up another.

I glance across the field, where Xaden walks patrol with Drake near Sgaeyl and Andarna. "They think one of them should always be with the group." It's as close to the truth as I'm going to get with her.

She glances at me like she can see right through the half truth.

Cue change of subject.

"Where did you go on leave?" I ask her.

Her mouth purses, like she's deciding. "I went to see Grandmother."

"You flew to Deaconshire?" I mean, that's a choice, I guess.

"You think I took personal leave to visit a burial ground?" She side-eyes me.

My eyebrows try their damnedest to reach my hairline. "You went to see Grandma *Niara*?" I end on a whisper.

Mira rolls her eyes. "You don't have to whisper. Our parents can't hear you."

I'm tempted to check our surroundings just to be sure. "She stopped talking to Mom and Dad…" I shake my head. "It must have been before I was born because I don't even remember her. Something to do with Dad marrying Mom, right?"

Mira shakes her head. "You were a toddler," she says. "Right around the age where your hair was coming in thick enough to pull into a little ponytail." She smiles at the memory, but it slips. "And it wasn't Grandma Niara who ended communication. Turns out it was the other way around."

"You know what happened, don't you?" Envy stabs quick and deep. Mom and Dad almost *never* spoke of his family. Is that where the bracelet came from?

"You should go up to Luceras." She looks at me with the oddest combination of worry and dread, her mouth tightening. "Talk to her yourself."

"With all the leave I get before graduation?"

"Excellent point." She scours the field for another rock.

Just not excellent enough for her to tell me. Fine. If the last year has taught me anything, it's that we're all entitled to our secrets. *But it's my family, too.*

"I brought Dad's books in case you want to read them." I offer another subject change and start looking for firepit rocks again. The ground is firm below our feet, so at least we won't be sleeping in mud.

Mira's brow knits.

"They mostly cover customs," I blurt. "But he devotes an entire chapter in every book to the unique flora and fauna of every isle. Very thorough." My own forehead puckers. I'm babbling, but I can't help trying to find *something* that bridges the space I can feel expanding between us. "Did Grandma Niara say how he found time to study things like the migratory patterns of terns and errisbirds? Or Fallorinia moths? He spends three pages talking about companion planting breeson root and kellenweed, then goes off about zakia berries and how if the birds migrate to Hedotis too late, they're overripe and the flock drops dead, their little yellow beaks stained blue."

"Thank you, but no. That sounds awful." She stiffens and shifts so both rocks are in her arms.

I clutch my rock. "Did Grandma Niara know he studied the isles?"

Her lips part, but then she looks away. "She knew. And he left the books for you alone, remember? I certainly don't need to know about bird migration or moths."

"Mira—" Fuck.

She quickens her pace, leaving me behind, and I blow out a slow sigh.

"That was embarrassing to listen to. Could you make it any more awkward?" Andarna chides.

"Go hunt something."

We set up camp with one eye on the forest at all times, cooking the rabbits Trager and Cat bring back, laying out bedrolls around the fire, and assigning watches before getting to sleep, encircled by two dragons and a matching number of gryphons at all times while the others accompany their riders and fliers on watch.

I take first with Maren and Drake, who I learn has a sarcastic sense of humor to rival Ridoc's.

Xaden takes second with Mira and Garrick.

The stars shine bright when Xaden finally slides under the blankets, fully clothed all the way to his boots just like I am. He wraps his arm around my waist, then tugs my back against his chest. I smile, half asleep, then burrow closer. Wood crashes, and I blink my eyes open as Dain throws another piece of timber onto the dying blaze, stoking the fire.

"Anything?" I whisper.

"Not yet," Xaden says against my ear, curling his body around mine, and any chill he's picked up on patrol is quickly warmed away. "They have to go."

I nod and fight the dread taking root in my stomach. Being bait settles like curdled milk.

He presses a kiss behind my ear, and his breathing evens out behind me.

"Wait for sunrise to disappear," I tell Tairn, already sinking into sleep. *"He*

needs as much rest as we can give him." Unnbriel is all about trial by combat, and he's the best among us.

Tairn grumbles his assent.

"Rise!" Tairn shouts what feels like an instant later, and my eyes spring open to see a line of pink and orange gracing the horizon.

I suck in a startled breath, and Xaden's hand splays over my hip, holding me in place. Grass rustles rhythmically behind us, and my heart starts to pound. This would be a *great* time to access that bond we share. My right hand fists the blankets that cover us, and Xaden's hand slips to my upper thigh sheath.

"It was a mistake to come," a man says in the common language, his voice low as he leans over us. "Your magic won't help you here, fire-bringer."

I rip back the blankets and Xaden draws my dagger, bringing it to the edge of the man's throat in a single smooth motion.

The soldier's brown eyes widen as I palm my next dagger and glance over his leather armor, spotting the weak joints at his elbows and beneath his arms. It's been dyed the same pale green as the leaves on the trees, and an emblem of two crossed swords over a horseshoe is stamped across his chest plate.

"That's fine." Xaden sits up slowly, keeping the dagger's edge at the base of the soldier's throat as he retreats. "We brought blades."

It is unwise to favor one god above another. Better to shun them all than show favoritism amongst a jealous, prodigious pantheon.

—MAJOR RORILEE'S GUIDE TO APPEASING THE GODS,
SECOND EDITION

CHAPTER THIRTY

Holding two daggers, I stand beside Xaden as the soldier backs away, joining what looks to be at least a couple dozen of his colleagues on horseback, all carrying swords at their left hips and daggers sheathed along their right arms.

Five others retreat from our squadmates' beds in the same manner, and everyone who isn't posted on third watch rises, weapons in hand. Looks like they sent an entire platoon to greet us, and they're all wearing varying degrees of the same bloodthirsty smile.

"Two full companies of cavalry lurk in the hills," Tairn tells me, and I chance a quick look around the field, spotting several pairs of golden eyes low among the tall trees.

"I would like to try an Unnbrish horse," Andarna muses.

"No," Tairn and I answer simultaneously.

Andarna sighs down the bond. *"One day I'm going to stop asking nicely."*

"You should take your fire-breathers and depart our isle," the soldier warns as the others fall into line ahead of the mounted cavalry.

"Two companies in the hills," I whisper to Xaden, careful to move my mouth as little as possible.

"Soon," Xaden tells the soldier and brushes the back of his hand against mine.

They're all so…similar. Every soldier in front of us, regardless of sex, stands roughly the same height—within a few inches of six feet tall, with the same muscular build and closely cropped hair. And all wear the same emblem on their leathers, though I'm guessing the different insignia at the bases of their necks denote rank.

"You speak the common language?" Dain reaches my right with Mira, and our squad faces down their platoon, keeping a civil ten feet of distance between our forces.

"My knowledge of your tongue is why I was selected to command this mission," their leader replies without taking his eyes off Xaden.

"Love wasting my time," Dain mutters, then shoves the small booklet I recognize as the language compendium for Unnbriel into the chest pocket of his flight jacket.

The blond, sharp-jawed soldier directly ahead of me gives me a once-over, his gaze catching on the daggers in my hands and the others at my thighs.

"We officially request an audience with your queen." Xaden steps forward, his hand still wrapped around my dagger.

"Denied," the captain answers. "She does not meet with those unworthy of her presence, and given how easy it was to walk up to your encampment, the chances of your worth"—his gaze skims over the line of us, and he scoffs after a quick appraisal of my stature—"are minimal."

Fuck him.

Branches sway as the dragons and gryphons walk out of the trees around us, loosely surrounding the platoon.

"We *made* it easy, Captain." I cock my head to the side and flip my dagger to pinch its tip as Tairn growls at my back, low and mean. *Just the way I like him.* "Rest assured, we can make it difficult, too."

To their credit, the platoon doesn't sprint away screaming, but a dark stain spreads down the green leather pants of the blond soldier who stares past me with wide eyes. He definitely would have been a runner after Parapet.

"Don't worry," I say with a quick smile. "It's not an uncommon reaction." But it does cause my heart to sink slightly. *"They've never seen dragons."*

"My family isn't on this isle," Andarna notes, frustration surging down the bond and pouring over me like a thousand pinpricks.

I roll my shoulders, trying to shake it off. The last thing we need is a dead soldier and a blown alliance. *"And please be careful with your feelings. I can't shield here."*

The soldier drags his gaze back to mine and narrows his eyes, saying something I don't fully understand, but I definitely pick up *weak* and *smallest.* I flip my dagger again and catch it by the hilt.

"He doesn't think you're..." Dain shakes his head. "You know what? Never mind." He lifts his middle finger to the soldier.

"Burning us will not grant you an audience with our queen." The captain raises his chin.

"No, but defeating your best in combat earns us entrance to court at the defeated opponent's rank," Xaden says, cocking his head as a smirk plays across his mouth.

The smile fades from the captain's face. "You know our laws."

"She does." Xaden gestures toward me. "And I'm with her. Seeing as I've already had my blade at your throat, I guess that means we should move up to someone with a higher skill set."

The captain slowly turns, his gaze sweeping high above our heads, and Tairn snarls. "The fire-breathers stay."

Sgaeyl lunges from the left and snaps her teeth close enough to a soldier that the woman's hair blows sideways as she gasps.

"She said to get fucked," Xaden replies to their captain.

The captain glances toward Sgaeyl without making eye contact. "Only half may come. Choose wisely. Final and only offer."

Xaden nods, then turns toward us and hands Garrick his sword. "Who do you want to take?" he asks me.

"Me?" I blink.

"Your mission," he replies.

Fuck. I draw a deep breath and look past Dain to Mira. "Xaden to challenge. Aaric to speak for Navarre. Cat for Poromiel…" My throat constricts, realizing I'm down to two.

Mira nods. "Solid choices. Stop stalling."

"Dain and me." Which leaves our second-strongest fighter behind as well as my sister.

"Aetos?" Garrick asks.

"Do not question command," Xaden warns in a tone that stiffens Garrick's back.

"Captain said he was selected for the mission because he speaks our language, so we can't assume it's common," I explain. "I can pick up a few words here and there, but I spent my time learning Hedotic and Dain took the rest."

Garrick's jaw ticks, but he nods once.

"Let me guess. I'm to stay here," Andarna snipes.

"You're learning," Tairn replies.

I lift my gaze to Mira's and find no judgment waiting there. "If we're not back by nightfall, burn the place to the ground."

．．．

Eistol, the capital of Unnbriel, is less than a twenty-minute flight inland, but it takes two hours for the cavalry to wind their way through the steep terrain and over the ridgeline to the heavily fortified city.

The city itself makes me second-guess bringing Tairn. Eistol dominates the countryside, consuming the tallest hill for miles. It's built in a series of terraced circles in various shades of stone, but the roofs of its structures are a uniform pale blue color. Each terrace is surrounded by a wall thick enough to sustain Tairn's weight, and the bottom one supports a dozen manned cross-bolts. The eight above hold decreasing but proportionate numbers, and unlike Deverelli, these swing in multiple directions.

This place is constructed to fight dragons, whether or not they've actually *been* here.

"I don't like you being this close to those bolts," I say along the bond, noting the platoon of cavalry as they ride single file through raised metal gates inside each ring. One order, and the city would be impossible to breach on foot...or escape.

"I don't like your selection in mates, yet here we are," Tairn responds as we approach the city from hundreds of feet above, leading the formation as a storm rolls in from the west.

"Third ring," I remind him as we soar over the fifth.

"I was there. I remember," he replies, tucking his wings and diving toward the third-highest ring in the city.

The belt of my saddle presses into my thighs as we dive, and I wait for the snap of wings I know is coming...but it doesn't.

"Tairn?" People run in the streets, ducking into the structures that line the rapidly approaching walls. If he doesn't slow soon, we'll take out the masonry. *"Tairn!"*

He sighs, then flares his wings and pumps once, jarring me in a bone-rattling shift of momentum before landing lengthwise on the wall of the third ring. Rock crumbles beneath his talons, and he lowers his head at the cross-bolt stationed less than a dozen feet away.

Two of the soldiers manning the station back up, but the third bravely stands partially hidden within the wooden base of the launching unit, one hand poised on the lever mechanism while the other slowly cranks the wooden wheel that pivots the weapon at us.

I undo the belt of my saddle and quickly rise for a better vantage point, dagger already in hand.

Shadow falls over us a second before Sgaeyl lands on the opposite side of the cross-bolt, and the soldier's head jerks in her direction as she growls low in her throat, her nostrils flaring.

The soldier lifts both hands from the weapon.

I leave everything strapped to Tairn's saddle except the weapons I carry, then move toward his shoulder, only pausing to be sure Cath, Kira, and Molvic have landed behind me.

"Watch where you dismount or you'll embarrass us both," Tairn warns, and my stomach lurches as I glance down. If I nudge even a few feet to the right, I'll fall off the edge of the fifty-foot wall.

"Noted." I aim inward and slide, landing on the wall between his first and second talon.

By the time Xaden and I reach them, all three soldiers have backed themselves into the cross-bolt turret. I open my mouth to assure them we only mean harm if they do, but a wooden door in the stone ground is pushed open on Xaden's left, and the cavalry captain's head pops through.

He lectures the soldiers, but the only word I pick out is *audience.* Then he beckons us toward the darkness with a motion of his hand. "Follow me."

Xaden walks in first, and I follow down the stone staircase. Natural light illuminates our path through small slits in the stonework, and we pass two doorways as we wind our way to the ground floor.

"They're inside the walls, too," I tell Tairn. Dad either left that part out or never saw the inner workings of the defenses. My bet is on the second.

"Smart," Tairn acknowledges.

The officer pushes open the door at the base of the steps, and Xaden and I walk into a shaded alleyway between stone buildings maybe a foot wider than Xaden's shoulders. The pommels of his swords come within inches of scraping rock. *"We could learn a few things from this construction. One soldier could hold off dozens."*

We reach the end of the alley and walk into the open cobblestone street. It looks to be thirty feet wide and, if Dad's records are correct, is part of the residential district, but there's nothing homey about the leather-clad soldiers lining the street, only a few of whom wear the muted green leathers. Soldiers in pale blue wear metal greaves along their legs. But the ones in silver stand in front of the next gate, swords drawn, the metal of their armored chest plates catching the morning light.

At least the portcullis hasn't been lowered.

"Wait here." The captain walks us into the middle, then leaves when one of the soldiers in blue shouts something from the left.

Xaden and I move to stand back to back.

"There're two dozen of them and only the both of us," I whisper, my gaze jumping from soldier to soldier, noting they have two stationed in front of every door.

Sgaeyl growls from above.

"Four," Xaden reminds me quietly, brushing his pinkie against mine. "And I'm really missing that bond right now."

"Me too." I keep my hands close to my blades without giving the guards reason to strike, fighting the fear that threatens to slow my judgment as the sky darkens with heavy clouds.

The guards at my right split, and the captain walks through, followed by Aaric, Dain, and Cat.

"Welcoming bunch," Cat notes when they reach us.

"This way," the captain orders, then strides toward the silver-wearing soldiers blocking the next gate.

"Stay close and don't get yourself killed," Xaden says to Aaric as we follow the cavalry officer. The soldiers walking on both sides of us alternate between watching us and glancing upward, as though Tairn and Sgaeyl might decide they've had enough of the wall.

The soldiers begin to argue as we approach the gate, but I only pick out *danger* and *holy.*

"They want the challenge held in this…station," Dain interprets from behind me as Sgaeyl and Tairn walk the wall above us, keeping pace. "They don't want us any closer to their primary temple."

"It's not their temple we're interested in," Cat mutters beside him.

The captain must win the argument because the guards part to allow us through. I glance at their chest plates and find the etched symbol of two crossed swords gripped in the center by a claw—the emblem of Dunne.

"It's similar to ours," I tell Tairn as we cross under the thick gate. *"They have a claw in her symbol, suggesting a common origin."*

"Focus now, analyze later," he demands as we enter the next section.

There are no residences here, only two sectors of terraced seating built into the walls on both sides, leaving an open plaza in front of the largest temple I've ever seen. It's easily the height of Tairn. The long, gabled roof is tiled in the same pale blue as the rest of the city, and the six wide pillars holding the front are all gray granite. The polished stones shimmer in the light, making them appear almost silver, and each has been carved with a different symbol. *Sword. Shield. Fire. Water. Claw.* My eyebrows rise when my gaze reaches the final pillar on the right. *Book.*

All tools of warfare.

Beside that pillar is a sculpted tribute to the goddess, a sparkling gray effigy of her likeness that reaches the lowest line of the roof. She holds a sword pointed in our direction in her left hand and a shield protecting the right edge of her temple in the other. Her long hair is braided down one side of her torso, and she's dressed in long, belted robes with an armored chest plate.

"Wow," Cat whispers as the uniformed guards filter in behind us, taking positions along the sides of the plaza as we move toward the darker stones between the terraced seats.

Blue-robed attendants rise on the temple steps, and my footsteps falter.

Every single one of them has silver hair.

Not gray.

Not white.

Silver.

Guardians are no longer permitted to dedicate children in service to their favored deity. The decision to serve the gods for life must be made after the age of majority and of one's free will.

—PUBLIC NOTICE 200.417
TRANSCRIBED BY RACEL LIGHTSTONE

CHAPTER THIRTY-ONE

"**A**re you dizzy?" Xaden asks in a low whisper.

"No." My gaze jumping from one attendant to the next as we walk toward them. They all have different heights, shapes, genders, and skin tones, but their hair color is as uniform as their blue robes.

One of the attendants on the top step claps her hands, and a group of children in light-blue tunics runs out from behind the statue of Dunne to race up the steps toward her. My gaze locks on the last of them, a girl who looks to be no more than ten. The brunette's silver-tipped braid swings against her back as she scoops up a younger child and is ushered inside.

Breath abandons me as she disappears.

"Violet," Xaden whispers. "Her hair—"

"I know." I wobble, and he steadies me with a hand on my lower back.

Never in my twenty-one years have I seen anyone with hair like mine. Does hers always end in silver no matter how short she cuts it? Do her joints fail her? Do her bones break? I need to know. I *have* to know.

The cavalry captain shouts up at the walls as Tairn prowls above us, and the attendants all draw blades from the belts at their waists, jarring me from my spiraling thoughts.

"He said, 'I've brought them,'" Dain translates from Xaden's left as we form a straight line on the cusp of what feels like a theater floor. Or a battle briefing stage.

"The blades are cute," Tairn remarks.

"The hair," I reply. *"Her hair looked like mine."*

"Survive first so you can be curious later. Focus."

Metal creaks, and a gate rises above the highest row on our left. A moment later, two people step out of the tunnel.

"Xaden's opponent?" I ask Tairn.

"Not unless he's fighting an aging general and a high priestess."

The middle-aged man with graying hair and rich brown skin on the left boasts the same uniform as the silver-dressed guards, and the older, light-skinned woman at his side wears not only the long pale blue robes of the temple attendants but a sword sheathed at her hip.

Her narrowed gaze sweeps over us, then fixes on me as the man calls out in Unnbrish at her left.

"He says he is the commander of the guard and asks if we truly wish an audience with their queen," Dain translates.

"Tell him we do, and we will comply with their customs to get it," I answer, sending up a prayer to Dunne that Xaden is ready for this.

Dain translates slowly, and the pair moves down the steps as the cavalry captain climbs to join them. The captain reports, and the commander's mouth flattens before he draws his dagger and slices through the shoulder straps of the captain's leather armor.

The green leather falls to the steps, and the captain lowers his head.

"I think that means demotion," Cat whispers to Aaric's right.

"In every language," Aaric agrees.

The commander's voice booms across the plaza and echoes off the rock as he descends the steps, and Dain translates as quickly as he can.

"'All we can achieve is death, but to...'" Dain pauses. "Shit, I think he said to provide our strongest warriors, and they will test our worthiness to speak with their queen."

Xaden nods. "Tell him I'm ready."

Dain repeats the message, and the commander claps twice. Three bare-armed soldiers step out of the tunnel, and my chest tightens. The woman in the middle has to be the same height as Sawyer, if not Dain, and the bulky men flanking her tower above with the same height difference I have with Xaden. I think they're twins.

The chill that races down my spine has nothing to do with the gusting wind or the disappearance of the sun behind the storm clouds overhead.

"Maybe we should rethink this strategy," Cat whispers.

Yeah, I'm with her for once.

"What you call strategy, they call law," Xaden replies.

My heart beats faster with every step the warriors descend behind their commander and the high priestess of the temple. By the time they reach the plaza, a hummingbird could time its wings to my pulse.

"Costa!" the guards along the walls cry out, and the warrior on the right lifts his muscle-laden arms.

"Marlis!" the rest of the guards shout, and the woman raises her chin.

"Palta!" Another chorus sounds, and the twin on the left cracks his neck.

The commander lifts his hand, and the soldiers fall silent before he speaks.

"He asks if this is our champion or our leader," Dain translates.

"Close but no. He asked if Xaden is our champion or our prince. Don't be embarrassed, Aetos. The words sound similar enough." Aaric steps forward, then replies to the commander in what sounds like *flawless* Unnbrish.

My jaw drops, but he speaks too fast to understand anything other than "Navarre."

Whatever he says gives the commander and the priestess pause before she replies, her gaze darting to me again.

"Are you fucking serious?" Dain snaps. "Why didn't you tell us you're fluent?"

"You never asked." Aaric reaches for the pommel of his sword as he turns back to face us. "I told them who I am and that I'd be the one fighting."

"You what?" My voice rises with my panic.

"I'm the one who needs the audience," he replies. "I'm not my brother, nor my father, and I won't hide while someone else—" He draws the first few inches of the sharpened steel.

"No!" I move toward him, but Xaden's there first, covering Aaric's hand.

"Prince or not, you're a fucking first-year and we both know I can put you into the ground. Your tutors are no match for real-life experience." He forces the sword back into its scabbard. "And no, you are not your father, nor your brother, which is precisely why you *will not* fight. We need you to live. Your *kingdom* needs you to live." Xaden grabs the collar of Aaric's uniform and pivots, forcing him back into line next to me. "Tell them I'm ready."

Fuck, I don't want *either* of them in that ring.

"Every possible path," Andarna reminds me. *"Even if my kind aren't here, they may have seen them. May know of them."*

"Do not consider the Dark One," Tairn chides. *"Navarre needs the soldiers from this alliance to defend the borders, freeing the riders to go on the offensive."*

Either way, someone's fighting.

"Same could be said for you." Color rises along Aaric's neck, and he shakes his head at Xaden.

"Tyrrendor is safe in Bodhi's hands should I fall." Xaden lowers his voice, and my stomach sours at the thought. "This isn't about honor. Consider it your revenge. Remember what I did to your brother and *tell them*."

Blood runs from my face. Xaden isn't talking about Halden.

Aaric says something in Unnbrish, glaring at Xaden the entire time.

Xaden lets go of him, then checks with Dain.

"He said you're the strongest," Dain admits, then translates again as the commander begins to speak. "And they have chosen Costa as your opponent."

One of the twins. I look past Xaden to see the warrior already standing in the middle of the plaza next to the priestess. He's more terrifying up close than he had been walking down the steps. Thick neck. Huge arms. Gleefully menacing smile. He's a walking arsenal, strapped with weaponry, and the scars up and down his tanned arms tell me he isn't a stranger to pain. The assumption is confirmed when the priestess scores the back of his forearm with a dagger and he doesn't so much as flinch.

Blood drips from the spot, spattering the dark stones beneath as the first rain drop hits my face, and the soldiers behind us *cheer*.

"That wasn't in my father's book." My stomach sinks with suspicion of *how* those stones became the shade they are and the ever-growing fear that Xaden may have met his match.

"Incoming," Dain announces, and Xaden turns to face the priestess as she approaches, passing by Marlis and Palta.

The tattoo of Dunne's emblem inked into her forehead crinkles as she lifts her silver brows at Xaden and holds out her hand. "The Goddess of War demands her payment before you may prove your worth," she says in the common language.

She must be at least seventy-five years old. How long would it take for such a tattoo to fade to the point it's unrecognizable? My stomach lurches into my throat. There's no way—

"*Focus,*" Tairn snaps like a frustrated professor.

Xaden shrugs out of his double scabbard, then his uniform top, leaving him in a short-sleeve undershirt as he holds out his left forearm. The high priestess draws the blade across his skin, and I sink my teeth into my bottom lip as blood flows, then drops onto the stones beside his boots. This isn't right. Every cell in my body rebels against the thought of him going out there alone. Xaden can't read Costa's intentions—he doesn't have the edge his second signet gives him. The collar of my uniform feels too tight, the leather too sticky in the growing humidity, its warmth too suffocating. I tear at the top button, then shove my sleeves up my forearms as thunder sounds in the distance, mocking my inability to wield it.

I want my fucking power back *now*. With them, Xaden isn't the deadliest in this plaza. I am. He's only out there because of me, and I should be the one taking on this fight.

Xaden faces me, then holds out his uniform top.

"He's huge," I whisper, our gazes colliding as I take the warm fabric from his hands and hug it to my chest.

"I know." He slides his arms into the double scabbard and buckles it across his chest. "Garrick is going to be pissed he missed this." He smirks, then cups the back of my neck and presses a soft, lingering kiss to my lips. "Be right back."

But what if he's not? Even the best fighters die in combat.

He's arrogant because he's the best. At least that's what I tell myself to slow my pounding heart as he walks toward Costa. The heat of anger swiftly replaces fear as the priestess moves to my side. I understand passing tests—I'd prepared my entire life to face the entrance exam for the Scribe's Quadrant—but this feels just as callous as walking the parapet on Conscription Day.

"You don't agree with Dunne's ways," the priestess surmises, her voice cracking with age as she looks down at me with dilated pupils. Oh *great*. Only Dunne herself knows what they're ingesting beyond those pillars.

"I find it a poor test of character," I reply.

"And yet character is always revealed in bloodshed, is it not?" The priestess looks my way and crosses in front of Aaric, her gaze appraising him, then Cat before turning her attention to Dain. "They'll negotiate weapons now."

"He's fighting without his greatest one." I watch Xaden's back as he approaches Costa and the commander.

"I think you may be right about that." The priestess glances up at the wall where Sgaeyl stands watch. "Which is why I have decided he should not fight alone." Before I can question her, she drags the blade over Dain's arm, cutting through his uniform.

Oh *shit*.

He hisses in surprise, then grabs hold of the wound. Blood flows through his fingers, dripping onto the stone.

"No!" I shout, reaching for Dain.

"Gods," Cat whispers.

"All right." Dain nods.

Xaden turns toward us, lines carved between his eyebrows, and I reach for our bond out of habit, coming up woefully empty again.

"I forbid it." Aaric moves closer to my side and draws his sword. "I'll fight in his stead."

"You can't." I shake my head. What is with the *fucking* death wishes around here?

The corners of the priestess's eyes crinkle with a soft smile. "See? Character is revealed in bloodshed." She looks at Cat. "You're an outsider, dressed differently than the others, yet your presence means they value you." Her gaze snaps to Aaric, and she tilts her head. "You are the prince of your people, honorable yet foolish to think you could survive our finest. Do you not know what would happen to those pretty green eyes should you step foot on *this* battlefield? Even if you accepted your death, Dunne has not chosen you to prove your skill this day."

Aaric's jaw ticks.

"You are the smallest," she says to me dismissively, then turns to Dain. "Which leaves you to fight beside your champion."

"Dain…" Words fail me. If anything happens to him because of my decisions…

"This just got interesting," Tairn notes.

"This is not interesting. This is terrifying." I snap my reply.

"I've got this." Dain slips out of his uniform top and hands it to me. "I knew what I was getting into when I agreed to come with you."

My ribs strain, but I nod. "Be careful." I add his top to the pile, and he starts toward Xaden, who's already moving to intercept him halfway.

"Palta!" the priestess shouts, her voice echoing off the stone. The guards clamor in approval as the second twin steps forward, blood already dripping from his fingertips.

My gaze flies to the remaining warrior, Marlis, but thankfully there's no cut on her folded arms.

"Tell me, did you choose this path yourself?" The priestess brings her weathered gaze to mine.

"My mother—" I start, but then I remember every time Dain tried to get me out of the quadrant, and I face forward as he and Xaden approach their opponents to negotiate weapons. "I chose my life."

"Ah, then it is good we did not complete your dedication."

"My *what*?" What kind of drugs do they provide in the temples here?

"But do you not yearn for temple? Usually the touch creates such longing that you can't help but return. Or perhaps you now favor another god." She glances up at Tairn, ignoring my outburst, and then her eyes slide to Xaden. "I still see *us* among your potential paths, should you decide to take it. Dunne will accept you. It is not too late to choose Her."

I raise my eyebrows at the woman. "I choose *him*." Whether she's talking about Xaden or Tairn, my answer is the same.

"Ah." She turns the dagger in her gnarled hand as the raindrops continue to fall. "So be it. Our goddess teaches that while battles may be won by the strongest warriors, they may also be lost by our weakest. Both must be tested today."

Pain erupts in my forearm, and a second later, she lifts the dagger as fresh blood races down its honed edge.

My blood. Looks like I get to fight after all.

With such wan coloring in the vegetation, it comes as no surprise that it requires four times the amount of indigo to dye even the simplest garment. I can't help but wonder if the colors of our Continent are the exception, or if the isles are.

—Unnbriel: Isle of Dunne by Second Lieutenant Asher Daxton

CHAPTER
THIRTY-TWO

Blood trickles down the top of my left forearm to drip from my fingertips. I'll have a scar to match the one Tynan gave me during Threshing. I grit my teeth through the burn of pain and look up.

"She faces Marlis!" the priestess shouts, and the soldiers behind us cheer.

Xaden whips in my direction, his eyes flaring with something that looks a little too close to terror to be comforting before he returns to whatever weaponry they're negotiating.

Marlis moves into the plaza, unfolding her muscled arms. Blood spills from her hand, splattering the stones. She moves like she's used to the weight of heavier armor, and she tucks the short strands of her flaxen hair behind her ears, coloring the strands red.

Three combatants. This had always been their plan.

"*Unfair!*" Golden anger courses down the bond and into my veins, heating my skin.

"*Your ire will not aid her. Control yourself,*" Tairn demands.

"No!" Aaric reaches for me, and I shove Dain's and Xaden's uniform tops into his hands.

"Yes." I quickly take off my own to free my arms and add it to Aaric's pile, leaving me in my armor and undershirt. It's almost a relief in the cloying heat. "Don't let him move," I say to Cat. She grimaces but nods. The scattered raindrops cool my skin as I walk toward the center of the plaza and whatever is about to be my *path*.

But Andarna's anger doesn't dissipate. It blends with mine, growing with every step I take. I am *not* weak.

Marlis sizes me up as I approach, then huffs a laugh as she rolls her shoulders.

"I've taken down bigger," I tell her as I step between Dain and Xaden.

She lifts an eyebrow, and I wonder if she speaks the common language.

Dain's mouth twitches, but he doesn't translate.

"It must be the same for all three," the silver-uniformed commander says to Xaden, eyeing me with pity.

"Then it's daggers," Xaden says.

My head whips at Xaden. "Your swords are your best—"

"Daggers," Xaden tells the commander, earning a smile from our trio of opponents.

"Agreed," Dain chimes in.

I could overrule them. This is my mission. But while choosing daggers gives me an advantage, it's not like they're not both lethal with the same form of weaponry. "Agreed."

"So it is." The commander nods, and the other three begin to disarm, handing their weapons to the temple attendants who scurry in our direction. "Best of three."

Xaden and Dain hand their swords off to an attendant.

I scan the blue robes quickly, but there's no sign of the girl with hair like mine. Movement catches my attention to the right, and when I look at the statue of Dunne, I would almost swear her eyes flash golden and glance my way for a second.

Just *once* it would be nice if Andarna would stay where I ask her to.

"Use your speed," Xaden instructs me as he removes all weapons but the four daggers he carries sheathed at his sides. "Aim—"

"Stop." I put my hand on his chest, and my brow puckers at how fast his heart races. A raindrop splashes on my forearm. "This is just a challenge without a mat. Dain wins his match. You win yours. I'll win mine."

Xaden's jaw flexes.

"Whatever you do, don't watch me. You can't afford the distraction." I tap his chest. "And don't die." Retreating three steps, just out of his reach, I unsheathe two of my daggers.

Then I face Marlis. My estimate was about right—she has at least ten inches and a good fifty pounds of muscle on me. Reach and strength are hers, too, so agility and speed will have to be mine.

Dain and Xaden turn toward their own opponents, putting enough distance on either side of me to give ample space to maneuver.

"Begin," the commander orders as all others step off the plaza.

My focus narrows to Marlis and the smug tilt of her wide mouth as she palms only one of her two daggers and starts to circle me.

This is just a challenge. Xaden and Dain are on the other mats.

Let's go.

I flip my left dagger to pinch the tip and rotate the other so the blade runs parallel with my arm as Marlis fake lunges twice, trying to throw me off-balance.

If I were a little more scared and a little less angry, that might have worked. Instead of falling for it and slipping on the wet stone, I flick my left wrist, throwing my dagger at her shoulder.

She dodges as expected, and the blade flies by. I take the opportunity to rush her, swinging my right fist toward her torso to slice across her chest—no stabbing here.

I don't want her to die, just to yield.

Someone shouts beside me, but I keep my gaze locked on Marlis. Dain can handle himself. He has to.

Marlis dances backward with a bemused smile, avoiding each of my swipes. *Faster.* I pour my energy into speed and lunge, finally making contact along the side of her ribs—the one area that isn't protected by her chest plate. Blood stains her silver uniform as I draw back, but I'm not fast enough on the retreat. She hisses at the same moment she strikes with her own dagger, stabbing into my side with so much force I *hear* my rib crack.

Her blade glances off my dragon-scale armor, and I stumble sideways from the blow, drawing controlled, deep breaths to try and block the nauseating pain that erupts under my left arm. No mental trick in my arsenal can contain the waves of star-bright agony, but I manage to stifle the scream that fights its way up my throat as steel clangs behind me. I will *not* be Xaden's distraction. Adrenaline kicks in, coursing through me like power.

Marlis glances at her blade in confusion, then lifts her gaze to mine, staring at me with macabre fascination and a small glint of what I think might be appreciation. "I'll remove my armor if you do, too," she proposes in the common language, giving me precious, necessary seconds to breathe through the worst of the pain.

"I'll pass." She's too tall for me to chance a leg takedown and too strong for me to expose myself any more than necessary. All I have is leverage, and that means getting closer to destabilize her. I crook two of my left fingers at her as rain begins to fall in earnest.

Her eyes flare, and she cocks her wrist back.

I'm already dropping to the ground when she throws.

The blade passes overhead so closely I can hear it whistle, followed by the rhythmic pounding of boots on the wet stone. Careful to keep control of my blade, I shove myself up with every ounce of strength in my arms and force my feet beneath me an instant before she arrives.

She slices for my throat, and I leap backward as I hear Xaden hiss in pain.

I fight every instinct to check on him and throw my right forearm up to block Marlis's next assault. She hits with bone-rattling strength and cuts into my forearm.

Now.

I drop my blade, using every second I have before the pain hits to follow her downward swing with my bloodied arm, reaching for her wrist. Rain slickens her skin, but I grab hold and throw my weight with my shoulder, driving her hand toward the ground and dragging the rest of her body along with her own momentum.

She stumbles and I take the opening, wrenching my torso upward and grabbing hold of her knee. I lock it against my chest, lacing my fingers, then quickly ram my shoulder into the pocket between her upper thigh and hip.

"Faster! Aetos is already unconscious!" Andarna warns as Marlis swings for me, her blade flying toward my face.

Fuck.

I hold tight to Marlis's leg and barrel my weight downward into her joint, throwing her completely off-balance and forcing her backward.

Her blade clatters against the ground and she falls like a toppled statue, her back smacking into the stone. She shouts, but I keep hold of her leg, and only when she tries to twist out from underneath me, flipping to her chest, do I let go, diving for her hands.

I wrench her wrists behind her back as the metal of her chest plate scrapes stone, then sit, locking her arms in place with my thighs. Light flashes in the sky above us, and rain comes down in sheets.

"No!" she screams, arching upward to buck me off.

"Yes." I draw a dagger and press the tip to the side of her neck as thunder rumbles. "Now, yield." A quick glance to my left confirms Andarna's assessment. Dain is unconscious on the ground, blood pooling around what I can see of his shoulder, and Palta's boot is against his neck.

"Never." Marlis tenses under me.

"I have you!" Blood runs down my arm with the rain, turning her tunic a mottled shade of pink.

"Perhaps," she admits, turning her face to the right and laying her cheek against the ground. "But Costa has *him*."

Holding my blade against her neck, I chance a glimpse to the right, then do a double take.

Costa has Xaden pinned to his back, his dagger inches away from Xaden's face. Xaden's fighting, both his bloodied hands wrapped around Costa's wrists to keep the blade from plunging, but it slowly lowers under Costa's weight.

NO.

"Keep me pinned? Or help him?" Marlis asks. "Choices, choices."

Xaden is seconds away from that blade meeting his face, and gods only know if Dain is even breathing under that boot.

Rage devours me from the scalp down, storming through my veins in a surge of heat that sizzles the rain on my skin. I yank my dagger from her neck, flip it, and throw in one smooth motion.

My blade lodges in the fleshy part of Costa's shoulder, and he bellows, his torso slackening for the one heartbeat Xaden needs to knock Costa's blade loose. It skitters across the stone, and I immediately look away, replacing the thrown blade with another from my thigh and pressing its tip against Marlis's neck in less than a second.

"Yield!" I demand, anger burning so deep it reaches my very bones. Out of the corner of my eye, I see Xaden throw a punch in Costa's face, then yank my dagger from his opponent's shoulder and bring it to his throat.

"No!" Marlis shouts, and the air charges in a way I'm all too familiar with.

We're in danger out here.

"Fucking *yield*!" The heat within me snaps outward and breaks with my voice.

Lightning streaks downward and strikes to the left and right. Rock cracks. Thunder immediately follows, rattling the ground and leaving only the patter of rain and silence in its wake.

I startle but manage not to nick her neck.

"I yield," Marlis whispers, her eyes wide beneath me. "I yield!" she shouts.

Costa's head whips in our direction, and Xaden slams his fist into his jaw. The fighter topples to the side, completely unconscious.

"She...yields!" the commander yells, and guards rush in.

I remove my blade and crawl off Marlis, then stagger to my feet as lightning cracks in the distance. Palta steps away, and to my relief, Dain appears to be breathing as Cat and Aaric race toward him.

Rain streams down my face when I look upward, finding Andarna between Sgaeyl and Tairn on the wall, her scales rippling with alarming speed in various shades of black. *"Are you all right?"* I ask.

"I am...angry," she says, her head swiveling in a serpentine manner as her front claws crack the edges of the wall's masonry. *"Their laws say* one *match, not three."*

"Was that you?" Xaden arrives at my side, and I busy myself with checking for injuries. He now has two cuts on his arms, one of which will definitely need to be sewn shut, and his jaw is already bruising. "The lightning. Was that you?" he repeats, lifting my chin between his thumb and forefinger and searching my eyes.

"No." I shake my head. "I mean…" The heat. The anger. The *snap*. Weird. "Just coincidence." *Or Dunne.* "There isn't any magic here."

"Right." Two lines appear between his brows and his gaze sweeps over me, then catches on my arm. "Fuck, you're cut."

"No worse than you are," I tell him as the rain lets up. "But I think she broke a rib."

His eyes slide shut and he cups the nape of my neck, then presses a hard kiss to my forehead. "Thank you. That throw probably saved my life."

"Good thing I didn't miss, or I don't think you'd be saying the same thing." My arm trembles as I sheathe my dagger and his hand slips away.

"You never miss." He glances over my head. "Looks like Aetos is going to need some stitches in that shoulder, but Aaric is bringing him around."

"I said I'm *fine*!" Marlis shouts behind me.

"Yes, Your Majesty," someone replies.

Oh no, no, *no*. My stomach lurches. Please tell me I did not just hold a blade to the Queen of Unnbriel's throat.

I pivot slowly to face what I'm sure is about to be a squad of royal executioners. A row of guards waits a respectful distance behind Marlis, who stands a few feet away with her arms folded over her armor.

"Well?" she asks, her mouth pinched in annoyance. "Two out of three victories. You've earned your audience."

My heart starts beating double time. "I didn't know who you were."

"You weren't supposed to." She cocks her head to the side. "Are you going to speak, or has this all been for nothing?"

"Aaric—" I glance toward our friends.

"I only speak with those who best me," Marlis interrupts. "And you are wasting my time, Amarali." She hurls the word at me like an insult.

Bolstering myself with a deep breath, I lift my chin. "We've come for two reasons. First, we're seeking the seventh breed of dragon."

Marlis narrows her eyes. "If there were such a thing, this isle hasn't seen fire-breathers in *centuries*. I'm afraid you've come looking in vain. What's your second purpose?"

It isn't quite a crushing blow, considering I'd already suspected as much, but the sorrowful pulse of disappointment coming down the bond tells me Andarna doesn't feel the same.

"Allies," I tell Queen Marlis. "We're in a war that might claim every life on the Continent, and we need allies."

"And you think we'll fight for you?" Marlis stares at me like I've sprouted another head.

"I was hoping for *with* us."

"Hmm." She glances at Xaden, then up to the top of the wall. "You can't afford our services."

"Try me." Hopefully Aaric forgives me for promising whatever is in the coffers.

"How did you do it?" Marlis asks.

"Take you down?" I reply as the storm blows past and the rain shifts to a drizzle. "It was a matter of leverage, targeting your joint to throw you off-balance—"

"I know what leverage is," she snaps. "You took me down for the simple reason that I underestimated your abilities and allowed you close enough to throw me off-balance. How did you do that?" She gestures behind me.

I turn, following the motion, and stumble for words. The terraced seats carved into the wall are cracked down the middle, and the rock is charred black where lightning struck.

"I didn't," I answer, pivoting to face her. "You have no magic here for me to wield."

Xaden moves to my side as Aaric helps Dain rise to his feet, holding the side of his head.

"And yet you've destroyed something that stood for seven hundred years before your arrival." Her eyes narrow slightly. "Perhaps it is truly Zihnal who blesses you. Good luck when you search that particular isle. They have a mean streak."

"So you won't fight with us?" I ask, trying to stay on topic and holding desperately to hope. No other army would be as effective.

"I think I prefer a Deverelli approach to an alliance for now," she replies. "You may take shelter in our jungles and have hunting rights for yourselves and your mounts should you need to rest on our isle. But as for fighting alongside you, I'm afraid the price is something you're unwilling to pay." She turns to leave.

"What do you want?" I call after her as Aaric, Cat, and Dain head our way. "At least name your price."

"The same thing everyone in the isles craves." She pauses and looks back over her shoulder. "Dragons."

Do not mistake a dragon's bond for fealty. If you expect a dragon to choose their rider over the well-being of their own kind, prepare for two things: disappointment and death.

—COLONEL KAORI'S FIELD GUIDE TO DRAGONKIND

CHAPTER
THIRTY-THREE

The plaza falls silent, but at least there are no flames erupting from the three dragons behind me, two of whom I know are *pissed*.

Xaden tenses, and our squadmates quickly form a line on my other side.

"You can't be serious." I shake my head at the Queen of Unnbriel's ludicrous suggestion.

"We want dragons," she repeats with an infuriating nod. "Not fully grown, of course. Your kind has let them become too headstrong, too arrogant."

"I will show her arrogance," Tairn threatens, and I wince at the godsawful sound he makes dragging his talons along the stone walls.

"Not necessary," I promise as Molvic and Cath land hard beside the others, straining the limitations of the wall.

The queen turns fully and arches an eyebrow as though Tairn just proved her point. "Bring us, say…twelve eggs—two of each breed—and I'll bring my army to the *Continent*."

Eggs? My stomach hollows, and I retreat a single step as Tairn growls in warning. *The second Krovlan uprising.* Dad was right. But they weren't looking for feathertails because of their gifts; it was because they thought they were… malleable?

Sgaeyl leaps from the wall, landing a few feet to Xaden's left. The scent of sulfur fills the air as she lowers her head, baring dripping teeth.

A handful of the guards bolts for the gate at the top of the steps, but most stay. Impressive.

Queen Marlis stares up at Sgaeyl, utterly enthralled. "What do you say?"

"If you want to be a rider, the quadrant accepts those who cross the parapet on July fifteenth." The ache in my ribs starts to throb as the adrenaline wears off. "And the dragons choose their riders, not the other way around."

"Surely a queen is worthy." She lifts her hand like she might actually try and *touch* Sgaeyl.

Sgaeyl's growl rises in pitch as she opens her jaw—

"Trust me, she's not impressed by titles." Xaden looks over at Sgaeyl. "If you want to, I understand, but her death would be incredibly inconvenient. Can you pick a guard or something?" The absolute lack of emotion in his voice lifts the hair at the back of my neck.

Golden eyes narrow in his direction, but she slowly clamps her teeth.

"Even thinking we might accept that offer makes you unworthy," I tell the queen. "We don't trade in *dragons*."

"That's what I thought." Marlis lowers her hand. "Hold on to that indignation, at least for now. But do visit again when you feel more desperate. From what I know of them, they're rather dedicated to protecting their own, and perhaps a dozen eggs aren't such a bad price for saving the rest of them." She leaves without another word, flanked by guards as she climbs the terraced seats to the gateway above.

Dedicated.

I look toward the temple, but there's not a blue robe in sight, and the platoon of silver-uniformed guards standing watch in front of the steps serves as ample warning that we're not welcome anymore.

Between finding our abandoned weapons and the time it takes to get back to the meadow, an hour passes before we arrive at the clearing. Trager rushes to Cat before she redirects him to Dain, across from where Tairn and Andarna land. Dismounting through the constant, pulsing pain in my arm and ribs takes me so long that I'm tempted to simply sleep in the damned saddle and keep my own field dressing on this cut, but I eventually make it to the ground.

Mostly because I know Tairn will never let me live it down if I don't.

"Did you wield?" Mira is in my face before I have a chance to take more than a few steps.

"What?" I hold my ribs and spot the Unnbrish soldiers retreating into the surrounding jungle.

"Did you wield?" Mira repeats, grabbing my shoulders and examining my face. "Aaric and Cat filled me in on what happened."

"Relax." I lift my brows at my worrywart sister. "We got caught in a storm. Lightning struck multiple times, and luckily a *really* close strike scared the shit out of the queen. There's no magic here. Why do I have to keep reminding people about that? Can *you* wield?"

"No, of course not, but you can still speak to your dragons." She sighs and drops her hands as Xaden approaches. "I'm sorry they won't ally with us. I thought an isle loyal to Dunne was our best chance."

"Me too." My brow furrows as I remember the priestess. "When did my hair turn silver at the ends?"

"Turn?" Mira's expression mirrors my own. "It grew in that way. Are you all right? I thought Dain was the one knocked unconscious."

"I'm fine," I assure her as Xaden reaches us. Of course my parents didn't *dedicate* me. That practice was outlawed in the two hundreds, and even earlier in Poromiel. "The high priestess just said some weird things that distracted me." And I foolishly let her. I'm supposed to be smarter than that.

"As I'm sure she meant to do," Mira says. "What does that have to do with your hair?"

"I saw a girl with the same hair as me."

"Really?" Mira's brow knits. "That's bizarre. It's not like we have family from the isles."

"Right? I'd never thought of it potentially being hereditary—" I wince when my ribs protest a deep breath.

"We need to get you wrapped." Xaden's mouth tightens. "We might not have a mender, but we can at least hold the bones in place to heal, and Trager should see if you need stitches."

"You're the one who needs stitches," I argue. "But yes to the wrap. Let's make sure everyone is ready to leave as soon as possible. I don't want to stay here a moment longer than we have to."

"Agreed."

• • •

After resting the gryphons for a full day at Drake's suggestion and a thirteen-hour flight, it's morning when we land on the rocky coast at the edge of Vidirys, the cream-stoned capital of Hedotis.

Have to admit, this is the isle I'm most excited to explore. A whole community built on knowledge and peace? Yes, please.

The weather is slightly colder this far south, and I strip off my gloves before dismounting. My wrapped ribs scream when I make impact, and I take a second to breathe through it before moving forward. *"The vegetation is even paler here,"* I say down the bond as I crush barely green sea grass under my boot.

Even the sporadic bushes are— *Wait.*

I crouch next to a wiry bramble bush and note the nine-pointed leaves, then lean closer. *"This looks like tarsilla, but the bark is nearly white."*

"Perhaps magic weakens the farther from the Continent one gets?" Tairn muses. *"Though I'm not sure how it can be much less than nonexistent."*

"I do not like this place." Andarna scrapes a single talon through the grass, revealing only damp sand. *"My kind would not settle here. We should leave."*

"Cover that. We have to at least ask. Besides, where better to find a cure for Xaden than on the isle of wisdom?" I stare up at the city as Xaden reaches my side. "It's beautiful but all so...uniform." There's a single row of merchants about fifty feet away, and then the three-story buildings begin. They're all the same color with equally distanced windows, each with the same muted flowers hanging in baskets beneath them. "They razed the original structures about a hundred and fifty years ago and rebuilt with what Dad called *intention*."

"That's a little unsettling," he agrees, looking back between our shoulders. The tiny cuts on his cheek and forehead have scabbed over, but the bruise along his jaw looks worse today. "And there's no port. It's a coastal city with no port."

The trading vessels are all anchored off the coastline, and we passed more than a few dinghies on the flight in. Small boats line the beachfront, pulled up onto the sand as if marooned here. For being the isle of wisdom, it's a far from logical approach.

"So, this one is all you, right?" Ridoc asks as he approaches from the left with Cat and Maren. "You have to take a test or something to enter?"

"One of us has to prove wisdom in order to meet with the triumvirate," I answer.

"I can't believe they elect people for high leadership," Cat mutters, glaring at the city like it might bite. "Town councils? Sure, but how can you confirm someone has the skills to lead if they're not trained from birth?"

"Being trained from birth doesn't make you any more qualified," Aaric retorts from the right, Trager at his side. "Any of you truly excited at the prospect of being led by Halden?"

Cat crinkles her nose.

"Valid argument," Trager points out.

Wait, is it just me, or did Cat actually grin at him?

"Not just you," Andarna notes.

"Let me see the arms." Trager moves to stand in front of Xaden and me, and *yep*, Cat totally tracks the movement.

I slip my left arm free of my flight jacket as Xaden does the same with his. My face puckers in a grimace when the blood-stained bandage catches on the cut beneath. I tug gently to remove it, and a bead of blood rises from the center of the cut, directly between the six stitches Trager sewed into my skin yesterday.

"Looks good," Trager notes, lowering his head to my arm, and I bite back a smile when I spot a mouth-shaped bruise on the side of his neck. "No infection, no swelling." He frowns at the last stitch, which is doing its best to tug straight through my skin. "That one doesn't seem to want to stay put, though."

"Happens." I rotate my arm. "You did a good job with the stitches."

"Thanks." He flashes a soft smile, then looks to Xaden. "Your turn— *Damn*."

"It's fine." Xaden's arm is red and angry along the deep gash that required fourteen stitches.

"It's not fine." I step into his space and examine the cut. "I brought some Lorin salve in Brennan's med kit. It will help with the inflammation and fight off any minor infection, but we need to get it on you in the next few hours." Wind gusts, peppering our legs with sand, and I turn my back to the breeze, sheltering Xaden's arm as much as possible. "Let's wait until we're out of the sand."

He nods and quickly wraps the wound.

"Because that wouldn't work," Mira snaps at Drake as they walk over with Garrick and Dain, who sidesteps a dead bird.

Yuck.

"It really would," Drake says to her with a grin that would probably charm anyone else but just seems to enrage my sister. "You pull a two-pronged Pelson flight formation—"

"And wyvern would pick you off twice as fast for dividing your forces in that environment." Mira shakes her head.

Xaden and I slip our jackets back on.

"You clearly don't understand Pelson." Drake lifts his hand toward his cousin. "Tell her, Cat. In a contained environment, a Pelson maneuver—"

"I'm not telling Mira *shit*." Cat shakes her head. "It's like arguing with Syrena."

"Oh, come on. Maren? Someone be on my side here," Drake pleads.

Maren winces. "Have you seen her right hook?"

"I have," Drake admits.

"I know Pelson," Mira argues, crossing to my left. "I've studied Pelson at length because it was my job to beat your maneuvers for *years*. And you have no real-world examples to prove your theory. Just stop talking." She looks me over like she expects new wounds.

"I'm fine," I tell her.

"Drake, you're starting to annoy me," Xaden warns with a sideways glance. "You should stop that." His tone ices over.

Garrick glances my way, and his mouth tenses.

Surely something *that* inocuous wouldn't trigger—

"We have company," Tairn alerts.

I yank my focus forward to find half a dozen people strolling onto the thick wooden walkway that connects the beach to the market. "Xaden."

He lifts his head and moves closer to me.

The group is dressed in tunics and gowns of various pastel colors, the one-shoulder fashion something I've only seen in history books or onstage. Fabrics billow in the breeze as they come closer, all staring up at the dragons in awe.

"They're incredible," the middle-aged man in front says in the common language with a toothy smile. His hair bears two strips of silver amid red curls. "And well worth the walk to the beach to welcome you." The intricate metallic embroidery of his tunic speaks to money, as does the sparkling red gem at the top of his cane.

It's the brightest pop of color I've seen on the isle so far.

"And you might be?" Xaden asks.

"Where are my manners?" The man places an empty hand over his heart. "I'm Faris, the second of the triumvirate. The other two enjoy standing on ceremony, of course, but I see no benefit in waiting to meet you and therefore am here." He bows slightly, then lifts his gaze as he straightens.

I blink and fight against the urge to stare. His eyes are so blue they're actually...purple. And here I'd thought Dad had written that part of the tome in hyperbole.

"Welcome to Hedotis." He turns his smile on me. "You have very unusual eyes. Not entirely blue or green or gold, but an amalgamation of all. Fascinating."

"I was just thinking the same thing about you," I admit.

"Mine are quite common on our isle," he says. "I've brought my household to formally make your acquaintance and escort you through our beautiful city. If you're amenable, we have room for you to rest at our home on the northeast shore." He gestures up the beach, then glances back over his shoulder. "Darling, won't you come say hello? I apologize for my wife. Talia seems to be overcome by your magnificent dragons."

"I'm here, my love," Talia says as she walks up the pathway behind him, her pale green gown and long black hair catching in the breeze. She moves to his side, then quickly laces their fingers before lifting her gaze. Her dark-brown eyes settle on Xaden immediately, and they flare in blatant, palpable shock.

"Is there a problem?" Faris asks.

She studies Xaden with a desperate intensity that puts us firmly in awkward territory, and Xaden must feel the same, given that he's practically petrified into a piece of stone beside me.

"Oh, *shit*." Garrick's face drains of color.

"Xaden?" Talia whispers, lifting her hand, then quickly dropping it. "Is it really you?"

My eyebrows hit my fucking hairline.

Xaden reaches across me and wraps his hand over my hip like I need protection. "Mom."

It has been the experience of my lifetime to spend these months with others who value knowledge just as reverently as I do. But though their intelligence and their wisdom inspire me, their artifice terrifies me.

—HEDOTIS: ISLE OF HEDEON BY CAPTAIN ASHER SORRENGAIL

CHAPTER
THIRTY-FOUR

O f all the ways I'd envisioned getting to know Xaden's mother, holding her at bay in a bedroom doorway of her own house while her son refuses to see her definitely never came to mind.

"This is very kind of you." I balance the silver tray of snacks she's just delivered on one hand and grip the golden doorknob with the other. "I'll be sure he gets these. And thank you for sending our missives."

Having seen renderings of Fen Riorson, I can definitely say that Xaden takes after him in looks, but there are traces of Talia, too. Xaden shares her high cheekbones, her long eyelashes, and even the shape of her ears, but it's the gold flecks in their eyes that make the biological link undeniable.

Hopefully Andarna's kind will know how to bring the gold back fully in Xaden's.

"It was lucky a ship bound for Deverelli was in the harbor to take your correspondence." Talia uses her considerable height advantage to peer over my head into our bedroom with eyes so full of longing that pity wraps around my rib cage, then constricts. "I was hoping he might want to talk?"

He definitely does not.

"He's resting." I force a quick, sympathetic smile and pull the door closer, narrowing her scope of vision.

"What about dinner? He should meet the rest of the family."

What an *awful* idea. He's been nearly catatonic since this morning, and she wants to throw a party with people he's never met? "I'll ask, but that might be a lot for him to—"

"We'll keep it small, then." Talia's face falls with her gaze and she purses her lips, forming little golden-brown lines around her mouth. "I was so young when he was born," she whispers, staring at the doorframe. "Still young when the contract expired. I never thought I'd get to see him again, and now that he's here…" Tears fill her eyes as she slowly looks at me. "You understand, right?"

What in Amari's name am I supposed to say to that? Of course I can't understand how anyone would leave him, but—

"Tell her the truth. He loathes her," Tairn suggests. *"As does Sgaeyl. The life-giver is lucky she wasn't scorched this morning, though I do believe Sgaeyl is still contemplating her options."*

Because that would be *great* for international relations, considering who Talia is married to.

"That's his mother," Andarna argues. *"What would you do, Violet?"*

"I'm not the person to ask about motherly relationships," I reply. Grief slices quick and deep, giving strength to the pity that's stretching its viny little tethers toward my heart. "I understand wanting to know him," I tell Talia. "He is spectacular in every way—"

"Then you'll let—" She steps toward me.

"Dinner," I say, standing my ground. "I'll see if he's willing to have dinner. But if he isn't, you're going to have to respect that, too. You push, and he'll shove back twice as hard."

She braces her hand on the doorframe and shifts her eyes in thought. "What if I can promise you'll get a meeting with the full triumvirate? That's what *you* need, right? Maybe I can give you some answers they'll look for to evaluate your acumen."

I blink, and pity recedes an inch. "What I *need* is for Xaden to be all right. If that means setting this house on fire and leaving without accomplishing anything else on this isle, then I'll hand him a torch." Damn, this tray is getting heavy.

Her posture softens and she steps out of my space, her hand falling to her side. "You must love him to prioritize his feelings over your mission," she says quietly, like it's a revelation.

"Yes." I nod. "It's nothing compared to the way he risked Aretia for me."

"He risked Aretia," she whispers through a watery smile. "Then he loves you, too. His father never would have…" She shakes her head, and her hair rustles against the back of her gown. "Doesn't matter. Having dinner with him would be more than I'd ever hoped for. I'll send someone up in a few hours to see if he's willing to join us."

"Thank you." I wait until she heads down the long cream-colored hallway, then shut the door and turn the lock just in case.

Then I take the tray in both hands and go find Xaden.

The room they gave us is obviously meant for guests of distinction. It has high, vaulted ceilings; intricately carved furniture; sophisticated artwork; and a bed that could easily sleep four people. Everything is cream with touches of pale green and gold, all perfect in a way that borders on too pretty to touch. Our black flight jackets look sorely out of place draped across the chair of the delicate desk, and our packs and boots are so dirty I insisted on leaving them in the attached bathing chamber.

The carpet is soft under my bare feet as I cross the spacious room and open one of the double glass doors onto the covered veranda. The high balcony links with the four other bedrooms to the right on this side of the house, so it's no surprise to find Garrick sitting on the edge of the balustrade with Ridoc, their backs to the ocean.

But it does surprise me to find the cushioned loveseat empty.

Ridoc lifts his brows at me and tilts his head to my left, and I take the cue, shimmying between the guys and the decorative table in front of the loveseat when they hop off the railing.

"Good luck." Garrick pats my shoulder, and the two retreat down the veranda.

I find Xaden on the shaded floor between the loveseat and the corner piece of railing where my armor is tied, drying in the ocean breeze. He sits in sparring pants and an undershirt with his back against the wall, bare forearms resting on raised knees, gaze fixed into the distance.

"Room for one more down there?" I ask.

He blinks, then forces a half smile. "For you? I'll move to the couch."

"Don't even think about it." I squeeze in next to the railing, careful not to twist my torso and anger my ribs, then sit and set the tray on the floor in front of me.

"These fell out of your pack." He opens his fist, revealing the two vials Bodhi gave me.

Shit. "Thanks." I take the vials and slip them into my pants pocket.

"That little one-two combo would definitely help me get my hands on you at home if I didn't think Sgaeyl would torch me for willingly blocking the bond, even temporarily."

I swallow. "I should have told you I had it—"

"You don't owe me an explanation." He looks me straight in the eye. "I'm glad you have it. I don't want to lose my connection to Sgaeyl, not when I can still use my signet to fight venin, especially since you have one obsessively hunting you. But feel free to shove that serum down my throat if at any moment I'm not...myself. I'd rather be powerless than potentially hurt you." He glances down at the tray. "My mother?"

Nice subject change.

"She brought you food, but really only wanted to talk to you." Through the gaps in the railing, I look out over the strip of sand that meets the ocean and press my lips into a tight line. While Tairn and Andarna sun their scales on the beach, Sgaeyl prowls along the waterline, her head low, her eyes narrowed.

"She's pacing for some reason," Xaden says as Sgaeyl passes by. "Not that I can ask her." He huffs a self-deprecating laugh. "Not that she'd answer."

"She's worried." I look over at his freshly salved wound. Good, the swelling has decreased a little already.

"Worrying isn't in her nature. She likes to solve the immediate problem and handle consequences later." He leans over and plucks a cinnamon-sprinkled dried fig from a crystal bowl, then studies it. "Of course there's fucking sugar on it. Like somehow remembering that one little fact from when I was seven years old is going to make up for the last thirteen years."

He leans again and drops it onto the empty plate, and I remain silent, hoping he'll continue. He's never really talked about his mom before.

"And all this time I figured she was living in Poromiel. She never even told me she was from Hedotis. Neither of them did." He leans his head back against the wall. "Makes sense now—why she never had family visit, why she was so infatuated with all things colorful, the bedtime stories told with arinmint tea when she would whisper about people with purple eyes who lived without war."

Waves crash against the beach below, and Sgaeyl turns, pacing back toward us.

"You should see if she'll hunt with the others," I suggest to Tairn.

"Feel free to ask. I'll watch. Be sure you're near the water so you can put yourself out when she sets you on fire," he replies.

"It's a mineral called viladrite," I tell Xaden as he flicks the sugar off his fingers. "Dad wrote that it's so prevalent on the isle that it's in everything they eat and drink. It turns paler eye colors purple."

"I love that you know that." He drops his hand to my knee. "Did your dad's eyes change?"

"Not that I know of. They were always hazel like mine." I smile at the memory. "Guess he wasn't here long enough." I still can't figure out when he had time to study the isles, but maybe my grandmother knows, if I ever get the courage to speak with her like Mira did.

"We'll only be here long enough to search the isle for Andarna's kind and speak with the triumvirate"—the bruise on his jaw ripples when he clenches his teeth—"and my mother is married to one of them. The irony is poetic."

I twist toward him and wince when my ribs object. "She wants to have dinner tonight."

"Fuck that." His expression shifts into the same impenetrable mask he used to wear around me last year.

"Xaden." I cradle the side of his face and stroke my thumb over the edge of his scar. "Don't shut me out."

His eyes flash to mine. "Never." Sliding an arm behind me, he grabs hold of my hips with both hands and carefully lifts me into his lap. "I can think of far better ways to spend my evening than dinner." He grazes his teeth along the shell of my ear, and a shiver rolls down my spine. "Can't you?"

I gasp at the sudden rush of heat that flares low in my stomach when he kisses the side of my neck, flicking his tongue at the spot he knows turns me into a puddle.

"No magic," he reminds me, sliding his hand down my stomach. "No danger of losing control."

A whimper escapes my lips as his fingers dip beneath my waistband, mostly because what he suggests sounds fucking fantastic, but partially because I want *all* of him. I miss the heightened rush from our signets, his shadows flaring, my lightning cracking, the intimacy of lowering every barrier and hearing his voice fill my mind. I need to feel him unravel under my touch. Losing control is part of what makes us…us.

"No lumpy bedrolls," he continues, slipping his hand into my pants. "No squadmates ten feet away. No awkward dinners. Just you and me and that bed."

I groan, instantly remembering what we're supposed to be talking about. "As utterly delicious as that sounds…" My fingers dig into his thigh as his mouth toys with my earlobe. "Sex is not going to fix the real problem."

He sighs, then lifts his head. "I know."

I scramble out of his lap before I change my mind and drag him to our bed. The quick motion has me hissing through the sharp sting as I stand and grasp the railing with both hands, facing the water.

"Fuck." Xaden jumps to his feet and wraps his arms around me gently. "I'm so sorry. I forgot about your ribs. You shouldn't be flying, let alone have me crawling all over you."

"Not flying isn't an option." I breathe in through my nose and out through my mouth as the worst of it passes. "And never apologize for touching me."

He drops his chin on the top of my head. "I hate that we can't get you mended."

"In a life without magic, the best medicine is time," I muse, a smile curving my mouth as I spot Cat and Trager walking down the beach, hand in hand. "Look at that."

"Good for them. He's been pining after her for years." His hands bracket mine on the railing, and his body heat staves off the chill from the ocean breeze. "How much pain are you in? I don't want to ask you to sit through dinner if it hurts."

I'm not about to be a barrier if he wants to talk to his mother, especially knowing what I would give to have the same opportunity with mine. "It's not too bad as long as I don't twist. Or breathe too deeply. Or lift Andarna." The joke falls flat.

"So you can sit through dinner." The conflict in his voice has me turning in his arms.

"Only if you want to." I look up at him.

"Do you want me to?" He swallows.

"I'm not making that choice for you." I bring my hands to his chest, trying to remember the last time he was indecisive about anything and coming up short.

His eyes narrow and he steps back. "You think I should, don't you?"

"It doesn't matter what I think." I shake my head. "And I'm probably not the best person to give you advice on this—"

"Because she charmed you in the three minutes it took for her to push a tray through the door?" He puts more space between us, retreating down the veranda.

"Because my mother just *died*."

He stills, and regret instantly washes over his face. "I'm sorry, Violet."

"You don't need to be. I'm just saying that I'm not the person to ask if you should spend a night talking to yours, because I would give *anything* for ten minutes with mine." I set my hand over my chest like it has a prayer of holding the grief inside where it belongs. "I have so many questions, and I would kill for a single answer. Maybe you should talk to Garrick, because any advice I give you would be poisoned by my own grief. You have to do whatever's best for you. Whatever you can live with once we leave here. Whatever choice you make will be the right one as far as I'm concerned. You have all my support."

"I don't know if there's a right choice. She's not like your mother." He laces his hands behind his neck as Sgaeyl passes by again, following her own footprints. "I absolutely understand you wanting ten minutes. I want them *for* you. Right or wrong, everything your mother did was to protect you and your siblings. She died protecting you."

"I know." I swallow the growing lump in my throat.

"My mother abandoned me." His hands drop to his sides.

"I know," I repeat in a whisper, my heart breaking all over again for him. "I'm so sorry."

"How does she"—he points to the door—"deserve *my* ten minutes when she fed me chocolate cake on my tenth birthday and vanished later that night?

I am the fulfillment of a contract for her. Nothing more. I don't give a shit how she looks at me, or whatever bullshit she undoubtedly spewed at you. The only reason we're in her house is because she's married to one of the triumvirate, and I have no problem using that to get what we need."

My chest cracks a little more with every word, then splits clean open. I knew she'd left, just not *how*.

"And don't think that has anything to do with this." He points to his eye. "I'm aware in the moments I lack emotion. You and Garrick don't need to share little *oh no* glances. I already feel it. It's like sliding over a frozen lake while a shrinking part of me screams that I'm supposed to be swimming in those pieces I've bartered away, and those feelings are right beneath the surface, but *fuck* is skating faster and a hell of a lot less messy. This shit?" He swings his finger back toward the house. "It's messy and painful and infuriating, and if I could choose to give this portion of myself away, so help me, Malek, I would. I get it now. It's not just the power that's addicting; it's the freedom to not feel *this*."

"Xaden," I whisper, all but bleeding out by the time he finishes.

Steam billows over the veranda, and our heads whip in the direction of the beach, where Sgaeyl stands the width of Tairn away with a curled upper lip, glaring at Xaden.

"Stop pacing and eat something," he begs her. "I know you're hungry and I can't stand that you're hurting this far from magic, so alleviate some of the pain and go hunt. I'm all right."

She drops her jaw and roars so loud my ears instantly ring. The glass doors bow and the little table trembles before she snaps her teeth shut. Three errisbirds fly out of the tree on my left, and two dark-haired boys come running out of the house to see what the commotion was.

"Sgaeyl," Xaden says softly, walking toward the edge of the veranda.

She backs up three heavy steps, and my heart stutters as her hind claw nearly tramples one of the boys before she launches skyward over the house. Her tail swings so close, it slices the leaves from the trees before she disappears.

Good thing the errisbirds left.

"At least she didn't set you on fire." Tairn quickly follows and Andarna trails after, fighting to fully extend her wing.

All of them are struggling without power.

"Fuck." Xaden's eyes slide shut.

"Simeon! Gaius!" One of the maids runs out of the house three stories beneath us, holding her skirts high as she sprints across the sand. "Are you all right?" she asks in Hedotic.

"That was amazing!" the older boy shouts in kind, lifting his fists toward the sky.

"We can leave," I offer Xaden, crossing the distance between us and winding my arms around his waist. "Right now."

"My mother is having our uniforms laundered." He brushes the loose strands of my braid behind my ears.

"So we'll be cold. Say the word, and we'll go." I turn my cheek and rest my ear against his heartbeat. "You're all that matters to me."

"Same." He drops his chin to the top of my head. "We can't just skip an entire isle," he grumbles, splaying his hands over my back. "We disobeyed direct orders to be here."

"We can." I listen to the steady rhythm of his heart and watch the maid fuss over the boys as they walk back toward the house. "The riot hunts, does a pass to make sure Andarna's kind hasn't chosen the blandest isle ever to call home, and we go. Hedotis hasn't entered a war or aligned itself with any kingdom *at* war in its recorded history. They aren't going to help us." I run my hand up and down his spine. "And you know where your mother is now. If you ever feel the need, you can come back. They're your ten minutes, too."

"And you're not hoping—" His words end abruptly as Talia runs out of the house beneath us, fisting the fabric of her gown.

"Boys!" she screams in Hedotic as she races to the edge of the stone patio, then yanks the children into her arms. "You're all right?" She pulls back and gives them the same once-over I usually earn from Mira after a battle.

"We're great!" the older assures her with a wide grin. "Right, Gaius?"

"Mama, you should have seen it roar!" the younger one adds with a bob of his head.

Mama. My stomach drops straight out of my body as I hope I have that word wrong.

Xaden tenses, and I hear his heart begin to race.

"I heard it roar, and that was excitement enough," Talia tells the boys, running her hands over their hair and down the sides of their faces. "But you're all right. You're all right," she repeats with a nod. "Elda, will you get them cleaned up? The triumvirate is joining us for dinner, and Faris's parents would like the boys to spend the night there."

"Of course," the maid replies, then ushers the children into the house.

Talia remains, her shoulders trembling as she catches her breath.

"What did she say?" Xaden asks.

"The triumvirate is coming to dinner." I start with the easiest part first. "And the boys…"

"They're hers, aren't they?" His tone slips into icy disdain.

"Yes," I whisper, holding him tighter as Talia returns to the house without looking up.

"The older is probably what? Eleven?" His arms drop. "No wonder she never came back. She didn't just marry; she built a whole new family." There's nothing amused about his laugh.

"I'm so sorry." I pull back to look at him, but his expression is flat.

"You did nothing wrong." He steps out of my arms, and it feels frighteningly poignant as he slips away. "This feeling is one I would gladly exchange."

It's not just the power that's addicting; it's the freedom to not feel this. His words play back in my head, and a new fear takes root, burrowing insidiously in the pit of my stomach. Does he know I've brought my new conduit? That there's a fully charged piece of alloy in my pack?

"Don't barter it away," I beg as he stares at the sea, and the words spill out of me faster and faster as his eyes harden and he resurrects the defenses it took me a *year* to break past. "The pain. The mess. Give it to me. I'll hold it. I know that sounds ludicrous, but I'll find a way." I lace our fingers. "I will hold everything you don't want to feel because I love every part of you."

"You already hold my soul and now you want my pain? Getting greedy, Violence." He brings my hand to his mouth and brushes a kiss over my knuckles before letting go. "Fuck it. Dinner with my mother sounds great. Think I'll wash up first."

He leaves me standing on the veranda, my thoughts racing more rapidly than Tairn could ever fly. The triumvirate is coming to dinner. They'll test us tonight. *They sent the kids away.*

Do they think we're dangerous? Or are *they*?

We need an edge. What would Rhi or Brennan do?

Shit. What did I bring with me? Brennan sent the med kit—

Brennan sent the med kit.

I need Mira.

"Andarna, when those boys leave the house, I need you to follow as invisibly as you can," I say down the bond.

"Are we scheming? I do enjoy scheming."

"We're planning."

Two hours later, I hold the precious glass vial with both hands as Mira and I head downstairs. Now is not the time to be clumsy. We quickly find Talia in the dining room, discussing dinner with a spindly man in a pale green apron who scrubs at his nails with a blue-edged towel.

"Violet?" Hope lights her eyes, and she dismisses the man before walking our way. "Did you ask him?" Her gaze darts toward Mira.

My sister folds her arms and studies the table.

"He said dinner sounds great," I tell Talia. It's not exactly a lie. My hands twist around the glass, shielding its contents from view. "The rest will be flying, but six of us can make it. And I thought this might serve as a peace offering between us, and maybe…" I press my lips in a line and look down at the vial.

"Stop debating and just give it to her," Mira orders with an exasperated sigh. "My sister is too polite to suggest that it might help smooth the waters and make tonight a little less awkward for those involved. Remind Xaden of home and all that."

Talia lifts her brows, and I hand over the vial and its dehydrated, light-green leaves. She takes the gift with a bewildered smile. "Is this…"

"Dried arinmint," I reply.

Gods bless Brennan.

The god of wisdom is the trickiest to placate.
Hedeon seems to only answer those who do not pray to him.

—Major Rorilee's Guide to Appeasing the Gods,
Second Edition

CHAPTER
THIRTY-FIVE

The dining room is just as monochromatic as the rest of the house, and the three people seated across the circular table would blend into the pale green wall entirely if not for their heads. Nairi, Roslyn, and Faris are dressed in what my father described as sacred ceremonial robes. They look a little too close to scribe robes for comfort, even if they're pastel green and their hoods aren't up.

Out of the ten people at the table, Talia seems the most on edge sitting next to Faris, and Xaden somehow appears completely in his element at my side. Gone are the quick flashes of smiles and tender touches.

The man sitting next to me in his freshly laundered uniform more resembles the one I met at the parapet on Conscription Day than the one I fell in love with. He's so cold I half expect the temperature around us to plummet.

Five servers are spread among us, each with a hand on a silver dome covering our plates. My stomach churns as Faris flicks his wrist. The servers respond to the nonverbal command, lifting the domes covering our dinner.

"Don't be a head. Don't be a head. Don't be a head," I chant under my breath, but from the sideways glance Aaric sends from my right, I'm guessing I'm not as quiet as I think. Thankfully, my plate steams with roasted chicken, potatoes, and some kind of stuffing mixed with what appears to be cauliflower. No heads.

"And we're served," Faris announces in the common language.

"We thank Hedeon for this meal," Nairi says, also using the common language. "For the peace in our land, the wisdom he sees fit to gift, and the satisfaction of thriving relationships. We offer to him private confession of our day's error in sacrifice. May only our minds know hunger."

"May only our minds know hunger," the Hedotics repeat, and I'm somehow not surprised when Aaric doesn't miss a beat.

"Let's eat," Faris suggests, picking up his crystal goblet teeming with chilled arinmint tea and gesturing in my direction. "And thank you for your gift. My Talia is quite delighted to serve it."

"I'm happy to bring her joy," I reply, and an awkward silence follows as he holds his goblet aloft like he's waiting for something.

"She's welcome." Xaden takes a deep drink of his tea and sets it down a little harder than necessary.

Faris's smile slips, but then he drinks, too. We all do, but it doesn't ease the awkwardness as we begin to eat.

"How do you find our city?" Roslyn asks, her brown eyes crinkling at the corners when she smiles.

"Hard to say, considering we haven't seen it." Mira plucks a lemon slice off the edge of her plate and tosses it into the glass.

"Hopefully we can change that tomorrow," Roslyn replies, studying Mira like she's found a worthy opponent for a chess match.

"After we pass your test?" I ask. "That's what this is, right? We're not in a formal setting as is custom, nor are there witnesses, but you're testing us."

Cat sets her silverware on her plate, but Aaric digs into his chicken, completely unfazed.

"Talia will serve as witness." Nairi slices into a potato. "And we thought an informal setting would be best given the...delicate nature of relations."

Talia's shoulders curve inward.

"You mean in case I embarrass my mother in a public setting with my lack of *wisdom*." Xaden leans back in his chair and extends his arm over the back of mine. "Is that your fear, Mom?"

"No." Talia's gaze jumps to Xaden, and her spine straightens. "My reticence about tonight is due to my own shame, in that I asked Faris for a personal favor so that you might be more comfortable during the conversation. I don't worry about your intelligence, Xaden. You were always a bright boy." Her hand trembles as she reaches for her goblet.

"Tell me something. When you die, do your dragons?" Faris asks, changing the subject.

"Depends on the dragon," I answer. "But usually, no."

"Gryphons do," Cat adds. "They bond for life."

Faris blinks. "To tie your life to another's, especially something as frail and easily breakable as a human, seems a foolhardy thing to do." His brow furrows. "You respect your gryphon for this choice?"

"I respect her for who she is and trust whatever decisions she makes," Cat replies. "Gryphons and their sacrifice to bond humans have allowed us to win the Great War and to survive centuries of war after that."

"Spoken like a royal." Nairi's eyes narrow on Cat. "Talia says you are in line for the throne of Poromiel."

"If Queen Maraya does not choose to have children, then my uncle will rule and eventually my sister will be an excellent queen." She picks up her fork and knife in a manner that dares them to argue.

Nairi's gaze flickers from Cat to Xaden to Aaric. "So many young royals here. So many potential alliances. Why are you not contracted to one another? It seems…foolish not to forge futures and provide heirs who could unite your kingdoms."

The chicken goes dry in my mouth, but Mira shoots me a *can you believe these people* look that steadies my heartbeat.

"My brother will be king," Aaric says, slicing through his chicken like this is any normal dinner. "Though a horrible one. Heirs and alliances aren't my concern. I will fight in this war, most likely die, and do so knowing that I protected others."

"Honor has never been the equal of wisdom." Nairi sighs, then looks to Xaden. "And your excuse? We received news months ago that your title had been restored to you."

Which means they have current information. They knew about the rebellion. About Fen's execution. I breathe deeply to help cool the instant, scorching anger that burns up my throat and level a less-than-friendly look on Talia. She knew and she *left* him there, didn't even go back.

Xaden stabs a piece of potato with his fork but keeps his arm around my chair. "Well then as you *know*, I'm a duke, not a prince."

"Tyrrendor is the largest province of Navarre," Talia tells the triumvirate, rushing to her son's defense. "Much of its territory lies beyond their wards, so its allegiance to the kingdom has always been…weaker than the others. It would not surprise me to find that in the course of this war, Tyrrendor regains its sovereignty, which is why a lifetime alliance"—her smile fades, and she glances at Xaden and me—"was secured. But you're not…"

Xaden chews slowly, then swallows as everyone stares at him. "I don't owe you an explanation about my love life."

Talia flinches, then sets her hands in her lap, but her focus strays to Cat.

"For gods' sake," Cat mutters, abandoning her silverware again. "I said yes, he said no. He met Violet, and now they're…them. They happen to be two of the most powerful riders on the Continent, so in that way, his alliance with her is perhaps *wiser*. The two of them could break and reshape the Continent if they chose to. And besides—I'm with someone else now."

My chest constricts in stunned gratitude, but she only rolls her eyes when I look her way.

"Breaking such an advantageous alliance is…" Nairi shakes her head at Xaden. "Unwise."

Oh *shit*.

Dinner churns in my stomach. They're not judging our intelligence; they're dissecting life choices.

"But easily remedied," Faris says, looking at Nairi and Roslyn. "It would show great wisdom and dedication to their respective titles were they to contract for three…say four years?"

Roslyn nods. "Long enough to secure an heir for Tyrrendor and put Poromish blood in the line."

I'm going to be sick.

Garrick huffs a sarcastic laugh. "If bloodlines equaled allegiance, we wouldn't be sitting here under interrogation." He glances to Talia at his right. "He *is* your son, right?"

She chugs the tea to the bottom of the glass.

"A contract marriage would be most wise," Nairi agrees with a nod, ignoring Garrick's words. "We could have the legalities performed in the morning at temple, and then hear what will, no doubt, be a plea for our assistance in their war tomorrow afternoon."

Wood creaks behind me. "Draw up the papers," Xaden says, gripping my chair.

Bile rises in my throat. What the fuck is he doing?

Cat's head snaps in our direction, Mira and Garrick both gawk, and Aaric continues eating.

I want the damned bond back *now*.

"Ah, there we go!" Faris claps twice. "What an excellent decision. Shall we go with three or four years?"

"Lifetime. Anything less is unacceptable." Xaden slides his hand to the back of my neck. "And her full name for the papers is Violet Sorrengail. Two Rs."

I'm torn between throwing a dagger at his chest and kissing the shit out of him.

Mira stifles a grin.

"My last name is tied to the title, but we could take yours," Xaden offers, and his eyes soften just slightly when they lock on mine.

"You could hyphenate," Garrick suggests. "Or combine? Riorgail? Sorrenson?"

"That is *not* what they meant," I whisper at Xaden.

"I don't give a fuck what they meant," he responds at full volume, and his fingers drift up and down the back of my neck as he faces the triumvirate. "You may question our knowledge, test our honor or dedication as riders and fliers. Serve up riddles, fake scenarios, chess games for all I care. But if you think I'm going to leave the only woman I've ever loved to contract marriage with a woman I do *not* get along with, then the lack of wisdom is yours, not mine."

"It's only three years," Talia begs, panic rising in her eyes. "And then you'd be back together. Surely the potential of our alliance, of sharing our knowledge would make that sacrifice worthwhile. Think of Tyrrendor."

Xaden leans forward, and his hand slips from my neck. "You cannot contemplate the things I have sacrificed for Tyrrendor. I lost my father, my freedom, my very—" He cuts himself off and I glance at the floor, half expecting to see shadows swirling at his feet. "Violet is the only choice I've made for *myself*. I won't sacrifice her for three years. Not for a single *day*. You would know that if you hadn't abandoned me, if you *knew* me at all."

"I didn't want to leave you!" She shakes her head, and Faris's brows knit in disapproval. "Your father wouldn't let me take you—"

"Do not speak of my father. I am the one who *watched* him die." Xaden points to the relic that stretches up his neck. "You left a child to face down a war you knew was coming, on a continent you knew was infested with dark wielders."

"I couldn't take you," she repeats. "You are Tyrrendor's heir."

"You could have stayed," he retorts, and my heart aches at the ice in his tone that I know masks his true hurt. "You could have been my mother."

I slide my hand onto his knee, wishing it was possible to take some of his pain.

"They would have executed me right next to your father, or in secret as was done to Mairi's husband. I did what I thought best!" she argues.

"For you." A mocking corner of his mouth lifts. "I'll admit, you've done well for yourself. Who needs to be the dowager duchess of Tyrrendor when you can be the wife to a member of the triumvirate? Mother of two? Live on a peaceful beach, in a peaceful city, on an isle that serves no greater good than its own."

"This heated show of emotion during an interview is unbecoming," Nairi mutters, then forks the last bite of her chicken.

"The interview ended before it began," Mira says, twirling the stem of her goblet between her fingers. "You don't care that Violet is the smartest person in this room. Or that Xaden tore apart Basgiath to save her, then returned to fight for Navarre because it was the right thing to do. Or that Cat lives in the most hostile environment possible to help her kingdom. You don't care that Aaric had to step into the light he hates so we'd have a royal representative, or that Garrick has stood by Xaden's side no matter the cost. We proved our lack of wisdom by coming here in the first place. You were never going to share your knowledge or ally yourself with us."

"True." Nairi pulls a jade stone from her robe and sets it in front of her plate. "And the first true piece of wisdom spoken here, which piques my interest. Now tell me, what do you think of our city?"

Mira glances at me, and I get the message. *My turn.*

"From the air, it seems laid out perfectly." I sit up straight. "It's a collection of exquisitely proportioned neighborhoods, all with central meeting places for markets and gatherings."

"It is perfect," Roslyn agrees, rolling her own jade stone over her knuckles.

"And cruel." I give my assessment with a flat tone Xaden should be proud of. He covers my hand with his and laces our fingers together.

Roslyn grasps the stone and places her hand in her lap. "Please, do go on." It's more of a threat than a request.

"You razed an existing city to build what stands now, did you not?"

"We improved our capital, yes." Roslyn's eyes narrow. "The smaller towns should have their rejuvenations complete by the end of the decade."

"And in doing so, you destroyed the historical base of the city, homes your citizens had lived in for generations. Yes, it's beautiful and efficient, but it also shows your intolerance for things that are not." I swallow hard. "I find it perplexing, too, that you don't seem to have a port."

"It is unwise to venture over water when we know next to nothing about what lurks within its depths—" Faris flusters.

They're…aquaphobic?

Roslyn holds up her hand. "Are we supposed to take criticism from a group who doesn't seem to know the name of their own continent?"

A deep breath disturbs my ribs painfully, and Xaden's hand tightens.

Amaralis. That's what both other isles have called us. Of course. Every other isle worships one member of the pantheon, and though we celebrate all, we hold one above all others. Amari.

"It's Amaralys, according to ancient royal records, though I believe Poromish records called it Amelekis. The only thing our kingdoms ever agreed on was calling it the Continent after the Great War," Aaric says, finally putting his silverware down after cleaning his plate. "Rather arrogant of us to simply refer to it as the Continent, as though there aren't others beyond the sea, but we've been torn apart by war for so long it's hard for anyone to think that we are one…anything."

For fuck's sake, what else is Aaric holding on to?

"You're rather quiet for someone who seems to know so much," Nairi remarks.

"I prefer keeping my mouth shut until I understand the rules of whatever game is aiming for my throat. Helps me judge the character and acumen of my opponent." He looks at each of them in turn. "Honestly, I find you lacking, and I'm not sure I want you for an ally. You have no army and you're stingy with the very thing that should be free to all—knowledge."

"And yet you seek our favor?" Nairi's eyebrows shoot up, and she blinks rapidly.

"Me?" Aaric shakes his head. "No. I'm just here because Halden can't control his temper and Violet didn't just bond one of our most terrifying battle dragons, but also an irid—the seventh breed. Dark wielders are spreading. People are dying as we sit here. Every day we're gone could change the battle map in ways we can't begin to predict. And my kingdom is full of assholes who won't take refugees under king's orders, so tracking down the irids is our best hope of not only adding to our numbers but maybe figuring out how we beat the venin six hundred years ago.

"If you fit into that solution, with all your wisdom, then great. If not, it seems all we're accomplishing here is dragging out family resentment and judgment, which we get plenty of at home. If it were up to me, we would thank you for the meal and get out before we discover what you do to people who don't pass your test."

"You are the highest member of nobility in your party," Roslyn notes, shifting in her seat with a grimace. "Is it not up to you?"

"Nobility doesn't play into rank, at least not for me." Aaric glances my way. "Andarna chose Violet, and though there are four superiorly ranked officers with us, it's Violet's mission. She's in command. And with the exception of her rather questionable taste in men, I've trusted Violet's *wisdom* since childhood."

Our eyes meet, and I shoot him a small smile.

The door opens, and servants pour in. The room falls quiet as they remove our dinner plates and disappear back into what I assume is the kitchen.

"You are truly bonded to a seventh breed?" Roslyn asks me.

"I am." I raise my chin. "She was left behind when her kind left the Cont—Amaralis, and we seek them. Now, are you interested in speaking to us about an alliance?"

"I am curious." Roslyn sets her stone in front of her plate.

"Two down. You're doing well." Faris grins. "Unfortunately, it must be a unanimous decision and I'm a little more…shrewd with my approach. Tell me, if you truly seek knowledge, why do you not worship Hedeon? Why would you not take up residence here like others who seek wisdom instead of allyship? Our libraries are unparalleled, our colleges centers for learning and culture, not death."

"I was taught that wisdom is never to be prayed for, but earned, and as much as I would revel in your library, I'm not interested unless it contains information on the venin." I shrug. "I'm not going to hide on an isle while the people I love are condemned to death by draining."

The door opens behind Faris again, and a server leans in. "Sir, are you ready for dessert?"

"We are," Faris answers, and the man returns to the kitchen.

"Please tell me you've done something with all that chocolate Talia has been stockpiling for weeks. I swear, she's bought every shipment that's come in, and you know how rare it is," Nairi teases, but a second later, her mouth purses and she adjusts in her chair. "Though I'm not sure I'm feeling up for sweets tonight."

"Me either," Roslyn agrees, holding her stomach.

"What kind of information?" Faris prompts me, his smile sharpening. "A weapon to destroy them, perhaps?"

"She already is one," Xaden remarks as the door opens, and Faris's eyes narrow on me slightly.

Servers stream in, then place our dishes on the table in front of us.

Oh…*shit.* A silver fork rests beside a perfectly sliced piece of chocolate cake.

Xaden's hand goes lax on top of mine.

"Is it still your favorite?" Talia's voice pitches up with excitement. "I know your birthday isn't until the end of the month, but you're here now."

Xaden stares at the cake like Halden stared at Anna's head.

"Phyllis," Faris calls out to one of the servants as they file back into the kitchen. "It seems the four of us are missing our forks."

"Of course. I'll fetch them immediately," the woman replies before the door shuts.

"Please, don't wait on our account." Faris waves at us. "Chocolate's an uncommon treat this far from Deverelli."

And she's been hoarding it for weeks. My mind begins to race.

Weeks. She knew we were coming.

I prefer a Deverelli approach to an alliance. That's what Queen Marlis said.

Courtlyn must have informed the other isles.

Talia knew *Xaden* was coming.

"If you don't like it anymore, that's all right." Talia's smile trembles. "I've been away from you longer than I was with you, and I know tastes can change. You're an adult now, after all. But just in case yours hasn't, we tried four recipes, and I think this one is closest to what we had in Aretia. You used to sneak into the kitchens when the cooks were baking—"

"I remember." Xaden drags his gaze to meet his mother's. "And it's still my favorite."

That scene on the beach where she acted so surprised was all…fake. My stomach sours. This is wrong. *Something*'s wrong. I've missed a detail I shouldn't have.

Her smile brightens, and Faris wraps his arm around her shoulder.

"You did well, my love." He kisses her cheek.

My gaze moves to Mira's, and her brow knits. She slides her hand backward on the table, and my heart begins to pound. We're being played. Talia knew Xaden was coming, which means Faris knew…and he's more *shrewd* in his approach to testing us.

The four of them conveniently don't have forks.

Something's in the cake.

Xaden reaches for his fork, and my fingers dig into his knee. His gaze snaps to mine, two lines forming between his brows.

I shake my head, then whip out my right and snatch the fork from Aaric's grip.

Cat drops her silverware, and it rattles on the plate.

"This tastes just like home," Garrick says, lifting another bite to his mouth.

Oh *Amari*, he's already eaten a third of it.

"Stop!" My heartbeat trips over itself.

Garrick pauses, then sets the forkful on the plate. "He said we could start—" He blinks once, then wobbles. "I feel…I feel—" Time seems to slow as his eyes flutter shut and he collapses, falling toward the table.

"Garrick!" Xaden shouts, shoving away from the table as Aaric lunges, catching Garrick's head before it can hit the surface.

Aaric's gaze swings wildly toward Xaden. "He isn't breathing!"

The citizenship test for those wishing to reside in Hedotis reminds me of the entrance exam for the Scribe Quadrant, but our test is designed to measure how much a potential cadet has learned, and theirs reads as though to prove how much one has not.

—HEDOTIS: ISLE OF HEDEON BY CAPTAIN ASHER SORRENGAIL

CHAPTER
THIRTY-SIX

hairs screech against the stone floor as Mira, Cat, and I stand. *"Get back here!"* I shout down the bond, and panic wraps its sharp-nailed hands around my heart and squeezes.

"Already en route," Tairn replies.

"Is Chradh—"

"Enraged but not suffering the loss of his rider from what I can tell."

"He just set part of the forest on fire," Andarna adds.

"Riorson, he's not—" Aaric starts to repeat.

"I heard you the first time." Xaden hooks his arms under Garrick's shoulders and hauls him from his chair, then lays him out on the floor and kneels by his side.

"What did you put in it?" I ask Faris, rounding the table.

His smile shifts from playful to cruel, but he doesn't answer.

"Get Trager!" Mira orders, and I hear a door open and shut behind me.

Xaden presses his ear to Garrick's chest. "Sluggish but beating."

"We need to get him to breathe—" Aaric starts. "He's fucking *blue*."

"Well aware." Xaden pinches Garrick's nose shut, then seals his mouth over Garrick's and exhales.

Garrick's chest rises.

I rock back on my heels and stand, finding Talia staring at Garrick with horror-stricken eyes. "What was in the cake?" I ask her.

She startles. "Nothing." Her brow furrows as she looks at Garrick's slice, then reaches for hers. "It's just—"

"Not for you, my dear." Faris takes her plate, then winces, tilting his head as he runs a hand over his stomach.

"What did you do?" Talia pushes back so quickly her chair falls into the wall behind her, leaving a mark on the pristine surface.

"I tested them as you asked," he tells her with a loving smile. "Here, in the privacy of our home, where they'd be comfortable."

Nairi and Roslyn both nudge their plates away, exchanging annoyed glances as Mira hovers, ready to strike.

"You poisoned my *son*?" Talia shrieks.

"Your son was wise enough not to eat it," Faris replies. "Our isle can be unforgiving. You should be proud, not angry."

I grab what's left of Garrick's cake and lift it to my nose. It smells like chocolate, and sugar, and maybe a hint of vanilla but— There. I breathe deeply, catching a hint of something sickly sweet. Like fruit that's been left in the sun too long.

"It's still slowing," Aaric says, and I glance back to see him lying with his ear against Garrick's chest as Xaden breathes again for his best friend.

My mind doesn't race—it *flies*. It could be anything. Powdered and added to the flour, liquefied and mixed in with the eggs or added to the glaze. It could be indigenous or imported. All I have is Dad's field guide. We're so far out of our depths here that I'm not even sure Brennan could help.

"Violet," Xaden pleads as our gazes collide. The panic in those onyx depths jars me like nothing else can.

I take a deep breath and steady my heartbeat to slow my thoughts. "I'll find it," I promise. "I won't let him die."

Xaden nods and breathes for Garrick again.

I smell the cake one last time and set it down, finding Faris watching us with rapt curiosity. Talia slowly backs herself against the curved wall, wrapping her arms around her middle as she watches Xaden.

"Is this the part where you draw a weapon?" Faris asks me, shifting in his seat. "Threaten to kill me if I don't tell you what your hasty friend ingested?"

"No." I lean my hip against the table where Talia should be sitting. "This is the part where I tell you I've already killed you."

Faris's smile slips. "And yet I breathe, and your friend does not." But his body rolls like he's trying to contain a belch, and he covers his mouth.

"Oh, you'll breathe just fine." I glance at the other three. "You all will. It's the vomiting until your bile turns to blood that will kill you. Should start in about ten minutes. Don't worry, it only lasts about an hour. Kind of a miserable way to go, but I worked with what I had."

Nairi lurches out of her chair and drops to her knees, retching onto the floor.

"Shit, my timing's off," I say to Mira.

"She had two glasses." Mira wrinkles her nose and retreats a step as Nairi empties the contents of her stomach.

"You drank and ate everything we did," Faris says, the blood draining from his face. "I watched."

"Not before dinner you didn't." I drum my fingers on the table. "Before dinner, it was just the six of us. Are you curious what I gave everyone for an appetizer as we walked down the stairs?"

His eyes flare. "You're lying."

"You wish." I glance sideways as Talia slides down the wall, muffling a cry with her fist. "Time for *your* test. Do you know why arinmint is illegal to export? Why it's against the rules to take it outside Aretia?"

"The fucking *tea*," Faris hisses, shooting a glare at Talia.

I lift his empty goblet and turn it upside down. "And you drank it all." I tsk at him, then set it back on the table. "I'll make you a deal. I was saving this for the unlikely event we failed your test and needed leverage, but you give me your antidote and I'll give you mine."

"You don't get to beat me." He shakes his head.

Anger prickles along my skin.

"And you don't get to poison my friend with impunity." I tilt my head, refusing to let *any* of the panic curdling in my stomach show on my face.

"Your friend will be dead in the next twenty minutes, and I will still have forty to see you slaughtered by my guards. You think we won't find the antidote in your room?" His voice rises.

The house shudders, and an ear-splitting roar rattles the forks against their plates.

"I wish you the best of luck." I manage to keep my voice level. "You have mediocre guards. I have ten lethally trained riders and fliers, four gryphons, and *seven* pissed-off dragons. The odds are in my favor."

Faris blanches. "How do I know you're not bluffing? That what you've given us is deadly?"

"You don't." I shrug. "But as soon as you or your wife starts vomiting blood, I'm afraid the antidote won't do you any good. Time's ticking."

The door swings open behind us, slamming into the wall.

"Oh *fuck*." Drake immediately sidesteps out of the doorway and Trager rushes in, the others close behind.

"What did they give him?" the flier asks, dropping to his knees opposite Xaden.

"Working on that," I tell him. *And I'm failing.*

Faris isn't responding to a threat to his own life, or even his wife's. It goes against every base instinct I have. I would have forked over the antidote as soon as I'd realized Xaden was in trouble.

"Stop thinking like you," Tairn orders. *"Think like him."*

"He'd rather die than lose." Fear drips off the edges of every word. *"He's not going to tell me."*

"Then stop asking him."

"Violet!" Xaden shouts.

"We have to get his heart beating stronger." Trager puts one hand on top of the other on Garrick's sternum, then forces all his weight down. "Keep breathing for him."

The door opens behind Faris, and a servant gasps, then slams the door shut and screams.

My gaze swings to Mira. "I need you to handle everything else in this house that can kill us." Then I look toward the doorway and find Dain standing behind Cat and Ridoc. "Get my dad's book on Hedotis. It's in my pack on the right side of my bed."

Dain nods and takes off running.

"We seal the house *now*," Mira orders. "There are three doors on this level. Cordella, take the front. Cat and Maren, handle the back by the patio. I'll go for the side. Ridoc and Aaric, stay with Violet." She draws her daggers and charges past the two sick women and through the servants' entrance to the kitchen.

The cook.

"Ridoc, with me!" I call back over my shoulder, then race through the door Mira left open and into the kitchen.

Five servants stand around a large, cluttered table, their hands up at their shoulders, palms facing outward. There are two more at the hearth, one at the wash basin, and two by a stone oven.

"Where is the cook?"

They stare back at me.

"Where is the cook," I repeat, switching to Hedotic.

The female servant who just found us trembles as she points to a doorway on her right. I draw two blades and trust Ridoc to watch my back as I storm past the workers and into— It's a pantry.

Shelves with jars and baskets of fruits line the walls.

The spindly man startles and nearly drops what looks to be a jar of pickled eggs.

"What did you put in the cake?" I ask in Hedotic.

"What I was instructed to." He slides the jar back onto the shelf, then reaches below and draws a knife from the block.

"Don't do that." I lift my blades. "Just tell me what's killing my friend and you live."

He charges me and I throw my daggers in quick succession, embedding them deep within both his forearms. Blood streams to his elbows and he drops the kitchen knife, then bellows, staring down at his arms as his hands shake.

"I told you not to do that!" I take three steps, then yank out both of my daggers by their hilts and kick him square in the stomach.

He stumbles backward into the shelves.

Debilitating pain explodes in my side, and I gasp, tensing every muscle like that might somehow rewind the last thirty seconds and spare my broken rib. *Fuck*, I did not think that through.

The cook brings his trembling hands together in a plea, revealing blue half-moons under his nails. "Please. No. I have a wife. And two children."

Blue.

He hadn't been using a blue-edged towel. He'd been scrubbing the blue off his hands.

I back out of the pantry slowly and find Ridoc guarding the door, flight jacket unbuttoned, sword drawn. "We're looking for something blue."

"You telling me there's actually something colorful on this isle?" We both stare at the pots, pans, and dishes covering the newly deserted worktable, then move toward it. Ridoc sheaths his sword, picks up a pot, checks its cream-colored contents, and sets it back down. "Even the freaking birds are white—"

Errisbirds.

Blue nails. The scent of overripe fruit.

That's it. "I know what it—"

The cook yells as he storms out of the pantry, and both Ridoc and I whirl.

My heart seizes as I catch sight of the cook's kitchen knife mid-flight. I dodge right, then surge forward toward the cook, walling off the pain like it belongs to someone else, and pull a move from Courtlyn's book. I throw the dagger with a snap of my wrist and pin the cook's bloodied hand to the fucking doorframe.

He has the nerve to howl like he doesn't deserve it.

"Stay there," I order in Hedotic, then turn back toward Ridoc.

Air gushes from my lungs as Ridoc looks down.

The cook's knife is lodged in his side.

I wish you and Sawyer were with us, but I'm grateful to have Ridoc, even if his sarcasm is wearing on Mira's last nerve.

—Recovered Correspondence of Cadet Violet Sorrengail to Cadet Rhiannon Matthias

CHAPTER
THIRTY-SEVEN

"Ridoc!" Fear pours into me, colder than a snow squall in January, as I stumble forward.

No. No. No. The words form a chant of pure denial in my head.

"That's…unfortunate," Ridoc says quietly, staring down at the knife that protrudes from his side.

Not Ridoc. Not *anyone*, but especially not Ridoc.

This isn't happening. Not again. Not when we're thousands of miles from home and he hasn't graduated, or fallen in love, or gotten to *live*. "You're all right," I whisper. "Just keep it there, and I'll get Trager—"

Ridoc reaches for the knife's hilt.

"No!" I lunge across him to grab his hand, but he's already yanked the blade free. I slam my palms over his side to stanch the flow of blood…but there isn't any. No hole in his shirt, either, just two slices through his flight jacket and a cut in the counter.

The blade caught the edge of his flight jacket…not *him*.

Ridoc flies at the cook, and my hands slip off his stomach.

"Asshole!" Ridoc shouts, and I pivot to see him plow his fist into the cook's face. "I have *four* uniforms, but only *one* fucking flight jacket, and I"—punch— "hate"—punch—"sewing!" Ridoc yanks my dagger from the cook's hand, and the man slides down the doorframe, his eyes fluttering shut. "For fuck's sake, you're supposed to be the *civilized* isle!" He wipes my blade on the cook's tunic, then turns and walks back toward me. "What is the wisdom in a kitchen cook attacking two trained killers?" His face falls. "Vi, you all right?"

I gulp for air and nod. "Yeah. I just thought…but I'm fine. And you're fine. And everything is…fine, except Garrick, so we should—"

Understanding softens his eyes, and he wraps his arm around my shoulders, pulling me into a quick but gentle hug. "Yeah, I love you, too."

I nod and we break apart. "I know what they put in the cake."

"Good." Ridoc gestures at the door, and we both head back toward the dining room. "And I want a patch for this shit, Violet. A quest squad patch. Understand?"

"Loud and clear." I make it into the dining room first and find two of the triumvirate retching while Xaden and Trager monitor Garrick as Talia sobs. Aaric waits on the edge of the table, dagger in hand, and Faris sits hunched over with his arms around his stomach.

"He's breathing on his own, but it's shallow," Xaden says. "Tell me you have good news."

"Almost." I try to smile.

"Book." Dain slides my father's field guide across the table. Aaric catches it, then hands it over.

"He'll be dead in ten minutes," Faris mutters.

"No, he won't." I flip through the book to the chapter I need, then run my finger down the flora chart Dad drew until I reach zakia berries.

Poisonous when allowed to ferment. Treat with fig or lime to the back of the throat within one hour.

Thank you, Dad.

"I've got it," I tell Xaden, then slam the book shut and look over at Dain. "Upstairs on the veranda by our room, there's a silver tray. Get the figs."

Dain nods, then takes off at a run.

I motion to Aaric, and he slides from the table. "I need five small cups filled with water. Fresh, not salt. One is for Dain."

He heads into the kitchen, and Ridoc follows.

"Figure out how to get him to swallow," I say to Xaden, then lean against the edge of the table, grimacing at the pain in my ribs as I lean down to Faris. "We're fighting a war for the future of our world. This shouldn't be a competition. Logic and wisdom dictate that you assist us so you don't *become* us."

"It is *your* war," he growls as Dain sprints back in.

"Crush it, dice it, whatever you have to do to mix it with enough water to get it down his throat," I tell Dain.

"On it." He steps onto a chair, then walks across the table, jumping off once he clears Garrick's head. Then he, too, disappears into the kitchen.

"It will be *our* war." I lean down as Faris shudders. "You think they won't come here once they've drained every last ounce of magic from our home?"

"We're safe." He glares up at me. "We have no magic here."

"Foolish, foolish man." I shake my head. "They'll drain *you*."

His eyes flare a second before he groans in pain.

Xaden and Trager have Garrick on his side when Dain returns with the fig slurry and a spoon. Aaric and Ridoc follow, each carrying two small cups of water.

I take them one by one and set them behind me, out of Faris's reach, then dig my nails into the palm of my hand to keep from panicking as the guys work to get the solution down Garrick's throat.

He has an hour, according to Dad, and it hasn't been—

Garrick sputters, spitting some of the slurry out, but his eyes flash open.

I sag in relief as Xaden yells at him to wake the fuck up and drink it. It takes him four big swallows before the cup is drained and he falls back, his head landing in Trager's lap.

Xaden's worried gaze snaps to mine.

"Give it time," I say gently. "We're under the hour mark. He'll be all right."

A muscle in his jaw ticks, making the bruise ripple, but he nods.

"Now is when you pray that Garrick wakes in the next few minutes," I whisper to Faris as Roslyn cries softly on the floor. "You pray to Hedeon, or whoever will listen, that you were not as clever as you thought you were, because that's the *only* way he's going to let you out of this alive."

Faris's purple eyes narrow up at me. "Why would I pray for him to wake and kill me?"

"Not Garrick." I shake my head. "Xaden. Sgaeyl is widely known as one of the most ruthless dragons in Navarre, and she chose him for a reason."

Fear streaks through his gaze.

I sit back and wait.

Three minutes later, Garrick groans and opens his eyes. "This is my least favorite isle."

A relieved laugh bubbles through my lips, and Xaden's head falls back like he's giving thanks to Zihnal, or perhaps Malek, for not claiming his best friend.

"You didn't win," Faris snaps.

"You're dying. I think that qualifies you as the loser." I slide off the table.

Xaden jumps to his feet and barrels past me, yanking Faris from the chair and shoving him against the wall.

Oh, *shit*. And here I thought I'd been bluffing. My stomach hollows as Xaden hits Faris with a bone-crunching right hook.

"You poisoned him?" He slams him into the wall again. "You tried to poison *her*?" He draws a blade from his thigh and sets it at Faris's neck.

"Whoa, whoa." Ridoc walks toward them. "We can't kill potential allies, even if they suck."

Xaden turns a glare on Ridoc that freezes the blood in my veins. That isn't him.

"No." I move without thinking, stepping between them and pushing Ridoc back with a hand against his chest. "No."

Ridoc lifts his brows but steps back, and Dain's eyes narrow as I turn to Xaden.

"Look at me." I take hold of his forearm, but he doesn't back off Faris's throat. A thin line of blood appears at the blade's edge. "Look. At. Me."

Xaden's gaze drops to mine, and my stomach flips. It's like I'm staring at a stranger dressed up as the man I love.

"Get off the ice," I whisper. "Pull your shit together and come back to me because I need you. Not this. *You.*"

His eyes flicker with recognition. A second later, he pushes away from Faris, lowers his blade, walks past me, past Ridoc and Aaric and Dain, past his own mother and Garrick and Trager, to lean against the wall by the door. He sheathes his blade and folds his arms, staring at the plate in front of my seat.

"You have a plan here?" Dain asks, his gaze swinging from Xaden to me. "Or are we winging it?"

"I have a plan." Sort of. That plan is just rapidly deteriorating the longer it takes Faris to buckle. Killing the triumvirate isn't going to secure the alliance we need, and naturally, Faris knows that. "Can you get everyone ready to fly?"

Dain nods. "Aaric, help Trager with Garrick and start moving him toward Chradh. Ridoc, let's pack everyone's shit."

They all move, leaving Xaden and me with the triumvirate and his mother.

"Sit," I order Faris, pointing to his chair, and to my utter surprise, he does. "What should I charge you for the antidote?"

"Meet Malek," he snarls.

"It's a shame you don't know more about Tyrrendor, seeing as your wife lived there for ten years." I move to the edge of the table. "Arinmint of all things. Ironic that it's your ignorance and not mine we discovered tonight."

"You'll never make it out of here alive," he swears.

"We will." I put the four glasses in front of me, then pull four vials from my left front pocket. "It's only a question of if we leave here with an alliance, an understanding, or a newly elected triumvirate."

He growls, but his gaze tracks my motions as I pour the vials into the water, one per glass. The clear liquid quickly turns black and grows sludgy.

"What's it going to be?" I ask Faris.

"My staff knows what's happened here. The city guards will shoot your dragons from the sky," he warns.

"I highly doubt that." I take Aaric's unused fork and stir the slurries. "Because in a minute, my sister is going to bring one of your guards in, and you're going to tell them to let us go, as we have a newfound allyship rooted in" — I glance at Talia, who has tucked her knees to her chest as she writhes in pain — "bloodline. Guess someone's contract marriage worked out as intended, because your wife's son is the Duke of Tyrrendor. Naturally, you'd want to nurture that relationship."

"You would never be able to trust me. I'll turn on you the second you leave."

"You won't." I shake my head. "Because like you said, your staff knows what happened here. You can certainly keep them quiet, but you can't keep *us* quiet. Do you truly think your isle would support your next bid for power if they knew you were outsmarted in your own home?"

He clenches his fists as his stomach heaves, but he doesn't vomit. "How did you do it?"

Now *that's* progress. "Arinmint looks just like regular mint, which is why its export is outlawed. By itself, steeped in milk, or turned into tea with lemon or a little chamomile, it works wonders for sleep and healing. But when you combine it with some other pretty ordinary herbs, say the shredded bark of the tarsilla bush, it becomes a deadly poison, and tarsilla grows all along your beaches." I lean down, careful not to jostle my ribs, so I'm at his eye level. "Ask me why we're going to fly out of here without you saying a single word."

"Why?" he grinds out.

"Because you love your sons." I smile. "That's why you sent them out of the house tonight."

Fear widens his eyes.

"Ask why there are only six dragons outside." I lift my brows and wait, but his breaths start coming alarmingly fast. "If you're going to be dramatic, I'll just give you the answer. It's because the seventh currently sits next to the window at your parents' house, where your boys sleep — where she'll stay until she knows we're out of range of any weapons you might be hiding."

Approval floods the bond, and I imagine Tairn's chest puffing with pride.

"That's impossible." Faris shakes his head. "Someone would have seen."

"Not when that dragon is an irid."

Sweat drips down his forehead, catching in his eyebrows. "You wouldn't. They're children."

"Do you really want to take that risk?" I stand and slide the first glass his way. "Or do you want to drink and live?"

"Faris!" Talia cries. "Please!"

"You didn't outsmart me. None of this happened." He reaches for the glass.

"I didn't outsmart you *alone*," I admit. "My father helped."

He clutches the antidote. "The eyes. I should have recognized your eyes. You're Asher Daxton's girl."

"One of them, yes." A slow smile spreads across my face. "And the other currently has command of your house. Make your choice."

He drinks.

Xaden doesn't so much as *look* at his mother when we walk away.

. . .

We hover out of cross-bolt range until Andarna joins us, then fly through the night, heading northwest along the trading routes. We only have two major isles left to search for the irids, and as much as I enjoy not being hunted by Theophanie, we can't stay out here long enough to thoroughly scour all the minor ones. Every day we fly lengthens the time it will take to get home, where the least of our worries will be the court-martial waiting for us if we don't bring with us the assistance we disobeyed orders to find.

By morning, there's still no sight of land.

My chest feels like it's clamped in a permanent vise. Gods, if I'm wrong, I won't have only almost gotten Garrick killed, I'll be the end of the rest of us, too.

I sleep on and off in the saddle, my exhaustion the only thing capable of outweighing the pain in my ribs. Luckily for me, the power in the sunshield rune I carry still holds, and my skin remains unburned as the temperature warms. By the time the sun is directly above us, we reach the southeastern tip of the archipelago that leads to Zehyllna.

"*Should be another hour until we reach the mainland,*" Tairn says as we sail over the first island, which looks small enough to be swallowed at the slightest hint of a storm.

"*Can the others make it that long?*" Andarna is already strapped at his chest.

"*I can't exactly ask them, but no one has snapped at my wings, which I find to be a good sign.*"

Or they're all too tired to.

I twist as far as my ribs will allow and see that the gryphons are mostly holding the center of the formation. "*Kiralair is lagging a little.*"

"*Is she?*" Tairn doesn't look back. "*Or is Silaraine?*"

I block the sun with my hand and focus hard on the second row of gryphons. "*You're right. It looks like she's fallen back to keep pace with Silaraine.*" But Cath and Molvic have their backs covered another row behind.

"*I know.*" We cross over the next island and the aqua water that surrounds it on all sides. "*Seems Catriona has found someone worth lagging behind for.*"

The thought brings a smile to my face as I settle in for the last part of the flight. True to his estimate, it's about an hour before we fly past the white sand beaches and their swaying palm trees…and their waving humans.

"That's…unusual." No one screams and runs or mans the wall of cross-bolts as we pass over the coastal town. They just…wave.

"It's unsettling," Tairn agrees.

"It's not a bad thing to be liked." Andarna clicks out of her harness and flies off to Tairn's right, tipping her wing when a group of children runs across a field, their arms extended.

I breathe a sigh of relief as we sail over green-leafed trees. Perhaps the color isn't quite as rich as the tones on the Continent, but it's definitely a welcome sight after the monochromatic scheme of Hedotis.

A sparkling river leads us into the hills, and we pass a sun-drenched waterfall before reaching a plateau, then continue due west along the winding riverbed.

Three more waterfalls and rises in elevation later, the capital city of Xortrys comes into view and takes my breath away.

It's situated at the base of an enormous, curved waterfall, and the way the river splits around the city makes it appear as an island of its own. The city walls look like they rise from the water itself, and the structures beyond defy any and all architectural logic, as though vertical additions were erected upon existing buildings as they were needed, growing the city skyward.

"The south bridge is the main gate," I remind Tairn, and he banks left along the southern branch of the river, flying toward the enormous structure that spans the water.

"Is that a gate? Or an amphitheater?" Tairn asks as a huge clearing comes into view at the end of the bridge.

"Uhh…both?" Along the western tree line sit rows upon rows of benched seating, enough to fit hundreds—maybe thousands—of people.

And they're half full.

"Do you think this is normal, or…" The other option makes me a little queasy.

"They're expecting us," Andarna replies with excitement, descending into the field before Tairn. Her left wing trembles as she flares them wide and she lands a second before we do, dead center in the field.

The crowd comes to its feet in a raucous cheer as Tairn tucks his wings in and prowls forward to Andarna's side. A few people dart from the stands and make a run for the bridge, too smiley to be fleeing for their lives.

"They're spreading the news." Tairn turns his head slowly, and I mirror his movement, lifting my flight goggles and taking in what is easily the oddest and potentially most dangerous arrival we've faced yet. We're more than outnumbered, though no one appears to be holding any weapons against us, nor do they approach; they simply watch.

The stands rise a good twenty feet over Tairn's head, and the people in them cheer louder as our squad lands in a single, long line. The earth shudders with each dragon's arrival, but the gryphons fit themselves into formation gracefully. The excitement in the air is a living, palpable thing, roaring in my ears louder than the waterfall in the distance, clinging to my skin with more tenacity than the stifling heat and humidity, humming along my veins as though their zeal is contagious.

"This is weird." I glance to the right and note Andarna scraping through the manicured grass with a single talon. *"Stay close."*

"Any closer and I'll be under *him,"* she retorts, her full claws flexing in the ground.

"Stop tearing up their grass before they—" Tairn lowers his head to the ground and inhales so deeply, his sides flare as his lungs expand. *"Do you feel that?"*

"Feel what?" The buzz from the crowd grows to a fever pitch, and a wave of energy rushes up my body, prickling the back of my neck in a feeling that reminds me of... I gasp.

Magic.

To live amongst the Zihlni, you must prepare to accept luck as your guide and chaos as your standard.

—Zehyllna: Isle of Zihnal by Major Asher Sorrengail

CHAPTER THIRTY-EIGHT

No wonder the leaves are almost fully green. Zehyllna has magic. Not enough to channel or even properly shield, and nowhere in the realm of wielding, but there are definitely two strands of power trickling down the bonds from Tairn and Andarna.

I shove my flight jacket into my pack so I don't sweat to death and make quick work of dismounting. Tairn dips even lower in deference to my aching ribs, and I pat the scales above his talon in thanks as I walk onto the field.

To my right, Andarna flicks her head left and right repeatedly, like she can't fully focus on one sight before another catches her attention, and on my left, Ridoc stares up at Aotrom, saying something I can't hear over the noise of the crowd. Just beyond him, Trager throws his head back in laughter, then reaches up to scratch under Silaraine's silver-feathered jaw.

The gryphon tilts her head to give him easier access and closes her eyes.

I can't help but wonder how long she's had that particular itch, since it's in a place she can't reach.

"Can they talk?" I move forward just enough to see down the line of our squad and watch the same scene playing out among riders and fliers. Even Xaden is paused before Sgaeyl, though it looks like any conversation they might be having isn't going his way.

"We all can," Tairn replies with a sound I'd almost call a sigh of contentment.

I give myself a second to smile, to revel in the happiness of my friends who have been denied the closest of their relationships for the last couple of weeks. Then I look up at the mass of people gradually quieting and taking their seats, and scan down the rows to the bottom without finding a single weapon out of its scabbard. Color fills the crowd, but everyone sitting in the front row is dressed in identical sleeveless tunics the shade of apricots.

For as much excitement as they're showing, none of them rush forward to greet us. In fact, the people joining climb the seats farthest to the right as they enter the field, as though not to obscure the crowd's view for even a second.

A wisp of a shadow brushes against my mind, and my smile deepens.

"Hi there," Xaden says as he strides toward me, the corners of his mouth curving. He's shucked his flight jacket, too, and pushed up the sleeves of his uniform to his elbows.

"Hi there." I grin, somehow having found *home* thousands of miles away from the Continent. *"Everything good with Sgaeyl?"*

"She's yelling, but I'll take it over silence any day." A muscle in his jaw pops as he reaches my side, then turns to face the crowd. *"Pretty sure she's spent the last week or so cataloging every one of my missteps, given how quickly she listed them."*

"I'm sorry." I brush the back of my hand against his.

"She has every right to be pissed." He laces our fingers and holds tight as he studies our surroundings. *"I need you to make me another promise, Violet."*

"That sounds serious." I smile at Ridoc as he heads our way with a definite bounce in his step. The others aren't far behind him.

"Look at me." Xaden softens the sharp command with a brush of his thumb over mine.

My gaze snaps to his and my smile falls at the intensity in his stare. *"What do you want me to promise?"*

"That you'll never do that again."

I blink. *"You're going to have to be more specific."*

"You put yourself between Ridoc and me—"

"It seemed like you might hit my friend." I lift my brows. *"And you weren't exactly yourself."*

"That's my point." Fear flashes across his face before he quickly masks it. *"There's no telling what I could have done to you. It's all I've been able to think about."*

"Is it just me? Or are we the equivalent of the circus coming to town?" Ridoc asks.

"You won't hurt me," I argue for the hundredth time. *"Even when you* wanted *to kill me last year, you never hurt me. Even when you lack your emotions, you're still…you."*

"Oh, we're definitely the show," Cat answers Ridoc.

"This might be my favorite isle." Trager takes Cat's hand. "What do you think, Violet?"

"Me, without any restraint or reason." Xaden lowers his brows.

"How about I decide when I think you're too dangerous to approach."

"I think I know when I'm too dangerous to approach." He leans in.

"Don't mind them." Ridoc's tone sings. "They're back to doing...whatever it is they do when they ignore everyone around them and pretend they're the only people in existence."

"This from the same man who thinks I need to know how to kill him?" I lift my chin. *"Which is it, Xaden? Am I too precious to get close? Or am I the one who needs to know which shadow is yours?"*

He gives me a look Sgaeyl would be proud of, and I hold his gaze. *"I wouldn't be able to live with myself if I hurt you."* The sun catches the amber flecks in his eyes, and I nearly relent at the plea in his tone.

"And I won't be able to live with myself if I stand there and watch you hurt Ridoc." I squeeze his hand. *"I take full responsibility for my safety. You are a giant battle flag waving in the wind right now, Xaden, but you're* my *battle flag, and you'd do the same thing in my position."*

"Hey, I hate to break up whatever moment you're having," Ridoc says, "but everyone's here and their emissary is headed this way."

"This discussion isn't over," Xaden warns as we turn our attention to the field.

"Happy to win the fight again later." I squeeze his hand one last time, then let go as a woman in an orange tunic and matching scabbard walks toward us, carrying a cone-shaped object half my height. *"I love you."*

"So fucking stubborn." He sighs. *"I love* you.*"*

All down the line, the dragons lower their heads in warning.

The woman doesn't flinch, but the crowd falls quiet.

I take a steadying breath and send a prayer up to Zihnal himself that this encounter goes better than our last.

"Welcome to Zehyllna!" the woman says in the common language, then grins as she approaches, her white teeth sharply contrasting her deep-brown cheeks. She's beautiful, with joyful brown eyes, a halo of black, airy curls, and thick curves. "I am Calixta, mistress of today's festivities."

Festivities? My brows scrunch at the term, and Ridoc rocks back on his heels. Xaden's head tilts.

Calixta pauses about five feet from my boots, then glances across our squad and begins to speak in Zehylish.

I blink. Any studying I did is completely useless. Nothing on the page could prepare me for hearing it spoken. It's a lilting, flowy language where one word seems to run into the next.

Dain replies slowly from my right, the words coming out like he's in pain.

Aaric sighs from beside Xaden, then proceeds to speak like he was freaking born here.

Dain looks ready to murder him.

"Excellent!" Calixta replies in the common language. "I am happy to speak in your tongue if it brings you joy." She turns to me. "Your translator says you are the leader of this glorious assembly."

I'm really starting to loathe that word. "I'm Violet Sorrengail. We've come in hopes of—"

"Securing an alliance!" She beams. "Yes! Word of your travels reached us a few weeks ago, and we have been waiting ever since."

"Here?" Ridoc asks. "You've all been waiting out here?"

"Of course not." She scoffs. "People come to the festival grounds as they have time in hopes they will be the first to see the dragons. And Zihnal is certainly with those of us who chose today!" Her gaze sweeps over the riot. "Which is the irid?"

I draw back. *"Courtlyn?"*

"Courtlyn," Xaden agrees.

Andarna lifts her head, and Tairn growls down the bond.

"Way to give yourself away." I narrow my eyes at her.

"It looks…black," Calixta remarks.

Andarna blinks, and her scales shift color, blending into the background.

"She," I correct Calixta. "Her name is Andarna and she's the only irid on the Contin—" I wince. "On Amaralys. We're searching for the rest of her kind and allies to hopefully fight alongside us in a war against those who wield dark magic."

"She is marvelous." Calixta bows, low and deep.

Andarna shimmers again, her scales returning to black, then lowers her head when Tairn huffs a breath at her.

"Our queen is delighted you've sought us out and is eager to come to your aid. We have always revered dragonkind." She tilts her head toward Silaraine. "And the gryphons, of course."

There's no fucking way this is *that* easy. Dad wrote about playing games picked at random to gain entrance. "May we speak to your queen?" I ask. "We've brought a prince of Navarre to speak on our kingdom's behalf."

"Of course!" Calixta replies. "But first—"

"Here we go," Ridoc mutters under his breath.

My thought exactly.

"—we must see what gifts Zihnal has chosen for you," she finishes. "If you are willing to play and accept whatever gift the god of luck presents you with"—she lifts a finger—"without complaint, then you will be granted entrance to our city, where our queen waits."

"I expected dice or even a board game, not gifts," I admit to Xaden.

"There's a trick here," Xaden warns. *"But there's not enough power to read her."*

"And if we…complain?" I ask.

All traces of amusement drain from her face. "If you do not accept that luck determines your fate, that Zihnal may gift you with great fortune or take it, then we cannot ally ourselves with you. We do not accept those who do not adjust their sails in a storm."

Not such a random choice of game, then. They want to see how we handle disappointment.

"No whining," Xaden remarks. *"I can respect that."*

Looking left, then right, I meet the eyes of every person on our squad, starting with Trager. One by one, they nod, ending with Mira on the right, who immediately rolls her eyes afterward.

"We'll do it," I tell Calixta.

"Wonderful!" She spins back to the crowd and lifts the pointed end of the hollow cone to her mouth before shouting into it.

The crowd roars.

"She said we'll play," Aaric tells me, leaning forward to see around Xaden.

"Where were these language skills when we were translating journals last year?" I ask.

He looks at me like I've gained another head. "I was raised to be a diplomat. Diplomats don't speak to dead people."

"You didn't think we should know you speak fluent everything?" I arch a brow.

"And nullify Aetos's reason for joining…what is it Ridoc calls us? Quest squad?" Aaric shakes his head.

"Let us see what Zihnal shall gift you with!" Calixta says over her shoulder, then walks toward the crowd.

Five people emerge from the right side of the steps, four carrying a table and one, a chair and a canvas bag.

"Guess we follow," I say to the others.

We walk as a line across the field, and I stifle a yawn. The sooner we get this over with, the sooner we can find our beds. I can't remember the last full night of sleep we had without pulling watches. Deverelli, maybe?

"I don't care if she hands you a steaming pile of goat shit," Mira lectures down the line. "No one complains. Got it? Smile and thank her. This is our last real chance to secure an army."

"What if it's cow shit?" Ridoc asks. "That's considerably heavier."

"No complaining," Drake snaps from the left.

"Fuck, it's like traveling with my parents," Ridoc mutters.

"What are you thinking?" I ask Xaden as the table is set on the field about twenty feet in front of the crowd.

"They'd better have an army worth handling cow shit for." His gaze continuously moves over the area. *"And I'm not a fan of it being two thousand to eleven, even with dragonfire at our back."*

"Agreed. Let's get this over with."

"Excellent idea. I'd like to find lunch," Tairn says.

Three of the furniture carriers scatter, leaving Calixta facing us in the chair behind the table and two men off to her right. The closest holds the cone.

"Stop," Calixta says, holding out her hand when we're about six feet from the edge of the table.

We stop.

I wave a bug out of my face and glance up at the sky, hoping for some form of approaching cloud cover to shade us from the heat, but there's none to be found. Guess Zihnal has decided we'll bake in our leathers while we wait.

Calixta reaches into the canvas bag, then pulls out a stack of cards as thick as the width of my forearm. They're the size of my face and have a bright-orange pattern on their backs. "Each card represents a gift," she says, mixing them with a skill that speaks to practice.

The closest man translates for the crowd, his voice booming through the cone, and the taller one to his right signs.

Calixta spreads the cards face down in a long arc across the table. "You will pull the card Zihnal inspires you to choose and receive your gift."

The men translate, and the crowd murmurs in anticipation.

"There's no way two thousand people gather to watch us open presents." My stomach turns at the looks of rapt fascination among the crowd.

"Don't pick the shit card," Xaden replies.

"Step forward and choose." Calixta points to Mira.

Every muscle in my body tenses and a wave of dizziness makes me brace my feet apart. *Not right now,* I beg my body.

Mira walks to the right edge of the table and plucks a card without pause.

Calixta takes it and smiles. "Zihnal gifts you wine!" She shows us the painted wine bottle, then rotates it for the crowd as the men translate.

The applause is instant, and a middle-aged woman with curly brown hair runs forward from the left front row carrying a bottle of wine.

"Thank you," Mira says as the woman hands it to her, and Calixta translates.

The woman bows her head, and Mira mirrors the gesture before turning toward me.

"I'm going to fucking need this," she says with a fake smile, then falls back into line as the woman hurries to her seat.

One by one, Calixta calls us forward, moving down the line.

Maren receives two orange tunics from a short, smiling man with a shiny bald head.

Dain's card reveals a hand, and when he offers his to the woman who walks over to him, she slaps him across the face so hard his head turns in our direction.

I swallow my gasp and force a blank expression onto my face when I catch Calixta glancing my way. Message received: we can't complain about anyone else's gifts, either.

Dain blinks twice, then thanks the woman and inclines his head.

Ridoc barely stifles a snort, but quickly schools his features when I glance sideways at him.

"Do not laugh," I warn Xaden, fighting off another tide of dizziness.

"I'm more worried about the implications of that hit," he answers without losing his professionally bored expression. *"And a little jealous of the woman who delivered it."*

Garrick is given a rusted steel bucket.

Aaric receives a fractured hand mirror that immediately cuts his thumb when the man hands it to him top first.

My heart pounds like I'm on the mat as Xaden chooses his card.

He's given an empty glass box the size of his foot, with pewter hinges and edges. *"Better than getting slapped."*

A smile tugs at my mouth, but it doesn't calm my racing heart as I step forward. I choose a card on the far left end of the arch, then hold my breath as I hand it to Calixta.

"The compass!" she announces and the men translate.

A tall man with bronzed skin and short black hair comes forward from the right, and I turn to face him. His dark eyes study me for a moment that quickly becomes awkward.

I lift my chin and his mouth tilts into a smirk as he nods subtly, as though finding my reaction worthy. Extending his hand silently, he offers me a black compass on a dark chain. I glance down as I take it and notice that the needle doesn't point anywhere near north. It's broken.

Now I understand the smirk.

"Thank you," I tell him and bow my head.

"Use it wisely," he replies, his eyes blatantly mocking me as he bows.

"Broken compass," I tell Xaden as I fall back into line.

"You can put it in my box of nothingness," he replies. *"We'll keep them on the bedside table."*

"I'm not carrying this thing home." But for now, I lift the chain over my head.

"It's bad luck to throw away a gift from Zihnal," Xaden lectures as Ridoc heads to the table.

Ridoc draws a card with a painted pair of lips, and the crowd cheers.

The way this is going, I half expect the lanky blond man approaching Ridoc to hand him a tin of lip rouge, or maybe a pair of lips that's been sliced off a dead cow. Instead, the man clasps both sides of Ridoc's face, then smacks a loud kiss onto each of his cheeks.

"Thank you," Ridoc says, and the two bow, then part. He lifts his brows at me before taking his place in line.

Cat is given a gold necklace with a dangling ruby the size of my thumb.

Drake draws next.

"The claw!" Calixta announces, holding the painted symbol high, and the crowd cheers when the men translate.

My heart jumps into my throat as a bear of a man marches forward from the right, huge fists swinging by his sides.

Drake doesn't flinch.

I ready myself for the punch that's inevitably coming and wonder if the man's nails have been filed into sharp points.

He stops in front of Drake, then reaches into the front pocket of his tunic.

And takes out a mewling *kitten.*

Drake receives the orange tabby with both hands, then thanks him and bows.

"What the fuck are we going to do with that thing for the rest of the trip?" Xaden questions.

"Keep Andarna from eating it." A bead of sweat drips down the side of my face, and I wobble as my head starts to swim, but I keep upright.

"Dizzy?" Xaden asks, sidestepping so my shoulder rests against his arm.

"I could use some sleep like everyone else," I answer but lean a little on him.

Trager draws a card from the center and hands it to Calixta.

"The arrow!" She holds it high, revealing a painted arrow, then turns it to the audience. The men translate, and the crowd falls silent.

Trager staggers backward. Time slows to a crawl as he turns toward us with three fumbling footsteps. His gaze lurches for Cat, and then he falls to his knees and sways.

An arrow protrudes from his heart.

He's dead before Ridoc and I can catch him.

Sometimes the best gift the god of luck can give is his absence.

—ZEHYLLNA: ISLE OF ZIHNAL BY MAJOR ASHER SORRENGAIL

CHAPTER THIRTY-NINE

No. No. NO.

I stare down at Trager's unseeing eyes as Ridoc and I lower him to his back, and a muffled sound comes from the left.

Ridoc's chest heaves and his fingers tremble as he presses them to the side of Trager's throat. He looks over at me and shakes his head, telling me what I already knew.

"No!" I shriek, but nothing works past my throat.

"Do not react!" Xaden's wingleader voice barrels through the roaring in my head, and his hands grip my shoulders.

Ridoc's eyes flutter shut and he bows his head as I'm lifted to my feet.

Trager's dead. It's my mission. My responsibility. My fault.

"Focus on me," Xaden orders, turning me in his arms. *"You react, and he will have died in vain."*

My head swims, and the world slows again, my thoughts drowned out by the sound of my racing heart. It pounds against my ribs and beats in my ears as I look right.

Drake's arms bulge as he holds Cat back, his hand covering her mouth.

That muffled sound.

It's her screaming.

Drake's face crumples for the length of a heartbeat as he whispers in her ear.

Her feet stop kicking, and she sags against his chest.

Garrick sets Ridoc back in formation, his stunned gaze locked on the ground. No, not the ground. *Trager's body.* Garrick's hands steady Ridoc's shoulders for another couple of heartbeats before he leaves him to stand on his own in front of the silent, waiting crowd.

"Violence," Xaden demands.

My focus drifts toward him, but it catches as I look past Ridoc and across the field. Every dragon holds their head lowered and aimed in our direction, but the gryphons are all facing inward—toward Silaraine.

She stumbles forward with her neck arched, her silver feathers shining in the sun. Three steps. Four. Five.

Kiralair follows, then moves to Sila's side, shouldering some of the gryphon's weight. Sila strains for one more step, like she can reach Trager if she just tries hard enough. But her ankles give, then her shoulders, and she collapses, her beak sliding down Kira's side before her head slams into the ground.

My eyes sting, and my fingernails bite into my clammy palms as the gryphons slowly turn to face the crowd, their eyes all narrowing in time with our dragons'.

Andarna roars down the bond in a tidal wave of grief and rage that rattles my soul.

"She is gone," Tairn says, and Kira extends a wing over Sila's body.

Something wet tracks down the left side of my face.

"VIOLET!" Xaden shouts, and his voice cuts through the haze. *"I can't do this for you. I wish I could, but they know you're in command."*

In command. I've never hated those words more.

I suck in one full breath, then another, and the world spins back to normal speed. Wrath stiffens my spine, and I cut off the part of me that cries for Trager and Sila, leaving only the weapon Basgiath forged me to be. But it's not my blade the situation calls for.

Fighting would be too easy. Killing them all for what they've done would be a fitting punishment.

The relentless sun beats into my leathers as I step out of Xaden's grasp and turn slowly toward the crowd. I look past Aaric and his clenched, bleeding fists, past Garrick as he moves back into formation near the bucket, and find Mira staring at me. Her eyes say what her mouth can't.

Handle this. Even with her arm wrapped around Maren, holding the flier upright, she's never looked more like our mother.

And our mother died so we'd have a chance to fight this war. If we fail here, we lose the army they offer. If I fail, we will have lost another squadmate, another *year-mate* for nothing.

With a nod, I square my shoulders and face Calixta, finding the archer at her side.

I take the two steps that bring me to Trager's body and lock eyes with the weathered man who took his and Sila's lives. The weight of the crowd's silent stares only serves to harden my resolve as I lift my chin before bowing my head.

And expel another piece of my humanity.

"Thank you."

Fuck them.

. . .

Eight hours later, Mira, Xaden, Aaric, and I return to the moonlit field where the rest of our squad waits with Trager's and Sila's bodies. A straggling group of onlookers still sits in the stands, drinking and celebrating.

Tairn opens one golden eye as I approach, then closes it, falling back asleep with Sgaeyl's head resting on his back. Andarna is passed out close enough to feel secure, but a wing's length farther away than when she was a juvenile.

Every gryphon and dragon but Cath sleeps, and the red flicks his swordtail as if to remind any onlookers who lurk in the stands that he's on watch. I can't blame them for their exhaustion. They've basically flown from Unnbriel without a break, and they swept over this isle today, looking for Andarna's kind while we negotiated.

And the irids aren't here. They aren't fucking *anywhere.* Fire burns in my stomach, and for the first time, I allow myself to consider what happens if we don't find them. Andarna will be crushed. Melgren will be furious. Aetos will throw us all into a cell for dereliction of duty.

We could lose the war to the dark wielders.

I refuse to let that happen.

"At least we're already in with the enemy," Tairn grumbles.

"Go back to sleep."

Xaden isn't the enemy. He's been infected by it.

We find Cat sitting against Kira's side, her head on Maren's shoulder, and the others hovering nearby. Everyone's gazes turn our way as we join them.

"Is it done?" Drake asks.

"It's done," Mira answers. "Aaric agreed to terms, which were oddly favorable to us. They'll send an advance party within the next couple of months and the rest of their troops whenever we're ready to receive all forty thousand of them."

Drake nods and looks Cat's way. "We'll be able to man thousands of cross-bolts, drive wyvern to the ground for a waiting infantry, increase patrols—"

"I get it," Cat interrupts without lifting her gaze.

She's better than I am, because I *don't.*

"Did you all eat?" I ask Ridoc.

He nods. "They brought us food and offered us beds in town, but…" His gaze darts left, to where Sila and Trager lie.

"Good choice," Xaden says, his hand resting on the small of my back.

"We have to bury him," Maren says, and her jaw trembles for a second. "And burn her. Gryphons...they prefer to be burned."

"We should burn him, too." Cat's voice is flat, her eyes vacant. "He would want to be with her." She blinks, then looks up at us. "Not here. No part of them remains here."

"Understood." I nod, my ribs threatening to crush the air from my lungs. I owe her whatever she wants. Maren, too. And Neve, and Bragen, and Kai and... A boulder wedges itself in my throat. I'll have to tell Rhi I lost Trager when she's worked so hard to keep us all alive.

"So we take them south to Loysam in the morning?" Dain asks, standing with his arms crossed next to Garrick. "The riot won't make it past the coast if they don't get some rest tonight."

"Not there, either. We can't trust anyone not to dig up whatever's left of her bones out of morbid curiosity." Cat shakes her head. "There are dozens of uninhabited minor isles within a day's flight north. Pick one."

"Cat, that's going to deviate us from the charted—" Drake starts.

"Fucking *pick one*," Cat snaps. "We can get back to all the good this"—she gestures around us—"is doing us after we burn them. I think they're worth losing a few days off the schedule."

Sova's head rises to the right, and he clicks his beak. Drake looks in his direction, then nods. "Fine by me."

"Will that mess too much up?" Maren asks me quietly, as if Cat isn't right next to her.

"No." I shake my head. "We can split up after they're given to Malek and search the minor isles three times as fast. Most will only need a flyover." I look Cat in the eye. "Then when you're ready, we'll depart for Loysam."

She nods. "It's kind of our last chance, isn't it? We're running out of isles."

I ignore the insidious kernel of truth her words shove in my face and straighten my spine. "That means we have to be close. The minor isles and Loysam border the edge of every map we have." The prospect of complete failure at such a steep cost is too heavy to swallow.

The group in the stands begins singing like they're in a damned tavern, like today's *festivities* are cause for celebration.

"Great, then we'll get to go home...if it's still there." Cat draws her knees to her chest and glares over at the stands. "We're sleeping out here tonight."

Everyone agrees.

"Cat, I'm so sorry—" I start.

"Don't be." She lays her head back on Maren's shoulder. "I'm the one who asked him to come."

A half hour later, beds are laid out within feet of one another inside the circle the dragons form, and watches are assigned. I can't remember ever being this tired before. The bone-weary exhaustion goes beyond fatigue, and my body is suffering for it. The dizzy flares, the screaming aches in every joint, the pain in my ribs, the urge to scratch out my stitches, and the knots in my muscles from trying to hold myself together are all getting worse by the day.

But it's my mind that fights me the hardest as I stare up at the stars from my back, reminding me of everything we have on the line and every way in which I'm failing. Mira called this a fool's errand, and maybe she was right.

Xaden pulls a light blanket over us as he lies at my side, then drapes his arm over my stomach. *"We have six hours before third watch. Try and rest."*

I turn onto my right shoulder, protecting my ribs, then lay my head on his biceps and look up at him. *"I froze today."* The admission is a whisper in my mind.

His brow knits and he splays his hand over my hip. *"He was your year-mate. You didn't freeze; you went into shock. It's understandable and why we travel as a squad."*

"Don't be nice just because you love me." I rest my hand on the thin fabric of his undershirt, right over his heart. Except for our boots, we're still dressed and ready to fly at a moment's notice if need be. *"This is my mission. Trager and Sila are dead. Cat's heartbroken. And I froze."*

"Everyone in leadership loses someone under their command." He strokes his hand absentmindedly up over my waist. *"You pulled yourself together and completed the mission."*

"At the cost of their lives." My chest constricts, fighting to contain the full confession that I can only give to him. *"I'm not meant to lead. Mira should be in charge, or even Drake. If they won't, then you."*

"Because my judgment is dependable right now?" He huffs a sarcastic sigh. *"The best leaders are the ones who never want the job. This is your mission because Andarna chose you. Tairn chose you."* His hand rises to my face. *"What they never tell us in the quadrant is that rank is well and good, but you and I both know that the moment we fly onto the battlefield, it isn't the humans giving commands. I hate to break it to you, but you were selected by a general among dragons. You can choose to step into leadership, or he can drag you. Either way, you're going to end up in front."*

My heart starts to race as his words pierce a shield of denial I wasn't even aware I'd been hiding behind, exposing a truth so blatantly obvious I feel foolish for not having seen it before. Tairn will always lead, and I will always be his rider.

Codagh speaks through Melgren, not the other way around.

"Then Tairn chose poorly." The lump in my throat grows, and I'm torn

between the pathetic instinct to wallow in self-pity and the opposing yet growing urge to channel a power greater than Tairn's—anger.

"Say that to him when he's awake and see how it goes for you." Xaden brushes his knuckles down my cheek. *"I've seen the moments you don't just rise to the occasion—you own it. Deverelli. Unnbriel. You poisoned the entire triumvirate of Hedotis, for fuck's sake. Imagine who you'll become when you finally learn to not just embrace that confidence but live it."*

"You?" I force a smile.

"Better than me." His thumb grazes my lower lip. *"You have to be. You promised to help me protect Tyrrendor, remember?"*

"I remember." I nod. *"I meant it. I'll stand by your side."* Exhaustion slows my breath and weights my eyelids. *"And between Andarna's kind and the research we're compiling about dark wielders, we'll cure you."* My eyes give in, sliding shut.

"There is no cure for me." He presses a kiss to my forehead. *"That's why you have to become better than me. There's only you."*

CHAPTER FORTY

We fly northwest at dawn.

Aotrom clutches Trager's body in his foreclaw.

Tairn carries Sila.

The ocean turns the blackest shade of blue I've ever seen as we soar over deep waters, leaving the safety of the trade routes and the major isles behind in hopes the map has been drawn correctly.

When night falls and the ocean only reveals the reflection of the moon, fear sours my belly. If we've erred, the dragons will be able to turn around and fly for Zehyllna, but the gryphons won't make it.

There's every chance that choosing to bury Trager and Sila on a minor isle will cause us to bury the others unless they consent to being carried.

By the middle of the night, I'm ready to give up and order our return when Tairn spots land.

Thank you, Amari.

Not sure I'll ever pray to Zihnal again.

The perimeter sweep of the tiny isle and its one, hollow-tipped peak takes approximately ten minutes, and after we're sure it's uninhabited, we land on a northern beach nearly as wide as Tairn's wingspan.

It could be a trick of the moonlight, but I'm pretty sure the sand is black.

Power ripples through me and energy crackles along my skin with about half the intensity that it does in Navarre.

We've found magic. And more than there was on Zehyllna, too.

The group seeks out fresh water from a nearby stream that runs through the beach, ensure the riot is hydrated, then make quick work of gathering wood from the edges of the jungle.

Sweat drips down the back of my neck as we carry load after load to the high point of the wide beach, halfway between the tide line and the forest behind us.

Once the pyre is built, we stand shoulder to shoulder, our backs to the jungle as Aotrom lowers his head and sets the wood ablaze. The fire lights up the night, and heat washes over my face.

Maren's shoulders shake, and Cat hooks her arm through her best friend's as she stares into the flames.

My throat tightens at the pain in their faces, and Xaden laces our fingers.

"Silaraine and Trager Karis," Drake says from the left, his voice booming over the roar of the bright fire and the crashing ocean waves behind it. "With honor, love, and gratitude, we commend your souls to Malek."

And so it's done.

We make camp close to the stream, and the fliers take turns keeping watch over the fire through the night. By morning, the flames rise no higher than a few inches.

I fill waterskins at the stream with Ridoc, and when we walk back to camp, we find the others in a somber discussion.

"I think we're off course," Drake says, fighting to hold the map with one hand and the squirmy kitten in the other. The paper's been folded so many times, holes have worn through the corners.

"Give me that." To my surprise, Mira takes the kitten, not the map, cradling it against her chest with one hand.

"Her name is Broccoli, not *that*," he mutters.

She looks at him like he's sprouted whiskers. "You named a kitten *Broccoli?*"

"No one really *wants* broccoli, but it's good for you, so seems fitting to me." He shrugs. "Now, that's clearly remnants of an old volcano"—he gestures to the peak high above us—"and the first marker for any such formation is here." His finger swipes over the detailed painting of a small archipelago on the northeast side of the minor isles.

I start comparing landmarks.

"We didn't fly that far," Xaden notes, folding his arms across his chest and studying the map.

"Why not Carrots?" Mira asks, scratching under the kitten's chin. "She's orange."

"Just to frustrate you, Sorrengail," Drake answers, glancing up from the map.

She scoffs. "I'd guess we're somewhere around here"—Mira taps an area of open ocean farther south—"and the map just doesn't show it. We haven't exactly been sending cartographers out this far."

"I can see another isle from the edge of the point." Aaric nods up the beach. "Molvic can make out two past it."

"Tairn?" I ask down our singular bond, letting Andarna sleep. She's utterly exhausted, and her wing trembled more than usual on the flight here.

"We are at the southern tip of an island chain of volcanic formations," he answers from high above us. *"It does not match anything on the map, though there is another mass of land an hour's flight due west with what appears to be sizable cliffs."*

I squeeze in next to Mira and examine the map, then locate the isle fitting Tairn's description, noting the mapmaker's symbol for cliffs. Then I track east with my finger and find only open water. "Pretty sure we're here, from what Tairn can see." I lift my head and look past Maren's shoulder out over the open water. "I'm guessing there are hundreds of islands out this way, not just the couple dozen the mapmakers recorded."

"And you think we should search them all?" Drake asks, incredulity puckering his forehead.

I look to Mira, but she just shrugs. "Not my call."

Xaden watches me just like he did last year, like he knows the answer but wants me to find it on my own.

"As many as we can today." I straighten my shoulders, and his mouth twitches upward. "We break into five groups. Maren and Cat take the unmapped islands to the north. Drake and Dain take this quadrant." I point to the nearest isles to our west, taking the gryphons' exhaustion into account. "Aaric and Mira, you go here; Xaden and Garrick, you take these; and Ridoc and I will take this section." I drag my finger to an eastern chain about two hours away. When I look up, everyone is staring at me. "What? I kept the gryphons close and paired dragons with similar flight strengths"—my gaze finds Xaden's, and he's not amused with my group pairings—"except for ours. Tairn and Sgaeyl have the best chance of staying in contact when separated if the rest of these islands have the same level of magic. It's better for the group if they split for the day."

He arches his scarred brow.

"Just you and me today, honey bear." Garrick swings his arm over Xaden's shoulder. "Don't worry," he leans in and whispers. "I'll take good care of you." He flashes a dimple.

"Sun should set a little after six, which gives us nine hours." I nod, pretty damned satisfied with this. "Meet back here before nightfall. If we find nothing, we go as a group toward the southeast isles tomorrow, then make the flight to Loysam." Where we'll have to resupply.

"Solid plan," Mira says.

"We can't go until the fire is out," Maren says. "No one leaves an offering to Malek unattended."

Cat shifts her weight restlessly, giving the impression that she needs to be anywhere but here.

"Ridoc and I will stay until it burns out." I glance back at Andarna. Her breaths are deep and even as she sleeps at the edge of the jungle, her scales a shade blacker than the sand. "That will give Andarna another hour or so to rest. Any other questions? Comments? Concerns?"

"Good to me." Drake folds the map, and the group breaks apart to ready their packs, leaving Xaden staring at me.

Ridoc glances between us. "I'm going...somewhere else." He walks off toward the dying fire.

"You can't tell me to lead and then get pissed at how I do it." I shrug.

He crosses the distance between us, leans down, and kisses me, hard and quick. "Be back by nightfall, love."

I grasp for his wrist, keeping him a second longer as I search his eyes. The flecks are still amber. "Are you all right?" I whisper. "There's magic and no wards."

"It's..." He grimaces. "It's tempting, and I don't even need it. But I can feel the power beneath my feet, and while I can wield enough to do this—" A whisp of inky black shadow curls up my leg, around my torso, and caresses the side of my face. "It's hard to know I could be at full strength if I just..." He swallows, and my grip tightens on his wrist. "But I won't."

"Not unless something triggers you." Unease rides the heels of the retreating shadow, sliding down my body and leaving goose bumps in its wake. "That's the other reason I sent you with Garrick."

Xaden tenses. "In case I channel?"

I shake my head. "So you don't. The last time you did, it was because of me. I'm a trigger."

He flinches. "You're not a trigger. You're the only thing I can't fathom losing. Wielding to protect you has always been an instinct, but now it's... uncontrollable."

"I know." I study the healing cut along his arm, then lift his hand and kiss the center of his palm. "Which is why you're going with Garrick. He carries serum, too."

"All right." He grips my waist. "I mean it when I say you own my soul. You're the only place I feel completely like me anymore. You're not a trigger," he repeats, then steals another kiss and walks away. "See you tonight."

"Tonight," I call after him. *"I love you."*

Warmth floods the bond in reply.

The teams launch, and Tairn stomps down the beach toward me with narrowed eyes.

"Don't start with me." I shake my head as Aotrom barrels past Tairn out to where the water covers his ankles, sprinting with his wings tucked tight. *"She'll be back tonight."*

"I'll say the same when you've been unable to communicate with your *mate for weeks and are then deprived by choice,"* he grumbles, stalking into the woods. Swaying trees mark his passing.

"Humans don't mate!" I call after him.

"Another sign of your inferiority." Wood cracks in the distance.

"Curmudgeon," I mutter, walking toward Ridoc standing at the edge of the water, where the waves don't quite reach his boots.

"I heard that."

Aotrom skids to a halt ten feet from Ridoc, driving his snout into the shallows and creating a wave that rushes up the beach and over Ridoc's shins.

"Why are you such a dick?" Ridoc flings his arms out sideways. "I brought one pair of boots—"

I halt in front of where Andarna sleeps along the tree line. Like *hell* am I getting near the water. Not when Xaden already wrapped my ribs today.

Aotrom lifts his head, then sprays water through his teeth, completely soaking Ridoc from the tips of his hair to the toes of his boots.

Yikes. I cross my feet and sit, resting my back against Andarna's shoulder.

"Not fair!" Ridoc wipes the drops from his eyes as Aotrom walks from the water up the beach and disappears into the woods. "I'm still winning. That doesn't count!" he calls after his dragon. A pause, and he yells, "Because we're on a mission!"

He shakes his head and slogs toward me, his boots squishing with every step.

"Do I even want to know?"

"He's getting me back because I won the last round." He flashes a grin. "I bought enough itching powder to fill a bucket, then dropped it between his scales on the back of his neck right after flight maneuvers a few weeks ago. He had to submerge his entire body in the river to avoid everyone in the Vale knowing I'd gotten the best of him."

"You guys are weird." I am suddenly *very* content with having bonded a grumpy old man, though I can't say what Andarna will be like in twenty years.

"Are we?" Ridoc tugs at the laces of his boots. "Or are the rest of you the weird ones?" He shrugs, yanking off his boots and setting them in the sand in front of Andarna. "Hopefully they dry out a little before we need to go. I'm going to get some fresh clothes on." He heads toward camp, then grabs his pack and walks into the woods.

"Don't get any ideas," I whisper to my sleeping dragon, laying my head back against her sun-warmed scales and closing my eyes.

The ground shudders.

"I swear to Amari, Tairn, if you spray me down with water—" The ground shudders again and again, and my eyes fly open.

Sand jumps. Water sprays. And in front of us lie fresh dragon tracks.

But neither Tairn nor Aotrom is here.

Apprehension climbs my spine and I rise slowly, favoring my ribs. I draw a dagger with my left hand, then turn my right palm skyward and open myself to Tairn's power. It seeps into my veins and hums along my skin as I sidestep around Andarna's shoulder to position myself in front of her neck, where she's most vulnerable.

Heat gusts against my face, and the scent of sulfur permeates the air.

"Tairn?" I swing my gaze along the beach, but there's nothing there, just the shimmer of the morning sun on the waves.

"I am busy with curmudgeonly things."

The sand ten feet in front of me moves, forming a series of furrows like the beach is splitting.

Like talons are flexing.

"TAIRN!" My heart jumps to a gallop as the air before me shimmers, then solidifies into gleaming sky-blue scales between two enormous nostrils.

"Hold fast!" Tairn demands. *"I'm coming!"*

The dragon before me inhales, then draws back, giving me a full view of pointed teeth before they tilt their head and narrow their golden eyes. Andarna rustles from her sleep, and motion at the edges of my vision makes me glance in both directions—then stare.

Six dragons of varying scale tones fill the beach, and all of them rival the size of Sgaeyl. Their massive claws dig into the sand as they lower their heads one by one.

My breath falters.

We didn't find the irids; they found us.

We did it. They're *here.*

Steam gusts across my face, and my stomach clenches. They're here and *really* close with *really* big teeth.

The one directly in front of us flares their nostrils, and a sound like a slide whistle fills my head, pitching from low to painfully high in less than a heartbeat.

"Hello, human."

What we know about dragonkind is nothing
compared to what we don't.

—Colonel Kaori's Field Guide to Dragonkind

CHAPTER
FORTY-ONE

What in the actual fuck. I draw back and *stare* at the irid, the knife loose in my grip.

Dragons don't speak to humans they're not bonded to, yet that deep, gruff voice definitely does not belong to Tairn.

"What is going—" Ridoc starts, coming up behind me. "Oh shit."

Half the dragon heads swing his way as he runs toward me, while the other half keep their eyes and enormous jaws pointed in my direction.

"Are we happy?" he asks as he reaches my side in his bare feet. "Are we scared?"

I nod.

"Why do you not answer me?" the dragon asks.

"Perhaps the human female lacks intelligence," a high voice chimes in, and the dragon on the right lifts her head.

My jaw drops. Guess arrogance is a universal dragon trait.

"She's just surprised." Andarna rises, but she leaves her head level with the others. *"And you're in her face."*

To my complete and utter shock, all six dragons take a step back.

"Thank you," Andarna says.

"You speak our language?" I ask the irids.

"We are magic," the male replies like it's the most obvious reason in the world.

"Did they just respect your personal space?" Ridoc whispers, then yanks his hands over his ears and flinches. "What was that?"

"It is rude to speak as though we cannot hear you," the female says from the right.

Ridoc's eyes widen.

"It is more offensive to lift a blade at us." The snappy schoolteacher voice comes from the left, I think.

"I don't know you, and I'm not going to let you hurt her." I glare at the one whose scales flicker to green.

"And you feel a dagger is sufficient." Her nostrils flare. *"I believe you are right, Dasyn. The human female lacks intelligence."*

Rude. But she's right about the first part. I sheathe the dagger.

"You are irid." The male in front of us changes the subject, his giant head tilting as he studies Andarna.

Her scales change from black to the green of the jungle, then ripple to blue, mirroring the sky just like the male. *"I am irid."*

"Holy shit," Ridoc says. "Was that Andarna?"

"I think when they make that whistle sound, it connects you to the irids," I mutter.

"Yet you choose black as your resting color?" the female asks Andarna from the right.

"It is acceptable in my ho—" She breathes out in a huff. *"In Navarre."*

The one diagonally to my left lifts their head. *"She is the criterion."*

The other five flinch and draw back.

"Is that a good thing?" Ridoc signs.

"I don't know," I sign back, my heartbeat easing slightly as they give us a little more space.

Wingbeats fill the air and the irids' heads lift skyward as darkness falls on top of us. Tairn lands hard, shaking the ground like thunder, his back claws digging into the sand to the left of Ridoc and the right of Andarna.

My heart stutters, and I can't decide if I'm more relieved that he's arrived or increasingly terrified at the thought of losing them both should the irids attack.

Dragons aren't exactly predictable, and I know *nothing* about the ones in front of us.

"My human," Tairn warns, swinging his tail. Trees crackle and crash behind us as he snaps his teeth at the irids. At least, I think that's what's happening, but all I can see is his underbelly and the legs of the irids.

"No!" Andarna scrambles out from beneath him and pivots as though staring him down. *"They won't hurt her. They're my family."* She turns in a circle. *"She's my human, too."*

My stomach twists. They might be her family, but she doesn't know them, and there's *every* chance they'll kill us all. We've been so busy trying to find them that we haven't given much thought to what would happen when we did.

"Are humans so rare in Navarre that you must share?" the female on the left snaps.

"Do you not have another one under there?" a different voice asks.

Something drips to the left, and my gaze jumps past a smiling Ridoc.

Aotrom slithers forward at Tairn's side, saliva dripping from his exposed fangs as he emerges from the trees. He growls low in his throat, giving a warning I don't need translated.

Mine.

"We have no interest in the humans," the male declares. *"And no quarrel with either of you. We've come only to speak to the irid."*

"Andarna," Tairn corrects him.

"Andarna," the female to the right says gently.

Tairn retreats step by careful step until Ridoc and I stand between his front claws, his back ones filling the space his tail just cleared.

"At least now we can see something before we die," Ridoc signs, then shrugs.

"We're not going to die," I sign back. My longing for Rhi and Sawyer to be here to see this equals my gratitude that they're not in danger.

Tairn's head hovers just above us, level with Aotrom's. Clearly, he's with Ridoc on this one.

Andarna swings to face us, her eyes dancing with palpable excitement. *"See? They won't hurt you."*

"I see." I nod, not wanting to kill the moment for her.

"Oh my." The female on the right gasps.

"What have you done to your tail?" The one on the left reels back.

Andarna cranes her neck to check her scorpiontail. *"Nothing. It's fine."*

My gaze jumps from irid to irid, my stomach sinking lower as I count from one to six.

They're all feathertails.

"Tell us what they've done to you," the male in front of us demands.

"Done to me? I chose my tail." Andarna's tone shifts defensively. *"As is my right upon transition from juvenile to adolescent."*

The irids fall silent, and not in a good way.

The male in the center lies down and wraps his tail around his torso. *"Tell us how you came to choose it."*

Andarna lifts her head to her full height as the irids lie down one by one.

"Is this really about to be story time?" Ridoc signs.

"You know as much as I do," I sign back.

A corner of his mouth quirks as his hands fly. "First time for everything."

Wood crunches as Tairn and Aotrom take the same position, leaving us standing between Tairn's outstretched claws.

Andarna sits just ahead of us to the right, her tail swishing across the sand. *"I blinked in and out of consciousness in my shell years—"*

"We're going to be here awhile," Ridoc signs, then plops his ass down in the sand.

I slowly lower myself to do the same as she tells her story to a captive audience.

It's only when she describes Presentation that the irids begin to throw questions at her.

"Why would you present yourself to a human?"

"No, they present themselves to us." Andarna's tail flicks. *"So we can decide if we should allow them to continue on to Threshing or turn them into char marks."*

The irids all gasp, and Ridoc and I share a confused look. I'm guessing they don't bond to humans.

"Seeing as I'm the eldest of my den in Navarre, there was no other to object to my Right of Benefaction," she continues with excitement and more than a little pride, which makes me smile. *"And so Threshing began."*

It's fascinating to hear it from her point of view.

"Why would you participate in harvest?" the female on the left asks.

"It's just what we call it when we select our humans for bonding," Andarna explains. *"So I went into the woods—"*

"You bonded as a juvenile?" the male to the right shouts.

Tairn cranes his neck forward and growls. *"You will not raise your voice to her."*

Andarna turns her head and narrows her eyes at Tairn. *"Do not ruin this for me."*

Hurt stabs through the bond and Tairn recoils, his head drawing back to cover Ridoc and me.

Ouch. My chest tightens, but there's nothing I can say to him and no way to say it without chancing the rest of them hearing me.

Andarna continues with our story. She tells them about Jack and Oren, about how I defended her, about Xaden and the rebellion.

"So naturally, I slowed time," she tells them when recounting the attack in my bedchamber.

"You used your juvenile gift for a human?" the female on the left questions.

"I don't like her," Ridoc signs.

"Me either," I respond in kind.

"For my human." Andarna tilts her head. *"She is part of me, as I am of her. You undervalue our connection."* That last bit reeks of adolescent snark.

"My apologies," the female says.

"Damn, this breed apologizes," Ridoc signs, lifting his brows. "Maybe we should have held out."

I roll my eyes.

"Do you not bond humans?" Andarna asks, and I lean forward, resting my forearms on my knees.

"We do not live with humans," she answers.

"Is it just the six of you?" Andarna's head swivels to look at them.

"There are hundreds of us," the male to the left replies, speaking for the first time. *"Please continue."*

The swirl pattern in his horns reminds me of Andarna's. Maybe they're from the same den.

More than an hour passes as she conveys every detail, as if forgetting one facet might alter whatever is about to happen.

When she starts to tell them about War Games, then Resson, my muscles tense, and I fight my own memories from interceding, fight the inevitable wave of grief that rises when she speaks of Liam and Deigh.

"And so I flew into the battle!" She pounces up on all fours.

There's more than one set of narrowed golden eyes.

"And Violet channeled my power—"

Two of them inhale sharply, and my stomach full-on knots.

"I don't think this is going as well as she thinks it is," I sign to Ridoc.

"Why? She's incredible," he signs back. "Brave. Fierce. Vicious. Everything the Empyrean respects."

But the way the irids look at her says otherwise.

"And we slowed time so that she could strike!" Andarna tells the story with an enthusiasm that belongs onstage. *"But it was too much magic to channel, and I was still small. My body demanded the Dreamless Sleep..."*

By the time she brings the irids to the present day without mentioning how we're trying to cure Xaden, several hours later, they've all stopped asking questions. In fact, they lie in eerie silence as she finishes.

"That's why we're here," she says. *"To ask if you'll come home to fight with us. To see if the knowledge was passed down of how the venin were defeated during the Great War, or if you know how to cure them."* Her tail flicks with expectation. *"And I'd like to know about my family."*

The male in the center narrows his eyes on me. *"And you allowed her to channel as a juvenile? You took her into a war?"*

My mouth opens, then shuts as guilt settles on my shoulders. He's not saying anything I haven't questioned of myself.

"It was my choice!" Andarna shouts.

The female to the right sighs, blowing sand down the beach. *"Show us your wing."*

Andarna tenses for a moment, as if deciding, then flares her wings. The left one buckles, and she forces it to extend, but the gossamer webbing trembles under the effort. *"It doesn't usually shake. I'm just tired from flying."*

The female glances away, the sun catching on her curved horns. *"We've seen enough."*

"I can fly!" Andarna snaps her wings shut. *"I'm just missing a second set of muscles and can't carry Violet. The elders said it has something to do with the delicate balance of wind resistance and tension on my wing, and her weight on the spinal discs that run under my seat. But that's all right because we have Tairn and he works with me every day—and the elders, too. And when I get tired, he carries me, but only on long journeys."* She glances down at her harness and shifts her weight nervously.

"Please permit the effrontery of our need for a moment of privacy," the male in the center says.

They're so rudely...polite.

Andarna sits, the irids' voices slipping out of my head.

The six of them walk into the water, their scales changing to colors only a shade darker than the ocean.

"I think we're blocked," Ridoc signs.

"I think so, too," I reply.

Andarna's head angles toward us, and I offer what I really hope is a reassuring smile.

A moment later, three of the irids launch straight from the water, then disappear into the sky.

"That's not good," I sign.

"Maybe they're just going to get the others," Ridoc signs slowly.

The three left are the quiet male with the horns similar to Andarna's, the one from the center, and the female from the right. They walk toward us, their scales changing back to shades of pale blue as they emerge from the water.

My chest constricts. They could have the answer to everything...or they could be as clueless about our history as we are.

"Did I pass the test?" Andarna asks.

The slide-whistle sound plays again, and I wince as it screeches so high I'm sure my ear is going to bleed.

"Test?" the male in the center asks, peering down at Andarna.

"You were just testing me, right? To make sure I'm fit to visit our den? Where is it, anyway?" The hope in her voice would cut my knees out if I were standing.

"You were never the one being tested." The female sighs and looks over at me. The hair rises on the back of my neck. *"You were."*

My head rears back and my stomach drops clean out of my body. "I'm sorry?"

"You should be." The female flexes her claws in the sand. *"You failed."*

Tairn growls, and this time Andarna doesn't stop him.

"Violet has never failed me," Andarna argues, thumping her tail against the ground.

I slowly rise to my feet. "I don't understand."

The trio blatantly ignores me. *"The fact that you defend her actions is a testament to their failure as a society,"* the male says to Andarna.

Ridoc stands and folds his arms beside me.

"Violet loves me!" Andarna shouts, her head swiveling between the three of them.

"She uses you." The female's eyes fill with sadness, and the scales of her brow scrunch. *"She took advantage of a vulnerable child. She used your power as an instrument of warfare, forced your premature growth—and look what you have become."*

I fight to swallow past the rock that suddenly fills my throat.

"You think I'm broken," Andarna hisses.

"We think you're a weapon," the male responds.

My lips part, and a rumble works its way through Tairn's chest.

"Thank you." Andarna's scales flicker to mirror theirs.

"It wasn't a compliment." His words sharpen. *"Our breed is born for peace, not violence like others."* He spares Tairn a single glance before returning to Andarna. *"You were left behind as the criterion. The measurement of their growth, their ability to choose tranquility and harmony with all living things. We'd hoped you would return to tell us the humans had evolved, that they had blossomed under the wardstones and no longer used magic as a weapon, but instead you have shown us the opposite."*

I wrap my arms around my waist as he slices her—us—to the quick.

"And dragonkind has not learned their lesson, either. While you"—the male in the center's gaze jumps to Aotrom—*"gifted your human with ice"*—he dares to shift his focus to Tairn—*"you armed yours with lightning."*

"That's not how signets work," Ridoc argues.

"And you"—the male lowers his gaze to Andarna—*"our very hope, have handed this human something far more dangerous to wield, haven't you?"*

While the enemy's advance throughout Krovla makes it impossible to station a full riot at Suniva, we offer you four dragons and their riders. In the spirit of our alliance, you may expect a shipment of our most valuable resource—weaponry—to be used at your discretion.

—OFFICIAL CORRESPONDENCE OF GENERAL AUGUSTINE MELGREN
TO QUEEN MARAYA

CHAPTER FORTY-TWO

Handed me *what*? I blink in confusion.

Ridoc glances my way, and I shake my head with a shrug. I haven't manifested a second signet from Andarna.

"You have weaponized your magic, even your tail," the tallest irid continues. *"You've become the very thing we abhor, the horror we fled from."*

He did *not*. Rage brings my power buzzing to the surface.

"She is not a horror!" I march forward as Andarna's scales turn black, unable to listen to one more second of this bullshit.

"No, you *are."* The male cranes his head in my direction. *"She is but what you made her."*

My nails bite into the palms of my hands and my chest tightens.

"I do not understand…" Andarna's tail flicks over the sand in front of me, and I step back, respecting the boundary. *"You will not return with us?"* she asks. *"You will not help us achieve the peace you worship?"*

"We will not." The male lifts his head, and I follow his line of sight. Chradh and Sgaeyl are back, just in time to witness our complete and total failure. *"We have watched some of your journey and feel it is not peace you seek, but victory."*

The male with the spiral horns stares at Andarna but remains quiet.

My heart starts to race. Oh gods, this is really happening. Our last hope is dwindling right before my eyes. We've risked everything, and they won't help.

"Peace requires the Aretian wardstone, which we cannot fire without you!" Andarna snarls.

"I fail to see how that is a mutual problem," the female replies.

"Do you not care that people will die?" Andarna curls her tail high above her back.

"Perhaps they should." The tallest male blinks. *"Perhaps the corrupted ones should devour the land in its entirety. Only when they're faced with starvation will they confront the evil they've become. Either they'll die off and the land will regenerate, or they'll confront the abominations they've become and change."*

Change. My heart launches into my throat.

"How do they do that?" Andarna asks, and apprehension trickles down the bond from Tairn as wingbeats fill the air. Xaden and Garrick are almost here.

"Their offspring could evolve, perhaps," the female muses, watching Sgaeyl and Chradh land near the stream twenty yards away. *"Others arrive. We should depart."*

No, no. Panic climbs my spine. We can't fail. This can't be *it*.

Xaden and Garrick dismount on the black sand beach, high above the tide line, and Tairn snaps his head toward Sgaeyl. Whatever he communicates keeps the two dragons from coming our way, but not their riders.

"Is that the dark wielder's cure?" Andarna asks, her head moving in a serpentine motion. *"To evolve?"*

My breath freezes in my chest.

The female's golden eyes narrow to slits. *"There is no cure."*

No cure? Her words hit like a physical blow, and my knees threaten to buckle.

"If they trade their soul, surely they can get it back," Andarna retorts.

"It is not a trade," the female lectures. *"The soul is not kept by the earth as dark wielders steal its magic. The power exchange kills the soul one piece at a time, and death has no cure."*

Xaden and Garrick keep their eyes on the irids as they stride our way without their flight jackets, swords strapped to their backs, the perfect example of warfare.

His soul isn't *dead*.

"Will you not at least tell us how the dark wielders were defeated in the Great War?" Andarna asks, her words flowing faster, like she knows her time is short.

"Apparently they weren't if you're here asking," the female replies.

The male with the spiral horns watches Xaden and Garrick as they carefully cross behind Ridoc and me, moving to my right side.

"Our kind must have helped," Andarna tries again. *"I can burn dark wielders. Are we the key to defeating them?"*

"*Hopeless.*" The tallest male backs into the water. "*Leothan, I have heard enough.*"

The other male flares his nostrils. "*I have not.*"

"They can hear us through the bond," I quickly sign to Xaden. "It's not going well."

He nods.

"Want to catch us up?" Garrick signs, studying the massive heads lowered in our direction.

"They think Andarna is a weapon, which is somehow a bad thing," Ridoc signs. "They won't come back to help us and pretty much think we all deserve to die because we can't solve mankind's oldest problem of how to stop killing each other."

"Got it," Xaden signs.

"And there's no cure for venin," Ridoc quickly continues, and it's all I can do not to grab his hands to stop him from saying more. "Their souls die, so there goes our save-them-to-defeat-them idea."

Fuck.

Xaden's head snaps forward as Andarna's talons flex in the sand.

"*You are magic,*" the female says, a note of sadness in her tone. "*And yet all you seek to use it for is violence.*"

"*You preach peace while only having known its privilege,*" Andarna hisses in retort. "*You are all a disappointment to me.*"

"*In that, we find common ground,*" the tallest male says.

What an ass.

Tairn growls, rumbling the sand and vibrating the trees, and Andarna's scales ripple to the darkest black as she retreats to his right foreleg.

"*We have a long flight ahead, and there is nothing to be gained here,*" the male continues, retreating another step into the water. "*The world was not ready for you, and though it is no fault of your own, we cannot accept you.*"

I gasp and clutch Xaden's hand.

"What's happening?" Garrick signs.

Maybe it's best they not hear this.

"*Leothan may feel differently*"—the tallest male glances at the other one—"*but our majority has determined you are irid in scale and name only, Andarna. You will not be allowed entrance to our isle nor instruction in our ways. We part here and wish you peace.*"

Peace? My grip tightens on Xaden's hand.

"*I wish I'd never met you,*" Andarna growls.

The tallest male crouches in the water before launching into the air, his scales shimmering for a heartbeat before he becomes the sky itself.

"What just happened?" Xaden asks.

"I think we lost," Ridoc whispers.

Andarna's snout dips, and bone-splitting agony courses down the bond, but it's the shame that hits in the second wave that pricks my eyes.

"Andarna, no," I whisper. "You are fierce, and smart, and brave, and loyal. None of this is your fault. You're perfect."

"I am…not," she snarls, whipping her head toward me.

"You did not know she was a juvenile when you bonded her?" Leothan asks, his golden gaze studying the four of us humans.

"I didn't," I answer out loud. "I should have, but the hatchlings and juveniles are kept hidden and safe within the Vale until after the Dreamless Sleep. Nobody had seen one for centuries, so we didn't realize that they're all golden feathertails until adolescence."

"What is going—" Garrick twitches. "Fuck, that hurts!"

Xaden grimaces, lowering his head and squeezing his eyes shut.

I'm guessing they just got the slide-whistle treatment.

"The uniformity assures all hatchlings are cared for without deference to breed or den—" Leothan startles as Xaden looks up.

The female recoils, baring her dripping teeth. *"How could you align yourselves with this?"*

Weird way to say "bond," but whatever.

"Again, I didn't know she was a juvenile," I argue. "Blame me, not her!"

"Abomination." The female hurls the insult, her eyes narrowing.

On Xaden.

My head snaps in Xaden's direction, and I gasp. The rims of his irises shine bright red.

"Your kind is beyond redemption." The female glares at Sgaeyl, then disappears.

Leothan studies Xaden for a heartbeat longer, then fades, and waves rush in where they'd been standing. Wind from invisible wingbeats gusts against my face, and I squeeze my eyes shut as sand blows all over us, their presence slipping from my mind just like before. When I open them, Xaden's eyes have returned to normal.

Or rather, his new normal. There are still spots of amber within their onyx depths.

"Fuck." His tone could cut scale as his fingers slip out of mine.

"You're not an abom—"

He slams his shields down, blocking me out.

Something heartbreakingly close to a whimper sounds to our right, and I look past Garrick to find Andarna retreating into the jungle, her scales shifting to gold.

"Andarna." I start toward her, but she blocks me out, too.

"I've got her." Tairn rises over us, and his tail takes out a tree to the left as he stalks into the jungle after her. *"Teine and Molvic approach."*

"I can—"

"Only one of us is fireproof," he reminds me, disappearing in the vegetation.

My fingernails dig into my palms. I've never felt so helpless.

"I'm guessing *he's* why you've been so hung up on finding a cure." Ridoc's accusation hits me like a bucket of ice water, and I snap my gaze to his.

Oh. *Fuck.*

"Yeah." He nods at me. "I saw his eyes turn red."

"Ridoc—" Xaden starts.

"Not a single word from you, *dark wielder*," Ridoc grits out, his eyes locked on mine. "Vi, you've got one chance to come clean and tell me what the actual fuck is going on."

If possible, hunt the enemy during the day. Their markings are so easily hidden by the shadows of night that it would not surprise me to find they walk among us.

—Venin, A Compendium
by Captain Drake Cordella, the Nightwing Drift

CHAPTER
FORTY-THREE

Ridoc listens to the shortest possible version of the story before the others land, and I promise to tell him everything if he can just wait until we get some privacy as Mira dismounts. "We have to tell them about the irids first," I finish in a hurried plea.

His mouth tenses and his brown eyes narrow on Xaden.

"Are the other four back yet?" Mira asks as she walks into camp with Aaric, her pack slung over one shoulder.

"Not yet," Garrick answers from behind me. "But we still have a couple of hours until it's fully dark."

"Please," I whisper to Ridoc as Mira drops her things near her bedroll.

"Everything all right?" Mira's brow furrows when no one answers, and her gaze flickers between the four of us before settling on me with an intense once-over that ends with her studying my eyes. "Violet?"

My throat constricts. I don't know what she'll do if she learns the truth.

"The irids are a bunch of assholes who rejected Andarna," Ridoc says. "So, it's been a rather shit day." He launches into the story, and my pulse slowly steadies.

"How's Andarna?" Mira asks.

"Devastated." I glance down the beach, but she and Tairn haven't returned yet. "I know we came in hopes the irids would help, or at least fire the wardstone, but she really just wanted to know her family."

Garrick's jaw ticks, and Xaden folds his arms.

"The others should be back soon," Ridoc says. "What do we do? Fly for Loysam tomorrow?"

"There's no point." I look to Xaden, but he keeps quiet. "Loysam has guards but no army. We can establish a diplomatic tie, but they won't help us win a war."

"So what do you want to do?" Xaden asks, the ocean breeze ruffling his hair as he looks over at me.

Gods, he really is beautiful, and not just on the outside. Everything about him — his loyalty, his intelligence, the softer edges no one else but me gets to see…even his casual ruthlessness holds me in thrall. And whatever parts are missing? *Dead*, according to the irids? We'll live without them.

He's still whole to me. As long as we can keep him from channeling from the earth, find a way for him to control that craving, we'll be all right. We have to be.

"We should go home." Saying the words brings a sense of finality, of failure that stabs hard and cuts deep. "Who knows what's happened in our absence." For all we know, the lines could have fallen and Theophanie herself could be waiting in my room.

"Court-martials for all," Mira quips sarcastically.

Garrick nods and stares out over the water. "Technically, on the map, if you were to fly northeast for two days, you'd hit the Cliffs of Dralor."

"The gryphons would absolutely *love* that." Ridoc scoffs. "Can't you see Kiralair snuggled up in Molvic's claw?"

"Only the larger dragons can fly two straight days," Xaden says. "Tairn. Sgaeyl. Molvic, maybe."

"We go through the isles," I decide. "It's the safest route to get everyone home…as long as we camp on a deserted coast when it comes to Hedotis. Pretty sure I'm banned there."

After the others arrive and our situation has been explained, Ridoc shoots me a look that says he's done waiting to chat.

Xaden and Garrick are less than thrilled when I take off with Ridoc into the woods under the guise of hunting for dinner. Taking the agate sound-shield rune Ridoc carries, we hike about five minutes uphill into the jungle, staying close enough to find our way back but far enough to assure privacy thanks to Aotrom's escort.

The Brown Swordtail isn't just nosey; he's pissed.

I'm nauseous telling Ridoc the full story about Xaden, remembering the entire time that Ridoc was the slowest to forgive when I kept my secrets at the beginning of the year. By the time I'm finished, the light has faded into dappled patches of color and he's pacing in front of me, looking anywhere but in my direction.

"I thought we agreed to tell each other the truth." His hands curl.

"It wasn't my secret to tell." I lean against a tree and watch Ridoc's short treks back and forth in front of me. "I know that's a shitty apology, but I'm not sorry for keeping Xaden safe."

"That's *not* an apology, Vi." He pauses in front of me, a million emotions crossing over his face too quickly to name.

He's right.

"I'm sorry I couldn't tell you, but if anyone finds out, they'll lock him up like Barlowe, or worse—kill him." I fold my arms.

He lifts his eyebrows and cranes his neck forward. "And there's not a single, tiny speck of you that thinks maybe they *should*?"

"No. He's not evil." I lift my chin.

"He's not *him*, either," he counters. "That's why you stepped between us in Hedotis. He's not fully in control and you know it."

"Are any of us ever in full control—" I start.

"Don't do that." He points his finger at me. "Not with me."

"He's not Barlowe. Not even remotely close. He's never hurt me. He's only ever channeled to save other people, first at Basgiath, then at a battle across the border, and then when Courtlyn tried to kill us in Deverelli." I leave out the slight discoloration on my headboard. That's a line I'm not crossing with Ridoc.

"Holy fuck, he's channeled *three* times?" Ridoc's eyebrows fly upward. "And managed to do it on an isle without magic?"

"I had a piece of alloy in my conduit."

"Oh, well, good to know you can keep him fed like Barlowe if you need—" He scoffs. "That's why you've been keeping Barlowe alive. Holy *shit*, Violet, do you have any respect for your own life? Or is it just Riorson we're concerned with now?"

"He's *never* hurt me," I repeat. "And he's still an initiate. He doesn't need to be *fed*." The word tastes like ash in my mouth. "As long as he doesn't do it again, he'll stay exactly how he is now."

"A dark wielder, just like the silver-haired one stalking you." Ridoc starts pacing again.

My head draws back. "He is *nothing* like her."

"Bonded to one of the most vicious dragons on the Continent," he continues, ignoring my defense. "That's...awesome."

"He doesn't control Sgaeyl." I watch as Ridoc pivots and starts the trek all over again. "In fact, she barely speaks to him right now."

"I don't blame her, either," Ridoc says after a pause, agreeing with Aotrom. "And she's kept this from the Empyrean—" He stops to my right, then slowly turns to face me. "Who else knows?"

"Other than Xaden and me? Garrick, Bodhi, and Imogen."

Ridoc blinks. "That's it? Just the five of you?"

"And now you."

"Well, at least the club is exclusive," he says sarcastically, then shoves his hands into his hair. "And they're all loyal to *him*."

"Well...yes." I shift my weight. "He's the one we're trying to save."

He rolls his eyes at the canopy. "Fuck me. How did we get here with the secrets again?" His finger shoots up. "Never mind, I already know—Riorson. *Again.* I sense a theme."

"Basgiath would have fallen if he hadn't killed the dark wielders' Sage," I remind him. "What he did give us—give my mother—was time to imbue the wardstone. We'd all be dead if he hadn't channeled for more power. The Continent would have fallen if not for him."

"Only to become the very thing we're fighting." He shakes his head. "The irony of it exists on so many levels, especially when you consider that he's the fucking *Duke* of Tyrrendor now." His arms fall to his sides. "He could tear our kingdom—our province—apart from within. He could deliver us to the venin on a silver platter. Barlowe was nothing. We have a dark wielder sitting in the Senarium."

Is that all he sees him as? Just another dark wielder?

"He's on our side. Fighting our battles." I push off the tree. "He killed more venin *after* the battle than any other rider, remember?"

"How can you be sure he's not playing you?" His brow furrows.

"Because I know him!" My voice rises.

"All right." Ridoc nods excessively. "I'll play along. Let's say he's still eighty percent Xaden."

"Ninety," I counter.

"Ehh." He shrugs. "There are four ranks to dark wielders, and your man's already channeled three times. I think eighty percent is mathematically generous, but sure, we'll live in your delusion for the purpose of the hypothetical. How long do we have until he's an asim? Until he's physically unable to deny the call of a Sage?"

"If he doesn't channel—"

"They always channel!" Ice forms at his fingertips. "Just because I like to crack jokes doesn't mean I'm not serious about reading the same shit you do. There are no accounts of initiates just walking away from the power."

"That's why I have to find a cure." My voice breaks.

"They just told us there isn't one." His arm swings toward the beach.

"And I've had about five minutes to process that information." Anger and fear war for control of my emotions, and both bring my power to the surface, sizzling my skin. "Everything I've done over the last few months, from securing the deal with Tecarus for books to searching for Andarna's kind, has been in service to the Continent, but also to find a cure for him, and hearing from the most likely source that there isn't one?" I shake my head as the heat rises within me, growing exponentially with my panic. "I don't know what to do with that yet. I don't have all the answers, Ridoc. I just know that I have to find them whether they're in a forgotten book or some dark wielder's head, because I've lost Liam and now Trager and my *mother* to this war, and I'm not giving up on the man I love!"

Power snaps within me and flares outward. Lightning slams into the tree behind Ridoc, and thunder booms instantly, shaking my bones.

"Fuck!" Ridoc shouts, covering his ears and whirling to face the tree.

My heart stutters as the trunk splits down the middle, and the halves waver... then fall. I lift my fingers, summoning lesser magic to soften the crash, but the heavy pieces are no match for my skills in this area. The halves smack into the ground in a line before us, then erupt into flame.

"Damn it." Ridoc flings his hands outward, and a thin sheet of ice races along the halves in both directions. The flames sizzle and die. "Now Riorson is *really* going to kill me," Ridoc mutters, but the joke falls flat. He turns my way.

"Thank you." I gesture to the embers, then sigh. "And I'm sorry."

"For which part?"

"All of it." The admission is a little stronger than a whisper.

He nods.

"I will save him." My throat tightens. "And not just because I can't fathom living without him. I'm selfish when it comes to loving him, and maybe a little self-destructive lately—"

"You think?" He gestures to the tree.

"—but if I don't save him..." My voice drops. "If I don't *cure* him, and he..." I can't say it. "I keep serum in case of emergency, but Ridoc, we have to keep him on our side, or this war is already lost. There isn't a rider alive capable of stopping him at full power now, let alone what he could become if he truly turns. And don't say that I can, because the truth is that I won't. Even if I hone my signet to his level, which would take the years he's had, I could no more hurt him than he could hurt me. He is...everything to me."

Ridoc's shoulders dip. "So where's the line? At what point is he too far gone for you to defend him?"

My mouth opens then shuts. "There isn't one. Not one he'd actually cross."

"Really?" He lifts his brows. "What if he hurts someone you love? Will that change your mind?"

"He wouldn't." I shake my head. "He hasn't in all these months. He won't."

He clasps my shoulders. "Not good enough. Give me a real, logical line he has to cross for you to walk away, and I'll keep the secret. I'll help you scour every fucking book you can find. I'm here for the I'm-going-to-save-my-man-at-all-costs mantra and will be on your side in this horrifically dangerous situation if you can just acknowledge there's a breaking point. You can put all your faith in him as long as you leave a little logic for yourself."

"I...I can't imagine not loving him." I bring my hands up to rest on his forearms.

"Never said you couldn't love him." He squeezes my shoulders gently. "You can still love someone after you let them go. But you have to tell me there's a line where you *will* let him go. Because if there isn't one, it's not just him we're going to lose, Vi."

My chest tightens. "I would never —"

"Would you channel to save him? Or is that the line?"

I swallow hard, remembering that breath of a second in the wardstone chamber where my power hadn't been enough to imbue the stone.

"If it makes it easier, then pick a line where I can turn him in," Ridoc whispers. "Tell me now, when you think there's no chance it will ever happen, so if he ever gets there, the decision isn't on your shoulders."

Every muscle in my body tenses.

"How about if he hurts Tairn or Andarna?" Ridoc suggests. "You have to help me here, Vi, or I'm walking straight to the only person I know will put your life above everyone else's on that beach."

Mira.

I try to look at the situation from Ridoc's perspective, and it's anything but pretty. "Fine. Hypothetically, he'd have to kill another rider without cause or hurt civilians. Hurt my friends, my dragons. Hurt...me," I end in a whisper. "If he hurts me, then he's not him anymore."

Ridoc nods, then touches his forehead to mine. "All right. Then there it is."

"There it is," I repeat.

His hands fall away, and we start back toward camp. "Stop keeping shit to yourself," he demands. "I don't want to have this fight again. The four of us are stronger together than we are apart. Don't fuck with that, even for Riorson. If you're too afraid to tell Rhi, Sawyer, or me about something you're doing because you know we're going to lose our shit, then either you shouldn't be doing it or you deserve to have shit lost on you."

"Noted." I sigh. "I miss them."

"Me too." He slings his arm around my shoulders. "Rhi gives better lectures."

"You did pretty well." A smile tugs at my mouth as we veer left around a giant tree the diameter of Tairn's leg.

And find Xaden on the other side, standing with one ankle crossed over the other, his arms folded as he leans his shoulder against the trunk.

Ridoc's hand flexes on my shoulder, but he doesn't let go as we abruptly stop.

Xaden arches his scarred brow, taking note.

"Quite the conundrum," Ridoc says. "You see, if I drop my hand, it looks like we've been caught doing something we shouldn't. Which we haven't. But if I leave it here, I'm not sure you won't go all blank-face on me in a fit of rage and—" He drags his left hand across his neck.

"Not helping," I tell him.

"I also don't want you to think that just because you're scary, I'm scared *of* you," Ridoc adds. "Which I'm not."

"You are. What did you decide?" Xaden asks, his face a perfect mask of boredom.

"You're not going to threaten to kill me?" Ridoc counters.

"I don't make empty threats."

I reach out mentally, but Xaden's shields are still locked tight.

Ridoc tilts his head. "Meaning you wouldn't threaten before you killed me? Or you wouldn't actually kill me?"

Xaden half shrugs. "You pick."

"Stop it." I look straight at Xaden and his gaze flickers to mine, warming slightly.

"She tells Rhiannon and Sawyer," Ridoc demands, then pauses, considering. "And Jesinia."

My heart practically stops. "Have you lost your mind?"

"Is that all?" Xaden asks, and I can't tell if he's being a sarcastic ass or a serious one.

"I'd prefer Mira and Brennan, too, but we can start with the first three," Ridoc states, looking at Xaden. "Everyone you've told values your life over hers—"

"That's not true," I argue.

"Everyone who knows has told Violet to run as far and as fast as she can," Xaden says. "Myself included."

"Good to know." Ridoc shrugs. "Rhi. Sawyer. Jesinia. That's my only condition for keeping your secret."

"That is not what we discussed," I hiss up at him.

"We discussed *our* terms," Ridoc says, then looks back at Xaden. "This is between us. Jesinia needs to know what she's actually researching in case there's a way to slow your progression. Sawyer, Rhi, and I are the only ones who can be with Violet during every class, and our dorm rooms are right next to hers. She's more than capable of protecting herself, but extra eyes don't hurt, considering what will come for her."

Xaden tenses.

"Yeah, you know exactly what I'm talking about." Ridoc nods.

My forehead crinkles. "Well, I don't."

"If he progresses and turns fully—" Ridoc starts.

"When," Xaden corrects him. "Denial and I don't keep company."

Ridoc's eyebrows rise. "All right then. When he turns fully, or when someone with the wrong rank realizes what he's become, they'll have to kill him for the very reasons you've already mentioned, Vi."

"What does that..." My stomach hollows as I follow his train of thought to its logical conclusion, then refills immediately with scalding anger. I drag my gaze to Xaden's. "Killing me is the easiest way to kill *you*." Just like my first year.

"I won't let that happen." Xaden's jaw clenches.

"*We* won't let that happen," Ridoc corrects. "You'll be off doing evil shit wherever evil shit gets done."

My lips part.

"Rhi. Sawyer. Jesinia," Ridoc repeats.

"Not Aetos?" Xaden questions. "Dain specifically."

"Absolutely not," I interject. "He'll kill you."

"He could try," Xaden replies. "The attempt would certainly make things awkward."

"I'm with Violet on this one," Ridoc chimes in. "While I'm proud of how far Aetos has come in the rule-bending department, he's not ready to graduate to this particular level. Rhi. Sawyer. Jesinia."

"Done," Xaden answers. "But let's be clear. I don't care who she tells when it comes to her safety."

"Good." Ridoc nods, then rocks back on his heels and takes a deep breath. "Oh, and just so *we're* clear, that strike up there wasn't"—he gestures between us—"you know. Us." He flinches. "I mean, it was us because I pissed her off, but it wasn't us...*us*, if you know what I'm saying."

I fight to keep from rolling my eyes.

"Well aware," Xaden replies. "First because I trust Violet, and second"—he glances at Ridoc in a dismissive once-over—"it wasn't a big enough strike."

Seriously? I scoff.

"Huh." Ridoc tilts his head as if deciding something, then shakes it. "Nope. You and I are not back to dick jokes yet. Not that we were ever there. I'm still pissed."

"You should be." Xaden pushes off the tree and walks toward us. "And I'm making sure Violet's capable of killing me when the time comes. If it's between her and me, I choose her. Kill the other guy I become."

My eyes narrow on the beautiful asshole I've foolishly given my heart to. "It's not going to come to that."

"Holy shit. Is that noble? Is that twisted? I can't decide." Ridoc pats me on the shoulder, then starts back toward camp. "I've never been happier to be single. You two have some serious issues."

"Garrick handled the *hunting* that you were supposed to be doing," Xaden calls out as we leave the trees.

Ridoc throws a thumbs-up as he walks down the hill.

Xaden studies my face, looking at me like he has to memorize every detail in this exact moment.

I step toward him and he retreats, shaking his head once.

My heart sinks. "You're going to put some space between us over the abomination comment, aren't you?"

He flinches, which is as good as confirmation for me.

"You're not—" I start.

"The other two irids stayed like they hadn't made up their minds yet," he interrupts. "And I think you had them because you didn't know how young Andarna was at Threshing." His jaw pops and he slides right back into that bored, unbothered mask he loves so well. "Then they saw me. I'm pretty fucking sure that this entire mission we've risked everything for just failed because of what I am. Because I'm here with you."

"That's not fair," I whisper.

"But it's true." Shadows scatter around the edges of his boots, and he looks down toward the beach. "I've *barely* made it a month without channeling beyond Sgaeyl." He shakes his head. "Had it just been you and Ridoc, or you and Dain, or you and…anyone else besides me on that beach, there's every chance you'd be on your way to whatever isle they've claimed, that Andarna would have a chance to know her kind, that they'd agree to come back and fire the Aretian wardstone and save my city, save my entire province." He drags his gaze back to mine. "So yeah, I think the abomination comment—and what it represents— requires taking a moment of space for us both to consider the undeniable fact that I am the worst possible thing for this mission, for my province, and for you."

My heart hurts for him, for how guilty he feels over something he can't control.

"All right." I fold my arms across my chest and debate whether to fight or comfort him, then decide to go a different route. "Facts are considered. I don't need the moment. You would have been on this mission regardless of our status because of Tairn and Sgaeyl. It's ridiculous that they passed judgment on you without even hearing you speak, but that's a statement on their character, not yours. And if you need some space to sort that out in your mind, fine." I tilt my head at him. "But it doesn't change a single thing about the way I love you."

His hands flex.

I turn away from him and start back toward camp. "Let me know when you're done brooding and we'll see how big my next strike is. Until then, we're flying home tomorrow."

• • •

The gryphons are exhausted, and it takes us ten days to reach Deverelli, where we spend an extra day fixing Andarna's harness when a piece of metal snaps.

Xaden keeps his distance the whole damned time.

Andarna is barely speaking.

Cat is heartbreakingly silent to the point that I *wish* she'd take a verbal jab or two.

And I'm about to break under the weight of failure.

We use the day to chart our path over Poromiel, choosing a route that brings us ashore between Cordyn and Draithus in order to minimize our chances of encountering dark wielders. By the time we launch for the Continent, Mira's asked me at least a dozen times if I'm all right, and though Dain has the annoying habit of continuously measuring how far Xaden and I sit apart with his eyes before meeting my gaze, he smartly keeps his mouth shut.

I scan our surroundings for venin constantly during the flight, too scared to sleep in the saddle. Every glint of sun off a lake makes my stomach lurch, and every distant thunderstorm has me gripping the pommels. Logically, I know there's no chance Theophanie is aware we're beyond the wards, available for her to pick off at will, but she shouldn't have known I'd be in Anca, either. Either our flight plan pays off or Theophanie chooses not to attack, and though we fly over patches of drained land, we make it to the wards without so much as a patrol of wyvern intercepting us.

The ease of it only serves to make me more anxious.

We spend a night under the stars just within the wards to evade the arrest for court-martial we all know is coming, and fly into Basgiath three and a half weeks from the day we left.

There's no sense of victory as I unload Tairn's saddlebags on the flight field, not even with having secured an army to come to our aid. The overwhelming failure of losing the irids feels like mold growing on my tongue, souring everything I drink and eat, infecting my words and the very breath in my lungs. The disappointment festers and spreads until I feel wholly, completely rancid as I dismount onto the muddy field.

Andarna flew straight to the Vale. She didn't even speak as she disappeared over the ridge. Her sorrow hurts most of all.

"Violet!"

I turn and am immediately devoured by Rhiannon's hug. Her arms close tight around me, and I drop the pack to return the squeeze. Maybe it's the sound of Kaori yelling at cadets across the field, or the scent of Rhi's hair, or the simple fact that we're back, yet not home, but the enormity of what we've lost immediately pricks my eyes and clogs my throat. "I really missed you. How did you know we were here?"

"Feirge told me you were headed in, so we ran out of dinner. I'm so glad to see you." Rhi pulls back with a watery smile. "Are you all right?"

I open and shut my mouth, unsure of how to answer the question.

"Rhi!" Ridoc slams into us from the side, wrapping us both in his arms, two weeks of beard growth scratching the side of my face. "Fuck, did we need you on that trip. Violet was out of control. She kicked a queen's ass and poisoned Xaden's mom *and* all three Hedotic heads of state, but secured us an army."

Rhi huffs a laugh as he sways us back and forth. "And what did you do?"

"Not much. Put out a couple of fires, punched a cook." He lets me go, then yanks Sawyer into the embrace when he walks over, leaning slightly on a cane. "This is good. This is right."

"Glad you're home, guys," Sawyer says, his face squished down next to mine thanks to Ridoc.

"Me too." I relax into the hug.

"There they are! Get over here!" Ridoc shouts, still in the embrace.

Maren laughs and runs to my other side, working her way in, but Cat just sighs as she walks over.

"No exceptions," Ridoc declares, then tugs Cat into the circle between him and Sawyer. "Sweet second-years, together again." He lets us go, but we stay circled up.

Rhi's gaze jumps from person to person like she's counting, and her smile falters.

"We lost Trager," I tell her softly.

"What?" Rhi recoils, her face stricken.

"How?" Sawyer's shoulders fall.

"Zehyllna," Cat answers, then clears her throat. "Arrow to the heart. But we got an army out of it, so—" Her voice breaks and she clears her throat again.

"I'm so sorry," Rhi says, her gaze swinging from Maren to Cat.

"We are, too," Maren whispers.

"And we failed." I say it out loud for the first time, looking Sawyer, then Rhi straight in the eyes. "We found the irids, and they won't come. We failed."

"Shit." Rhi's face falls entirely.

"That's disappointing to hear, given the current political climate."

We break apart and turn toward General Aetos, who stands a respectable distance from Tairn, glowering at us. He doesn't even glance at Dain as the others make their way over.

Xaden pauses between Garrick and Drake, and our gazes collide for a heartbeat before we both focus on General Aetos. *Court-martial coming in three...two...*

"We will discuss your punishment for disobeying direct orders later." General Aetos glances at Drake. "It's too bad you were born on the wrong side of the family." His gaze snaps to Cat. "The good news is that you're one step closer to your throne."

Cat blanches. "Syrena?"

My stomach plummets, and I spot Mira white-knuckling the strap of her rucksack.

"Is that your sister?" Aetos asks, reaching into the pocket of his uniform and walking toward us.

"Yes," Maren answers so Cat doesn't have to.

"Ah. Right. The infamous flier." Aetos retrieves a missive and hands it to me without really answering Cat *or* Maren. "This perplexing read came for you about an hour ago. Looking forward to discussing it during your debrief."

I clasp the parchment, noting the broken seal. "Is Syrena Cordella alive?" He's cruel to drag it out like this.

"Last I heard, she's fine." Aetos glances meaningfully at the paper.

Thank you, Amari.

Cat sways, taking in a deep breath, and I unfold the already opened missive. "What happened?" she asks.

My skin chills as the blood runs from my face at the sight of *her* handwriting.

Violet—

I do hope you had a marvelous time on your journey, though your riot looked a little haggard when you flew over Pavis. I do wonder why you went to so much effort when I have the one thing you seek above all else. Do enjoy the time you have with your friends until our next rendezvous. Don't worry, I'm making all the arrangements.

—T

I crumple the parchment on reflex, and my gaze jumps to Xaden.

"What is it?" He tilts his head.

"Theophanie." It's a struggle to draw a full breath. *"She knew we were gone. She saw us fly over Pavis and somehow delivered this here before we arrived."*

His mouth tightens. *"She can't get to you here."*

"And yet she did." I shove the paper into my pocket and notice General Aetos watching me like a hawk.

"Is my uncle all right?" Cat's voice rises. "Just tell us already."

Tecarus. Oh *shit.*

"While you were out doing gods know what on the isles for three weeks," Aetos says, his eyes hardening, "Suniva fell to dark wielders."

Maren gasps, and dread hangs on the momentary silence.

"Queen Maraya is dead."

Your Majesty, unfortunately I can find no law that supersedes the Unification Scrolls. The Provincial Commitment under Queen Alondra the Bold (207.1)—consolidating the provinces' armies under the queen's standard for the Poromish conflict—expired with the Second Aretia Accord, and control of all forces ~~should~~ must return to the provinces from which they hail. I recommend ~~demanding~~ asking for a new Provincial Commitment covering our current conflict. ~~The provinces will never agree after the rise in conscription rates. My advice: do not anger Tyrrendor's duke, who now commands the largest portion of our army. Screw this. I hate my job.~~

—Unsent, Drafted Correspondence
of Colonel Agatha Mayfair, Royal Archivist

CHAPTER
FORTY-FOUR

Leadership separates us completely after we put our things in our rooms, then questions us for twelve hours each with scribes. When Aetos accidentally lets slip his annoyance that King Tauri is so grateful to have Aaric back that he's forbidden *any* form of punishment, the emotional relief results in an immediate sense of overwhelming exhaustion, but I don't ask for a reprieve from the endless debrief. I made the decisions, and if this prolonged interrogation is my only collegiate repercussion, I'll take it without complaint, especially knowing the other members of the squad are safe, too.

They go over the trip's details so many times, for so many hours, that I start to worry if they're looking for holes in our stories or if they suspect we had more than rare texts to guide us. It's tedious and exhausting, but at least I get to see Markham's face twist with jealousy from across the room on the few occasions he sits in on my sessions.

I've seen things he never will, touched pieces of history he didn't know existed.

Just like my father.

Mira and Garrick are released back to the front on March twenty-eighth, the last day of our inquisition. Drake departs for Cordyn. Brennan arrives from Aretia to mend my ribs. Xaden is hauled into Senarium meetings while being returned to his position as a professor.

And the rest of us go back to class.

For having missed more than three weeks, I'm only completely lost in physics and mildly confused in history, since all my studying prior to the trip had nothing to do with Braevick absorbing Cygnisen under Porom the First. If not for Rhi's notes, the three of us would drown academically, and I'm sure Aaric feels the same about Sloane.

But it's Battle Brief on our first day back that shows just how much damage can be done in three weeks. Suniva is far from the only city to have fallen. In fact, geographically speaking, it's an outlier.

"That's not possible," I whisper, staring at the map from my seat. How many dark wielders would it take to cover that much territory this quickly? Rhi and I spent the early morning hours debriefing, but this hadn't come up.

"It's happening fast." Rhiannon takes out her pen and paper.

"If by fast, you mean that half of Krovla has been painted red while we were away, then yes, I'd say *fast* is a good term," Ridoc notes from Rhi's right.

"You guys didn't see any of it on your flight in?" Sawyer asks.

"No." My grip tightens on my pen. "We flew over the ruins of Pavis." There are so many patches of red that they blend into one. Only the southern tip and west of Krovla have been spared. Cordyn still stands, but for how long? "Civilian casualties?"

Rhi's mouth tightens. "Unknown, and the borders are a mess. People are fleeing in every direction. Draithus is facing major supply shortages. Too many people too fast."

My stomach knots. Mira and Garrick were both sent to Draithus.

"Because your king won't let anyone in." Cat seethes.

A few heads turn in her direction before quickly looking away. It's been like that all day, cadets whispering and staring at us.

"What?" I lean forward to look past Maren as the stragglers take their seats. "We're still not taking civilians?"

"Guessing they skipped that part of your debrief," she replies.

Or I'd only been interviewed by Navarrians.

"Welcome back to our travelers," Professor Devera says as she takes her position at the front, alongside Professor Kiandra. "From my understanding, they have secured us an army of forty thousand soldiers from an alliance with Zehyllna." She gives me a subtle nod, and I force a smile. "Which may help turn the tide of this war."

But we failed to secure our primary objective. And lost a squadmate. I'm going to need to get back into the gym with Imogen to carry all this fucking guilt.

"I'd settle for a stalemate," Maren says from my left.

"Also, welcome to our new guests." Devera's gaze flicks to the two captains in rider black standing watch at the end of Aaric's row. "Please make yourselves as uncomfortable as possible."

Aaric glares past Sloane and Baylor, then faces forward.

"On to battle strategy," Devera announces. "Where should we put our forty thousand troops?" she asks the room, then calls on a first-year from Second Wing.

"They should be stationed here to protect the wardstone," the curly-haired guy replies.

"Yes, because *that* is where venin seem to be headed," Imogen quips from above us.

"Next," Devera orders.

"They should be sent to the south to hold the line so Cordyn doesn't fall," Cat says without being called on.

"That would be one excellent usage of them," Devera agrees, "though I wonder if your bias comes into play with that kind of decision, seeing as it's now the seat of power for your uncle."

King Tecarus.

"What do our other travelers think?" Devera inquires, her gaze skimming over us.

I stare at the western line that's creeping closer to Tyrrendor and keep my mouth closed so the same point can't be made to me regarding bias.

"They should be split," Dain answers from above us. "Half to the south to defend the new king and what's left of the territory, and half to the western line."

"You would deploy all the troops within Poromiel?" she questions, sitting back on her favorite spot on the table.

"It's where they're needed," he answers with a certainty I envy. "And before the riders in here get defensive, remember that protecting Krovla's western line keeps the dark wielders off Tyrrendor and Elsum, and we're bound by our alliance to defend King Tecarus."

"And it was a flier who paid the cost of that army," Cat adds.

"Solid points," Devera admits. "Personally, I'd divvy the troops into thirds, putting most along the lines Aetos suggested and the rest at our outposts." My brow furrows. Why would the outposts need more troops within the wards? "If we start losing wards, there will be no safe harbor on the Continent."

"Safe for who, exactly?" Maren mutters.

"Hard for outposts to fall or lose wards when they're already protected," Sawyer muses.

Unless they think the arsenals are at risk. All it takes is a disruption in the power supply and the wards will fail.

"We'll see what leadership decides." Devera pauses, and her hands trip on the edge of the desk. "It is not lost on me that today's subject will be a sensitive one—I know many of you had family there—but it is critical that we discuss Suniva's fall now that the intel reports are in."

There's an immediate hum of tension within the room, as if half its occupants can't help but channel.

"How many of you know how it happened?" Devera's gaze sweeps over us.

A second-year flier from Third Wing raises her hand, and Devera nods at her. "I don't think any of us have all the details, but we know they were taken by surprise. I heard twenty venin—"

"I heard it was more like thirty," someone counters from the right.

"Which is why we have this briefing." Devera lifts her brows. "It does us no good to train with misinformation and rumors." She looks back at the flier.

"They dropped out of the sky, which made Suniva's fifty-foot walls obsolete," the flier continues, "then started a…fire. Is it true most everyone burned to death?"

My stomach pitches. I can't think of a more horrible way to die.

"Unfortunately, yes." Devera nods. "The fire started in the famous textile district and, with the help of what we think were wind-wielding venin, quickly devoured most of the city, despite the efforts of the four drifts in permanent residence, all of whom perished. We had a riot of four stationed there to protect the queen. One rider and two dragons made it out alive, which is the only reason we have facts instead of rumors to build on. Estimated casualties are somewhere around twenty-five thousand lives."

Holy shit.

A flier two rows down hangs her head, and her shoulders shake.

"The fire did most of the work for them," Devera continues, "allowing their horde of approximately twelve wyvern to split into three coordinated units."

"There's no way twelve wyvern took out Suniva!" a flier to the right yells.

"Twelve wyvern. Twelve venin," Devera answers without batting an eye. "Four to hold the perimeter, four to fly directly to the palace, and four to concentrate on the barracks and armory. Twelve of them took out twenty-five thousand people. Putting your feelings aside," Devera instructs, raising her chin, "ask the questions that will allow you to hypothetically change the outcome of this loss."

The room falls quiet, and not a single hand rises.

Twenty-five thousand people. We've never studied a modern battle with so many casualties before. How in Amari's name are we supposed to dissect one that not only killed some of our classmates' families but took the life of their queen? It hasn't even been a week.

Devera looks to her right, and Professor Kiandra moves from the edge of the room to the desk in the center of the stage.

"If we do not rip apart this tactic," Kiandra lectures, "they will use it again, and the next town they come for will be yours. Suniva was our kingdom's capital but our fourth-largest city. You honor the dead by making sure no others fall in the same manner. We have to learn from this. I know it's hard, but in a matter of months, you third-years will be on the front lines. That will mean *you* defending Diasyn." She points to someone above us. "Or you"—her finger swings left—"defending Cordyn."

"Start asking," Devera orders. "Start thinking, or we're all dead."

"What was in the armory?" Xaden's voice carries over the hall.

I look back and find him standing in the doorway next to Bodhi, his arms folded and jaw locked. My heart leaps. It's been three days since I've seen him. The beard he grew on the journey home has been shaved, and the name tag is back on his uniform. Instinctively, I reach for the bond, but his shields are up.

His gaze darts to mine and warms for the millisecond he holds contact before we both turn our attention to the front of the room.

"They have to think for themselves, Professor Riorson." Devera arches a brow.

"What was in the armory?" he repeats.

Kiandra nods. "Six crates of freshly delivered alloy-hilted daggers, and yes, the venin took them all."

Everyone's interest shifts forward, and it takes conscious effort to pick my jaw up. There are maybe *two* crates kept at each outpost.

"Why didn't Poromish forces use the damned daggers?" Ridoc asks.

"Because the *damned* daggers had only arrived a few hours earlier," Devera answers. "And the armory was the first target hit. Our best guess is that there was simply no time to distribute them."

"Why would six crates be sent there?" Caroline Ashton asks.

"Suniva was only supposed to be a distribution site. Drifts were set to take the crates to other cities in the morning," Kiandra answers.

Shit. The venin knew about the shipment. That's the only logical explanation.

"How many people knew the distribution schedule?" I ask.

"Right there." Devera points at me. "The answer is too many. We have traitors in our ranks."

My pulse launches. How many Barlowes are out there, hiding among us? Just waiting for their opportunity? The cadet turning in the Signet Sparring pit proved some of us are willing to turn under the right circumstances. Maybe even in *this* room.

"How did they get to Suniva without being detected?" Rhiannon asks. "The area surrounding the city was clear for hundreds of miles. Fliers and our riot had to be on patrol."

"What's common in Suniva in March?" Kiandra asks in answer.

Fuck if I know. That hasn't exactly been a part of our education to this point.

"Thunderstorms," Kai answers from Aaric's right. "From March until about June, they roll in around five and are gone by midnight."

Kiandra nods. "They flew in with the storm."

"You mean above it?" a first-year asks.

"No, dumbass," another first-year from First Wing counters. "They can't survive at that altitude."

"Some storms *are* low enough to fly over," Devera corrects, "which is why you should pay more attention in class, Payson. In this case, they flew *within* the cloud."

Within the cloud? That would require… No way. It's impossible. *Not with enough years of training.*

"That doesn't make sense," a third-year calls out from above us. "It's an unacceptable risk to fly in those conditions unless absolutely necessary due to the prevalence of lightning. We're taught that in the first month of flight maneuvers."

Most of the room mutters in agreement.

"Which is why the patrols were grounded." Devera stares at me like she knows what I'm thinking.

"Maybe they don't give a shit how many wyvern die," Imogen counters.

My heart races, and I shift my weight in my seat.

"What's wrong?" Rhiannon whispers.

"I know how they did it," I reply just as quietly, my grip tightening on my pen.

"Then say something," Rhi prods like it's first year all over again.

"I don't want to be right," I reply just as quietly.

"That's a first," Cat mutters.

Devera cocks her head to the side, calling me out without saying a word.

My stomach hollows. Gods, I'm really going to have to say it.

"They'd give a shit about wyverns if they're riding them," the other third-year retorts at Imogen. "They might not have souls, but they value their lives, and no reasonable rider flies within a thunderstorm."

"I do." Fuck, I actually said it.

Every head turns my way, and Devera nods.

"I can direct my strikes within a cloud just like I did during the battle here in December," I continue. "Which means I could theoretically control the natural strikes and move a riot within a thunderstorm with relative safety...after about twenty years of practice." I abandon my pen on my notebook. *Theophanie.* "She was with them—their lightning wielder. I'd guess that's how the textile fire started, and probably what took out the other dragons."

"That's what the report suggests," Devera answers.

Shit. Shit. *Shit.* "To do all that after moving a horde through a storm..." I shake my head. "She has to be a Maven." And I'm a fucking second-year who just spent three weeks chasing a mirage of hope on isles without magic when I should have been training.

"Most likely," Devera agrees, giving me the same look Mira had on Zehyllna: expectation. Then she glances away. "So now let's discuss how we defeat this particular assault. What signets could have made the difference? Nothing's off the table. Who do you send to guard your most valuable targets with this kind of threat?"

"Water wielders could have helped the fire," someone suggests.

"You send Riorson," Caroline Ashton says. "He's the most powerful rider we have, and he's held back more than just a dozen wyvern. If Riorson's there, this doesn't happen."

True, but at what cost? Would he have channeled from the earth to keep it from happening? I glance over my shoulder, but Xaden is already gone.

"Don't we have a fire wielder powerful enough to have controlled the flames?" Baylor asks. "He's a major stationed with the Southern Wing."

"Major Edorta is stationed at Athebyne," Devera confirms.

Rhiannon glances sideways at me, then looks away.

"Your turn to say something," I whisper. "Don't hesitate."

"No way. Not even in hypotheticals." Sawyer shakes his head at Rhi as people call out different signets around us. "You don't send a cadet against—"

"You send Sorrengail," Rhiannon announces.

"—a Maven," Sawyer finishes in a whisper. "And yet you just did. Gods*damn.*"

Cat and Maren both gawk at Rhi, and Sawyer sinks lower in his seat.

"You said nothing was off the table," Rhi adds, keeping her eyes forward. "Sorrengail could have taken out a chunk of the wyvern on approach by striking into that same cloud, including their lightning wielder, as long as they don't know Violet's there."

"And if they do?" Devera questions. "Remember that someone told them about the daggers being moved."

Rhi swallows, and her breaths speed up.

"Do your job." I whisper the reminder. "It's just a hypothetical."

She straightens her spine. "Then Sorrengail needs to be the better of the two."

And I'm not. I'm distracted the rest of the hour, thinking of different tactics I could use to even the playing field between Theophanie and me and coming up empty-handed, with the exception of one fact. She wants me alive.

Battle Brief ends, and we have two precious hours before our next class, which Ridoc uses to cajole Sawyer, Rhi, and me into going down to the Archives.

Not that Sawyer needs much of a push.

"We really couldn't have waited another couple of days?" I whisper at Ridoc as we walk through the tunnel, passing the stairwell to the interrogation chamber.

Rhi and Sawyer are far too into arguing about her decision to send me off to the front to pay attention.

"No," Ridoc says. "We couldn't. One day, Battle Brief is going to cover how a shadow wielder took out Cordyn, but you won't be sitting in your seat because they will have already killed you to stop him."

"Not much of a Battle Brief if you already have the answer." I flash a fake smile.

"Basgiath was a unique case," Sawyer argues with Rhi at my left. "We were defending the school, and we kept the first-years out of it for the very reason you can't just order Violet into battle. They weren't prepared."

"Stop," I tell him. "It's her job as a squad leader to see me as an asset and not just her friend."

"I still think it's bullshit," Sawyer mutters as we walk past the scribe on duty at the Archives door.

"It's war," Rhiannon reminds him as we reach the table at the front. "And I think it's bullshit you haven't even thought about flying yet."

Ridoc and I exchange a look of *oh shit.*

"I can't," he fires back in a whisper, tapping his cane against his prosthesis. "Not with this thing. It's not ready yet."

There's no need to ask for Jesinia. The class of scribes sitting at their perfectly lined-up desks sends someone running to the back the second they see us.

"You could ask Sliseag to—" Rhiannon starts.

"Sliseag isn't Tairn," Sawyer hisses. "I'm not about to ask him to make exceptions for me—not when he risked bonding a repeat in the first place."

A few scribes pick their heads up, then quickly look away.

"You'd rather spend your time consulting with the retirees?" Rhi counters. "You're still a rider, Sawyer."

"Maybe we should ease up," Ridoc suggests.

Sawyer's face flushes. "All respect, but you have no idea what this is like, Rhi."

I lean into Rhi just enough to get her attention, then shake my head subtly. "Subject change," I suggest in a whisper.

Her mouth purses, and she sighs. "What's going on with you and Riorson?" she asks, keeping her voice just as low as mine. "You didn't so much as smile when you saw him during Battle Brief."

"He's brooding." I shrug.

"That's a word for it," Ridoc says, pressing down a corner of his ice-wielding patch that's come unsewn.

Jesinia emerges from the back of the Archives, holding a small paper bundle tied with twine. She quickly makes her way toward us, immediately gifting Sawyer with a smile as she sets the book-size package on the table and pushes it toward me.

"Hi," he signs, and damn if his grin doesn't tug at the corners of my mouth.

"Hi," she signs, then turns toward us. "Your reports have been fun to read, but it's good to have you back so you can tell me about the trip in person." Her gaze meets mine. "That was delivered for you by courier this morning—I intercepted it before Aetos could open it like he does all of your mail."

"Thank you," I sign, then pick up the package. It's far too soft, too malleable to be a book, and the tag labeled with my name and quadrant is from a seamstress in Chantara.

Weird.

"We need somewhere private," Ridoc signs.

Rhi's brow furrows. "What's going on?" she signs.

"Please," Ridoc signs to Jesinia.

She nods, then leads us to one of the private, windowless study rooms that line the front wall of the Archives and motions us inside.

I head in first with Sawyer, and the others follow. "I know Sliseag isn't Tairn," I whisper as we make our way around to the back of the table. "And I also know it can be hard to do things differently, especially in an environment that demands perfection and uniformity."

"An environment that *produces* perfection and uniformity." Sawyer stiffens, glancing across the table at Rhi and Ridoc as she quizzes him again as to why we're here.

Oh. I get it now. "For me, flying...differently is worth it," I say under my breath as we sit. "But whether you feel the same about asking Sliseag for help is a question only you can answer."

"I think I could keep my seat," he admits quietly. "Most of that is thigh work. It's mounting that intimidates me."

"Anything I can do to help?" I ask him.

Jesinia peeks through the doorway as if checking to see that we weren't followed, then closes the door.

Sawyer shakes his head. "I've been working toward the run and making adjustments to the prosthesis for the climb. I just need to get it right, make sure it works before I let myself hope." His gaze flickers to Rhi.

"You could never disappoint her," I rush as Jesinia turns toward us.

"Our friend? Never. Our squad leader?" He grimaces.

"You shouldn't be in here," Jesinia signs, "so make it quick before they come kick you out."

Ridoc leans all the way back in his chair and stares at me.

"What is happening?" Rhi signs, looking between the two of us.

"Tell them," Ridoc signs. "Or I will."

I sigh. There's no point being nervous. Either I trust my friends, or I don't.

"Xaden is slowly turning venin," I say and sign.

Rhi's eyes widen, and she leans forward. "Talk."

I think I started falling for you that night in the tree when I watched you with the marked ones, but I began tumbling the day you gave me Tairn's saddle. You'll give some self-serving excuse, but the truth is you're kinder than you want people to know. Maybe kinder than you know.

—Recovered Correspondence of Cadet Violet Sorrengail to His Grace, Lieutenant Xaden Riorson, Sixteenth Duke of Tyrrendor

CHAPTER
FORTY-FIVE

I hang in the air, suspended by an invisible hand around my throat as lightning strikes in the distance. Fear pumps through my veins, but the harder I fight, the narrower my windpipe becomes, the harder it is to draw breath.

"Quit fighting it," the Sage orders. "Quit fighting *me*."

You're dead. This isn't real. I repeat the phrases mentally when my lips refuse to form the words. This is only a nightmare.

A very visceral, terrifying nightmare.

The fight drains out of me, and I fall to the ground before him, hitting my knees and gasping for charred air.

Andarna screams, bellowing with rage and pain, and my head snaps toward the ridgeline...toward the storm. Blue fire licks up the hillside, reaching for the city walls of Draithus, devouring the fleeing civilians in its path.

"Such emotion." The Sage tsks, crouching down in front of me. "Don't worry. It will fade in time."

"Fuck you." I lunge forward, only to be shoved back to my knees by an invisible force.

"I'll allow you to help her this time," the Sage promises, pushing his robes up the length of his tanned arms. "Just submit. Come to me. Accept where you belong, and you'll find a freedom like no other."

"And if I don't?" I ask, playing into the dream.

"Then you'll find I have ways to bring you to heel." The Sage draws a sword from his robes, and the next flash of lightning reflects in the emeralds adorning the top of the hilt.

Whisps of silver hair blow in the breeze at the edge of my vision, and the sword of Tyrrendor rushes toward my chest.

WAKE! I scream, but my mouth won't work—

My eyes flash open and my hands jolt upward, my sweaty limbs tangling in the blankets as lightning crashes outside my window.

Heart racing, I shove away the covers and run my fingers over my sternum. "Of course there's no cut, you fool," I mutter. It was just a damned dream. A very visceral one, but a dream nonetheless.

I swing my feet to the floor, then wrap my arms around my middle as I rise and walk toward the window. Rain assaults the glass in sheets that obscure the view over the ravine toward the main campus.

Tairn and Andarna are asleep, but there's a stirring along the bond I share with Xaden. His shields are down, but the foggy barrier of sleep stands between us.

I breathe in through my nose and out through my mouth, counting to twenty as my heart slowly calms. The Sage is dead, but *she* isn't.

Theophanie is very real, and if she can get to me here at Basgiath, she can get to my friends, too…the ones who are justifiably disappointed that I kept yet another secret from them. Thank gods they understand that Xaden's not the enemy, that he's still fighting on our side.

How long will it be until Theophanie goes after *Xaden*?

My throat tightens, but this time it's my own fear clogging my windpipe. How the hell am I supposed to fight a dark wielder who's had decades to perfect a signet I still need a conduit to control?

It's the end of March. I've barely had my powers for a year.

The last day of March.

I glance down at the package Jesinia handed me the day before yesterday. It's right where I left it on the sill, one end undone. At the opening of the paper, the edges of a delicate Deverelli silk nightgown and robe spill out with a handwritten note.

For the nights I can't sleep next to you. — X

My chest clenches just like it did when I opened it. He'd somehow seen me eyeing the fabric in Deverelli, bought it, then placed the order to have it made before we left to search the other isles.

"I love you," I whisper down the bond, then lean forward and rest my forehead against the cold glass, using the sensation to solidify my certainty that the nightmare has ended. *"I need you. Quit brooding."*

Maybe it's time I try one of his own techniques.

I reach for pen and paper.

. . .

"**T**he purpose of this maneuver, as you remember, is to spend as little time on the ground as possible," Kaori lectures that morning as he stands beside Xaden, amplifying his voice across the flight field as the riders of our entire section sit mounted like we're in formation...mostly.

Sawyer stands between Sliseag's claws two rows back, and Tairn waits next to Feirge, both their wings tucked for proximity's sake, instead of standing behind her where we belong.

"I am precisely where I belong," he counters.

"Kind of wish you were a gryphon so we could have sat this one out."

"Kind of wish I'd sat out Threshing two years ago," he counters.

The corner of my mouth rises. *"You sure you don't want to join us?"* I ask Andarna.

"No point when I can't carry you." She shuts the bond.

Awesome. My heart sinks to a new low. I pushed too hard again. Or maybe too little.

Tairn sighs like he's in his elder years.

"In this new type of warfare," Kaori continues, "it's more important than ever that we spend less time on the ground, but there will be moments when you cannot accomplish your mission while mounted. You must be prepared to dismount in a running landing, wield to defeat your opponent, then be ready to take to the sky in what we're calling a 'battle-mount' if you are unsuccessful... or outnumbered. Every second you remain on the ground endangers not only your life, but your dragon's, should they remain on the field." Kaori lifts a hand and conjures a projection of a robed figure at the far right end of the field. "Professor Riorson?"

Shit. I haven't mastered a run-on landing like the rest of my year-mates, let alone whatever a "battle-mount" will entail.

"For the sake of the first exercise," Xaden says, his voice booming across the field, "your opponent's signet is unknown, and you are alone. Once you've shown you can complete the maneuver, we'll work in teams. First-years, we just want you to get the tactic down so you can practice while on your upcoming Aretia rotation. Don't worry about wielding; I know not all of you can." Xaden surveys our line, and I can't help but notice the dark circles under his eyes. He might be sleeping at night, but it's not well, and I hate that I can't do anything about it. "This is your fighting pit today." His gaze finds mine. "Try not to incinerate it."

"Ha. Very funny."

"Never know with you," he surprises me by replying.

Bodhi goes first, nailing the running landing like it's part of his everyday workout, then uses the momentum to continue into the projection, twisting his left hand and swinging the sword with the other, decapitating the fake model.

Cuir banks hard to pivot back to Bodhi, but it's too steep, and his green swordtail takes out a small section of boulders halfway up the hill as he pulls the turn.

Bodhi breaks into a run from the projection, and Cuir returns, extending his left foreleg as he slows his speed. The two are parallel just long enough for Bodhi to leap onto Cuir's claw, and the dragon is already accelerating, gaining altitude as Bodhi climbs up to the seat.

Oh...we're fucked.

"I can't do that." It's not self-doubt talking. It's just fact.

"You will," Tairn decrees. *"It just won't look like that."*

Right. Because I'll be dead, lying face down on the muddy flight field from the impact.

"Sometimes I forget just how nearly perfect Bodhi is at everything," I say to Xaden. No one thought of him during Battle Brief yesterday, and he should have been the first name that came to mind. Countering signets might not be the best offensive tool, but damn if it isn't a hell of a defense.

"He's my cousin," Xaden replies, locking eyes with me. *"Of course he's exceptional."*

"Hmmm. Just like you, but without the arrogance." I cock my head to the side. *"Maybe I fell for the wrong—"*

"It would be a shame to kill my last living relative." Xaden tilts his head to mirror mine, then straightens, and on today of all days, I choose not to remind him that he has two half brothers. "And that is how it's done," he calls out. "In this scenario, the smaller dragons have the advantage. Maneuverability is key, so do yourselves a favor and talk out your approach before the attempt. We only have one mender on campus."

And I'd rather fly to Aretia than let Nolon touch me.

"Maybe we should wait a month and try when we're on the Aretia rotation," I suggest to Tairn.

"Or you could simply not break anything," he suggests oh-so-helpfully.

First Squad begins. The initial two maneuvers are successful. The next cadet breaks her leg on impact.

"Ouch," Rhi hisses through her teeth and glances my way. "You all right to do this?" she asks as the first-year stumbles off, cradling the appendage.

"I'm never all right to do this," I reply. "I just do it anyway."

"Sounds about right." She nods, then her eyes narrow at something across the field.

I track her line of sight to Xaden and shake my head. "Don't." I can't say more out in the open, but it's not like she doesn't know what I'm talking about.

"It's hard not to," she admits without apology. "But I'm trying."

"I know. Thank you." I adjust my new saddle strap and pray the stitches I finished this morning will hold. Instead of keeping my thighs at the seat like the original one I've left fastened in front of me, this one wraps around my waist like a belt and buckles in front with three different notches I can tighten or loosen depending on how much maneuverability I need.

A second-year nails the running landing but misses the leap for his Red Morningstartail's claw and slams into the mud.

I wince. Movement catches my eye, and my gaze runs up the hill behind Xaden, finding Andarna perched on an outcropping fifty feet overhead, her scales the same color as Tairn's. *"Change your mind?"* I ask with what I hope is the right amount of encouragement.

"No." Her tail flicks a second before she launches, leaping from the outcropping with sure beats of her wings, climbing up and over the ridge of the box canyon.

Fuck. I blow out a frustrated sigh. I can't say or do *anything* right to help her.

"She's adjusting," Tairn says.

I glance across the field and find Xaden watching me. *"It's going around."*

First Squad ends with five successful maneuvers, four failed attempts at landing, and two failed launches, resulting in a total of three broken bones and one bloody nose.

"This does not bode well for us in battle," Rhi says.

"Let's hope we have time to get it right." It's the most supportive comment I can come up with. "You're the squad leader, so you'd better go set the example. Good luck. Don't die." I flash a smile her way.

"Thanks." She fights the smile she returns, then pretends to puff out her chest. "I will bring honor to the patch."

"See that you do." I watch as Feirge steps forward and launches once she's clear of Tairn.

Xaden looks my way, and for a second, the mask falls, giving me a glimpse of longing that tightens my chest.

"You getting any sleep?" I ask.

"I sleep better when I'm next to you," he admits.

"You know where to find my bed. Professor or not, I'm pretty sure you know how to sneak in." I run my hand over my flight jacket pocket, making sure my little parcel is secured. *"Unless you're still brooding."*

"It's a full-time occupation at the moment."

"Does that schedule allow for giving me a moment after class?"

He nods.

Feirge approaches, and Rhiannon moves to her foreclaw as she descends, then executes a perfect running landing. She lifts her hand, and a blade appears. The projection wavers as she slices through it, then races back as Feirge returns.

I can't help but grin. Rhi doesn't miss the jump. Damn, she's good.

Tairn waits for Imogen and Quinn to take their turns, then fires off a series of orders to me as Ridoc lands with a particularly showy somersault. Ice flies from his hands through the projection, and he turns to the squads with a bow befitting any stage performance before racing for Aotrom. There's a heartbeat where I think he won't make it, but he swings his body onto Aotrom's claw and the two take off.

"You really think that's going to work?" I ask Tairn, pulling down my flight goggles as he crouches.

"I think it's the only way to accomplish the mission without breaking your neck." He launches with powerful wingbeats, and the ground falls away. *"Wait for the last second so you don't embarrass us."*

"So encouraging," I tease. Tairn climbs, then I adjust my weight as he banks hard left at the top of the canyon. My heart begins to pound when we dive toward the target, and I grip the conduit in one hand and reach for the buckle of my saddle with the other.

"Not yet!" he snaps.

"Just preparing." I throw open the Archives door and let his power flood me, focusing on concentrating the energy at the center of my chest as the walls of the canyon rise quickly around us.

"Unbuckle," Tairn orders as colors blur on either side of me, but I keep my gaze homed in on the target and undo the leather that keeps me in the seat. *"Move."*

Holding the belt of the saddle in my right hand, I stand, nearly stumbling at the wind resistance as he descends directly at the target, not leveling out like the others.

"What are you doing?" Xaden growls.

"Busy right now, love." I slam my shields down and my heart threatens to leap through my throat as the ground approaches at terrifying speed.

"Now!" Tairn shouts.

I release the belt and run for his shoulder, then leap.

For a dizzying heartbeat, I'm airborne, the sounds of the world completely drowned out by the rush of air, the drumbeat in my chest, and the *snap* of wings. I plummet toward the field, my stomach rising to the roof of my mouth as I fall. The power gathering within me is useless to slow my descent, but I throw out my arms to the side like they have a chance and lock every muscle in my body.

Talons clamp over my shoulders and tighten, locking me in place.

Wind gusts, and momentum shifts as Tairn stops my fall a few feet from the ground, then releases me. His wings beat once, and I barely have time to bend my knees before my feet hit the field. A ripple of painful protest shoots from my toes, up my spine, and bursts in my head like a rung bell as I land six feet in front of the target.

Holy shit, I'm not dead.

"Faster!" Tairn snaps with another beat of his wings.

I focus on the projection, lift my right hand, and release a *crack* of power, then draw my fingers downward, dragging the energy from the sky. Lightning strikes, so bright it robs me of vision, and thunder sounds immediately, echoing off the walls of the box canyon.

When the light recedes, a scorch mark flares outward from the base of the projection.

Yes!

I throw up my arms, and talons wrap around my midsection. Tairn secures me in his back right claw and continues to climb.

My stomach lurches as I get an up-close view of the hillside, and a few seconds later, we're clear, nothing but air around us. He ascends another hundred feet to give us room, and I welcome the adrenaline flooding my system because we're not done yet.

"Now."

He swings his body to a vertical position and *throws* me.

It's just like first year, except we mean to do it. I rise as he falls, and it's all I can do to not look down. That way lies death. This is all about trust.

I rise over his shoulder, and he pumps his wings.

My feet meet scale, and I grab on to the base of his nearest spike, careful to steer clear of its sharp point as he surges forward.

"I trust you can find your seat," he says with a note of pride, leveling out as we fly above the field.

"I've got it." I navigate my way back to the saddle, then grab hold of both flapping ends of the belt and buckle myself in. We did it.

My heart is still galloping when we land, then take our spot in formation.

"That was...unorthodox," Kaori says.

Tairn rumbles low in his chest.

"And it worked," I counter, shouting across the field.

"It did," Xaden replies, a corner of his mouth rising. *"I fucking love you."*

"How could you not?" I don't bother fighting my smile.

He scoffs.

Kaori looks like he wants to protest, but then he motions the rest of the group forward.

Baylor skins his knee on landing.

Avalynn fractures her collarbone.

Sloane completes the entire exercise with a grace that reminds me of Liam but doesn't even pretend to wield.

Lynx comes up with a face full of mud and a broken nose.

Aaric lands twenty feet from the projection without breaking a sweat, but instead of rushing the target, he whirls toward Xaden and Kaori and hurls a palm-size axe.

My heart trips as it flies end over end, but Xaden doesn't even flinch as it lands a foot in front of Kaori, the blade embedded in the mud. The projection disappears.

"I think he won," Rhi says.

Xaden nods once before Aaric backs away, then breaks into a run to mount Molvic.

"I'd definitely say so," I agree.

After maneuvers are done for the day, the dragons launch, and I hang back to catch Xaden alone, even after a few reproachful looks from my year-mates.

Kaori walks up, looking like he wants to say something, but a Red Swordtail lands farther down the field, catching his attention. He simply tips his chin and walks toward the dragon, leaving me alone with Xaden on the far end of the field.

"That was fucking terrifying to watch." Xaden's gaze bores into mine. "And magnificent."

"I feel that way about you every day." I smile, then dig my hand into the pocket of my flight jacket and remove a parchment-wrapped parcel and a letter. "I got you something. Present is for now, letter is for later."

"You didn't have to." His brow furrows, but he takes them both and pockets the letter.

"Open it." My heart flutters. I hope I made the right choice, since it's definitely too soon to bring out anything that resembles a cake.

He untucks the folded parchment, then stares at the black metal wrist cuff.

"It's onyx," I tell him as he studies the clasp and flat, rectangular stone mounted within the band. "And that's a piece of the turret on top of Riorson House."

His gaze jumps to mine, and his fist closes around the cuff.

"You mentioned it needed repairs, and I asked Brennan to have that made for you from one of the broken pieces. When things get…shitty, I hope you can look down at it and imagine us sitting there together when this is all over. That's the vision I'm going to cling to: you and me, holding hands, looking over the city." I close the distance between us, take the cuff from his hand, and secure it around his wrist, then flick the metal closure. "Thank gods it fits. I had to guess—"

He takes my face in his hands and kisses me. It's soft. Tender. Perfect. "Thank you," he says.

"Happy birthday," I whisper against his lips.

"I love you." He lifts his head, and his hands slip from my cheeks like a caress. "But I'm only going to get worse. You really should run."

Not done brooding. Message received.

"Come find me when you're ready to accept the fact that I won't." I back away slowly. "That I never will."

"Forty-seven days." He searches my eyes and lets his breath go. *That's how long it's been since I channeled from the alloy in Deverelli.*

"That's longer than the month you lamented about before we came home."

"Not long enough." His eyes spark with determination, and hope flares brightly within my chest.

"You have a number in mind before you feel…in control?"

His jaw flexes. "Control is probably just prolonging the inevitable, but I've got one that might indicate…stability."

"Feel like sharing?"

He shakes his head.

"As much as I hate to break up whatever's happening over here—" A voice booms across the area, and we both turn, finding Felix walking toward us with a full pack strapped to his back as Kaori leaves the field.

I blink three times to make sure I'm not seeing things. "I thought you said you wouldn't leave Aretia?"

"I do hate Basgiath." He scratches the silver cloud of his beard. "But not as much as I hate dying." He pulls a tied bundle of missives from the pocket of his flight jacket and hands them to Xaden. "Those are yours, *Your Grace.*"

"News from Aretia?" Xaden takes them.

"Provincial affairs." Felix nods. "And two wyvern came through the wards yesterday."

My stomach pitches.

"How far did they get now?" Xaden asks, and my head swings in his direction. This isn't the first time.

"About an hour before they skidded into the side of a mountain." Felix lifts his silver brows. "That's about ten minutes farther—"

"Than last week," Xaden finishes, and I start to understand the circles beneath his eyes.

"The wards are weakening." I state the obvious.

"They're failing," Felix corrects, turning to me with a look that already makes my arms ache. "And since I've been informed that you won't let Carr instruct you, I suppose we'd better get back to work."

"I'll be in Aretia in about a month for rotation. You didn't have to come all the way up here." Guilt gnaws at me.

"And if I was sure we'd have a month, I would have waited." He narrows his eyes.

Oh.

When this is over, we should take as much leave as they'll give us and spend it all in Aretia. We can figure out what life is supposed to look like without the daily threat of death. You can govern the province you love during the day, then slide into bed with me at night. Or I can always join you in the Assembly chamber. You do some of your best work on that throne.

—Recovered Correspondence of Cadet Violet Sorrengail to His Grace, Lieutenant Xaden Riorson, Sixteenth Duke of Tyrrendor

CHAPTER FORTY-SIX

Three weeks later, I can barely lift my arms as our squad walks back from Signet Sparring. Gods, I hate when Carr rotates in to teach. Countless muscles in my body ache, and there's a permanent knot between my shoulder blades thanks to the work Felix has me doing. Every single second that I'm not in class, eating, or working out with Imogen, Felix has me on the mountaintop, wielding. But as my aim improves and my strikes increase, the rest of the world seems to go to shit.

Xaden and I talk most nights through the bond, but he still broodily refuses to spend physical time alone with me.

The western line falls back, and dark wielders surge toward Draithus at a daily pace that has me holding my breath during every death roll. At this rate, they'll reach the city walls in a matter of weeks. Or they could change tactics and simply fly directly for the city.

The entire quadrant is well aware that we're in trouble when Xaden is called to Tyrrendor, and that pit of worry only grows with every day he's gone. Now that it's been more than ten days, I have a stack of letters for him to read, and Tairn is impossible to be around.

And Andarna simply…isn't around.

Exactly how long am I supposed to give her before I march into the Vale itself and demand she at least *talk* about what happened?

"You did well today," Imogen says, breaking through my spiraling thoughts as Aaric and Lynx enter the main campus from the Infantry Quadrant just ahead of us. Aaric's obnoxious guards stalk behind us as usual. "Though I wondered if Ridoc was going to take you down during that last match."

"Finally, I rise to Imogen's standard!" Ridoc says, falling behind so we can fit through the door.

Quinn laughs.

"Don't let it go to your head," Imogen lectures over her shoulder.

"Oh, he will," Rhi replies from my right with a smile that doesn't quite reach her eyes. It seems to be her permanent expression, since none of us—including Jesinia—have found anything to help Xaden. I hate that they're burdened with the truth.

Between Xaden's status, the western line retreating toward Draithus, and growing resentment between the Aretian riders and Navarrians over the debate of whether or not to open our borders, this whole place feels like a bow with its string pulled tight, just waiting for the order to be fired. And we're the arrows.

"Too bad Carr had to teach today," Sawyer says, walking behind us with Ridoc. He hasn't used the cane in a couple of weeks now, but no one is pushing him to wield.

"You keeping Tavis locked up in your bedroom or something, Cardulo?" Ridoc teases.

Imogen tenses, and her eyes calculate the cost of murder.

"Not worth it." I shake my head, then glance over my shoulder at Ridoc. "He's still in Draithus."

"Oh." His tone completely shifts. "When do you and Quinn head back out?" Third-years filling midland posts is becoming so common, it's practically a class.

Voices rise as we walk closer to the great hall.

"We're with you through the Aretian rotation," Quinn answers. "You're stuck with us for *weeks*," she teases.

Imogen's gaze slides my way. "No slacking on your training. Gym tonight."

"Oh, good, I was wondering when I'd get sore again," I retort. "We still leaving for Aretia the day after tomorrow?" I ask Rhi.

"Movement is at five a.m." She nods, then glances over to Sawyer. "Make a decision yet?"

"Working on it," he replies and flexes his jaw.

"All right." Rhi looks my way. "And I think Kaori, Felix, and Panchek are coming with as our leadership," she adds gently.

"Those three?" Not Xaden? My brows jump. Felix is understandable, and

Kaori's one of my favorite professors, but I suspect he's chosen to escort our group in hopes of seeing Andarna. And she's not in the mood to be seen. Maybe Xaden will already be there? At least for Sgaeyl and Tairn's sake.

"I'm sorry, I know you were hoping it would be—" Rhi starts.

"You will abide by the decision set forth!" a man shouts from the great hall.

Aaric tilts his head, then pauses just before the door, bringing the squad to an awkward stop.

"What are you do—" Lynx starts.

Aaric throws his arm across Lynx's chest and drags him back, bumping into Sawyer just before the door bursts open and the Duke of Calldyr flies through.

He lands on his ass in the middle of the carpet, tangled in his bejeweled overcoat.

Holy shit. My eyes widen.

"Say it again," Lewellen demands, marching through the doorway.

What is he doing here?

Every infantry guard steps off the wall, but Calldyr waves them away and climbs to his feet, raking a hand over his face and blond beard. "The desire of one province may never outweigh the good of the kingdom!"

Ah, Lewellen must be serving as proxy for Xaden's Senarium seat...but they usually meet in Calldyr. Are they here for a war council?

"I don't want to serve a kingdom that leaves civilians to die!" Lewellen snarls.

"You let them in, and there will be no kingdom to serve." Calldyr lifts his nose. "We have already weakened the outposts by stripping them of all but the necessary alloy, and look what that got us in Suniva. We have sent riders. *Lost* riders. What more would you have us do? Starve when we cannot feed double our current population?"

"You are a pretentious, spoiled child who has never known suffering a day in your—"

"Enough." Xaden walks through the door, and my heart stops. His gaze jumps to mine like a compass pulled north.

He's *here*. I drink in the sight of him, then swallow. Hard. The amber in his eyes seems brighter, but not lighter. A new, sharp ache spreads in my chest. Has he channeled from the earth again? Or are we on day sixty-six?

"The discussion is over," Xaden says, ripping his eyes from mine before passing by Lewellen on his way toward Calldyr. "You were informed as a courtesy. Tell the Senarium, don't tell them. I don't particularly care."

"You cannot." Calldyr retreats until his back rattles a shield display on the wall.

"And yet, I'm going to." Xaden stops a full two feet from Calldyr, but shadows curl at his feet and spread down the hall.

Calldyr notices, then glances at one of the shields like it might actually help him.

"Do we worry?" Rhi asks under her breath.

I catalog the anger in Xaden's eyes and shake my head. He's pissed, but he's him. Still, just in case, I watch the shadows, spotting the darkest one.

"I forbid it." Halden strides into the hallway, followed by two guards.

He's here, too? Oh, this is bad.

"I don't give a fuck." Xaden pivots so he can see both men.

"And *boom*, it's a show," Ridoc whispers.

"My money's on Riorson," Sawyer chimes in.

Halden glances our way, his gaze jumping from me to Aaric, then stiffens when he sees the rest of the squad. "This discussion is better had in private."

"This discussion is over," Xaden counters.

"Ooh, he used the wingleader voice," Ridoc says under his breath.

"You will *not* open your borders!" Halden's face blotches.

Tyrrendor is going to take in civilians? My chest constricts and warms all in the same second. *"I love you."*

"I will do as I damn well please with *my* province." Xaden's eyes narrow dangerously on Halden. *"Even if I'm about to start another revolution?"*

"Especially then."

"*Your* province?" Halden squares his shoulders. "It's *my* kingdom!"

"Yes, you're first in line to rule a large amount of territory," Xaden agrees. "But I rule mine *now*. Draithus has *weeks* before they attack, and Tyrrendor will open her borders. We will take any and all Poromish civilians willing to climb the Medaro Pass. Would you truly condemn thirty thousand people to die?"

Draithus has weeks? What new intel has come in?

Mira. I sway, and Rhiannon grabs hold of my elbow, steadying me.

"You're choosing their people over ours?" Halden's fists curl.

"They are not endangering our people," Lewellen argues. "This is not a them or us situation. They are not risking our wards, nor are they raiding—"

"You don't have to defend my decision," Xaden interrupts, turning his full focus to Halden. "We're opening our borders."

"Will you be quite so sure of yourself when I bring my troops into Tyrrendor?" Halden threatens.

He wouldn't fucking *dare*.

Every cadet around me straightens, even Aaric.

The shadows darken and emotion drains from Xaden's eyes, leaving only cold, cruel calculation as he takes a single step toward Halden. "You are *a* prince, not *the* prince. Bring your troops into Tyrrendor, and Aaric will suddenly find himself first in line for the throne."

Fuck.

Guards draw their swords.

"Get off the ice," I shout down the bond, and scalding power surges within me.

"Not smart to threaten a prince. And Cam?" Halden's gaze swings our way. "What *does* my little brother have to say about this?"

"Aaric," Aaric corrects him. "And I'm on his side." He gestures to Xaden. "Aretian, remember? And unless Riorson here is going to sign another provincial commitment, I believe I'm under *his* chain of command now, as are probably a third of your *troops*."

Halden's jaw flexes once. Twice. Then he glares at Xaden. "You've been warned."

"And you've been informed," Xaden replies in a tone that makes me fear for Halden's existence.

Halden pivots on his heel and storms past us, his guards and Calldyr on his heels.

"Proud of you." Lewellen thumps his fist against Xaden's shoulder and heads toward the hall. "I'm going to tell the others."

"We're taking civilians?" I slip past Lynx to get to Xaden. *"Come back to me."*

His cold eyes glance my way, chilling my blood, and then he does a double take.

"We are." He nods, his voice softening. He blinks hard twice, like he's at war with himself, and then the shadows dissipate and the ice in his gaze thaws. He's back. "Not that it will do them much good. A wyvern made it halfway to Aretia yesterday before falling out of the sky. A dozen more tried—" He pauses. "Your rotation should be fine, but we don't have long. A month at most."

That's horrifically sooner than Mira estimated.

"The riot can stay in Aretia—" I start.

"We'll all stay," Rhi agrees.

"No." Xaden shakes his head. "It was one thing to take cadets to Aretia when we were a relatively safe distance from combat, but it's another to keep them there if we become the front lines."

"But—" I pause as whisps of shadow spread from behind me in an unfamiliar pattern.

Maren gasps.

"What the fuck?" Ridoc whispers.

Xaden glances behind me, and his eyes flare.

"That's not possible," Imogen says.

I turn around, reaching for a dagger, and freeze completely.

Lynx stands in the middle of the hallway, shaking from head to foot, staring at the darkness that envelops his hands.

"It's all right." Rhiannon rushes to Lynx's side. "Breathe. You're just…"

"Manifesting," Xaden says, putting himself in front of Lynx. "Don't be scared. They're defending you. Fear. Anger. Whatever it is, level out your emotions, and they'll recede."

Manifesting? *Shadows?*

"I can't—" Lynx shakes his head, and the shadows creep up his arms.

"You can," Xaden assures him. "Close your eyes and think of the place you feel safest. Go ahead."

Lynx slams his eyes shut.

"Good job. Now breathe deeply and picture yourself there. Calm. Happy. Safe." Xaden watches as the shadows recede.

Lynx's breaths even out, and his hands reappear.

"Get him to Carr *now*," Xaden orders Rhiannon, and she nods.

The squad ushers Lynx down the hall, but I stay behind, shock gluing my feet to the carpet. "I don't understand. You're our generation's shadow wielder."

"Not anymore. Magic knows." Xaden's shoulders dip as he turns slowly to face me, his brow scrunching in apology before he schools his features. *"He's the balance."*

A chill runs down my spine.

"I should…go." His voice comes out like it's been scraped over hot coals. "Aetos asked me to resign my professorship due to my extended absence on provincial matters, and for once, I agree with him, especially after seeing that. I shouldn't be here."

He doesn't mean to his room. He means *leaving*.

Panic seizes my heartbeat. "Stay." I reach for him, but he shakes his head and retreats a step. "Please," I whisper, more than aware of the guards stationed down the hallway. *"Please stay with me. Fight for the future that's beyond all this. Sixty-six days, right?"*

He can't leave, not now. Not like this. Not when the hope has drained from his eyes.

"I'm needed in Lewellen. Melgren's demanded we double our Talladium output for alloy, which is straining the miners, and there's unrest after that conscription announcement. There's more to Tyrrendor than just Aretia." He glances left, toward the nearest window. *"I told you—control is just prolonging the inevitable. Maybe stability is a fool's hope."*

Lewellen is beyond the wards, unless we've moved two cases of daggers there I don't know about. If he leaves the wards in this state of mind…

"You have an entire assembly to help with that." I move, putting myself in his line of sight. *"You can't give up. I don't care if Lynx manifested shadows. You have to fight. If you won't do it for yourself, then you do it for me."*

His gaze snaps to mine.

"What happens to me if you turn?" My hands curl at my sides. *"What happens to Tairn and Sgaeyl if you give in?"*

Xaden's jaw flexes.

"Do venin get once-a-week visits?" I take a step closer and lift my chin. *"Does their bond survive you turning? Does ours? You and I are tethered for life, Xaden Riorson. Am I expected to turn with you? Is that the only way to keep our dragons alive if you give up?"*

A thousand emotions flit across his face...and then they're gone.

He's on the ice.

My stomach flips.

"Stay," I demand. "Or meet me in Aretia. The man I love stays. He fights."

"Riorson?" Lewellen asks from the doorway of the great hall. "Luceras wants a word regarding mining production."

"You have to accept what I already have," Xaden says to me. "The man you love no longer fully belongs to himself." He walks past Lewellen into the great hall, taking my heart with him.

I just fought with every weapon in my arsenal, and it wasn't enough.

My shoulders slump in defeat as I lean against the wall.

"I'm not entirely sure what that was about, but I've seen how hard it can be to love someone in power." Lewellen grimaces sympathetically. "Wearing a title like his can sometimes feel like you're a fraying rope, being continuously ripped apart between what you personally want and what your people need."

"What about what he needs?" I ask.

Lewellen pauses, as though choosing his words carefully. "He needs *you* to keep him from fraying, which can sometimes mean putting what *you* want— or need—aside for the good of the province. It's horribly unfair to ask that of anyone, let alone the first lightning wielder in a century." Lewellen's voice softens. "I have the utmost respect for you, Cadet Sorrengail, but this is a crucial time that will determine the path of the province for the next millennium. Your purpose is as great as his in a wholly separate arena, and if that purpose makes it impossible for you to be what Tyrrendor needs—"

"Tyrrendor, not Xaden?" I'm fighting for both, but he doesn't know that. To his ears, he stumbled into an argument where I just asked Xaden to stay with me instead of tending to Tyrrish business.

A guard shifts, reminding us both that we're not alone.

"They are now one and the same." He says it with such kindness it's hard to be angry. "You are both so young, with such formidable signets. And if you choose not to adapt to the changes his title brings—" He stops himself, then sighs. "I just hope you two will figure out the balance between it all."

Like hell am I giving him up, even though nothing about what he laid out sounds equal or *balanced.*

"By balance, you mean Tyrrendor comes first, Xaden second, our relationship fights for third, and my personal needs are a matter of convenience." Saying it aloud puts it all in harsh perspective.

"Something like that." Sadness pulls at the corners of his mouth.

"Xaden comes first for me." It comes out so self-sacrificial that I half expect my mother to appear and smack me upside the back of my head. "Just so we're clear. But I will never stop being the woman he fell in love with in order to morph into whatever doormat you *think* he requires. We're already balanced because we're *both* strong for ourselves and each other. He needs me to be *me*, and I'm telling you I promised to help keep Tyrrendor safe, but *not* at his expense."

"He'll say the same about you. It's what makes your relationship so dangerous." He sighs. "Like I said, it's hard to love someone in power, and that goes both ways." He slips back into the hall and shuts the door.

But Xaden isn't *in* power. He *is* power.

And he's slipping.

"Let me know if he leaves," I tell Tairn, and then I head to class.

Xaden flies out two hours later.

A dragon determines its last flight, and its rider's.

—ARTICLE ONE, SECTION TWO
THE DRAGON RIDER'S CODEX

CHAPTER
FORTY-SEVEN

"You're sure you only want me here the first time you try this?" I ask Sawyer two days later as we stand in the middle of the flight field with Tairn, Andarna, and Sliseag at four thirty a.m. "I'm not exactly the best one to catch you if this goes poorly."

He tightens the straps on his pack. "No, but you're the only one I want seeing if I fall on my ass."

"Or going for help if you break your leg?"

A small smile plays across his mouth. "Let's hope that doesn't happen."

"Do you want to talk about this?" I gesture to Sliseag.

"Thanks, but I've been talking to Jesinia. I'm ready. I need *you* for the more practical side of…this." He nods toward Sliseag, then crouches down, then pulls a lever on the inside of his prosthesis. A flat, two-inch-wide piece of metal with a curved end pops out of the toe of his boot. "And it's not my first time. I need a second opinion because it didn't go so well for me yesterday."

"You made that?" It's pretty damned cool.

"Yeah." He stands, then stares at Sliseag's left front leg. The Red Swordtail is smaller than Sgaeyl, but his talons are still enormous given what Sawyer's about to try. "His scale pattern in this one row doesn't overlap." He points upward. "And in theory, the hook should just catch the top of each scale as I climb, but I can't get there without fall—"

Sliseag lifts his head over us and breathes out a huff of steam that I'm going to have to wipe off my goggles.

Ugh. It's too early to be sticky.

"I wasn't talking *about* you," Sawyer argues. "It's not like we haven't discussed the scale pattern, and you don't have to—"

Sliseag steams us again, the heat stinging my face. If he gets it any hotter, he's going to blister my skin.

Tairn stalks forward and tilts his head at Sliseag in a way I never want to see aimed at me, and Andarna is quick to follow.

"Because I don't want you to have to!" Sawyer shouts up at Sliseag, who narrows his eyes.

This would be a really ridiculous way to die.

"He wouldn't dare," Tairn warns.

"Just let me try it," Sawyer argues.

Sliseag bares his teeth.

Sawyer bares his right back.

"I will never understand the relationships other riders have with their dragons," I say down the bond. I barely understand my own, but giving Andarna a wide berth seems to be working, since she's here. Not that she could stay behind for the length of our rotation, but I'm declaring it a victory.

"You're not supposed to," Tairn remarks.

"Here we go." Sawyer rolls his shoulders, then runs toward Sliseag's claw.

He makes it two steps before the tip of his boot catches in the mud and he falls forward.

Shit. I lunge for his pack and grab hold with both hands, yanking Sawyer upright before he yucks a set of flight leathers. My shoulders both pop, but the joints have the decency not to subluxate on me.

"Thanks," Sawyer mutters, staring at the boot. "See?"

"I do." I crouch to peer at the device. "Can you kick the lever open?"

"In theory," he answers. "But it's probably a little small for that, and I don't have time to make changes before movement today."

"Well, let's try it as it is. You can modify in Aretia. None of us want you to stay behind." Mud squishes under my boots as I stand. "You can run, right?"

Sawyer nods. "I wouldn't try this if I couldn't. My gait is off because I can't quite get the flex right, and I'm just not nimble enough to run the full length of his leg like I used to."

"We can work with that." I nod. "How about you run just like you'd mount before, and right when you feel your momentum shift, like you're about to fall back, kick the lever open. It should catch your foot just like you designed it to, and you climb the rest of the way."

Sawyer looks down at me. "That's how you did the Gauntlet, isn't it?"

"Kind of. I waited until I felt my weight shift backward, then stabbed a dagger into the wood and pulled myself up. But I somehow doubt Sliseag would be appreciative of that approach." A corner of my mouth lifts.

Sliseag huffs another breath—this time without steam—as if in agreement.

"I'll give it a shot." Sawyer pops the lever closed, then nods to himself. "Here we go." He takes off running, and Sliseag flexes his talons, flattening his claw. Sawyer's long legs eat up the first half dozen feet of the climb, and I hold my breath when his progress stalls.

He kicks the lever, then clings to Sliseag's leg about halfway up, his foot scraping the scales for a place to grip for a heart-stopping second before it catches.

"You've got it!" I shout. "Climb!"

His left boot holds steady, working as he'd designed, but his right slips, leaving a streak of mud down Sliseag's red scales.

My chest clenches as he tries again, then again, with the same result.

"Fuck!" he yells, then lays his forehead against Sliseag's leg.

"I can flatten the tip of my tail and boost him," Andarna offers, having crept closer.

Now my ribs tighten for a whole different reason. It's the first positive thing she's said since our return.

"That's an honorable offer," I tell her, then repeat it to Sawyer.

"No!" he shouts. "Thank you, but no."

Sliseag rumbles low in his chest, and I stand there helplessly, knowing there's nothing I can do.

"Because it's not the same," Sawyer argues, frustration rumbling through his tone and I know he isn't talking to me. "You're the one who took a risk on me, and I won't ask you to dishonor…" He falls quiet.

"Is that how you feel when you dip your shoulder for me?" I ask Tairn. *"Dishonored?"*

"I am the second-largest dragon on the Continent and a revered warrior. My tales are legendary. My mate unparalleled. My feats unmatched—"

"Doesn't change my question." I cut him off before he starts to list his accolades.

"It would take a great deal more than a change of posture to dishonor me," he replies.

"But you never had to lower yourself before me, did you? Not for Naolin, or—"

"We do not speak of the one who came before." Agonizing pain floods the bond, and I immediately regret my choice of words.

Andarna lifts her head and narrows her accusing golden eyes at me.

"I know." I put my hands up in the universal sign of surrender.

"You know that's not how I feel about it," Sawyer says as his arms start to tremble. "We've been over this! Any rider would have done the same in my position." He shakes his head and reaches for the next scale, then pulls himself upward, gaining a foot of hard-fought distance. "Of course I don't blame you! That's not—" His head whips sideways, toward Sliseag's. "No, I'm not punishing— For Amari's sake, will you just let me get a word in?"

From the silence that follows, Sliseag does not comply.

I shift my weight as my pack grows heavier by the minute, and my lower spine stops whining and starts shouting.

"Because my leg was and still is worth your life!" Sawyer snaps when he can't reach the joint of the next scale. "Of course you're allowed to feel the same—" His hand slides back to its previous hold. "Oh."

Sliseag huffs, then extends his left leg, sliding his claw through the mud. Slowly, it lowers to a walkable degree of incline.

My throat tightens as Sawyer lets go and slowly rises. He extends his arms outward, like a cadet on Parapet, then trudges upward step by step as I catch movement in my peripheral vision.

"Your year-mates arrive," Tairn says.

I keep my eyes locked on Sawyer as he reaches the top of Sliseag's shoulder and lowers his arms. His next movements look like a routine he's performed thousands of times, and with a few quick steps, he finds the seat.

Sliseag rises to his full height as Sawyer settles in, and I back away for a better view.

"Looks like you've been up there a time or two," I call to him as he relaxes in the seat.

"Feels like I never left," he shouts down with a grin. "I can ride."

"You can ride," I agree, my smile instant and wide. "Now, does it matter how you got there, or only that he chose you?"

"You know the answer to that already." His smile softens.

"I do." I nod, then turn to Andarna, narrowing the pathway to just her. *"Look at me."*

She spares me a glance.

"You can grieve." If my words don't work, maybe *hers* will.

Golden eyes lock on mine.

"You can grieve," I repeat. *"And when and if you're ready to talk about it, I'll be here."*

"You do not talk about your grief," she counters. *"Neither does he."* Her tail flicks in Tairn's direction.

She has a point. *"I'm getting there,"* I say slowly. *"And he's not perfect, either."*

Her nostrils flare and her scales shimmer to the purple-toned black she usually prefers.

I nod and let the subject drop, but it definitely feels like progress.

"Thank Amari," Rhi whispers as she comes up on my left side, grinning up at Sawyer.

"Sawyer! Look at you!" Ridoc runs forward, his arms up in victory.

Sliseag swings his head and snaps his teeth shut a few feet in front of Ridoc.

"Look at you from a distance!" Ridoc retreats, his arms still held high. When he bumps into Maren, he turns and sweeps her into a hug as she laughs.

"I couldn't help," Rhi says quietly as Sawyer focuses on reacquainting himself with the seat. "Did I fail him?"

"No. You were exactly who he needed you to be." I slip my arm through hers. Fuck, this pack is *heavy*. "You're our friend, but you're also our squad leader. He doesn't want to fall in front of you; none of us do. We want to make you proud. And I know you're used to being responsible for us, and you're truly exceptional at your job…"

Ridoc puts Maren down, then reaches for Cat, who accepts his hug with straight arms and an annoyed eye roll.

"But?" Rhi glances at me sideways.

"But you couldn't have made this happen any faster." We walk toward the others. "Not you, or me, or Ridoc, or Jesinia. It was always down to the two of them. It was only ever going to be on their timeline."

Ridoc spins toward Neve, and the third-year flier looks at him like he's grown another set of eyeballs as she dodges his embrace and bumps into Bragen. He whirls toward Imogen, who puts up her hand as she walks by with Quinn.

"Don't even think about it, Gamlyn," she warns.

"You're so warm and fuzzy!" Quinn says, slinging her arm around Imogen's shoulders.

"Only to you." She looks up at Sawyer. "Nice to see you where you belong, Henrick!"

Ridoc spins and throws his arms around Dain, who lifts his brows, then slowly brings his hand up and pats Ridoc's back twice in an awkward exchange. "Looking good, Sawyer!" Dain calls up, then continues on toward Cath.

"Good job, Matthias," Bodhi says to Rhi as he walks by. "Got your cadet back in the seat."

"I didn't—" she starts, and I squeeze her arm with mine. "He did it himself, but we're proud of him. Thank you, section leader."

Bodhi nods with a smile that looks so close to Xaden's my whole rib cage draws tight. Neither Bodhi nor Dain had a chance to take the rune course because of their duty schedules and our failed mission, so we get them both on our rotation.

"Look at him!" Ridoc races our way and smooshes us in a hug. "All is right with the world!" His arms slacken and he draws back, his gaze soaked in apology. "I mean, other than what's going on with Riorson."

"I know what you meant." I shift my pack and force a smile. "And hopefully, I'll see him there."

Hope stows away like a little windproof passenger as we launch for Aretia, and somehow lives through the night when we make camp just inside the Tyrrish border. Have to admit, it's freeing to fly without worry that we're about to be spotted by a wyvern patrol or found by Theophanie. Only once we're sure the gryphons can still handle the altitude after being gone for months do we start the final leg of the trip, entering the lone protection of the Aretian wards.

Landing in the valley above Aretia that evening feels like coming home, but Xaden isn't here. Or Sgaeyl isn't, which means the same thing.

"This sucks," I tell Tairn with a heavy sigh.

He growls in agreement.

Andarna snaps at Kaori when he walks a little too close over Panchek's blustering protest, then takes off after a herd of sheep as I dismount from Tairn.

"I'm sorry," the professor says, knitting his dark, slashing brows. "I didn't mean—"

"You did," I interrupt. "And I sympathize with why you've come, but she's not going to let you study her. Not even here."

"I understand." Kaori nods, then looks around the high hanging valley with its lush green foliage and snow-tipped peaks. "Selfishly, I also wanted to see how this Empyrean functions. I suspect it's why Panchek has tagged along as well."

A smile tugs at my mouth. "Good luck asking them."

"You ready?" Rhiannon asks as she approaches with footsteps that border on bouncing.

"Yeah." I flat-out grin at my friend's happiness. "Let's get down there so you can see your family."

"I'd prefer we hold formation—" Dain starts as he comes up on my right.

Rhiannon and I both level a look on him.

"—tomorrow morning," he quickly corrects course. "Family first, and all."

"Family first," Rhiannon agrees with a quick smile, and he passes by, heading toward the rocky path down to the house. "I get that he has to come for rune training, too, but why our squad?" Rhi whispers.

"Same reason I'm here." Bodhi pops up on our left and lifts his face to the sun like he's greeting an old friend. "This is the best squad."

"I forgot how fucking hot this place is," Ridoc says, unbuttoning his flight jacket.

"It's a hatching ground," Rhiannon reminds him with a wide grin. "I bet it's almost the same temperature as the Vale with how many dragons are here now."

"We beat the storm, but I bet it lowers the temperature tomorrow." I flick the buttons open on my jacket, well aware I'll be freezing the second we cross the magical barrier that defines this territory as the hatching grounds.

Sure enough, it's glacial by the time we make it down to Riorson House.

Gods, just the sight of it makes me miss him.

The squad files past the guards and through the front doors, into the massive entryway that looks up five full stories set into the mountain like giant steps. It's quiet for this time of day. Or maybe it just seems empty because the halls are no longer bustling with cadets.

Kaori turns around with a stunned look of disbelief.

Felix pats him on the back, then says something to Rhiannon before leading Kaori away.

"Eyes on me!" Rhiannon's voice echoes, earning everyone's attention. "Find your bunks as previously assigned. The night is yours to do what you want, but formation is at seven tomorrow, so I'd think twice about finding a tavern."

We break and climb the first flight of stairs.

"Let's get out of here as quickly as possible," Rhi tells Maren just ahead of me.

"I can't wait to see my brothers." Maren claps excitedly, light catching on the long silver scar on the back of her hand. Pretty sure there's not a single one of us who has come through the last few years unmarked in some way. "Cat, are you coming?"

"I wouldn't mind seeing the little terrors," she says with a nod as we reach the landing.

"Vi?" Rhi asks over her shoulder.

"Sure," I answer with a quick nod. "I love your family."

"Sawyer and I are going, too." Ridoc heads up to the third floor.

"All right," Rhi calls up the stairs as she climbs. "Whoever wants to go to my house, we meet in the foyer in forty minutes, which should give you a chance to bathe and change. My mother will boot you out of her house if you walk in smelling like sulfur, and I'm not even kidding."

I pause on the landing, my gaze flickering from the steps ahead to the hallway on my left.

"Please don't tell me you're lost," Bodhi says, coming up the steps last.

"Of course not." I shake my head slowly. "It's just that I don't have a room here, and I'm not sure where I should sleep."

He scoffs and gestures down the hall. "You have a room. It hasn't moved."

"It's his room," I correct him quietly. "And he's all broody."

"We're home, Vi. Act like it." He grins, then turns around me, walking backward down the hallway on the right. "Sleep in your bed. He'll just brood harder if you don't."

I sigh when he disappears into his room, and then turn left and head to mine—ours.

The handle won't turn, so I flick my wrist and picture the mechanism opening, using lesser magic to unlock it.

Walking in is surreal. Magic tingles across my skin when I step through the wards. It looks just like we left it in December, except most of our things are now at Basgiath. After shutting the door, I swing my pack from my shoulders and set it on the chair Xaden waited in for all those days while I slept after being stabbed over Resson.

The bedding is the same dark blue, the curtains beside the massive windows are open to the evening light, and every book in his collection is exactly where it belongs on the built-in shelves to my right.

There are a few pitiful attempts at tempered runes on the desk, left from my last lesson, along with a forgotten notebook in the top drawer. I check the armoire and find one of my sweaters, a uniform for each of us, and the blanket his mother made him tucked up in the right-hand corner.

And *gods*, does it smell like him. My chest threatens to split straight open at the sudden, acute stab of pure longing. I've left my mark here, too. The bathing chamber still smells like the soap I use on my hair, and I find the bar right where I left it. I take a few minutes to clean up, then dress in a fresh uniform, half expecting Xaden to walk in at any second and ask me about my day.

It's almost like this room is removed from time itself, a tiny corner of the world where we simultaneously live together yet don't. The only indication months have passed is the glass box from Zehyllna on his nightstand, and the emerald-hilted Blade of Aretia resting within. It's missing a single stone near the top, but looks no worse for wear after having been in Navarrian possession for six hundred years.

Someone knocks on the door, and I glance at the clock. Has it already been forty minutes?

I swing open the door and find Brennan on the other side. His eyes are tired, but his smile is bright as he gives me the standard sibling once-over.

Can't help it—I do it, too, coming away satisfied that he's not wearing any new scars.

"Pull me in." He holds out his hand. "He fucked with the wards the last time he was here."

"Of course he did." I grab my brother's hand and pull him through. He immediately yanks me into a hug.

I soak up the rare moment of peace until he steps back, having lost his smile some time in the last ten seconds. "Do you need anything mended?"

"No." I shake my head.

"Are you sure? Because every time you show up here you're an inch from death." He studies me like I might be lying.

"I'm sure."

"Good." He kicks the door closed. "Sound shield only works with the door shut, right?"

"Right." I retreat a few steps in apprehension. "What's wrong?"

Brennan's face falls, and he stares at the ground. "I can't mend him."

"I have no idea who you're talking about." I lift my brows in utter confusion. "We're all healthy. No one was hurt on the way here."

He looks up, and the sorrow in his eyes sends me staggering backward. "Xaden. I can't mend him, Vi. I tried every day that he was here last week."

I struggle to draw adequate breath. "You know."

"I know." He nods once. "He must be further along than Jack had been when Nolon started working with him. I'm so sorry."

That unit of measurement is unfathomable. "Me too."

"We tried silent offerings in every local temple, pushing magic back into the earth, even sitting with the eggs in the hatching grounds. We've tried everything either of us could think of, though the letter he sent from Lewellen yesterday had a weird—" He looks at me like I've grown horns. "Are you...smiling?"

"Yesterday?" I don't even try to fight the hopeful little curve.

Brennan nods. "He wants to try mending *the spot* at Basgiath."

"Good idea." There's nothing small about my grin now.

He might be broody, but he hasn't given up.

472 AU, Willhaven, Braevick: With the exception of one house, the village was desiccated overnight by a single venin estimated to be a Sage. The only adult amongst the three survivors described her as, "Astonishingly ageless. Hair as black as the day we married, but in place of the age lines I'd expected were bulging scarlet veins branching outward from her red-ringed eyes."

—THE RESURGENCE OF EVIL, A TIMELINE, BY PIERSON HALIWELL

CHAPTER
FORTY-EIGHT

Thunder rattles my bedroom windows the next night as I pore over the pages of the latest book Tecarus sent, letting my hair dry.

He hasn't forgotten our deal even now that he's king, and I'm not giving up on Xaden, especially when it's clear he hasn't given up on himself. The answer is out there somewhere, and we'll find it. Having Brennan in the know only bolsters that hope. Maybe he can't mend Xaden, but there's never been a problem my brother couldn't solve.

I glance over at the mess of practice runes on my desk and momentarily debate working on the delayed-activation rune Trissa spent most of the afternoon drilling into us. Its purpose is to take an existing, dormant rune and turn it "on" by tempering more magic into it. Its actual use? Nothing, since I can't make the damned thing work.

Cat got it right on the first try.

Imogen followed quickly after.

Kai singed the ends of his spiky black hair.

Dain, Bodhi, Rhi, Ridoc...everyone eventually mastered one except me. Even Aaric, who has yet to manifest a signet, managed the intricacy of the lesser magic.

Whatever. We're here for two weeks. Eventually I'll get it right, and if I don't, then that's why we work in squads. I don't have to be good at everything.

I tug the perpetually slipping strap of my Deverelli silk nightdress back up my shoulder and flip the page in Tecarus's book. My brows rise at the next passage I read, and I go over it once more to be sure I've caught on to a pattern. *That makes three.*

Thunder sounds again, and power rises within me like it's been called by a friend to come play. I watch the rain that seems to be coming in sideways from the east, then grab the conduit off my nightstand and let it flow.

Felix graduated the alloy in the center to the same size as those that power the daggers, and I may as well multitask and get his homework done while I read. Dunne knows he's going to expect at least three of them to be imbued before hauling me up the mountains tomorrow for yet more practice. He's training me like I'm the only thing standing between the venin and Aretia, and with the wards declining every day, I can't fault him. With Xaden handling province matters in Lewellen, I'm the best we've got against Theophanie...at least offensively.

Someone knocks at my bedroom door.

I close the book and stash it on my nightstand with the conduit, then climb off my bed to answer the door. It's after ten, which means it's either Rhi wanting to chat like last night or Brennan looking for a partner to raid the kitchens. Either way, this gown is practically see-through, so I grab a robe from the armoire on my way.

Glittering onyx taps against my shields a breath away from the threshold, and I abandon the robe's tie to yank open the door. My heartbeat stutters, then *flies.*

Xaden stands in the doorway in flight leathers, soaked to the bone, rain dripping from his hair. War rages in his eyes, like this is both the last and only place he wants to be.

"Hi." My hand flexes on the door handle. *"Why didn't you tell me he was here?"* I ask Tairn.

"You didn't ask to be made aware of his arrival, only his departure."

Fucking semantics.

"Tell me to go, and I will," Xaden says, his voice coming out like it's been scraped over coals. "It's only been seventy-three days."

"Come here." I let the handle go and step back to make space. "You must be freez—"

One second he's standing in the hallway, and the next, his hands are in my hair and his mouth is on mine.

Gods, *yes.* His lips are cold, but his tongue is deliciously warm as it strokes into my mouth. The kiss wakes up every nerve ending in my body and reminds me just how long it's been since Deverelli. Between traveling, our close confines with other riders, and his fear of losing control, it's been too many weeks since I've felt his skin against mine.

One kiss from him is all it takes for power to hum along my skin, for need to override any and all thoughts besides *closer* and *more*. It's always *closer* and *more* when it comes to him.

The door shuts somewhere in the background and I hear the click of a lock, the thud of his pack hitting the floor, the drag of wet leather as he undoes the clasp of his back scabbard, then slides it over his shoulders, never once breaking the kiss. He takes my mouth just like he did the first time, wholly, completely, like he's given himself permission to be reckless and he's going to make the most of it.

He sucks my tongue into his mouth, and I whimper at the frenzy whipping through me, at how much I've missed the physical contact between us. My hands rise to his chest, and the chill of his jacket sends a shiver down my back. How long was he flying in that storm? I push gently. "Wait."

He immediately pauses, lifting his head just enough to look in my eyes. "I shouldn't be here, I know. Not yet, at least."

"That isn't what I meant." I slip my fingers between the buttons of his flight jacket and hold on to the fabric like we can solve every problem in the world if he just stays in this room with me. "Of course you should be here. I just thought you were in Lewellen."

"I was." His focus drops to my lips and heats so quickly that I almost regret stopping him. "Then I launched for Tirvainne and ended up in our home." The words come slowly, like they're being ripped from him. "Or at least it will be after you graduate and we're both assigned here."

"It's already home." My pulse jumps. I can't remember the last time he talked about the future with anything but dread. "You flew nine hours in the wrong direction," I tease, undoing the top button of his flight jacket, then the next.

"Well-the-fuck-aware," he whispers with a hint of a smirk. "I'd been pissed and skating that mental ice in Lewellen—but I held my shit together instead of punching the two men who raised me after Dad died." He searches my eyes like I might condemn him for the admission, but I simply work my way down his buttons and listen. "We were beyond the wards, but I didn't reach for any form of power because even in that state, I knew it could take me back to day zero, and day zero doesn't give me *you*. I clawed my way back to myself and left."

"You kept your control." Pride has a smile tugging at my mouth as I free his last button.

He nods. "I'm not ignoring my fate. I know there will come a point in time where I'll become more *it* than me." He swallows. "But as dangerous as hope is, you're right—I have to fight for this. I think I'm stable for now, and I know it's only day seventy—"

"What is this magical number you have?" Gods help me if we're looking at triple digits.

He tucks my hair behind my ears. "Seventy-six. It's twice Barlowe's longest stretch without draining after his first significant channeling—the cliff incident. I didn't want to get your hopes up, but I figure that making it seventy-six days will indicate that I can stall the progression."

I blink. "Three days?" My hopes don't just rise; they soar.

"I told myself I'd wait until day seventy-six to show up at your door, but Sgaeyl changed course once I realized if I could keep control beyond the wards..." He leans in, hovering inches above my mouth.

"Then you can keep control with me?" I shamelessly finish the sentence the way I want it to end. My breath catches when icy-cold water drips onto my collarbone, doing nothing to dispel the rising temperature of my body this close to his.

"Under the right circumstances." He nods, then retreats a step, stripping off his soaked flight jacket, and I follow suit, shrugging out of my robe so the garments hit the floor at the same time. "This might be as good as it gets, and I want every single second we—" He stops mid-sentence as his gaze rakes over the full length of me with blatant, palpable hunger, warming every inch of my skin that it touches. "Oh *fuck*," he groans.

"What would those circumstances be?" My heart starts to race. Whatever he wants, whatever he needs, it's his. I'm his.

"Are you wearing..." He lifts a hand toward me, then pulls it back, clenching his fist.

"The nightdress you had made for me? Yes. Don't get distracted. What circumstances?" I repeat, then drag my tongue over my swollen lower lip. That kiss wasn't nearly enough. I'm starved for him, and if he's ready, I'm happily willing to feast.

"Not distracted. Obsessed. You look..." His eyes darken as he studies my curves like he's never seen them. "Maybe we should wait until day seventy-six." He retreats and reaches for the door handle.

Absolutely *not*.

"Open that door, and I'll pin the edge of your pants to the wood and leave you there for the next three days." I glance meaningfully at my daggers on the dresser. "We can curl up in our bed and just sleep if that's what you want, but please stop running from me."

"I *definitely* don't want to sleep." He pushes off the door, and my pulse thrums as he consumes the distance between us. "And I'm entirely incapable of running from you." His fingers spear through the hair at the nape of my neck and he tugs, tilting my face toward his. "Even when I'm not entirely...me, whatever I am still craves you, needs you, only wants *you.*"

That's a feeling I'm more than familiar with.

"I love you, too." I brace my hands on his chest, my fingertips grazing the patches of soaked fabric near his collar as I surge up onto my toes and kiss him. The need that had simmered comes back in a rush twice as strong, and what starts as soft and sweet turns mind-blowingly hot in a matter of seconds. Our tongues twine, our hands roam, and everything outside this room slips away, overpowered by what really matters: us.

He hooks a hand around the back of my thigh, then lifts. The world spins, and I find the wall at my back as he raises his head. "If I loved you in the way you deserve to be loved, I'd ignore that you're the only form of peace I've ever known and put a thousand miles between us because *stable* still isn't *whole.*" His gaze drops to my mouth. "Instead, I'm here plotting, thinking of every possible way to mitigate the threat I pose so I can tear this very translucent silk from your incredible body and bury myself inside you."

"Yes, please." I push the thought down the bond and wrap my legs around his waist, gasping at the chill that meets my thighs.

"Violet." His moan fills my mind as he stares at me, flexing his jaw.

"I decide what I deserve." Right now, my body definitely knows it deserves him. I lock my ankles and accept the cold with a small shiver. I'll have him warm in no time. "What risks I'm willing to take. Now, *what* circumstances, Xaden?"

"I'm making you cold." His brow furrows a second before he reaches behind his head and tugs his shirt off.

Mine. *All* mine.

"And yet you somehow think you could possibly hurt me." My arms wind around his neck as the shirt hits the floor, my entire body drawing tight at his bare chest and that scar above his heart. I want to lick every line of his torso. "Tell me what you need so I can have you."

He palms my waist, then dips his head and sets his mouth to my neck. "Fuck, you smell good."

"It's just soap." Then my mind turns to mush and my head falls back against the stone. Each press of his mouth is a shot of electricity that floods my bloodstream, mixing with my power and pooling between my thighs.

"It's just you." He kisses up the side of my throat, then down my jawline until his lips hover over mine. "I need you to give me the one thing you love breaking."

I force my brain to work through the haze of lust he's creating. "Control."

"Control." He nods.

"Done." I suck on his lower lip and then graze my teeth across it as I let go. "You have it already anyway." I'm as malleable as putty the second he puts his hands on me.

"If you only knew." He shakes his head and slides his fingers up over my ribs to cup my breast. My breath stutters as he drags the silk of my nightdress over my sensitive nipple again and again. "My control when it comes to you is an illusion. You are the temple where I worship. I live for the clench of your thighs, your breathy little cries, the feel of you coming around my cock, and above all else, the sound of my favorite three words from this mouth." His thumb skims my lips before he cradles the back of my head and looks into my eyes. "Keeping my hands off you has been the feat of my *life*, and you have the power to shred my discipline with a single fucking touch."

I *melt* and arch into his hand. It's a good thing he has me pinned against the wall, because I know my knees would have given out halfway through that confession, let alone what he's doing with his fingers. "Don't touch you. Got it."

"Do you?" Bands of shadow stream over his shoulders to wrap around my wrists, and a heartbeat later, my hands are anchored to the wall above my head. "Is this something you can take if I need it?"

The shadows flow over my palms and through my fingers in a continuous caress that steals my breath.

"Yes." I swallow hard. "It's disturbingly hot, actually."

A corner of his mouth rises into a slow smile, and bands of shadow stroke over my legs like hands, pushing my hemline up my thighs. "I'll keep that in mind."

My back bows as those shadows firm along my inner thigh. He hasn't so much as lifted a finger to wield. He's doing all of this with his mind. The casual display of power is even hotter. "What else? Because if you don't actually start touching me soon, I'm going to do it myself and make you watch."

"We should have done that months ago." His eyes flare, and he rolls my nipple between his thumb and forefinger.

"That feels so damned good." My hips rock against him. He's hard and right *fucking* there, just a few layers of fabric away from where I desperately need him.

He covers the peak of my breast with his mouth, using the wisp of silk and his teeth to make me whimper.

"Xaden," I blatantly beg, my thighs tightening around his waist.

All traces of teasing leave his eyes as he lifts his head. "Do you have serum?"

"In my pack. Do you want it?" Now we're making progress.

He shakes his head. "Sgaeyl would eviscerate me. But I want you to shove it down my throat if you—" He winces. "Fuck that. How many daggers do you have in here?"

"Two." No need to ask which daggers he's asking about.

"Make that four." He unsheathes one at his thigh and sets it on the bookcase to my right, then uses lesser magic to float his other one to my nightstand. "Scared yet?"

My lips curve at the reminder of his words from *months* ago.

"Nope." I brush a kiss across his lips, knowing I won't need to use the weapons. "It wouldn't be the first time I raised a blade to you."

He stares, utterly bewildered, then flashes a grin. "I'm not sure what that says about us."

Is it toxic? Maybe. Is it us? Absolutely.

"That we've debated killing each other multiple times and have always abstained?" I kiss him, flicking my tongue over the seam of his lips because he's mine and I can. "I'd say that bodes well for our future. If we'd actually tried to draw blood, I'd be worried."

"You threw daggers at my head." His hands clasp my hips, and his mouth slides down my throat, lingering to suck on the juncture between my neck and shoulder.

Gods, that's *nice*.

I draw in a breath as my temperature rises at least a degree. He's going to have me molten before he even starts. "I threw daggers *next* to your head. Big difference." Rolling my hips earns me his low groan. "If it makes you feel better, if at any time I think you're actually going to kill me, I'll stab you, all right? Just put my conduit in my hand and fucking touch me already." Holy shit, I just said that.

And I'm not even fazed.

"No conduit." His hands flex, pulling me against the hard length of him, and he kisses every inch of bare skin he can get his mouth on.

I'm going to combust right here, dangerously close to these books, but at least rain still pelts the glass. "I mean, it's your house. If you want to set it on—" My heart clenches. "You want me at full power."

"I'm not taking chances with you." He loosens the shadows at my wrists, and my hands fall to his shoulders as his mouth whispers along my collarbone in a sweep that sends tingles of pleasure straight down my spine. "Would you like to hold the dagger, too? Or is within reach acceptable?"

"Don't need it. *I* am the weapon." I use his very words from the sparring pit and plunge my fingers into his hair, trying desperately to hold one of the most important conversations of my life while he systematically unravels me.

"I know." He ghosts his lips over mine and draws back when I lean in for more. "It's the only reason I let myself knock on your door. Want to change your mind?" He studies my eyes like there's any chance I'm going to deny what we both desperately need—each other.

"Our door," I correct him. "I choose you. I choose whatever risk this brings.

I see every part of you, Xaden: The good. The bad. The unforgivable. That's what you promised, and that's what I want—all of you. I can handle myself, even against you if I have to."

His gaze darkens. "I don't want to hurt you."

"Then don't." I skim my fingertips down over his relic, relishing in the feel of him while he'll let me have it.

"If I slip…" He shakes his head. "Fuck, *Violet.*"

The way he says my name—part moan, part prayer—wrecks me. "You won't. Day seventy-three, remember?" I run my thumb down his jawline. "But we can wait to seventy-six if it makes you feel better."

His jaw ticks against my fingers. "No more waiting."

While most deities allow temple attendants to choose their timeline of service, only two require a lifetime of dedication: Dunne and Loial. For both war and love change souls irrevocably.

—MAJOR RORILEE'S GUIDE TO APPEASING THE GODS,
SECOND EDITION

CHAPTER FORTY-NINE

Our mouths collide and we ignite. There's no more teasing. No more doubt. His tongue sweeps past my lips with arrogant ownership and I moan, sliding my fingers into his hair to hold him to me. He takes my mouth over and over in deep, drugging kisses that have me arching for more and nipping at his lower lip when he doesn't give it fast enough.

Stone grates against my back as he rolls his hips, but all I feel is searing pleasure as he hits the perfect spot. *"Again,"* I demand, then whimper into his mouth when he delivers.

The fever he's worked me into threatens to devour me, and there are still *so many* clothes between us.

His hand glides under my thigh and the rumpled hem of my gown, and he runs the backs of two fingers between my thighs, right over the fabric of my underwear. *"You're fucking soaked for me,"* he growls.

The tantalizingly light touch rouses a surge of power that only adds to the crackling heat gathering low in my belly.

"Well-the-fuck-aware." I smirk, rocking against those fingers, and kiss him like I might lose him if I surrender his tongue. *"Have you seen you?"*

He huffs a laugh against my lips, and then we're moving. I expect to feel the bed against my back at any second, but he surprises me by unhooking my ankles and setting my feet on the floor in between the high-backed armchair and our bed.

Then his mouth is on mine again, stoking the fire that already rages too hot to survive much longer. Clothes fly.

I reach for the button at his waistband.

He breaks the kiss only long enough to tug my nightdress over my head.

I shove at the water-logged leather of his pants.

He strips me out of my underwear.

If undressing is a race, I definitely win, but he's startlingly quick with his boots. All it takes is one look to remind me just how *much* I've won.

"Mine," I whisper, tracing the carved edges of his abdominals with my fingers. "I keep waiting for it to wear off," I mutter as he palms my lower back and tugs me toward him.

"What?" he asks, sitting in the armchair and lifting me into his lap.

My knees bracket his muscled hips, and my heart flutters impossibly fast. "The complete awe I feel when I remember that you're mine." I stroke my hands over his shoulders and down his chest. "That by some miracle, I'm the one who gets to touch you."

"Hasn't worn off for me yet, either. Don't think it will." His gaze drifts over my unbound hair and body with a hunger so sharp it could slice through dragon scale. *"This is all I thought about last time I was here without you."*

Oh, *yes*. I start to lower myself, more than ready to feel every inch of him inside me.

He hisses through his teeth when the head of his cock slides between my thighs, and I do the same when he rubs against my clit, sending sparks skittering along every cell in my body. "Not yet," he says through gritted teeth.

My fingers dig into his shoulders. "I might actually die if you make me wait—"

"Never said you'd be waiting." He lifts one of my knees to the top of a padded chair arm, then the other, and stares up at me with a wicked smirk as his hands slide to my ass.

"Grab hold, love."

Before I can ask *where*, shadows tug my hands to the top of the upholstered chairback and hold them there. "What are you—"

"Worshipping." He lifts my ass and brings my hips straight to his mouth.

I cry out at the first sweep of his perfect tongue, and it's only his hands and shadows that keep me from collapsing. White-hot need streaks through me like lightning, and power rises to a frequency that vibrates along my skin when he does it again. And again. And again.

"I'll never get enough of you." Xaden licks and lashes and sucks like he has no other plans for the night, driving me absolutely mindless, holding me in place as my hips rock for more.

"Xaden," I moan. Pleasure and power spiral, hot and urgent, winding within me so tightly that my muscles lock and my thighs start to shake. "Don't stop."

He sends me right over the edge.

Lightning crashes, illuminating the room, and thunder immediately follows as I break into uncountable fragments, shattered by the waves of bliss that come, and come, and come. Instead of letting up, Xaden slides two fingers inside me and moves in time with his tongue, and the orgasm that should wane kicks into a second that's just as bright, if not slightly sharper.

"You're so slick, I'll be inside you in one thrust," he says as I start to descend, falling limply against the back of the chair, my arms trembling in the aftermath. "Stay right there." He kisses my stomach, then slips out from underneath me.

I tug at the shadow bonds, but they hold fast. Fuck, I want to touch him, kiss him, devote myself to his body the way he just did mine. But if this is what he needs—

"You are every fantasy I'll ever have." His lips brush the shell of my ear, and I shiver. He draws my right knee down to the seat, and the chair creaks as he sets his left behind me. "Give me your mouth."

I look back over my shoulder and he curls over me, kissing me hard and deep.

He slides the head of his cock into position, then lifts his mouth from mine. "Last chance to change your mind."

"Never going to happen." I look into his eyes. "Fuck me. Make love to me. Take me. I don't care what you call it as long as you get inside me right now." "Need" isn't a strong enough word for the way I'm feeling, how desperate I am to hold all of him.

"You can reach the dagger on the dresser if you—" he starts, and I silence him with a kiss. He groans, then takes my hips in his hands and pulls me downward, into the long, rolling thrust that takes me inch by magnificent inch. *"Fuck, you feel like home."*

We both cry out when he pushes all the way in. The pressure, the stretch, the depth he's hitting at this angle are all sublimely perfect. I stop tugging at the shadows at my wrists and grip the back of the chair so I can rock into his next thrust.

He starts a deep, pounding rhythm that's as merciless as it is exquisite, and every time he returns is better than the last. Thank gods there's a sound shield on this room, or they'd hear us all the way in the Assembly chamber. We can't kiss deeply enough, can't get close enough, and our efforts only serve to bead sweat on our skin. I descend into keening cries as he drives us onward, his breath panting against my lips, one of his hands tangling in my hair while the other pulls me into every snap of his hips.

That spiraling tension is deeper this time, tugging at my power, intertwining pleasure and electricity until the air charges around us. "Xaden," I whisper. "I need...I need..."

Gods, I don't even know.

"I've got you," he promises, his voice hoarse. *"My power, my body, my soul—it's all yours."* He slips a hand down my stomach and lightly strokes my hypersensitive clit. *"Take whatever you need."*

Just him. That's all I need, and I have every possible part of him.

I shatter, my hips bucking as the release takes me, hurling me from my body into whatever realm exists beyond, then drowning me in cascading avalanches of pleasure. Lightning strikes again and again, and I catch the scent of smoke before Xaden mutters a curse and shadows fly.

Oh *shit.*

"Just the desk. It's fine," he swears, and I'm absolutely boneless as he plucks me from the chair and flips me so I'm straddling his lap again.

I sink down onto him, watching his eyes slide shut, and I wrap my arms around his neck. "My hands—"

"Not your hands I'm worried about now." He grits his teeth and reaches to grab hold of the edge of the dresser. That explains the shift in positions. The furniture isn't the only thing he's holding on to, either. Sweat coats his brow, his pulse thrums in his throat, and his abs are so rigid against my stomach that he might as well be stone.

"Let go," I order, rising up on my knees and sinking again, riding him at a faster pace that I know makes him feral.

"Fuck." He throws his head back, and the muscles of his neck strain. "Violet. Love. I can't—"

"You can." My hands move to the sides of his neck, and I drop my forehead to his. "My body. My soul. My power is all right here. You love me. You will never hurt me. Let go, Xaden." I call on just enough power to hum along my skin, enough to tell him I'm not defenseless in this moment, and then I shamelessly take every ounce of how good this feels and shove it down the bond.

"Oh *shit.*" His arms tense, and his hips snap once, twice, and on the third, shadow fills the room, plunging us into darkness and sending metal clanging to the ground. He drops his head to my shoulder and groans into my neck as he finds his release. *"I love you."*

I sag against his chest, happily limp with exhaustion, and the darkness fades, revealing the room—and the storm raging outside—once more.

"The wood—" he starts, lifting his hands.

I begrudgingly raise my head just so he doesn't worry us into an early grave and peek over the back of the chair. "Not a mark in sight." My heart swells.

"Not even a fingerprint?" He tenses beneath me.

"Not one." I look into his eyes and smile. "You're stable."

"For now," he whispers, but his eyes light up. "And I'll take it." He wraps his arms around me and surges to his feet, carrying me along our bed.

"Are we going somewhere?" I hold on even though I know he's more than capable of carrying me.

"Bathtub," he says with a devious grin. "Then the dresser. Then the bed."

I completely ignore the homework I have yet to finish. "Excellent plan."

Your Majesty, Tyrrendor hereby officially declines your request for a Provincial Commitment of troops for our current conflict. Having resigned my professorship at Basgiath War College, I am now in rightful command of all Tyrrish citizens in military service.

—Official Correspondence of His Grace, Lieutenant Xaden Riorson, Sixteenth Duke of Tyrrendor, to His Majesty, King Tauri the Wise

CHAPTER FIFTY

Spring-green meadow grass bends under my boots as the first drops of rain fall. I shouldn't be here. I know what happens here. And yet, this is where I'm called time and again.

This is the price of saving her life.

Lightning splinters the sky, illuminating the high walls of Draithus and its spiraling tower in the distance and outlining dozens of wings in the sky. If I move fast enough, I'll get there this time.

But my legs won't obey, and I stumble, just like I always do.

He steps out of nothingness, straight into my path, and my heart pounds, as though increasing the speed of its beats will cease it from sinking through my chest.

"I grow weary of waiting." The Sage pulls back the hood of his robe, revealing red-rimmed eyes and scarlet veins branching at his temples like roots.

"I am not yours." I flip my palms, summoning the power that's come to define me, but nothing rises except my own panic. Before I can reach for my blades, I'm yanked into the air. Icy fingers wrap around my neck, too vaporous to fight yet substantial enough to nearly cut the flow of air. Pain sears my throat.

Asshole.

My magic never works here, but his always does.

"You are ours." The Sage's eyes narrow with malice. "You will bring what I want" — his grip tightens with every word, allowing only a trickle of air into my lungs — "or she dies. I'm through waiting, and I will *not* allow her to win such a prize."

I sweep the sky for a familiar set of wings as I hear her scream but find none as the rain begins in earnest.

He's bluffing.

"You." I force the word out. "Do. Not. Have. Her."

He drops his arms, and I fall to my knees on the grass, pulling breath after breath to replace what he'd denied me.

"But I will," he vows. "Because you'll bring her to me."

The fuck I will. Anger cuts through the fear, and I slam my left hand to the ground. Rain runs off my flight jacket and courses over the edge of my relic in rivulets as I flex my fingers in the wet grass, splaying my fingers wide.

My hand…it doesn't look like mine —

There it is. Power courses through the earth beneath me, ready and willing to annihilate their forces if I have the courage to let go of the impossible dreams I've clung to and accept the fate Zihnal has dealt me.

I only have to reach, and they'll be safe. *She'll* be safe.

No. This is wrong.

This is a dream. Only a dream. And yet he holds me here night after night. Fighting through the weight of the nightmare, I wrench my hand from the ground.

"Wake!" I scream, but no sound emerges.

"This city will fall. Yours will be next," the Sage promises.

"Wake!"

I jerk my head up, only to find the Sword of Tyrrendor at my throat. The Sage draws his arm back —

My body jolts and my eyes fly open. There is no field. No Sage. No sword. Just gentle raindrops hitting our window, the warmth of the blankets tangled at my legs, and the weight of Xaden's arm draped over my waist. The worst of the storm has passed.

Filling my lungs to capacity persuades the pounding in my chest to ease, but the breaths against my ear only come faster, growing more ragged with every second.

"Xaden?" I twist toward him and lift my hand to his face. His skin is damp with sweat, his brow furrowed, and his jaw clenches so hard I *hear* his teeth grind. I'm not the only one having nightmares tonight.

"Xaden." I sit up and slide my hand to his bare shoulder, then tap gently.

"Wake up."

He flings himself onto his back, and his head begins to thrash.

"Xaden." My chest tightens at the visible pain on his face, and I throw myself down the bond. *"Xaden!"*

His eyes open and he surges upright with a full-bodied gasp, then plants his hands beside his hips on the mattress.

"You're all right," I say gently, and his gaze snaps toward mine, wild and haunted. "You were having a nightmare."

He blinks the sleep out of his eyes, then swings his head in a quick sweep of the space. "We're in our room."

"We're in our room." I draw my fingers across his shoulders, and the muscles soften.

"And you're here." His shoulders dip as he looks my way.

"I'm here." I pick up his left hand and press it against my cheek.

"You're clammy." His brow knits. "Everything all right?"

Go figure he immediately asks about me.

"I had a bad dream, too." I shrug. "Must be the storm."

"Must be." His gaze flickers past me toward the window. "Come here." He pulls me closer, then lays us down to face each other. A second later, he draws the sheet—but not the blanket—over us and settles his hand on my hip. "Tell me about yours."

I tuck the sheet under my arm and slide my other hand under my pillow. "It's the same one I've had since Resson."

"Same one?" He brushes my hair back over my shoulder. "You told me you had bad dreams but never said they repeated."

"I have a recurring nightmare. It's nothing." Thunder booms in the distance, and he stays quiet, waiting for me to continue. "It's usually in a field, and there's a battle in the distance. I can hear Andarna scream but I can't get to her." My throat tightens, and I lift my hand to his chest. "The Sage is there, and he always levitates me like I'm nothing heavier than a pocket watch. And I can't kick, or scream, or move. I'm just stuck there as he threatens me."

He tenses. "You're sure it's the Sage?"

I nod. "He held the Sword of Tyrrendor to my throat after demanding I bring him something. It's like my subconscious is trying to warn me that they're going to use you against me."

"What else?" His heart starts to pound beneath my fingers.

I blink, trying to remember. "I can't explain how I know, since I've only ever seen it from a distance, but the last couple of times, we've been near Draithus."

"Are you sure?" His eyes widen. "What did it look like?"

"It's usually pretty dark, but I could make out tall city walls on a raised plateau, and a central, spiraling tower."

"That's Draithus." His breathing picks up again.

"What's wrong?" I slide my hand to the side of his neck.

"What else?" He palms my hip.

He's oddly intense about this, but if it helps him talk through whatever plagued him while he slept, then I'll play along. "Tonight was...weird. Different."

"How?"

"When he dropped me, I had this second where I thought about channeling from the earth, and when I looked down..." My gaze slides to his relic. "I had a relic on my left wrist, right where yours all start. And my hand didn't look like *mine*. Now that I'm thinking about it, it looked like...yours. Who knows. What was yours about?"

He stares at me silently, and worry creeps up my spine.

"Why are you looking at me like that?"

"Because it's my hand."

My fingers slip off his neck. "I just said that."

He sits up and I mirror the motion, holding the sheet to my chest. "It's *my* hand," he repeats. "You were in my dream."

• • •

It's not possible, is it?

Two hours later, I've told him about every dream I can remember with the Sage, and Xaden's had every single one.

There has to be a reasonable explanation.

"You think we're sharing the same dream?" I ask slowly, sitting in the middle of our bed with a blanket wrapped over my shoulders, watching him pace the short length of our bedroom in his sleeping pants.

The move reminds me of Sgaeyl on Hedotis.

Is sharing dreams even possible? Some effect of our bond?

"No. They're *my* dreams." He rubs the skin beneath his lower lip. "I've had them at least once a week since Resson, and more frequently since Basgiath, but I almost never realize they're nightmares when I'm in them. When I do, I wake up feeling like someone was there with me, watching." He looks over at me and pauses his steps. "Like tonight."

"That doesn't make sense." I tug the blanket closer. "I've had the dream on nights you aren't with me. Nights you were *hours* away."

"Maybe it's the bond." He leans back against our dresser. "But they're definitely my dreams. You've never been to Draithus, and that scenario...it's exactly what happened on the edge of the river when I fought him at Basgiath."

I blink. He never talks about that.

"The dark wielder Andarna scorched behind the school pulled the same move." I tilt my head. "But that dark wielder wasn't him. Do you know what the dream's about? What he wants you to bring to him? Because it's all vague to me, like I'm walking in mid-conversation..." My words die as my mind flies through the possibility that he's right, no matter how *impossible* it is.

"Because you are." Xaden lifts his brows. "And he wants me to deliver you."

"They have their own lightning wielder," I argue like I can reason with Xaden's subconscious.

"But it's my nightmare, and I only have one *you*," he says. "It's getting harder and harder not to go to Draithus just to prove to myself that it's all in my head." His eyes flare, then narrow. "But it shouldn't be in yours. Has it ever happened with anyone else?"

"How would I know?" I shake my head. "I don't think so, but I don't remember all my dreams." Still...there's the nightmare I had in Samara—that one still sticks with me. It's as visceral as a memory. As visceral as these nightmares. "How much do you know about the fall of Cliffsbane?"

He grips the edge of the dresser. "You dreamed about Cliffsbane?"

"When I was in Samara." I nod. "In the dream, I was in my room—at least I think it was mine—and the fire was coming, but I wouldn't leave without the portrait of my family, and..."

The family in the portrait. The honey-brown eyes. The burn on my hand.

"And what?" He walks toward me slowly, studying me like he doesn't already intimately know every inch of my body.

"I..." My heart rate picks up, and nausea racks my stomach. "I told Cat she had to live because she's the future queen of Tyrrendor, and the way Cat looked at me..." I swallow the bile that rides the fear rising in my throat. "It was like I was precious to her. What if"—I fight the urge to be sick—"what if I was Maren?"

Xaden sits at the foot of the bed, and the muscles of his back ripple as he tenses. "You were in Maren's dream." He turns to face me, and something that looks eerily like terror widens his eyes before he can mask it.

"That's not possible." I wrap my arms around my stomach. "Maybe with you because of the bond, but there's no way to trip into someone else's dream."

"There is if you're a dream-walker." He nods thoughtfully, and my heart pounds as I guess what he's about to say. "It must be your second signet—the one being bonded to Andarna gives you. It would make sense. Her kind are peaceful, and the ability itself would be passive, even a gift in a culture like that."

A what? My back stiffens. "There's no such thing as dream-walking, and the irids told her that she gave me something more dangerous than lightning. It was one of the reasons they were so angry with her."

"There is such a thing." Xaden's voice drops. "It's absolutely more dangerous than lightning. It's a form of inntinnsic," he ends on a whisper.

"I don't read minds. That can't be right." I shake my head.

"You don't read them. You walk straight into them when unconscious."

My jaw slackens, and I reach for Andarna. *"Is it true?"*

Tairn rustles but stays silent.

"I did not choose it any more than Tairn chose lightning," she says defensively. *"But you have been known to wander while dreaming. It's harmless. You're mostly drawn to him."*

The blanket falls from my fingers.

"And you said nothing?" Tairn growls.

"You did not inform her the first time she wielded lightning!" Andarna argues. *"She needed to discover it herself."*

"Oh gods." I start to shake.

"Shit." Xaden tucks the blanket around me, then pulls me into his lap. "It's going to be all right."

"It doesn't make sense. Signets are based on our unique bond and the power of the dragon." My thoughts tumble over themselves as I babble. "And what we need most, so it's logical that you needed to know everyone's intentions when you manifested. You had to keep the marked ones safe. But there's no part of me who wants or needs to know what anyone else is dreaming—" The trembling stops as it clicks and I understand. "Except when I did. I was cut off from her while she slept all those months."

"Andarna." He nods. "That makes sense. My signet doesn't work on dragons, and I'm guessing yours doesn't, either, so you unknowingly developed it on a human."

"On you." I search his face for any sign of anger but find none. "I'm so sorry."

"You have nothing to apologize for." He strokes my hair and holds my gaze. "You didn't know. Didn't do it on purpose—"

"Of course not." I would never purposely violate his privacy that way—or Maren's.

"Which is what makes you exceptionally dangerous." His jaw flexes twice. "I can only read someone while they're awake, and I'm limited by their ability to shield. No one can shield while they're sleeping. You could potentially walk straight into Melgren's own dreams and he couldn't stop you. Probably wouldn't even know." His face twists for a heartbeat before he quickly masks it. "Violet, they'll kill you if they find out. It won't matter that you're the best weapon they have against the venin—against *me*. They'll snap your neck and call it self-defense."

Well, that's…terrifying.

"Only if it's true." I slide off his lap and start pulling on my sparring uniform, leaving my armor draped on the back of the chair. "It's just dreams, right? *If it's dreams? It's like tripping into someone's fears, not their actual thoughts.*"

"Except I think you meddle, because I wanted to channel on that field and found myself raising my hand instead— What are you doing?"

Meddle?

"I can only think of one way to confirm for sure, and don't worry, I'll be careful." I button my pants, then stare as he rises and pulls a set of dry clothes from his pack. "What are *you* doing?"

"Going with you, obviously."

There's no point arguing, so we both dress. A few minutes and several stairs later, I knock on Maren's door.

It takes her a minute to answer, and when she does, her eyes are groggy with sleep. "Violet? Riorson?" she asks with a jaw-cracking yawn. "What's going on?"

"I'm sorry to wake you, but I need to ask you something completely…weird." I rub the bridge of my nose. "There's no other way to say it, and I need you to not ask me why."

"Tread carefully," Xaden warns.

"All right." Maren folds her arms over her robe.

"Did you happen to have a portrait of your family?" I ask.

"I still do," Maren answers, her forehead puckering. "Is something wrong with my brothers? I just saw them a few hours ago."

"No." I shake my head vehemently. "Nothing like that." Maybe we're wrong and this is just some weird effect from the bond. If Maren still has the portrait, then it couldn't have caught fire. Then Xaden can't be right—I didn't walk into her dream.

"Here, I'll show it to you," Maren offers, then disappears into her room. She's back within a few seconds and holds out the portrait.

Recognition hits with all the subtlety of a dagger. *"I've seen it before."* The soft smiles, the honey-brown eyes. Gods, no wonder the boys looked familiar to me. I was just in too much pain to register *why* the first time. "It's beautiful." I force myself to swallow.

"Thanks." She draws back her hand. "I keep it with me wherever we go."

"You're not worried about losing it?"

"That used to be my worst nightmare, actually," she says, staring down at the miniature. "Until I lived through losing them."

Worst nightmare. It takes every ounce of self-control I have to keep my expression flat. "I can understand that all too well. Thank you for sharing that with me—"

"Silver One!" Tairn bellows.

Xaden's head tilts, and Maren stiffens.

"I'm right here—"

"A horde approaches from the east!" he shouts.

Bells peal, the loudest of them straight overhead.

We're under attack.

For maximum potential, riders should be stationed close to their villages if possible. Nothing is a more effective motivator than seeing one's home on fire.

—TACTICS PART II, A PERSONAL MEMOIR BY LIEUTENANT LYRON PANCHEK

CHAPTER
FIFTY-ONE

"*How many?*" I ask Tairn as we race down the steps. Doors open on every floor we pass, and people pour out of their rooms, most still tugging on their uniforms. Only a small percentage are in black.

"*A few dozen. Hard to tell with the weather. Twenty minutes out, maybe less. I'm on my way to you.*"

"Andarna—" I start as Xaden makes it into our bedroom first.

"*Do not tell me to stay put!*" she shouts. "*I can scorch the dark wielders.*"

I'll take yelling at me over silence any day.

"*Guard the wardstone.*" I dart around Xaden as he shoves his arms into his flight jacket, then grab my own out of the armoire. Fuck, I'm in sparring gear and lack armor, but it will have to do. At least my boots are on.

Within minutes, we're both armed and running down the hall, into a growing crowd.

"How many on patrol?" Xaden shouts to Brennan when we make it to the foyer.

"Six," Brennan answers, buttoning his flight jacket. "The horde outflew the two on the Dralor route, and the other four are twenty minutes due west."

Well, that's the wrong fucking direction for what we need.

"If they outflew two dragons, they have to be greenfire wyvern," I say, looking up as a conglomeration of riders, infantry, and my own squadmates races in our direction with thundering bootsteps.

"Noted. Riders in residence?" Xaden asks, his gaze sweeping over the staircases as I weave my hair into a simple three-strand braid to keep it out of my way.

"Fifteen retired, ten active — with you, eleven," Brennan replies. "Taking over all outposts in Tyrrendor from Navarrian riders left us undermanned."

"Suri?" Xaden scans the foyer.

"In Tirvainne." Brennan flinches. "And Ulices —"

"In Lewellen," Xaden finishes. "So neither of the generals of my army are present."

"Correct," Brennan confirms.

His army. My fingers stall in my hair as it hits me. Xaden isn't the ranking officer here, but he's in command. The weight of that responsibility would buckle my knees, but he simply nods at my brother's catastrophic news.

"That's irksome." Xaden looks up the stairs. "All right. We work with what we have. Felix, keep the first-years safe and your eye on that one." His finger swings toward Aaric. "Infantry, get to your posts and take out any wyvern we drive to the ground. Riders, run *faster*." He pivots toward Brennan, and the others scurry to follow orders. "Thoughts?"

"Wards are still up here, or we would feel it." Brennan tilts his head.

I tie off the end of my braid.

"Considering the stone's in the backyard, that's not saying much," Xaden replies.

"They haven't spotted any venin among the patrol flight," Brennan adds as Rhi reaches my side, Imogen close on her heels. "But it's fucking *huge*, so they must be expecting to breach the city walls. Their course was noted as due west."

Aaric pauses on the landing above, his brow furrowing before Felix practically shoves him down the hall.

"If I'm them, I'm flying in small-batch waves to test the barrier of the wards," Brennan continues. "My recommendation is to station the officers two to five miles east, put the squad of...older riders at the city gates, and assign the cadets to the wardstone as a last defense."

Holy shit does this feel familiar, and I wasn't exactly thrilled with how the last time played out.

Xaden's jaw ticks and his gaze darts back and forth for a second as he thinks. "I'll join the officers," he tells Brennan, and my heart jolts. "The older riders might be skilled, but half don't fly —"

"I'm your best weapon," I interject. "If you won't put me on the first line, then station me at the gates."

"Absolutely not!" Brennan snaps, leveling a horrified look at me.

"She's right." Xaden grimaces, then schools his features. "Split the retired riders. Half to the wardstone, half throughout the city in case civilians need to flee for the caves. You're on the wall, Cadet Sorrengail."

"Send all of us," Rhi adds. "It's not like second- and third-years haven't seen combat. If it's fight and die or don't fight and die, we'd rather fight."

Xaden nods. "Only those who are willing."

"We're willing," Dain answers from the step beside Bodhi.

Every second- and third-year crowded near them nods.

"Fine. Aetos, your wing, your command," Xaden says, and Brennan takes off to relay orders. Wind gusts through the front door as people rush out to take their positions.

"Third-years, you're with me at the east gate to the city. Second-years, you're with Matthias at the north. Work in pairs," Dain orders.

"I'm here," Tairn announces. *"Enemy is ten minutes out."*

Holy shit. That's the closest any wyvern has come to Aretia.

"I'm coming with you." Bodhi jumps the last two steps, landing beside Xaden.

"You're staying with the first-years," Xaden immediately counters.

What? My eyebrows fly upward.

"The fuck I am." The absolute wrath on Bodhi's face has me retreating a step. "I will be at your side—"

"You will be as deep within this house as possible." Xaden gets right up in his face.

"Because I'm not a weapon like you are?" Bodhi argues. "Cuir and I are just as deadly in the air."

"Because you're first in line!" Xaden clasps the back of his cousin's neck. "Neither of us have an heir. We're all there is, Bodhi. I don't have time to argue, and you will do as ordered. Our family just got Tyrrendor back, and we will not lose her because of your ego. Understood?"

Bodhi's eyes narrow. "We'll lose her because of *yours*. Understood." He pivots and disappears into the crowd.

"That didn't go well," I mutter.

"Fuck," Xaden says under his breath, then turns to me and leans into my space. "I love you more than this city. Do not die defending it." He crushes his mouth to mine and kisses me quick and fierce.

Tyrrendor. Xaden. Our relationship. Me. *It's hard to love someone in power.*

I pull back. "As motivational speeches go, that was not your best." My gaze sweeps over his face, memorizing every line. "I love you. Stay out of the clouds, off the ice, and come back to me whole."

He nods, his eyes flashing as he catches my meaning, and then he's gone.

There's no time to contemplate if that was our last kiss.

"Do not worry for him," Tairn orders. *"He wins no matter how this battle goes."*

"Don't be an ass." I follow Rhi and Cat toward the front door.

"Sorrengail!" Aaric shouts, and I look back over my shoulder to see him sprinting down the steps. "Wait!"

"Don't have a lot of time here," I reply, letting the other second-years pass.

"You have to protect Dunne's temple." Aaric runs across the foyer, followed by two exasperated guards.

"I have an entire city to protect."

"The temple is outside the walls." He glances toward the open door.

"If that's where our orders—"

"No." He shakes his head, then seems to fight for words. "You have to protect the temple."

Is he *fucking* kidding me right now?

"Did you make some alliance I'm not aware of?" I ask, backing away. Singling out Zihnal's temple in the spirit of alliance is something I could understand, but Dunne? So help me Malek, if another Navarrian aristocrat has been making deals behind my back, I'm going to lose my shit.

"It's not—" he starts as a group of soldiers races past.

"Violet!" Rhiannon yells. "We have to fly!"

"Coming!" I call back over my shoulder before addressing Aaric. "Dunne's temple attendants are skilled in protecting themselves."

"It's how you save Tyrrendor." Aaric's voice drops to a whisper.

"By favoring Dunne?" I shake my head. "The time to weigh in on strategy was about five minutes ago. Go be with your year-mates." I leave without waiting for his response and join my year-mates filing through the doorway.

"Orders?" Sawyer asks, cracking his knuckles.

"Fliers at the base…" Rhi blinks, then looks over us quickly as we walk into the blustery vestiges of the dying storm. The rain has eased, but what it lacks in intensity, it makes up for with ice-cold chill. The courtyard is teeming with dragons and gryphons. They wait on the walls, on the ground, and in the street beyond the gate. "No. Fliers on top of the wall for easier maneuverability," Rhiannon orders with a nod. "We're splitting strengths, so Sorrengail and I will hover at a hundred feet. Everything above that is ours. Henrick and Gamlyn will cover from the ground to our sector," she shouts over the wind. "Most of us have family here, so fight like it."

We all nod in agreement, then split to mount.

I pull my flight goggles down and find Tairn front and center. *"You couldn't wait off to the side like the others?"*

"No." He dips his shoulder and I mount quickly, my boots keeping their grip despite his rain-slick scales. *"You must get faster at reacting to attacks like these."*

"I can't tell leadership to make decisions faster." I settle into the wet saddle, then buckle the water-laden strap with quickly cramping hands.

"Then perhaps we need to make our own decisions," Tairn grumbles, then launches without preamble or warning.

I'm thrown back in the seat as he catapults upward at a vertical trajectory, so close to Riorson House that I cringe, expecting to hear claw collide with stone.

"I am not an amateur," Tairn reminds me as we crest the top of the house, then bank hard right to join the others as they take to the skies. His little maneuver may have pushed my heart through my spine, but it gave Feirge, Aotrom, and Sliseag time and space to launch northward out of the courtyard.

I ignore the instinct begging me to look east to catch another glimpse of Xaden, or even Sgaeyl's wings. My focus is needed here and now. Xaden is more than capable of taking care of himself…as long as he doesn't channel magic that isn't his.

The city rushes underneath us as we soar toward the north gate. Infantry races through the mage light–illuminated streets to their positions. Civilians scurry from house to house. Temple attendants dart into their sanctuaries—except those who serve Zihnal. They're on the front steps of their shrine, *drinking* as we pass over. Only when I verify that Rhiannon's family has light shining through their windows do I scan the cloudy skies ahead of the northern wall.

"Have to love fighting in the dark," I mutter, dragging my sleeve over my flight goggles to clear them.

"I've heard you have quite the solution to that," Tairn counters.

Good point. I retrieve the conduit from my left pocket, fasten the strap at my wrist, and palm the glass orb. Then I crack open my Archives door.

Tairn's power rushes in, heating my skin and my rain-chilled hands.

Energy hums in my veins, condenses in my chest, and when it crackles into the conduit, I lift my right hand to the sky and wield, splaying my fingers wide as I push the power upward and it erupts through me.

Lightning streaks through the cloud overhead, branching out in dozens of directions and illuminating the field for the length of two heartbeats.

Pairs of gray-winged wyvern fly toward us on dozens of different flight paths from dozens of different altitudes, disappearing into the darkness as the light collapses and thunder booms. Brennan was right about the wyvern flying in small batches to test the wards. He just failed to anticipate that they'd do so in such a wide arc, and it's going to cost us.

"They aren't in formation like Basgiath," I note to Tairn as we reach the northern gate and climb to hold a hover with Feirge. Steam rises from my skin, but I keep my Archives door open, allowing the power to gather within me so I don't have to reach for it next time.

"Either they've traded the security of formation in hopes smaller pairings will get through," Tairn muses, *"or they know you're here and formations make*

a bigger target."

"That would require one of the dark wielders to have escaped Basgiath." I glance downward and see Sliseag and Aotrom land at the gates, a row of gryphons manning the walls above them.

"It would," Tairn agrees, then rumbles low in his chest. *"The officers have made contact."*

Xaden. Worry fights like hell to worm its way into my chest. *"You'll tell me if something…"*

"You'd know," Tairn replies, then snakes his head right toward Feirge. *"Your squad leader requests light."*

I know Rhi isn't talking about the glow from the orb, so I twist my hand upward and wield again. Heat whips through me and lightning strikes overhead, spreading through the cloud. I hold my fingers in their splayed position and push another wave of energy outward, prolonging the strike in a way I've never managed before.

Rain sizzles when it hits my cheeks, and I quickly count four pairs of wyvern flying in our direction unimpeded. My fingertips *burn*, and I drop my hand, effectively cutting the strike.

Thunder roars louder than any dragon I've come across.

"Impressive," Tairn says.

"Impressive but foolish." I wince, then hold the conduit over my right hand. Two blisters bubble the skin on the outside of my forefinger. *"What are our orders?"*

"The squad leader," he growls, *"incorrectly instructs to stick close to the walls, but it's the wrong call. Your power should not be wielded in such proximity to civilians."*

"Not until I'm a hell of a lot better at controlling it," I agree. *"Relay that."*

"She hesitates." Tairn's head swivels toward Feirge. *"We cannot afford to do so."*

Fuck. The *last* thing I want to do is go against Rhi or leave my squad, and now *I'm* the one hesitating because Tairn is right. *"Go."* I breathe in deeply. *"Tell them to stay back as ordered, but you and I have to go."*

"Agreed." He launches forward. *"A wind wielder has been assigned to bring moonlight. Now, ready yourself. We have two minutes until they're on us."*

My heart begins to pound. *"Did the officers' line fall?"*

"They circumnavigated it." His head tilts again. *"We're taking the pair on the high left. Feirge has joined us."*

"Let's go." Fighting in pairs makes sense, but Rhi has never left the squad.

Tairn beats his wings in three consecutive hard pumps and we surge forward, gaining altitude immediately with Feirge close behind.

"It's too dark ahead. I can't see," I warn Tairn. There's a stark line of black to my left I know belongs to the mountains, but the farther we fly from the city lights, the fewer shapes I can spot in the sky ahead of us. Everything blurs in the dark.

And miles away toward the east, flames erupt in streams of orange…and green.

"We are the dark. Drop the conduit," he orders.

"I won't be able—" My chest clenches as magic ripples. We've passed the protections of the wards.

"Drop it!"

I release my fingers, and the orb falls to the end of its chain, the light dying as the glass thumps the back of my arm. There's nothing left to do but make myself the smallest burden possible, so I grip the pommels and lie as flat as I can while smothering Tairn's power. *"Tell me you made it to the wardstone,"* I call back to Andarna.

"It is well protected," she promises, and her words lift the hair at the back of my neck.

"Are you at—" I start.

"Prepare!" Tairn orders.

We hit a fucking *wall*.

At least that's how it feels as I hurtle forward, my momentum giving zero cares that Tairn has all but stopped in the sky. Claw and teeth collide with scale as I'm whipped backward, my weight driving into the seat.

Gravity pulls from the left, and air rushes from the ground as my stomach rises. All I can do is hold tight and trust Tairn.

A shriek threatens to pierce my eardrums before it ends abruptly, only to be followed by the wet sound of flesh tearing, then a series of snaps. Tairn levels out and two wingbeats later, I hear a thud beneath us.

"It's been ages since I've honored the color of my scale in such a manner," Tairn declares with a pitch of pride.

"You blended in with the night." Andarna scoffs. *"Hardly an accomplishment."*

"You sound closer than you should be!" Why won't she ever stay where she's supposed to?

Tairn rumbles low in his chest, and fire streaks ahead of us. Feirge's flame outlines the shape of the wyvern's partner a second before she surges for its gray throat. The Green Daggertail's body swings forward as her teeth sink into the wyvern's neck.

The creature screams, and its wings beat frantically as it tries to escape.

"Hold tight." Tairn increases his speed, and I do exactly as he orders, bracing for another impact. My body is going to hate me tomorrow if we survive the

night. Clouds clear just enough for the moon to shine as Tairn flies straight at the flailing wyvern.

Tairn tucks his left wing as we skim by Feirge's claws, passing so close that my eyes lock with Rhi's for a scant second. Then I whip my head forward, and Tairn barrels into the wyvern's barbed tail, opening his jaws and taking hold with his teeth.

Then he *rolls.*

Holy. Fucking. Nausea. I pitch forward with Tairn and the sky turns into ground. The saddle strap digs into my thighs as we flip, and small pinpricks of light blur beneath me—above me—I can't even tell. They disappear before I can process the pull of gravity.

Bone snaps as the sky appears again, and Tairn lets go.

The wyvern falls, smashing into the ground a few seconds later.

"We broke its neck," he announces, flaring his wings to halt our momentum.

My head swims, and my stomach threatens to release its contents. *"Let's never do that again."* I check to make sure Rhi's all right, and she lifts a hand in acknowledgment.

"It was an effective maneuver," Tairn argues. *"The opposite force twisted the creature's spine—"*

"I get how it worked. Never again." The moonlight makes it possible to scan the field fully, and my heart drops at the sight of piled wings near the north gate. I can't differentiate among them in the dark, but I can make out the gaping hole in the top of the wall.

"Your year-mates have brought down two pairs themselves, but the bodies have caused destruction," Tairn says in explanation. *"The wards have not been reached by wyvern. They'll continue to send waves to test the boundaries."* His head whips back and forth between the horde holding off to the east and those engaged in combat before them.

Xaden. My feelings get the best of me, and I reach down the bond. Instead of warm, shimmering shadow, I'm met with a wall of onyx ice so cold it burns to the touch.

I inhale sharply and throw up a shield. *"Is Sgaeyl all—"*

"She copes," Tairn interrupts, his head snapping left. *"Look below."*

The muscles along my stomach tense. Four wyvern skim the ground at dizzying speed, keeping low as if trying to get by undetected. I swing my gaze, projecting their flight path, and find Andarna waiting in front of a lone structure in a field beyond the walls, flicking her tail. Terror steals the breath from my lungs.

"Go!"

Tairn tucks his wings, and we dive.

Wind tears at my hair, and I fight gravity to palm the conduit. Then I forget the fall and focus only on the wyvern, power rushing back to my surface. I gather it, condense it, burn with it, then summon more and more until I am light and heat and energy itself.

"Not too much!" Tairn warns as I lift my right hand against the wind.

But how can it be too much when I am the very thing I wield?

I keep my eyes on the wyvern as we approach the inevitable point of intersection and spool power like thread as the ground flies up to meet us. We can stay ahead of them if we get there fast enough.

I just need five seconds. We have fifty feet of altitude on them and the same in distance.

Five. Tairn snaps his wings to slow our fall.

Four. The bones in my spine grind at the abrupt change in momentum, but he's brought us close enough to see the tips of their clawed wings. And they're only getting closer.

Three. My body *burns* as I twist in the saddle and wield, releasing the coil of energy with a flare of my hand in one heartbeat, then dragging it downward with two scalded fingertips in the next.

Two. Tairn beats his wings, lifting us as lightning rends the sky—and maybe time. Everything seems to move slower as I force my fingers apart, splitting the bolt in two. Heat devours my breath and pain becomes my entire existence as I direct the scorching blasts into the wyvern's flight path.

One. The strike hits the lead pair, and they burst into flames, missing Tairn by a matter of feet as they fall out of formation in streaks of fire, revealing the remaining two.

And one carries a silver-haired rider.

Zero. Thunder shakes the alloy in the conduit, and my hand falls as Tairn drops onto the nearest wyvern.

The creature screeches, and the world spins in a flurry of black and gray wings.

Tairn bellows, and his pain replaces mine.

Dedicating oneself to temple work isn't just a noble pursuit. Becoming
high priest or priestess is the closest most of us will
get to touching the power of the gods. The rest are riders.

—Major Rorilee's Guide to Appeasing the Gods,
Second Edition

CHAPTER FIFTY-TWO

"*T*airn!*" I scream, and my mouth floods with the bitterness of newfound
terror.

"*No!*" Andarna yells.

We skid to a halt in the prairie grass, and I lift my head just in time to see
Feirge fly after Theophanie's wyvern, who's taken to the sky. Dunne, no. As
strong as Rhi is, even the two of us together aren't a match for a Maven. And
we aren't together.

"*Andarna! Tell Feirge not to chase!*" Bone crunches beneath Tairn, and I
draw a breath of pure fire. "*Are you all right?*" I ask him, fumbling the buckle at
my waist so I can see how badly he's hurt. Heat sears my lungs, and I reach for
power in preparation to fight Theophanie. There's no way she's going to leave
this field without getting what she came for, which I suspect is *me*. She'll be back.

"*Cut it off!*" Tairn demands, and something else snaps beneath him. "*You'll
burn out!*"

"*But Theophanie—*"

Ice pierces through my shields like they aren't even there. "*Violet!*"

Not ice. Xaden.

"*I'm fine. Stay in control and don't get distracted. Theophanie is here.*" I
slam the Archives door shut in my mind and breathe in the cold night air,
extinguishing the flames licking the inside of my lungs. It was too much, too
fast, but I'm not burned out, just a little singed.

"Get Tairn back to the wards as soon as you can." The ice slides away.

"On it."

"That wasn't fine," Tairn snarls and walks off the corpse of the wyvern, favoring his left hind leg.

"Says the one who's wounded!" I counter as Feirge flies back toward us. *"How serious is it?"* Thunder booms to the east, and it's not mine.

Oh *shit*, the storm. That's how they got this far undetected.

"Its wingspur broke off in my leg. I will live. It does not." He swivels his head toward Andarna and stalks her way, limping slightly. *"Your inability to follow simple orders will get her killed, and I will not lose her as I did the one who came before!"*

"I'm fine!" My temperature lowers with every breath, and high, intricately carved marble pillars come into view. *"I didn't burn out. I wasn't even as close as I was the day—"* The words die as Tairn stops, then lowers his head, clearing my field of vision.

Andarna stands in front of the steps of Dunne's temple, flanked by a half dozen sword-brandishing attendants who look between us as if they're not sure who to be more wary of—the reckless dragon beside them, the massive one in front of them, or the snarling Green Daggertail arriving to my left.

"What could you possibly be doing here?" I shout at Andarna, finally ripping my buckle free. I have to get that wingspur out of Tairn's leg before Theophanie returns.

"The prince said to protect Dunne's temple!" she argues, flicking her tail and knocking over a vat of burning coals that hiss as they hit the wet marble. The embers narrowly miss the twenty-foot-tall statue of the goddess, which looks almost exactly like the one in Unnbriel.

"Aaric said that to me," I counter, moving to Tairn's shoulder, but he doesn't lower it. *"Not you. And I denied his suggestion!"*

"How are you angry? Princes do not make suggestions, and I am an extension of you." Andarna marches forward, lowering her head in threat. *"Am I not everything you wanted me to be? Am I not as fierce and courageous as he is? Is this not what I am supposed to do? Sharpen my claws on the scales of the enemy?"*

The wind picks up, and something in my chest cracks.

"Your tantrum is ill-timed, Golden One," Tairn growls.

"Do not call me a child." Andarna's scales shimmer but remain black.

"Do not act like one!" he snarls.

"What was that all about?" Rhiannon shouts from Feirge's back. "We could have caught them!"

And died. "That was Theophanie," I call back.

"And?" Rhi throws her arms up.

"And I couldn't fly with you—Tairn's wounded," I reply. Does she have a death wish? *"Let me down so I can get that thing out of your leg. Or I'll just jump."* Tairn dips his shoulder with a grumble, and I dismount a few feet in front of Andarna. *"I don't need you to be* anything *but who you are."* I yank my flight goggles to the top of my head and look straight into her golden eyes. *"Clearly we need to have a conversation when we're not in the middle of a battlefield. You always say that you chose me, but I stood in front of* you *on that Threshing field. And I would do it again."*

She huffs a breath and we head for Tairn's hind leg, keeping one eye on the sky.

I will never understand what goes on in an adolescent brain.

My stomach lurches as the wound comes into view. Holy shit, the wingspur is easily half my size and embedded in his thigh. There's no way he can launch with it in, and even out, the wound might cause too much pain. Moonlight catches on his blood as it drips down his scales. How in Dunne's name am I supposed to get that thing out? *"I'm so sorry."*

"It looks worse than it is. Merely the tip is embedded."

"How much pain are you in?"

"Mentally or physically?" he growls.

"Your sarcasm *is ill-timed."* I reach to the full extent of my height but can't come close to the wingspur.

"Where is he hurt?" Rhiannon asks, jogging over. Mercifully, she looks unharmed.

"There." I point up at his thigh, and she gasps. "You should get back to the others. We're vulnerable out here."

"I'm not leaving. You don't always have to do everything on your own." She backs up a handful of steps and lifts her arms.

"Sometimes, I do," I counter.

She shakes her head. "We can handle this."

"Are you really—" I start, my eyebrows rising as she tenses.

A moment later, Tairn roars, and I flinch.

The wingspur appears in front of Rhiannon.

My mouth drops as she shoves it away, and the hooked piece of claw topples to the ground. "How did you just do that?"

"I practice." Rhiannon grins and drags the back of her hand across her forehead, wiping away a sheen of sweat. "Though it's the biggest thing I've ever retrieved."

"Thank you." I grab her into a quick hug, then look up at Tairn's wound. *"I can't see much in the dark. We need to get you back to the valley."*

His head swivels toward us, and Feirge turns, too. *"It is too late for that. We have minutes."*

Wingbeats fill the air, and I spot three wyvern on approach, a blur of more in the distance.

Rhiannon and I lock eyes for one telling second, and then we both *run*. She sprints toward Feirge, and I bolt underneath Tairn, racing toward his foreleg.

"Fly back, now!" I order Andarna.

"They'd be defenseless," she argues, and my heart drops when I emerge under Tairn's chest.

Dozens of white-haired temple attendants and their high priestess wait at the top of the steps behind Andarna, their attention focused on the night sky. "Get inside!" I shout. Some shelter is better than no shelter, right?

"So we can burn inside?" the high priestess asks, her voice eerily calm as the wingbeats grow louder.

Shit. There's no time to argue, and I can't abandon them. Andarna's right—if we take to the skies, we leave them defenseless, and Tairn is already wounded.

But I don't need to be mounted to wield.

"Tell Feirge to go," I say down the bond, then run up the rain-slick marble steps for a higher vantage point, palming the conduit. *"I'd ask you to go with her, but I know better."*

"And yet you still mentioned it." Tairn slowly turns to face the incoming wyvern with Andarna and lifts his tail high. *"Be warned. Should Theophanie appear, I will choose your life over the attendants'."*

Should Theophanie appear, we're all fucked. If any venin report to the others that they've gotten this close to Aretia's gates without being halted by wards, they'll skip over the undrained territory of Krovla and come for our hatching ground.

We can't afford to let a single wyvern escape.

"Will you at least consider taking cover?" I ask the high priestess when I reach the landing.

"We will not." Her gaze assesses me in two seconds, then lingers on the silver half of my braid. "Do you use lye and the juice of the Manwasa flower on your hair as we do?"

My eyebrows hit my hairline. Does she realize how much danger we're in? Now can't be the right time to have this conversation. "It just grows like this."

"Does it?" Her tattooed forehead crinkles. "You have journeyed far to come to our aid." The priestess draws the shortsword sheathed at her hip. "Either Dunne protects us, or we meet Malek as her worthy servants."

"Dunne isn't going to appear and take up arms," I argue, even though I know it's pointless, then turn to stand at her side. Tairn has prowled to the left, giving me a clear view of the three approaching wyvern, while Feirge stands ready to fly to the right of the steps.

"Of course not." The priestess scoffs, and the wind picks up. "She sent you."

"Well, she's never been revered for her judgment." I add temple attendants to the growing list of thought processes I'll never comprehend, and open my Archives door just enough to test. Power fills my veins like hot water poured over a sunburn, and I breathe in slowly, accepting the pain and setting my new baseline. *"Why hasn't Feirge launched?"*

"The squad leader will not leave you," Andarna replies.

Damn it. I lift my right hand—

"Let's not do that," a familiar voice says from my left.

My head snaps in that direction, and dread anchors my feet to the temple floor. I unsheathe both my daggers.

Theophanie.

Tairn's head swivels, his growl rattling what's left of the spilled coals, and attendants gasp all around us.

"Launch before she drains you," I beg Tairn and Andarna, but true to their nature, they stay put.

"Lift a blade or a hand to wield, and I'll kill you all. Come with me, and I'll let the rest live," Theophanie says from the base of the steps, her dark-purple tunic contrasting the pallor of her skin. The red veins beside her eyes pulse in time with a heartbeat as she offers a weary smile that's all the more unsettling for its exhausted satisfaction. She cocks her head to the side. "Let's not fight, Violet. Doesn't all this violence tire you? Come with me. I'll give you what you want most."

"You have no idea what I want most." My stomach curdles, and the high priestess sidesteps me.

"Heretic! You are not welcome here," she shouts, her voice breaking with a rasp.

Heretic? My gaze darts between the two women as my mind races in time with my heartbeat. The faded forehead tattoo. Theophanie was a *priestess* of Dunne. Her silver hair matches the attendants' on Unnbriel...matches mine—

My thoughts stall as the white-haired priestess raises her sword toward Theophanie with a trembling arm.

Oh shit. Power floods my body in a scalding rush of fire. There are too many people around for me to miss, and if she drains this close—

"Perhaps *I* am not welcome," Theophanie muses, her feet planted in the grass, "but they are."

Two more venin, men wearing red robes, walk through the grass behind her, and Andarna leaps over Tairn's tail, blasting a stream of fire Theophanie's way. The scents of ash and sulfur fill the air, but when Andarna lands at the base of the steps to my right, Theophanie still stands untouched.

"*Why?*" Andarna shrieks.

"Marvelous," Theophanie says with a smile. "Did that make you feel bet—" Theophanie's gaze rises to the sky behind me, and she backs away, her eyes widening. "Leave them and go!" she shouts to the approaching dark wielders and breaks into a run toward them. "Now!"

All three grasp hands, and the one in the center takes a single step and *vanishes.*

Just like Garrick.

"*Incoming!*" Tairn roars, and my focus swings east.

There's no time to ponder what in Malek's name just frightened Theophanie so badly that she fled. The four wyvern still on approach descend in a wing formation, one taking point with the others closely following. And they're headed straight for us.

I lift my right hand again. Gathering more energy feels like I'm picking up the glowing coals Andarna scattered with my bare hands, but they'll be here in less than thirty seconds.

"*Any time now, Silver One,*" Andarna prompts, moving back to Tairn's side and stalking forward as Feirge crouches, ready to take the fight to the sky.

If darkness has thrown off my depth perception, if they're flying faster than I estimate, we're all about to be cooked. I target the lead wyvern and send up a prayer to Dunne. Then I wield, releasing a blast of energy and flicking my finger downward. No holding on this time. I learned my lesson.

Magic washes over me, prickling my skin in a familiar wave, and lightning strikes the first wyvern. It drops from the sky in a ball of fire, but we can't celebrate with three still—

What the fuck?

They're no longer flying toward us; they're *falling.* My heart beats wildly as they plummet like projectiles. The ground shudders as the one on the right hits about sixty feet ahead, its momentum driving it into the dirt.

"*Prepare!*" Tairn shouts, leaping at the one on the left. Pain shoots down the bond as he knocks it off course, and dirt flies to the left of the temple when it lands.

Leaving one that rivals Feirge's size still falling.

It slams against the ground twenty feet in front of Andarna, then skids toward us with all the grace of a battering ram. And it's not stopping.

"*Go!*" Tairn orders, and fear clenches my chest as Andarna holds her position.

"*It's too big for you!*" I shout.

Feirge takes a single step and swings her head like a mace into Andarna's side, heaving her out of the wyvern's path just before it careens across the very ground she'd been standing on.

The wyvern barrels toward us, eyes sightless, teeth exposed.

"Move!" I grab the high priestess's elbow and *pull*, dragging her out of the way as the carcass crashes toward the marble stairs. Screams erupt as attendants scatter, and the wyvern's shoulders take out the bottom portion of the steps at the same moment its head crashes into the intricately carved central pillar.

Oh *shit.*

The column explodes on impact, and chunks of marble fly. Throwing up my hands, I push with all the lesser magic I'm capable of, but there's no stopping the claw-size pieces of rock hurtling in every direction, including ours.

But then they do just that...stop.

The one a few feet from my face hangs in midair, its flame-inspired etched edges suspended by a single black band of shadow.

Xaden.

Relief weakens my knees, and the remnant of the destroyed pillar slowly lowers to the ground, settling with a *thunk.* All around us, attendants scurry out of the way as the other pieces descend gently.

My head swings right, past the remaining pillars and the high priestess, following the retreating shadows to their wielder.

Xaden climbs the only intact section of steps two at a time, lowering his right hand while blood drips from the sword in his left. There's no trace of red in his eyes, just determination and quickly fading fear as he glances down my frame, looking for injuries.

I do the same to him, and my heart jolts at the blood streaking the side of his face.

"It isn't mine," he says a second before he pulls me against his chest. I drop my forehead, breathing deeply to steady my heartbeat, and he presses a hard kiss to the top of my head. "And it *is* always you."

There's no benefit to arguing given the circumstances. "How did you get here so quickly?"

"You let this happen to him?*"* Sgaeyl snaps.

I step out of Xaden's arms and find Sgaeyl's narrowed eyes and sharp teeth unsettlingly close. "I'm sorry—"

"She bears no responsibility," Tairn argues. Sgaeyl's head whips in his direction, and a thick wall of shields immediately blocks our connection. Cue fight.

"She refused to hold her position once she felt the wound," Xaden replies, surveying the temple. "And I'm glad, or it looks like we'd both be dead. We were almost here when the wards went up."

The wards? My eyebrows rise. That explains the ripple of magic, the wyvern falling from the sky, Theophanie's fear. "But how?"

The sound of a slide whistle screeches through my head, and both Xaden and I pivot, putting our backs to the temple.

To the left of the wyvern's body, behind Tairn and Sgaeyl, darkness transforms. Scales the color of night ripple into a shade that's not quite black or purple, forming the dragon whose horns carry the same swirling pattern as Andarna's.

"It seemed necessary to fire your wardstone," Leothan says.

My stomach bottoms out.

The irids have come.

CHAPTER
FIFTY-THREE

If the irids fired the wardstone as the seventh breed, then Aretia is *safe*. Most of Tyrrendor is.

It's too surreal, too easy. Emotions beyond names hit me from every side, but fear replaces them all when Feirge swings her body to confront the irid, lowering her head and baring her teeth.

"No!" Andarna bounds from Tairn's side, leaping over the wyvern to put herself in front of Feirge. *"He's of my line!"*

The Green Daggertail retreats a single step but leaves her head near the ground as Rhiannon dismounts, jumping straight to the platform of the temple.

Xaden tenses at the sight of the irid, even though there's no sign of red in his eyes. "You handle that, and I will see what needs to be done…here."

Considering what happened the last time he met with an irid, I nod.

"Give him my gratitude," Xaden says quietly as Rhi races our way.

"I will," I promise, locking eyes with Rhi.

She bobs her head in acknowledgment, and then we walk down the stairs.

"No weapons," I tell Rhi as we walk between Tairn and Sgaeyl. "They're pacifists."

"Got it," she notes, keeping pace at my side. "So he shouldn't burn us to death, right? I refuse to tell Feirge that she was right. She'll never let me live it down, even if I'm dead. And I really want to know what just happened with those dark wielders."

"I'll fill you in," I reply as we approach Leothan and Andarna. "Just be prepared for—"

Rhi gasps and covers her ears.

"That," I finish with a wince.

Leothan glances at Rhi, then turns his back to the corpse of the wyvern with a look of what can only be called disdain.

Andarna moves to my left when we reach them, flooding the bond with a mix of apprehension and excitement.

"I would expect a warmer greeting from a green," Leothan lectures Rhi, then turns his golden gaze on me.

"Thank you," I blurt awkwardly, craning my neck to look at him. "You've saved everyone in this province."

"I did not do it for you," he says, peering down at Andarna.

"Harsh," Rhi whispers.

"I give my thanks," Andarna replies, her head high.

"Your human is as dangerous as we feared." He studies her with a tilted head, and my stomach sinks. Whatever he's seen has only confirmed the reasons they denied Andarna in the first place.

"She defends her people," Andarna retorts, her claws flexing in the rain-soaked grass. At least the weather has eased to a drizzle. *"And ours."*

"As do you." Leothan's voice softens. *"I have been watching you since my arrival."*

And no one knew. Tairn bristles, and my throat grows tight.

"And what have you seen?" Andarna's tail flicks overhead. *"What judgment have you passed?"*

Her caustic tone certainly isn't going to help, and neither is the growl rumbling in Sgaeyl's throat.

The irid narrows his eyes. *"Your behavior is abhorrent and your actions misguided—"*

"She is a credit to our riot," Sgaeyl hisses.

"As we hoped she would be." He swivels his head toward Sgaeyl, and Tairn angles into a striking position. *"Yet in none of the ways we value."*

Rhi steps closer to my side.

"None of which is her fault," I interject, and he looks my way. "You set her up for what you consider failure when you left her here to be raised in the ways of the Empyrean."

"You really want to yell at the massive unknown dragon?" Rhi whispers.

"I do," I answer, looking straight at him. "There is *nothing* wrong with her. We can never thank you enough for what you've done tonight in firing our wards, but if you've only come to point out all the ways you believe her to be lacking, you'll find Feirge's greeting *warmer* than mine."

He tilts his head, then dismisses me, swinging his gaze to Andarna. *"Your motives are honorable,"* he says. *"That was what I was going to say before I was interrupted by the blue."*

"Sgaeyl," Andarna corrects him, her tone a knife's edge softer than before.

"Sgaeyl," he repeats, then focuses on Andarna. *"We are separated by many generations but share the same bloodline. Unlike the others you encountered who are of a more distant line, we are of the same den, or would have been had you been raised among us."*

He's her family. My heart clenches.

"Your human may stay," he replies to Andarna. *"The rest may not participate in our conversation."*

My eyebrows rise.

"I will not leave them unprotected." Tairn's claws flex next to Rhi.

"The fact you think they need protection is why my words are only for them." Leothan keeps his focus on Andarna. *"I will only offer once."*

Andarna tenses, then whips her head toward Tairn and Sgaeyl. *"I must hear him."*

Sgaeyl startles, and Rhi's hands jump to cover her ears.

Tairn snarls, and I reach down the bond, but there's a stronger shield than his blocking us. Leothan.

It's oddly similar to the effects of the serum they dosed us with during RSC. Every part of me rebels at the disconnect, but I owe it to Andarna to stay with her.

"We will begin once they depart," Leothan promises.

"He's cut us off from you," I say to Rhi, then look up at Tairn. "I'll be all right."

Sgaeyl bares her teeth, then pivots abruptly and turns toward the temple, toward Xaden.

"You're sure?" Rhi asks, worry knitting her brow.

"I'm sure." I swallow the growing boulder in my throat. "I won't be the reason she can't hear him out."

Rhi looks like she's going to argue for a second, then nods. "We won't be far." She follows Sgaeyl, and Tairn growls in warning at Leothan before pivoting.

Andarna's tail curves over my head.

"It did not sit well with me that you were judged by the shortcomings of others," Leothan states, dipping his head to Andarna's eye level. *"Even the dark wielder you seem…fond of."*

Hope flickers in my chest, burning away the expected insults, and Andarna's scales ripple in shades of black.

"You should be given the chance to learn our ways," he continues. *"To choose our ways."*

"You will stay and teach me?" she asks.

"You will come home with me," he answers, holding her gaze. *"It may take a few years, but the others will accept my decision. By then you will have learned enough to know your truth."*

Years? My stomach launches straight into my throat.

"We cannot leave for years." Sorrow drenches Andarna's words.

"You can," he rebuts.

"By myself?" She freezes.

Oh gods. My spine stiffens, and a terror I've never encountered before locks my muscles. He means to separate us.

"I have saved the human you care for by firing the protections in place," he states, like he's checking off boxes that might impede her departure. *"She will be safe from all but her own kind under the wing of your mentor."*

"I cannot leave her!" Andarna's head draws back.

My heart thunders a dangerously quick beat.

"You must. This was not meant for you, nor any of our line. Look at what happened tonight. Had I not interfered, you would no longer exist." His scales flicker, taking on a pearlescent sheen. *"There is nothing here for you but war and suffering."*

And me. And Tairn. And Sgaeyl. It takes all my self-control not to scream it, not to ruin this moment for Andarna.

"I am bonded." Andarna's tail lowers, curving around me. *"Our lives, our minds, the very energy that forms us is intertwined."*

Right. That. Exactly. I find myself nodding.

"So end it." He angles his head, and the scales above his eyes furrow into a single line. *"Bonds are merely magical ties. You are irid. You are magic. Bend it, shape it, break it as you see fit."*

Wait. What?

"I cannot." Andarna's tail winds closer.

Air becomes scarce, and my head starts to swim.

"And yet you already did." He glances down at me. *"Who bonded you first?"*

This can't be real. Maybe I'm dreaming. Or in Xaden's dream. Though we've definitely stumbled into nightmare territory. "They chose me the same day."

He sighs in annoyance, and steam gusts over me. *"Who spoke to you first?"*

My eyes shift, and I throw my thoughts back to Threshing.

Step aside, Silver One. Tairn's voice rumbles through my memory.

"Tairn," I whisper, turning my face toward Andarna. I take in everything about her, from the pattern of her scales, the slope of her nose, the angle of her eyes, up to the swirls on her horns that match his. "You didn't speak to me until you gave me your name on the flight field."

She blinks.

"*See?*" Leothan shifts his focus to Andarna. "*Humans should only be capable of bonding a single dragon, and yet you forged a second connection where there shouldn't be one. Only an irid can do that. Your instincts are excellent, but you need instruction. Break the connection and come with me.*"

My heart thunders like hoofbeats in my ears.

"*But Violet…*" Andarna's tone shifts from denial to… Amari help me, is that worry?

I blanch as it hits me. She wants to go. Of course she does. He's her family—the only dragon of her kind willing to accept her. I'm the one holding her back.

"*Her other bond will sustain her life,*" Leothan states like that's all there is between Andarna and me. "*Should you choose to return, you can always reforge the bond.*"

When she doesn't respond, he lowers his head to my eye level. "*She is emotionally ensnared because of her age. What would you have her do?*"

Andarna ducks her head.

"I…" Warmth drains from my face, but I keep my eyes on her, memorizing every detail like it might be the last time I see her. The possibility is unfathomable—I developed my signet out of sheer need for *her*—and yet it feels like we're hurtling toward some kind of precipice. "I love you and I want you to feel complete," I tell her, and she slowly meets my gaze. "I want you happy and safe and thriving. I want you to live." My voice breaks. "Even if it's not with me."

"*Admirable,*" Leothan says. "*I understand your choice.*"

Yearning floods the bond, so deep it aches within my own chest, and the pain of it sucks the breath from my lungs. I force my head to nod, feeling everything she can't say.

"*I do not know how—*" she starts.

A shrieking whistle sounds in my head, and then only silence remains. I reach for the bond and find only a wall…then nothing.

Andarna whips her head toward Leothan.

He launches without warning, springing high above me. His wings snap open, and wind blasts my face as he gains altitude. His scales flicker, turning the color of the cloudy night sky, and he begins to disappear.

Andarna roars up at him, and then her gaze swings wildly, focusing behind me, then to the right, then landing on me for the length of a heartbeat. Her eyes flare like she wants to say something, and I throw myself at the wall where our bond should be.

But it's gone.

A breath later, so is she.

All that's left is a gust of wind as her scales blend into the sky.

A roar vibrates my very bones, and my ears ring as the edges of my vision darken. My heart stutters, and my lungs cease their struggle. There's no air and no reason to seek it. I was infinite yet moored, and now I'm hollow and adrift in waters too vast to comprehend.

My knees buckle, then collide with the ground.

"Violct!" someone shouts, and racing bootsteps register a second before she crouches in front of me, her brown eyes searching mine for answers I don't have. "Are you all right?"

I'm nothing.

The sky darkens, and the ground trembles. I look up into the black void, and my vision narrows in an ever-shrinking circle. Not the sky. A wing.

Stern, demanding golden eyes appear.

"You will breathe!" His deep, gravelly voice fills my head, and unyielding strength barrels down the pathway that connects us.

Tairn.

He exists, therefore I must, because we are bound. Never alone. Always connected.

I gasp and air rushes in. My heart pounds in an erratic, painful beat, but the edges of my vision clear. *"She left us. She left us. She left us."* It's all I can think.

"We *remain*," Tairn orders, as if I have a choice not to.

"What happened?" Someone hits his knees beside me, and my gaze swings, meeting amber-flecked onyx. Not someone—Xaden. *"Violet?"* Worry and fear slide down the bond that tethers us, and the connection anchors my heartbeat.

I exist for Tairn, but I live for Xaden.

"I don't know," Rhiannon answers, and I find her watching me with heartrending worry that I instantly want to soothe.

Rhi's still here. So are Mira, and Brennan, and Ridoc, and Sawyer, and Dain, and Jesinia, and Imogen, and Aaric…everyone is here but *her.*

"How could she do this?" Sgaeyl snaps, fury sharpening the words to daggers.

"She's gone," I whisper to Rhi, then crumple under the weight of the unbearable truth. Xaden catches me, tugging my shoulder against his chest, and his brow furrows as our gazes collide. "Andarna's gone."

No rider has ever survived the loss of their dragon.
I can't imagine wanting to.

—Colonel Kaori's Field Guide To Dragonkind

CHAPTER
FIFTY-FOUR

*A*ndarna is gone.

I don't leave our room for the next three days. I barely leave our bed.

Andarna is gone.

But I'm never alone.

Brennan reads in a chair by my bedside in the mornings while I drift in and out of sleep. My squadmates take over in the afternoon, but their voices barely cut through the fog of exhaustion. They are an endless stream of company that doesn't know what to say, which is fine by me, since I don't have it in me to answer. Xaden holds me at night, wrapping his arms and his mind around me.

Andarna is gone.

Tairn leaves our bond wide open, giving me unfettered access to him in a way I've never had. He's always been with me, but now I'm with him, too. I hear his side of the conversation when he tells the elders about Andarna's departure. I hear him bickering with Sgaeyl over what he calls her *excessive hovering*, and I'm privy to the lecture he gives Xaden about making sure I eat.

That's not all I hear. For the first two days, every time the door opens, there's an air of celebration, sounds of happy voices and laughter that fade the second someone walks in.

Of course they're happy. Aretia's safe. The very thing we were desperate for a few months ago has been accomplished. I don't blame them for celebrating—I just can't join them. That would require feeling something, anything.

I sleep, but I don't dream.

Andarna is gone.

The atmosphere shifts on the third day, but I don't ask about the tension in my squadmates' silence. Not because I don't care, but because it takes all my energy to perform what should be the natural act of breathing.

She'll come back, right? She has to. She isn't dead. Leothan will ensure she makes it across the sea. And if she returns to find me like this, huddled in on myself, I won't be worthy of her relic. If this is an emotional Gauntlet, I'm failing, but there's no rope to grab to prevent my fall this time.

On the fourth morning, I wake when the mattress dips behind me.

"I did not fly through the night to watch you sleep. Wake up."

Her voice jars me like nothing else can. I roll over and find Mira staring at me from Xaden's side of the bed, her legs stretched out on top of the blankets, her stockinged feet crossed at the ankles. Dark circles linger under her eyes as she studies mine, but I don't spot any new wounds, thankfully.

"I don't want to." Lack of use makes my voice scratchy.

"Yeah." She studies my eyes with a creased brow and smooths my hair back from my forehead. "But you have to. You can cry, or scream, or even break shit if you want, but you cannot live in this bed."

"I was whole and now I'm not." My eyes sting, but I don't cry. That stopped days ago. "She's really gone."

"I'm so sorry." Sympathy fills Mira's expression. "But not sorry enough to lose you to your grief. You just have to start by getting up." She wrinkles her nose. "Then you can graduate to bathing."

Someone knocks, and my focus jumps to the closed bedroom door. "How did you get in here, anyway?"

"Riorson let me in." Her hand slides from my head as the door opens. *Of course he did.* "She's awake," Mira calls over her shoulder.

Xaden looks in, worry etching lines across his forehead until he spots me. "Look who's up." A corner of his mouth rises.

"Unwillingly," I admit.

His eyes flare, and I realize it's the first time I've spoken to him in days, too. *Shit.* I need to pull myself together.

"How did you replace the power you lost?" Mira asks quickly.

I wrench my gaze back to hers. "I…didn't. What are you talking about?"

"If she's awake, then let me in," Brennan argues from the hallway behind Xaden. "They're *my* sisters!"

"I can kill him if you prefer," Xaden offers, raising his scarred brow.

"And give him another opportunity to fake his own death?" Mira scoffs.

"He can come in." Pushing with both hands, I force myself to sit up. I've been in Xaden's sparring shirt and a rolled-up pair of his sleeping pants for so long, they're practically embedded in my skin.

Xaden pulls Brennan through the doorway, and my brother immediately frowns at Mira.

"What are you doing?" Brennan questions as he shuts the door behind him.

Xaden leans back against the bookshelves and stares at me like I might flee at any second or worse—disappear back under the covers. *"Hi."*

"Hi." I don't have it in me to smile, but I drink in the sight of him.

Mira's eyes narrow at Brennan in warning. "You sent me a missive saying our sister was a breath away from catatonic, so now I'm here. What does it look like I'm doing?"

"I wanted you to get her out of bed." Brennan gestures at me. "Not crawl into it with her."

"I've been here less than half an hour and she's already speaking, so I think my methodology is pretty sound." She levels him with a look that reminds me of Mom. "What exactly have *you* been doing?"

Mom would definitely be horrified by my inability to function.

"Sitting in that chair"—he points beside the bed—"figuring out how to house and feed the thousands of people currently climbing the Medaro Pass, while overseeing a massive increase in forge output, in addition to spending my evenings mending every wounded rider capable of flying here from the front."

"You don't have to tell *me* about the front." Mira taps her chest. "Raising the wards must have pissed them off, because they are kicking our ass out there and all we can do is fall back. I can see Draithus from the line."

"You really opened the border." My eyes widen on Xaden as my siblings continue to argue in the background.

He nods once. *"It's what my father would have wanted."*

But Fen didn't actually do it. Xaden did. And I've been too lost in my misery to even know, let alone support him in an act of blatant treason. My face falls.

"Whatever you're thinking, stop," Xaden says, tilting his head.

"I've left you to deal with it alone." Lewellen would be heinously disappointed in me. I'm heinously disappointed in *myself.*

"You've been breathing, and that's enough for me." The relief in his eyes is palpable, and that somehow makes me feel worse.

I'm supposed to be stronger than this. What else have I missed?

"She lost a *dragon*," Mira shouts. "Not a boyfriend. It's not a breakup." Her gaze swings to Xaden. "No offense."

The emptiness threatens to overwhelm me again, but Tairn inundates the bond with a deluge of defiance and indignation. *"Focus on now, on him if you have to."*

I still have both of them: Tairn and Xaden.

"None taken." Xaden folds his arms but doesn't look away. "We're past the breakup stage."

"Point is," Mira lectures Brennan, "the deficit of power has to be staggering, let alone the emotional impact of severing a bond."

"Stop talking about me like I'm not here," I whisper.

"I didn't imply she has to bounce back like a toy," Brennan retorts.

"Stop!" My shout brings the room to a standstill. I have to get out of this bed, if only to escape from their arguing.

Brennan's entire body sags. "Thank the gods. You speak."

"I told you she speaks!" Mira throws up her hands.

"No wonder Dad spent so much time in the Archives," I mutter, then peel back the covers. Step one, get out of bed. Step two, bathe off four days of misery.

"And now you're telling jokes?" Brennan's mouth drops.

"She likes me more than you." Mira brushes a piece of grass off her uniform.

"Nothing about this is funny." My feet hit the floor. "You two have *got* to stop fighting. Work it out, because other than Niara, we're all that's left." I slowly stand.

Xaden moves to push off the bookshelves, and I shake my head at him.

"I need a moment." I make my way to the bathing chamber, reminding myself to breathe. The argument dims as I shut the door, then disappears when I start the bath after relieving myself. *"Moment over."*

Xaden walks through the door in a matter of seconds and quickly shuts it behind him, cutting off Brennan's and Mira's raised voices.

"Are they still arguing?" I sit on the edge of the tub and reach in to test the water.

"They're your siblings," he answers, rolling up his uniform sleeves as he comes my way. "Let me do that." He dips his hand in the bath, then adjusts the lever that brings water in from the aqueduct system. "Can I help you?"

I nod.

He strips me out of my clothes, and I get into the tub. Warm water rushes over me as I lean back, and I start pulling apart the strands of my braid. Kneeling beside me, he lathers soap on a small cloth and begins to wash me, starting at my feet.

"You have other things you should be doing," I say softly, watching his eyes as his hands move with a gentleness that would shock everyone but me.

"Everything else will wait." He moves to my knee.

But it can't. Not if he's opened the border against the decree of the Senarium, though I love him all the more for saying so. It doesn't matter how impossible everything feels; the world is still spinning beyond these doors. And I have to catch up to it.

I'm a master of pain, and Andarna's loss is the deepest I've ever had to mask in order to survive. But I don't have to pretend with Xaden.

"I've missed three days of rune instruction," I whisper when I'm nearly clean. Best to start small when it comes to what's lacking in my life. Plus, it's one of the only areas in my life where I've never allowed him to assist.

"Hate to break it to you, love, but three days was never going to help you in that subject." His lips twitch, and he moves the cloth down my arm.

"Will you help me?" The words are easier than I thought they'd be.

His gaze snaps to mine. "Ask me nicely."

The corners of my mouth quirk as I remember the last time he made the same demand and ended up kissing me against the foundation wall. "Will you please help me?"

"Always." He finishes with my hand. "May I wash your hair?"

"Please." I duck my head under the water as Xaden moves behind me. Then I rise and search for the right words. The simple pleasure of his hands working soap through my hair gives me a flicker of hope that I might just be able to feel something positive again. "I think I know why riders die when their dragons do."

His fingers pause before he continues. "Why?"

"It's not just the deficit of power," I muse, cupping the bathwater with my hand, then letting it flow out between my fingers. "In that moment, I didn't know who I was, where I belonged, or why I should bother breathing. If Tairn hadn't grounded me, I think I would have willingly floated away. I still can't comprehend the enormity of her absence. I don't know if I ever will. I can't see past it."

"You don't have to yet." He moves to my side and sits on the edge of the tub.

"Yes, I do. I'm pretty sure I just heard my siblings say the western line is crumbling and you have thousands of people fleeing into your province." I tilt my head. "Is there more?"

"Yes," he answers without hesitation. "But no rider has survived what you just did—"

"Except Jack Barlowe," I interrupt.

"Glad to see your sense of humor is intact." He lifts his scarred brow. "No one expects you to be anywhere close to fully functional."

"I do." Keeping busy will prevent me from falling back into that bed. I lean into Tairn and try to ignore the gaping void where Andarna should be.

"Then here's the question." He grips the side of the tub and searches my eyes. "Do you need me to take care of you or kick your ass? I'm fully capable of and willing to do both."

"I know it." My lips press into a tight line. I want him to take care of me, but I need him to kick my ass, and *need* beats *want* every time. I sink under the water and work the soap from my hair, lingering in the absolute silence a moment longer than necessary to rinse. When I emerge, Xaden is leaning forward like he was one second shy of coming in after me. My body remembers to breathe on its own. "Can you grab me a uniform from the armoire? I need to get dressed."

He nods, then presses a kiss to my wet forehead. "Be right back."

By the time he returns, I'm drying my hair and body while the water drains.

Reluctance mars his face as he hands over my things. "I'm going back out there to make sure they don't kill each other. Who is Niara?"

My eyebrows shoot up. "My grandmother."

"She's apparently a sore subject." He grimaces and heads into the bedroom.

I get dressed quickly, leaving my hair wet and unbound as I burst through the bathing chamber door into our bedroom.

Mira and Brennan look one step away from drawing weapons and are utterly oblivious to my arrival. Shadows curl at Xaden's feet as he leans on the edge of our desk, arms folded, eyes narrowed on my siblings.

"She hated our mother." Brennan shakes his head. "I can't believe you would go there."

"Violet has Dad's books. You have Aretia," Mira hisses. "I went to the only other living member of our family because all I have are a few of Mom's journals, and there are *months* missing, Brennan."

"He recognized the bracelet as belonging to your grandmother, and it went downhill from there," Xaden fills me in.

"So Mom didn't journal for a couple of months. So what." He shrugs. "Did you ask Violet if she has—"

"The months are missing in the middle of the book," she counters. "And they're from the summer Mom and Dad left us with Grandma Niara. Mom purposely didn't write anything."

Wait. I've read that journal, too.

"That doesn't mean—" Brennan starts.

"I was eight," Mira interrupts. "And it was just you and me, remember? Violet was too little to stay. When they returned, Grandma stopped speaking to them."

"Want me to figure out…" Xaden lifts a brow and glances in my direction.

"No." I shoot him a warning look.

"That doesn't mean they hauled her to Dunne's temple and dedicated her." Brennan shakes his head with disgust. "That's been illegal since the two hundreds."

Dedicated. Gravity pitches and my balance shifts, like the stone beneath my feet has suddenly become sand.

It is good we did not complete your dedication. The Unnbrish high priestess's words ring through my head, as does the memory of her silver hair, just like

Theophanie's, just like mine.

"Violet?" A band of shadow wraps around my hips, steadying me for the heartbeat it takes Xaden to reach me and replace it with his arm.

"Then they went to Poromiel to do it!" Mira shouts. "You *will* believe me, Brennan, because it happened! It's why she refused to speak to either of them. The priestess started the process, then told Mom and Dad that they only accepted children whose futures are certain, and Violet still had paths to choose from—"

"Since when do you believe in drug-induced hallucinations spit out by oracles?" Brennan throws up his hands, revealing the rune-shaped scar on his palm. "Or the ranting of our grandmother?"

Tell me, did you choose this path yourself? That's what the priestess asked me.

"—and one of those paths…" Mira runs him right over, shaking her head. "They refused to take her. And I've been requesting temple records for months, but of course none of them would list a child, let alone a *Sorrengail.*"

My mind races, putting together pieces of a picture that I have no desire to see but am somehow a part of.

Brennan glances my way and blanches. "Mira—"

"The priestess spoke all cryptically but basically said if Violet chose her future poorly, she could still earn their mentorship, but she'd turn—" Mira continues.

"Mira!" Brennan gestures toward me.

Her startled gaze whips in my direction, and she flinches. "Violet," she whispers, shaking her head. "I didn't mean for you to… I'm sorry."

"Turn what?" I demand. There's only one *turn* that comes to mind.

She looks at Xaden. "Do you want to give us a second?"

"Stay." I lean into him as my thoughts spin.

"No," he answers Mira.

"Turn venin?" I guess.

Mira presses her lips into a tight line.

"You wouldn't find any records at our temples," I say slowly, heaviness settling in my chest.

"Because they never tried to dedicate you," Brennan assures me, glaring at our sister.

"They did." I nod sluggishly. "It just wasn't here. They must have taken me to Unnbriel. It explains why you think my hair grew in like this, and the wild things that priestess said to me before she sliced my arm open."

"No." Brennan puts his hands on his hips. "Dad thought you were perfect, and he said that parents *used* to dedicate their infants to a particular deity's service when they thought the touch of a god would help that child—" He quickly shuts his mouth.

My stomach hollows. "They tried to *fix* me by giving me to Dunne?"

"No chance. Mom was never temple-minded," Brennan argues. "And you've never needed fixing."

I'm not sure I'll ever forgive him for what he's done to her.

Oh gods. They'd never seen dragons until our squad arrived.

"Mom didn't take me." My eyes sting at the unexpected betrayal. "Dad did." A horrified laugh bubbles up through my throat. "It's why he told you that little piece of history, Brennan. In case you needed to put it together. It's why he *sent* me there with those books." I look to Mira. "I don't think any of us actually knew our parents." I blink. "Is that why you've been so distant lately? Why you constantly look at me like I'm going to grow a set of horns? Because you think I'm going to turn at any second?"

"No. Yes. Maybe. I don't know." She moves toward me, but Brennan blocks her path.

"What did she say?" Brennan asks Mira. "What were the priestess's exact words?"

Mira twists the bracelet, then looks me straight in the eye. "She said the heart that beat for you—or within you—would do the wrong thing for the right reason, reach for unspeakable power, and turn dark."

My lips part.

"*Within* her or *for* her?" Brennan asks.

"Isn't it the same thing?" Mira challenges. "Violet's at risk of turning, and with power like hers—"

"Stop," Xaden says, and my head snaps in his direction. "It's not Violet. It's me."

"*No!*" I shout down the bond, fear grasping me so tight my head lightens.

"My heart beats for her," he tells Mira without so much as flinching. "I reached for unspeakable power. I turned. I'm the dark wielder she warned your father about, not Violet. Stop treating her like she's a liability. I'm already the problem."

Oh *fuck*.

Mira's eyes sharpen on him, then me. "He's not serious."

"He is," I confess, my voice barely a whisper. "He's the reason we survived Basgiath."

"Since *December*?" Her eyes bulge as she unsheathes the alloy-hilted dagger at her thigh.

"No!" I move in front of Xaden. "He's stable."

"He's venin!" Mira lifts her blade.

"I don't take kindly to blades being lifted toward Violet." Xaden sweeps me to his side.

"Like *I'm* the dangerous one?" She flips the dagger in readiness to throw, and power rushes into me. "Brennan, are you—"

"Don't," my brother says softly.

Mira pauses and turns at the tone of his voice, understanding creeping over her face. "You knew?" Mira's gaze jumps from Brennan, to Xaden, to me, hurt and shock mixing in a lethal combination. "He'll kill you," she says to me finally. "It's what they do."

"He won't." I pour every ounce of my certainty, my trust into the words.

"I won't," Xaden vows. "And yes, I'm stable, but all we can do is slow the progression."

Mira's breathing stills, and her eyes harden on mine. "You kept this from me."

"You kept things from me, too." My fingernails bite into my palms. "Things about myself that I deserved to know."

"She doesn't intend to tell anyone about me," Xaden says.

He cut through her shields?

"You taught her well." She glares over at our brother and sheathes her blade as she walks away. "Good luck keeping her alive." The door slams on her way out.

As our largest province, Tyrrendor provides the most conscripts for our forces. However, the strength of Navarre isn't only found in Tyrrish soldiers, but also in the province's most valuable resource: Talladium. Losing it would doom Navarre.

—ON TYRRISH HISTORY, A COMPLETE ACCOUNTING, THIRD EDITION BY CAPTAIN FITZGIBBONS

CHAPTER FIFTY-FIVE

Two days pass without Mira telling anyone, and I start to believe that Xaden was right and she won't, even if she isn't speaking to me.

Navarre is one step away from declaring war on Tyrrendor for defying the Senarium. Halden has troops stationed along the Calldyr border, just waiting for his father to give his order, which prompted Xaden to cut off shipments of Talladium until King Tauri confirms their alliance stands without the Provincial Commitment and the Aretian riot is safe at Basgiath, all but stalling the war college's forge. The only positive is that I find myself back with my squad during the day and in Xaden's bed at night.

Turns out Panchek doesn't actually care where anyone sleeps. Quinn spends every night with her girlfriend, too, since Jax happens to be stationed here.

The best part of Professor Trissa's all-day runes class is being outdoors in the valley. The gaping hole in my chest feels a little smaller when I'm closer to Tairn. The shitty part? I'm worse than ever at runes. There are more than a dozen discarded practice disks on the ground in front of me as I sit cross-legged in the circle our squad has formed, and those are only my mistakes since lunch.

A few months ago, I'd barely gotten by using the more delicate threads of magic from Andarna's power, but Tairn's is unruly and hard to separate. No wonder my signet is pretty much all-or-nothing. Tairn doesn't do anything in half measures, and neither does his power.

"Was that Teine I saw launching before the break?" Rhi asks, setting a messy yet no doubt effective unlocking rune in front of her as Professor Trissa walks the opposite side of the circle, inspecting Neve's and Bragen's work.

I nod and press my lopsided trapezoid with its four unequally spaced knots and overlying oval—which I've managed to make look like an egg—into the practice disk, tempering the rune. The wood hisses, and the shape appears, burned into the disk. "They only gave Mira seventy-two hours of leave, which, from the sound of it, is more than they could afford." My forehead puckers as I study the rune. Every day, the line retreats closer to Draithus, and the atmosphere around here feels like the air before a thunderstorm, charged with inevitable violence.

"I'm sorry you two didn't have more time." Rhi offers me what I'm starting to call the *careful* smile. It's half sympathy, half encouragement, and a hundred percent please-don't-go-catatonic-again.

It's become the trademark expression of our squad since I showed up for class the day before yesterday.

"At least you got to see your sister," Cat says from the east end of our circle beside Maren, shaping a yet-to-be-seen rune in the air with both hands. "I haven't been with Syrena in months." She doesn't bother with the careful smile, and I weirdly appreciate it.

"I'm sorry." I genuinely mean it. Cordyn is all but blockaded. The only way in without crossing venin territory is by sea.

"I'd say it's all right, but we both know it isn't." She sets a perfectly shaped unlocking rune down in front of her. "And neither is whatever you just attempted, because that isn't going to unlock…anything."

"Be nice." Maren throws a sideways glance at Cat.

"Good thing I excel in other areas." I flash a fuck-off smile.

Ridoc snorts to Rhi's left, and before I can tell him I didn't mean it that way, Sawyer jabs him in the ribs.

Professor Trissa moves down the line to the first-years, and I prepare myself for the inevitable sigh of disappointment she'll give once she gets to me. She's been in a foul mood since spending most of yesterday afternoon with Mira, going over which runes did and didn't work on our failed quest. So far the only consensus is that certain materials can carry magic beyond the Continent and others can't.

"It's better than the last one." Rhi nods at my rune and brightens the careful smile.

"It's not." My heart leaps as an outline of wings casts a shadow on the south side of the valley, then plummets when an Orange Clubtail lands to the west, near where Tairn lies sunning his scales. *At some point I'll stop looking for her, right?*

"*Perhaps,*" Tairn answers.

So comforting.

"Here, let me help you." Quinn scoots over at my right.

"I've tried. She doesn't want help," Imogen remarks, finishing another perfect rune.

"Maybe she doesn't want help from *you*," Quinn says, her tone overly sweet.

True.

"Odd, considering I'm one of the best out here," Imogen replies with just as much sugar. She, Cat, Quinn, and Sloane are our strongest, with Baylor and Maren coming in a close second. Bodhi's right up there with Cat, but he's missed afternoons the last two days, not that I'm one to judge. And I have to admit, it's fun to see an area where Dain doesn't head the class, either.

"Which might be the issue." Quinn swings her gaze to mine. "It's hard to take advice from someone who's been doing them for so long that they come as second nature."

"It is," I agree. Marked ones have been studying for years. By the time they reach the quadrant, they already know the patterns; they just need the magic. "I'd love your thoughts."

Quinn tucks her blond curls behind her ears, then reaches for my disk. "I don't remember you struggling *this* badly before. What's different?"

"I've always used Andarna's power," I admit softly. "Tairn's is too strong to break pliable threads from."

"Sounds right. It's not like Melgren is running around tempering runes with Codagh's power." She sets the disk down. "Maybe you need to manhandle it. Really snap the angles instead of bending. Don't coax it into the shape you want—try a more assertive approach. Aggressive, even. Get rough when you break the edges, pull hard when tying the knots." She mimics the motions.

"Harder. Rougher. I can do that." I nod, then reach into my Archives and yank a strand of Tairn's power loose.

"I'm sure you can, considering who you're sleeping with," Ridoc teases.

I roll my eyes and do as Quinn suggested, forcing the power into shape and tying the knots with a pull that's almost brutal. When I temper the rune into the disk, it's not perfect, but it's not the worst, either. "Thank you."

"No problem." She grins, then slides back toward Imogen. "They're going to be hopelessly lost when we leave them in July."

"*Going* to be?" Imogen scoffs.

When Professor Trissa makes her way to our side of the circle, she gives Imogen a nod of approval, then Quinn, and then pauses over my disk. "It will do in a pinch."

It's the highest praise she's given me this trip.

An hour later, Felix walks up from across the field, his flight jacket draped over his arm.

My stomach sinks. Using strands of Tairn's power is one thing, but wielding feels like another.

"Let's go," he says to me, motioning down the field. "Trissa, I'll have her for the rest of the afternoon."

Oh joy. I rise to my feet and brush the grass off the backs of my legs.

"Felix, do you think now is the time to push her?" Trissa asks, addressing the very question everyone is thinking but no one has dared to ask.

"I think now is better than a battlefield," he counters, already walking away. "Come on, Sorrengail," he adds. "You may have lost your little irid, but you still have Tairn."

"I'll hold on to your disks," Rhi assures me.

"Thank you." I grab my flight jacket and pack, then catch up with Felix. "I didn't lose her. She left." Not sure why, but the wording makes a difference.

"All the more reason to practice." He strides toward his Red Swordtail. "If the irids aren't coming to save us, then you'd better be ready. All it takes is another Jack Barlowe and they won't just be approaching Draithus—we'll have venin at our front door."

Right. The wards protect us, but they're not infallible. And I have to stop looking for miracles. Leothan fired the wardstone. All I can control now is me.

"I'm not going to coddle you like others when war knocks at our doorstep. None of this training matters if you can't follow orders," he lectures. "Your inability to do so during the attack nearly cost civilians their lives when those wyvern bodies came crashing through the walls." His brow furrows in disappointment. "Your squad leader has already been spoken to. You were correct to engage farther from the battlements but should have immediately returned to your post and intercepted those wyvern instead of gambling your lives at the temple."

"There were civilians at risk." My spine stiffens.

He pauses. "Did you ever consider that they wouldn't have been were you not there?"

I blink as my throat constricts. "Because she's hunting me."

He nods, then continues toward our dragons, leaving me scurrying after him. "Your squad needs to learn some boundaries. You are not just any cadet, and they have to realize they cannot go chasing after you when you make mistakes, be that here or through the isles. Between you taking unnecessary risks and Riorson leaving *his* post for you, we would have lost, had the irid not fired the wardstone."

Guilt twists in my stomach. "I understand."

"Good. Anything new to report from your skirmish beyond the walls?"

Felix asks.

"I split a bolt into two branches." I lift my chin, and Tairn stands ahead of us. The wound on his thigh has scabbed and is healing at a rate I envy. "And not into a cloud. From the sky."

His silver brows rise. "But did you hit your target?"

I nod. "Both of them."

"Good." A satisfied smile curves his mouth. "Now show me."

By the time I make it back to Riorson House that evening, my arms feel like dead weight, I've sweat through every piece of my uniform, and my right hand is covered in blisters.

But I can wield.

And I do so the next day, and the day after that.

"You go straight from bedbound to burnout," Brennan mutters after he finishes mending my arm muscles for the third time in three days. "Can't you pick a nice middle ground?" His voice echoes in the empty Assembly chamber.

Almost every officer from Aretia has been stationed on the outposts, including the Assembly members. If Brennan wasn't needed to run the place when Xaden isn't here, he'd be gone, too.

"Apparently not." I lift my hand from the end of the long trestle table and flex my fingers. "Thank you."

"I should let the healers tend to you and see how quickly you run out to do it again." He rubs the bridge of his nose and sits back in his chair.

"You could." I tug the sleeve of my uniform down. "But I'd just be out there again tomorrow. I've already taken too much time off." Theophanie isn't going to give up just because the Aretian wards are in place.

"If I could stand to see you in pain, I'd give it some serious thought." He drops his hand. "What are you going to do when you're back at Basgiath? I can't just fly eighteen hours every time you overdo it."

"I have almost a week left to figure that out." My forehead scrunches. "Do you think we'll go if Tauri hasn't confirmed he won't burn the place down like he did six years ago?" There's a growing part of me that wouldn't mind staying.

I love sleeping next to Xaden at night and waking up to the feel of his mouth on my skin in the morning. I love how uncomplicated we are here, and *really* love that General Aetos isn't lurking around every corner, looking for a reason to make us miserable. But mostly, I love that Xaden seems more like himself in the last few days. He's still icy in moments, but he also carries an air of peace and purpose, and for the first time, I don't just dream about our future here.

I can see it.

"Keeping a squad of Basgiath's cadets would complicate—" Brennan starts to answer.

"You're an asshole." Bodhi strides into the room, tearing at the buttons of his flight jacket.

"That's not new information," Xaden retorts at his heels, ripping the flight goggles off his head and pinning his cousin with a stare I wouldn't wish on my worst enemy. His hair is windblown, and his swords are strapped to his back, but I don't see any blood—not that he's turned fully in my direction at the opposite side of the room. "And the answer is no. Stop asking."

Brennan lifts his brows at me, and I shrug. Fuck if I know what they're arguing about.

"You need every rider you can get," Bodhi argues. "I could be manning an outpost—"

"No." Xaden's jaw ticks.

"—or patrolling Draithus, which we both know is about to fall—" Bodhi's hands curl into fists.

"Absolutely not." Shadows gather around Xaden's boots. "You can't just take Cuir and leave school because you decide you're fully educated. You have to graduate."

Wait. Bodhi wants to drop out?

"Says who?" Bodhi challenges.

"Besides the Empyrean and every regulation recorded?" The shadows spread. "Me!"

Bodhi shakes his head. "If it's that fucking important I finish, you wouldn't be pulling me out of class every day."

"Because I need you to know how to take over," Xaden snaps.

"Because I'm now first in line?" There's more than a little sarcasm in Bodhi's response.

"Yes!" The shadows flee, racing for the walls.

"Xaden?" My stomach clenches.

He glances my way, then takes a deep breath and relaxes his shoulders. "The answer is no, Bodhi."

"I'm not your backup plan." Bodhi retreats two steps, then looks down the table at Brennan and me before glaring at Xaden. "You are the duke. I am the rider. That's how it was always meant to be until our parents got themselves executed. I will stand by your side and be your right-fucking-hand for the rest of our lives, but if you want a member of our family to hold that seat"—he points to the throne—"you'd better hold your own shit together." He walks out of the room without another word.

But he'd meant for me to hear every single one he said.

An ache unfolds behind my ribs. That's why Xaden is so peaceful, so driven here. He's putting the pieces in place, training his replacement. He's accepted a different future than the one I envision as I walk these halls and continue following every possible path to a cure.

Xaden strides the length of the table, and Brennan pushes back, his chair squeaking against the floor of the dais.

"There's a stack of things requiring your signature on the desk in the study," Brennan says, intercepting Xaden. "And these came for you." He retrieves two missives from his front pocket and hands them over. "Oh, and I'd love to know why the King of Deverelli referred to my sister as your consort in his last offer."

"I'd say it's a long story, but it's really not." A corner of Xaden's mouth rises, and he takes the missives.

Gods, I love that arrogant, wicked, sexy little smirk. How in this world does he think I'm supposed to live without seeing it every day?

"Right." Brennan shakes his head and leaves the hall.

"How was your day, love?" Xaden asks, breaking the wax seals on both parchments.

"Is that what you're doing?" I ask, leaning forward on the table. "Preparing for your own demise?"

"Mine was interesting." He ignores my question and reads over the first letter, then frowns at the second. "Flew out to the cliffs to check on the evacuation, which is going slower than we estimated." His eyes meet mine as he shoves the letters into his pocket and walks up the steps. "And now, Melgren warns me not to fly into battle or we'll lose—just a few days late with that warning, but the high priestess of Dunne's temple has written to say that Dunne holds you and Rhiannon in her regard, and that she is in my debt and owes me whatever favor I see fit." He pushes Brennan's chair aside, then leans on the edge of the table, facing me. "So how was your day?"

He wants to exchange pleasantries? Fine.

"I read a book on the emergence of venin. Almost managed to split a bolt in three, but my accuracy was questionable. Two seems pretty solid. And I managed runes that both harden surfaces"—I arch a brow—"and soften them. Are you preparing for your own demise?"

"Yes." He slides his hands into his pockets. "But I'm not embracing the fall, if that's what you're thinking. I won't give up a single day I have with you. Not without a fight."

Days. Not weeks or months or even years. I'm hit with the sudden urge to never sleep again, to use every minute I have with him. "Do you want to go sit on the roof?"

"I had something else in mind." He glances toward the throne.

"Yes, please." I flick my wrist and shut the door using lesser magic, then lock it.

His smile instantly becomes a core memory.

CHAPTER FIFTY-SIX

I stand in the field in front of Draithus, surrounded by the peaks of snow-topped mountains, and even though I shouldn't, I take the first step toward the city. I'm too far. I'll never reach Tairn, and he's my only chance at finding her.

Battle erupts in the sky over its spiral tower, and the outlines of wings pop through the ominous clouds hovering over the canyons to the south before descending into darkness once more. The storm gives me the one thing I can never really afford—hope. The rain might make flying a pain in the ass, but it will give her the edge she needs.

Fire erupts along the high walls, and flames of blue and green rise, climbing the guard towers like ivy. Shit. I have to get there *now*. I can put it out. Shadow beats flame every time.

My footsteps falter, and I pause.

Shadow?

I don't wield shadows. Xaden does.

My body fights to lurch forward, to run toward the city, but I shouldn't continue across this field. It only ever ends one way, with the Sage yanking me into the air—

This is Xaden's dream. Awareness prickles the back of my neck.

I'm *in* Xaden's dream.

The realization does *something* that feels like a snap across the back of my skull. Suddenly, I'm no longer a part of him as he takes off running ahead of me, dressed for battle.

"Xaden!" I shout before he can make it a half dozen steps.

He stops, then slowly turns to face me in the grass-covered field. His eyes widen when he spots me, then narrow as he glances left, then right. "You shouldn't be here."

"That's an understatement." I take in our surroundings with a quick glance. The field is barren, but if this dream is anything like his others, it won't be for long.

"You aren't safe." He shakes his head and stalks toward me. "I can't keep you safe."

"This isn't real." I take his ice-cold hand in mine, then startle. I can *feel* that. "Why can't you escape this place? What keeps you here?"

"I do," the Sage answers from behind Xaden.

Xaden whips around, reaching over his shoulder for a blade that disappears, and I move to his side.

The Sage pulls back the hood of his maroon robe, revealing the freakishly young face that haunts my—Xaden's—dreams, and smiles, cracking the skin of his chapped lips. The veins along his temples pulse crimson as he folds his gnarled hands like this has the possibility of being a civil encounter. "It's so nice of you to join us, lightning wielder." He tilts his head. "Or should I call you dream-walker?"

My lips part. Xaden's nightmares are eerily on point. "We should go," I whisper.

"He can't." The Sage's smile widens, and he lifts his bony hand.

Xaden rises and claws at his throat.

"Wake up!" I shout at Xaden.

"I told you, he can't. And here I'd hoped you'd be a quick learner. How disappointing," the Sage lectures, then slits his eyes like a snake toward Xaden. "You lost something I wanted, but you will bring *her*," he demands.

"Never," Xaden forces through his throat, and his feet kick for the ground.

"Don't worry," the Sage says with a twisted smile. "I'll be a more merciful teacher than Theophanie."

Fear races down my spine, and I reach for power—

Stop. This is a dream. It isn't real. He isn't losing air. He's breathing just fine in our bed. I have to wake up, but that only ever happens once the Sage strikes.

His sword coming down on me...

Pain. I need pain. I reach for my thigh but only find a smooth layer of leather.

"I am done waiting," the Sage snarls. "Done playing this little game. You may have raised your wards, but they won't save you. We have the advantage, and if you will not deliver her, then she will come herself." He closes his fist, and Xaden wheezes. "It's simple, dream-walker. You come or she dies."

She *who*?

This is a dream, I remind myself, and if it were mine, I'd be armed.

I slide my hand down my hip and find the hilt of a dagger. Before I can second-guess my plan, I wrench it free.

The Sage's eyes widen on the polished, wooden handle, but I'm already swinging it toward my arm. The blade sinks into my skin—

I jolt upright in bed and gasp for breath, blinking furiously to clear the haze of the nightmare as dawn breaks outside our bedroom window.

Xaden.

His spine is arched beside me, his head thrown back in pain as he strains for the very air he's breathing.

"Wake up!" I put both my hands on his chest and shove with my body and mind. *"Xaden! Wake up!"*

His eyes flash open, and he falls flat against the mattress as his heart pounds beneath my fingers.

"It was just a dream." I shift my weight to kneel beside him, then push his hair off his clammy forehead. "We're in Aretia. In your room. It's just you and me."

He blinks at me a few times, then blows out a small breath. "That sounds like a much better dream." His hand splays over my hip and his heart rate slows as he looks up at me. "You were there."

"Yeah." I nod, tracing the scar above his heart.

"I saw you pull the dagger. I knew *you* were there. That's never happened before." He sits up, bringing our faces closer.

"I…" How do I explain it? "You know it's not the first time I've recognized it as a dream, but it *is* the first time I knew it was *your* dream—that it wasn't mine. The second I realized it, I became myself, separate from you." My brow knits. "I just don't know how."

"It sounds like you figured it out pretty quickly." He searches my face.

"I shouldn't have been able to do it." My voice fades to a whisper. "Andarna's gone."

His thumb strokes the top of my hip. "Maybe the power's gone but the ability still remains."

"Tairn?" I reach down the bond.

"I have encountered this as many times as you have." His reply is gruff with sleep.

Not helpful.

Before I can sink any deeper into my thoughts, someone *pounds* on our door.

It's too early for anything positive. "That can't be good."

"Agreed." Xaden throws back the blankets and heads for the door in nothing but his sleeping pants, and I scramble for the armoire. "Garrick? You look like shit."

What could Garrick possibly be doing here at this hour? I grab my robe, then tug it over my cotton nightdress before hurrying to Xaden's side.

He wasn't kidding. Garrick looks like shit. Blood drips from his hairline, and his left eye is rapidly swelling shut from what appears to be a fresh hit. Instead of his swords, he carries a *massive* shield on his back, the size and weight of which would absolutely crush me.

"We were on patrol when she found us." Garrick's gaze flickers my way, and the instant pity that fills his open eye sours my stomach. "I wasn't strong enough. Or quick enough. She ripped us straight out of the sky like a pair of pigeons in a windstorm."

"Who?" Xaden asks, steadying his friend's arms when he wavers.

"Their lightning wielder," Garrick answers. "She let me go to deliver a message."

Theophanie.

"To me?" Xaden asks, his brow furrowing.

"For both of you." Garrick retreats a step, then swings off his shield. "They've reached the walls of Draithus. She said if that isn't threat enough, you have five hours to bring Bodhi and Violet or she dies." He glances at me.

You come or she dies. Isn't that what the Sage said? But why Bodhi? And who could she possibly—

No. I shake my head, and my stomach lurches. There's no possible way the irids would let her put hands on Andarna, if Andarna is even still on the Continent.

"Who—" Xaden starts, then falls silent and stares at Garrick's shield. "Fuck."

I drop my gaze to the shield, too, and my heart drops out of my chest.

It isn't a shield; it's a green scale that matches the exact shade of my armor.

Not Andarna…Teine.

Theophanie has Mira.

But even harder than taking a life is doing nothing while one is extinguished beside you. Keep your eyes forward, Mira.

—PAGE SEVENTY-ONE, THE BOOK OF BRENNAN

CHAPTER FIFTY-SEVEN

"We fly for Draithus. They'll attack as soon as they get what they want."

"And leave Sorrengail to die?"

"Who says she's even still alive?"

The voices of arguing, armed riders blur as I stand between Xaden and Brennan near the center of the dais, staring at the updated map on the Assembly chamber wall.

"There are thousands coming up the pass out of the city. If Draithus falls, they're all dead."

"We have a six-dragon riot stationed there—"

"Ten now that the line has fallen back."

"Don't forget the nightwing drift."

"Against hundreds of wyvern?"

"And at least a dozen dark wielders."

"Whoever goes isn't coming back from that."

"Then you send *us*."

"We're not sending cadets into combat!"

"It was our dragons who woke us. End of debate. We're going!"

I barely hear any of it. Only one thought matters: Theophanie is done waiting for me, and she has Mira.

She has my *sister*.

And our last words were in anger.

Fear threatens to worm its way past the rage boiling in my blood, and I fight to deny it entry. Mira doesn't have time for my fear. It's a four-hour flight to

Draithus, and if we don't leave in the next half hour, we'll be too late—not just for Mira but for the thousands of civilians as well.

How did this happen? A harsh red line on the map spans from what had been the eastern front directly to Draithus. They've surged in the last twenty-four hours, ignoring everything else along their path, concentrating on this one target when easier, comparable cities remain untouched.

"Not all signets are equal. I know she's a Maven, but is she more powerful than you?" Brennan folds his arms at my right as the others continue to argue.

"Yes," I answer. There's no point lying.

"We'll be walking into a trap." His gaze locks on the flag representing Draithus.

"Flying, and who said you were coming?" I counter. The space between the flag and the Cliffs of Dralor seems impossibly small for so many people to flee, and the climb is hellacious. They won't all make it.

"She's my sister, too," Brennan states.

He has a point.

Xaden stands silently in front of the throne, his arms crossed as he studies the field to the north of Draithus, where Theophanie has demanded we meet. "We don't have enough riders to retrieve Mira, defend Draithus, and protect the pass."

"No." Brennan sighs and examines the map more closely. "We'll have to prioritize an objective. Maybe two."

Xaden nods.

"We can't just leave people to die," I protest.

The arguments between cadets and officers grow louder, and the pit in my stomach deepens. I should be with my squad, but I'll be damned if I stand patiently and wait for others to decide my sister's fate.

"What would you do if they were your citizens on the other side of the border?" Cat yells across the room from where our squad stands in loose formation. "Or are you thinking like true Navarrians now that you're tucked in safe behind your wards?"

A smart-ass captain snaps something back at Cat that I can't hear over the din, and Sloane charges. I nearly jump over the table, but Dain gets there first, hooking his arm around her waist and hauling her back as she swings. The second he sets her on her feet, those fists are aimed in his direction, and I wince as he lets two make contact before trapping her wrists and leaning in low. Whatever he says must register, because she gives a curt nod, then retorts with a glare and walks back into formation, where Rhi is waiting with what looks like a scathing lecture.

Dain lifts his brows at me, and I grimace in apology before he moves to

Bodhi's side.

"How long are you going to let them fight?" Brennan asks, glancing at Xaden.

"Until my tactician gives me a plan that doesn't make me choose between objectives," Xaden answers. "The volume of their delivery doesn't make their points any less valid."

"I can't guarantee two, let alone three." Brennan's mouth purses.

"Live up to your reputation and try," Xaden orders.

Brennan curses, then looks over the room. "I need Tavis and Kaori!" he shouts. Both men quickly separate from the crowd and make their way up Brennan's side of the dais. "Have you been to Draithus?" he asks Kaori.

"Once." The professor nods.

"Can you give me a roughly scaled projection of the territory?"

Kaori lifts his hands, and a three-dimensional projection of Draithus and its surrounding areas appears over the table. The room falls quiet as Brennan leans forward, bracing his palms on the table to study the image as Garrick points out where our current defenses stand. The gash on his head and black eye are both gone thanks to Brennan.

The city sits at the southwestern edge of an intermontane plateau that spans a couple dozen miles. It's surrounded by peaks on every side and accessible only through a winding series of valleys, the western river that flows south to the Arctile Ocean, or air—which Theophanie commands due to her signet. And if Garrick's reports are accurate, the eastern field is theirs, too.

"Whatever calculations you make, just know that I'll be going with Violet," Xaden says.

"I figured," Brennan answers.

My chest tightens with enough pressure to crush a dragon. *"You'll be risking your life."*

"It's risked the second you cross the wards, and we both know you're going after Mira. I'd rather be at your side than hunting you down after you sneak out." His jaw flexes.

"Theophanie doesn't want to kill me, or she already would have." I memorize the topography of the field, feeding the information to Tairn. Between the jagged peaks, lines of forest, and the row of vertical rock formations along the western edge, it's basically nature's own fighting pit.

"That's exactly what I'm afraid of," Xaden replies as Felix and Professor Trissa walk in. *"There are worse things than dying."*

"Is now a good time to point out that Tyrrendor can't afford to lose her duke on what amounts to a death wish?" Felix asks, heading to the front of the dais with Professor Trissa.

"I have no intention of dying," Xaden replies. "Panchek has already launched to request reinforcements."

"Which we know Melgren won't send. Apparently that *late* warning was actually an *early* warning for this," Trissa counters, keeping her voice level and glancing at me, then Brennan. "I'm sorry for the loss of your sister, but Melgren has already proclaimed this battle a defeat, and he's never been wrong."

A lump the size of my conduit forms in my throat. I'm not giving up on Mira, on any of them. "Choice determines our future. Melgren's only seen the outcome of one path." I glance at Xaden. "Which couldn't have had three rebellion relics."

"Cadets belong in formation, not battle planning," Trissa snaps at me.

My spine stiffens, and my hands grip the edge of the table.

"She stands at my side." Xaden's voice drops into that lethally calm wingleader tone, and he places his warm hand over mine. "Remember that."

The compliment and the pressure of it aren't lost on me.

"Starting to understand the consort missive," Brennan mutters under his breath, then looks at the model from a different angle. "We lose if we only take the officers."

"Absolutely no cadets." Felix shakes his head. "Not after what happened last time. We're still repairing the walls from when those two went rogue." He looks my way.

Xaden glances toward my squad, his gaze lingering on Imogen, then Sloane, then Bodhi.

"Make a different choice, get a different outcome," Garrick suggests. "They'll have to live with themselves, so let them make their choice, too. Gods know we did."

"Only volunteers. First-years stay behind the wards," Xaden orders.

"Put us where you need us," Bodhi calls out, then glances at Dain. "With the permission of our wingleader, of course."

"Given," Dain agrees.

Rhi takes count of every hand in the air, which is all of them. "Second Squad stands ready."

"This cannot be happening," Trissa argues.

"It is." Xaden's tone doesn't invite interpretation. "The Assembly wanted me in that chair, and now you'll deal with my decisions while in it."

"You're not ready." Felix shoots the insult my way.

"Even if Draithus and fleeing civilians weren't under direct threat, she's my sister. I'm going to do everything I can to rescue her." I lift my chin.

"*Our* sister," Brennan corrects, studying me with a tilted head. "Which means that dark wielder knows way more about us than we do her."

Xaden looks toward the back of my squad's formation, where Bodhi stands with Dain. "Garrick, tell me *exactly* what her demand was. Why does she want Bodhi?"

"I don't know." Garrick scratches the stubble along his chin. "She said to bring Violet and your brother, and they'll let Draithus stand."

Stand or live? Anca was standing when they left it, too.

Xaden tenses. "She said 'brother'?"

Garrick nods. "Everyone knows you were raised together."

"It's certainly the fastest way to wipe out Tyrrendor's ruling line," Trissa notes.

"Right." Two furrows appear between Xaden's brows, and his mouth tenses.

"What are you thinking?" I ask.

"Venin don't care about succession."

"You have another who calls you by the name," Sgaeyl chimes in, her words sharper than her teeth.

"Another—" I frown. The only other person who would have qualified for that title was Liam. *Wait.* The very first time I met her, she didn't kill me, but she didn't achieve her rescue objective, either. My stomach hollows. *"She wants Jack."*

"That's my guess." His gaze darts to Kaori, who's solely focused on his projection, then jumps to Garrick. "You up for a little walk?" he asks quietly.

Garrick glances at Kaori, then nods.

"Use me," I whisper to Brennan so Xaden won't hear. "Once I rescue Mira, I'll station myself between the pass and Draithus. I can wield in both directions if wyvern get past me."

"That's it." Brennan's eyes slide shut. "Everyone but the seven of us out. *Now*," he orders, his voice booming through the room. "Stay in the hallway for quick recall."

"We don't have time for this," Felix argues as the crowd moves into the hallway.

"You're the variable I'm missing, and worse, you make Riorson one, too." Brennan swings his gaze to mine as the Assembly chamber empties.

I draw back. "I'm sorry?"

"Tread carefully," Xaden warns.

"That right there, for starters." Brennan stares at me while pointing at Xaden, and I don't think he's just talking about this discussion. He gestures to the model. "Violet, pick one objective to win."

"People will die if we only choose one." My heart starts to pound.

"Yes." He nods. "Welcome to leadership."

"Why me?" I stare at the model. Mira has to come first, but the thought of leaving civilians to be desiccated, our own riders and fliers to die with their bonded ones? It's too much to fathom. Losing Liam was battle. Mom was her own sacrifice. Trager was…luck. Being responsible for the deaths of thousands?

"Because I don't think you can," Brennan answers gently. "Theophanie knows you'll try to save everyone like you did in Resson, or at Dunne's temple, or Basgiath before Mom…" He swallows. "That's why we'll fail. Because you will choose everyone over yourself, and he will choose you over everyone."

My stomach hollows.

"You're not playing fair," Xaden replies, his voice sliding lower.

"In all the years we've known each other, *fair* isn't a term I've ever heard you argue." Brennan holds up a single finger. "Prove me wrong so we can go get our sister, Violet. The only way we're walking out of the trap this dark wielder designed for you is if *you* don't fall for it. One objective. One path." He lifts his brows, and the words hit me square in the stomach.

Tairn would select one in a heartbeat.

Andarna would choose them all.

But she's gone. What's the objective with the biggest impact? Setting Xaden aside…Draithus will only hold as long as we can defend it. The same goes for the pass. And if I rescue Mira, there's every chance Theophanie will—

This isn't about Mira. She's hunting *me*.

"Theophanie." I take a steadying breath. "I guess I would kill Theophanie."

"I'm impressed. That was *not* on my list." The table creaks as Brennan sits on its edge. "And if Cadet Sorrengail is abducted while securing her objective?"

Shadows spread at Xaden's feet. "Bodhi will make an excellent duke."

"At least one of you can be taught." Brennan rubs the scar on his palm. "Do you trust your squad leader to hold a position this time?" he asks me.

"With my life," I answer instantly.

"All right." Brennan nods. "I have one idea." He looks at us all in turn. "I'll unlock the armory. Trissa, we need you to open up that little cache you keep of runes and maorsite arrowheads. Xaden, we need you to trust Violet not to get herself killed." He doesn't wait for Xaden's response before staring me down. "And above all else, we need *you* to understand that you cannot save everyone and you cannot stray from your orders."

I'll do whatever it takes to save Mira. "Fine."

Most cadets believe their ability to recite historical fact will usher them onto the adept path, but it is actually the ability to observe and recount it that separates the librarians from the scribes.

—COLONEL DAXTON'S GUIDE TO EXCELLING IN THE SCRIBE QUADRANT

CHAPTER
FIFTY-EIGHT

Tairn can fly to the nearest edge of the Cliffs of Dralor in two hours, but it does us no good to leave Sgaeyl, Cuir, and Marbh behind, so by the time we reach the ten-thousand-foot drop, we're cutting it close to Theophanie's deadline.

Gods, if we miss it, if we're too late and she kills Mira—

My throat threatens to close.

"We'll make it," Tairn promises as we descend the cliffs in a steep dive between the falls and the crowded Medaro Pass. It had been a treacherous, deadly climb in autumn, and we were cadets. I can't begin to imagine how civilians—how *children*—are making the ascent.

"Do you agree that it's a trap?" The words spill out before I can stop them.

"Of course," he replies. *"But you already know that. Otherwise, we would have discussed it over the last three and a half hours."*

Guilt wedges itself between my ribs as we plunge into a thick layer of fluffy white clouds.

"Do not dishonor me with such emotions," he lectures.

"And how does Sgaeyl feel about me endangering Xaden?" I scan the clouds as best I can for the outline of wyvern, but the cover is thick and we're moving too fast to be thorough.

"Had she not agreed, she would still be in Aretia, and your Dark One would be walking."

Excellent point. *"Theophanie took Mira because of me. I'm the reason she's going through this."*

"You are our lightning wielder, and while your life may not matter more than other riders', your signet does. You are the weapon and will have to learn to accept the sacrifice of others in your name if you want to win this war."

Nausea churns in my stomach.

"And you think I should have accepted Mira's death as a sacrifice?" We burst through the clouds, and the field comes into startling view.

"If I did, I would still be in Aretia and you would be walking."

My heart sinks as I survey the landscape. The eastern fields approaching Draithus are covered in hordes of gray wyvern, setting siege against a line of dragons and gryphons perched between the guard stands along the city walls. They outnumber us in a ratio I don't even want to calculate. For the first time, I'm relieved that Andarna chose to go. Brennan is brilliant, but this feels unwinnable. *"Our estimates were off."*

"It appears so."

But none of them launch to attack as we descend, nor do they impede the thick line of evacuees streaming from the city's western gate.

"Molvic has been spotted along the cliffs," Tain warns as he flares his wings, slowing our momentum.

Fucking Aaric. *"If he gets himself killed—"*

"He was seen flying south, away from conflict." He spits every word in disgust.

What in Amari's name could he be doing? *"It's not like Aaric to run away."*

"Nor Molvic." Tairn levels out as we approach the northern field, where at last I spot a horde of a dozen wyvern waiting in a circle around Teine.

In. Out. I force myself to breathe. It's unnatural to hold a dragon…captive.

The wyvern are perched on heavy chains that loop around Teine's tail, bind his legs and his snout, and pin his wings to his thrashing body. Each line of metal is coated in his blood, and several of his scales litter the ground.

Theophanie stands in front of them, silver hair shining, holding one blade to Mira's throat and another against her ribs.

My grip tightens on the pommels, and I can't tell if it's Tairn's rage or my own stampeding through my veins, but it tramples every last ounce of my fear, my doubt, and my guilt until I am nothing but wrath.

How fucking *dare* she.

"She dies for this," Tairn demands, his impact rustling the green meadow grass as we land twenty feet in front of Theophanie, who welcomes us with a smile.

She hasn't drained the field…yet, but she has beaten the shit out of my sister. The right side of Mira's face is purple and swollen, her throat carries a necklace of bruises, and blood drips from her left hand, but her leathers hide its origin. Theophanie's scarlet long-sleeved tunic and pants aren't helping with contrast, either.

"Agreed. Can you carry Teine if he can't fly?" I unbuckle from my saddle as the others land on either side of Tairn.

"Not without sinking my claws into him." He growls low in his throat. *"Spend no more time on the ground than necessary."*

"I'll stick to the plan." Leaving my bag strapped behind Tairn, I adjust the leather-capped quiver and holstered crossbow at my back, check to make sure my conduit is tucked safely in my pocket, then dismount.

All Theophanie has to do is set her hand to the ground, and we're all dead.

"I'm here, just like you wanted." I hold out my arms, and power rises within me, heating my flight-chilled skin. Out of the corner of my eye, I see Brennan approach from the left, while Xaden and Bodhi walk in at my right.

"So you are." The wind whips Theophanie's long, silver braid as her smile cracks her chapped lips, and my gaze catches on the pulsing veins at her temples and faded remnants of the tattoo on her forehead. "And yet, you seem to have lost your irid. How inconvenient."

"No," Mira garbles, and Theophanie tightens her gnarled grip on the blade, pressing it harder against Mira's throat. Another ounce of pressure and her skin will split.

"Shhh. Speak again, and I'll spill your dragon's blood all over this field," Theophanie says into Mira's ear as the others reach me.

My sister stills as the men reach my sides.

"Let them go." I will slaughter the dark wielder where she stands. Energy hums in my veins, ready for the first opportunity to strike.

"Stay calm," Xaden says, shadows curling over the toes of his boots and drifting south as we start to walk closer. *"Stay in control."* He glances toward the doomed city.

Keeping the promise I made to Brennan means not looking, so I don't.

"That's usually my line." I keep my eyes off Mira, focusing solely on the dark wielder.

"Not yet. And four on one hardly seems fair." Theophanie glances at Brennan, then Bodhi. "I didn't ask for either of you to attend."

"I thought you requested brothers? Next time be more specific about who's invited," I suggest.

"And yet you didn't bring the brother he wanted." Theophanie sighs. "Berwyn will be disappointed." A thin line of blood appears along the edge of her knife.

"He's on the way," I say quickly.

"Berwyn." Xaden tenses, and his focus swings south toward the city again. That's where he needs to be—in position to save as many people as possible—but he's made it clear he doesn't want to leave me.

"Yes. Hence the term *brother*." Theophanie glances my way. "I won't make the mistakes with you Berwyn made with Jack. He spills his Sage's secrets too easily."

"I'm not turning." My hands curl into fists.

"You are," she states like it's certain. "In just a few minutes, in fact. I'm intrigued to see what the actual catalyst will be." Her eyes light up. "Saving your sister? Defending your lover? The trite-yet-always-popular revenge? I'm betting on a combination of all three." Her head tilts, and she rests her cheek against the top of Mira's head. "Speaking of which, time is up—"

My heart lurches, and a gust of wind blows from the north.

"He's here!" Garrick shouts.

I glance left and find Chradh standing where there had only been empty space moments before, his foreclaw clutching a familiar runed armoire. They made it, but the knife still at Mira's throat makes it hard to feel any sort of relief.

"Show him to me," Theophanie orders.

Xaden rolls his neck, and the shadows around his feet drift past Bodhi's.

Garrick dismounts, then walks to the Rybestad chest with slower steps than usual and pulls the key from his pocket. It only takes a few seconds for him to open the chest's doors.

"There he is." Theophanie smiles, but I don't risk taking my eyes off her to examine how Jack is doing, especially not when Mira looks like she might pass out at any second. "Just one little matter of business to attend to, and then we'll begin."

"He is emaciated and wan," Tairn tells me. *"Suspended in air as the chest intends, and he appears...sedated. I can show you through my eyes if you prefer—"*

"Description is perfect, thank you." I lift my chin. "Both Jack and I are here. Our end of the deal is fulfilled, so let Mira and Teine go."

Brennan's hands flex at his sides.

"That wasn't the deal." Theophanie tsks. "I said we'd let Draithus stand, not that your sister would live." Her mouth curves in a sadistic smile. "First thing to learn about us is that we're careful with our words. And the second? We also lie."

She draws the blade across Mira's neck and slits her throat.

It was not without risk that the first dragons bonded humans, for though they clearly hold the power, their bonded riders made them the one thing they could not tolerate: vulnerable. Many dragons suffered the loss of their bonded riders in the name of self-preservation.

—THE SACRIFICE OF DRAGONKIND BY MAJOR DEANDRA NAVEEN

CHAPTER
FIFTY-NINE

"Mira!" I scream louder than a dragon's roar as crimson blood streams from the laceration in my sister's throat.

Everything seems to happen at once, like a group of musicians cued for a performance.

"Time to play, Violet." Theophanie hurls the dagger—at Jack.

A sea of gray wings rises in the south, and my boots pound across the field.

Xaden projects a stream of shadow toward Theophanie, but the bands fly southward.

What the fuck? No time to think. I'm already running at the dark wielder, alloy-hilted dagger drawn, when the closest wyvern launches and plucks Theophanie from the ground as it flies overhead.

Mira collapses to her knees in the grass, grabbing for the fatal cut with both hands, and suddenly nothing else matters. Not revenge. Not Draithus. My sister only has *seconds*.

Malek, please, no.

"It's all right." My voice breaks, and I discard my dagger and hit the ground, catching her as she falls. Blood streams through my fingers as I press my hand against the pulsing wound at her throat. Pressure. She needs pressure.

Not Mira. I yell at whatever deity will listen and press harder, like I can force the blood back into her body. My breath comes in stuttered gasps, terror cutting off the flow of oxygen.

Mira stares up at me, her brown eyes wide with shock, and I force a smile so she doesn't meet Malek in fear. "You're going to be all right." I nod, my head jerking as my eyes blur.

"Move!" Brennan hits his knees, and I barely have time to yank my hand away before his is there. "You will live, do you hear me?" He slams his eyes shut and sweat immediately beads on his forehead as he leans over Mira.

Is it even possible? Brennan's powerful, but I can't think of a single rider who's been saved on the battlefield with an injury this extensive. She goes limp and my heart seizes, but she's still breathing despite the blood coursing down the sides of her neck.

Shapes blur and snarls sound from every direction. I look up, and the dragons leap over us, claws filling the sky before they land on the circle of wyvern. Four of the gray creatures launch at the onslaught, shrieking their way into the sky. The daggers of Sgaeyl's tail swing just a few feet above us, and I throw my body over Mira and Brennan as the navy-blue blades cut so close I can feel air rush against my skin.

Xaden casts a wall of shadow, blocking us from the fray, and to the right, I see Garrick pull the venin's dagger from the door of the Rybestad chest as Bodhi forces the other one shut.

Screeches fill the air and my muscles lock as I look back over my shoulder at the impenetrable darkness. *"Tairn!"* I can't see him.

"They die," he says, fury saturating the bond.

I take that as the only good sign on this field and sit back on my heels, giving Brennan room to breathe.

"Come on, come on," Brennan mutters, his brow furrowed in concentration just like Dad's used to, but he's swaying slightly and losing color in his face.

It has to work. It just has to.

Blood trickles down the column of Mira's neck, crossing her scar as her eyes flutter shut.

"You can't have her," I whisper up to Malek, and I swear the clouds darken slightly in acknowledgment, or maybe mocking, as two reds approach from the south at tremendous speed.

Wait. Why are they flying away from the city?

I strain to identify the dragons. Thoirt? The tear pattern in her right wing is unmistakable, but that would mean...

Oh gods, Sloane is here.

Liam, I'm so sorry. My throat tries to close as I throw my head back and search the sky for gray, but there's only Thoirt and— I blink. That's Cath on her tail.

Sweat drips down Brennan's neck at the same alarmingly fast pace as blood from Mira's wound, and his breathing becomes labored. "There's too much damage," he whispers.

"There isn't," I argue, glancing between Mira's slackened face and the strain on my brother's. "Brennan, you can mend anything, remember?"

Marbh roars.

"Your brother nears the limit of his power," Tairn warns.

And I can't give him mine. My heart races.

"Get the chest out of here," Xaden shouts to Garrick. "If she wanted him dead, he obviously knows things they don't want us to."

"Chradh!" Garrick yells, and the Brown Scorpiontail bounds over the shadows to Garrick's side. A second later, they disappear, along with the trunk.

I feel a rush of air as they go, and glance toward the sky as the two reds approach.

"How much are we trusting Aetos these days?" Bodhi says as he runs toward us.

"Not enough for what he just saw," Xaden answers, his shadows blocking what looks to be the tip of a wyvern's tail from hitting me.

Wind from wingbeats blows back Brennan's hair, and the reds land so close their heads hover over us as they skid to a halt, their talons dragging up clumps of grass.

"Violet, I'm sorry," Brennan whispers.

"Don't say that." I shake my head. "The blood flow is slowing. It's working." Though it hasn't stopped.

"What the fuck are you doing here?" Xaden calls up at Dain as he dismounts, but my focus firmly locks over Brennan's shoulder.

"Following her ass," Dain replies, then winces at the crunch of bone coming from behind the wall of shadows Xaden holds in place with both hands. "She's under my command, and Cath alerted me the second they crossed the wards *against orders*." He aims that last part in Sloane's direction.

Sloane. A shard of hope pierces the terror wrapped around my heart.

She races our way, reaching into her flight jacket and retrieving a cylindrical parcel the length of her hand. "Aaric told me you'd need this—" She stumbles as she catches sight of Mira.

I don't give a shit *why* she's here. Only that she is.

My eyes prickle. "Please."

Sloane's fearful gaze snaps to mine.

"Mira?" Dain runs, then drops to a knee beside me. "Oh *shit*."

"Please," I blatantly, shamelessly beg Sloane. "Brennan needs more power, and we're going to lose her."

She takes one tentative step, then another as Brennan trembles, his hands on Mira's neck. "I don't know how. When your m —" She stops herself. "Transferring is different than imbuing. I know that much."

"Whatever you're going to do, you'd better do it fast," Bodhi warns, drawing a sword and standing guard, his eyes on the sky.

"Try," Dain urges, shoving the sleeve of his uniform up his forearm. "It's dangerous to use your own power if you haven't trained, so take mine. I'm the only one here who doesn't have to wield today. Just *try*."

A wyvern snarls behind me, and a distinctive *snap* follows.

Sloane lowers herself between Dain and Brennan as Mira's blood soaks into my leathers.

"One hand on my wrist," Dain says gently, like he's talking to a skittish horse.

She stares at the gray handprint that scars his forearm. "I don't want to do *that*. Become *that*."

"You won't." He lifts his brows. "You can hate me later, but trust me now or she dies."

Sloane wraps her fingers around Dain's wrist. Her eyes flare, and she swallows. "Someone like you shouldn't have this much power."

"Good thing for Mira I do. Put the other hand anywhere his skin is exposed," he orders.

Sloane drops her little package and lifts her hand to the back of Brennan's neck.

I brush Mira's hair off her forehead, leaving a bloody smear behind. She's so damned pale. I should have told her about Xaden. She should have told me about my dedication. We've wasted so much time keeping things from each other, when Dad warned me to only trust her. If I had, would this still have happened?

"Do not blame yourself for wounds you do not inflict," Tairn lectures.

"Eyes here," Dain says, and Sloane looks his way. "Pull from the excess you feel in me, and push to the deficit in him. You're not a weapon of destruction. You're not venin. You're the artery power chooses to flow through. You're life."

Her brow knits, and Dain flinches. "I'm going to hurt you."

"Gods, don't I know it." He nods. "But you're not going to kill me, no matter how badly you want to. Now do it."

Her mouth tightens, and Dain grits his teeth.

Precious, long seconds pass before Brennan breathes deeply and color flushes his cheeks. I glance back to Mira, expecting the worst, but her chest still rises and falls. Blood ceases to drip, color returning to her cheeks.

"Brennan?" I whisper, too scared to even hope.

"It's messy, but she's alive." My brother sits back, his frame drooping as he drags the back of his arm over his sweaty brow. "Thank you, Mairi."

She lets go of both men, then lifts her gaze to mine. "She'll be all right?"

"Thanks to you," I say to Sloane.

She blows out a swift sigh of relief as Brennan reaches for the waterskin clipped at his hip. He quickly uncorks the top, then pours the water over Mira's neck. A thick, angry pink scar straddles her throat.

I push her hair off her forehead again and give myself exactly three seconds to feel *everything*. My chest threatens to explode.

One. She's alive.

Two. I won't have to navigate a world where she doesn't exist.

Three. Brennan is a fucking miracle worker.

"We have to get Mira out of here," I say to my brother as the snarls and sounds of tearing flesh diminish behind me. A shape comes flying overhead but is yanked back by a rope of shadow. Pretty sure it was a talon.

"Agreed." Brennan looks toward Draithus, where an outright battle has begun. Dragons and gryphons hover above the city walls as enormous cross-bolts fire into the cloud of approaching wyvern. "You all right, Aetos?"

Dain twists his hand around his wrist. "I'm good."

My stomach clenches. The hardest part of this will be trusting everyone to do their jobs, and the city isn't mine to hold. I glance at Xaden, then Dain. "You both have to go. They'll be out of cross-bolts soon."

Dain rises to stand and offers his hand to Sloane.

"Fuck off, Aetos." She rocks forward and up to her feet.

He pauses like he's counting to three. "Get back across the wards, Mairi, and stay there."

She turns on her heel and stalks toward Thoirt, lifting a middle finger.

Bodhi snorts.

"Fucking *first-years*," Dain mutters as she mounts. "Riorson, I'll meet you down there." He heads toward Cath's foreleg.

"Dain!" I shout, and he looks back over his shoulder. "Thank you."

"Don't thank me. Just tell me later how the fuck Garrick and Chradh disappeared into thin air." He takes off at a run, and within a matter of seconds, both Thoirt and Cath fly in separate directions.

Bodhi helps Brennan to his feet.

"I don't want to leave you." Xaden drops the wall of shadow. I glance over my shoulder and find dead wyvern scattered in the field, and Sgaeyl, Tairn, and Marbh examining the chains strapped around Teine.

"I know. But you have to."

"I'll carry her." Brennan bends and scoops Mira's unconscious body off my lap.

"You're all right?" I locate my alloy-hilted dagger in the grass and put it back in place as I rise, then grab the package Sloane left behind, too. It's addressed to Aaric and bears the unbroken seal of Dunne.

Why in all that's holy would he send Sloane into a war zone to give me his own mail? I'm going to throttle him…as soon as I figure out what the fuck he's currently doing.

"Mairi gave me a little more than she needed to. I'm fine." He adjusts Mira in his arms.

"I know you were supposed to stay, but take Mira," Bodhi says. "We'll figure out how to free Teine so she can follow."

"Agreed." Brennan's mouth tenses, and he looks at me. "I have more than a dozen runes I can leave—"

"Thanks, but I'll pass," I interrupt. "Better I stick to what I'm good at."

He nods. "*Stick* to the plan, Violet—no matter what goes wrong. We're counting on you." His gaze jumps to Xaden. "That applies to you, too." He doesn't waste time waiting for a reply, just heads toward Marbh.

I slip Aaric's package into my flight jacket pocket and watch as Brennan walks away. Weird. There's no mark at the back of his neck like he carries on his palm. There hadn't been one on Dain's wrist, either.

"You'd better go," Bodhi urges Xaden. "We've got wyvern trying to round the north side of the city, and the pass is just beyond. Whole battle just a few miles away, remember?"

"I'm going." Xaden grabs Brennan's discarded waterskin, then pours its remaining contents over my right hand, washing away the majority of Mira's blood. The water runs off my fingers, slowly fading from crimson to pale pink before he drops the skin. "Concentrate." He cradles my cheek, and our eyes lock. "Use only Tairn's power. Do not turn. Do not die. Accomplish your mission, and I will find you after."

He kisses me breathless, and for just that second, time doesn't matter. My heart races, and I wrap my arms around his neck, pouring everything I feel for him into my response. It's chaotic and desperate and over far too soon.

"Come back to me," I demand as he moves away.

"Only ever you." He holds my gaze for another few steps, then turns to Bodhi. "Stay with her, but remember your promise."

Bodhi nods. "I don't want your fucking province."

"Noted." Xaden clasps Bodhi's shoulder, then breaks into a run for Sgaeyl. Her golden eyes swivel toward mine.

"*Get off the ground and stay with him,*" she orders, and we both know she doesn't mean Bodhi.

"*Same goes to you.*" I lift my chin.

They're airborne within seconds, flying south toward the city. I look away before fear has a chance to grab hold. He's the most powerful rider on the field, and she's merciless. Their survival isn't a question.

Bodhi and I will give them enough time to save the city.

"Now that the Duke of Angst is gone," Bodhi says, his voice rising, "we have a problem."

Of course we do.

The only thing more stubborn than a dragon is its rider.

—Colonel Kaori's Field Guide to Dragonkind

CHAPTER SIXTY

"What's the issue?" I walk back to the carnage surrounding our dragons. *"He does not wake,"* Tairn announces, and Cuir lowers his green snout to Teine's.

Oh *shit*. Fear comes racing back.

"We have to get him off this field before Theophanie returns." Bodhi studies the clouds.

"Can Garrick get Teine up the cliffs?" I ask.

"Under normal circumstances? Yes." Bodhi winces. "But he's already exhausted from walking all over the Continent in the last few hours. There's no chance."

"The plan is going to shit fast." And we're miles away from everyone except the lethal dark wielder who wants to kill us. But there's another option. My head swings to Tairn. *"You're the only one strong enough to get him out of here. You can carry him if you use the chains."*

"I will not leave you on this field—" he growls.

"If I leave, everything falls apart. Dragonkind protects its own, even above a bonded rider," I remind him.

His eyes narrow, and steam billows from his nostrils. *"Do not lecture me on the laws of my kind or you will learn how comfortable I am breaking them."*

Cuir quickly removes himself.

"Please," I beg Tairn. *"If not for Teine's own sake, then for Mira's. I've already lost Andarna. I can't lose my sister, too. Do not ask me to find that strength or I will fail you. I will fail us both."*

A snarl rips from his throat and metal clangs as he positions himself over

Teine, gripping the four ends of chain wrapped around his torso in his claws. *"You will not move from this field,"* he orders.

"Thank you." Wind gusts across the side of my face as his wings beat harder than I've ever seen, and Teine's limp body slowly rises from the field. His shadow engulfs me as he flies overhead, carrying Teine toward the safety of the cliffs.

"Bold strategy," Bodhi notes, watching them depart. "Sending our biggest dragon away is definitely not going to bite us in the ass."

"He'll be back." I look up to the sky and slowly rotate to better survey the space, but there's no sign of Theophanie or the wyvern she prefers. My heart starts to pound. I'm not fond of being the prey.

Breathing out slowly, I deny the impulse to check the city skyline for Xaden. This doesn't work if I can't focus here, now. I force myself to cut off all thoughts of the others and step into the headspace where I am no longer a sister, a friend, or a lover. I exist only as a rider, a weapon.

"You want to wait to start hunting our silver-haired friend?" Bodhi says as Cuir stalks toward us, wyvern blood dripping from the tip of his swordtail.

"We don't have to hunt." I strap my conduit to my wrist, then reach over my shoulder and flip the cap open on my quiver. "As long as I'm here, she'll come." And I'll get the chance to kill her before she attacks anyone else I love.

"Waiting feels...anticlimactic." He puts his back to mine.

"Always does." Simultaneously torturous, too, like the moment in flight when Tairn's muscles shift beneath me and I know I'm about to lose my stomach in a dive, or those long minutes on the ridgeline above Basgiath, waiting for the horde to arrive. "You think this will work?"

"Has to. Magic requires balance, right?"

"It's the oldest rule there is." Theophanie walks out from behind the carcass of a wyvern. "But once a century or so we get a chance to skew the scales in our favor, and I will prove myself to him this time."

We whip toward her, shoulder to shoulder, and I reach for Tairn's power, but barely a trickle answers the call.

Shit. Tairn's out of range. It's not going to be a quick jaunt to haul Teine the many miles to the wards and up ten thousand feet, either. But Mira's safe, and that's what matters. Bodhi and I can keep ourselves alive.

"Where the fuck did she come from?" Bodhi whispers, drawing his sword.

"She's fast," I reply just as softly, remembering how she disappeared from the brig at Basgiath.

"There're only a few of us who are faster," Theophanie replies, walking along the carcass of the wyvern, grazing the ridges at its back as she saunters toward us. "Older, too."

My lips part. She heard us from twenty feet away.

"Pity you had to kill them." She clucks her tongue. "They take *forever* to generate. Are you ready to tip the balance, Violet?"

Having two lightning wielders on any side wouldn't just tip a balance; it would destroy it.

The same as shadows.

Cuir lowers his head and growls at Bodhi's right.

"I'm ready to kill you." I reach for a dagger out of reflex and throw so hard my shoulder pops but thankfully doesn't subluxate.

Theophanie waves her gnarled fingers, and the blade falls aside before it reaches the halfway mark. "Disappointing. Have you learned nothing since the last time you tried that? No need to be embarrassed, though. We'll work on it. I'll be happy to mentor you."

My eyes flare. Was this the path the priestess foresaw for me? Not their mentorship but Theophanie's?

"Fuck," Bodhi mutters. "That's another problem."

Probably makes the arrows at my back useless, too. Awesome. I'll have to get up close and personal to kill her.

"Odd choice of companion, seeing that you reek of his kin." The veins beside her eyes pulse and she appraises Bodhi, her pace completely unhurried as she strolls toward the head of the dead wyvern. "Tell me, do you not grow tired of being a less-powerful version of your cousin?"

"I'm not the one out here trying to prove myself," Bodhi counters, his head tilting in the same way Xaden's does when sizing up an opponent.

No sword. No staff. She's unarmed with the exception of a row of blades at her hip. I search her stride for weakness and find none. She's faster, too, which means I'll get one shot.

"Witty." Her smile cracks another line in her lips. "You're almost done waiting. He'll be gone soon. The crown will be yours."

Come on, get closer.

"We don't have a crown." Bodhi switches his sword to his left hand, freeing his right. "You don't know me well enough to try and fuck with my head. I'm doing exactly what I've always wanted—protecting my cousin, my province."

"And her." She pauses just in front of the wyvern's bloody snout and cuts her gaze to mine. "A weapon like you will only submit to someone stronger, so come, let's get this farce over with so you can begin your real journey. He's waiting." Glee lights her smile.

"Berwyn?" I guess.

"As if I would answer to that fool? I think not." She glances skyward. "Pity you sent your dragon away, but don't worry, there's plenty of power beneath your feet. Now, show me what my patience has bought." She lifts her arms as the breeze picks up, sweeping off the cliffs at our back.

No more stalling, then. Here we go. As long as Bodhi counters her signet, we can end her before Tairn even gets back.

Bodhi raises his right hand and turns it as though clasping a doorknob none of us can see. The sky darkens and wind gusts, and though no lightning strikes, the temperature and humidity rise in a way I've only ever felt around one other person.

Theophanie's smile sharpens.

Gravity shifts, and my perception of *everything* changes.

"It's working." A smile tugs at Bodhi's mouth.

"It's not," I whisper, all the hope leaving my body like water out of a bathtub drain. "You can't counter her. You have to go. Now." I palm the next blade. Maybe I can't throw it, but I'm not going down defenseless, either. I can hold out until Tairn returns.

"There's no lightning," Bodhi argues, his knuckles whitening on the pommel of his sword.

"I was wrong. She's not a lightning wielder." It had struck in both battles, and I'd conflated its presence with hers when it was simply a byproduct of her true signet. She hadn't controlled the lightning during their assault on Suniva.

She'd controlled the very thing causing it.

"Of course I'm not." Theophanie flicks a finger, and the clouds above us begin to rotate. "There is only one exception to the rule, Violet Sorrengail. Imagine my surprise when it turned out to be *you*. If it was going to be one of her daughters, I'd have bet on your sister."

"Amari help us." Bodhi's hand slowly lowers, and his gaze jumps skyward. "She isn't the dark wielder version of you."

"No." I shake my head as the next gust of wind nearly pitches me forward. I've prepared for the wrong fight. I know the feel of lightning charging, recognize the crackle in the air just before it strikes. I understand the limits, the boundaries of wielding it. Each strike requires its own burst of energy, and once it's over, it's done. But what Theophanie's doing will take on a life of its own and carry forward long after she's given it her power.

This is so much worse than battling myself.

"She's their answer to my mother." Saying it out loud snaps the shock from my system, and my mind begins to race. Only Aimsir's exhaustion or a physical illness weakened Mom. Not even the strongest wind wielder could diminish Mom's storms.

"She was the answer to *me*," Theophanie hisses, and the clouds start to *swirl*.

The tornado. My chest clenches. My mother had never accomplished that particular feat. No wonder I hadn't recognized Theophanie for what she is—I'd never met a more powerful storm wielder than Mom. Until now.

"You have to get out of here." I shove at Bodhi's arm. "Go before Cuir can't launch in the wind!"

"My signet is always the balance," Bodhi argues, lifting his hand as the wind rises to a constant roar at our backs. "I can stop her!"

"You can't!" I push again, and this time he stumbles sideways. "Your signet must only work on our magic, not theirs. Now go! You promised Xaden!"

"Come with me!" he shouts.

Somehow, Theophanie knows you'll try to save everyone... Brennan's words fill my head.

"I can't." If I go, she'll follow, and we'll lose. If I stay, I can be the distraction the others need.

"Then I'll fight beside—" Bodhi starts, but Cuir wraps two talons around his midsection and launches before he can finish. His green wings beat in giant sweeps as he carries a loudly protesting Bodhi from the field, heading south. No doubt he'll clear the wind before ascending the cliffs.

Tyrrendor's succession is safe, but there's no time to feel even an ounce of relief.

A howling gust of wind forces me forward, and I fall to my hands and knees in the grass, narrowly missing the conduit that dangles from my wrist. Something groans behind me, and I look over my shoulder just in time to watch a tree taller than Tairn lean in my direction from the edge of the field, pausing at an obscene angle before it's completely uprooted.

Oh *shit*. I push to my feet and throw my body weight to the left, racing to get clear. The wind takes me down again in less than ten steps, and my stomach lurches as the tree plummets toward me. My feet slip over a group of loose rocks, but my boots hold my ankles in place as I scramble for another few feet of distance.

The tree crashes, hitting the ground with the force of a dragon. Heart pounding, I stare at the branch lying less than an arm's reach away.

"Channel, and we'll walk away together!" she promises, her voice rising over the wind even though the tree has hidden her from me.

Come to think of it, the tree has also hidden *me*, at least until she shifts position.

I need to work fast.

The wind is too strong to make a straight shot possible—it will fly right past her without some weight to it. I grab a dagger, lift my flight jacket, and slice a strip of cloth from the bottom of my uniform. The wind fights to rip the fabric away, so I stick it between my teeth and bite down, then sheathe the blade. Faster. I need to move *faster*. Reaching over my shoulder, I grip the maorsite-tipped arrow's shaft as tightly as possible, then pull it free from the stabilizing quiver and drag it in front of me.

The wind dies slightly as I tie the arrow to a conduit-size rock from the field.

"Reach for the power and wield!" Theophanie steps into view twenty feet ahead of me.

I rise up on my knees and throw the rock as hard as I can with the wind.

The gale carries it, but Theophanie knocks it off course three-quarters of the way there. "Have you *still* learned nothing?" It lands a couple of feet to her right.

And explodes.

Dirt, grass, and rock fly, and the impact flings Theophanie half a wing length through the air. The wind dies before she smacks into the ground.

Thank gods the storm isn't strong enough to hold without her yet. I surge to my feet and charge, drawing my last alloy-hilted dagger. I can't risk losing it in a throw.

Grass clings to her braid as she shoves herself upright, and her eyes struggle to focus as I flip the dagger parallel with my wrist and hurl myself at her. My knees hit the ground a second before I swing.

She catches my forearm and squeezes with a strength that threatens to crush the bone. "Enough!"

A debilitating wave of pain crashes over me, but I hold on to the dagger like my friends' lives depend on it, then pull a black-handled knife from my left and stab down, embedding the blade in her thigh.

Her lips crack as she screams, but instead of releasing my forearm or removing the knife from her thigh, she grasps my throat and drives me backward, slamming my spine against the ground. My eyes widen and I wait for the explosives in my quiver to kill us both, but the cushion somehow sustains the impact.

"Foolish woman." She rams her knee into my stomach and forces the air right out of me.

I struggle for the next breath, but it comes, and she pins my other hand to the ground with a speed I could never beat.

"Your mother knew at your age that she was no match for me. That's why she hid behind those wards. Perhaps you should have followed her example." Theophanie's jagged nails dig into my skin and the veins beside her eyes bulge as she looks south. "A few seem to have gotten by. Whatever will you do?"

I follow her line of sight, and every muscle in my body locks to keep from thrashing. A horde of wyvern has cut north, bypassing the city and flying straight into the valley that leads to the Medaro Pass. I should be there...but then I couldn't keep her *here*.

Dunne, be with them. I look away and find Theophanie staring at me, her eerie red eyes so close she consumes my vision.

"The horde is hungry. How many innocents climb the pass? A thousand? Two? You can still save them. Reach for it. Take the power at your fingertips." She flips my hand so my palm presses into the grass, and I consciously keep my senses closed. "So stubborn. It must be killing you, realizing you don't have every answer, aren't the solution to every problem. You're just another lightning wielder, mortally incapable of being everywhere at once." The metal eases from my throat. "Go ahead. It will be entertaining to watch you try."

I glance south just long enough to witness the horde disappearing into the valley. "You're right. I can't be everywhere." Theophanie's eyes widen as I arch my neck against the blade. "I don't have to be."

When push comes to shove, I'm not the best of us.

She is.

Command is built on respect, rules, and obedience.
Squads are built on trust.

—LEADERSHIP FOR SECOND-YEARS BY MAJOR PIPA DONANS

CHAPTER
SIXTY-ONE

RHIANNON

mogen. Quinn. Violet. My heart pounds. I don't know how to protect the pass when we're down three of our most powerful, battle-hardened squadmates, but failure isn't an option.

Thank Zihnal, the infernal wind stopped. For a moment, I thought we'd all be blown to Cordyn. I inspect what I can of the Medaro Pass from its entrance and sigh with more than a little relief that none of the civilians fell in the squall.

"The cliff blocked the wind for them, as it did us." Feirge steps away from the safety of the base and pivots sharply to face the winding valley that leads to Draithus.

"Tell the others to form a line. If we can fly now, so can they." A horde of gray had just rounded the last curve of the valley when the windstorm hit, driving the wyvern to land.

According to Cath, every dragon was forced to hunker down in Draithus, too.

"Done," Feirge responds, and rain splashes at the base of her neck.

Great. Rain is the last thing anyone on this damned cliff needs.

I remind myself of what Raegan always says — *Zihnal gives what he sees fit.* No use thanking the god for one blessing and cursing him in the next breath. I'd like to see her say it under these circumstances, but she'd probably pull it off. She's always been the more graceful twin.

Tara, on the other hand, would tell me to make my own luck.

I check right, making sure the others weren't harmed in the freak windstorm. Maren and Cat fall into line, and neither they nor their gryphons look worse for wear. Beyond them, Sliseag swings his tail, keeping his wings tucked for proximity, and Sawyer nods my way. Then I look left and find Neve and Bragen both in position, with Aotrom shifting his weight impatiently.

Ridoc stares at the northern peak, not the path through the valley just south of it, like he could see straight through the thing if he tried hard enough.

Part of me screams that we should be on the other side of that peak, but we have our orders. *And half a squad.*

I clear my throat and my feelings. This isn't the Squad Battle. I make a mistake here, and innocent people *die*. We lucked out when the wyvern that crashed through the holes I left in our defenses only took out the wall and not my parents' house. No matter how much Violet means to me, she's one life. We're guarding thousands who are fleeing as my family had, and we owe them the same protection.

"Gamlyn!" I shout across the gryphons. "I need your focus *here*."

He looks like he might give me the finger for a second, but nods.

"Acknowledging your fear for the lightning wielder does not compromise you." Feirge calls me out just like always. *"Ignoring it does. Accept the emotion and move on."*

My grip tightens on the raised ridges of green scales that form the pommel. *"Of course I'm worried about Violet."* She's out there in the one condition I never want any of us—alone. Tairn flew into the cloud cover moments before the windstorm hit, carrying Teine in chains and escorted by Marbh, and the last status report from Cath had both Riorson and Durran spotted near the city walls. At least I haven't seen any lightning. *"But we have a job to—"*

A dozen wyvern—maybe more—rise along the valley floor a few hundred yards out. My heart begins pounding. *"Ask Veirt how many Baylor can see."*

Screams sound in a chorus from the evacuees, both those waiting to climb and the ones already on the cliff. Rain. Wyvern. Panicked civilians. The situation has real shitshow potential. Gods, the first-years better be pulling the civilians to safety at the top of the pass as instructed. Graycastle and Mairi are already on my lecture list. Fuck knows what either of those two were thinking.

Undisciplined. I need to rein everyone in with a quickness.

"Baylor sees seventeen," Feirge responds a second later.

Seventeen. Against three dragons and four gryphons. Shit. *"That's a little menacing,"* I admit to Feirge.

"Then let us *be menaces,"* Feirge snarls, her head weaving in anticipation. *"Ready to relay your orders."*

My orders. No pressure. We need to intercept.

"Riot, launch in a thorn formation," I tell her. I learned my lesson in Aretia—we have to engage far from the cliff. *"Drift, guard the evacuees under Bragen's command."*

Feirge takes three steps, and I tighten my thighs to hold my seat as she launches into the cloud-soaked sky. *"Kiralair is disgruntled with the decision."*

What else is new? I debate the choice for all the time it takes to blink. *"Tell Kira they have better maneuverability against the cliff than we do and a full arsenal of runes. We can't stop seventeen wyvern with three dragons. They need to be ready."* Just once, I'd like to give an order that Cat doesn't feel the need to fight.

I settle my flight goggles over my eyes as we fly headfirst toward the wyvern, Feirge, Aotrom, and Sliseag forming three points of a triangle. We need to engage as far from the cliff as possible. Plenty of room to move forward, not a lot of room to retreat against sheer rock.

The enemy are roughly arranged in three columns, two deep.

"Continue thorn—" Wait. *"No, vertical. Switch to vertical formation."* It will give us the best shot at taking down as many as possible.

"Second-guessing your choices makes me do the same regarding Threshing," Feirge lectures, climbing in altitude as we approach the steep walls of the valley.

"Very funny." I wish I could see directly beneath us.

"They're in position." Feirge answers my unspoken question, but I have a feeling Aotrom is going to deviate as soon as he gets the chance.

"Check in with Sliseag." We've got less than thirty seconds, and this will only be his second encounter after nearly losing Sawyer at Basgiath.

"He's insulted you asked," Feirge responds.

"Naturally." I lock the toes of my boots between her scales and make ready for impact once I can see the shape of their teeth. *"Top center first."*

"I thought we'd go bottom left," she replies with mock innocence.

"No time for your sarcasm."

Our target screeches, then climbs out of formation. Feirge breaks away to pursue, and my whole body clenches as a stream of blue fire erupts in our direction.

"Hold!" Feirge shouts, and I do exactly as she orders, locking my muscles as she rolls right. My body weight shifts, and I push with my right leg to balance out as she pulls a near-vertical climb.

"You're going to do the thing, aren't you?" I hold on to the pommel like a lifeline as our momentum stalls at the zenith she's chosen.

"Maybe." She pitches back left, falling into a dive so steep my stomach tries to dig its way out through my feet.

"You have to warn me!" I shift my grip and push at the pommel, readying

myself for what inevitably comes next as we barrel toward the wyvern from above.

"Why? You were prepared." She soft-snaps her wings, slowing our descent a second before we make impact just enough that I won't go hurtling over her head.

The collision shakes my grip, and the rain isn't helping.

Feirge digs her claws into the wyvern's back and clamps her jaw at the base of its skull, where the neck is thinner, weaker. Its scream rattles my eardrums.

Then we fall, despite the frantic beat of Feirge's wings. Fear rears its ugly head, and I try to swallow it. She has the advantage of being clear of the wyvern's claws and teeth, but agility has always been her biggest asset, not strength. Her claws shred through the leathery gray wings, then she breaks their bones as the mountain rises to my right.

"Getting close to the ground!" I warn her.

"Your situational awareness never fails to leave me awestruck." She heaves her weight forward, then wrenches the wyvern's head back, snapping its neck as a blur of gray flickers through my line of sight.

"In that case, would you like to know about the one above us?" I ask.

She releases the wyvern into the mountainside below, and both our heads snap upward.

Aotrom flies by in pursuit, and a curl of green fire rushes up his tail. I cease breathing until the brown outruns the flame, saving Ridoc from a painful death, and then I face the source.

"Hold," Feirge warns a second before we collide with the greenfire wyvern. She snaps for its neck, taking a bloody chunk away as it dives, spraying blood over the mountainside.

She sinks her claws into another and dissects its throat.

Where is the rest of the squad? I search with a quick swing of my head and find Aotrom flying vertically alongside the other wyvern above us. My mouth drops as he rolls, putting his spine—and Ridoc—against the creature.

"What in Malek's name is he doing?" I shout as Ridoc claps the pommel with one hand and extends the other toward gray scales. Is he trying to get himself crushed? He can't be seriously—

He is.

The wyvern shrieks, and a paler shade of gray spreads along its scales, emanating from Ridoc's hand. The beast tenses, then ceases to beat its wings... and *falls* directly toward us.

Feirge surges forward, banking left to avoid the ridgeline, and I turn in the seat to watch the wyvern impact the rocky terrain. Holy shit, I think it cracked in half.

"Did you see that?" I ask as we round the corner of the mountain, finding Sawyer finishing a kill hundreds of feet below us. We need to regroup. If it's this hectic back here, how outnumbered are they beyond the valley in Draithus?

I glance up at the sky and, in a moment of weakness, scan for any sign of Tairn. How long can Vi be out there by herself?

"Focus." Feirge's head swivels toward the pass, and I put my head where it belongs.

Shit. Seven of the wyvern got through. Cat has one by the throat, Kira's talons tearing into the spaces between scales as it lies immobilized beneath her, while Maren takes aim at another with her crossbow. A second later, its wing is on fire. Impressive rune.

Bragen and Neve each chase their own up the cliffside, leaving four to pick off screaming civilians one by one.

"Regroup," I order, determined to save as many as possible. *"Shield formation."*

"Are you sure?" Feirge asks in that sweetly mocking way of hers.

We're down three, but the strength of the squad is in the whole, not the individual. We *will* hold this pass, even in this godsforsaken rain.

"Positive. Let's go."

There is no goddess more wrathful than Dunne. Entering Her temple will slice the soul from any attendant who has shunned Her grace.

—Major Rorilee's Guide to Appeasing the Gods,
Second Edition

CHAPTER SIXTY-TWO

VIOLET

Rain splatters against my forehead as Theophanie's dagger scrapes the skin of my throat, but I hold fast and keep my eyes on her. My mind flips through every possible way to get out of this hold alive, and I settle on the simplest, but it's a risk. "My friends will continue to fight long after I meet Malek, and I'll meet him with my soul intact. Do your worst."

The red in her eyes pulses as surprise ripples across her face, and she lifts the blade just enough to give me the inches I need.

This is going to hurt.

I slam my forehead straight into her nose. Bone crunches as her head snaps back, her body rolling with it. The second her weight shifts, I yank my right knee to my chest and kick up as hard as I possibly can, catching her in the pit of her arm and breaking her grip on my wrists.

"Shit!" she shrieks, then uses her speed to appear twenty-five feet to my left, clutching her nose. "That's never going to straighten out!"

I rock to my feet.

"You think I won't do it—take your life." She studies me with a malice she'd previously lacked and draws a green-tipped dagger from her belt.

My stomach turns. Being inflicted with that particular poison once in my life was quite enough. "I think you exposed your desperation with your once-a-century comment." I keep my eyes on her as I grab my runed dagger from the rain-slick grass. "You need me."

"Another will come along," she warns. "You are not special."

"But I'm the only lightning wielder you have to *prove yourself* now." Pretty sure I've pressed her to the limits of her patience and shit is about to get real. Gripping the conduit out of habit, I reach for Tairn. The growing drip of power and parchment-thin bond tell me he's getting closer but still out of range.

"Which meant a lot more when you had your irid." She crouches and runs her hand over the meadow grass. A single tap of her finger turns the spot gray.

Oh, shit. If I overplayed my hand, all she has to do is lower hers, and I'm dust. Panic winds its way around my heart and digs her nails in, but I shove the insidious bitch straight out before she can get a good grip.

"Violence?" Xaden asks. Exhaustion and urgency mixed with a little pain slide down the bond. He's in combat.

"I'm all right. Focus on you." I chance taking my eyes off Theophanie for a heartbeat and glance toward what I can see of the city through the thickening storm. Dragons, wyvern, and gryphons fill the sky above the spiral tower, but I don't let my gaze linger long enough to search for blue in that sea of chaos.

Xaden is the strongest of them. He'll be all right. I have to keep my focus—and Theophanie—here to give them a shot at saving Draithus. They just need *time*. I turn my back on the city and face Theophanie as rain begins to fall in earnest, pelting the ground with heavy drops.

"Ah, you worry for the shadow wielder," Theophanie says with a cruel smile and continues to skim her hand across the tips of the grass. "Do you not want to have forever with him?"

"I already do." I scan our surroundings for any advantage and find none.

"Not in the way you want." She tilts her head. "We're excellent actors, but our kind doesn't feel what you call *love*."

That gets *all* my attention.

"You're lying." I would know.

"Ah, there it is." A cruel smile tilts her mouth. "Battles are lost by our weakest warriors, and that's what he makes you—weak. Now that I know where you're vulnerable, we can begin."

"Fuck you." I've proved to Dunne's favored isle that I'm anything but the weakest, while she no longer carries Dunne's favor.

"Lesson one. To survive in our world, you must protect the magic that sustains you. Do you know how to keep from being drained by this method?" She splays her palm on the ground, and the earth slowly desiccates. Grass turns gray and crumbles. Ground shrivels and cracks, swallowing the rain. The infection oozes outward from her hand, slowly devouring inches, then feet.

I retreat a single step, then realize how wrong that instinct is. She can turn up the speed at any second. She's just playing with me.

"It's simple, actually. Occupying ground that has already had its magic repurposed creates a barrier." She lifts her silver brows. "The easiest solution is to drain it yourself. If you do so before I get there, you'll live. You'll keep your love—at least what it masquerades as—and your power, and even your dragon if you wish."

"And if I don't?" The desiccation spreads and wingbeats fill the air, but Tairn's still out of reach, so I'm guessing I'm about to meet more of her wyvern.

"You die." She leans onto her hand, and the ground withers at four times the speed, the magic draining in a circle of gray that approaches like a tidal wave. "I can wait for another lightning wielder, but you're too dangerous to be left alive, so choose quickly."

Fuck. I have seconds—

Already had its magic repurposed. I need a barrier.

I break right, then sprint like hell, dropping the conduit. It smacks my forearm with every stride as I unsheathe another dagger from my thigh, and my foot slips on the rain-slick grass, just enough to throw off my pace. My left knee screams, and I block out the pain, keeping one eye on the spreading circle of death that races toward my feet and the other on the nearest wyvern carcass. Ten more feet. I can make it. I have to make it.

I'm not dying on this field.

My heart pounds and my lungs burn as I leap those last three feet, soaring toward a wall of gray. I slam into the fleshy area between the wyvern's talons and stab my right dagger deep, then immediately pull up and thrust the left as high as I can. My feet kick for purchase on its slick, leathery skin, but I manage to get a foothold and use the daggers to climb.

I scramble to the top of its claw, then race up its scaly leg, over its ankle, and find the shredded meat of its thigh.

The wave of desiccation ripples underneath me, then passes right by on the other side of the wyvern's carcass, and I lift my hands to my chest to feel the drum of my heartbeat. If I was dead, I'd know it, right? I definitely wouldn't still hear wingbeats.

"My, aren't you clever." Theophanie focuses on something behind me. "No!"

The curve of talons appears in the corner of my eye, and I throw out my arms. A claw closes around me, then jerks my body into the sky. *"Tairn."*

"Not quite."

Rain bombards navy-blue scales. *"Sgaeyl?"*

"You are an inconvenience for which there is no adequate measurement," she snarls, flying west as the clouds churn above us, darkening with an abysmal quickness. *"But you have done an excellent job keeping the Maven occupied."*

West is the wrong direction when Xaden is south.

"You can't leave him!" I shout.

"Which is why I'm leaving you." She swings her foreleg forward, then releases her grip. *"She's all yours."*

I careen into the storm with as much grace as a flailing drunkard held hostage by physics, and I lock my jaw, swallowing the scream that rises in my throat. Fear grips my lungs, and power rushes through my veins in response, coursing with a hundred times the force of adrenaline.

That's Tairn.

The fear that summoned my power evaporates into the storm, and I throw my arms outward. A gargantuan void of black cuts through the rain ahead of me as my trajectory shifts and gravity takes hold, pulling me back to the ground.

"A little help here?" I begin to fall faster than the rain around me.

"I told you to stay on the field." Two talons hook over my shoulders, and every bone in my body grates on the others as I'm jerked upward. *"But in this case, I'm relieved you did not listen."*

"Sgaeyl made that choice, but me, too." I'd be dead if she hadn't. *"Teine?"*

"Quickly recovering under Brennan's care at the top of the pass." Tairn swings me up toward his snout, then tosses me onto his back.

I land at the base of his neck and skid. My left knee buckles, but I hold my arms out for balance and rapidly navigate the spikes of his back against the will of the wind and rain. *"Mira?"* I settle into the saddle and breathe a little easier once I'm buckled in and my goggles are in place.

This is how we're meant to face combat. Together.

"She lives," he replies as we descend. *"We're approaching the field."*

The clouds above us start to rotate counterclockwise.

Fantastic.

"Watch the weather. Theophanie's a storm wielder. She'll try to force you out of the sky." I grasp the conduit in my left hand and throw open my Archives door, changing the stream of power to a deluge as the field comes into view.

"She may try," he growls.

The field bears the circle where she drained the magic from the earth, but she's nowhere in sight. *"She's gone."*

"She recognized her loss of advantage. Look south," Tairn announces, and my head swivels.

"I can't see that—" My vision shifts just like it did after Threshing, and the battlefield comes into startling clarity. But it's not Andarna's eyes I'm looking through; it's Tairn's. *"Far."*

Whatever hordes had waited to launch have taken to the sky a mile from the city gates, leaving behind a line of a dozen—no, eleven—venin-carrying wyvern on the ground behind them. I can't make out the dark wielders' features, but it isn't hard to spot Theophanie's silver hair or the enormous wyvern she rides.

My heart lurches. The one in the center looks bigger than Codagh.

"Because it is," Tairn relishes. *"It would be my finest kill to date."*

I blink, and my vision returns to my own. The last thing I want is to put Tairn anywhere near that enormous wyvern, but there's no way the city can withstand the coming assault. If Kaori and the others fail *their* orders, none of us will survive without falling back and abandoning the civilians.

"Our orders are to occupy or kill Theophanie." I draw and hold more power, heating my skin to a noticeable burn. *"The fact that there are more than a hundred wyvern between us and her that also happen to threaten the city—"*

"Agreed," Tairn interrupts and banks right, soaring toward Draithus.

"Why would riders develop farsight if you can see that clearly, anyway?" I ask.

"The privilege of our sight is afforded to few," he comments.

Go figure.

Rain sizzles as it hits my face, and I spot Glane and Cath high above a line of gryphons on the northern wall while Cuir flies lower in formation, all picking off wyvern trying to dart by the city on their way to the valley beyond. Rhi and the rest of the squad will stop them before they get to the pass. Wait…Cuir? *"Isn't Bodhi supposed to be—"*

"We all make our own decisions."

Xaden's going to be pissed.

I scan the horizon for him. The officers have a dozen dragons in the sky, but there's only one blue above the southern end of the city, and it's not Sgaeyl. *"Where are they?"*

"She has withdrawn from me," he admits with a mental growl.

A string of curse words flows through my head as we approach the city, and I gather more power, letting it scald and smolder deep within me. *"Probably doesn't want you worried."*

"Which has the opposite effect," he retorts as the horde passes a line of stacked wyvern carcasses to the east. They'll be at the gates in less than a minute, and there are too many to target.

At least I don't have to aim.

"Pull the riot back to the airspace above the city." I drop the conduit, letting it fall against my forearm, and lift both hands to the rain as energy sears my lungs, building to a burn I can't contain for much longer.

"Done." He banks slightly left so our course is set for the horde and not the city, and the multitude of color in the sky shifts, concentrating above Draithus.

I'd bet my life that not a single dragon in the sky questioned Tairn's immediate authority over the airspace.

"Carr's teachings might actually come in handy." I focus on the horde, then

splay my hands wide and release the built-up energy. Power erupts with a white-hot *snap*, jolting my spine as I drag my hands downward, and I let go as lightning cleaves the sky in too many columns to count.

"Ten bolts," Tairn announces with a swell of pride as thunder reverberates through my body and wyvern fall. *"Seven struck."*

Determination expands my chest. Yeah, I can do this. I lift both hands, draw power voraciously, then wield again just like before. Columns of lightning crash, though not as powerful as the first strike, and I take out five wyvern, according to Tairn.

"Four," he announces after the next strike.

Again and again, I draw energy recklessly, counting on volume, not accuracy. Everything in my body burns like I've been tied to a pyre, but I push onward.

"Six. Three. Eight!" Tairn keeps count with each wield.

We have time for one more as we near the northeast edge of the walls, and I draw in Tairn's scorching power like breath, then wield.

"Six!" he announces, and I fall forward, my head swimming as the ones I didn't kill fly at us in a swarm and breach the city airspace. *"Hold tight!"*

"We can't—" I grasp the pommels, and Tairn pulls into a climb so steep the edges of my vision blur. The wind feels so fucking good against my face, but it doesn't touch the fire in my lungs. I fight for breath against the force crushing my chest and only manage once Tairn clears the cloud of wyvern and levels out for a precious second.

"You cannot fight if you burn out. Water!" Tairn orders, and I rip the waterskin from its strap behind the saddle, pull the cork, and chug. It hits like butter on a frying pan, and my stomach instantly rebels. *"Keep it down."*

As if it's that easy.

I breathe in through my nose and out through my mouth, quelling the urge to vomit, then shove the waterskin back into position as my body absorbs the offering. Heat burns behind my eyes, which means my temperature is still elevated, but the searing pain is gone. I'm getting better at this. *"Let's kill their makers."*

"Let's," Tairn agrees, and we dive toward the line of venin sitting atop their wyvern.

Wind roars in my ears, and they launch at the sight of us. Six surge for the city, two fly our way, and three retreat into the mountains—including Theophanie and her *monstrosity*.

Fuck.

"We kill those in our way and then pursue their storm wielder," Tairn decrees.

"I only have one alloy dagger left." I grasp the conduit in my hand as we race toward the dark wielders. Instead of gathering more, I draw on the power already thrumming through my veins with care, excising only what I need with precision.

"Then I suggest you not throw it."

The venin on the left flicks his wrist, and a spear of ice hurtles our way. Tairn rolls right, and the projectile flies within feet of his wing, too close for comfort. That one needs to die first.

Power snaps through me and I draw it downward with the tip of my finger, searing my skin as I aim. It strikes the venin right through the fluttering hood of his purple robes, and he and his wyvern fall from the sky, instantly dead.

I shift focus to the other dark wielder, only to hear Tairn's teeth snap in that direction as the pair flee in retreat.

The roaring wind crescendos like a river that's burst its dam, and a gust catches Tairn's wing, propelling us sideways for a startling heartbeat before he levels us out and turns into the wind.

Oh, fuck.

A tornado spouts at the northern edge of the field where I'd faced Theophanie, dropping from the clouds in a narrow cone. Earth churns as it spins slowly toward Draithus, its path too precise to be natural. It will rip the city apart.

"Ground the riot!" Tairn shouts so loudly my vision shakes, and I get the feeling the message didn't go just down our pathway, but *every* pathway.

Theophanie.

"Our prey waits on the mountain beyond the field," Tairn says as we cut a route toward the northeast corner of the city.

Wingbeats sound behind us, and I pivot in the saddle. Hope surges at the sight of blue wings— *"What the hell is he doing?"*

My brows rise as Molvic emerges from one of the southern valleys.

"The Spare brings the advance party from Zehyllna." Tairn's head swivels as he relays the information. *"A thousand soldiers and their horses. They landed at the port of Soudra by accident instead of Cordyn and will be here in less than half an hour."*

The city has reinforcements if it can last that long, but wyvern outnumber riders and fliers fleeing for cover. Our forces will have to drive the wyvern to the ground for the infantry to kill in order to make a difference. My stomach pitches. Where are Xaden and Sgaeyl?

I reach through the bond, only to be met with a wall of black ice.

Cuir disappears into the fray above the city, and my breath stutters.

"We have to—" I start.

"One objective," Tairn growls as we near the battle. *"Decide our fate."*

Glane launches toward Cuir despite the order to shelter.

I nod to myself, then rip my gaze away, focusing northward on the tornado and its creator.

Time to do what Imogen suggested months ago and delegate. She'll rip the very sky apart before she and Glane accept defeat.

One objective. *"Fly for Theophanie."*

Fuck you. My daughter and I will meet Malek with clean consciences. Will you and *your* daughters be able to say the same when they come for you?

—The last words of Tracila Cardulo (redacted)

CHAPTER SIXTY-THREE

IMOGEN

If chaos were a place, it would be Draithus.

Rain beats against the glass of my goggles as Glane climbs toward the three wyvern trying their best to rip Cuir apart. The steep angle of her chosen approach makes it hard as hell to stay seated, but I'm not going to tell her to slow—not that she'd listen anyway. Bodhi's in trouble.

I grit my teeth. He doesn't get it. If we lose both him and Riorson, Tyrrendor falls to whomever the king appoints. I'd rather die than see a Navarrian aristocrat on the burned throne Mom and Katrina died defending. The flame of perpetual rage that lives in my chest burns hotter. Fuck that horde. Fuck the venin who ride them. Fuck that unholy vortex of a tornado at the end of the northern field, and fuck the orders to stay grounded in these winds. We're not losing Bodhi.

There are still too many wyvern despite the inhuman amount Sorrengail just dispatched, and where the *fuck* is Riorson? He'd better be helping in the northeastern tower, because I haven't seen a trace of a shadow in the last twenty minutes.

"Cruth reports we did not bring a sufficient supply," Glane warns, relaying Quinn's message from the armory in the turret below.

Gods*damn* it. *"We brought* two *cases!"* Enough to start a war within our own kingdom, considering Riorson has been withholding our forge's weapons from King Tauri.

"Nuirlach says they've sent for more." She doesn't sound hopeful.

"From four hours away? How—" Oh shit. Felix knows about Garrick. Gods, he has to be nearing burnout at this point. *"Then we hold out and pray Sorrengail can stop that fucking storm."*

"Cruth also relays that you should be drinking more water, as we've been in combat longer than hoped for."

I scoff. *"Tell Cruth to tell Quinn that I'm perfectly fine."* It figures she's worried about me while she's the one doing all the work.

Glane's head snaps upward. *"Cuir suffers,"* she warns me in that gnarring tone that usually means she's about to do something impetuous, and sure enough, she angles her wings and climbs even higher, at a nearly ninety-degree angle.

Shit. I slip my boots back to the next scale ridge and adjust my hold. Lying along Glane's back, tucking my head beneath her pommel, and pressing my cheek to her scales helps cut the wind resistance against my torso as we climb.

It's a mistake to look down at the burning city, but I can't help but track two wyvern crossing our airspace below. Cath launches, and I blink in surprise. Guess Aetos is all about breaking rules now.

"Brace," Glane warns.

It's more than I usually get.

Her momentum shifts, slowing for a nauseating second, and I clamp every muscle and mold myself to her spine, changing our shape from rider and dragon to one being. She's pulled this maneuver too many times for me not to recognize how shitty this is about to be.

She attacks from underneath, all teeth and claws, then tucks her wings to protect them and swings her tail upward.

I concentrate on moving with her, fighting gravity as I'm hung upside down and her daggertail slices into the next wyvern. Blood sprays, coloring the rain red. My grip loosens despite my rubber-coated gloves, and I grimace, forcing my fingers further between her scales. *"Anytime now!"*

"Fine," she sighs. Then we plummet.

The force of the fall pushes me against her scales, effectively holding me in place as she drags the wyvern from the sky. Bone cracks, flesh rends, and she tosses the carcass like yesterday's trash. The gray mass falls like a stone to the right, and Glane rolls, putting me on top of her back instead of under it.

"Seventeen," she counts.

"Pretty sure it was sixteen." I pull myself upward, using her scales like a ladder until my ass hits the seat, and I drag my arm across my goggles to clear the rain. There has to be a rune somewhere that will keep the fucking lenses clear.

"The first one counted!" she argues as we surge toward Cuir and the

remaining wyvern.

"Cath took that first one."

"Only after I wounded it!" Glane snaps.

"Still not a kill." My stomach tenses as I get my first good look at what we're up against. Cuir swings his swordtail again and again, keeping the wyvern at his back at bay, but there's a deep, bleeding furrow cutting diagonally across his chest, no doubt gifted by the claws of the wyvern at his front.

"I want them all." Glane's head swivels in both directions.

"Go for the one at his back," I suggest and hope she's in the mood to listen. Never know with her.

"Excellent choice," she agrees with a macabre tone of glee.

Bodhi has his sword in hand, but there's no clear shot for him as the trio starts to spiral downward. At this angle, we'll intercept them head-on.

I draw my own sword and clench Glane's pommel scales with one hand. My thighs are strong enough to hold on their own, but she's anything but predictable, and I'm not in the mood to die.

Blue fire engulfs Cuir from snout to horns, and Bodhi ducks his head as the remnants of flame roll down Cuir's neck, extinguishing to smoke before they reach him. I inhale swiftly to dispel the sudden tightness in my chest. That was way too damned close.

Then I focus on the top wyvern, looking for areas of weak—

Glane diverts, banking left to follow Cuir's spiral, then lunges at the wyvern clawing at his belly. *"Changed my mind."*

"Obviously."

Glane hits the wyvern like a battering ram, and I hold tight, whipping forward, then back at the sudden shift in velocity. My pulse jumps as we push forward to the unmistakable sound of ripping scales, but there's only determination and rage pouring down the bond—not pain.

An enormous head appears over Glane's shoulder, and for a split second fetid, dripping teeth are all I can see snapping toward me.

Fuck that nonsense.

"Stay level," I tell Glane, standing on the seat beneath me. Then I run up the slippery scales of her neck, passing the snarling teeth that part long enough for a jet of blue fire to rush across Glane's back.

Good thing I moved.

Before it can go for her throat, I thrust my sword into its eye and shove with all my strength. The blade plunges through the softer flesh with a sickening *squish.* Its high-pitched scream rings in my head like a bell, and I debate my life choices when it wrenches its head back, nearly taking me with it. My fist catches on the steel ball at the top of the sword's hilt, and I lock my grip as the wyvern falls away.

Glane dives after the plummeting heap of scales and wings, and I fall backward, my ass hitting every ridge of her neck before colliding with her pommel scales.

"Are you kidding me?" I heave myself into the seat, then lock into a position my muscles are more than familiar with, sword still in hand. Red flashes by on the right. Cath.

"Did you fall off? No. I did not bond a whiner." She chases the wyvern down through the rain, then latches on to its neck and rips its throat out.

I throw my weight left and narrowly miss being sprayed by blood.

"Eighteen!" she declares, flaring her wings to pull out of the dive and point us back to the northern wall.

"Seventeen if we're going by your measurement, since I wounded it first." Another lump of gray falls in a blur ahead of us, and I look up to see Cath and Cuir descending toward us. There's a hole in Cuir's right wing, and the laceration on his chest is going to leave a scar, but I can't tell at this angle if Bodhi is wounded.

Glane's head swivels as a bluefire wyvern circumvents the city to the south, sending a row of trees up in flames. *"That one."*

"Not our airspace." Kaori and the other officers hold the eastern, southern, and western territory, which is swiftly becoming the epicenter of the battle due to the winds, but they're down their most powerful rider—Garrick. And there's no sign of Chradh in sight.

"For someone so decisive, you have yet to act on that—" Glane starts to lecture.

"Stop right there and I'll agree your kill count is eighteen." My ribs tighten as we descend toward the city. The venin are done fucking around—they've come themselves. Blue flame swirls down the spiral tower, courtesy of two wyvern climbing its sides, and the fire whips outward as a dark wielder in gaudy scarlet robes sweeps her staff in a circle from the top of the landmark. Gryphons launch with their fliers toward the threat.

A sinking feeling pools in my stomach. There are too many of them, and we're already exhausted. Beyond the three felled dragons, four more lie wounded along the walls to the west beside innumerable gryphons. Their bleeding riders do their best to tend to them, and I look away from what's likely a fatal wound on a severed tail on a large brown.

"Orders?" I've always known I'll die in combat. I just don't want it to be today.

"The tower!" Glane shouts.

Quinn.

My head snaps toward the left, and my heart somersaults. One dark wielder in purple robes strides down the eastern city walls like he owns them, and another in crimson fighting leathers approaches along the northern. Both are headed for the turret where the only person I truly love on this battlefield is working, and she probably doesn't even know they're coming. *"Relay to Cruth!"*

"Already done." Glane's wings beat as quickly as my heart as we move toward the walls. There's nothing we can do from the air. I'm going to have to dismount.

Glane growls.

"You know it's true, and I'm not leaving her to die." I sheathe my sword and move to her shoulder despite the roaring wind shoving at my back. Orders can come later; I have to go *now*.

Infantry soldiers fight to intercept the dark wielders and are flung from the walls like inconsequential dolls. The guards plummet fifty feet to their deaths, clearing the path for the venin.

Terror saturates my lungs, and my heart *pounds*.

"You are to defend the tower from the walls with the wingleader," Glane relays with a disagreeing snarl, banking left for a parallel approach.

"Great. Get me on the wall, now." The dark wielders are less than thirty feet from the door of the turret, and the two remaining guards in the cross-bolt launch platform above look ready to flee.

Damn it. They were supposed to be *safe*. No one was supposed to know, but the purposeful strides of those dark wielders prove they know what's happening in that tower.

"Your death would annoy me." Glane slows just enough so I'll survive and extends her foreleg as she flies along the northern wall.

"Same." I *race* down the scales of her unwounded leg. There's no time for fear, no room for mistakes, not when Quinn is being hunted. Reaching Glane's talons, I leap into the rain without hesitation.

My pounding heart fills my ears while I'm airborne, and the northern wall rushes up to meet me. I bend my knees to absorb the coming impact, then *run* the second my boots hit the stonework so the momentum doesn't kill me. I hurtle forward and narrowly avoid falling on my face on the wet expanse of cobblestone as I sprint toward the back of the venin in crimson.

There's forty feet between us.

Thirty. Commotion erupts from the base of the tower, but I focus on the dark wielder and the staff he carries in his right hand.

"They are evacuating the weapons by foot," Glane says from somewhere above me.

Good. My lungs burn, but I breathe a little easier. Quinn will be safe.

Another set of footsteps joins mine, and a flash of metal sparks in the corner of my eye. Aetos catches up on my right, half his face drenched in blood, bearing his own dagger and a shield half his size.

Shit. That's not good.

Twenty. I channel my rage, rejecting any notion of fear, and draw one of my alloy-hilted daggers from the sheath at my arm in preparation to strike. We're almost there—

The dark wielder pivots, whipping to face us with an unnatural speed even I can't match, and swings his staff in our direction. Fire erupts, barreling toward us in a deadly stream, and I weigh our options for all of a millisecond as we skid to a halt. It hits? We die. Jump? We die.

"You will not burn!" Glane demands.

Fuck, I really didn't want to have to do this, but I mentally open the door to my childhood home and flood my body with her power.

"Get—" Aetos starts to yell.

"Get behind me!" I shout, ripping the shield from his grip. His eyes flare wide, and he lets go. We have *seconds*, so I flip the shield, then slam its flat top between the row of stones at our feet and drop behind it, keeping my hand on the leather strap.

Aetos jumps behind me as power rushes into my fingers so quickly I clench my teeth to keep from screaming. Heat surrounds us and the leather hardens in my grip as the shield turns to stone. Fire roars, blazes, flows around us. We are the rock in the river, demanding the water part.

The heat dissipates as the blast ends, and Aetos dives to the left and *throws*. An alloy-hilted dagger sails from his hand and I rise, clutching my own.

The dark wielder's expression of shock remains permanent as he desiccates a few feet away and falls off the wall.

One down, but the guards are missing from the top of the turret, and I see a flash of purple disappear into the tower. Worse, another dressed in crimson strides along the eastern wall.

Aetos jumps to his feet and draws his remaining dagger. "I'll take that one. You get the one in the tower." He glances at the stone shield, then breaks into a run, and I follow, sprinting as fast as I can. "And we're going to talk about whatever the fuck *that* just was later," he shouts over his shoulder, but I've already passed him, using lesser magic to boost my speed.

Cruth roars, sweeping from the sky to the city below, but Draithus is just like other Poromish cities, designed to keep dragons from landing within its narrow streets.

Two women carrying crying toddlers stumble out of the turret's doorway, horror etched on their faces. The taller one's gaze swings to mine as I reach them. "You have to help her! We got lost and went into the wrong tower and she—"

"Go west!" I shout, pointing in the direction I've just come from as Aetos runs past to intercept the other dark wielder. "And *run*."

They nod and do just that.

I fling myself through the doorway into the tower and blink, struggling to adjust to the dimmer lighting as I descend the spiral staircase down and down and down, looking for whomever they left behind.

"Where are you?" A raspy roar of frustration fills the tower and my heart surges into my throat as I round the bend of the third story.

Purple robes spin as the venin turns on the landing, swiping a green-tipped dagger at Quinn as she flashes in and out of space, appearing in front of him only to disappear within seconds and pop up somewhere else. There are two of her—no, three—circling the dark wielder.

She isn't here. She's projecting. Relief nearly cuts me at the knees.

I pause just out of sight and lean over the railing to scan the stairs below, but I don't see her. She's probably buildings away with Felix, setting up a new armory. I adjust my grip on the dagger, then creep down the steps to get within throwing distance.

Wait. The Quinn a handful of stairs beneath me has her labrys strapped to her back and is actually moving closer to the infuriated dark wielder who thrashes wildly with his dagger while other versions of Quinn dance around him, serving as the diversion.

I flip my dagger and throw at the same moment Quinn lunges with her own and the pale-haired venin spins. His eyes light up, then glass over as he turns gray and shrivels, collapsing at Quinn's feet with two daggers in his chest.

"Got him!" I lift my hands in victory and hop down the rest of the steps as Quinn turns toward me, her dark-green eyes impossibly wide as she looks at her chest.

No. The venin's blade is lodged between her ribs in the vicinity of her heart.

The world around me slows as she sways toward the wall, her horrified gaze finding mine.

"No!" I shout, throwing myself at her so it's me she falls against, and my back scrapes stone as we slide to the floor of the step. I cradle her as carefully as I can, locking my right arm around her back so she doesn't fall. "Quinn, *no*."

"Did they make it?" Her voice breaks as she stares up at me, blood spreading into the layers of her uniform through her flight jacket along the blade.

"We can fix this," I promise, and suddenly it's so *fucking* hard to breathe. "We just need to get you to a mender—"

"Did they make it?" she repeats, resting her head against the top of my arm.

The women. The kids. They hadn't been telling me they'd left someone behind. They were telling me she'd *saved* them. "Yeah." I nod as my eyes burn and my throat tightens. "They made it. You got them out."

"Good." A soft smile pulls at her mouth.

"Hold on, all right? We need to get you some help." I look up and down the staircase, but we're alone. Someone has to be close by. Aetos, maybe? *"Get us some help!"* I scream toward Glane.

"I'm sorry," she says more gently than I've ever heard, ever wanted to hear.

"There's no helping me," Quinn whispers.

"That's not true." I shake my head, and my vision blurs. Quinn will be fine. A world doesn't exist where she isn't fine, isn't laughing with Jax or hanging off my bed with her curls hitting the floor so she can get a head rush while she lectures me about *feelings*.

A roar vibrates the stone at my back. Cruth.

"There are no menders here, and no runes for this," she says with that damned reassuring smile of hers. "This is one thing you can't fix, Gen." Her face contorts with pain and I swear I feel it in my own chest, rending muscle and stripping my veins before it passes and her breaths grow shallow. "I need you to tell Jax that I love her."

"No." I wipe away the tear that slides from my eye before it can reach her hair. "You tell her. You're going to graduate in a couple of months, and then you'll marry her in that pretty black dress you picked out, and you're going to be happy."

"Tell her she's been the best part of my life—" Her mouth curves and she glances past me. "You don't count, Cruth. You *became* my life." She brings her gaze back to mine, and the color drains from her face. "Please, Gen. She's with the officers in the south, and I won't…"

I nod. "I'll tell her." This can't be real, can it? How can this be real?

"Thank you," she whispers and relaxes against me, her blinks slowing. "Tell my parents it was worth it. I'm glad it's you with me. Parapet to Malek's own doorstep. I'm so sorry I have to go first this time." Her breathing garbles. "And you should tell him, Gen. Tell him, and *you* find some happy."

"Quinn—" My voice shatters. "Don't go. Don't leave me," I beg, wiping another tear as my vision blurs and clears. "You're my best friend, and I love you. Please stay." This is *not* how she ends, not in some dark stairwell in Draithus. It can't be. I'm the one who's supposed to fall. She's supposed to live forever.

"You're mine, and I love you, too." Her smile slips and another tear falls. "I'm scared. I don't want to be scared."

My face twists, but I mask it. "Don't be scared." I shake my head and force a smile. "My mom will take care of you. And Katrina, too." My mouth quivers. "She's a little bossy, but she'll be thrilled to have another little sister. I talk about you all the time. They'll know who you are. Don't be scared."

Her next breath is strained and watery. "They'll know me."

I nod. "They'll know you and they'll love you. It's impossible not to love you."

"Imogen," she whispers, and her eyes flutter shut.

"I'm right here," I promise, but I can't force the words any louder as my throat closes.

"We made it a good one." She falls limp, and when I lift my shaking fingers to her throat, there's no pulse. She's gone.

My hand slides to the side of her head, and I hold her tight.

The scream that forces its way through the tangled mess of my throat shreds my soul on the way out and reverberates off the stone, shaking the foundations of my world until it doesn't just slow, it stops. I stop.

Hi! I'm Quinn Hollis. I've decided we should be friends. That's what she said to me as we climbed the turret on Conscription Day.

You do realize we're about to cross the walkway of death.

Well, then it might be a short friendship, but we'll make it a good one.

I stare at the other side of the staircase, locked in the memory, watching as the stones begin to pale, then lose their color one by one, each loss higher than the last. My heart somehow continues to beat, marking what I used to think of as time, and color disappears from the stones in the bend beneath us so gradually that I can't help but wonder if Quinn simply took the color with her.

"Quinn!" someone bellows from above, and footsteps thunder. "Where are you? We have to go—" There's a deep intake of breath to my left. "Imogen? Oh, fuck."

My head turns slowly toward the voice and Garrick crouches on the step above us, his hazel gaze locking on mine and filling with so much misery, so much *sympathy* that it overflows my own eyes and wetness streams down the sides of my cheeks. "She's dead."

Saying it doesn't make it feel any more real.

His face falls. "I'm so sorry." He glances down the staircase. "But we have to go. There's half a dozen of them with their hands on the city walls, draining the life out of the stone. It's time to go."

I hold her tighter, unable to fathom the concept of moving, like there's some miniscule chance she'll return if I just wait here long enough. "I can't. Just leave."

"I am with you. You may not die," Glane growls.

Garrick's square jaw flexes. "You have to. *We* have to go, or they'll drain us, too."

"I'm not leaving her!"

"I'm not leaving *you!*" He leans in and slides his hand behind my neck. "I'm not leaving you, Imogen," he repeats, softer this time. "We'll take Quinn, but we have to go *now*. Let me have her."

I notice the circles beneath his beautiful eyes, the unusual pallor of his complexion. He's exhausted, and for the first time in my life, I don't care that he's seeing me at my weakest, because he's right there, too. My chin tips in a nod.

"All right." He moves quickly to the step beneath us, kicking something out of the way and gathering both of us into his arms. I lock mine around Quinn so she doesn't slip as we're lifted off the floor, and the landing beneath us loses its color. "Let's get you out of here."

He takes a single step.

Heat and light force my eyes shut as my stomach careens.

When I open them, we're somewhere else. Rain falls through an open doorway, and the scent of smoke and sulfur fills my lungs.

"Oh gods!" Professor Trissa gasps as Garrick sets Quinn and me down on a warm stone floor in a nondescript building. A store, maybe? Quinn's body slides, and he helps lay her beside me, cushioning her head with his hand.

"Venin." Garrick explains her loss with a single word. "Are you weaving?" he asks Trissa.

"We're starting." Her gaze darts over me. "They'll be weak until we can bolster with more power, but they're our best shot."

"It's still not enough." Garrick's head hangs as he stands. "I can't…" He sighs and strides through the door.

I obey the simple instinct to follow, shoving myself to my feet and forcing my body to move. There's a battle. We're in a war. Malek might claim more lives. I follow him past the little room where Felix works beside cases of alloy-hilted daggers, all imbued, all humming with power.

Then I step outside into the rain and stare. Houses burn. Wyvern and gryphon bodies lie in the middle of crumpled rooflines. Civilians scream. Cruth sails through the sky and takes a wyvern straight to the ground. Bodhi is on his hands and knees across the town square, retching.

If dark wielders are draining the city walls, we're next.

"Where are you going?" I shout at Garrick's back.

"I can't walk again. Even if I made it to Aretia, I'd never be strong enough to get back," he calls over his shoulder. "So, I'd better find some fucking way to do something."

I unsheathe my last alloy-hilted dagger and stare up at the wyvern-filled sky. Then I make my way back inside, slip Quinn's last dagger from her thigh sheath, and reach for Glane. *Tell every rider within the walls to get over here and disarm. It's the only way we're living through this.*

Outside, the sky darkens further. Sorrengail better take their leader all the way the fuck out, or this will all have been for nothing.

A gift from one servant of Dunne to another. I must warn you—only those touched by the gods should wield their wrath. I will pray to Her that she need not use it to avoid reacquainting herself with the other who curries her favor. Her path is still not set.

—RECOVERED CORRESPONDENCE OF HIGH PRIESTESS DESERVEE TO HIS ROYAL HIGHNESS, CADET AARIC GRAYCASTLE, PRINCE CAMLAEN OF NAVARRE

CHAPTER SIXTY-FOUR

VIOLET

I swear the tornado slows as Tairn battles the wind at the eastern edge of the field, flying for the mountainside ahead of us.

"It is slowing," Tairn agrees.

"She used it to get us here." Theophanie's holding it like a nocked arrow, waiting for our arrival.

Trees are uprooted a mile to the left, turning into low-flying projectiles that hurl across the field like cross-bolts. The tornado may have slowed its progress, but it's doing far more damage along the way.

The wyvern launches ahead of us, moving our way, and for a split second, I can't help but wonder if I've just invited Malek to our doorstep.

She's a Maven, and I'm a cadet.

She wields storms with expert precision, and I need a conduit for my lightning.

She's already felled Tairn once before.

The smartest thing I could do is fly for the wards and save us both—all four of us, considering Xaden and Sgaeyl—but I can't leave those people to die, even if it means we're desiccated alongside them.

Riders don't run. We fight.

"Now, preferably," Tairn remarks. *"If you're done accepting our deaths."*

"Not accepting, just calculating." I draw power through my charred veins as the distance between us grows smaller and smaller, gripping the conduit in my left hand and raising my right.

Energy rips through me as I release it, dragging the bolt downward and letting go before it can blister my fingers. Lightning strikes as Theophanie's wyvern rolls to the right.

I missed. My stomach clenches.

"Again!" Tairn demands, banking right to follow her down as rain turns to ice.

Hail hits in stones the size of peas, then cherries, hitting me with the force of a thousand blunt arrows as wind tears at my face, but I lift my hand—

The conduit shatters.

Glass slices into my palm, and I gasp in pain as blood wells.

No, no, no! I can't aim without it.

"You have to!" Tairn orders as we spiral downward.

Right. Dying up here isn't an option I'm willing to entertain, and I'm not about to let her kill my friends—or Xaden, either. I quickly undo the strap holding the jagged remnants to my wrist and let what's left of the orb, and the fist-size chunk of ice that destroyed it, fall away. My hope plummets with it.

I'll have to kill her just like I did those wyvern—with volume. I unsheathe my last alloy-hilted dagger and grasp it with my bleeding hand so I'm ready for anything, lift my right hand, and wield again.

I miss as she rolls in the opposite direction and begins to climb. We follow, and I draw power again and again, but it becomes harder with every strike. She avoids every single one as we fly along the mountain, hugging the terrain. Tairn surges with sweeping beats of his wings, gaining on her.

Heat singes my lungs, then burns, then fries, until I feel nothing but fire and rage.

Rock flies as I hit the ridgeline to the right, missing her by ten feet as we fly into the sun.

The sun.

I jerk my head left. The tornado has stalled midway toward the city, and the sky above us is clear all the way to the east.

"She's killing the storm to make it harder for me to wield!" That explains why I'm burning hotter than before. I jerk my focus back to our prey before it can wander toward the city I'm desperately fighting to save.

"Do not take more than you can channel," Tairn warns as he lunges forward. His teeth snap closed a few feet behind the wyvern's tail.

They're too fucking fast.

The wyvern dives, curving along the ridgeline to the right, and Tairn follows.

A roar of unfettered agony fills my head, so loud it vibrates my bones and shrill enough to pop my ears.

"Sgaeyl!" Tairn bellows, his wings losing their rhythm, and my heart skips a series of beats.

Oh Malek, *no*.

I hurl myself at the bond, but the wall of ice doesn't just stand firm; it repels me with brute force. Dread nails my stomach to the floor as we lose speed—

I hear the *snap* a second before the shadow falls over us. No, not a shadow. A massive net with weights the size of desks attached along the edges.

Tairn roars and banks left, but it's no use.

"Tairn!" I scream as the net hits, smashing my torso downward onto the pommels and covering every scale I can see. He'd be able to bear the weight of it easily on his torso, but it smothers his wings, and the weights... Oh gods. *"Tuck your wings or they'll break!"*

His roar of indignation shakes the rocks loose from the mountainside, but he snaps them closed, tangling in the net.

And we fall.

"Prepare yourself!" Tairn warns as the mountain flies by in a blur.

Andarna. Xaden. Sgaeyl. Mira. Brennan. My friends. They slip through my mind in a whirl of pictures I can't grasp on to, flickering too fast to fully feel. All I can do is ease off the pommels, lean right to spare the inevitable impact to my abdomen as the thick rope of the net digs into my back.

"You have been the gift of my life," I tell Tairn.

"It is not over!" he shouts.

We hit with a jarring impact, bone crunching against rock, and my left arm *snaps* and the dagger falls.

A scream forces its way through my lips as we slide down the mountain... just like the first time we encountered Theophanie. The sound of claws scraping over stone consumes my existence as I fight to block out the pain, and Tairn swings his body weight so we skid headfirst through the trees in an endless, terrifying plunge.

I keep my head down to avoid any low-hanging branches as something digs painfully into my ribs, and eventually our momentum slows.

Holy shit, we just might survive the fall.

"Of course we'll survive!" Tairn growls.

"Are you hurt?" I ask Tairn as we come to a stop at what appears to be the edge of the forest.

"Nothing that won't heal after we free ourselves and separate her sinew from bone." The scent of sulfur fills the air as Tairn breathes fire through the net.

Wood crackles and net *thwangs*. Then he surges forward and the net slips just enough for me to sit up through the opening that's clearly designed to hold dragons, not riders.

"We have to get to Sgaeyl." Which means getting him free, but it will take too long to cut through these ropes with the runed daggers I have. And even if I do, I'll still have to wield to kill her without my alloy-hilted one, and I'm already edging burnout. My arm throbs mercilessly, and every breath I take scalds my lungs.

"Sgaeyl can handle herself," Tairn grits out, but bowstring-tight tension and worry radiate down the bond as fire streams again and he fights to get us loose. *"And the dark wielder descends ahead."*

Sure enough, Theophanie's wyvern glides down toward the field like they have all the time in the world, like we're pinned exactly where she wants us.

Gods, she's *relentless.* It doesn't matter that my arm throbs with excruciating intensity—we have to get out of here right fucking now. Time to use the runes I brought in case of an emergency and pray I tempered them correctly, because *this* is definitely a crisis.

"We have to get out from under this thing." Cradling my left arm to my chest, I twist for my pack, but something pushes into my ribs as I dig into the bag one-handed. I discard the ones I don't need, then snag the one for softening surfaces and shove it up against the rope. *Here's hoping it's right.*

Magic ripples, and the fibers stretch and give way.

My eyebrows rise. It *works.*

"Rip what you can!" I shout to Tairn.

"Stay seated so we can fly," he orders, shredding the net on the edges of his spikes, and I take the opportunity to grab whatever's jabbing me in my pocket. *Aaric's package.* I catch the hastily scrawled message on the edge of the package I'd missed when Sloane handed it to me.

For when you lose yours. Strike in the dark, Violet.

What the fuck? The fall has broken the wax seal, and the parchment unrolls as I loosen my grip, dropping a carved piece of gray marble in my lap—a ceremonial-looking dagger with familiar flame-shaped etchings along the hilt. I glance at the accompanying note from the high priestess of Dunne's temple in Aretia, but the letters blur as the pain in my arm flares and Tairn thrashes to free us.

A gift from one servant of Dunne to another. I must warn you—only those touched by the gods should wield their wrath. I will pray to Her that she need not use it to avoid reacquainting herself with the other who curries her favor. Her path is still not set.

My stomach pitches. How would Aaric know I'd lose my dagger, let alone think that some piece of rock could replace—

"Ahead of us!" Tairn snaps, and I jerk my attention forward and sheathe the marble dagger out of instinct.

Theophanie stalks toward us from the tree line, her hair fraying from its braid, and there's nothing patient or amused on her face.

I frantically scan what sky I can see. Theophanie's wyvern waits in the field beyond the trees, and the only other wings I find are locked in battle over Draithus in the distance, which hopefully means she's alone.

"How much time do you need to free yourself?" I ask Tairn, wrenching the buckle of my saddle free and climbing through the hole in the net. Pain shoots up my left arm, but I pretend it belongs to someone else and keep going. Pain doesn't matter if you're dead.

"Moments," Tairn shouts. *"Do not—"*

"I'm not going to let her kill you like a trussed pig!" I retort, fear and wrath fueling me as I scramble for his shoulder, struggling to keep my arm stable until he stills. He must have thrown his claws out before the net hit, because his forelegs are already extended, bracketing his lower jaw.

I draw a runed dagger, then slide down, dragging the edge of the blade along his leg as I go. The blade won't cut scale, but the net falls apart in its wake.

"Brought low by a *net*?" Theophanie mocks, striding toward us. "How easy it was to catch the pair of them."

The pair? *The scream.*

"They have Sgaeyl, too." Tairn's rage washes over me like acid.

I put myself in front of Tairn and open the floodgates to his power, welcoming the scorch of heat and flame in my blistered veins.

"Silver One," Tairn growls in warning to the accompaniment of the sound of shredding rope.

"If I burn out, so be it, but she won't touch you," I say aloud just so Theophanie will know I'm not fucking around.

"Have you made your choice, then?" Theophanie asks, coming closer by the step.

"I have." I flick my right hand skyward and let the energy *snap* through me, yanking it down with the tip of my finger.

Theophanie races ten yards to the right, moving faster than I've ever seen. "You'll have to be—"

I wield again before she can finish and strike the very place she's standing, earning an immediate clap of thunder.

But she's already twenty feet to my left.

"Faster," she finishes, and I strike again, only for the pattern to repeat.

Again and again and *again*.

My lungs scream as I breathe the very thing I've become, heat and power and rage, but she's still too fast for me to catch and moving closer to Tairn with every failed strike.

"Almost there," he assures as ropes snap behind me.

I need to throw her off her game *now*.

I hold my next strike when she appears twenty feet ahead. "Tell me, do you miss Unnbriel?"

Her eyes flare, and she startles.

Victory. I gather more and more power, spooling it like molten thread. "Do you not yearn for temple?" I use the words the high priestess had on me.

Her face twists with an emotion that almost looks like longing, but it's quickly masked with anger. "Do *you*?" she counters. "Or are you immune, having only been touched, but not dedicated?" She charges forward. "Do you know the pain of never being allowed to return, of knowing that it would sever the very thing that's kept me untouchable all these years?"

I let a fraction of my power release, striking the ground in front of her, and she skids to a halt. *Touched.* Shit, the priestess in Unnbriel had said *that*, too. So had the note wrapped around Aaric's gift. "As a high priestess, you would have had immeasurable power on the isle. How was it still not enough?"

"Why serve a god when you can *be* one?" Theophanie snarls.

Putrid *fear* consumes the bond, followed by another roar that nearly buckles my knees.

Sgaeyl. My head jerks upward, my heart lurching against the cage of my ribs as Tairn snarls, his talons furrowing in the forest floor. *"Don't!"* Terror clogs my throat as I shout for Xaden, but he can't hear me.

Draithus is enveloped in darkness, and the shrieking cries of wyvern soon follow, racing across the field and echoing off the rock above.

"What—" Theophanie pivots toward the noise.

Shadow spreads like a ripple on a lake, devouring the field in the fury of an onyx storm and sweeping toward us at a speed that squeezes the hope from my chest, then outright shatters my heart. The pain hits like a physical blow to the center of my chest.

He's terrifyingly powerful with Sgaeyl, but not like this.

This is the kind of force that ends worlds.

And it's almost here.

"I love you," I whisper down the bond, and the ice cracks, but it's not enough to halt the approaching wave of darkness.

Shadow throws Theophanie to the ground a second before it rushes over me, whisper soft against my cheeks, tossing us into pitch-black night.

"Strike!" Tairn snaps, and I hear the net give way.

Exhaustion grabs hold and refuses to be ignored. I'm too tired. Too close to burning alive. What's the point if I can't catch her?

"Use the darkness!" Tairn orders.

My heart stutters. Use the very thing that's taking Xaden from me? I never dreamed that taking every possible path to cure him would lead to his *choice*. The fire devouring me from the inside out threatens to consume my very bones, and for a second, I debate letting it. I couldn't stop my mother, and I can't stop Xaden. I can't save him.

Wait. *Strike in the darkness.* That's what Aaric's note said…

Like he knew this would happen.

I gasp as all the pieces click in one overwhelming heartbeat. The reinforcements. Telling me to guard Dunne's temple. Yanking Lynx out of the way before the doors even opened to the great hall. He *knew*. He's been manifesting this entire time.

"He's a fucking precog," I whisper in awe. A *real* one—not like Melgren, who can only foresee battles. If Aaric wields true precognition, he saw *this*, and he gave me a weapon made of the fractured temple—a temple Theophanie can't step inside. I don't believe in oracles, but I *do* believe in signets.

I unsheathe the marble dagger with my right hand, then mix my pain into the searing power that scorches what's left of my beating heart, lift my broken arm, and release the agonizing burn of energy skyward.

And hold it.

The continuous strike lights up our surroundings and branches out through the shadow, revealing Theophanie's back. She stumbles to her feet and whirls toward me, her eyes flaring wide, and she dives left, smacking into an invisible wall and falling backward.

A wall that *snarls.*

Scales shimmer to the same silver-blue as my strike, and a small dragon stalks toward Theophanie, her head low, teeth bared.

And just like that, my stammering heartbeat stabilizes.

Andarna.

Theophanie reaches out her hand, wonder lighting her red eyes.

I don't care what her intentions are—she's not getting her hands on Andarna. Pain wraps me in a broiling vise and fire sears my lungs, but I hold the bolt and *sprint.* Andarna leaving was one thing; losing her to the touch of a dark wielder is incomprehensible.

"Irid," Theophanie whispers with reverence, straining toward Andarna. I lunge, driving the dagger straight into her heart. Fire breathes through me, until I am char and cinder and agony.

She staggers backward and starts to laugh.

Then she sees the blood and stops. "How?" Her eyes flare, and she topples to her knees. "Stone doesn't kill venin."

"You were never just venin," I reply. "Dunne is a wrathful goddess to high priestesses who turn their backs on Her."

She opens her mouth to scream, then desiccates in an instant.

I release the bolt, plunging us into darkness and surrendering to the fire burning me alive.

"*Violet,*" Andarna whispers.

And then I hear nothing.

The only thing more unpredictable than the volatile province that is Tyrrendor is her duke. There is a reason reigning aristocracy should never wear black.

—JOURNAL OF GENERAL AUGUSTINE MELGREN

CHAPTER SIXTY-FIVE

XADEN

It was one thing to beckon me, call me, *summon* me to this hidden, sun-soaked canyon south of Draithus against my will, to drag me from the walls of our defenses and force me to walk away from my friends and a city full of civilians. It is wholly another to have wounded and ensnared *Sgaeyl*.

Blood drips among her scales, coursing down her shoulder, and the sight of it soaking the forearm-thick ropes that bind her cuts me to the quick and floods me with power in a way nothing else could. I take it all, then draw more, but she's already depleted from holding off so many wyvern at the walls of Draithus.

Wrath courses like a current under the ice I willingly skate onto, cutting my emotions free like the burdens they are so I can be the weapon she needs. She was the first to choose me, to elevate me above all others, the first to see every ugly side of me and accept it all, and every single person in this fucking canyon will die before they remove a single one of her scales.

Violet will free Tairn. That's the only outcome I allow to exist.

The two venin standing guard ahead of me at the mouth of the canyon in their ridiculous robes aren't an issue. I'll have them desiccated within heartbeats as soon as Sgaeyl can regain enough power. But the one who walks forward toward Panchek's cowering, traitorous ass, putting himself between Sgaeyl and me… He's a problem.

Not because he's more lethal.

Not even because he's supposed to be *dead*.

But because I. Can't. Kill. Him. I could no more raise a blade to his throat than I could Violet. The bond between Violence and me is the kind of magic that has no explanation.

The bond between Berwyn and me is the kind that should never exist, and now that my Sage has another *sibling* he can use against me…I'm screwed.

"Watch carefully, my initiate," Berwyn says to me over his shoulder, baring the scar down the middle of his face from when I threw him into the ravine at Basgiath.

I glance past Berwyn, past Sgaeyl and the venin, to my new brother and the unconscious dragon lying in the valley beyond the canyon, guarded by seven wyvern. How could *he* do this? Choose this after watching me stumble and fall over the last five months. How could he willingly walk the path I've fought like hell to leave? He's the last person I ever would have expected to turn, and yet here we are.

I can't let Sgaeyl die. Can't leave *him* to stumble down the same path I did. Can't allow my friends to perish because I selfishly want to keep Violet by my side. A clamoring, consuming emotion pounds at the ice, but I can't let it in. She has her own path.

No matter what I choose, it's wrong.

But only one path leaves Sgaeyl alive.

"This is not what we agreed to!" Panchek shouts, stumbling backward toward his own shrieking, netted dragon.

I don't bother looking in their direction. Fucker deserves to suffer for selling us out. Whatever the Sage—what *Berwyn*—does is of no consequence to me. How much information has he sold to the enemy? Certainly enough to lure us *all* to Draithus. How many times did he give them Violet's location?

He dies. The decision is made without debate.

"*Do not lose yourself,*" Sgaeyl warns, thrashing against the net that has her pinned to the rocky ground twenty feet in front of me. "*You have not turned as a result of his ploys this afternoon. Do not give in to this one!*"

But he hadn't had *her*, and now he does.

"*There's no other way,*" I reply, slowly unsheathing the two alloy-hilted daggers I keep at my thighs and earning a glare from the dark wielder standing at the tip of Sgaeyl's tail, his fingers splayed in obvious threat.

"Did you not ask for power?" Berwyn snarls, holding two alloy-hilted daggers of his own as he approaches Panchek. "Have I not provided?"

"Put those away. We both know you're not going to hurt me." Panchek reaches for the net over his dragon. "I'm the only one who can give you access to your *son*."

"I have another." Berwyn stabs deep between the dragon's scales, and it *desiccates*, green draining from its scales and shrinking in on itself to a husk.

Terror busts through the ice.

Berwyn just killed a dragon with a *dagger*.

How the *fuck* is that possible?

"Were you watching? Because that's exactly what's about to happen to yours." He turns to me and saunters toward Sgaeyl as she thrashes futilely under the net. "You'll have to channel deep to replace the loss of her power." He lifts the blade, and I don't just skate over the ice.

I become it.

"*Stop!*" Sgaeyl roars, blowing back Berwyn's robes. "*Do not do this to save me!*"

Do this? It's already done.

How fucking *dare* they pull my dragon from the sky, snare and hurt the one who anchors my existence.

I throw my blades into the air, fall to one knee, splay my hand over the canyon floor, and *break*.

In my final act of resistance, I become the very thing I despise. Maybe it's good that I can't feel a single damned thing.

I breathe in the power that pulses beneath my hand like a living, breathing creature, and exhale darkness. Shadow streams through the canyon, thick as tar and black as ink, blacking out the afternoon sun and turning the space pitch-black. Shadow plants my daggers in the chests of the two venin standing guard. Shadow drags Berwyn from Sgaeyl and knocks both him and my new brother unconscious. Shadow brings *quiet*.

My soul departs like pieces of ash from a fire, flaking free and drifting away as power consumes the space it once inhabited. I'm no longer on the ice—I *am* the ice.

And still I feed, tunneling deep into the source of magic itself and surging outward simultaneously, finding the identical heartbeats that mark wyvern and slicing through scale with shadow, ripping their runestones free. I start with the one who dared set its teeth in Sgaeyl's shoulder, skim past the one who now thinks himself my brother, then destroy the six blocking the entrance to this canyon.

Save them, the last remaining pieces of me beg, holding on with teeth and claw to keep from being torn away, too. My shadows surge from the canyon, over the city, ending every wyvern in the air and on the ground. I'm everywhere at once, shredding the net that ensnares Sgaeyl, tearing the heart from the wyvern who has Dain and Cath backed into a corner, rushing over Imogen as she looks to the sky. I'm at the pass, plucking wyvern off one by one, listening with satisfaction as their bodies hit the ground in front of the people *she* loves. I stream up the cliffside, fall back at the magic that burns to the touch, and surge north.

"I love you." Violet's voice cracks the cold, and a silken thread of warmth wedges itself in the opening before it seals shut, locking it in place.

No. *Wait.* I grab for that thread with desperate hands, clawing to keep her as more of my pieces are blown away, lost to the void. She is warmth and light and air and love.

My shadows consume the valley she stands in, dagger bared, defending Tairn from the same style of net that caught Sgaeyl. I shove the Maven to the ground, regardless of her rank, then slide over Violet with a gentleness that takes all my concentration.

I love her. That is the emotion I cling to, the fire of pure power burning at the feeling's edges, and I know if I take it any further, it will be the next and final piece to float away. I bare my teeth and yank my hand from the ground, gasping for a full breath as my heart thunders.

I've never felt so strong and so defeated at the same time. This was the only way. I rise to my feet and release the shadows, and the canyon comes into view.

Sgaeyl struggles to stand upright ahead of me, blood dripping from the bite marks in her shoulder. The net falls in tatters and she expands her wings to their full width, taking nearly every foot in the canyon. She glances over the destruction, the bodies, and narrows her golden eyes in silent rebuke.

"Will you forsake me now?" I ask, walking over Berwyn's unconscious body. I'd kill him if I could. Fuck, I thought I *had.* I wonder how many initiates feel the same about their Sage? At least one that I know of. But beyond the physical impossibility of it, he has something I need.

And I'm no longer an initiate.

"What is there left of you to forsake?" Sgaeyl lowers her head and steam gusts down the canyon, reminding me of the moment she found me in the forest at Threshing.

"You tell me." I lower the ice and let her in.

Her next breath is laced with sulfur, and her eyes widen. *"You cannot mean to—"*

"You saw what happened. It is the only way."

She glances over her shoulder. *"And you think she'll help?"*

"She loves me."

"Tairn does not, and you haven't looked in a mirror yet. The red veins branching from your eyes look like her lightning."

"She'll help." It comes out with a hell of a lot more certainty than I feel. *"She promised."*

"*Even if she agrees, no one will—*"

"*Someone owes me a favor.*"

"*He'll never let you near her.*" Her tail flicks. "*Especially while she lies in a vulnerable state.*"

"*Is she hurt?*" The beating organ behind my ribs stumbles, and I reach down the bond that connects my mind to hers, but it's muddled with unconsciousness.

"*Yes,*" Sgaeyl says slowly, her head moving in a serpentine motion. "*But she will survive.*" She pauses. "*They have completed the wards, but they extend no farther than Draithus.*"

That's good. Bad. Fuck, I don't know. What even *am* I?

Hers.

"*Persuade Tairn,*" I beg.

Everything depends on it.

"*We will ask,*" Sgaeyl finally says, flexing her claws in the rocky soil. "*And her decision will determine our fate.*"

Those are terms I can agree to.

We're airborne in less than a minute.

While cadets are strongly encouraged not to form romantic attachments while studying in the quadrant, lieutenants are permitted to marry whomever they choose upon graduation.

—ARTICLE FIVE, SECTION SEVEN
THE DRAGON RIDER'S CODEX

CHAPTER SIXTY-SIX

VIOLET

"Violet!" Brennan shouts, racing down the steps of Riorson House and into the moonlit courtyard.

Sounds of celebration stream through the open doors.

I groggily rise to my feet beside Imogen, and a shape moves in the shadows to the right.

"I will not let them burn you," Andarna vows.

"What?" My head whips her way. *"Why would my brother burn me?"* And why in Dunne's name would I be sitting on gravel in the courtyard? My thoughts are…slow. Something's off.

Something's wrong.

"Are you all right?" I ask Brennan as he reaches us.

"Am *I* all right?" His eyes bulge, and he looks me over for injury. "It's three o'clock in the morning! Where have you been?" His voice rises, and a group of riders I don't recognize comes through the gate at our left. "Weilsen?" Brennan asks, and the taller one walks our way. "Report." He glances over his shoulder. "Quietly."

My mouth opens, then shuts. Where *have* I been?

"We've—" The officer's gaze darts over me.

"It's fine," Brennan assures him.

"Official numbers are four riders, their dragons, and three elders murdered in the valley in what we're estimating is the last few hours," Weilsen says. "And we still have five riders missing—four now," he adds, looking at me. His mouth tenses. "But after that display, we all know Riorson did this. I bet the other three are already dead."

My stomach lurches, and Imogen tenses so hard she might as well be stone.

Wait. Is this a dream? I clench my right fist and prick my palm with my fingernails just enough to feel pain, but I don't wake.

"The wards are holding in Draithus as of the last report, but who knows how many of those desiccations during the battle were actually him," Weilsen continues. "And so far, the tally is at six missing eggs from the hatching ground, but they're double-checking."

Missing eggs? I reach for Tairn, but the bond feels foggy, like he's asleep.

"He needs a cycle of rest to recover," Andarna clarifies.

"Recover from what?*"* He was fine when I saw him last, which was about five minutes ago, in the woods at the edge of the field—

Where I killed Theophanie.

Xaden.

The wall of shadows… My heart sinks. What the fuck is happening? How did I get here? Why is my head so hazy? Am I concussed?

"You're dismissed," Brennan tells the rider. "Keep this classified until we have a full report."

"Just because she's your sister doesn't mean she's not the fastest way—"

"Dismissed!" Brennan snaps, and the rider backs away.

"Do you know where he is?" Brennan asks me softly once the other rider is fully out of earshot. "Riorson? You heard what Weilsen said. We have dead dragons and riders and missing eggs, and if you've seen Riorson, I need to know, Violet."

"I…" Words fail me. Why can't I *think*? "I don't know." I raise my hands to my mouth, and a piece of parchment in my front pocket catches on my arm, then falls.

Brennan catches it. "Cardulo?" He lifts his eyes to Imogen.

"I haven't seen him since yesterday," she says, her voice low, almost monotone. "Lieutenant Tavis?"

"Among the missing," Brennan answers gently, then glances my way and does a double take. "Holy shit, Violet."

"What?" I lower my arms. Garrick is missing, too? Who else makes up the four riders Weilsen mentioned?

"Your finger," Imogen says, then stares at the ground.

My finger? *The snap.* Right. "I think I broke my arm." I glance down and stare.

My left arm is splinted, and a beautiful gold ring with an emerald the size of my thumbnail sits on my hand. Oh gods, I know that stone. It matches the others from the Blade of Aretia upstairs on Xaden's nightstand. Is it the missing one? "What is happening right now?" I ask slowly.

"You don't know?" Brennan lowers his voice.

I shake my head.

Brennan turns to the paper from my pocket. "This carries the seal of Dunne," he says. "May I open it?"

I nod, gawking at the ring. It's not just any ring on any finger. It's *the* finger. But how? I was in the field battling Theophanie this afternoon, and then she desiccated and I burned myself straight into unconsciousness. Now it's three a.m. and I'm in Aretia, and there are murdered dragons and riders, missing riders and missing eggs? Xaden wouldn't do that.

Would he?

The storm of shadows. My blood chills. How far had he gone? I fling myself down the bond, but there's nothing there. It's *gone.*

Or he's too far away to feel it, I remind myself to keep from panicking. When had he put this ring on my hand?

"It's an official blessing of your legal, binding marriage," Brennan whispers, stunned, then quickly rolls the parchment. "By the head priestess of Dunne's temple."

"To Xaden?" Gravity bends, warping everything I thought I knew into whatever this reality is.

Brennan nods.

My eyes flare. We're *married*? A thousand emotions try to force their way through my jumbled thoughts, but the immediate rush of awe trips right over the logic of *how*. There's no fucking way I'd forget something like that. Why isn't he here? Where did he go? And why?

"I think the note on the outside is meant for you." Brennan hands back the parchment.

I flip the missive over to see two sentences written in Xaden's handwriting.

Don't look for me. It's yours now.

He's gone.

I try to fumble my foggy brain through the overwhelming shock, but I can't think straight. It's like someone has fucked with my—

No.

My chest draws tight. "How long have I been missing?"

"Twelve hours," Brennan answers.

"What did you do?" My head snaps toward Imogen, and a deep sense of foreboding takes root in my chest.

She slowly lifts her gaze to mine. "What you asked me to."

ACKNOWLEDGMENTS

Thank you to my husband, Jason, for being my gravity. For getting me to every doctor's appointment and managing the overwhelming calendar that comes with having four sons and a wife with Ehlers-Danlos. Thank you for holding me together with hugs and regular deliveries of chips and queso over the last few years of chaos. Thank you to my six children, who are quite simply my everything. You continually astound me with your grace, your tenacity, and your laughter. To my sister, Kate, who never complained when we were holed up in a London hotel room with edits instead of sightseeing...AGAIN. Love you, mean it. To my parents, who are always there when I need them. To my best friend, Emily, for being the easiest part of my life and the keeper of secrets.

Thank you to my team at Red Tower. Thank you to my editor, Alice Jerman, for pouring your time and heart into this book and always being up for a Zoom no matter what time zone I was in. Thank you to Liz Pelletier for giving me the chance to write my favorite genre. To Stacy Abrams for your endless wisdom. To Lizzy Mason for always picking up the phone, taking the picture, and soothing my anxiety. To Ashley, Hannah, Heather, Curtis, Brittany M., Brittany Z., Molly, Jessica, Katie, Erin, Madison, Rae, and everyone at Entangled and Macmillan for answering endless streams of emails and for bringing this book to the marketplace. To the wonderful beta and sensitivity readers for your eagle eyes. To Julia Kniep for always going out of your way. To Becky West for the endless encouragement, McDonald's, Coke, and T Swift calls. To Bree Archer for this phenomenal cover and Elizabeth and Amy for the exquisite art. To Meredith

Johnson for being the GOAT. Thank you to my incredible agent, Louise Fury, for always standing at my back and Shivani Doraiswami for being my wondrous film agent! Endless thanks to the teams at Outlier and Amazon Studios. You guys are absolute dreams to work with!

Thank you to my business manager, KP, for holding my fragile sanity in your hands and never dropping it. Thank you to my wifeys, our unholy trinity, Gina Maxwell and Cindi Madsen—I'd be lost without you. To Kyla, who made this book possible. To Shelby and Cassie for keeping my ducks in a row and always being my number one hype girls. To Rachel and Ashley for being the smartest, kindest women I know. To every reviewer who has taken a chance on me over the years, I can't thank you enough. To my reader group, The Flygirls, for being the happiest place on the internet. To my readers: your excitement keeps me at the keys.

Lastly, because you're my beginning and end, thank you again to my Jason. You and me against the world, love.

Kai wakes in the woods with no idea who she is or how she got there. But when she sees the village blacksmith fight invaders with unspeakable skill, she decides to accept his offer of help. Too bad he's as skilled at annoying her as he is at fighting. As she searches for answers, Kai only finds more questions, especially regarding the blacksmith who can ignite her body like a flame, then douse it with ice in the next breath. And no one is what—or who—they appear to be in the kingdom of Vinevridth, including the man whose secrets might be as deadly as the land itself.

Leith of Grey thought volunteering to fight in the gladiator arena—vicious, bloodthirsty tournaments where only the strongest survive—would earn him enough gold to save his dying sister. He thought there was nothing left to lose. He was wrong. They took *everything*. Then a princess offers him the chance to win the coveted title of Bloodguard...and his freedom. But in a kingdom built on lies, hope—and revenge—doesn't come cheap.

AVAILABLE NOW WHEREVER BOOKS ARE SOLD

CONNECT WITH US ONLINE

@redtowerbooks

@RedTowerBooks

@redtowerbooks

RED TOWER
BOOKS™

THE CONTINENT

EMERALD SEA

NAVARRE

LUCERAS PROVINCE

MORRAINE PROVINCE

ELSUM PROVINCE

IAKOBOS RIVER

THE VALE ✧ ✧ BASGIATH

✧ CALLDYR CITY

CALLDYR PROVINCE

DEACONSHIRE PROVINCE

TYRRENDOR PROVINCE

✧ LEWELLEN

✦ ARETIA ✧

ATHEBYNE

CLIFFS OF DRALOR

MEDARO PASS

DRAITHUS

ARCTILE OCEAN